THE CRUSADE OF VENGEANCE

The Earthborn Saga Vol. V

Steven Bissett

Copyright © 2023 Steven Bissett

All rights reserved.

No portion of this book may be reproduced in any form without permission from the publisher, except as permitted by U.S. copyright law.

This is a work of fiction. Names, characters, places, and incidents either are the products of the author's imagination or are used fictitiously. Any resemblance to actual persons, living or dead, businesses, companies, events, or locales is entirely coincidental.

CONTENTS

Title Page	
Copyright	
Chapter 1	1
Chapter 2	63
Chapter 3	122
Chapter 4	192
Chapter 5	269
Chapter 6	327
Chapter 7	402
Chapter 8	466
Chapter 9	527
Chapter 10	582
	651

CHAPTER 1

"Quick! Quick! We must be quick!" Flammeldiagbozzforhan insisted for the thousandth time, as Captain Julius Bardol struggled to keep up.

"Get it moving, human," *Dogentaradok* said in his surly way, annoyed to have been drawn from the safety of the cave just to escort an organic like Bardol. "If you don't pick up your feet, we're gonna leave you."

"Don't say that!" *Rhizamorobalafan* shot back, taking the captain's hand and helping him keep moving. She looked at him, her eyes surprisingly tender and warm despite the rapid pace they were setting. "I won't leave you to the *Ahsahklahn*," she assured him.

A thunderous roar a couple hundred feet behind made them all jump.

"Quick!" the eldest of the *Dehlengohl* repeated. "They're going to catch us at this rate! Oh, why couldn't Krancis have landed one of his ships *closer* to us?!"

"Because he's an organic," *Dogentaradok* remarked sourly, slowing to a stop. "They're always screwing things up."

"What are you doing?" his sister asked, as she bolted past him, all but dragging Bardol.

"Buying *him* some time," he retorted, stabbing a finger in the captain's direction. "Now get him out of here before they catch up."

"Be careful," she pleaded, though her pace did not slacken.

"Sure," he muttered, rolling his eyes and spreading his feet a little to face their pursuers.

Doubtfully *Flammeldiagbozzforhan* slowed down, looking between his daughter and his son. Certain that both needed him to survive, he couldn't decide which one to help.

"Go with her!" *Dogentaradock* barked, making him jump. "Make sure they get out alright."

Though uncertain, he nevertheless nodded wordlessly and followed in her wake. Disappearing through a thick wall of leaves, it took only a quarter minute for the *Ahsahklahn* to encounter *Dogentaradock* and bellow from the depths of their souls. The sound carried for miles.

"Father, we must go!" *Rhizamorobalafan* said, seeing that he was still moving with hesitation. "*Dogentaradock* has made his choice. He must bear the risks alone. If our way is just, we shall see him again. You must believe in that."

Steadied by her words, he took the captain's other hand and likewise pulled him forwards. All but dead on his feet after a morning of running, it was all he could do to keep his legs from collapsing under him.

"You must hurry, Julius," *Rhiza* said earnestly, trying to urge him on as he stumbled over a succession of vines and roots. "Your people are near. And then you will be safe."

"What…about…you guys?" he managed to gasp.

"We cannot leave this world," she replied with regret. "It was never our purpose. The task given us by the Reformer remains: we must shepherd and protect the living things of this world." Another roar rumbled behind them. "Especially now that the parasite has drawn so many of the *Ahsahklahn* from their dens. This world will be tormented by them, and it is our duty to lessen that burden as much as possible."

"But you…can't fight…them," he countered. "They're…too strong."

"We must try," she replied bravely, though her tone of

voice bore a finality that made his heart ache. "It is the only way. It is our *purpose*."

Lowering his head as he ran, the notion weighed heavily upon him. But he knew that in her place he would act no differently, and he refused to insult either her or her father by trying to persuade them to neglect their duty.

"We are almost there!" *Flammeldiagbozzforhan* said encouragingly, his hope rising that they would actually be able to reach the egg Krancis had dispatched. "Just a little bit–."

Suddenly an enormous bear made of dark black smoke burst from the trees beside them, knocking the apparitions over backwards without striking Bardol. Torn from their grasp, he tumbled forwards and slid across the ground, his face scraping against dead sticks and fallen leaves. Gaspingly he put his hands under his body and pressed himself upward, turning in time to see the creature raise its claws towards *Flammeldiagbozzforhan* and take a swipe. Dashing between the beast's mighty legs, he pointed at Bardol and snapped his fingers while looking at *Rhizamorobalafan*.

"Run! Go! Get him out of here!"

"No! I can't leave you!" she replied desperately.

"Go! He's your mission now! Only his people can stop this!" he insisted, dodging the ferocious swipes of the bear. "They must survive if life is to triumph in this galaxy!"

Looking between the impish old man and his enormous opponent, Bardol could only gape in wonder. The monstrosity's eyes burned orange, while its body was made of the blackest smoke imaginable. Constantly it shifted and evaporated, as though fed by an invisible fire just beneath its feet. Its claws were like iron spikes, nearly a foot long and built to savage and maim in a single swipe. Yet it moved with a quickness that was at odds with its fearful size. It would take all of the remarkable being's guile and cunning to grapple with such a foe.

"Go!" he repeated, barely slipping beneath another

swipe from the creature's terrible claws. "I can't hold him forever, you know!"

Shaken from his stupor, Bardol struggled to his feet and took *Rhiza's* hand.

"Come on," he uttered urgently, pulling her away. "We've got to go."

Slowly yielding, she allowed herself to be drawn from her father, moving hesitantly until he was out of sight. Turning away from the scene, her lower lip began to tremble as tears formed in her eyes.

"Goodbye, Daddy," she said softly, closing her eyes to force the tears away. Squeezing Bardol's hand a little tighter, she pulled him into a quick run once more. "Hurry," she uttered, gathering steam.

Struggling to keep up, Bardol was nevertheless driven on by the creature he'd just seen, his body finding energy it hadn't had moments before. The continued roars and howls of entities yet unseen further motivated him. He could hear them crowding in on the sides, hemming them within a tunnel that was quickly closing.

"They're nearly upon us!" *Rhiza* gasped, looking over her shoulder at branches that rustled just behind them. "Oh, I think we're too late!"

At just that moment they burst through the foliage into an open area. In the middle of it rested an egg, piloted by a man with an artificial hand.

"Duck!" he shouted, leveling a massive pistol on the runners' backtrail. No sooner had they hit the dirt than a trio of bullets flew over their heads, causing the creatures to halt just short of open ground and snarl from the safety of the bushes. "Come on!" he bellowed. "It ain't gonna take 'em long to figure out this thing doesn't work on 'em!" he added, wagging his pistol.

Jumping to their feet, Bardol and *Rhiza* made for the craft and halted beside it. Looking into each other's eyes, they knew they had only a fraction of a second to convey a lifetime of meaning. Utterly lost for words, they drew each other into a desperate kiss.

"Stop trading spit and get aboard!" ordered Pinchon, cracking off another pair of shots to keep a smokey being at bay. It had only poked an arm out, but it looked to him like some kind of nightmarish vision of a humanoid demon. Spikes of smoke quivered from the top of the briefly visible limb, its hands fitted with vicious claws. Tearing at the air, it drew back at the sound of his bullets crashing into the branches around it. "*Now!*" he reiterated.

"Go!" *Rhiza* urged Bardol. "I cannot come."

"I can't leave you like this!" he insisted, glancing back at the monster that had once again poked its arm out. The colonel fired another pair of bullets. But the entity knew better than to heed them this time. Pressing the branches aside, it stepped into the clearing, revealing itself, much like the bear, to be a being of smoke with fiery orange eyes.

"Forget this!" Pinchon said, dropping his pistol and seizing the controls. "It's now or never, kid," he said to Bardol, shaking his head to indicate there was no turning back.

Pressing a final kiss to his lips, *Rhizamorobalafan* turned and dashed past the creature, just dodging its claws as she disappeared into the jungle. With a horrible screech the entity followed, pushing the branches apart and likewise vanishing. Riveted in place, Bardol could only watch helplessly as *Rhiza* took her life in her hands to guarantee his.

"Get aboard!" Pinchon instructed, snapping him back to reality. "Krancis said to bring you back. He *didn't* say in how many pieces."

Looking up the side of the ship, the captain saw the pistol leveled on him now. Nodding dully, stunned by the self-sacrifice of *Rhiza* and her kin for his sake, he dragged himself up the side of the egg and dropped into the back seat. Instantly Pinchon took to the air, lowering the canopy as the craft rose above the jungle. Searching the treetops for any signs of movement, Bardol could only detect the rustling of the wind. The fatal drama unfolding beneath their bows was hidden from him.

"What was she thinking, anyhow?" Pinchon asked in exasperation. "What were you *both* thinking? If you'd just gotten aboard right away, we could have all flown off!"

"She can't leave this world," Bardol uttered sadly, still fruitlessly searching the foliage below. "She's not a normal being, like you or me. She's a *Dehlengohl*, an entity left behind by the Reformer to shepherd life on Hubertus."

"A *what* left behind by *who?*" Pinchon queried.

"Nothing," he shook his head, drawing a breath and letting it out slowly. "Nothing at all. Not anymore."

"Well, she ran pretty quick," the colonel replied, trying to soften the blow a little now that he'd had a few moments to cool off. "Could be she'll outrun that thing. Whatever it was."

"That was an *Ahsahklahn*."

"That clears things up," Pinchon replied with a hint of sarcasm.

"I don't know what they are," Bardol said frankly. "That's just the term *Flammeldiagbozzforhan* used for them. They're some kind of evil entities. They can run like the wind and will stop at nothing to crush any life that they encounter. That big Devourer mass was drawing them towards it."

"You don't say?" Pinchon asked quietly, the trees beneath them turning into a solid mass of green as they moved away from them. "As if that thing hadn't been up to enough already."

"What?" Bardol inquired. "What else has it been doing?"

"You'll have to talk to Krancis about that," Pinchon punted, not wishing to get on Krancis' bad side by revealing too much to a mere captain of militia. "He'll tell you what you need to know."

Reaching *Sentinel* after a wordless interval, the colonel landed it just as a pair of men reached the hangar. Security types, they wore body armor and expressions of granite.

"Am...I in some kind of trouble?" Bardol asked Pinchon, as the latter shut down the egg and raised the canopy.

"Search me," he shrugged. "Our lord and master works in mysterious ways."

"What?" he asked, confused by this irreverent quip. But he had no time to reflect.

"Captain Bardol?" one of the security men inquired. "We're here to escort you to a room for immediate evaluation. Please come with us."

"What kind of an *evaluation?*" he asked, not liking his word choice.

"Please come with us, sir," his partner repeated, broadening his stance a little, his hand hovering a bit closer to his sidearm. "I'm afraid we must insist."

"Go with 'em," Pinchon advised. "They've gotta be doing it on orders from Krancis. He runs this behemoth like it's his own private yacht. Nothing happens without him knowing about it."

"That is correct, Colonel Pinchon," the first security man uttered. "We are here on Krancis' explicit instructions."

"Told ya," Pinchon chuckled mirthlessly, climbing down first to the visible consternation of the escorts. "What? He's coming!" he protested, as they brushed him out of the way and were about to climb up after Bardol. "Right, kid?"

"Uh huh," the Hubertan nodded, eyeing them for another doubtful moment before throwing a leg over the edge of the cockpit and scrambling down the meager ladder that automatically manifested itself from the side of the egg. The second his boots hit the hangar floor the little foot and handholds melted back into the craft, leaving its hull perfectly smooth.

"Don't worry about a thing, kid," Pinchon said, moving beside Bardol as the security men followed right behind him. "Krancis does this to everybody. Treats us all like criminals until he's certain we're alright. Then he just ignores you or sends you halfway across the empire to get your head shot off."

"Take a right here, sir," the first escort said. "You needn't come along, sir," he added to Pinchon. "We've been instructed to take him to a holding cell until he can be examined. No visitors."

"Well, I'll just come along all the same," the ex-pirate said casually. "Who knows, might be fun to watch."

"Watch what?" Bardol asked, concerned that he'd merely traded one set of problems for another by coming aboard. "What are they going to do to me?"

"Oh, I wouldn't worry about it too much. He'll probably just have one of his psychics kick around inside your head for a while."

"What?!" demanded the impulsive captain, halting where he stood and causing the escorts to move back and draw their sidearms. "What's he think I am? Some kind of terrorist?"

"Keep moving, sir," the second escort ordered, his weapon leveled on Bardol's chest.

"Relax," Pinchon said, grabbing the younger man's shoulder and twisting him forwards again. "He just wants to make sure you're not gonna be a danger to the ship."

"How could I possibly endanger *Sentinel?*"

"I'm sure I wouldn't know," the colonel replied, as they approached the holding facility. "But like it or not, the old bird's usually right. That's the trouble."

Forced to part inside the facility, Bardol was searched and placed within a small cell with smooth metal walls. The ceiling was high, featuring a ventilation grate that was several feet out of reach. Looking at the door, he kicked it several times just to test it. It was unmoveable.

"What have I gotten myself in for?" he muttered under his breath, spinning around a couple times and trying to make sense of what had happened to him. Fully anticipating a hero's welcome after radioing what he'd discovered within the Devourer mass, he was flabbergasted to find himself a prisoner.

But he didn't have long to wait. Within minutes his cell opened, and a young woman stood before him.

"My name is Soliana," she uttered in a quiet voice that was both ethereal and authoritative. Stepping inside the small room, she waited until the door closed before continuing. "Krancis has asked me to examine you."

"Why?" he asked, equally hurt and dumbfounded.

"I can understand your pain," she replied sympathetically. "But you must believe me when I say this was a necessary precaution. To pass psychically into the parasite's mind is no light thing. It may have left a residue behind that will influence you at a later date."

"What, like an infection?" Bardol queried.

"Something of that nature," she nodded, finding the analogy accurate enough for the moment. "The parasite is immensely powerful, and we are not altogether certain of its limits. Especially now that the dark world *Eesekkalion* is no longer able to hold it in check."

"The what?"

"That's neither here nor there," she shook her head, taking a step closer and gesturing for him to sit upon the floor. "It will be easier if you are at rest," she explained when he stood fast. "To explore your psyche from a standing position puts you at some risk. A powerful impulse may pass through your mind and cause you to lose balance. We don't want you to hurt yourself."

"And just what are you going to do?" he asked skeptically, crossing his arms and leaning against the wall. "Read my thoughts? Make sure I'm not lying?"

"I'm going to probe the depths of your unconscious, searching for any signs of the parasite," she answered. "And that process will go much more smoothly if you are cooperative," she added with a slight edge in her soft voice. "There is no reason for you to be apprehensive," she assured him after a moment had silently passed without a change in his posture. "All of us aboard *Sentinel* wish for the same thing: the destruction of the parasite. You are among friends."

"Friends who've locked me up!" he snapped.

"I've already explained why that was necessary. You must understand that we are subject to the exigencies of war. We cannot be too careful."

"Fine," he said, throwing up his hands in exasperation and sliding down the wall to the floor. "Dig around inside my brain," he added tartly.

"I'll be as quick as I can," she told him. "The procedure will be painless."

Smoothly descending to her knees, she moved up beside him and placed her thin fingers on his temples. The instant contact was made the captain was pulled into a fantasy realm of dark, swirling clouds in an expanse of pure blackness. Snapshots of past memories fluttered past, borne on a wind he couldn't feel. Down he fell, tumbling over and under these images until he hit rock bottom. Stopping suddenly on a floor of white mist, he looked around him and saw only darkness. And then he looked up. With a gasp he saw the massive octopus with its many tentacles. Each of them shot forth at once to grab him. But they passed harmlessly through his body.

"It's alright," Soliana commented from behind him, making him jump and turn around. "This is merely an image. It doesn't have an active presence in your mind."

"*That* isn't *active?*" he asked incredulously, stabbing a finger towards the octopus as it drew back its limbs to strike again. In lieu of responding the girl merely snapped her fingers, causing it to disappear at once. "H-how did you do that?" he stammered, again wondering what kind of world he'd stepped into when he'd radioed *Sentinel*.

"I am a very powerful psychic," she replied factually,

her voice still serene. "There is very little that I can't do within the confines of your mind. And that's why we must be so thorough in examining you for the parasite's residue: it is likewise very powerful, much more so than I. If I can manipulate your inner experiences in this way…" her voice trailed meaningfully.

"Then it can, too," Bardol finished. "Or could have."

"Precisely. Now do you see the importance of our task?"

"I do," he nodded reluctantly, a frown nevertheless on his face. "But that doesn't mean I like it."

"Most people do not," she told him, taking a step closer. "It is a terrible violation of one's privacy. It also bears the risk of bringing us into contact with portions of ourselves that we'd rather keep hidden. There are many dark depths within the human soul that each and every one of us would rather leave buried."

"Even you?" he replied with an ironic grin, finding it hard to believe that there could be anything untoward in such an ethereal person.

"Especially me," she answered, the sudden gravity in her voice and expression telling him he'd struck a nerve. "There's a great deal in me that I pray will never see the light of day."

"Look, I didn't mean to…" he began, feeling he'd taken a step too far but unsure how to repair the damage.

"Come, we have little time for talk," she shook her head, dismissing the matter. Taking his hand, she led him along the misty floor into unfathomable darkness.

"Where are we going?" he inquired, curious why she was holding his hand.

"We must travel together, or there is a risk we'll be separated," she replied, explaining her conduct before answering his question. "We must find the portions of your mind that the parasite would be likely to target and search them for harm."

"Then it wouldn't just be lying around anywhere?" he asked. "I mean, it would be targeted?"

"Yes," she said distractedly, her eyes searching the gloom around them. Carefully they moved from one point to the next, as though evaluating the proper course. "Here, this way," she said suddenly, pulling him off to the right.

"What way?" he queried, seeing nothing but more darkness.

"You will simply have to trust me," she responded. "There are markers within your psyche that any good psychic can follow, though they're invisible to you. I see stretched before me dozens of paths we could take. But only one shows any trace of the parasite."

"Then it *has* been knocking around in here?" he asked, his heart clenching at her words.

"Do not be alarmed," she soothed him at once, pausing and looking up into his face with gentle eyes. "The parasite has been within you, as you have been within it. But that does not *mandate* that you have been infected by it. The trail it left behind is akin to bruising in that it is visible but not permanent. It will lead us to anything that might have been implanted within your psyche if indeed anything *has*. But it would equally be here if the creature merely passed through, looking you over before moving on."

"A bull in a china shop," he muttered in summary, glancing around the dark expanse, mystified that she could see things within his mind that he could not.

"In essence. Nothing that large could move through such a store without knocking at least a couple of teacups over. The same is true of a mind as potent as that of the parasite. Despite its best efforts, it would leave marks behind that it doesn't even intend to. That, incidentally, is another reason we were in such a hurry to examine you: like bruising, the trail would fade, which is precisely what the parasite would like to have happen if it *has* implanted anything."

"I understand," he nodded, still averse to his

treatment but gradually coming around. "We had to jump on it while the trail was fresh."

"Yes," she assented. Then she gestured forwards. "This is the jumping off point for another part of your psyche. Are you ready?"

"Ready as I'll ever be," he said with some misgivings.

Wordlessly she stepped forward into what appeared to be empty space. Following slightly behind, drawn ahead by her small hand, he suddenly found himself within a bright room of pure white that assaulted his senses and made Soliana scream in despair. Losing hold of her hand, they tumbled away from each other, suspended in thin air by an unseen force.

"Where are you?" he shouted, his voice echoing off the walls of his mind as every nerve in his body howled with pain. He could hear Soliana whimpering, but the constant shifting of his body kept him from laying eyes on her. "Are you hurt?"

Instantly the space disappeared, and he found himself back inside the small cell with the psychic still kneeling beside him. But there was another man in the room now, one dressed all in black. His hands had been placed over Soliana's when Bardol awakened. Slowly he drew her fingers from the captain's temples, returning them to where she knelt, her head hanging low as if in deep contemplation.

"Krancis?" Bardol asked with wonder. He tried to stand up and salute. But his body was strangely uncooperative, his movements uncoordinated. His muscles, seemingly, had forgotten how to function.

"That'll pass in time," Krancis said, seeing his consternation. With a scowl on his face, the emperor's right hand regarded the young captain for a few moments. "You're going to be a difficult case."

"I...I don't mean to be..." he stumbled, wishing above all else to be an asset to the great Krancis.

"It's not your fault," he assured him. "It's merely

that the parasite has found in you a perfect host for its wicked mind. It wants more than anything to infiltrate *Sentinel* and find a way to destroy it. The exposure you suffered during your contact with the mass allowed it to penetrate your psyche in subtle ways. Were it not for her talent." he explained, glancing at Soliana who yet rested in her contemplative pose, "it would have been perfectly concealed."

"But…what happened, sir?" Bardol inquired, afraid to ask but far too curious not to. "What was that bright space we passed into? And why did it hurt so badly? Soliana was screaming as soon as we were inside."

"You stepped into a fragment of the parasite's implant," Krancis answered. Then he nodded towards Soliana. "She carried you right into a fiber of its thought. Typically one would view it from without, and thus there would be a certain distance. But by placing yourselves right in the middle of it the full force of its evil intent was able to burn its way into your psyches. Being in the presence of such hatred is not easy to handle. It begins to press itself into your mind, in effect countering every impulse that drives creatures such as ourselves to live."

"I don't understand," he replied meekly, still in awe.

"The human mind is both guided and fueled by unconscious directives that are embedded in our very natures. These directives include the drives to live, procreate, avoid harm and loss, and so on. We often think of them as static, unchangeable forces that we couldn't get away from if we tried. But that isn't true: they *are* mutable. They can be changed. And that is what ever-so-briefly began to happen when you were faced with the parasite's implant: the force of its mind began to override the fundamental notions that are hardwired into your genes. It began to rewrite *you*, and your body screamed in agonized protest. It was, as with all painful reactions, attempting to protect you from harm."

"I could feel it," Soliana uttered, her voice trembling,

her body shaking as she twisted her head and looked into Krancis' cool eyes. "I could feel it pressing itself into the gaps between *my* implants, trying to exploit the divisions in my psyche. It could sense my weakness and acted upon it *instantly*." She shook her head, "What kind of intelligence are we trying to grapple with here?"

"One incomparably ancient and powerful," Krancis told her, before looking back at the captain. "You're going to have to remain under lock and key for the time being. We can't afford to risk you in the rest of the ship. *Sentinel* is far too important."

"Of course," he assented readily, seeing the necessity after having the Devourer's immense power shown to him firsthand. "I'll do anything you say, sir."

Wordlessly Krancis nodded. Taking Soliana's arm, he helped the quivering girl to her feet and made for the door.

"Sir?" Bardol inquired as he was about to step out. "Is she going to be alright?"

"Don't worry about me, Captain," Soliana replied, forcing a faint smile. "I've been through worse than this."

"That's debatable," Krancis commented, once they'd gotten outside the detention facility and were moving along the corridor to the nearest teleportation room. "Even your brief possession by the parasite didn't rattle you like this."

"I had to tell him something," she responded. "I didn't want him to feel it was his fault. I *was* in his mind when this happened, after all. It would be entirely too natural for him to take responsibility for it." She glanced at him as they walked, his lean hand wrapped tightly around her arm for support. "Is that really the best we can do for him? Lock him away in a tiny cell with the parasite moving around beneath the surface of his psyche? He'll feel awful in a few hours under such conditions, constantly afraid that it'll rear its head and take possession."

"It's the best for the moment," he answered. "The only thing that comes close in that beast's priority list to destroying *Sentinel* is getting its hooks into me, so I must be cautious in my dealings with the captain. That leaves just you, and you're much too distressed to do him any good at present. No, Julius Bardol will have to bide his time."

"But couldn't we put him in a different room? Something a little less sterile?"

"Security must come first," he said, opening the door to the teleportation room and ushering her inside. "If the implant should do something unexpected, he won't be able to threaten either *Sentinel* or its crew in there."

"I understand," she replied quietly, stepping into one of the chambers and turning around.

"Sleeping quarters," Krancis ordered the technician.

"Yes, Krancis," she nodded, whisking Soliana away.

Moments later he followed.

"What am I going to do now?" she asked, once they'd left the receiving room and were once more walking the halls of the ancient warship.

"You'll rest for a time," he responded, though his mind seemed to be on something else as he guided her unsteady form along the corridor. "You need a chance to reject the influence of the parasite and recenter yourself."

"Then you think I've been harmed?" she asked with some concern.

"No. I think you've been jostled and need a chance to return to a place of equilibrium. The best thing to do at this time is to remove the burden of consciousness from your psyche and to allow the forces at the back of your mind to smooth out the wrinkles."

Stopping at her door, he opened it and helped her inside. Reluctantly she sat on the side of her bed, looking up at him with doubtful eyes.

"I don't feel very much like resting," she admitted, wrapping her thin arms around her stomach in a self-hug as she continued to tremble. "I–I don't feel very much like being alone, either."

"I'm hardly one to seek comfort from, Soliana," he responded factually. "It's not in my nature."

"I know," she said quietly. "But you're the only one I can speak to frankly."

"You've got Hunt and Gromyko," he pointed out. "The former's protected you from day one, and the latter's the only one, beside myself, who's seen the inside of your mind."

"Gromyko doesn't respect or understand the complexities of the human soul," she uttered with some regret. "He's enthusiastic but shallow. And Rex is much too busy to bother with me. I wouldn't think of asking him to wait with me. I'd feel silly."

"But I have nothing better to do with my time?" he asked with a touch of a smile on his lips.

"Oh, I didn't mean it like that," she shook her head with a frown, blaming herself.

"I know that," he assured her, putting his long, thin hand on her shoulder and squeezing it ever so slightly. "But each of us must bear up as well as we can. Already numerous affairs have been placed on hold so I could look after you and the captain. They cannot be neglected any longer."

"I understand," she whispered, looking down.

"You alright in here?" Pinchon asked from the still open door, poking his head inside. "I heard there was some kind of ruckus down in detention. Bardol give you trouble?"

"It wasn't his fault," Soliana informed the colonel as he closed the door and approached. "He was infected with a strain of the parasite's thought. It was so powerful, so *intelligent*," she uttered with amazement, her eyes clouding as she mentally returned to the bright white room and all its pain. "I never thought such a thing was possible."

"You've seen stuff like that before, haven't you?" he asked, sitting on the edge of her bed with avuncular concern.

"In category, yes," she stipulated. "But not in degree. The fragment the captain and I encountered of the creature's thought was incredibly potent. It caught me completely off guard. I–I don't know if I could have broken contact on my own. It seized me as if by the throat, paralyzing me in place. I lost all ability to maneuver in Captain Bardol's mind."

"Then how'd you get out?"

"Krancis saved me," she answered, looking up at the man in black. "He saved both of us."

"Surprise, surprise," the ex-pirate muttered, pleased that she was alright but wishing that rescue had come from some other quarter, the further reinforcement of Krancis' seemingly boundless insight and power troubling him. "Well, is she gonna be alright now?" he asked, twisting his head towards him.

"She's in no danger," he replied flatly, not appreciating the colonel's dislike. "She's suffered no lasting harm. But she needs rest."

"Then we'd best get out of here and leave her to it, don't you think?" he asked, standing up and looking down at her with a small smile. "Anything you need, kid, just let me know." Then he looked towards Krancis. "Unless you've got something planned for me?"

"Not at present."

"Would you stay with me, Colonel?" Soliana asked as they made to leave, the thought of being alone frightening her. "Just for a little while? Until I fall asleep?"

"Sure, if that's alright," he replied, glancing at Krancis. "Any objections?"

"None whatsoever. But don't keep her talking. She needs to rest."

"Oh, yes, sir," he replied with a touch of sarcasm, as the emperor's right hand opened the door and left.

"I wish there wasn't such friction between you two," Soliana said as Pinchon once more sat on the side of her bed. "During times such as these we all need to pull together."

"Just a conflict of personalities, honey," he said with a shrug. "I don't like him, and he returns the compliment. I'm just a little more vocal about it, is all. But I bet you every dime

I'm worth that he'd throw me into the nearest ditch if he didn't need every good pilot he can lay his hands on. He's got no use for pirates, former or otherwise."

"I think you've misjudged him greatly," she countered. "I don't think he'd do anything of the sort. He's ruthless, yes. But he would never go out of his way to eliminate someone for personal reasons. He's much too objective, too rational for such a petty act."

"I suppose you're right," he nodded, seeing her point. "Anyhow, enough about him and me. What about *you?* Are you really alright, or was Krancis just brushing me off?"

"He *says* I'm alright," she began cautiously. "But I'm not so certain. The parasite left an infection in Captain Bardol's mind, and it tried to force itself on me. Krancis believes that I was extracted from the captain's mind in time. But I'm afraid. It was such a terrible experience that I feel some kind of lasting harm must have been done. One is in such a *vulnerable* state when perusing the layers of another's mind. Care must be practiced at all times." She covered her face with her palms and sighed. "I can't believe I just walked right into that trap like I did. The implanted material must have been laughing at me the entire time I was guiding Bardol. Oh, how could I have been so *stupid?*" she demanded of herself, grinding her teeth as her face flushed. Forming a fist, she smacked herself on the forehead.

"Hey, hey, whoa," Pinchon cut in, grasping her wrist and pulling her hand away. "No more of that, little honey. You did the best you could. Shoot, if it took *Krancis* to pull you out of Bardol's skull, that thing must have had a pretty good hold on you. That's not the kind of thing just anyone can deal with."

"I should have known better," she said. "I knew we were stepping into one of the few places that were likely to have implants, if indeed he had any. I should have been more cautious. But I just jumped right in. I–I've never been *reckless* before. I don't know what came over me."

"Well, don't worry about that now," he soothed her, loosening his hold on her wrist and rubbing it for a moment before letting go. "You know better for next time."

"I most certainly do," she agreed gravely, looking off into space as she thought. Half a minute passed before she came back to herself and looked at him. "I think I can sleep now, Colonel. Thank you for waiting with me."

"What, just like that?" he inquired with a laugh. "Sure you don't want me to wait?"

"No, I'm alright now," she answered, her voice calmer and more steady, as though she'd reached a realization. "I just need a chance to rest now."

"Okay," he uttered doubtfully, rising as she climbed under the covers. "Don't forget to call out if you need anything."

"Thank you," she replied almost mechanically, clearly distracted by inner reflections. Feeling that he'd dropped off her radar completely, the colonel snorted quietly and left. Stepping into the corridor, he all but collided with Girnius.

"Watch where you're going, Pinchon," the surly pirate boss remarked, narrowly stepping around him and continuing on down the hallway.

"Yes, sir, Mister Chairman," he shot back sarcastically, following after him. "I'll be sure to do that."

"And just what do you want?" Girnius queried, glaring over his shoulder at him as he moved.

"Just happen to be going the same way, Your Excellency," he retorted, his concern for Soliana putting him on edge. "I'm looking for Krancis."

"As am I. We have arrangements to make about the infrastructure I need to run the Black Fangs."

"You mean for *Wellesley* to run the Black Fangs," he corrected, all but telling him about the AI's backup plan to subvert his leadership and take over the organization if needed. The notion still gave him the willies, especially since Wellesley, despite his independence of mind, would essentially be ruling in Krancis' name. A sizable part of the ex-pirate wanted to warn Girnius to behave himself, to keep on his toes and avoid giving either the man in black or the alien construct an excuse to push him aside and assume control. But his behavior tipped him far enough away from the battered crime lord that he couldn't bring himself to do it. Despite the risk engendered to the one major group he could hide within should things go pear-shaped with the government, he preferred to see Girnius hang himself with his own narrowness of spirit. "After all," he changed tack, "he's the facilitator, the link between you and the organization."

Glancing over his shoulder once again, but this time with a hint of puzzlement in his expression, he digested the colonel's words before responding.

"Wellesley will be acting exclusively on my orders," he informed him. "There won't be any distance between my wishes and his actions. The Black Fangs still have a chairman at their head, and he's not an alien AI."

"Of course," Pinchon agreed, trying to keep the sarcasm out of his voice.

Reaching the teleportation room, the two men chose different places to search for Krancis. Both felt he was on the bridge. But Pinchon happened to call out his destination first, which drove Girnius, irritatedly, to select the library instead to get away from him. With a faint grin the colonel disappeared in a flash of blue.

"I thought I'd find you here," Pinchon said upon reaching the panoramic bridge, where Krancis, seemingly as always, stood with his hands clasped behind his back. Thoughtfully he eyed the lush surface of Hubertus below. "Not a bad view, is it?"

"Indeed not."

"Was that true, what you told Soliana?" he inquired, drawing up beside him and crossing his arms. "Is she really gonna be alright?"

"Of course," he responded without enthusiasm.

"How can you be so sure? She seems pretty shaken up by the whole thing."

Slowly he turned his head towards the colonel.

"If I wasn't certain, why did you bother to ask?"

"Just making sure," Pinchon shrugged. "That little girl's been through a lot. Be a real shame for anything to happen to her. Well, anything more than what's already happened." Giving the air a moment to clear, he changed subjects. "How much longer are we gonna stay here? From what I understand the civilian population is all but spent, along with half the animals."

"Not long. The survivors that remain are being supplied from our excess stores. Once they've been seen to, we'll depart."

"And go where?"

"Are you in a hurry to leave?" he queried, gazing upon Hubertus once more.

"Well, it's not like there's a lot for me to do around here," Pinchon evaded, not wishing to explain that his motive for asking was the man standing next to him. "The empire's aflame, and about the only thing I can do about it is fly a ship. I'm no use to anyone outside the pilot's seat."

"How public-spirited of you," Krancis remarked blandly, the topic exciting not the slightest interest. Pinchon's eyes narrowed a little as he looked at the side of Krancis' face, sensing that he in fact knew precisely why he wanted to depart and wasn't the least impressed with him for it. "But you'll get a chance to act on your noble impulses soon enough," he added, turning towards him again and searching his face with his cool eyes. "There are many tasks that will require your skills as a pilot – dangerous tasks that will leave you wishing for your present state of inactivity. Just relax for a little while and leave the fighting of the war to others. It'll be your turn again quickly enough."

"Reckon I can live with that," he said, as Krancis

pressed a finger against the small radio in his ear and listened for a moment.

"Understood, Captain," he replied. "I hope you enjoyed your rest," he said with the faintest irony in his tone.

"What, my number's been called up already?"

"The mass of flesh that we destroyed has awakened an entire host of nightmarish creatures from the depths of Hubertus. They're besieging what's left of the capital city of Milet. A handful of people have managed to survive the invasion by concealing themselves in the ruins. But the creatures are chasing them from their hideouts and consuming them."

"What do you mean *consuming* them?"

"Precisely what I said. They're consuming them as a fire does kindling. From what we've briefly been able to observe, it's a slow, painful process, taking several minutes per victim. It seems these entities have only a very limited ability to cross into the physical plane of existence and assault its denizens. This results in a relatively slow method of killing. But they'll destroy what's left of the population if we don't extract them at once." Pausing, he again pressed a finger into his ear. "Captain, inform Minister Radik that he is to bring his fleet down here at once to assist in removing the population."

"Even between *Sentinel* and Radik's carriers we won't be able to extract everyone. Why don't we just finish off these monsters?"

"There's too many. It would take countless years to hunt down every last one and destroy them. Especially given that Hunt is the only asset we can deploy against them. He's needed elsewhere, as is *Sentinel*."

"Then we're just gonna leave the rest of the Hubertans to die?" Pinchon asked pointedly.

"There's nothing else to be done," Krancis replied factually. "There are always casualties in war. The unfortunates who are left behind will have to take their chances."

"Some chance," retorted the colonel.

"Then I suggest that you make for the hangar at once and give them the best one you can. Hunt is already en route to meet you there. Depart immediately. Milet will be directly beneath us within minutes."

"Fine," the colonel replied, heading for the door.

Moving quickly, he soon reached the hangar.

"Off on another mission for our lord and master, eh, Rex?" Pinchon asked sourly as he approached the Deltan, the latter leaning against the side of the egg. "Sounds pretty dangerous this time. Nightmare creatures Krancis called 'em."

"Yeah, I've gotten the rundown already," Hunt responded, climbing aboard the egg after the colonel and fastening himself into one of the back seats. "Sounds pretty bad down there."

"You hear we're just gonna leave some of 'em to die?" he queried, dropping the canopy and slowly raising the craft. "Can you believe it? Why'd we bother rescuing this planet in the first place?"

"Hubertus isn't the only place that needs our help, Philip."

"Yeah, I know that," he replied, guiding the vessel out of the hangar and into the bright sunlight. "But he doesn't have to be so miserably *cool* about the whole thing. You'd think we were leaving so many vials of bacteria in a lab. These are real human beings who prayed and pleaded that *Sentinel* would come and deliver them from the Devourers. No sooner do we do that than we leave them to something that burns 'em up like twigs. 'Consumes them like kindling' was Krancis' way of putting it."

"I know," he said with displeasure, frowning as he looked down the side of the small craft. "But we've got to pick our fights. Especially with those other masses out there. We've got to take 'em down before they do the same thing to their planets that the one here did to Hubertus. Or what it did to Soliana, for that matter."

"Reckon you're right," Pinchon said unwillingly, thinking of all the other people who must have been suffering and dying that very moment. "Guess he had a point after all."

"Guess so," Hunt seconded quietly, not wishing to pile onto the colonel.

Without further comment the craft descended towards Milet, the shattered remains of the modest city taking away their words. Everywhere was rubble and dust. Twisted metal supports stuck up into the sky at odd angles, while entire streets were covered in broken walls that had tumbled over. Scarcely a single structure was still intact, except for a few small shops that were concealed between larger buildings. Water freely gushed down many of the roads, the underground network of pipes broken in many places. Trees everywhere were splintered to bits, casualties of stray blobs from Devourer fighter craft as they'd strafed the ground, suppressing the movements of the fleeing population. But there wasn't a single alien ship to be seen. The battle for Hubertus had first been lost and later won in space. Only a handful of craft had remained planetside, and these were quickly turned to dust by *Sentinel's* weapons.

"*Esiluria* has informed me that the remaining refugees are gathering in the northern end of the city," the egg's AI told Pinchon, standing upon the dashboard, her little hands clasped behind her back as she bobbed up and down on the balls of her feet. Her behavior was incongruent, given the gravity of the situation. But he appreciated her light touch. "I'll place a waypoint on your display."

Looking over Pinchon's shoulder from the backseat, Hunt saw it was only a few hundred yards away. Glancing back at *Sentinel* to see if other ships were on the way, he was surprised to see a fleet of carriers rapidly dropping out of the sky towards the beleaguered city.

"Looks like we've got company," he commented.

"Yeah, Krancis said Radik and his experimentals were gonna be helping us out. Moving the survivors, that is. You'll still have to deal with those creatures."

"Looking forward to it," Hunt remarked with quiet bitterness, seeing several of the entities bolt along the streets beneath them, all of them headed in the same direction as the egg. "He say how many there are?"

"Lots. Just lots and lots. Honestly you'd better watch yourself. We can't afford to lose you down there."

"It's not exactly high on my priority list, either."

"Heh, yeah," Pinchon chuckled dryly. Then he stabbed a finger at a point on the ground just ahead. "There they are," he said in a heavy tone, watching as panicking civilians climbed atop mountains of rubble to try and get away from the *Ahsahklahn*. "Just in time."

Popping the canopy, Pinchon lowered the craft as Hunt stood up and began gathering a cloud of darkness around his fingers. Casting bolts from both hands, he shocked the creatures and drove them momentarily back.

"Gonna take more than a few zaps to get rid of these guys," Pinchon shouted, the wind howling around them and all but stealing his voice. "Get down there. I'll ferry off as many as I can."

Wordlessly Hunt jumped from the craft as the colonel got it on a level with the highest part of the rubble. Instantly he was surrounded by petrified Hubertans, each of them fighting to get aboard the small ship.

"One at a time!" he heard Pinchon shout, as he waded through the crowd and cast a succession of dark streaks down at the smoky entities. Howling with pain, their orange eyes burned all the brighter, their mouths opening so wide that they could have swallowed a man whole. All of them looked like the humanoid demon that *Rhiza* had led away from Bardol and Pinchon. There was something horribly familiar about them to Hunt, yet he had no notion of having encountered any such beings before. They seemed to have been drawn straight from his worst dreams.

Charging up a large bolt, he cut it loose and knocked the closest demon off the mountain, sending it tumbling head over heels to the ground below. Shrieking in fierce outrage, it balled its undulating hands of smoke into fists and bounded up the mountain once more.

"Are you the best that Krancis could send?" an old woman asked as she stumbled past Hunt. "You can't hold them back! You're just making them angry!"

"I'm just getting warmed up, lady," he replied gruffly. Closing his eyes, he opened himself up to the dark realm, allowing its power to flow through him more freely. Opening them again, the old woman saw his eyes replaced by orbs of fearful blackness. With a snarl he cast thick smoke against the front rank of *Ahsahklahn*, disintegrating several and sending the rest down the mountain. Reaching the bottom, they looked up at him doubtfully, weighing another attempt. "Is that good enough for you?" he shot at the refugee, his voice thunderous. Struck to her core with terror, she could only vigorously nod her approval.

In the few moments that this exchange required, the air had thickened with eggs from *Sentinel* and transports from Radik's fleet. Pinchon was already halfway back to the flagship, his craft a mere speck against Hubertus' slowly declining sun. All around him people were shouting and arguing and begging, trying to be among the first to depart.

"Mister Hunt! Help!" another woman called from the opposite end of the mountain's flat top. "They're working around to this side!"

Forcing his way through the crowd, he got to the other side just as a dozen *Ahsahklahn* reached the top and seized several of the refugees. Horrific screams escaped their lips as the foul beings wrapped their enormous mouths over their victim's heads, muffling their shouts for help as their bodies began to shake and twitch with agony. With a roar of angry vengeance Hunt unleashed a wave of blackness against the attackers, breaking their hold on their targets and sending them down the mountain. Standing over the battered, horrified refugees, he gestured sharply for them to retreat from the edge of the mountain and then drew another deep blast from the dark realm and sent it flying down the ragged slope of broken concrete and twisted metal. Many of the attackers fell at once, though a handful managed to withdraw down to the streets and scatter.

More screams called Hunt back to the first slope. But now the *Ahsahklahn* were much larger, at least half again the size of their predecessors.

"Keep beating on 'em, Rex!" he heard Pinchon shout over the noise, having just made it back. "We're extracting as many as we can! We just need more *time!*"

Nodding, Hunt swirled his hands before his chest and struck the largest monster with a beam of darkness. Howling with rage, the being threw aside the man it had seized by the throat and advanced on the Deltan. Scowling at his much larger opponent, Hunt surrendered yet more of his mind to the realm of shadow, allowing its might to flow through him as flood waters break recklessly down a dry canyon. The being halted in its tracks, the power too much to bear. It began to retreat, one halting step following another in reverse. But a final push from Hunt caused it to freeze and open its mouth wide in a roar of pain as it disintegrated into the air.

Seeing the difficulty with which one had been destroyed, the remaining three giants cast away their victims and strode heavily towards him. Aware that he could give no more ground to the shadow element without risking a total loss of control of himself, Hunt backed slowly into the crowd that stood at his elbow, many of them touching and holding him for strength as he cast his power against their pursuers. Like triumphant conquerors the entities followed the Earthborn champion part way across the mountain, hemming him and his wards in as another group of *Ahsahklahn* pushed from the opposite slope.

Suddenly a trio of small black streaks shot from an egg and struck the lead demon. Twisting his head to look, Hunt was surprised to find Girnius floating just above the mountaintop in an egg, making small, ineffectual gestures with his hands. Leaping from his ship, he gestured for the refugees to pile in with the pilot and get out of danger. Then he ran behind the massive *Ahsahklahn*, discharging one tiny bolt after another at them.

"Get moving!" he roared at the petrified survivors, their eyes locked on the fearful beasts. "You've got one chance to get out of this alive!"

Snapped out of their collective trance, they poured towards his transport and quickly overwhelmed it. Many tried to hang onto its smooth sides as it pulled away and returned to *Sentinel*.

"Get out of here, Girnius!" Hunt ordered, as another wave of creatures followed on their larger cousins' heels. "Or you're dead meat!"

Ignoring him, the pirate boss ran between the closing walls of *Ahsahklahn* and reached the other side. Bracing his feet, he reached as deep as he could and cast a modest blast of smoke at the smaller attackers, trying to draw them off. In this he succeeded, quickly finding himself surrounded.

Inwardly cursing, Hunt cast a much larger bolt at the pirate leader's assailants, the pain of the blow seering its way through their strange forms, blinding them to Girnius and drawing them to the Deltan.

"Now *beat it!*" Hunt ordered, as the mass of smoky forms gathered around him, crushing him against the remaining refugees. Glancing up at *Sentinel* as he poured forth everything he had to slow the oncoming wave of darkness, he wondered why in the world the mighty warship wasn't firing countless black bolts at the monsters.

"What are we going to do?" a woman pleaded behind

him.

"We're gonna die! We're gonna die!" a small boy exclaimed, every nightmare he'd ever had replaying itself before his very eyes.

The terror of the youth struck something deep within Hunt, pushing him past the restraint he'd exercised heretofore. Surrendering yet more to the dark realm, his eyes went pure black, and the scene faded from before him. To his regret he found himself once more suspended above the sea of the dead, the dull red sky glowing as ever above him. As before the invisible hand of that mysterious essence gently held him aloft, carrying him slowly over the immense floating graveyard. Unable to help himself, he scanned the faces of the dead until he found Milo. Instantly a deep rage filled his soul, causing him to cry out at the sight of his fallen brother. The agonizing reality that he was the last Hunt in the galaxy; that his family had been battered and manipulated by the malignant plans of outside forces; that they were each of them pawns in an enormous, ancient game – it drove him out of the dark realm and returned him to Hubertus. Like an enraged lion he bellowed his righteous fury, sending a tidal wave of shadow against the *Ahsahklahn*, destroying all the smaller once in a flash and paralyzing the giants. Aware that they faced a force that was suddenly insurmountable, they attempted to retreat but couldn't. In a matter of seconds they likewise disintegrated.

With the mountaintop free of adversaries, Hunt dropped to his knees and breathed. It was only then that he noticed black streaks running through his arms. Raising his exhausted limbs before his eyes, he realized that his larger veins had all been darkened by the experience. Rubbing them with his fingers as Girnius approached, he wondered if the color would fade.

"I've never seen anything like that," the pirate uttered in awe. "I thought we were all dead."

"We were," Hunt replied, still studying his arms.

"That's why the dark realm took me."

"Took you?"

Looking up at him, the pirate's features obscured by the light of the sun over his shoulder, Hunt shook his head.

"Nevermind," he said quietly, as multitudinous hands began to press themselves against his back and shoulders. Turning to look, he found the refugees embracing him in speechless admiration. Standing with effort, he turned around just as the little boy from before wrapped his tiny arms around his leg and hugged him for all he was worth. Patting his small head wearily, Hunt nodded and waved and spoke what spare words sprang to mind for the occasion. Unused to such adulation, he quickly found himself at a loss. Recognizing this, and respecting him all the more for it, the crowd gradually left off and began to move in an orderly fashion towards the transports.

"You're a hero, Mister Hunt," Girnius observed. "These people will spread what you've done here far and wide."

"They won't have to," he responded, turning from the diminishing crowd and making for Pinchon's egg. "Krancis'll have this spread across the empire by the time we reach *Sentinel*."

"You sound as if you regret that fact," the pirate remarked, walking beside him across the rubble. "Most wouldn't."

"I'm not most people."

"No, that's certainly true."

With a puff of air Hunt stopped and glared at him.

"I'm not interested in your flattery, Girnius," he said pointedly, the fatigue of his exertions wiping away what little sense of politeness he felt may have been due the chairman. "If you're trying to butter me up, you can forget it."

A faint, smug grin appeared on his face.

"You don't think I'm capable of any kind of respect or admiration at all, do you?"

"I don't," he answered without hesitation. "You push

buttons to get the result you want." He took a step closer. "And I don't like that," he uttered quietly. "Do you understand that?"

"I do," the chairman replied, not batting an eye. "But remarkable though it may seem, I'm also capable of appreciating both power and skill. And you've got both. More than that, you've got the dark realm in your back pocket. That's something I could only ever fiddle with, as you've seen." He shook his head. "That little demonstration of yours back at my house on Petrov should have been enough to convince me, but sometimes I'm a little slow."

"Nobody has the dark realm in his back pocket," Hunt said, resuming movement towards the egg. "It's always the other way around."

"And you don't appreciate that?" he queried, certain of his own stance if such power was his to wield.

"I don't appreciate having my life taken from me," he told him in a smoldering tone. "I don't like being made into a weapon."

"We're all tools," Girnius opined. "Each of us serves someone or something else. Why should you be so different?"

In lieu of answering, Hunt reached the egg a moment later and climbed up its minimalist ladder.

"That was good work, Rex," Pinchon congratulated him, as he dropped into one of the rear seats and leaned back. Glancing into Girnius' eyes as the latter came aboard, he couldn't resist snorting at the meager assistance his paltry powers had brought to the battle. "Next time stay home, Girnius," he chuckled scornfully, glad to twist the knife in his former boss's ribs.

Much too moved by Hunt's demonstration to be offended, Girnius simply strapped himself in and watched the rubble of Milet shrink beneath them as they rose to meet *Sentinel*.

"What happened to the others?" Hunt suddenly asked,

searching the mountaintop for the *Ahsahklahn* that had been pushing against the crowd from the other side.

"They took off once they saw what happened to their brothers on this side of the battle," Pinchon informed him. "Guess they didn't want to push their luck."

"They should each be hunted down and killed," Hunt said implacably, his voice low and dangerous as he contemplated their many victims. "Each and every one of them."

"I know," Pinchon said quietly. "There'll be another time for that. Right now we've got to look after the handful of little lost sheep we've managed to save. Too bad they didn't all wait…" his voice trailed.

"What do you mean?" the Deltan all but demanded.

Drawing a breath, the colonel reluctantly let it out before answering.

"A bunch of 'em pitched themselves off the east and west sides of the rubble, trying to reach ground level and scatter. But they just smashed themselves to pieces and ended up dead by the time they hit the bottom. The drop was just too steep. But with the north and south slopes covered, I guess they thought it was better to take a chance at surviving the fall than being eaten up by those things."

Roaring a mighty oath, Hunt slammed his hands against the seat.

"*At least we won't have to leave anyone behind now,*" Pinchon thought grimly, as a group of eggs flew past to ferry off the last of the survivors.

"But what about the rest?" he queried after a few moments, seemingly reading his thoughts. "Krancis said there'd be too many to take. That can't have been every last soul on Hubertus up there on the rubble."

"They must have been taken down by those monsters," the colonel replied. "Right before you boarded a message came over the radio from *Sentinel's* captain ordering all transports to pick up the supplies that had been dropped off once we were finished with the refugees. Doesn't seem there's anyone left to use 'em."

"I'm going to come back here when this is all over," Hunt vowed. "And when I do, I'm going to destroy every last one of those things."

Too solemn for further words, the other two men left him to his thoughts as they approached *Sentinel*. To the surprise of none, Krancis was in the hangar waiting for them.

"What happened down there?" he asked Hunt as he strode past, so pointedly ignoring Pinchon and Girnius that they knew better than to follow.

"We lost a lot of good people," Hunt answered, heading through the doorway and down the corridor behind it.

"You're quite aware of what I mean," Krancis said, nodding towards the black marks that covered the younger man's veins. "You've been changed."

"The dark realm took me," he explained, still walking but slowing down, certain that Krancis wouldn't let the matter drop until he'd gotten a full explanation. "Something triggered me down there. I guess it was the despair of this little boy that stood behind me. I let myself go – gave myself completely to the shadow. I lost contact with this plane of existence for a few moments, until I saw my brother floating in the sea of the dead." He shook his head. "I was so *angry…*" his voice trailed, finding further words difficult.

"And that brought you back here," Krancis elaborated after a moment.

"Yes. That was when I finished the *Ahsahklahn*. Well, the ones in front of me, anyway."

"It's an incredible feat, even if some of them managed to escape."

"None of them should have," Hunt said sharply, turning his head towards the man in black and stabbing the words at his imperturbable face. "Not a single one."

"The fact remains that many did," Krancis replied evenly. "Their peculiar form of life will continue until they are individually snuffed out." He glanced at the fuming Deltan. "Of course, you've already made up your mind to see to that."

"I have," he confirmed, before casting a curious look at the emperor's right hand. "How did you know that?"

"It's in your nature," Krancis responded. "It doesn't take a psychic to deduce the spirit of vengeance that runs through you. It's part of who you are. It's that very drive for revenge that caused you to emerge from the dark realm after seeing your brother. Were it not so strong, it's an open question whether you'd be standing here right now. Though even with your consciousness absent, it's likely that the dark realm would have looked after your body."

"You mean it might have possessed me?"

"That remains to be seen," he answered evasively, stopping before a teleportation room. "There's little for me to do until the refugees are loaded and we're ready to depart, so I'm going to examine young Miss Aboltina. I imagine you'd like to be present?"

"You said Soliana was going to do that," Hunt pointed out, as the lean man led the way into the room and instructed the technician on duty on his desired location.

"She will be indisposed for some time now," Krancis said once they were both on the other side and heading for the sleeping quarters. "Her work with Captain Bardol has upset her greatly, and that will likely continue to be the case for some time. He has been implanted with a seed of the parasite's thought, and slow, careful handling is absolutely essential. She has no time to perform such a routine task as this."

"And you do?"

"Of course not. But if she *is* genuine in her desire to change sides, she could be of great value to us."

"Why do I get the feeling you're not telling me

something?" Hunt uttered, suspicious of Krancis' sudden change of tack with the unfortunate Erduian. Clearly hostile to her upon their first meeting, something had come into the picture to shift the arithmetic in her favor.

"There's a great many things that I don't tell you or anyone else," Krancis replied factually, as they turned down the corridor that contained Mafalda's room. Instantly the guards before her door stiffened when they saw a familiar dark outline in their peripheral vision. Paying them no mind, Krancis stepped between them and knocked once to announce his presence. Giving Mafalda half a second to prepare, he opened the door and went inside, Hunt right behind him.

"Krancis," she said at once, rolling out of the bed. Embarrassed to have been half-asleep when he'd knocked, she ran a nervous hand through her tumultuous red hair and glanced between the two men and the floor. Still dressed in the clothes Chrissy had given her on Petrov-2, she felt herself to be both a charity case and an unwelcome houseguest. The fact that years of fringe propaganda had taught her to hate and fear the very sight of Krancis made matters all the more confusing. Though the guilt she felt for her actions had more or less effaced the hate, the fear palpably remained.

"Don't be alarmed," Krancis instructed her unsympathetically, moving slowly across the room, his eyes fixed on hers as Hunt closed the door and quietly followed. "I'm here to determine if you're truly in earnest about supporting the empire."

"Oh, yes," she nodded anxiously, her eyes unable to break from his as he paused before her. Though desperate to look anywhere else, she was held as though in a trance. "There's nothing I want more–."

"Your assurances are of no value," he informed her flatly. "Given both your history and your potential usefulness, only a deep dive into your psyche will suffice. Regretfully Soliana is unavailable at this time, so I will perform the examination."

"You?" she asked in horror, the thought of every act of treason she'd ever committed passing before the emperor's most powerful servant terrorizing her. "But...but I..." she sputtered, shaking her head impotently.

"You needn't alarm yourself," he said clinically. "Your past actions will not be held against you. All that matters in the current struggle is what you can bring to the table. And whether you're honest in your desire to employ both your knowledge and talents in the emperor's service."

"I am," she replied, finding a bit of strength in that determination.

"That remains to be seen," he said, unconvinced. "Mister Hunt, if you would be so good," he added, pointing towards a pair of chairs that stood on the other side of her bed. "We must have a stable place to work."

Frowning to be put to work in this way, Hunt nevertheless did as he was bidden and lugged the chairs to where Krancis and Mafalda stood looking at each other. Dropping them none-too-ceremoniously, he pointed them at each other, more or less, and stepped back.

"Take a seat," Krancis told Mafalda, nodding slightly towards one of the chairs. Hesitantly she broke eye contact and moved nervously to the place indicated. Waiting until she'd seated her spare form on the very edge of the cushion, Krancis took the opposite chair and gazed at her for a moment. Then, likewise moving to the edge of his own cushion, he rested his elbows on his knees and raised his fingers towards her temples. Automatically she drew back. "You can cooperate, or we can do this the hard way," he uttered censoriously.

"It was just reflexes," Hunt interjected. "She's not fighting you."

Unamused with his interference, Krancis nevertheless let it slide.

"Lean forwards, and place your head between my

fingers," he instructed her. "Given your work in the fringe, you ought to be familiar enough with this process."

Wincing at this painful reminder of her guilty past, she wilted a little and shifted her weight forwards. The instant her temples slid between his hands her eyes shot upwards and then closed.

"Now the real work begins," Krancis muttered, as Hunt drew a little nearer to watch. "Don't crowd me," he ordered, his own eyes closed as he searched within the young woman's mind. "Leave me a little room to breathe."

"Like the room you're giving her?" the Deltan shot back.

"You spread around your sympathy much too easily," the man in black remarked, both his eyes and those of his prisoner moving rapidly under their lids as he calmly spoke. "You ought to be more cautious with it. Much sooner than later it will cost us dearly."

"Meaning?" Hunt queried, crossing his arms and leaning on one leg. Before receiving a response Mafalda whimpered. Glancing at her, he saw tears flowing out of her closed eyes. "What are you doing to her?" he all but demanded.

"Examining the depth of her conviction," he answered, as though studying an insect through a magnifying glass. "There can be absolutely no doubt as to her–." A scream pealed from her lips, interrupting his sentence. "As to her loyalties," he finished.

"Do you have to *torture* her?"

"She's the one torturing herself," Krancis replied, his eyes still closed. "I have given her the initial impetus. But she's very much in charge of the direction we've been taking. It's part of the game one must play when examining a difficult case. It isn't enough to simply jump deep, though you must do that, too. You must also render the mind unconscious, and watch carefully where it drifts. So far it has drifted in a laudable direction. She is utterly overcome with guilt for her treason, to say nothing of the immense grief she feels over Amra Welter. The path we've followed is the one she wishes to pursue."

"Well, what are you seeing?"

"The tongue isn't fast enough to render it into anything intelligible. The mind is quicker than any physical organ. Besides, it's nothing more than a tapestry of blood. This little one has been up to her knees in it."

"Haven't we all?" replied Hunt, wishing to take a little of the heat off the Erduian but unsure how to given her undeniable past.

"Indeed."

For a time Hunt fell silent, content to watch Mafalda's unconscious yet highly expressive face. By turns she was consumed with remorse, filled with anger, and softened by sadness. Over and over tears dribbled down her cheeks and moistened the expensive shirt Chrissy had given her. As soon as they dried new ones took their place, leaving glistening streaks on her skin. Gradually she slouched, her strength slowly fading.

"Krancis?" Hunt queried, seeing she was close to falling over.

"Mm-mm," he responded, shaking his head slightly to indicate he must concentrate.

Moving to where she sat, Hunt stood in readiness to catch her. Just as she tumbled forwards he shot his hands out and seized her shoulders, causing Krancis to exclaim and jump back in his seat with surprise. With his eyes wide open he searched Hunt's face for several seconds, the Deltan returning his gaze with confusion as he kept the unconscious girl in her seat.

"What's the matter?" he inquired, slipping his hands under Mafalda's arms and dragging her against the back of the chair. As he gently let go, she slumped over the back rest. "You get zapped or something?" he followed up when Krancis didn't respond.

"No," he replied contemplatively, looking between Hunt and Mafalda. "*She's* the one who got a charge out of that."

"What do you mean?" he asked, surprised that Krancis should happen upon the same word he'd used the first time he'd touched her. "What did you see?"

"It's not what I *saw*," he replied with a shake of his head, his eyes still moving between the two of them. "It's what she *felt*. There was a cosmic click, a touch of destiny about the contact you shared with her. And it wasn't the first time. It's happened before."

"We've felt a charge pass between us," Hunt confirmed. "But we didn't know what to make of it," he added, his tone suggesting his willingness to learn more.

"That's a question nobody can answer right now," the man in black replied, dashing his hopes. "All we can do is wait and see how matters unfold. But one thing we can be certain of: the connection between the two of you isn't an accident. It was placed there by design."

"By whom?"

"The correct question is *by what*."

"You mean the dark realm?"

Krancis nodded.

"But what purpose can there be for the two of us?" he objected, though the notion had crossed his mind more than once since meeting her. "We're on totally different paths."

"Perhaps that needs to change," Krancis replied with satisfaction, a faint smile on his lips.

"Now we're back to that thing you're not telling me about," Hunt speculated, pointing a finger at him. "Something's just clicked together for you."

"It has," he confirmed.

"Then why all this mystery? Just spill it."

"There are many reasons why a high official of state would conceal information," he explained evasively.

"Oh don't give me that garbage," Hunt fired back.

"I've given enough of my blood and sweat to the empire to demand the crown jewels without blushing."

"Rest assured that you'll know all you need to very, very shortly," Krancis told him, rising from his seat and looking down at Mafalda. "As will she."

"How much longer are you going to keep her here?" Hunt asked, as the older man made for the door.

"I'm not," he replied, opening the door and dismissing the guards. "She's perfectly pure in her intentions. We needn't apprehend any danger from her. The greater risk is that which she poses to herself. Crushed by grief, she has very little will to go on. She's going to need to be built up, supported and secured by those she trusts. That means you and Colonel Pinchon."

"You mean she may try to hurt herself?" Hunt clarified.

"No. But she may not fight hard enough to save herself should she fall into the wrong circumstances. If she ever were to fall into the hands of the *Pho'Sath* again, they'd break her without even trying."

"I won't let that happen," Hunt uttered, his words as forceful as a solemn oath.

"You'd better not," Krancis said, closing the door and returning to where she lay draped across the chair. Thoughtfully eyeing her, he dropped his voice. "She's been through torture like you've never imagined was possible. They killed her, more or less, and brought her back again and again. Turned her heart on and off, seared her mind, battered her body. It's a miracle that there's anything left of her."

"You think the dark realm had a hand in that?"

"Partially," he replied, still watching her. "Her own talents have flown towards the realm of light, though that's just the product of her training. She has a much, much stronger affinity for the dark realm than its opposite. Given time, and the correct teacher, she could develop quite nicely into an effective conduit for its power. But the true credit for her survival in that dungeon rests with *Deldrach*. He knew exactly, and I do mean *exactly*, how far he could push her without ending her life. He carried her well beyond the breaking point, leaving her limp form pressed right up against death's door without actually opening it. It's a question whether any lifeform is as skilled in torture as the *Pho'Sath*. Even the ghastly terrors of the parasite fall short, given its lust to destroy. It won't patiently savor the snapping of each individual fiber of its victim's body and mind. It just goes for the kill, most of the time."

"So you're saying she would have been better off dead," Hunt commented.

"It would have been far more merciful. It's precisely why *Deldrach* held her back from that. Now she'll spend the rest of her life putting the pieces back together." Raising his eyes to the Deltan's, he spoke more pointedly. "That's why it's imperative that she be given all the help she can get. You must build her up."

"I intend to," Hunt replied, more curious than ever by his shift in attitude.

"Good," he nodded, as Mafalda began to stir. "Keep her company for a while. The deep dive will have jostled a host of bad memories to the surface. It's no time for her to be alone."

"Just one thing," Hunt said, as the man in black reached the door and laid a hand upon its knob.

"Yes?"

"Why didn't you cut loose with *Sentinel's* guns down there?" he asked, nodding towards the floor. "It could have chopped them down in seconds."

"Don't you think we would have tried that *before* deploying one of our greatest assets?" he queried. "The fact is we *did* cut loose. But the beams didn't have any effect. The creatures were able to dodge the dark realm's energy and carry on. That's why they couldn't stand before you: the essence of that realm cooperates with you, lending itself to your aims. When a bolt of shadow bursts from one of our guns, it lacks that intelligent element."

"Then my power is as much my own as it is the dark realm's?"

"To a point. It has a peculiar affinity for you. It moves and flows for you in a way that it doesn't for other people. The same is true of *Sentinel*. Being a mere warship, it cannot *guide* the application of the dark realm with its will. Moreover, the darkness doesn't have any affection for it. That latter quality is something you must have felt when in its presence."

"I have," Hunt confirmed, as Mafalda yawned and then gasped. Sitting up straight, she was at a loss for what to do.

"See to your new friend, Lord Hunt," Krancis said to him, looking at her one final time before walking through the door. "We'll speak again soon," he said without looking back, closing it behind him.

"What happened?" Mafalda asked, as Hunt took the opposite chair and drew it a touch closer. "D–Did he find anything bad?" Her eyes as big as peaches, she feared the worst.

"No, no, he didn't," Hunt assured her, taking her trembling hands in his and squeezing them. "He's given you a clean bill of health. He even ordered the guards to leave."

"But he was so suspicious of me," she protested. Remembering none of the journey through her psyche, it seemed to her as if a mere moment had passed, leaving her situation inexplicably reversed. "How could he have changed his mind so quickly?"

"He didn't," Hunt shook his head, releasing her hands and leaning back in the chair, still tired from his exertions atop the mountain of rubble. "It was only after a very thorough examination that he came to see your sincerity. That, and witnessing the charge that passed between us when I touched you."

"What, it happened again?" she asked earnestly. "Did he say what it was? What it meant?"

"If he does know, he's not talking," Hunt frowned, annoyed at Krancis tight lips. "But I think it was a major part of him changing tune."

"I just wish we knew what it meant," she said with chagrin, looking down and thinking for a moment. Then, seemingly for the first time, she noticed the black marks on his arms. "What are those?"

"A little present from the dark realm," he answered, raising his arms and twisting them back and forth. "Picked 'em up when I was planetside fighting some kind of demon."

"Demon?" she queried anxiously.

"Yeah. They're called *Ahsahklahn*. Would've killed me and what was left of the refugees if I hadn't dropped into the dark realm and gotten charged up. Once I came back, I leveled the ones in front of me and sent the rest running for the hills. I only wish I could have taken them all down."

"I know what you mean," she said. "I feel the same way about the *Pho'Sath*. I wish we could drive every last one of them from this galaxy."

"We will," he assured her, seeing her wilt once more as her mind went back to Amra Welter. "And you'll have an important part to play as we do it."

"It's hard to believe that I'll be able to do anything important after what *Deldrach* did to me," she uttered, raising a hand that still trembled from seeing Krancis. "I'm so rattled that I can barely keep my teeth from chattering. It took every bit of my strength to keep from coming apart when Krancis and Soliana went against me when I first came aboard. Once they locked me in here, I just cried and cried until I fell asleep. It was like my nerves just couldn't take any more strain."

"Well, you don't have to worry about that now," he said, once more reaching out and squeezing her hand. "If *Krancis* is convinced of your goodness, that'll be enough for anyone else."

"Now if only *I* could be convinced," she chuckled with

mirthless self-consciousness, smiling queasily and glancing downward.

"*I* am," he uttered sincerely, the power of his words drawing her eyes to his. "I haven't a shadow of doubt in my mind. Try and draw strength from that."

"I will," she whispered, nodding subtly. "So what happens now?" she asked, her voice a little calmer. "Do I stay here?"

"You're free to roam the ship," he answered, leaning back again. "Anywhere you're not supposed to access will be impossible to get into. So don't worry about stumbling into anything by accident." Then his tired eyes brightened with an idea to get her mind off her troubles. "Would you like me to show you around? It'll be good for you to get a feeling for this place."

"Oh, I don't want to be a bother," she shook her head. "You look exhausted."

"It's not like I can sleep, anyhow," he replied, standing up and gesturing for her to follow suit. "Too tense. Come on: it'll do us both good to amble around for a little while."

Unwilling to argue with her rescuer over anything, she pulled on her shoes and followed him out the door. Hunt intentionally rambled the sleeping quarters for a time, giving her a chance to get her equilibrium back before running the risk of encountering many people. Eventually he took her to a teleportation room and instructed the technician to send them to the cafeteria.

"There won't be a lot of people there," he informed her, noticing the way she shrank into herself at his words. "We're between meal times. Shouldn't be more than a handful."

In this Hunt was absolutely correct. But he didn't know that a certain smuggler would be among that handful.

"My friend!" he exclaimed upon seeing him and his beautiful charge. "Oh, you wound Gromyko to recoil in that fashion!" he added when Hunt reflexively drew back and rolled his eyes, too tired to censor himself. "Nice tattoos, by the way."

"We're busy, Antonin," Hunt said pointedly, as the smuggler drew up and eyed Mafalda with undisguised admiration. "We're just gonna grab a bite and move on."

"Three's company, as they say," he replied by way of justification.

"That's not how they mean it."

"Well, what do *they* know, anyhow?" he countered, his eyes not leaving Mafalda for so much as an instant. "My dear, I can't tell you how *fascinated* I would be to learn more about you. There's something…" his voice trailed, as he raised his hands and massaged his palms with the fingers of the same hand. "Something *magical* about you. You're no mere passenger aboard this vessel. No, sir."

"I really don't want to be made a fuss over," she said shyly, as Hunt frowningly guided her towards the food. "I'd like to keep a low profile," she added in a small voice.

"But how could one *not* make a fuss over someone like you?" the smuggler asked with a laugh. "You're a breath of sunshine," he explained, his enthusiasm making him mix metaphors. "The soulless halls of *Sentinel* are enlivened by your presence."

"You heard her, Antonin," Hunt nearly snapped. "She just wants to lay low for the time being. She's been through a lot. Now, I can see you're about finished with your meal," he observed, looking towards the table the smuggler had occupied upon their entry. "Why don't you polish it off and get about your business?"

"Oh, what business?" he asked breezily, dismissing the notion with a wave of his hand as he leaned upon the cafeteria's counter.

"Get your elbow off there," a woman holding a ladle snapped, clearly of a mind to use it. "Haven't you ever heard of sanitation?"

"Oh, bah!" Gromyko likewise dismissed her, pushing off the counter and moving past Hunt to crowd in on

Mafalda's other side. "No, Rex, I think I should stick around. She can use all the friends she can get."

"That's right," Hunt agreed, his tone irritable as he seized Gromyko's collar and dragged him several feet away. "*Friends*, not breathless admirers. Now finish your food and beat it."

"My friend!" Gromyko protested, shaking loose of his hand and straightening his collar. "Why do you treat Gromyko this way? Haven't we been through every possible danger together? Are we to be split apart now because of this undeniably beautiful girl?" The smuggler smiled when he saw Mafalda's cheeks blush at his compliment.

Sensing that his last human friend from the old days was about to make a comment both of them would shortly regret, Hunt took a step closer and glared down into his eyes. A hint of the dark realm's powers circulating around his eyes was enough to set the smuggler aright.

"But, perhaps you're correct," he uttered with a hint of nervousness in his voice, finally remembering the last time he'd pushed things too far with him. "I wouldn't want to encumber you, anyhow," he added as he retreated, suddenly bolting for the exit as the comment left his lips. Disappearing into the corridor before Hunt could make up his mind whether to strike him or not, he managed to get away with his little barb.

"What did that mean?" Mafalda asked, joining him as he stood fuming.

"It means that Antonin Gromyko has too much personality for his own good," he said in a growl. "Sometimes I'd like to grind a little of it out of him."

"Oh," she replied guiltily, feeling she'd come between two close friends.

Sensing the tone in her voice, he turned and saw her looking downcast as she took a metal plate and gingerly placed a few items upon it.

"Don't you *dare* take responsibility for that," he

ordered her, his voice softened by a hint of a good-natured chuckle. "You're not to blame for what that numbskull gets himself into." Snatching a donut from one of the wells, Hunt put a hand to her slim back and guided her towards a corner table. "Besides, he's been in and out of trouble since the day he was born," he added with a bite of donut in his mouth, taking a seat across from her. "Most of it self-inflicted. He just can't stand anything approaching normalcy. Life's always got to have more zap if he's gonna be happy."

"Then he's like this all the time?" she queried, surprised that anyone could maintain such a high output of energy.

"You'd better believe it. He's a walking circus."

Despite her low mood she chuckled.

"There, that's a little better," he said with pleasure. "A little more laughter and a few less tears."

"I've brought so many of the latter that I don't think I have much of a right to the former," she replied, her face slowly sagging again.

"Don't talk like that," he told her, shaking his head and fixing her with his eyes.

"I'll try," she promised softly, before looking down to her plate. "Don't think I've eaten this well in years," she commented, changing topics. "It'll be a nice change after all those cold meals in Biryth." With this the image of Amra Welter passed before her eyes, the memory freshened by Krancis' perusal of her psyche. Unable to help herself, she suddenly burst into tears and covered her face.

"We'd better go back to your room," Hunt said, rising from his seat and rounding the table to help her up. "This has been too much for you."

"No, no, I'm alright," she insisted, wiping her eyes as he stood over her. "I'm sorry. It was just a…bad memory. Something I've got to learn to grapple with."

"Don't push yourself too fast," he cautioned her.

"I won't," she shook her head. "Please, just sit down

here beside me for a little while. I've got to try and get my bearings."

"Alright," he assented, taking the place next to her and crossing his arms on the table before him.

"So, have you and Gromyko known each other long?" she asked with a sniffle, trying to move forward.

"Oh, for years and years," he said without too much interest. "Sometimes it seems like *decades and decades*," he chuckled, trying to brighten her up a little. "Like I said, he's got too much personality. This isn't the first time he's nearly gotten his head stepped on."

"How does he get along with Krancis?" she inquired, taking a small bite of her food. "They don't seem like they'd be in sympathy with each other."

"They're not. But Krancis can work with anyone who'll make himself useful to the empire. I guess you could say that's one of his talents: putting his personal feelings utterly outside the equation."

"Is that true of his dealings with Girnius as well?" When he merely replied with a pleased smile at her perceptiveness, she elaborated. "Oh, I noticed that they didn't seem too friendly when we were all together on the bridge."

"They're not," he confirmed. "Honestly Girnius is as close as Krancis has gotten to allowing his feelings to affect his behavior. When he first came aboard *Sentinel* they made it clear how little they cared for each other. His usual coolness warmed a little. For once you could see something of how he personally felt about someone else."

"I noticed much the same reaction from Soliana towards me," she remarked.

"Oh, that was just because you'd been a separatist," he said. "She hasn't got anything against you personally."

"I don't think that's true," she replied with as much certainty as she could muster. "I could see it in her eyes whenever she looked at me. It was more than just suspiciousness: she viewed me as a kind of threat."

"Well, Krancis'll put that to rest once he talks to her."

"No, I meant a *personal* threat. Like I'm coming between you and her. I don't mean to be impertinent…" her voice uneasily trailed.

"Please," he said, gesturing for her to continue.

"Do you two have a past?"

"Only in her head," he replied quietly, his tone indicating that she was to keep it in confidence. "She's had a thing for me since we first met. Tried to force her way between me and someone I care very much about. I thought she'd gotten the message, but given what you're saying, I might need to have a little talk with her. I don't want friction aboard *Sentinel* because she's toying with fantasies about the two of us."

"Then you don't feel anything like she does?"

"Not at all. She's a good soul. But I could never see her as anything more than a bizarre kid sister. The fact she's got a half dozen different personalities swimming around inside her head doesn't help that."

"You're joking?"

"Not at all. Well, not *half a dozen*. I don't know the exact count. But she's got a bunch of them. Gives her all sorts of insights, but also makes her helpless as a kitten half the time. That's one of the reasons she's aboard *Sentinel*: she's valuable, but a ready-made victim for anyone with intent and opportunity. She can't take care of herself."

"But Krancis places so much faith in her abilities," she responded.

"Sure – her abilities as a psychic. Offhand I'd guess that she's second only to Krancis himself in that department. But you should have seen her back in the Black Hole. Kept wandering towards a signal that was being sent out by one of the *Prellak* worlds. And that signal just so happened to be calling her to the most dangerous part of the base. No, practically speaking, she's little more than a child most of the time. I don't know just when, but some people seem to have kidnapped her and put all those different personalities in her mind. How I can't imagine."

"Nor can I," she seconded. "I've never heard of anything like that before, even among the *Pho'Sath*. Of course, we were little more than puppets for them, so they wouldn't have shared their more arcane secrets with us." Suddenly her face lit up with fear, and she turned sharply to look at him. "You don't think *they* could have done that to her, do you?"

"I don't think so," he replied with a shrug. "Krancis dove into her mind once and together they saw a scene of blurry humanoid people working upon her. I think if the *Pho'Sath* had been present in their suits and whatnot, that they would have noticed."

"But the memory was already distorted, right? I mean, that's why the people were blurry, so they couldn't be seen?"

"I imagine so."

"So why couldn't they have planted the image of *people* too? Maybe it's just a false trail to hide the truth."

"But what truth would that be? Soliana's had her problems. But on the whole she's been an enormous asset. Even helped us start up *Sentinel* that first time. Why would the *Pho'Sath* help us activate a *Keesh'Forbandai* warship?"

"I don't know," she shook her head, finding some small comfort in that.

"You're still afraid of them, aren't you?" he queried, noticing the way her face had flushed upon mentioning them.

"Yes," she nodded quietly. "They were such a constant presence on Erdu that I feel like they're shadowing me everywhere I go. I constantly expect to turn around and see one looking at me, its mask right before my face." A tremor passed through her body. "Even *Sentinel* doesn't feel safe from them."

"It is, believe me," he assured her easily. "And besides,

Krancis and I are here. The *Pho'Sath* don't want to mess with either of us."

"You mean he's powerful enough to stop one?"

"I think he must be, given all his other powers. Shoot, even if he's not, I'm sure he's thought of a dozen ways to deal with a *Pho'Sath* if one ever got on board. He stays on top of things."

"Most assuredly," she agreed somewhat uneasily, still uncomfortable that he'd gotten an unvarnished look into her psyche. "How much longer do you plan to stay aboard?"

"That depends on Krancis," he shrugged again, leaning back in his chair. "Presumably we're gonna go after those other Devourer masses. But he's been hinting at some other mission for me, so I can't say for sure. At least a few days, I reckon."

"Good," she uttered with relief. "I don't want to be alone with him. He frightens me."

"I think he has that effect on most people."

"Oh, but you must understand how hard this is for me," she explained, shifting in her seat to face him more easily. "I was trained for years to hate him. Any of us separatists would have gladly given our lives to kill him. In many minds he was more important than the emperor himself, because he's so much more potent. Even before he assumed dictatorial power we knew that he was the man of the future. Especially the *Pho'Sath*. They sensed his destiny long before any of us humans did. I can't tell you how many plots were hatched against him. Yet somehow they've all failed." She shuddered. "He's almost like a god in that way – he seems to know everything and never makes a mistake. I think that's most of the reason we hated him so much: his quasi divinity called into question both the power of our allies and the rightness of our cause."

"Well, he's not a god, I can tell you that," he replied with a faint smile, finding the notion ridiculous but not wishing to hurt her feelings.

"Oh, I know," she assured him quickly, not wanting to sound like a quack. "I just meant that he was very disturbing. Even the *Pho'Sath* treated him like he was in some fashion on their level. And given their own god-complex…" her voice trailed meaningfully.

"I see what you mean."

"But it's more than that," she continued, looking off into space as she spoke. "When I look into his eyes I see something that I've never seen in anyone else's: I see fate, death, the end of all things. He's like some kind of…dead end. The final chapter." She glanced at him with an apologetic little smile. "I'm sorry. That must sound awfully silly. But I can't escape the feeling that I'm looking at a man with no future. It's as if tomorrow doesn't exist for him. Or that it's already happened, and he's come back from it like a ghost in order to review it. I think that's what truly unsettled the *Pho'Sath*: it was as though he knew their moves in advance, and even their great insight couldn't help them around that. It cast doubt on their own divinity."

"That reminds me of something I've been meaning to ask you," he said, likewise turning a little more towards her. "I've heard them talk about some kind of journey that they're going to take. What's that all about?"

"We were never allowed to know much about it," she shook her head. "Oh, they talk about it endlessly, but never in detail. It's secret knowledge that only they're really allowed to have."

"But they wag it around and you're supposed to be impressed with it?" he summarized.

"Yes, that's right. They never made any bones about the fact we couldn't participate in it. Honestly a lot of us were rather awkward about it and tried to avoid the topic as much as possible. It was the one thing that made us feel they weren't altogether sane. Our best guess was that it was some kind of salvation from death."

"That explains their fanaticism," Hunt murmured to

himself, thinking for a moment. "Tell me, how do we fit into this whole picture? What's their beef with us?"

"To be honest I'm not sure. Oh, I know what they *said* the problem was with the empire. Allegedly it constituted an aggressive threat to the entire universe and had to be destroyed. We were all too ready to believe something like that, given our experiences on the fringe. But the last thing they'd care about is peace in the universe. I think it must be connected to this Journey of theirs somehow."

"It's hard to imagine how. If they have found some way to transcend, what could we do to stop it? We don't have either the technology or the psychic gifts to stand in their way. If it wasn't for the treaty with the *Keesh'Forbandai* we'd have been swept away ages ago."

"Maybe they're not ready yet, and they're afraid we'll gradually grow into a threat. They *are* allied to the light realm, and we're more strongly affiliated with the dark. Given your emergence, to say nothing of Krancis and *Sentinel*, they may fear that we're going to grow under the aegis of the *Keesh'Forbandai* into a major dark power. You've already proven capable of destroying their operatives."

"I'm just one man," he objected quietly. "I can't threaten an entire race of fanatics."

"All it takes is one man to start a revolution," she replied. "A single voice can multiply infinitely. Your dark power could easily be the inspiration that carries humanity on the next step of our development."

"Krancis seems to think so," he said with aversion, thinking of the dynastic ambitions he had for the Deltan.

"But you don't?"

"I don't want to be some kind of figurehead for humanity," he answered. "I play the part Krancis has marked out for me, more or less. But I never wanted any of this. Shoot, it wasn't so long ago that I was scraping a living out of the snows of Delta-13. I was an exile, a forgotten nobody. I'd have preferred that in a lot of ways."

"But your life is so much better now," she objected, visibly confused.

"It's more *active*, but I'd hardly call it better. I've lost my father, my brother, and the world I knew ever since childhood. It's true, I've gained a relevance for the empire that will ensure I'm never forgotten. But moving from one battle to the next isn't my idea of the good life. Countless worlds lay shattered, denuded of their populations; two alien threats are battering our people; and somehow fate has singled me out as the answer to the whole problem. It started with me activating *Sentinel*. For a time that seemed like it would be enough. But then I keep getting dragged deeper and deeper into this. Now Krancis is trying to get me to abandon the woman I love so that I can have an heir to carry on the dark legacy of the Hunt family."

"Why does he want you to leave her?" she queried quietly, aware that the topic would be sensitive.

"She has an incurable disease named Valindra," he confided quietly. "What, you've heard of it?" he asked when her face tightened.

"I have," she nodded. "Someone very close to me once had it."

"Who?"

"My sister Arida," she answered regretfully, thinking of the last time she saw her alive before *Anzah* disintegrated her body before her eyes. "We searched everywhere for a cure. But we could only find it in one place."

"Where?" he asked earnestly.

Slowly she turned her head to look at him.

"Among the *Pho'Sath*. Only they have the power to cure something like that. But they're the last people who would heal her."

"I wouldn't be so sure about that," he replied. "When I fought those assassins to protect Girnius, one of them broke my leg. I compelled her to heal me on pain of death. I'd say they can be brought to the table if the right motive is held out for them."

"That sounds very unlike the *Pho'Sath*," she commented. "I've never seen one barter for life like that."

"Well, she was also buying time for her Journey Partner to sneak up behind me and slug me."

"Oh, that makes sense of it," she replied. "I don't think any of them would trade their lives by giving in to extortion with one of us. They pretty much think of us as bacteria. It would debase them to do so. Of course, if it was all just part of a ruse, then they'd still feel they were on top of the game."

"That could be manufactured easily enough. I could tell 'em that I'll go into exile or something if they heal Lily first. Make a trade that would have them come out the absolute winners as far as they're concerned."

"And then?" she asked hesitantly, worried that he'd actually go through with it, leaving humanity to its fate.

"Well, I'd have to welch on it, wouldn't I?" he asked. "Not that I break my word easily. But if it's gonna save someone's life, you couldn't do otherwise. And I sure wouldn't do anything else for Lily. Any price is worth paying if it saves her."

"I wouldn't set my hopes too high for deceiving the *Pho'Sath*," she cautioned him meekly. "They have peculiar powers of insight. They'd probably see right through it."

"There's got to be *some* limits for what they're capable of," he objected. "They can't see their way through *every* deception. Honestly I think half of the talk of their powers is just superstition."

"A great deal of it is," she confirmed. "But not all of it. They know things they shouldn't, and you can never tell just what it's going to be. It put all of us on edge lest we think thoughts that could've displeased them. It made us all the more fanatical as a way of driving anything from our minds that they wouldn't like. It was probably the single most powerful motive for conformity that we had."

"Sounds like you guys were almost prisoners of

theirs."

"Oh, yes," she nodded. "Not that any of us would've admitted that to ourselves at the time. But it never escaped our minds how we were caught between two points. On the one hand was the empire and the certainty of retribution if we were caught. On the other was the *Pho'Sath*, and their terrible powers of both insight and torture. In the middle we stood, with what we *thought* were ideals of liberty and justice for the fringe. Of course, now I can see that we were just pawns in a larger game, never strong enough to stand on our own. The *Pho'Sath* had their hands on our strings the whole time, each of our moves just part of a dance that they controlled."

"And how does that make you feel?" Hunt queried, genuinely curious.

"Honestly? Like an idiot. I can't believe all the time and energy I spent on a cause that had nothing to do with either the fringe or the ideals I thought I served. I wish I could take it all back for those reasons alone. And when you add in all the suffering I caused in their name…Well, it doesn't make it easy to sleep at night, I can promise you that."

"I know," he sympathized quietly, reaching over and giving her shoulder a modest squeeze. "That'll pass in time, once you've had a chance to pay some of it back."

"You don't believe that," she said gently, looking at him with broad eyes.

"I was hoping *you* would," he grinned mirthlessly, releasing her shoulder and resting his elbows on the table, clasping his hands as he looked out across the cafeteria. "I've both hurt and killed people, Mafalda. I know what you're going through. You never get *over* it, you just get *past* it. The images are always going to be in your mind, and they'll guide you, making you the woman you'll be tomorrow. That's a part of life. Probably the most important part. It's our *mistakes*, it's the things we do *wrong* that shape us more than anything else. And we can't reject the memory of them, or we'll be nothing. We can't let them go, because they're part of us. You need to draw on those failings to guide you when you're unsure where to turn. You need them to fuel you as you reach higher and higher, striving to achieve something good. Take the things you've done and make it your mission to learn from them. In place of pain, bring healing and peace. Instead of suffering, give hope to those who have none. I know that a gentle heart beats in that chest of yours. Give it a chance to ache, to regret its choices, and then to make them good."

"I never dreamt you were such a philosopher," she smiled appreciatively, comforted by his words.

"Oh, that's because of my time on Delta," he said with a dismissive shrug. "You get an awful lot of time to think when you're surrounded by nothing but snow. You either think, turn to booze, or go nuts. A lot of Deltans took the middle choice, and a few the latter. Almost none took the first option. It was too painful in the absence of hope."

"You did," she observed.

"I never had it in me to hide from the truth," he uttered almost regretfully, that attribute having burdened him for years. "A fact is a fact, and I'm compulsive about facing them. Especially when they're negative. I'd have been far happier washing my cares away with third-rate moonshine like the rest of them. But I could never cut loose like that." Quietly he snorted at himself and then looked at her. "I *was* a bit of an adrenaline junky. Half the time I hunted artifacts just to get away from the monotony of life in Midway."

"Did you find anything really rare? Well, besides Wellesley."

"Not really. Most of the good stuff had been taken long before. Probably even before humans set foot on Delta. By the time I went digging through the snow it was mostly trinkets. Finding Wellesley was a miracle. I still can't believe no one else snatched him first."

"Maybe the planet orchestrated that, guiding others away from him and you *towards* him."

"I've thought about that," he agreed. "You're probably right. Too bad we'll never know, now that the Devourers have finished it off." He shook his head, feeling sorry for the ancient being. "Too bad," he repeated.

"What about the other living worlds?" she queried. "Are any of them left?"

"I can't say," he shrugged. "You'd have to ask Krancis. I've been too busy with other things to pay attention. There *are* some *Prellak* worlds left, but they're not likely to be of use to anyone, even themselves. Without their leader they're rudderless. Just marbles dropped in a big black pond."

Just as she was about to respond, a group of disheveled refugees entered the cafeteria, led by a guard. Quickly more groups followed, until the room was filled with the sounds of their shoes upon the floor and their quiet comments to one another. Every inch of the ship was searched by their eyes, the wonder and majesty of *Sentinel* holding them in awe. In short order the reclusive Deltan and his fiery-haired companion were noticed, drawing respectful nods and hesitant waves. Sensing that he wished to be left alone, they did their best not to gaze too openly. But this determination was shattered when a little boy shot across the room, dashed under Hunt's table, and seized his lower leg in a bear hug.

"Thank you for saving us, Lord Hunt," he said with a lisp that melted Mafalda's heart and made the Deltan smile from ear to ear. Reaching under the table, he drew the tot up and set him on the table before them. "What are these?" he asked, putting his little hands on the black marks that ran up and down the veins of his arms.

"They're a promise," he answered, as the child's mother neared the table in a fluster. "A promise to never let anything hurt you, or your mom," he nodded towards her, "or any other human ever again. They're my commitment to our people. Can you understand that?"

"I think so," he uttered, his little eyes wide as he gazed into the weary face of the Earthborn champion. "You've crossed your heart," he translated, drawing an X on his chest with his tiny index finger.

"Yes, I have," he confirmed, nodding sincerely to the boy. "I absolutely have."

"I'm sorry, Lord Hunt," his mother apologized, taking her son and lifting him off the table. "I hope he didn't bother you."

"Not at all," he assured her, smiling as she took the little fellow away. Then, in a lower voice, he added to Mafalda, "That boy saved our lives today."

"How?" she asked, looking between him and the child.

"Somehow, over all the noise and screams I heard him say that we were all going to die. And that triggered something in me. I knew I couldn't let that happen. That little guy has only begun to taste life, and I had to make sure he had a chance to see the rest of his natural days. I wasn't about to let those smoke creatures get to him. It was then that I surrendered even more of myself to the dark realm. Filled with its power, I came back with these marks. Even now I can feel it coursing through me more potently than it ever has before. Honestly," he concluded in a whisper, "I think I may have gone too far."

"Too far?" she queried, shaking her head.

"I think it might be pulling me in, taking me over," he explained, his voice surprisingly calm. "I don't know for certain. But it stands to reason, given these marks," he added, rubbing his forearms. "What started as an ability to inspire fear has turned into a power so great that it defines me more than anything else does. People no longer see Rex Hunt, exile of the government. They see the man of dark power riding upon a steed of shadow to their rescue. And that's because of the ever increasing role that this element has in my life. There may well come a time when the dark realm pushes me aside completely, using me as nothing more than a vehicle for its expression."

"Have you talked to Krancis about it yet?" she inquired softly.

"No, I haven't felt like it," he replied. "I've had enough things going on today without adding this on top. Once I've gotten a good night's sleep I'll be in a better place to hear bad news."

"Then your mind's already made up?"

"Pretty much. Unless the dark realm decides to stop part way, it seems that it has to take me over sooner or later. I can feel the solicitousness with which it views me every time I visit it. Like Krancis says, it's got a special affinity for me."

"But maybe that'll stop it from consuming you," she pointed out hopefully. "You can't appreciate something if you absorb it into yourself. You have to let it be itself."

"I don't think the dark realm agrees with you," he responded, again holding up his arm, illustrating his point with the marks. "I'd say it's put its brand on me. It remains to be seen how much further it'll go." Glancing up at the ever expanding crowd, he nodded towards the entrance and slid his chair back. "We'd better get out of here while we can still squeeze through the door. There's gonna be a lot of hungry people coming this way."

Making their way through the packed hallways of *Sentinel*, his lordly status permitted them to cut through the line at the teleportation room and jump for the sleeping quarters.

"I'm sorry you had to spend so much time with me," Mafalda apologized as they neared her room, though she'd been very glad for his company. "I should have let you go much earlier. You must be exhausted."

"Nothing a few days in the sack won't fix," he chuckled, stopping before her door.

Looking up into his tired eyes, she opened her mouth to speak but could find no words. Nodding his understanding, he squeezed her shoulders again.

"Just try and get some rest. You've got a long road ahead of you, but I know you can make it if you give yourself a chance." Letting go, he was about to turn away when she put her hands on his shoulders and pulled herself up high enough to give him a peck on the cheek. Then she disappeared into her room. With a smile he turned towards his own room.

CHAPTER 2

"Mister Welter, I'm afraid that we must have an answer much sooner than later," Doctor Keelen insisted, his voice firm though respectful. "Kren-Balar is in danger of coming apart at the seams if we don't quickly replace Seldek with a leader who can inspire confidence among our people. That places us in the crosshairs of not only the discontents within the base, but also those of the many enemies that are outside of it. Should even a single dissatisfied Kol-Prockian manage to escape Kren-Balar, he would put us immediately at risk of being found out."

"Then I suggest you keep the door locked 'round the clock," Welter replied flatly. "But you're not talking to the emperor until he's in the kind of condition that will permit him to judge this matter calmly. He's been through far too much lately to weigh the potential ramifications hastily. When he's ready to make a decision, you'll be the first to know."

On the verge of arguing, Keelen thought better of it and nodded his defeat. Turning towards the antcroom's entrance, he reached the door and then stopped. Thinking for a moment, he looked over his shoulder.

"I hope for both our sakes he acts quickly. Already I've been forced to change several of the guards that I'd stationed outside this room for fear of disloyalty among them. For his own safety he must assume command at once."

With this thought he left Welter alone.

"Always has to get in the last word," he remarked, crossing his arms as he sat in his usual chair beside the chamber's door. Settling in for a long wait, he quickly discovered this was unnecessary when the door popped open and Tselitel's worried face poked out.

"Gustav, we've got a problem," she uttered gravely, gesturing urgently for him to enter.

Rising from his place, he walked into the large space and glanced around. In one corner of the room he saw *Karnan* sitting on the floor as always, his back against the wall, his arms loosely folded over his chest in a doze. On the other side lay Rhemus, his eyes closed, his breathing slow and relaxed.

"What's the deal?" he whispered to Tselitel, who stood nervously wringing her hands beside him.

"What do you *feel*, Gustav?" she urged him.

Pausing again, he allowed the sensations of his body to fill his mind. At that moment he noticed it.

"The chamber's offline," he said at once.

"Yes," she nodded anxiously. "I think something must have broken. What are we going to do?"

"Wake up Mister Genius," he said factually, moving to where *Karnan* sat and taking a knee beside him. Not particularly well disposed towards the ancient scientist, he put a hand on his arm and shook him a little more roughly than he truly needed to.

"What...what's going on?" he asked, as though emerging from an inebriated haze. Momentarily he glanced between the two humans, before gazing off into space and uttering an oath in *Kol-Prockian*. "The chamber's offline," he said with profound anger, shutting his eyes to hold in his outrage. "Why does technology always break down just when you wish it wouldn't?"

"Fate," Welter replied unsympathetically. "Can you fix it?"

"That depends on what's wrong, doesn't it?" *Karnan*

shot back. "Could be something simple like a fried wire. Or it could be half the machinery has finally broken down. With a piece of tech this ancient, you can't rule anything out."

"Then you'd better get to work, hadn't you?"

"Does he always point out the obvious?" *Karnan* asked Tselitel.

In response to this the burly bodyguard seized his upper arms and dragged him to his feet.

"Alright, alright," the old scientist uttered, shaking off his iron grip and moving unsteadily towards the door. "I'll get my people in motion. Should know more within the hour."

"I wish you wouldn't be so hard on him," Tselitel fretted to Welter once the alien had gone. "He's terribly frustrated and embarrassed to see the once great technology of his people fail at such a decisive moment in their history."

"Can't say I'm a big fan of it myself, Doctor," Welter replied, crossing his arms and watching Rhemus as he slept. "How's he been?"

"Quite well, in fact. Though I'm not sure how long that will last. If *Karnan* can't get this thing running again soon…" her voice trailed.

"We'll cross that bridge when we get to it."

"Of course."

"Stay with him," he instructed, turning for the door. "I'm gonna make sure *Karnan* and his monkeys get it into gear."

As the door quietly clicked shut, Tselitel padded on bare feet to where Rhemus lay. To her surprise his eyes opened at once.

"How long will it take them?" he queried.

"*Karnan* isn't sure. He says he'll know more in an hour or less."

"I guess that'll have to do," he replied, closing his eyes and taking a deep breath. "How are you holding up, Doctor?"

"Oh, I'm fine," she answered a little too quickly,

drawing a modest frown from him. "Well, I've been better."

"I think that's true of us all," he remarked, shifting a little where he lay. "Even Gustav seems more tart than usual."

"He's worried about conditions inside the base," she informed him, having spoken with their escort some time before *Keelen* had. "The situation is deteriorating rapidly. Despair is filling *Kren-Balar*."

"Which means they need an answer from me," he observed with a heavy sigh.

"Yes," she agreed quietly, though the earnestness of her desire that he would assume command was palpable in her voice.

"It's not the sort of decision one should make lightly," he told her. "These *Kol-Prockians* seem to do everything on impulse, so they can't understand why I'd make up my mind at any speed but instantly. But given the instability within the base, I'm not completely convinced that the announcement that I'm taking over wouldn't plunge what's left of the population into anarchy. I'm alive to their assurances to the contrary, but I can't believe that a proud people would accept a foreign ruler without at least *some* misgivings. I don't want to shatter what's left of order by sparking a civil war between those who agree with the takeover and those who don't. What would happen if the opposing forces should take control of the infrastructure that keeps the base habitable? What if they cut the power or damaged the air purification system and then abandoned the base? No, this requires careful planning. We'd have to be utterly certain that all essential portions of the base are under our control first. And that means relying on Doctor *Keelen*. He's the only one in a position to know who among his people is loyal and who isn't. And I must say, given his utter failure to recognize what *Seldek* was doing, I'm not filled with confidence in his abilities."

"There's a great deal of risk no matter which course is pursued," she agreed.

"But you think I should assume control of *Kren-Balar*?" he inquired, opening his eyes and looking at her.

"Yes, I do. I think it's the best chance we have."

"You're probably right," he said, closing his eyes again. "But I'm not ready to sign off on it yet. I need more time to think."

"Of course," she replied, taking his hint and quietly making for the door. Seeing Welter and *Keelen* arguing with quiet passion on the other side of the glass, she tapped against the window thrice to stop them before stepping out.

"How is he, Doctor Tselitel?" *Keelen* asked at once, glad to put Welter on hold.

"He's fine," she responded, crossing her arms against the relative chill of the anteroom and joining them. "He said he needs more time to consider the situation in *Kren-Balar*," she added, aware of what was truly on his mind.

"*How much more time–*," he nearly exploded, barely catching himself and taking a breath. "I hope you pressed upon him the seriousness of our situation."

"I have."

"Then why is he waiting so long?"

"Perhaps that assassin in the hangar had something to do with it," Welter fired at him.

"If that were so, the dozens of *Kol-Prockians* who put their lives on the line to escort him *away* from there should have tipped him the other way," *Keelen* shot back. "No, I fear that your emperor has simply grown infirm from his disease."

"It wasn't so long ago that you thought he was more than tough enough to run our empire and your little base."

"Perhaps it was all just wishful thinking," he uttered with self-pitying flippancy, his emotions carrying him away. "Perhaps this truly is the twilight of my people."

"I doubt that," Welter remarked caustically. "You couldn't keep your mouths shut long enough to stay dead."

His pride wounded, *Keelen* looked poised to strike him.

But half a moment's thought reminded him of the ease with which Welter had dispatched the assassin in the hangar. Emitting a snort, he could only glare at the surly human.

"Where's *Karnan?*" Tselitel asked, trying to cool the temperature of the room.

"He's consulting with his engineers as we speak," *Keelen* replied sourly, still eyeing Welter. "Most of the machinery for the chamber is accessible from outside the room, so it shouldn't be necessary to disturb your emperor during this process." Just as he was about to say more the lights flickered and went dim.

"What's wrong?" Tselitel asked anxiously, fruitlessly looking around the anteroom.

"One of two things," *Keelen* replied. "Either our power plant is in trouble, or the chamber is coming back online." He pointed towards the chamber's door, his eyes bouncing around the room as he thought. "Check and see if it's working again."

Making for the door, she paused when the lights once again shone brightly. Glancing back at Welter and *Keelen*, the latter urged her on through gesture. Reluctantly sticking her head inside the chamber, she was profoundly relieved when she once more felt its healing charge filling the air.

"It's running again!" she exclaimed, covering her mouth when she remembered Rhemus. Quietly closing the door in apology, she rejoined the other two. "I'm glad they were able to get it running again so quickly."

"*Karnan* is a brilliant scientist," *Keelen* uttered proudly, as though the repair had been a foregone conclusion. "It's natural that he should have found the answer quickly."

"Yes, of course," Tselitel replied, noticing the roll of Welter's eyes as he walked past her and settled into his chair once more. The tension between the other two still palpable, she decided to wait with them until *Karnan* returned and made his report. But the wait was brief. She'd barely settled into a chair by the table when the door burst open, swinging 'round on its hinges and slamming against the wall. Through it shambled *Karnan*, his body trembling with rage as one of his engineers endeavored to help him.

"Oh, let go of me!" he all but shouted, shaking off his assistant who melted back into the corridor, quickly closing the door behind him.

"What's wrong?" Welter asked, his arms crossed and a leg thrown over the other. His tone indicated he already had more than an inkling of what it was.

"Sabotage!" the alien exclaimed. "Sabotage, pure and simple! And in a form that wasn't easy to find, either! Whoever did this knew what he was doing."

"Then how'd you find it so fast?"

"Because I know that chamber like the back of my hand!" *Karnan* snapped. "I've lived and breathed it for so long that I've got a sixth sense about it. But anyone other than me would have spent at least a week trying to figure it out."

"Then it's one of your engineers," Welter observed.

"Obviously."

"But if even the engineers have turned against us..." Tselitel murmured gravely, more to herself than to them.

"The *engineers* haven't turned, my dear," *Karnan* assured her, holding back enough of his seething temper to calm her fears. "If all of them did, the chamber would be broken for good. No, this was a lone actor. Or perhaps two at the very most. Any more than that and the job would have been much more thorough. They had to act quickly but discreetly to avoid getting caught by the others. Hence why they didn't have time to do any meaningful damage to the machinery. It was a simple fix, once discovered."

"But the fact remains that the chamber is both vulnerable and on their target list," Welter said. "Sounds like they don't want Rhemus hanging around here any longer."

"Yes, that's clear enough," *Karnan* replied, making for the table and feebly settling into a seat. "Neither Doctor

Tselitel nor myself would justify destroying one of the last great artifacts of our people. They must have gotten wind of our proposed power transition."

"I don't see how they could have," Tselitel chimed in. "I mean, we're the only ones who know about it, right? Unless *Seldek's* office was bugged or something."

"Or *someone* can't keep his mouth shut," Welter said accusingly, glaring at *Keelen*.

"It was hardly a matter of choice, Mister Welter," the *Kol-Prockian* shot back. "I had to test the waters among the higher–."

"You should have kept silent!" cut in *Karnan* sharply, smacking his frail hand against the table beside him. "Why is it that *none* of this present generation..." his voice trailed as he ground his teeth, looking down at the floor with a mixture of anger and exhaustion. "*Why is it...*" he began again, laboring for breath.

Wordlessly Welter arose, looking at Tselitel and nodding her towards *Karnan*. Taking one arm in his powerful hands, he waited for her to take the other. Together they helped the weakened scientist back into the chamber, his protests continuous but lacking any kind of energy at all. Then they returned to the anteroom.

"Well, *Keelen*, looks like you've done it again," Welter remarked. "By now every ten-cent revolutionary in *Kren-Balar* will have his sights on Rhemus."

"What can we do?" Tselitel interjected before the doctor could respond, trying to keep the conversation productive.

"There's only one course of action open to us," Welter told her, leaning against the wall beside the chamber's door and crossing his arms. "What's left of *Kol-Prockian* society is in tatters. Neither the soldiers nor the engineers can be trusted. From bottom to top it's riddled with mold. All we can do is contact Krancis and have him send a garrison we can actually trust."

"What! Invade *Kren-Balar!?*" *Keelen* exploded. "You would take a bad situation and make it disastrous. What greater fuel would the discontents require than an expanded human presence?"

"You were all for an expansion of our presence when you were arguing with *Seldek*," Welter countered.

"That was before I knew how deeply the cancer ran," *Keelen* protested. "I thought it was just the lower echelon that harbored such notions. To find that even our brightest minds aren't immune to such madness has changed the face of the matter entirely. If *they* can't see the advantages of Rhemus assuming command, then there's little doubt that many others won't be able to, either. We'll simply give a stimulus to those individuals who haven't turned yet, and further motivation to those who have. No, it's much too dangerous."

"It's much too dangerous *not* to," Welter replied. "But I agree that there is risk involved, which is why we'll conceal what we're doing until the last possible moment."

"And then what? Just spring the trap? Fill the landing pad with human soldiers and overrun the base?"

"No. First you'll put people you can actually trust in charge of the hangar entrance to ensure that our forces can get inside. Then you'll be on hand to greet them, explaining to your people the necessity of their being here. They'll be stunned and frightened, but the sight of one of their own luminaries going along with it will keep them from panicking. We'll break our forces into small groups, each of them led by a *Kol-Prockian* soldier who will take them to the most vulnerable portions of the base."

"And what happens when news spreads of this invasion, Welter?" *Keelen* objected. "Your soldiers can't move instantly. The discontents will learn of their presence and damage the chamber or any other number of critical systems. Indeed, they probably already have plans set in place for just such an eventuality. They're well aware of your aggressive stance towards problem solving."

"That's another chance we'll just have to take," Welter answered. "Put the best troops you can find around the chamber and the other systems. Besides, in their panic, their first thought will be to attack Rhemus personally, cutting off the problem at the source. Damaging the base isn't their goal."

"You mean to say you're comfortable putting your emperor in harm's way to carry out this plan of yours?" he asked pointedly.

"You're the one who put him in danger by blabbing to the wrong people," Welter retorted. "I'm just picking up the pieces. Besides, I'll be on hand to ensure nothing happens either to the emperor or Doctor Tselitel."

"What is your position on this, Doctor?" *Keelen* queried.

"It's really not for me to decide," she objected, her absence from the chamber coupling with the recent strain to make her more nervous. "Gustav was appointed by Krancis because of his combat expertise, and thus I must defer to his judgment. I'm no more qualified to speak–."

"This is no time to worry about credentials, Doctor," Welter cut her off. "Just give us your thoughts."

"I think either course is desperately risky," she admitted. "To attempt to seize the base is like running through a powder room with a lit match. But as morale crumbles with the passage of each and every hour, there's no question of waiting for the situation to improve. The only other option, potentially, is for the emperor to announce his intention to annex *Kren-Balar* without further delay. That may inspire enough confidence for the remainder of the *Kol-Prockians* to hold fast, gradually isolating and eliminating the discontents. But if it just throws fuel on the fire…" she shook her head.

"We could end up overwhelmed, only a handful of soldiers and myself between the emperor and an early grave," Welter finished for her.

"Precisely. We might incite them to violence while we're at our lowest ebb. At least if they rebelled at the sight of our soldiers, we'd only have to wait a few minutes for reinforcements to arrive and secure the chamber." She looked between them for a moment. "I'm afraid the entire matter hinges on how the *Kol-Prockians* react to our actions. And given the desperate situation they've lived in for so long, there's no question that their nerves are at the breaking point. They may behave completely unpredictably."

"In your opinion as a psychiatrist, Doctor," *Keelen* began slowly, watching her shrink as yet more responsibility for the fateful decision was given to her, "how do you feel my people would react?"

"Not being intimately familiar with *Kol-Prockians*–."

"We don't need the disclaimer, Doctor," Welter told her. "We're all shooting in the dark on this one. Just give us the best assessment you can."

"My *feeling*," she carefully stipulated, her head ducking a little as her eyes shot between the two of them, "is that the *Kol-Prockians* won't let us down if we place our trust in them. I believe, given how they responded to the emperor in the hangar, that they'll by and large accept him as their ruler. But I think it must be accompanied by an act of good faith on our part."

"You mean announcing it without bringing in troops?" Welter clarified. "A leap of faith to build rapport?"

"It's worked many times throughout history," she explained quickly.

"Yes, on humans," Welter specified. "Not on a bunch of desperate, half-crazed aliens that we hardly understand."

"Please remember what happened in the hangar," *Keelen* reminded him. "Their collective move to protect one they respected was neither desperate nor crazed. It was an act of both courage and generosity. Willingly they put their lives into the hands of any other would-be assassins who might have been hiding in the crowd, "

"That's true," Tselitel assented.

"But it doesn't change the fact that there's enough traitors in our midst to both damage the chamber and force you to change the members of our guard detail," Welter pointed out, nodding towards the door. "All it takes is a sizable minority to both damage *Kren-Balar* and potentially kill the emperor. Even if the mass of *Kol-Prockians* go along with us, there could still be enough rebels to destroy everything we're trying to do here."

"I'm afraid I must agree with that," *Keelen* uttered quietly, his temper slowly cooling as the conversation grew, not civil, but calm.

"Then what can we do?" Tselitel asked, her voice anxious.

"I believe the only thing we can do is place the matter before your emperor and let him decide," *Keelen* shrugged, his arms crossed as he looked down at the floor and thought. "After all, it *is* his decision whether or not he assumes command of *Kren-Balar*. In truth, we ought to have done that already, instead of arguing out here as though it were up to us."

"That's true enough," Welter allowed.

Quietly Tselitel padded across the floor in her thin robe and looked through the window. To her surprise *Karnan* had gotten up and moved to where Rhemus lay. Quietly they conversed, the scientist sitting with his back against the wall as always.

"*Karnan* is talking to him," Tselitel informed them in a half-whisper, turning from the glass before they noticed her.

"If they're pleased to talk, we should let them," *Keelen* opined. "Both have been through enough for the moment. Let's not throw yet more troubles onto them."

"A decision has to be made now," Welter disagreed. "Those troops can't get here instantly if he chooses to go that route."

"No, but I can begin to rearrange the garrison to

protect us in any eventuality," *Keelen* replied. Briefly he looked through the window before continuing. "That will be necessary no matter which path your emperor takes."

"Even a small delay might be too much," Welter shook his head, making for the door. "We don't have any longer to wait." Glancing through the glass just as he was going to open it, he noticed the two aged figures coming towards him. Waiting until they drew near, he pulled the door open for them and stood aside.

"Majesty," *Keelen* said respectfully, bowing a little as he passed into the anteroom.

Together the sovereign and the scientist went to the table, sitting down before gesturing for the others to join them.

"*Karnan* has informed me of what happened to the chamber," Rhemus began gravely. "There can be no question that the situation within this base has reached the tipping point. We are all of us, both *Kol-Prockians* and humans, in danger because of the actions of these mutinous elements. I have spent a great deal of time thinking over this matter, and with the able counsel of *Karnan*, I have reached a decision."

Everyone, including Welter, held their breath.

"I have decided to assume the rulership of both *Kren-Balar* and its residents immediately. I shall extend my hand over these people in the hope that they will receive such a gesture favorably, gaining both courage and strength from it."

"And what of bringing in reinforcements?" Welter queried.

"No reinforcements," Rhemus shook his head slightly, his tired eyes finding those of his bodyguard. "The relationship between our two peoples must begin with trust, and I am the only one who can extend it, given the circumstances. The *Kol-Prockians*, I'm sure, will rise to the occasion and prove themselves worthy allies, both within the confines of *Kren-Balar* and beyond."

"As you wish," Welter nodded slightly, his active mind already working out how best to protect the emperor. "When will the announcement be made?"

"Once I have had a chance to recuperate," he replied, rising from his seat with difficulty and leaning his hands on the table for a moment. "I must be at my strongest if I am to win both their affection and their confidence. But soon. Very soon."

With this he and *Karnan* returned to the chamber.

"I'll begin reorganizing the garrison at once," *Keelen* said quietly to Welter and Tselitel. "I am both proud and refreshed to have so much faith placed in my people. But I fear he has underestimated the true danger we face. Every precaution must be taken."

"Be discreet," Welter told him as he walked away.

"Aren't *Kol-Prockians* always discreet?" he replied, pausing just short of the exit and smiling faintly before disappearing into the corridor.

"Didn't think he could poke fun at himself," Welter uttered.

"Do you think the emperor has made the right decision?" Tselitel inquired now that they were alone, her thin fingers knitting and unknitting themselves before her on the table.

"Doesn't matter what you, me, or anyone else thinks at this point," he shrugged. "The decision's been made. Now it's up to us to help him pull it off." Silently he thought for a moment before looking at her. "You'd best get back in that chamber and get your strength up. I'm gonna need you later."

"For what?" she asked nervously. "I'm no good as a bodyguard."

"But I know I can trust you," he pointed out. "And even you can fire a gun at close range. If this deal goes pear-shaped, we might be left with only ourselves, *Keelen* and *Karnan*. In that case we'll need every willing hand we can get."

"I understand," she nodded, sitting a little straighter

and trying to brace herself for what was to come. "Do you think it *will* go that way?" she asked after a few seconds, searching for hope.

"We'll know soon enough," he answered with a thoughtful scowl, looking across the table at the wall as he mused.

The passage of an hour found Tselitel back in the chamber and Welter back in his usual chair. His pistol was drawn and in hand, resting on his lap as he sat with his left ankle propped on his right knee. Staring at the entrance to the anteroom, he wondered how many discontents *Keelen* had managed to accidentally tip off while trying to be secretive. Rolling his eyes at the notion, he wished that *anyone* besides the vain doctor could have been put in charge of the task. Or, better still, that *Kren-Balar* had been thoroughly in human hands from the get-go. Though possessing great faith in Krancis' ability to appropriately judge almost any situation, he couldn't help but wonder if he'd over-stepped common sense by dispatching the emperor to a desperate, foreign people with only a single man to protect him.

Thrice he tensed as a *Kol-Prockian's* head passed before the outer door, entirely expecting one of the mutineers to kick it open and try to kill the emperor. But each time the head merely bobbed past without so much as looking inside. Indeed, they seemed indifferent to the chamber and its occupants.

Reflecting on his two charges, he was particularly glad that Krancis had chosen him when he reflected on the soft-hearted vulnerability of Tselitel. Though he would never admit it to another soul, the idea of her being on her own in any scenario involving danger made him cringe inwardly. He knew she was capable of taking care of herself, or she wouldn't have risen to such heights within the psychiatric community. Or rather *had* been, he reflected, before Valindra had stolen so much of her energy and confidence. She seemed at times little more than a shaking leaf ever since he'd first laid eyes on her. It made him wonder how she'd managed to grapple with everything that had happened to her since she'd first reached Delta-13.

"Hunt must have looked after her," he reasoned.

Another *Kol-Prockian* head floated by, Welter only catching it out of the corner of his eye. For half a second he paused, feeling he'd seen that particular face before. But having only seen it blurrily in passing, he could only shake his head and let his suspicions drop.

Another hour passed without either a word from inside the chamber or *Keelen*. In the back of his mind Welter began to wonder if he'd been discovered by the discontents and killed, or at least taken prisoner. Were that the case, he would have no warning at all before a contingent of mutineers appeared at the door, ready to slaughter the visitors to their base.

A gentle tapping at the window beside him drew his attention. Twisting and looking up, he saw Tselitel mouthing the word *Keelen*, obviously curious about his whereabouts. She frowned with concern and disappeared when Welter merely shook his head.

"You and me both, Doctor," he murmured quietly, resettling himself and once more staring at the door.

Just as he did, a head passed which caught his attention. A peculiar gleam in the alien's eye betrayed more than a volume could have. Kicking the door open, he leveled a small pistol on Welter just as the guards beside him seized his arms and jerked them upward, causing him to discharge his fire into the ceiling. Shouting and writhing in a frenzy, the would-be assassin dropped his gun and continued to struggle. Breaking free of the guards just as Welter reached the door, he tore off down the hallway towards a loose group of civilians.

"Get down!" Welter roared, gesturing towards the floor.

Instantly taking his meaning, the shocked *Kol-Prockians* hit the deck just as two bullets tore through the air, striking the mutineer in the back and dropping him to the ground. By the time he'd slid to a stop on the smooth floor he was dead.

"Bring him back," Welter ordered the guards beside him, unwilling to leave the chamber unprotected for so much as a second. When they failed to move he recalled the language barrier and managed to communicate his wishes through sign. Nodding earnestly the moment they understood, they seized the ankles of the corpse and dragged it back to him as though hauling a dead pig. Indicating that they should move him into the anteroom, he dismissed them once they did so, returning them to their post.

"Are you alright?" Tselitel asked from the chamber, the door only partially open as she stuck her head out.

"We're fine for the moment," Welter answered without looking, his back to her as he searched the body of the assassin. "But I'd say *Keelen's* been whispering in the wrong ears."

Gingerly she stepped out of the chamber and joined him, kneeling on the floor beside the corpse. His mouth hanging open, his eyes wild and charged even in death, she was shocked by the bizarre sight.

"Thought so," Welter said grimly, his hand thrust into the alien's collar. Drawing out an artifact, he held it out before Tselitel. "These guys just can't get enough of these things."

Carefully wrapping her thin fingers around its chain, she raised it and swung it back and forth a little.

"Looks like the same kind that *Seldek* was wearing," she observed, trying to recall it in detail. "But I'm not sure. Guess we can ask *Keelen* when he gets back."

"*If* he gets back," Welter remarked, searching the body further. Finding nothing of interest, he seized the light corpse with his powerful hands and dumped him outside the door, making signs to indicate he ought to be gotten rid of. At once the guards agreed, and he went back inside.

"You think he's in trouble?" she queried, already knowing the answer.

"Most likely. We ought to have heard something by now. The base isn't *that* big."

"Maybe he's just finding it harder to shift the garrison around than he thought."

Frowning at her, he shook his head.

"Yeah, I don't believe that, either," she said, standing up and swinging the artifact a few more times. "Kind of pretty, in its own way."

"Pretty *dangerous* I'd say," he replied, watching her gaze upon it for a few seconds before taking it from her and setting it on the desk. "That's enough show and tell."

"Oh, of course," she agreed quickly. "I wasn't implying we should use it or anything. I was just admiring the *Kol-Prockian* tendency to ornament their works. Even AIs are given–," she halted, realization crossing her face. "We've forgotten about Frank again!"

"I haven't," Welter uttered, leaning against the desk and crossing his arms, keeping the door in view. "We just haven't had a reason to consult a second-rate bureaucrat."

"Oh, well, *I* forgot him, then," she corrected herself, stepping closer and holding out her hand. "Can I have him, please?"

"What for? He's just gonna gripe about collecting my pocket lint."

"That's why. I don't want him to be angry about how he's being treated."

"Suit yourself," he shrugged, taking the medallion out and giving it to her.

"Frank? Are you okay, Frank?"

"Sure," he answered flatly.

"I'm sorry if you're angry," she began, her eyes searching those of her implacable bodyguard, trying to find some kind of justification. "Um, how have you been?"

"Just dandy. You should try it sometime. Nothing like being stuck in some guy's pocket for hours on end."

"Look, we've just been so busy–."

"That you haven't needed me. Yeah, I got the picture. I'm an AI, remember? I'm good at putting stuff together. Chamber goes offline? No way I could help with that. Weighing the pros and cons of a given course of action when intimate knowledge of the psyche of the *people who made me* is necessary? Nah, couldn't be any use there, either. Overall I'm just a fancy paperweight. Or lint collector, as Welter would have it."

"Frank, I know you're very upset," she said, moving away from Welter and taking a seat at the table. "And personally I'm really, really sorry that we forgot you." She dropped her voice. "But I've been feeling very poorly, and I just simply forgot. I apologize."

"Well," he grumbled, his anger softening. "Couldn't you at least keep me on you, so that brute can't keep stuffing me in his pocket? It's like a black hole in there. I never know when I'm coming out."

"Sure, I'll keep you with me," she assured him. "Incidentally, what *do* you think about the course the emperor has chosen?"

"Well, to quote someone I'm not *exactly* enthused with at the moment, that doesn't matter anymore. We need to bend all our thoughts on keeping Rhemus and the rest of you safe. That'll be hard enough with *Keelen* the chatterbox bending the ear of every gossip in *Kren-Balar*. Honestly, and I truly can't believe I'm saying this, but I wish more *Kol-Prockians* were surly and uncommunicative like Welter. At least then news wouldn't travel with the speed of *thought*. We're gonna be paying for *Keelen's* big mouth for the foreseeable future. I just hope each of you makes it out of this okay."

"Even Gustav?" she asked quietly, a little smile on her

face as she glanced at her escort, his gaze vigilantly on the door as ever, his pistol held loosely in his hand as he thought.

"Yes," Frank said with a loud, exasperated sigh. "Even Welter. He grows on you in his nasty way. At any rate he's the best fighter we've got by far. I'd take him over half a dozen *Kol-Prockian* guards. Unlike them he still believes in what he's doing, even if he's bloodied and battered. He's got a strong spirit. Probably half the reason Krancis sent him."

"And the other half?"

"The fact that he's deadly as a cobra," he answered. "I couldn't *see* what happened with that assassin just now. But hearing it was all I needed to know he dispatched him with his usual efficiency. He's the last man I'd want to be crossways of."

"I agree."

"But, enough of our laudable companion," he said tartly, feeling he'd expressed quite enough appreciation. "The fact remains we have to ensure Rhemus lives long enough to assume genuine control of *Kren-Balar*. I think by and large my people will go along with the transition. Probably most of them will heave a big sigh of relief when it happens. But it'll take time for the ashes of discontent to cool. Especially given that they're likely to flare when the news is generally known. Those who have lost hope will jump for joy. But the others, the ones who hate the idea of a human ruler, well, they'll be driven to desperate acts of violence. We're gonna have to be on our toes. I just wish *Keelen* wasn't our only meaningful contact with the rest of the base."

"I agree," she nodded thoughtfully, reflecting on the problem.

"Assuming we've still got *Keelen*, that is. He's been gone an awful long time."

"Too bad we haven't got more people with us," she sighed, leaning back in her seat. "Gustav can't go. And I'd just be a ready-made hostage if I started wandering the halls."

"There's *Karnan*," Frank offered. "Granted, he's feeble

as a day-old kitten. But I don't think the mutineers would lay a hand on him. They'll try to break his chamber, sure. But he seems to be held in universal regard."

"No, we couldn't risk that," she disagreed. "What if they even just captured him? They could do whatever they wanted to the chamber and we'd have no chance of repairing it. Then the whole reason for coming here in the first place would be lost."

"You're right. Silly thought." A few moments passed silently. "I guess that leaves me."

"You?" she asked with half a laugh, uncertain if he was serious.

"Sure. I can hitch a ride with one of the guards and tell him where to go. I speak *Kol-Prockian*, unlike you and Welter, so I can easily find my way around the base and ask the right questions. Besides, the mutineers wouldn't think much of a guard rambling around. And they *certainly* wouldn't think to search him for an ancient AI that hardly anyone would think could have lasted this long. I'd be perfectly incognito. Of course, that *would* take an extra guard off the door..." his voice trailed briefly. "But I think Welter can take up the slack."

"You think?"

"Well, I *know* it. But I don't want to give him *that* much credit."

Fighting off a smile, she arose and explained the AI's plan to Welter.

"At least he'd be putting himself to good use," was his initial comment. "And it's not like we need him around here."

"I love the way he makes you feel valued," Frank said sarcastically to Tselitel.

"Just have some common sense about the whole thing, Frank," Welter continued. "They've got to have a pretty good idea who's on their side and who isn't. They wouldn't hesitate to jump one of the loyal guards if they could do it without making a big stir."

"He'll be careful," Tselitel relayed for the AI, his disc still held in her hand.

Welter gestured towards the door.

"Go to it, then."

Opening it, Tselitel motioned for one of the guards to enter. Preparing him with a few brief signs, she handed the AI to him and watched as his eyes lit up with wonder. For several minutes all he could do was gape at the medallion and utter brief responses in a tone of awe. Eventually the shine began to wear off, and he composed himself enough to make a few signs to the humans that he was going. Then he departed.

"Guess it's up to him now," Welter said dubiously, frowning at the door. "How's the emperor been?"

"He's resting," she replied, seating herself on the desk a few feet away. "He heard the gunshots, of course, but seemed unalarmed. He's got a great deal of faith in you."

"Nice to be appreciated," he responded indifferently. "And *Karnan?*"

"As well as can be expected," she said with concern. "Repairing the chamber took a lot out of him, or rather the emotional strain of betrayal did. He really shouldn't be outside of it anymore. I think he dies a little bit each time he leaves it."

"Most likely, given how old he is." Then he glanced at her robe, looking for any sign of a bulge in her pockets. "Where's the gun I gave you?"

"Oh, I left it–."

"Keep it on you constantly," he cut her off, his eyes deadly serious. "Right now there's me and a single guard standing between the emperor and who knows how many mutineers. We need every gun we can get."

"Alright," she nodded, sliding off the desk and retrieving her weapon. Holding it with some aversion, she returned to the desk and sat in the chair behind it. "I'm not sure I could even hit the door from this range," she commented, gesturing towards the entrance with the pistol. "I've never been much of a hand with weapons. Or even tools."

"No better way to learn than when your back is against the wall."

"That's true. But there are a great many less nerve-wracking ways," she smiled faintly, to which he nodded.

"Just hold it with both hands, point it straight at the target, and start squeezing the trigger. It's about like pointing your finger at something."

"Just a lot deadlier."

"Yeah."

"Oh, I wish Rex was here," she uttered softly, holding the weapon and recoiling at the idea of taking a life. She knew it was necessary sometimes. But the softness of her healer's heart revolted at the idea. In truth, she felt uncertain she could even do it to save her own life. Probably, she reflected, she couldn't. But to save another she would have no choice. She'd *have* to act.

"I wish he was here, too," Welter replied. "It'd make things a whole lot simpler. Probably hold the base in awe with his power. Then we wouldn't even need to think about having the emperor take over. But there's no point in wishful thinking."

"You're right, of course," she assented, still eyeing the weapon as she felt it's cold, hard surface with her gentle fingers. "But I can't help missing him. It feels like it's been years since I saw him last. It's awfully hard being apart."

"I know," he sympathized as much as he could. "But you'll see him soon enough."

With this the conversation died, neither of them wishing to say more. Tselitel went back into the chamber for a little while but was far too restless to remain. She had to stay near the seat of action until at least *some* news, good or bad, was received about *Keelen*. Settling in behind the desk once more, her pistol resting upon it for easy access, she eyed the entrance and reflected.

After nearly two hours a respectful knock was heard at the door, the familiar face of Frank's guard standing before the window. Immediately Welter ushered him in, taking the medallion and sending him back to his post.

"Well, what've you got for us?" he asked, leaning against the desk and holding the medallion so Tselitel could touch it, his gun still in his other hand as he watched the door.

"*Keelen's* evaporated," Frank said without varnish, his tone fatally serious. "We walked up and down the halls of *Kren-Balar* and couldn't find hide or hair of him. Everyone we asked either said they didn't know or evaded the question. They're afraid. Very afraid."

"They've got plenty of reason to be," Welter scowled, still watching the door as he calculated their odds of survival.

"And there's more," Frank continued. "*Seldek* isn't in his cell anymore. They got him out."

"What?!" Tselitel exclaimed. "Why in the world would they want him? He's just a nut."

"Maybe they're as nutty as he is," the AI suggested. "Either way, he's vanished, too. It was like nobody knew he was ever locked up. I checked the computer and the record of his confinement has been deleted."

"Great, so they're ideological about it," Welter remarked, glancing at Tselitel who was visibly a little confused. "If they're deleting records, it means they're making it like it never happened. It isn't enough to break him out: they have to erase his wrongdoing from history."

"Oh," she nodded, taking his meaning.

"Yeah, that's what it looks like," Frank seconded, wishing he'd made the observation first.

"So *Keelen's* out of the picture, *Seldek* is on the loose, and as far as we can be reasonably certain, there's only two guards we can depend on?" Tselitel summarized.

"That's the size of it," Welter confirmed.

"Then what are we going to do?" she queried. "We can't just stay in here. Who knows how much longer it'll take them to make another move against the chamber. If the base has passed over into fear of these guys, they might strike at any time."

"That's right," Welter assented.

"All we can do now is contact Krancis for troops," Frank opined. "The situation is too desperate for anything else. The good ones among my people are all but cowed by the bad. We'll just have to take our chances on how they'll react to seeing human soldiers flood *Kren-Balar*."

"But how fast can they get here?" she asked.

"It'll take some time," Welter told her gravely. "Krancis stationed some troops nearby in case we needed them. But they're just a handful of special operations forces. They *might* be enough to tip the scales in our favor, but it'd be pretty close. To truly dominate the base, we'd need a transport ship either from home or one of the bases here in Quarlac. And that'd be certain to draw the unwelcome attention of watchful eyes."

"Then our backs are still against the wall even with reinforcements," she concluded.

"Yep."

"So what's our next step?" she queried.

"Tell the emperor and see what he says," Welter told her. "We can't move without his consent."

"Alright," she agreed, heading into the chamber.

"Gotta say, this isn't how I imagined our stay would work out," Frank uttered after a few moments. "I never thought my people would degenerate this far. Weak on one hand and vicious on the other. It's like they've lost all their civilization and are turning into animals, driven by fear and suspicion."

"That's what happens when your hope has been gone for too long," Welter observed.

"Yeah, I guess so."

A few silent minutes passed before the door to the chamber opened. Welter stood up when he saw Rhemus, Tselitel, and *Karnan* coming out.

"Doctor Tselitel has made me aware of the situation," the emperor began. "And it's my conclusion that an announcement must be made now, before the situation can deteriorate any further."

"We don't have control of any of the base's vital systems," Welter objected. "They could fatally damage this place."

"That's something we'll just have to risk," Rhemus replied. "We don't have time for reinforcements to arrive, even if they're close by. Besides, one of us would have to reach the egg and use its radio to try and contact them. What are the odds that person would be coming back alive, given our circumstances?"

"The only possibility is to win over the fearful among my people with a show of imperial dignity," *Karnan* added. "Appearing before them in the hangar and announcing the emperor's intention is our one shot. Anything else will take too long and is fraught with mortal risk."

"And this isn't?" Welter countered.

"We're out of time," Rhemus declared, his tone ending the discussion. "We move at once."

"Follow up the rear, Doctor," Welter instructed Tselitel, moving to the front of the group. "And keep that gun handy."

Stepping out into the corridor first, Welter glanced up and down it before signaling for the two guards to flank Rhemus. Falling in at once with perfect obedience, their presence and discipline offered some reassurance to the outnumbered humans. Proceeding down the corridors with as much caution as the emperor's surprisingly rapid, martial pace would permit, Welter's eyes were everywhere at once, scanning the faces of every *Kol-Prockian* they encountered for signs of mutiny. But each of them watched with a mixture of bland disinterest and surprise that both Rhemus and *Karnan* were once again abroad, walking the halls of *Kren-Balar* so soon after the last attempt to assassinate him in the hangar. With his typical decisiveness Welter gestured for passersby to move far out of the way, not willing that any should come into close proximity with the emperor.

Nervously Tselitel watched their backtrail, her trembling hand gripping her small pistol for strength. She started when a *Kol-Prockian* appeared some distance behind, rounding a corner and watching them. But he simply gazed at the procession, curious what the incisive treading of feet meant. Glancing ahead to Rhemus for a moment, she wondered how long he could maintain such a pace. Sweat already glistened on the back of his neck, gently moistening the collar of his thin robe. She hoped he would have the strength to carry off whatever speech he had in mind for informing the *Kol-Prockians* of the annexation.

Turning into another corridor, Welter instantly pulled back, his arms spread wide for the group to retreat. A short distance ahead stood a crazy-eyed rebel with a pistol leveled on them.

"Look out!" he barked, getting them back before leaning around the corner and casting a pair of bullets down the hallway. As he did this a trio shots sailed towards him, bouncing off the wall that protected him as the assassin dropped to his back. Slowly he pushed off the wall and took a couple of steps into the open, confirming that the corpse wasn't playing possum. "Alright, come on," he ordered, waving them on with his free hand when he was sure. "*Karnan*, tell your boys to get in front of the emperor."

Quickly the old scientist relayed his wishes, which were instantly obeyed.

Nearing the hangar, the hair on Tselitel's neck stood up just as she looked over her shoulder at the corner they'd hidden behind moments before. Seeing a weapon poke around it, she screamed Welter's name and twisted around. Leveling her pistol on the assassin's gun, she closed her eyes and squeezed off three rounds. A fourth sounded from beside her, and she turned to find Welter standing between Rhemus and the assassin, his pistol held at arm's length. With a groan the assassin fell into the corridor, Welter's bullet having caught him in the bit of his head that had been exposed by looking around the corner to aim.

"Keep moving," Welter said imperturbably, laying a hand on one of the *Kol-Prockian* guards and positioning him behind Rhemus to catch wayward bullets. Resuming the lead, he got them into the hangar and guided them towards the egg that stood in the middle of it, beside the elevator. All around them were curious onlookers, drawn by the sounds of gunfire.

"Where are we going?" Rhemus asked, alarmed to see them approaching the egg for fear that Welter had decided to evacuate them on his own authority.

"You need to be up high if they're gonna hear you," he answered grimly. "And it'll make it easier to see threats."

Calling out to the egg's AI, he had her pop the canopy and produce the minimalist ladder that was embedded in the side. Laboriously the emperor and the aged scientist managed to climb it, followed by Tselitel and Welter. The two guards remained at the bottom.

"Take Frank," Welter told Rhemus, handing him the disc as he continued to scan the curious onlookers for threats. "He can interface with the egg and use it to magnify your voice. He'll also translate what you're saying into *Kol-Prockian*."

"I'm at your service, Majesty," Frank confirmed the moment skin contact was made.

Looking out across the strange faces that surrounded him, Rhemus suddenly felt a quiver of fear run through his stomach. He'd never given a speech to an alien audience before, and he was unsure how to proceed. He had to strike the right note, or it would all be for nothing. It wasn't enough merely to give a good speech: he had to win over their hearts, convincing them that their destiny lay with him.

"*You have no doubt heard of the fate of Seldek by this time,*" he began, a little jarred to hear his words magnified tenfold and rendered into *Kol-Prockian*. "*In serving his people, he made the ultimate sacrifice of both his mind and body. The artifact that robbed him of his sanity was, I am sure, utilized only out of a desire to see good come to his people. But the fact remains that it has destroyed him as an individual, and that he is no longer capable of governing your affairs. It has been proposed to me by several of your most lustrous luminaries, among them Karnan,*" here he paused, allowing the scientist to take a step forward within the cockpit and nod, confirming his words, "*that I should assume command of Kren-Balar, ruling your people as I rule my own. After much reflection, I have decided to do exactly that, provided–,*" here he was cut off by an explosion of cheers. "*Provided,*" he continued, when they'd quieted a little, "*that it met with the approval of you all.*"

Again the hangar thundered with applause, many *Kol-Prockians* jumping up and down for joy, their limbs shooting in every direction as they all but burst in ecstasy.

"*Many hard miles lay before us,*" he resumed after several minutes of deafening noise. "*We must hold together if we are to grapple with the many threats that face us. But I am certain, that with the strength of my people, and the genius of yours, we shall prevail against all who range themselves against us. Under the aegis of the human empire the name Kol-Prockian will once more be heard throughout the universe. Together we shall stride forth, stronger and more capable than ever before. In unity we shall find the strength to not only survive, but to thrive. The sacrifices of your sojourn within Kren-Balar will never be forgotten, nor shall they be regretted in the days to come. They will be looked back upon by your children and grandchildren as the long night through which, with indomitable courage, your people struggled to preserve the genius of your race. It shall* not be the final chapter of your kind, but a new beginning – the birthplace of a renewed and revitalized Kol-Prockian civilization."

Pausing once more as applause drowned him out, Rhemus could see tears in *Karnan's* eyes. Indeed, most of the *Kol-Prockians* were gushing as they cheered, their weary souls refreshed to hear that their long pilgrimage in the dark had finally passed.

"*But we must remain vigilant,*" he continued. "*There are those among us here in Kren-Balar who do not agree with this course of–,*" again his words were overcome, but this time it was by a hair-raising hiss. Instantly the joyful faces of the *Kol-Prockians* had been transformed into scowling, angry visages. Fearing that he had stepped on a live wire, Rhemus held back from speaking for several moments. Then *Karnan* whispered in his ear.

"They're hissing at the mutineers," he said.

"*Felen-kor! Felen-kor! Felen-kor!*" the crowd chanted.

"They're condemning them in the strongest possible terms," Frank informed him. "*Felen-kor* is an ancient term used for only the most despicable of offenses. It derives from the ancient *Kol-Prockian* religion called *Delek-Hai*."

"You should speak again, Majesty," *Karnan* confided, as the crowd grew frenzied. "Soon they may lose their heads and seek out the rebels to exact retribution."

"*We must all of us,*" he began, as Frank pumped up the volume to a staggering level to overcome the noise of his audience. "*We must all of us remain dedicated to our duty, which is the preservation of our two peoples. Now is not the time for vengeance, but for unity. We must not permit suspicion and violence to tear apart the peace we will bring to Kren-Balar. But equally we must not allow a handful of renegades to sabotage the life that your people have bravely carved from the hard rock and molten rivers of this world. Thus guards will be placed to protect the most important systems until every heart within this sanctuary beats as one, devoted to our mutual survival.*"

Again the crowd cheered, this time with a finality that assured Rhemus his object had been totally, unequivocally obtained.

"With your permission, Majesty, I'll organize them into groups and dispatch them to protect the base," Frank uttered.

"Do so," Rhemus commanded him, suddenly exhausted now that his goal had been achieved. Using all his strength to remain on his feet, he listened as the AI relayed his wishes to the eager crowd. Quickly they formed up into groups of four and six, dispersing into the base.

"Are you alright?" Tselitel asked, standing beside him and speaking as softly as the noisy hangar would permit.

"I'll be fine," he answered, breathing as subtly as he could for the crowd's sake, his face red and perspiring. Closing his eyes for a few seconds, he reopened them and straightened up. "Let's return to the chamber now," he said, handing her Frank. "My task here is finished."

Barely making it down the ladder, the emperor was pleased to find an honor guard of a dozen *Kol-Prockians* had elected to escort him. With six in front and six behind, their bodies shielded him completely, permitting Welter to stride a few extra feet ahead to anticipate threats. He had little time to wait, for no sooner had they reached the corridors than another mutineer, his eyes wild and bulging, leapt from a corner fifty feet away, a gun held in his outstretched hand. Instantly Welter snapped up his pistol and fired, shattering the attacker's arm and causing him to fall backwards, dropping the weapon. As he struggled to get up, Welter looked over his shoulder, held up three fingers, and then pointed at the assassin. Like wild dogs a trio of *Kol-Prockians* broke from the honor guard and tore the bleeding rebel to pieces.

"Tell them to save his limbs," Welter ordered *Karnan*. "We're not finished with him yet."

Carrying the remnants of the assassin with them,

they deposited the emperor and *Karnan* inside the chamber, positioning a small host of guards outside the anteroom to protect him.

"What are you going to do with him?" Tselitel asked Welter, horrified by the sight of the dismembered *Kol-Prockian*.

"We're going to hang what's left of him up in the hangar, so that any other would-be killers will know that the *Kol-Prockian* people will no longer tolerate their treasonous acts."

"That's why you had them rip him to bits," Tselitel concluded, as Welter took Frank from her. "You wanted them to take responsibility for the safety of *Kren-Balar*."

"That's part of it," he replied, pausing to convey his wishes in more detail to Frank. Then he handed the medallion to one of the *Kol-Prockians*, who led his fellows away with the decentralized corpse. "It also gave them a chance to serve their new ruler. Acting in their sovereign's service will weld them more completely to him. With pride they'll remember how they dispatched a traitor mere minutes after Rhemus assumed command. They'll consider themselves the very first patriots of the new order."

"Very wise," Tselitel said, though the sight of the savaged *Kol-Prockian* made her nauseous. "Are we in for more displays such as that?" she queried, gesturing towards the door.

"A few," Welter told her. "We still haven't settled up with the boys who broke *Seldek* loose, nor *Seldek* himself. There's bound to be some diehards who'll fight to the bitter end. We won't have any choice but to kill them on sight. But they'll have some followers around them who aren't as hardcore. Those are the ones who'll be persuaded by a display like that. They'll melt away from their ringleaders once they realize they can't stem the tide."

It wasn't long before the *Kol-Prockians* returned with Frank. Handing him back to Welter, they lingered with a look of concern on their faces. When Welter signed for them to leave and guard the door from outside, they modestly shook their heads and pointed to the disc that he held by its chain.

"You got something to say to me?" he inquired, making skin contact and looking away from the aliens with an impatient expression on his face.

"You could say that," the AI began, as Tselitel likewise touched him to listen. "On our way back we ran into one of *Seldek's* followers. *Keelen's* alive, but he's got a knife to his throat as we speak. If we want to save him, we've got to turn the base over to *Seldek* and depart at once. He's given us thirty minutes to decide."

"He's out of his mind!" Tselitel declared.

"Literally, in fact," Frank said. "Doubtless they've hooked him up with the artifact he was using before, so he's got a few of his marbles back for the time being. But he's capable of anything at this point."

"Can he threaten the base?" Welter asked.

"As far as I'm aware, no. His messenger said nothing about damaging any of the vital systems, which I should think he would have if his bunch had access to them. I guess the emperor's message of hope spread quicker than we could have imagined possible. Almost to a man *Kren Balar* is ours."

"Then we don't have anything to worry about," Welter concluded.

"But what about *Keelen?*" Tselitel queried. "We can't just leave him in the hands of that madman."

"It's not as if we can turn over the base just to save him, Doctor. He knew the risks, and he's going to have to pay the price. If we try to rescue him, they'll just cut his throat."

"This can't be the only way," she shook her head. "There's got to be something we can do."

"It's hard to imagine what," Frank chimed in, reluctantly agreeing with Welter. "The messenger strictly warned us not to try anything heroic, or he'd be dead before we got halfway to him. We were to avoid the rear of the base completely, proceeding straight from the chamber to the hangar. Once there, Rhemus was to announce his abandonment of *Kren-Balar* and then depart with us all aboard the egg."

"I don't believe it," Tselitel fretted, leaning her spare form against the desk, still touching the medallion. Looking down in anguished consternation, she contemplated her feet for several seconds before looking up at Welter. "I thought we'd cut the Gordian Knot when the emperor made his speech. But all we've done is cranked the temperature up to the boiling point. We can't leave because then Rhemus'll die. And we can't stay, or they'll murder *Keelen*."

"Life's full of hard choices," Welter uttered unsympathetically. "But there's no question which way this has to go."

"We have to tell the emperor about this," she said, pushing off the desk and making for the chamber's door. But Welter's strong hand shot out and seized her wrist.

"Don't bother him," the bodyguard ordered, drawing her back. "He's been through enough to kill him. Besides, his answer can't be any different. He can't fail the empire by surrendering to extortion."

"It's a difficult decision," Frank seconded. "But only one course is just and right. We have to let *Keelen* go, and try to organize the loyalists to prevent the rebels from taking their actions any further."

"But we can't sacrifice *Keelen* like this," she objected. "At any rate, it's the emperor's right to decide for himself. He's the master of *Kren-Balar* now, and not you or I."

"Go ahead," Welter relented, releasing her wrist. "But the answer is going to be the same either way."

"I wish she wasn't quite so emotionally involved," Frank confided, as she passed into the chamber and disappeared. "She's already got enough on her mind to twist her in knots. She doesn't need to add to her burdens."

"I agree," Welter replied, surprised to hear his own

words once they'd left his mouth. The talkative AI was the last individual with which he expected to establish any kind of rapport. For his own part, Frank was equally surprised but wisely said nothing, aware that Welter would not appreciate his remarks.

Leaning against the desk as Tselitel had done, his eyes periodically moved from the *Kol-Prockians* to a bare place on the wall. As she had been, he was deeply frustrated to find that the situation within *Kren-Balar* hadn't been largely solved by Rhemus' announcement. He'd anticipated difficulties, naturally. But nothing quite so dramatic as the threat against *Keelen's* life. Glancing over his shoulder at the chamber's door, he hoped that the soft-hearted psychiatrist wasn't bending the emperor's ear with her words. Instantly he dismissed the notion, aware that such a thought did him a disservice. He was much too grounded to be swayed by an emotional appeal, no matter how fervently Tselitel might argue it to him. Crossing his arms and looking back at the aliens before him, he frowned and waited. Finally, after the passage of several minutes, the chamber opened behind him. Turning, he saw Rhemus and Tselitel coming out.

"Doctor Tselitel has explained the situation to me," he began, taking a few weary steps before resting his hand on the desk. Out of respect, Welter stood up, letting his hands fall to his sides. "There is no question that *Keelen* must be saved if at all possible."

"*Seldek's* holding all the cards on this one," he replied. "His people have orchestrated it so we've only got one way to play it if we want to keep him alive. There simply isn't any way to reach them without being spotted."

"Then we offer him something in return," he replied, leaning a little more heavily on the desk before straightening up. "We will offer him me."

"You?!" Welter and Tselitel exclaimed simultaneously. Had it been possible, Rhemus would have heard Frank utter the same word.

"We can't do that, Your Highness," Tselitel objected after half a moment. "The risk is much too great. He wouldn't hesitate to kill you if given the chance."

"She's right," Welter agreed. "You're everything they hate at this point – the symbol of their decay. Killing you, in their minds, would prove that they don't need human help to survive after all. They'd eat their own mothers for a chance like that."

"Then you'd better not give them that chance," Rhemus replied, growing irritated by both his fatigue and their spelling out of the obvious. "I don't intend that either *Keelen* or myself should be sacrificed to satisfy these fanatics. I am going to suggest a trade, filling his mind with all sorts of notions of extorting concessions from Krancis to allow us to stay here while I act as a hostage to ensure our good behavior. If I read him right, his diseased mind won't be able to resist the idea of dragging the great human empire around by its nose. It will appeal far too much to his pride and vanity. Even in his right mind he wouldn't be able to turn such a chance down."

"But, Your Highness, what can we do to ensure your safety?" Tselitel all but pleaded, her tone fervently opposed. "You'll be walking into a trap."

Rhemus watched her as she spoke, and then turned to Welter.

"That's where you come in," he said, dropping his voice a little. "Right about the time *Seldek* thinks I'm in the palm of his hand, I want you to cut down every last rebel in the room. No survivors."

"That'll be a hard job," Welter responded, calculating the odds. "And if they keep their guns on us the whole time, it'll be impossible. I'd be lucky to kill two of them before I was cut down myself."

"That's why we'll meet in a neutral place, accompanied by only two attendants apiece." Taking a step forward, he partially grasped Frank. "Is there such a place within *Kren-Balar?*"

"Sure. There's loads of rooms in the back that would be perfect."

"He's not gonna go along with this," Welter shook his head. "Not when he's got a knife to *Keelen's* throat. He thinks he's got the odds in his favor, and he's right. He's not gonna move."

"I think I can convince him," Frank commented.

"How?" Rhemus queried.

"Simple," he audibly smiled. "I'll just say that that hard-headed bodyguard Welter won't let you meet with him on anything other than neutral turf. He's well aware of how stubborn he is, so that won't be a hard sale."

"And if he stipulates that I'm to be left behind?" Welter asked.

"Then I'll tell him that you're holding the emperor here more or less by force," he responded, before adding more tartly, "He won't have a hard time believing that, either."

Frowning at the medallion, he raised his eyes to Rhemus with a question in them.

"Do it," he said at once. "Say whatever you must. Ensure beforehand that *Keelen* is actually still alive by demanding to see him. But get me that meeting."

"I'll do my best," Frank assured him, before being handed off to the waiting *Kol-Prockians*. They stood still while the AI communicated in their native tongue. Then, with a deep bow to the emperor, they turned and departed.

"Let me know the instant we have an answer from *Seldek*," the emperor instructed, making his way back to the chamber and disappearing inside.

"This is the worst idea he's ever had," Welter told Tselitel once they were alone. "It's at least even money that he gets his head shot off."

"He has faith in you," she replied quietly, drawing a little closer.

"As he should. But I can't work miracles, Doctor."

Cursing under his breath, he slammed his hand against the desk, making her jump. "I'd keep him here by force," he told her, his eyes aflame. "I'd do so without so much as a second's hesitation. But these *Kol-Prockians* are sharp, and the moment they realized I was forcing Rhemus to do something he didn't want to do, they'd lose all faith in him and crumble to dust. He's the only thing keeping their spirit alive at this point. Break his image, and everything we're trying to do here collapses." Looking at the anteroom's exit to ensure they were still alone, he smacked the desk a second time. "So I've got to let him go ahead with this. I've got to let him stick his head into the noose and jump off the platform. I just hope I'm fast enough to catch him."

Aware that she could utter nothing that wouldn't sound like air-headed pap, she chose instead to lean on the desk beside him, silently offering what support she could. Like Rhemus, she didn't want to see *Keelen* hurt. But like Welter she felt his chosen course was little short of madness. Now she wished she'd listened to him when he'd grabbed her wrist minutes before. Inwardly she feared that the rigors Rhemus had been subjected to had pushed him over the edge, at least for the short term. It wasn't possible, she felt, that such a fatal risk would be run by a man who was in complete command of his faculties.

From time to time she glanced anxiously at the door, afraid that time would run out on the original ultimatum and that *Keelen* would be lost before they could so much as lift a finger to help him. Such thoughts also filled the mind of the man beside her, but with a twist: he hoped to run out of time, sacrificing the irascible doctor to save the emperor from an all but certain end. It was with another curse under his breath that he saw the *Kol-Prockian* who bore Frank appear at the door, hope in his widely-spaced eyes.

"Looks like we've got our answer," he said sourly to Tselitel, pushing off the desk and taking Frank from the alien.

"I'll say we do," Frank said at once. "I couldn't believe he actually went for it! Boy, you should have seen his face light up when I started going over the value Rhemus would have as a hostage. You'd think he'd found a kantium mine in his basement. Gotta say, the emperor sure knows how to play the game."

"Good for him," Welter answered irritably, handing the medallion to Tselitel. "Go pass along the good news," he told her, again crossing his arms and staring at a blank space on the wall. He was all but ready to explode, to burst from the room and force *Seldek* to kill *Keelen* by storming the room he was in. But a little voice in the back of his mind held him back. So far Rhemus had proven expert in handling their alien hosts, which was a great deal more than could be said for Welter. It was just possible that he was right.

It was also true that the *Kol-Prockians* who'd escorted Frank knew of the change in plans. He couldn't interrupt them without utterly destroying the emperor in their eyes. No, the game would have to be played just as Rhemus had intended.

Moments later Tselitel returned with him, this time accompanied by *Karnan*.

"You'd better believe that I'm going!" the aged scientist declared, following behind them with as much alacrity as his brittle bones could manage. "None of these boys will do you any good!" he insisted, waving a hand at his fellow *Kol-Prockians*. "They don't speak your language. They couldn't follow your lead. No, you need to be on the same wavelength for an operation like this."

"Frank could translate," Tselitel suggested.

"Oh, sure," *Karnan* shot back. "Welter tells him, and he passes it along? It won't wash, Doctor. Reaction time would be too slow."

"Which is why we'll bring Doctor Tselitel," Rhemus declared.

"No," Welter said at once, too inflamed to care about

protocol. "She'll just get herself killed. She hasn't got any experience at all for something like this."

"He's right," she seconded, the notion driving her heart into her throat and nearly choking her.

"You handled a gun well enough earlier, Doctor," the emperor uttered with finality. "Your target would have been eliminated had he been closer and not concealed around a corner. In this case, your targets will be right across the room from you."

"But what if I hit *Keelen?*" she objected. "I could end up killing the whole reason we're going."

"Then I suggest you don't," he answered with annoyance, the burdens of the day adding up. "I've made my decision. The three of us shall proceed at once. Arm her," he ordered Welter, "so that we may depart."

To all appearances Welter hesitated for a moment. But in truth his body twitched forwards ever so slightly, his intent being to seize Rhemus and shove him back into the chamber before forcing *Seldek* to kill *Keelen*. Just as he was about to do so, the little voice spoke up again, arresting his movement and causing him to lock eyes with his sovereign. Somehow the latter seemed to grasp what was going through his mind, for he just barely nodded his head, assuring him that he knew what he was doing. With a subtle nod of his own, he reloaded Tselitel's sidearm and handed it to her.

"Let's go," Welter uttered gravely, signing for the *Kol-Prockians* to remain and taking the lead.

All along the way *Kol-Prockians* stood aside and watched the procession. Most of them bowed, still in awe that Rhemus was now their emperor. But a few stood and watched, sensing that something was very wrong within *Kren-Balar*. Why, after all, was the emperor traveling without a stronger guard detail to protect him? And why was Welter wearing a murderous expression on his face? They couldn't understand it. But they knew far better than to annoy Welter by attempting to inquire. Observing the small group from a respectful distance, they waited until they were out of sight and then chatted among themselves as to what was afoot.

"Take a left here," Frank told Welter, dangling from his neck. "It isn't too much farther."

Guided by the AI to a nondescript door, he opened it slightly and saw *Seldek* and his attendants inside. Both were armed. Both flanked a bloodied *Keelen*.

"You're insane for coming here!" the hostage exclaimed, before being smacked on the head with an alien pistol. Losing his balance as stars appeared before his eyes, he fell against the attendant on the right, knocking him off balance.

Seeing his chance, Welter kicked the emperor to the ground, threw open the door, and hit the deck, cranking off shot after shot into the mutineers. Both the attendants grimaced and fell to the ground, leaving only *Seldek* standing. Dropping to the floor behind *Keelen* just as a bullet tore through his arm, the crazed alien drew his knife and held it against the doctor's throat.

"You want me to kill him, Welter?!" he demanded, his voice a mixture of rage and triumph. "You want me to spill his blood all over this floor?!"

"Don't hurt him!" Rhemus said, limping into the bare room and away from the door, supporting himself with the nearby wall.

"You're in no position to negotiate, *Emperor Rhemus*," *Seldek* retorted nastily. "You've already shown bad faith by having your killer here murder my escorts."

"Don't let any more blood be shed within this base," Rhemus said, drawing a little closer and buying time to think. "Too many lives have already been lost."

"And *Keelen's* will be among them, if you don't come over here at once and take his place!" *Seldek* shouted, his eyes wild. "The entirety of your empire shall lay at my feet! Even mighty Krancis will do my bidding! *Sentinel* will come out here at once and remove my people to your galaxy, where we shall carve out a new life for ourselves. Never again will we be forced to live like maggots! Proud and strong, we shall stand tall, fearing no one! Glory shall once again be ours!"

"You will have both glory and honor," Rhemus told him. "They shall be yours by *right*, and not by extortion. I only wish that which is best for both my people and yours. There is no reason why we shouldn't cooperate for millennia to come."

"And why should we *cooperate*, when we can merely *demand* that our will be done?" *Seldek* shot back. "Your high and noble words may confound the lower strata of our people. But do not believe that we have all been deceived!"

At this they heard a trio of shots from Tselitel's gun outside the room. A fourth explosion sounded, and seconds later she fell through the door and hit the ground hard, blood rapidly staining the left shoulder of her robe.

Feeling *Seldek* loosen his grip ever so slightly at the sight, *Keelen* seized his knife arm and rolled onto his stomach, exposing the mutineer to Welter. A quartet of shots rang out, jerking *Seldek's* body as he lay helplessly exposed atop his hostage. With a gasp his life escaped through his lips, and he went limp. Growling in disgust, *Keelen* rolled him off onto the cold floor.

The instant he'd done for *Seldek*, Welter twisted where he lay and covered the door with his pistol, expecting more mutineers to burst in. But half a minute passed without any sign of them. Carefully getting to his feet, he poked an eye outside as *Keelen* dragged Tselitel out of danger and examined her wound.

"She alright?" Welter inquired, still looking through the door, a pair of fallen mutineer bodies justifying Rhemus' faith in Tselitel's ability to shoot at close range.

"She's taken a very bad hit," *Keelen* informed him gravely. "She needs medical attention right away."

"Then give it to her," he snapped, sliding a fresh magazine into his pistol in a flash.

"No, I mean we need to get her to the hospital at once. She won't last long here on the floor."

"Well, we're not moving until we've secured the area," he responded. "We need reinforcements immediately."

"I'll get them," *Keelen* volunteered, gesturing for Rhemus to approach and kneel beside Tselitel. "Keep pressure on her wound," he instructed, taking the sovereign's hand and placing it against the moist hole in her shoulder. "The first thing we must avoid is loss of blood." Taking one of the mutineer's pistols, he slipped past Welter and disappeared.

"I hope he hurries," the emperor said with deep concern, looking into Tselitel's unconscious face. "She's in a bad way."

"She'll be alright," Welter replied, though without much faith in his own words. "We won't be here long."

As he said this a shot echoed down the hall back towards them.

"*Keelen's* found some trouble," Frank remarked. "Hope he can shoot straight."

Scowling his doubts, Welter mutely watched the corridor outside the room. Soon he heard the sound of many feet tramping towards them, and he knew they were either saved or about to be massacred.

"Welter! Emperor Rhemus!" *Keelen's* voice called, just out of sight. "I've brought help back with me. Don't shoot."

Stepping carefully into view, he hastened his pace when Welter waved him on. Followed by a dozen armed *Kol-Prockians*, he led them into the room and quickly got Tselitel off the floor and into the arms of four of them. Carrying her carefully while the rest formed a wall of bodies around her and the emperor, the group made for the hospital.

Many hours later she awoke inside the chamber. Opening her eyes slowly, she found herself in Rhemus' usual place upon the floor. Her throbbing shoulder was tightly bandaged, reminding her at once of the last thing she had seen before losing consciousness: a pair of *Kol-Prockian* mutineers advancing on her. Closing her eyes, she'd pointed the pistol where she remembered them to be and squeezed the trigger thrice. Opening them again in horror as a searing pain shot through her chest, she realized she'd been hit just before tumbling through the doorway and smashing her head on the floor. With that she'd lost consciousness, though a faint sense of the events that followed lingered in her mind. Or was it her imagination? She didn't know. But a feeling of being surrounded by many people pervaded the time between being shot and awakening in the chamber. Help must have arrived from some quarter or other. In any event, she'd been well taken care of.

Realizing voices were speaking quietly on the other side of the room, she tried to sit up but found the pain in her shoulder intolerable. Dropping back to the floor with a gasp, she attempted rolling onto her side, gathering her legs under her. But this likewise left her in such agony that she could only lay back and breathe. Shutting her eyes and drawing air for a few moments, she didn't notice the sounds of approaching feet.

"So you *are* awake," Rhemus said, smiling fondly as he rounded the curtain with *Karnan* at his side. "I thought perhaps you were struggling in your sleep."

"I struggle enough in my waking hours," she chuckled, trying to mask her chagrin at having another disability to labor under.

"We are all of us held back by some handicap or other," *Karnan* told her, aware of her true feelings despite her attempt to hide them. Pressing his back against the chamber's wall, he slid down to her side and sighed. "Sooner or later, whether by age, genes, or pure accident, we all end up with a stone in our shoe. It's just a part of life."

"Tell me about it," she muttered, pitying herself momentarily because of her Valindra. Shaking her head, she tried to take back her words. But *Karnan* held up a hand before she could speak.

"It's all right, little one," he smiled. "You're among friends here. Each of us has felt that way at one point or another. It just means you're human." Then he chuckled. "Or *Kol-Prockian*, I guess."

"Did Gustav come through it all okay?" she asked, suddenly remembering him. "I hope he wasn't hurt."

"No, he's fine," Rhemus assured her, sitting down near her head. "Came through it without a scratch. Which is more than I can say," he added, rubbing where Welter had kicked him in the leg. "Saying he has a kick like a mule doesn't *begin* to describe what that man can do with his feet. I'm surprised he didn't break any bones."

"Well, he just wanted to ensure you were safe," she quickly replied.

"Oh, you don't have to apologize for him," Rhemus said with a wave of his hand. "I know why he did it. That's the whole reason Krancis sent him: he knows what he's doing, and he doesn't hesitate. Just hurts to be on the receiving end of it."

"And *Keelen?*" she inquired after a few quiet moments. "Is he okay, too?"

"Just fine," *Karnan* answered. "A little shaken up. But in some ways that's a good thing. He's made it his personal mission to scour every last one of those artifacts *Seldek* was using from the base. Probably won't be more than a handful left by morning."

"You mean they'll *still* hang onto some of them after all *Seldek* has put us through?" she asked in surprise. "Haven't they had enough?"

"Some *Kol-Prockians* have less sense than they ought to," he replied with a frown. "I guess that's true of all races. But when you take a people as proud as mine and drop them this low, well, the temptation to put an ornament around your neck and amplify your capacities is all but irresistible for some. Even just having the *option* to do so will ensure that a few of those artifacts remain within *Kren-Balar*, hidden in little out-of-the-way nooks. But don't worry about it," he continued, seeing the concern on her face. "Emperor Rhemus has just announced that the possession or use of such artifacts is a capital offense. That will all but eliminate their use. I consider it very unlikely that we'll run into any trouble from them in the foreseeable future."

"But what about down the line?" she queried.

"By then the base will be locked down tighter than a drum," Rhemus said, aware that she was slowly beginning to spiral into worry. "We're already in control of every major portion of the base. It's just the odd renegade that we have to deal with. Once they're out of the way, *Kren-Balar* will be a very safe place for us."

"Good," she uttered in relief, closing her eyes and breathing for a moment to recenter herself. Opening them, she found the emperor's. "I don't think I can stand any more excitement," she added with a little smile.

"You've done admirably, Doctor," he assured her. "Much more than could have been expected, given your condition and the utter strangeness of your circumstances. Those rebels would have gunned us down if you hadn't stopped them."

"I'm just glad it's over," she responded, blinking her eyes to drive away the memory of the dying mutineers. Despite their intent to kill, it troubled her to have ended their lives. "I hope I never have to do it again."

"My hope is the same, for your sake," *Karnan* seconded. "It's much better that a man such as Welter should handle such work. His inner hollowness robs him of any sense of consequence. He doesn't see the ending of a life when he guns down a killer. For him, it is simply an obstacle that has been eliminated. The softness of your heart always leaves you hoping that another path could have been held out for the evildoer. You wish everyone could be redeemed."

"I do," she assented apologetically. "I guess it's just the

way I'm made."

"Oh, I didn't mean that critically, my dear," *Karnan* hastened to add. "It's a wonderful thing to wish life and growth to all living things. But some of them don't want that – they want to tear down and kill and destroy. And for people like that, only Welter's way will do. Some beings are simply wild dogs, and you've got to destroy them before they have a chance to tear you up."

"I don't think Gustav is hollow inside," she remarked after a moment. "I think he's just hurting inside. He lost–," she paused, just as Amra's name was on her lips. "Um, he lost someone very important to him shortly before coming out here. It's made him cold and incredibly hard."

"A man like that's always been cold and hard," *Karnan* replied wisely. "It's just the way he's made. More than likely the person he lost kept the hope alive in his heart, preventing him from reaching the ultimate conclusion of his personality. With her gone, he's given up in a sense. He doesn't hope for life and growth anymore. All his thought is bent upon the coldest definition of justice now."

"I hope that isn't true," she replied, ruminating momentarily before starting. "How…did you know it was a female he'd lost?" she asked, afraid she'd somehow betrayed information that had been shared in confidence.

"It's clear enough," *Karnan* answered, lifting his head and eyeing the chamber's door. "A man doesn't seek fulfillment from his own sex. He recognizes in the female his other half, and wants to see her grow. When she's destroyed, it likewise destroys his hope. But not just any woman," he continued. "She has to be special to him. Part of his flesh, in essence. Recognizing the symptoms of his loss at once, I knew, more or less, what had caused them. Naturally I had the sense not to bring this to his attention. He's not very sociable where his private affairs are concerned."

"Indeed not," she agreed, glad that he'd kept the matter to himself. "You know, it's funny," she remarked. "I never had any idea that there was a sort of…I don't know, *aspirational* quality in how men view their women."

"It's a pretty subtle thing, easy to miss," *Karnan* shrugged.

"It's not the sort of thing that a psychiatrist *ought* to miss," she responded. "I've got to be able to view things from all angles, not just my own."

"How are you going to manage that?" he asked with a tolerant smile. "We're all locked into a given perspective by our nature, little one. If there's one thing I've learned from a century and a half of life, it's that we can never truly escape our own heads. We can only approximate minds that differ from our own. We can't play God and be omniscient. So don't be too hard on yourself. We're all born with blinders on our eyes. If we're smart, we take account of those things that differ from us and give them space to live. But we must all accept that we'll never achieve omniscience."

"I think you might want to take up psychiatry," she replied with a generous smile, impressed by his wisdom.

"I've had a lot of time to think," he said modestly. "Not like there's been a lot else to do, sitting in here year after year."

"Tell me, does this aspirational quality hold true for *Kol-Prockian* relationships as well?" she asked, excited at the idea of a common link between the two races. "Do *Kol-Prockian* males view their females like that?"

At this question his face slowly fell, and he looked out across the chamber.

"Indeed they do," he answered somberly, his eyes distant as he thought. "Indeed they do."

Inwardly kicking herself for asking, she tried to think of something to say but no words came to mind. Awkwardly letting the matter drop, she tried to fold her hands on her stomach but had forgotten her shoulder. Gasping with pain, she kept her left arm on the floor beside her, placing her right hand on her abdomen.

"Got to remember that," she said with a little smile.

"It'll take some getting used to," *Karnan* replied, getting unsteadily to his feet and returning to his side of the chamber without another word. Anxiously she looked at Rhemus. But he merely shook his head.

"Let him go," he told her in a whisper. "Only he can deal with whatever's troubling him."

"But I hurt him," she protested gently.

"No, something else did that," he answered. "Something long ago. It's not your fault for reminding him. Just leave it alone. It'll pass off with some time."

"Sometimes it's the hardest thing in the world to do nothing," she responded, her healer's heart going out to the ancient alien.

"That's usually when it's the best course to take," he replied, stretching out beside her and heaving a tired sigh. "Now take a little rest for yourself, Doctor, and stop worrying about other people's problems. You've been through enough lately."

"Alright," she assented reluctantly, shifting on the floor a little and closing her eyes.

Despite her concern for any emotional distress *Karnan* might be suffering, she nevertheless quickly drifted off to sleep, the calming effects of the chamber easing her out of consciousness. The dreams that followed were multitudinous, gentle, and meaningless – simple rearrangements of pleasant experiences she'd had over the course of her life, starting from her earliest days. Even in her sleep she sought some kind of purpose behind them, a hidden message that would guide her in some way. But they were nothing more than pictures being paraded within the theater of her mind. Gradually she grew frustrated by their lack of import and wished to awaken. But sleep held her like a giant in the palm of its hand, and refused to let her go. Even techniques she'd used many times before to emerge from the deepest of slumbers failed her. Slowly it dawned on her that there was a purpose behind the lack of purpose. And then, all at once, wisdom appeared in the form of Rhemus voice speaking to her from all around.

"*At times, the best course is to do nothing,*" he said.

And then she awoke.

Once more forgetting her shoulder, she sat up and looked around, though this time it didn't hurt her very much to do so. Realizing this, she felt her wound and found it painful but tolerable. Aware that she was the only one in the chamber, she lay back for a few minutes and allowed the fog to clear from her mind before attempting to rise. With difficulty she did so, finding it harder to balance than she'd expected, having only one wing to work with. Peeking through the chamber's door, she found the anteroom empty, save for Frank's disc on the desk. Stepping out of the chamber, she sat down on a corner of the desk and lifted the AI in her hands.

"What are you doing here all alone?" she inquired.

"Oh, they figured you'd get up at some point or other, so they left me behind," he explained, a hint of annoyance in his voice. "Given you don't speak *Kol-Prockian* and all, I guess they had a *small* point. But I think mostly Welter just wanted to get rid of me."

"How long have I been asleep?" she asked, yawning and stretching her back as much as she could without hurting her shoulder.

"Two and a half days."

"What!?" she exclaimed. "How's that even possible? Shouldn't I have needed to eat or drink or something?"

"The chamber works in mysterious ways," he answered humorously. "It's taken a lot of the healing load off your body, so you haven't had the same need for resources. Although I imagine you're pretty near starving at this point."

"Am I ever," she agreed, her stomach rumbling as if on cue. "Well, what's been going on? Is everyone still okay?"

"Oh, sure," he said easily. "But hang on just a…second.

I'm scanning your vitals." Half a minute passed. "Okay, you're looking pretty good. I mean, for someone who's been shot, smacked her head against the floor, and all but tortured with strain."

"Am I safe to go walking the hallways?" she queried.

"Well, medicine isn't exactly my forte, but I suppose you're strong enough," he said with some hesitation.

"No, I meant is *Kren-Balar* safe? I want to find the others."

"The emperor said for you to stay here," he answered. "He felt you might get a little lonesome. But he didn't want to risk you over-exerting yourself."

"Oh, I'm fine," she replied, sliding off the desk and making for the door.

"Given he *is* the emperor," Frank cut in, his tone just incisive enough to stop her, "isn't it prudent to set a good example for his new subjects? After all, if one of his own people doesn't see fit to follow his instructions…" his voice trailed.

"I suppose you're right," she assented half-heartedly, nevertheless drawing a little closer to the door and peering out the window for a moment. Seeing one of the guards' heads, she was reminded at once of the difficulty with which the *Kol-Prockians* settled themselves down to do anything at all. Given that they regarded Rhemus very nearly as a figure of religious devotion, she couldn't bring herself to endanger that kind of respect by setting a bad precedent. In lieu of this, she opened the door and, Frank acting as interpreter, arranged to have some food sent her way.

"That's a good idea," Frank said once the door was closed and she was moving towards the table. "Organics always feel better after eating something."

"I still can't believe I slept for so long," she replied, easing into a chair and grimacing as she rested both arms on the table. "My dreams just went on and on forever. I can't tell you how bored I got, how *alone* I felt."

"The chamber must have put you into a more relaxed state to facilitate recovery," Frank opined. "The longer, and the more peacefully you slept, the better."

"I imagine so," she replied. "But it's so weird to be out of control like that, to feel yourself just drifting from one fantasy to the next for days on end. It's like having no will of your own. Especially for me. I've never just floated along so helplessly."

"Maybe that's good," Frank offered. "Could be you're growing in a new direction."

"I guess so," she responded somewhat morosely, feeling yet more alone despite his company. Aware that something was suppressing her mood, she leaned back in her seat and tried to figure out what it was. Then it dawned on her. Pressing her fingers around her wound, she found a very thin disc. It was held tightly against her skin by the bandages that had mummified her shoulder. "What's this?"

"What's what?" he asked a little too brightly.

"*Frank*," she said rather pointedly.

"Okay, fine. It's an artifact."

"Like one of the ones *Seldek* used?" she asked with worry.

"No," he laughed. "Certainly not. It's a medicinal artifact, one that improves healing. It won't make you crazy like *Seldek's* did."

"Then why the secrecy?" she asked. "And why's it making me feel so funny?"

"Oh, well, to heal the body, energy must be taken from other places. So instead of supporting your mood and a wakeful state, it inadvertently suppresses those things so that you can repair yourself more effectively. It's not magic, you know. It has to work with what's available. It can't just *beam* health into your body."

"And the secrecy?"

"What secrecy?"

"*Frank!*"

"Okay! Fine! I wasn't supposed to tell you this, but it belongs to *Karnan*. He uses it to suppress–. Hey, where are you going?" he asked, as she pushed her chair away from the table and made for the door.

"To give this back," she said at once, passing into the corridor and signing for one of the guards to take her to Rhemus. Shaking his head, he managed to convey that they had orders to stay put. "What, am I under house arrest?"

"More or less," Frank said. "Look, it was *Karnan's* own free choice to give you that artifact. Can't you just accept it and be grateful?"

"Not when he's giving away his life in the process," she responded, padding off down the hall in her bare feet. But she'd scarcely made it twenty feet when a few of the guards darted past her and blocked the way. Angrily she moved her hands as though parting a wave, but they wouldn't budge. "Frank, tell them to move," she insisted, holding out the medallion.

"I'm sorry, Doctor," he said. "But I've got my orders, too. Now, you *really* need to get back into the room before this becomes an incident. Remember what I said about setting a good example?"

"And what kind of example is *Karnan* setting?" she shot back. "Putting himself at risk for me? Without him we don't have the chamber anymore. Where would that leave the emperor, to say nothing of the empire he serves? We can't afford to play favorites, Frank. He needs to take this device back right away."

"Lily, you would have *died* without it," he replied reluctantly. "That's another thing I wasn't supposed to tell you. The only reason *Karnan* turned it over was because you wouldn't have seen the end of the day if he hadn't. Besides, it was *Keelen's* professional opinion that he could safely part with the device for a few days without undue harm. Nobody walked into this with their eyes shut."

"Except me!" she protested, rattled by the news of her

near death. "When was I going to be told about this?"

"You weren't," Welter replied from behind her. "There wasn't any reason."

"Why?" she demanded, growing overwrought. "Haven't I got a right to know?"

"Yes," he assented. "But rights don't count for much in a war like this."

"Why?" she repeated, drawing near and looking angrily up into his eyes. "You can't single me out like this and leave that poor old scientist to suffer and decay."

"We most certainly can," he responded, taking her arm and turning her around. At once the guards parted for them. "Besides, he's not in any danger at present."

"You're still not telling me why you did it," she pointed out, fruitlessly pulling against his grasp.

"Because you're important to Rex Hunt," he answered without looking at her, striding as quickly down the corridor as she could manage. "That makes you of importance to the entire empire. *Karnan* recognized this and at once volunteered the artifact of his own free will. He said we couldn't gamble with what losing you would do to Hunt."

With a gasp of realization she stopped.

"That's what he was talking about," she said to herself, her eyes darting all around as she connected the dots. "He doesn't want Rex to go through the same thing y–," she paused, glancing at Welter. "The same thing he did," she finished, resuming movement.

"Evidently not."

Proceeding the rest of the way in silence, they passed through a heavily guarded door into a large room. Clearly a command center of sorts, it had a number of desks situated near the door, manned by *Kol-Prockian* technicians who monitored the vital systems of the base. Towards the back stood a much larger desk at which Rhemus sat. Both *Karnan* and *Keelen* were with him, seated on either side.

"How are you feeling, Doctor?" *Keelen* inquired, rising

from his place and solicitously placing a hand on her arm.

"Much better than I ought to, from what I've been told," she replied, looking at *Karnan* with concern. "Are you okay?"

"I gather our little friend has been blabbering away all of our secrets?"

"He has," she nodded.

"Why, of all the AIs who could have survived…" his voice trailed ruefully, his eyes going to the ceiling in annoyance. "I knew you would take the news poorly, Doctor, which is why the entire matter was supposed to be a *secret*," he said pointedly, glaring at the medallion in her hand. "It was a necessary step, though one I was certain you couldn't see your way towards accepting. So we had to act without either your knowledge or your consent."

"Then take it back now," she insisted, reaching for her bandages as though to pull them off through her robe.

Instantly *Keelen's* thin hands shot to hers.

"Don't do that," he ordered. "Your wound has made a rapid recovery. But do not presume too much on your present state of health. You could easily undo all the progress of the last few days. You still need time to heal."

"And what about him?" she queried, pointing at *Karnan*. "When does he need the artifact back?"

"Not yet," the aged scientist assured her. "My condition is not such that it requires constant exposure to the artifact."

"Then why do you carry it with you all the time?" she countered, not buying his story. "You can't tell me you can do without it if the only thing that caused you to part with it was me lying on my deathbed."

Carefully standing up, he walked unsteadily towards her and lifted his own robe to just below his thighs. She gasped in shock at the sight of ugly sores on his skin.

"I have a condition that would have made my life hatefully miserable had it not been for the artifact. But it takes time for the condition to work its evil. Time that I can give to you, to save you alive for your own sake, and that of the man you love. Don't worry," he continued, lowering his robe once more. "I'll take the medallion back in time for it to reverse the effects I've suffered. But that'll only be possible if you rest and allow both it and the chamber to do their work. Otherwise I will have suffered for nothing."

"Are you in pain?" she asked, still stunned by the sight.

"Immense pain," *Keelen* answered for *Karnan*, as the latter moved slowly back to his chair and sat down. "The sores run up and down his legs and torso. No treatment beside that of the artifact has ever proven effective. Which is why, as he said, you must allow it to work as effectively as it can. Rest and be calm, and don't take more onto yourself than you absolutely must. Your every energy must be bent upon healing yourself so that he can resume use of the artifact at once."

"I understand," she replied, unable to say more.

"Mister Welter," Rhemus said after a silent moment. "Would you escort Doctor Tselitel back to the chamber?"

Wordlessly he took her arm and guided her slowly away. Several times she looked over her shoulder at the old scientist as she and Welter retreated, the spell of his condition not broken until he was physically out of sight.

"I had no idea," she uttered, shaking her head once they were alone in the corridor.

"That was the idea. You should have left well enough alone."

"I know. I'm sorry."

Silently they returned to the chamber.

"Wait," she pleaded, as he released her arm and turned to leave. "Don't go yet. Just keep me company for a little while. I've felt so strange over these last few days, even though I've been unconscious. Like I've been desperately alone. I know I'm not exactly your favorite person right now," she concluded apologetically. "But please don't leave me here by myself."

"You've got Frank," he replied, nodding towards the medallion she still held. "He's chatty enough to hold down both ends of a conversation on his own."

"Yes, but he's not exactly human companionship," she said, grimacing slightly since the AI could hear her.

"Thanks a lot," he replied tartly.

"Look, Doctor, the best thing for you right now is rest. It won't heal you any faster to stay awake talking."

"Oh, I know that," she replied anxiously, turning away and taking a step farther into the chamber, gently wringing her hands. "But I'm too tense to sleep. I just feel…like I'm on the edge of some kind of precipice." She faced him again. "I guess that's why I overreacted about being kept in the dark. I was just freaking out, latching onto the first thing that passed in front of me. Have you ever felt that way before?"

"No."

"I have," she continued. "Many times. Like the whole of my life was about to drop off into an impossibly deep canyon. One in which nobody would ever find me. It's what I imagine quicksand to be like: all of a sudden you're trapped, and you're just sinking and sinking and you can't do anything about it. You know it's going to pull you under; that you'll disappear into the muck and never see the light of day again; that you'll suffocate helpless and alone." She shuddered. "It's a horrible feeling."

"You seem to be doing your best to refine it," Welter replied, crossing his arms and leaning against the chamber's wall. "You've painted quite a picture. It's like you *want* to think about such things."

"Believe me, I don't," she shook her head. "It's just that…I don't know, I've always needed a way to *physically* represent what I'm going through mentally, as a way of making myself intelligible to others. Even if I don't share such images, I like knowing that I can – that my experiences aren't mine alone, that someone else can share in them, no matter how terrible. It makes me feel like less of a looney."

"You're the farthest thing from a looney," he assured her frankly. "*Seldek* was a looney. Shoot, even *Karnan's* got a few brain cells that are out of place. But you're solid as they come, minus Valindra."

"Minus Valindra," she repeated, nodding to herself. "Don't you see that's what I'm talking about? That's the monkey that's been riding my back ever since I was a little girl. That's what's always made me feel so terribly afraid and alone – my special condition, the one that really no one else had, no one could cure, and, half the time, no one could even pronounce. It was the worst form of being unique, because it meant nobody could really understand what I was going through. It forced me to face death alone from such a tender age, and I wasn't up for it. I-I couldn't handle it. It broke me. It was only years later that I picked up the pieces, but not completely. I'm like a piece of pottery: you can glue it back together, but the cracks remain. And now," she shook her head, "seeing my life flash before my eyes these last few days as I dreamed, I was reminded of just how close to the edge I am. That's why I had to seek out you and the others. Sure, I was upset about *Karnan* and this," she said, tapping her bandage to indicate the artifact. "But more than anything I needed an excuse to be with you all. I can't stand being alone like this. It tortures me so."

"Doctor, I know you've been through a great deal," he began, pushing off the wall and approaching, his arms still crossed. "But you've got to be strong like the rest of us. Everyone within *Kren-Balar* is holding on by the skin of their teeth. Even the emperor."

"And you?" she queried.

"My case is different," he replied. "I don't have anything to hold on for anymore. But you do. And so does every other soul in this base. You have to keep the flame alive within you."

"But *I* need you, Gustav," she protested. "And so does

Rhemus. We couldn't have made it half this far without you. And we'll be certain to fail if we were to lose you. You mustn't consider your life's work over and done with now that–," she hesitated, seeing his eyes flare. "Now that–," she began again, trying to be brave but melting under his gaze.

"Don't say it, Doctor," he told her. "That's not something to be talked about. It's much too sacred."

"We've spoken of it once before," she pointed out gently, trying to soften his anger.

"Which was once too many," he responded. "Now let it drop," he added in a tone of warning.

"I'll let it drop," she agreed, glancing away for a moment to regain her equilibrium.

"Remember that the next time you want to bring it up," he said, turning towards the door.

"Gustav, I'm truly sorry," she said, following him out of the chamber and into the anteroom. "But please don't leave me alone. Not yet."

Without turning he paused halfway through the room.

"You're alone every time you're with me, Doctor. There's nothing inside me to give. Not anymore."

With this he left her.

"I don't think I'll ever understand that man," Frank said after a moment. "You'd think he was already dead. But he's still sharp as a knife and quick as a viper. I don't get how he can keep it up if he's got nothing inside him to drive him on."

"He's got something to drive him, alright," she replied, still watching the door through which he'd left. "Something terrible."

"And what's that?"

She watched the door a moment longer, and then turned back towards the chamber.

"Revenge, Frank," she answered. "He's waiting for revenge."

CHAPTER 3

"I can't believe I ever signed up for this," Captain Roland Bessemer murmured inwardly, unwilling to speak aloud because of the eerie feeling he was getting off the orb behind him. For days he'd been alone, surrounded by a tunnel of blackness as he traversed warp with nothing to keep him company save the mysterious cargo that, he felt, was somehow watching him.

Shifting uncomfortably in his seat, he wished that Krancis hadn't insisted on his wearing a spacesuit. After all, he reflected, the eggs were feats of engineering perfection. He hardly needed an extra layer of protection. But the hasty alterations to the rear seats had made the man in black question the ship's integrity, and he'd been forced to give his solemn word to keep the suit on until his mission was complete.

"Just once I wish I wasn't so honorable," he thought without self-consciousness, watching the darkness stream by. The wonder of the dark realm had long since lost its appeal. Now, more than anything, he wished for a little bit of color. Even just a tiny flower in a vase would be enough. "Oh," he said aloud, remembering the AI and activating her hologram. At once a sprightly little figure appeared on his dashboard. She looked like a woman in her early twenties, her body made of bright pink light.

"Yes, Captain Bessemer?" she asked pleasantly.

"Oh, just keep me company for a while," he said with

a sigh, shifting again in his seat, trying to make himself comfortable.

"Of course."

He knew better than to engage her in conversation. The moment he'd learned of his assignment, he'd anticipated many long, fascinating discussions with an alien intelligence that had seen all sorts of things that he'd only ever dreamed about. But she seemed to know almost nothing of interest. It was as though her memory had been erased, save for the bare essentials. Conversation always ended in frustration, so he did his best to satisfy himself with her mere presence.

"Sir, we're approaching our destination. Estimated time of arrival is fifteen minutes."

Before he could respond, the hair on the back of his neck stood up. Swallowing hard, he could have sworn that a field of some kind was reaching out from the orb and touching him. It felt intelligent, like a kind of psychic gravity that was pulling him back towards it.

"Very good," he answered the AI, trying to sound normal.

"*Why did I sign up for this?*" he asked inwardly, all but certain that the orb was somehow haunted. "*Wasn't enough for me that it can roll, or not roll, at will! That should have been my first clue. Wasn't until I mentioned the Gate of Zeruc that it decided to move!*"

He wished he could go back and turn Krancis down. But then he frowned, for he knew he'd never turn down anything that the emperor's strong right hand asked him to do. He'd sooner die in his service than disappoint him. So he was stuck with the orb.

"Are you alright, Captain?" the AI queried, making him jump. "Your vitals are showing abnormalities. Your heart rate is quickening, and your–."

"I'm fine," he cut her off. "Perfectly fine. I'm just tired of being cooped up in this ship. The sooner we reach the *Gate of Zeruc*, the better."

He named it again in the hope that the orb would be appeased. To his relief, it was, the power of its field of influence weakening once more.

"*Thank God,*" he thought, sighing as he melted into his chair. "*Just a few more minutes and I'll be rid of this thing for good.*"

With nothing else to bend his thoughts upon, he began to wonder just what the orb was. Was it a kind of weapon? Or perhaps an ancient artifact, like a power generator? That could be, he reflected, given the energy it gave off.

"*Maybe it's got an AI running it from the inside, channeling its output,*" he reasoned, his hopes growing that it was merely a technical product of an advanced civilization, and not some supernatural being held in some kind of stasis. As this latter notion flitted through his mind, his heart sank again, for that was exactly what he feared it to be. Swallowing hard once more, it suddenly occurred to him that Krancis might have had another reason for putting him in a spacesuit. "*What if this is all some kind of trick?*" he asked himself, starting to sweat despite the temperature controlled suit. "*What if the suit is meant to protect me from* it?"

The temptation to look over his shoulder at the orb suddenly became all but irresistible. It was like a fire drawing him in after a long night in the cold. It bore, dare he say it, charisma? No, that wasn't quite it. Awe? Nobility? Desperately he wanted to turn and face it, to lay his hand upon it and feel its impossibly smooth surface. He wanted to get closer to it, to sit beside it and soak up its aura.

"Captain," the AI cut in on his thoughts, making him jump again.

"Yes?"

"We are ten minutes from our destination."

"Thank you," he replied gratefully, aware that he'd been slipping under the orb's influence and thankful for her interruption.

"*This ain't any power generator,*" he reflected. "*It's something a whole lot different than that.*"

Unconsciously he began to drum his nervous fingers on the dashboard. He ceased the instant the orb started expanding its influence again, apparently noticing his anxiety.

"H-how much further?" he asked the AI, as evenly as he could.

"Seven minutes until we reach our destination, Captain Bessemer."

"G-good," he nodded emphatically. "Very good. Can't wait."

"Captain, your pulse is nearly one-hundred and fifty," she pointed out. "And your blood pressure–."

"Sometimes I get claustrophobic after long journeys in warp," he lied. "I can't help it. No matter how many trips I take, I usually get a little taste of it towards the end. It's like I can't quite believe the journey is nearly over, you know? It's silly, of course. But I've always been that way."

"Oh, I didn't realize." she responded, her voice automatically growing more serene in an attempt to calm him. "Would you like me to turn on some music to distract you?"

"No, no, that's alright," he shook his head. "I'll just wait it out. What doesn't kill you makes you stronger, right?"

"Of course, Captain," she agreed.

"*I hope,*" he added internally.

Within the privacy of his mind he counted off the minutes, growing more agitated as they dwindled. Could the orb read his thoughts? Was it aware that he was on to it?

"*No, that couldn't be,*" he tried to assure himself. "*Or it wouldn't have been tricked by mentioning the Gate of Zeruc. But still...I feel like it might reach out at any time and–.*"

"One minute to our destination, Captain," the AI announced, jolting him again.

"Excellent," he said hastily, the word smearing out of

his mouth in a blur.

"And then your claustrophobia will be at an end," she added reassuringly.

"Absolutely," he replied.

"Krancis must have known something was up with this thing," he reasoned as the seconds evaporated. "That's why the AI doesn't know spit! He made sure she couldn't give anything away by accident. But give it away to who? Or what?"

Suddenly feeling very alone in the universe, he reflexively glanced around him to get his bearings. But there were none in the black tunnel through which he was traveling, and he lowered his eyes back to the dashboard, where the AI had helpfully transformed into a little pink countdown clock. At the thirty second mark his heart climbed into his throat, and it took all his will not to deathgrip his seat with his fingers. With fifteen seconds to go he stopped breathing and began to feel faint, the last few seconds ticking away in a slowly gathering haze.

Then suddenly the dark tunnel terminated and he was deep within a nebula of shadow. In wonder he looked around, for he knew it was no ordinary cloud in space. Glancing at his instruments, he received no signal whatever.

"This is where the Gate of Zeruc is?" he asked aloud, curious how he'd ever manage to find it. Able to see scarcely a dozen feet in any direction, the dreadful thought filled him that he might be forced to fly up and down the nebula for days, perhaps even weeks in search of where he was to discard his mysterious cargo.

But as he thought on this the orb began to rumble. Not physically, for he could feel the ship was quite stable. But *psychically*. At once his head began to hurt. Anger surged inside him, but not his own: it was the orb's. Or rather, he felt immediately certain, the being held within it. He was all but blinded physically, as the entity's power pushed aside his faculties and asserted its rage, using him as an antenna to communicate with the world outside its prison.

"Gyaaaaah!!!!" he screamed, unable to help throwing his head back as orange light beamed from his eyes. Desperately he slapped the dashboard, hoping to find the switch that opened the canopy. To his amazement the AI stood passively as before, the stripping of her personality so complete that she hadn't the least inclination to interfere. The orb was completely off-limits to her artificial psyche.

Gasping for breath, sensing that his mind must disintegrate at any moment, he lucked into the right combination of key presses and caused the canopy to pop open. Immediately upon doing so he seized the controls and thrust the craft downward, causing the orb to float away and disappear into the shadows that surrounded him. Rapidly he felt its influence wane, the blackness around him insulating him like a blanket. In merely a half minute the nightmare was over.

Closing the canopy, he sat back in the seat and breathed. Certain of the spacesuit's purpose now, he tore its helmet off and angrily threw it into the rear of the craft.

"Is this what you sent me out here for, Krancis?" he demanded, quivering with rage. "So I could be some kind of dead-on-arrival delivery boy?!"

"I–I–I'm af–aff–afraid that it was n–n–necessary to keep you in the dark, Captain," the AI spoke in a fragmented voice.

"Oh, shut up!" he barked, believing she was merely glitching from the effects of the orb.

"You m–m–must give me a moment," she replied "Releasing the o–orb has begun to alter my database."

"How?" he snapped.

"Please look behind you," she uttered haltingly, holding out a trembling hand towards the rear of the craft. Irritably he looked over his shoulder, and was surprised to find that the place vacated by the orb was covered in strange writings. "Th–th–those are inscriptions made in the t–t–tongue of the *Keesh'Forbandai*. My psyche has been del–

deliberately fragmented to ensure that…the…being could not understand our purpose. Those writings contain… instructions on how to recover myself. Please permit me to complete the fusion of my–my–my–my mind. Then I will be happy to explain all that it is in my power to disclose."

Bessemer was little inclined to wait for anything after such an ordeal. But the AI's air of intelligence, despite her glitchiness, was at such sharp odds with her previous empty-headedness that he decided to give her a chance to explain. Pointing the craft down and away from the orb, he accelerated to an easy cruising speed to put some more distance between it and himself.

"The process is now complete, Captain," she uttered with poise after several minutes.

"About time."

"You have every right to be upset," she replied. "You have been sent on a mission that was almost certain to end in your death. Indeed, the likelihood of your survival was merely twelve percent by my estimation. That you have come through it alive is a miracle that must be attributed to both your self-possession and the efforts of the dark realm. Had it not reached forth its great power to protect you from the being within the orb, you would have certainly been consumed by it."

"You call that *protection?*" he shot back. "I could feel it boiling my mind like soup! I probably have brain damage!"

"You may," she allowed. "Regrettably this vessel's instruments aren't capable of ascertaining the state of your brain in detail. But you may rest assured that I do not detect any superficial damage. Though understandably your pulse and blood pressure are still very high."

"Who would have guessed it? I almost get killed, and I'm a little shaken up!"

"Krancis wished me to express his personal regret that this course had been forced upon us," she continued. "He recognizes both your skill as a pilot and your devotion to the empire. It was for these reasons, in part, that you were chosen for the task. A lesser man would have certainly died. Although there were other motives as well, such as the fact that the being within the orb would have been tipped off had we made any weaker effort in moving it."

"So you had to make the deception good," he summarized with annoyance. "Had to make sure the butler had on his tux and fancy shoes! Couldn't let that–that *thing* get the wrong idea!"

"That is an accurate reformulation of my words, Captain," she replied. "It has been withheld from me why such secrecy was necessary. Indeed, I have no information about the being held within the orb except the tiny fragments that Krancis has seen fit to give me. And they are as follows: that the being is incomparably ancient, devastatingly powerful, and subsequently can never be allowed to leave this place. The nebula that surrounds us is an oddity – a vast cloud of shadow left behind by the dark realm. It will conceal the being for the foreseeable future, working in tandem with the orb itself to muffle his voice and contain his power."

"His?" Bessemer queried, his anger diminishing a little as he came to see the stakes that were involved. "Just what kind of being is it?"

"I'm afraid I have no further information to share," she replied, causing him to turn his head sharply away in disgust.

"So I put my neck on the line, and all I'm told is 'This guy is dangerous, we had to get rid of him'?"

"That is correct. You may rest assured that the less you know, the far better off you will be."

"And how do you know that? You don't know any more about him than I do!"

"Because that's what Krancis told me," she explained, clasping her hands behind her back. "I do not mean to be lecturesome, Captain, but that ought to be enough for any of us."

"Not after what I went through," he shot back sharply. "Do you have even the *slightest* idea what that was like? To feel its rage shooting through me like I was some kind of, uh, of a *water pipe?* It was beyond terrifying – it was mind-cracking! I'm surprised I didn't have a nervous breakdown! That's not the sort of thing you can just slap a *Top Secret* label on and walk away from!"

"Nevertheless that's precisely what you must do," she responded, her tone gaining a bit of iron as he persisted. "Krancis stipulated that you must give your word never to pursue this topic further."

"Or what?"

"Or I have instructions to disable this vessel and leave you here to die," she answered evenly.

"*What!?*" he exploded. "Wasn't it enough to send me on a suicide mission without finishing the job *himself?!*"

"My next course of action is entirely in your hands, Captain," she pointed out. "Krancis does not wish to sacrifice so much as a single life unnecessarily. But if you force his hand, he will act without hesitation."

"*You* will, you mean."

"To act on Krancis' behalf, upon his express wishes, is the same as if he were to perform the act himself," she reasoned. "Believe me, I do not wish to do this to you, either. But I will perform my duty."

"What choice have you left me?!" he snapped, smacking the dashboard and accidentally hitting a button. When it produced no effect, he glared at her. "You've disabled the controls!"

"That is correct," she replied, causing the craft to decelerate and then ease to a stop. "Before we proceed any further, I must have your word. The quality of your character is obvious to all, hence another reason why you were chosen for this task. If you *did* happen to survive, you could be counted on to remain silent about what you'd done. Provided you bound yourself with a solemn oath."

"Krancis is pretty old fashioned if he believes something like that," he replied, buying a little time to think.

"Krancis is an impossibly shrewd judge of character," she replied, standing a little straighter as pride edged its way into her voice. "He doesn't make mistakes in matters such as these. Of that you may rest assured."

He was assured, alright. In truth it frustrated him that the man in black had him dialed in so perfectly. Had he been wrong, he could have easily dashed off an oath to get control of the ship back. But that was not in his nature, as Krancis knew all too well.

"Captain?"

"Don't prod me," he said. "I'm thinking."

"There's only one course of action open to you," she continued. "Either swear, or suffer the consequences."

"Thank you for pointing that out," he responded acidly. "Can't you understand that it's a little humiliating to have my head put in a noose, have the chair kicked out from under me, just so the rope can break and I can be told to walk away and never look back? It's like being a puppet with no will of my own! No curiosity!"

"Curiosity can be fatal," she said gravely. "You must remember, there was a reason that the orb was hidden so well on Jennet. It was never intended to be found."

"Then why wasn't it just destroyed eons ago?" he countered. "Why bother with all this hide-and-seek? If the galaxy is in half the danger–."

"*Universe*, Captain," she corrected. "And not half of it. Should the being held within that orb be released, there is literally no limit to the damage that he could do. No one would be safe. Even the mightiest empires would fall – empires vastly more powerful than that which we now both serve. It would make the threat from both the parasite *and* the *Pho'Sath* appear trivial."

"I can't believe that," Bessemer shook his head.

"Nothing's that bad."

"You must believe it," she uttered, her artificial eyes boring into his own. "It is the entire reason for your task – why it was so important that the right man be chosen to carry it out. It is furthermore why this vessel's navigation equipment was partially damaged the moment I reassembled my psyche."

"What?!"

"In this way, no one will be permitted to find this location. Even you. Should even the *Pho'Sath* manage to capture and torture you, they would find out nothing. They already know that the being exists. Indeed, they search for him daily, hourly. But all you could communicate to them is that he exists, and that he dwells within a cloud of shadow. One which even their great insight cannot reveal to them."

"Why?"

"Were I to tell you that, they may find a way to locate it," she replied.

"Oh, you're kidding!?" he exclaimed.

"Hardly. There are many secrets in this universe, Captain Bessemer. Secrets which almost no being has a right to know. You should count it a privilege that fate has permitted you to see even this far into the dark background upon which all our petty lives play out. Constantly we are at risk of being swept aside by elements much larger than ourselves. It is only through our intelligence, our cohesion, and our devotion to duty that we can, and have, survived."

"You sound like Krancis now," he said sourly.

"There is no greater man to echo, Captain," she responded with complete certainty. "He is captain of our affairs by virtue of his capabilities. Were all the Earthborn to place their utmost faith in him, our chances of survival would improve considerably. As it is, your people still hesitate. We must hope that they will see the error of their ways and throw themselves utterly behind his every command."

"You mean deify him."

"That is not in the least what I mean, nor does he desire that. He wishes only to serve his people and, once the threat to mankind is vanquished, disappear forever. He has no personal ambitions whatsoever. He wants neither monuments nor even to be remembered in the history books, though that, of course, is a given. A star cannot shine so brightly as he has without being recorded for the rest of time. Alien eyes already watch his movements and decisions with a mixture of awe, fear, and respect. Not merely will the Earthborn remember him: all civilized life shall."

"Good for him."

"And now, Captain, I'm afraid I must bring matters to a head. Either you will accept the terms held out to you by Krancis, or I will be forced to sabotage this craft. What is your decision?"

For a long moment he hesitated. He knew there was only one answer. But despite the good sense, indeed, the frank necessity of the steps taken by Krancis, he couldn't help being riled. A man who'd seemed all but divine before appeared a great deal less likable now that the captain's own neck had been put on the line in such a ruthless fashion. Though inwardly he knew that wasn't truly the case. Deep down, the fact remained that he was still scared almost to death of what the being inside the orb had done to him. Its power; its malice; its pure, ancient rage, refined through countless years of forced isolation — all of them had passed through his mind when it reached out to him. He'd faced many fearful things in his time. But nothing so…godlike. It had rattled him unlike anything he'd ever encountered. And that was his real beef: not simply that Krancis had put him in danger, but that he'd put him in the presence of such a terrible being.

"I would be well within my instructions to strand you here, Captain," the AI cut in. "But I recognize the incredible trial through which you've just passed, and I believe, were he here, that Krancis would permit you a few moments' grace to finally speak.

"I give you my word I won't pursue this any further," he finally conceded.

"That's excellent. But there was a very particular oath that I was ordered to extract."

"Aren't you satisfied?" he demanded, his voice a mixture of anger and something akin to grief. "Haven't you put me through enough already? Forcing me to go up against that thing?!"

"I understand your trauma," she answered. "And the resultant cascade of emotions that are bursting through your mind. But my instructions are absolute. You must swear, as an officer in the service of Emperor Rhemus, that you will never attempt to uncover more about the entity that you have this day delivered into safekeeping."

Reluctantly, he did so.

"Thank you, Captain," she uttered, her tone growing more pleasant as she shifted and stretched her little hologram. "That was the final step. I'm sorry to have been so hard on you. But I was specifically programmed to have a tiered psyche. In order to move beyond the rather punitive personality that I evinced a few moments ago, you, and only you, had to speak the proper oath."

"So what, now more fragments can come together?" he asked with annoyance, though it was moderated by a blanket of fatigue that was quickly draping itself over him. "More…secrets?" he yawned.

"A few," she responded, her voice growing gentle as his eyes became heavy. "But now is not the time to speak of such things," she added, slowly accelerating the craft. "The ordeal with the entity has left you exhausted. You need to rest. I'll pilot us slowly out of the nebula."

He noted, with sedate, depersonalized surprise, that he couldn't respond. The words were in his mind, but the energy to move his tongue was gone. Totally spent. The oath, he reflected, had put some kind of cap on the whole affair, and now he was free to collapse from the burden of the experience. Scarcely half a minute passed before he slumped back in the seat, fast asleep.

"Rest now, Captain," she said tenderly, watching him. "Rest and recuperate. You will be needed again soon. Very soon."

His sleep was anything but restful as nightmare images tormented his every unconscious moment. Chased about by unseen forces, the very air around him seemed filled with fiery, bright orange demons shaped like griffins. He felt intent hanging over him like a cloud – intent to do him harm in the worst possible ways. Then he heard a voice whispering his name. It was sweet and pleasant, such a contrast to the evil that surrounded him. Slowly his sleeping brain recognized it as belonging to the egg's AI.

Aware of his dreamstate, he wished above all to awaken and leave it behind. But the encounter with the being had been so intense that he lacked the strength to be anything more than an observer within his own mind. Even as he attempted to dash away from the air demons across fields of dead, brittle grass, he made no headway. The ground slid beneath him as though it were a treadmill. Darting down from the sky, the griffins scraped their flaming feet along the ground and ignited the grass. With cackling laughs they hemmed him in with a rapidly forming circle of fire.

Again he heard the AI whisper, and this time a little spark stirred inwardly. The will to fight back asserted itself, and with effort he managed to push away both the demons and the circle of flame. Halting where he ran, still standing on a vast expanse of dead grass, he looked to the sky and realized it was blindingly bright. Covering his eyes too late, he rubbed them for a few moments and then looked at his feet. But all he beheld was darkness. Recoiling in horror, he moved backwards, stumbled, and fell. The grass pricked him mercilessly, drawing blood from a thousand points. About to shout in anguish, he suddenly found himself back inside the cockpit of the egg. Gaspingly he looked around, truly feeling claustrophobic within the small space. All but mad with fright, he jerked to and fro in the chair, desperately wishing to run to escape the griffins that he felt must still be right behind him. But there was nowhere to go. All he could see, in any direction, was the black warp tunnel.

"You're alright, Captain," the AI assured him, once he'd had a moment to get his bearings and had laid eyes on her. "It was just a nightmare."

"That wasn't *just* a nightmare," he asserted, wiping the back of his hand across his sweat-soaked lips. "That was from that being."

"What being?" she queried, tilting her head in confusion. "Is it something that's haunted your dreams before?"

"What are you talking about?" he asked incredulously, his eyes bulging at her. "The being! The entity! The one who–." He paused. Upon her face was an expression of such complete ignorance that he realized at once what had happened. Just as her initial persona had been shallow and ignorant to mislead the orb's prisoner, so too all that had been experienced after it asserted itself had been erased. Sometime while he'd been asleep her programming had completed her transformation. Crushed by the realization that he'd lost the only one who knew anything about what he'd gone through, he could only sigh and wave his hand to dismiss the question entirely. "How long was I out?" he queried after nearly a minute of stunned silence, gazing blankly across the dashboard into the ever-spiraling tube of blackness.

"Approximately one day, three hours, and forty-two minutes," she replied in a chipper voice, glad to have something factual to contribute, hoping it would ground him somehow. "You must have been very tired after your last mission."

"You can say that again," he murmured, leaning back in the seat and drawing a big breath. Exhaling it raggedly, he allowed his eyes to fall back down to the AI. "What now? More adventures?" he asked bitterly, all but despairing in his loneliness.

"In fact, there is another task for you to complete before returning to *Sentinel*," she confirmed. "You are to retrieve an artifact."

"What kind of artifact?" he queried dubiously, concerned that it may be yet another ancient monstrosity in disguise.

"I was given only very limited information about it," she replied somewhat apologetically. "But it resides within an ancient temple of some sort. I've already entered the location into the ship's navigational computer."

"So just more sitting and waiting," he groused. Though hardly regretting a chance to rest after all he'd been through, he wished it could have been in more comfortable surroundings than a modified egg equipped only with an amnesic AI. "Is it dangerous?"

"There are no reports of hostile populations surrounding the structure. It appears to be utterly vacant."

"How long until we get there?"

"Ten hours, nineteen minutes, and fifty-three seconds."

"Out of the frying pan," he mumbled. Suddenly deciding he was sick of his spacesuit, he peeled off the rest of it and threw it into the rear of the craft. The activity did him good, his aching muscles burning for action. But he regretted the decision once he looked up at the huge tunnel of darkness and felt that much less protected from it. It was peculiar, he knew. But he felt an odd aversion to the shadowy element that hadn't been there before. Like it was watching him, or sought to do him harm. Shrugging the notion away, he dismissed it as a holdover from his dreams.

Thus began Bessemer's long wait. Unable to sleep

after so many hours unconscious, he was forced to make what conversation he could with the earnest but uninteresting AI. Gleaning what he could from her about the temple, he put together that it was scarcely more than a pile of stones on some neglected little jungle moon nobody had given a thought to in over a century. Once upon a time it had been the site of a modestly successful kantium mine. But it was so far out of the way of every other kind of civilized life that the population abandoned it once its raison d'etre had sent its last gleaming coin into the imperial treasury. The only company he could expect, outside of the local wildlife, were the ghosts of past miners.

Eventually sliding into a light doze, he awoke with a jolt when the ship emerged from warp.

"What the–?" he exclaimed, looking around and finding himself surrounded by a curtain of stars. Looking down at the little AI he frowned. "Could have let me know we were about to drop into normal space."

"I'm sorry, Captain Bessemer."

Waving away her apology, he exhaled his annoyance and took the controls. Straight ahead lay a lush moon in orbit around an orange gas giant. It's hue brilliant, it looked like a massive ball of cheese floating in space. Instructing the AI to place a waypoint on the temple, he made for the moon, soon penetrating its atmosphere and descending through layer upon layer of clouds.

"*Not a bad place*," he reflected, impressed with the sense of life and vitality that presented itself. "*Like some kind of farmer's paradise.*"

Indeed, it did appear that every kind of plant imaginable was capable of sprouting from its fertile soil. As far as he could see, in every direction, there waved in the wind such a variety of flora that no two plants seemed to be alike.

"*Like some kind of garden. Doesn't seem natural*," he commented inwardly, doubtful that such an incredible array of species could be found in nature. In times past he would have scarcely made time to so much as note such a fact before moving on. But his encounter with the orb made him suspicious that perhaps there was more to the mission than merely the retrieval of an artifact. He started to wonder what he wasn't being told. "Where's the mining town?"

"Approximately eighteen miles from our objective," she answered, her hands clasped behind her back, her little shoulders held straight.

"Put a waypoint on it."

"But…that's not our objective," she said. "Our mission–."

"Is to recover an artifact, yes, I know," he responded. "But I've got a funny feeling about this place. I want to explore a little."

"I don't think we should spend any more time on this moon than is necessary," she objected. "Our instructions were to land, retrieve the artifact, and depart. If there were other things of value to be found, I'm sure they would have been included in our orders."

"You're carrying blind faith to new heights," he remarked, still flying towards the temple but lowering his speed. "Put up that waypoint. I want to check over the town first."

"Very well," she relented, her orders being to assist him in whatever he elected to do, so long as it didn't directly impair the mission. She placed a small gray waypoint on his IIUD while leaving a much larger green one hovering over the location of the temple. Rolling his eyes at this not-so-subtle attempt to modify his decision, he turned away from the temple and dropped still further. Flying just above the trees, he could all but smell the plant-infused moisture outside his canopy. Longing to land and stretch his legs, he dashed across the treetops, snapping off a few branches as he passed. "I strongly advise–."

"The ship can take it," he cut her off, rapidly

approaching his desired waypoint. Slowing as he neared it, he was surprised to find no trace of it from the air. "Alright, where is it?" he asked pointedly.

"Right here," she replied.

"All that's here is trees and trees."

"Captain Bessemer, this site has been abandoned for over a century. The jungle has simply reclaimed what little civilization had been carved out of it. Considering the almost violent passion for growth that has been evinced by every form of plant life that we've seen since entering the atmosphere, I doubt that the miners ever really did much more than live around it, anyway. It would have been too much work to clear a large area and then hold back the encroachments of nature."

"So where can we land?" he queried, looking over the side of the craft for even a small opening.

"This is the best spot, according to the ship's instruments," she replied somewhat reluctantly as she updated the waypoint's location, still wishing to bypass the town entirely. "But the fit will be tight. You'll have to descend blindly through a canopy of leaves into a space between a pair of buildings."

"Good enough," he answered, maneuvering to the place indicated and slowly pressing the egg into the trees' open arms. Loudly they snapped and crashed to the jungle floor, jerking their parent trunks to and fro.

"Wait a moment," she said, causing him to pause. "You'll have to turn the craft thirty degrees to the right, or we'll clip the edge of one of the buildings."

"Alright," he assented, doing as she said and resuming his landing. Glancing up through the hole he'd carved in the boughs, he saw that the canopy of leaves was so thick that scarcely any of the setting sun's waning light made it through. Flicking on the egg's external lights, he touched down, the craft resting a little off-balance on the uneven ground. Shutting it down, he popped the canopy and savored the first non-recycled air he'd breathed in what seemed ages. "Threat assessment?" he queried, pulling on a pair of boots and taking a small automatic pistol from a storage compartment beneath his seat.

"There are no indications of developed life on Balian," she replied.

"Balian?"

"That's the name of this moon. According to the data at my disposal, there is, however, a very significant animal population. It would seem that the fertility of this world is not limited to its plantlife. Given the very large food supply for herbivores, there consequently are a great many of them. This, naturally, means there's a great many carnivores as well. And they're not too shy about taking what they consider to be theirs."

"Sounds dangerous," he remarked with a hint of sarcasm that made her little artificial heart tighten. Standing up, he told her to unfurl the minimalist ladder of indentations so he could climb down.

"Be careful, Captain Bessemer," she said with concern as he threw a leg over the side and found a foothold. "There's no telling what you'll find down there. Keep your pistol at the ready."

"Just keep an eye on this ship," he answered. "And close the canopy once I've gone."

"I will," she replied quietly, as his head dropped out of sight.

Surrounded by a thick darkness that was only broken by the egg's external lights, he reached into his pocket and drew out a pair of light enhancing glasses that he'd been told to take back on *Sentinel*. Though at the time he thought nothing of the peculiarity of such equipment for what was supposed to be a purely space-based mission, he rolled his eyes at Krancis' fore-planning.

"*You knew I'd be here*," he thought, scowling as he put the glasses over his eyes. "*What else do you know that I don't?*"

Striding away from the ship, he drew his pistol and held it lightly in his hand. In every direction he could hear the evidence of the AI's warning. The bushes were vibrantly alive with creatures big and small. In fear they skittered away as he moved towards them, a thousand little eyes watching from the safety of the plants that obscured them.

The buildings, if they could be called that, were mere wooden shacks that had nearly collapsed after a century of neglect. Thrown up in haste, they were crooked, lopsided, and so rotten that they were soft to the touch.

"*Don't know why she had me land between 'em,*" he thought, easily pressing his thumbnail into a corner post. "*Would've crushed 'em like a grape, anyhow.*"

Pressing on into the town, the glassless window frames of many homes gaping at him in silent agony, the sense began to grow that he wasn't alone. Something seemed to be watching him from the houses. Something other than the myriad creatures that had called them home for generations. There was an aura in the air, an essence both old and wise. It seemed weary, as though countless years had worn away its strength, leaving it a mere shadow.

"*Or a ghost,*" he thought, his stomach tightening at the notion.

Glancing back over his shoulder towards the egg, now hidden behind a wall of foliage and old buildings, he wondered if he ought to turn back. His fear was gone – the being in the orb had stamped that out of him, at least for the moment. Nothing, he felt, could truly throw him after an experience like that. But he could feel his nerves tightening all the same, as though, on some deep level, his body was aware of a danger that he wasn't. Looking around again, he saw lizards and snakes and little monkeys hanging from branches, each of them curiously watching him. But nothing that could put him into any real danger, so long as he kept his wits about him.

It was then that he heard a faint echo on the wind. He

twisted his head to try and catch it before it disappeared. But the fraction of a second this took was too long. Like a snippet of sound it appeared and then vanished, having neither lead up nor wind down. He couldn't be sure, but it sounded like laughter.

Tramping down the middle of what had once been mainstreet, the buildings on either side began to thin out. Nearing the end of town, he was about to turn back when he heard the sound again. This time he was certain it was a laugh, a big, hearty one, like that of a sailor who's just come into port after months at sea and was eager for some time ashore. Hurrying after it, his boots splashing in pools of mud left by a recent rain, he passed out of town and into the surrounding jungle. All but thwarted by its incredible density, he had to fight his way tooth and nail to make any headway. Two hundred feet into it, he paused for breath and to listen.

"Where are you?" he murmured, slowly twisting this way and that to find the sound again. As if in answer he heard it fifty feet behind him.

Turning towards town again, he moved cautiously, trying to make as little noise as he could. But his environment defeated him. Giving up any attempt at stealth, he shoved his way through the greenery and reached the source of the laughter. Bleeding from several cuts to his arms and cheeks, he brushed the dribbling wounds on his face with the back of his hand and waited for another clue. Jumping at the sound of a stick snapping straight ahead, he dashed, more or less, through the foliage that separated him from his goal, bursting once more into the relative open of what was left of the town. Heaving for breath as he looked left and right, he wondered how he could have missed his quarry.

Then he heard the laugh burst out directly behind him. With a start he jerked around, aiming his pistol into thin air. Backing several steps away, he again glanced left and right.

"*So it is a ghost*," he reflected, continuing to retreat towards the egg.

Certain that the pistol was of no use with such an entity, he lowered it to his side and moved as casually as he could, hoping not to provoke even more outlandish antics from it. Turning around, he jumped at the sight of a tall, lean skeleton fringed by an orange glow. At once its fleshless mouth popped open, emitting a now horrible laugh of scorn mixed with anguish. Reflexively Bessemer raised his weapon and cranked off a trio of shots. But they passed harmlessly through the apparition.

"So they have sent another sacrifice to this lonely world," the ghost uttered, advancing towards him as he moved backwards. "Or perhaps you have come of your own accord?" he queried rhetorically. "It matters not. Your purpose shall be the same in either event."

"What are you?" Bessemer asked in shock, as the glowing skeleton continued to back him out of town.

"Like you, I am a sacrifice," he replied. "Food for the light master's soul. A scapegoat for the sins of humanity. A substitute for his terrible rage against our people."

"You were human?"

"I *am* human!" he bellowed, causing the captain to jump. "I have always been human. I will always *be* human, whether in body or spirit. Nothing can ever take that away from me. Even the Lord of Light."

"What are you talking about?" Bessemer asked, sensing great misery in the apparition and hoping to buy time. "Tell me about it."

"You can delay the inevitable," he replied cannily. "But you cannot prevent your fate. The same dark destiny that sent me to this world has now sent you. There is no escape for you. Your hope ended when you landed in the village. You ought to have kept away."

"Look, if you think I'm gonna–."

"There's no question of what you're going to do," the apparition cut him off, snapping his fingers and causing several more skeletons to appear. "You've been delivered into our hands for the purpose of the sacrifice, as were we in our turns. Now you shall share in our fate."

Turning to run, Bessemer found himself surrounded by the other ghosts. Though incorporeal, the orange glow that surrounded them gave off a field of energy that was palpable even from a half dozen feet away. Nevertheless he intended to try his luck and barrel through them. But just as he was about to, something hot touched the back of his head, and he lost consciousness.

Many hours later he awoke, lying face down on a floor of roughly cut stones. Spitting away some of the drool that had accumulated by his mouth, he twisted painfully onto his side and looked up, finding himself surrounded by his ghostly ambushers. Mutely they watched as he struggled to his knees and then his feet.

"You have awakened at last," the lead ghost uttered, his deep, tortured voice instantly recognizable despite the haze in Bessemer's head. "We thought perhaps we'd damaged you in the process of rendering you unconscious."

"That'll be the day," he replied, unphased by their presence.

"You would do well to show respect before your new master," the apparition scolded, gesturing behind him. "Turn and behold."

Expecting a trick, Bessemer scowled and turned very slowly. That's when he saw it: an exquisitely detailed figure carved from a solid piece of stone was embedded in the wall. Over seven feet tall; humanoid, but impossibly muscled; his body square, his hands enormous. His eyes were cold and merciless, his brow furrowed with an anger that had burned for generations. An unusual sword was in his right hand, and a scepter in his left. At once Bessemer knew that a great warlord was before him.

"Kneel to your lord!" ordered the apparition, driving him to his knees by placing a searingly hot hand upon his shoulder. "Kneel, and prepare to surrender your life to him."

He made to rise. But the other ghosts surrounded him and likewise placed their burning palms against his body, preventing him. Then, with a low chant that seemed to come from the depths of their nonexistent bellies, they pressed him towards the figure's sword. As he neared, the weapon's point on a level with his eyes, its tip glowed orange. Desperately he fought his captors. But their power was inexorable. When he was mere inches away they shoved him forwards, his skull colliding with the stone, the sword's tip landing squarely between his eyes. Instantly he felt a rush of unthinkable pain that was accompanied by a blindingly bright light. Then he lost all awareness of the room, his mind carried away into another land, another place. He felt his entire psyche searched from one end to the other. He saw the figure no more, but instead beheld a cloud of bright orange light. Twice as tall as it was wide, it floated through a version of his mind. He recognized the memories that it proceeded to rifle through, but they were presented in a fashion he could scarcely comprehend. Then he realized they were mere fragments of his memories, pre-selected portions that held some kind of relevance for the figure, but none for himself.

Soon he sensed that the examination had moved from his storehouse of memories to his personality. He could feel it, like a worm burrowing into his skull and working its way about inside his brain. Above all he wished to escape. But he was utterly powerless, forced to watch as it digested his psyche in full.

And then he felt something peculiar: the figure recoiled before something. Contemplating it for several seconds, it moved near it and likewise withdrew a second time. He could tell at once that it had been shocked. But more than that, he knew it had been *disturbed* by what it had found. Moving about inside his mind, looking for different angles from which to view the item in question, it again and again pulled back. Then it paused and seemed to think for a long while.

He wished to speak, to challenge the lordly ease with which the figure made itself at home within him. But an invisible hand was upon his mouth, stopping his tongue. For what seemed to be hours he watched the cloud in silent contemplation. Then, without the least hint of warning, the vision ended, and he was once more upon his knees within the stone chamber. Falling away from the sword's tip, he landed on his back and smacked his head, sending a dizzy blur through his vision as the boney faces of his ambushers hovered over him.

"What has happened?" one inquired of the leader.

"He has been sent back unharmed," he replied.

Bessemer, painfully gasping as he struggled to rise, could have challenged that notion.

"No," the apparition cautioned, once more laying a hand on his shoulder. But this time it didn't burn him. "You must rest."

"What kind of circus is this?" the captain demanded, shoving away his glowing hand and bolting upright just so he could lose his balance and fall into the arms of the surrounding skeletons. To his surprise they set him down gently upon his back. "First you attack me, then you sacrifice me, and now you're worried about my *health?!*"

"The Lord of Light has returned you unharmed," the leader answered. "He would not have done so without a reason."

"Maybe he didn't like how I tasted," he retorted.

Angrily one of the skeletons raised his foot to kick him. But the leader stopped him.

"No! Leave him alone," he ordered, putting his arm across the attacker's front and shoving him away. "The master doesn't wish him to be harmed, or he would have done the deed himself. For some reason this man has been preserved when no other has. We must respect the master's wishes."

"Then he must respect the master as well," snapped the kicker, his voice a raspy whisper. "He must not denigrate the Lord of Light."

"He will learn the proper way," the leader assured him. "But woe to any who lays a hand upon one set aside by the master."

Struck by these words, the other skeleton moved a little way back and watched sullenly. His face, of course, was capable of no form of expression. But Bessemer felt certain that he was being scowled at.

"And why would he do that?" queried the captain after a moment, straining as he moved to his side. Rolling onto his hands and feet, he stood like a dog for several seconds before attempting an upright posture a second time. His head already throbbing from striking the floor, to say nothing of the trauma of the examination he'd just undergone, it was all he could do to keep his footing. Placing a hand upon the wall, he let his head hang for a quarter minute before looking up at the assembled ghosts and repeating his question.

"We cannot say at this time," the leader replied. "It remains to be seen if the master will reveal his thoughts to us."

"So what? I'm free to go?"

"No. You will remain until the matter has been made clear. For the time being you will reside with us here. We mustn't tempt the master's anger by acting prematurely. Once we know his pleasure, you will be informed."

"And what happens until then?"

"You'll be kept under close guard," the leader answered, snapping his fingers. Somehow knowing his desires perfectly, a pair of the skeletons stepped forward and placed their boney hands on his arms, drawing him firmly, but not aggressively, away from the figure and farther into the structure.

"Just where are we?" Bessemer queried, looking around as they passed stone walls covered with ornately engraved writings. But he received no response. Taken to a room in the back, he was pushed into it. Lacking any kind of door, the skeletons walled him in with their bodies, their eyeless sockets watching him minutely. The space, no bigger than a large closet, was just roomy enough to permit him to pace. Choosing to do so in the hope of limbering up his stiff muscles for a dash should the chance present itself, he quickly felt like a bug under glass. "Haven't you guys got peripheral vision?" he asked, annoyed to see their heads following him up and down the room. "Look, I can't push past you, and I sure can't bore through this," he argued, clapping his open palm against the rear wall. "So stop watching me like I'm about to jump overboard and swim away." Deaf to his words, they continued to follow him up and down.

After an interminable period under their watchful gaze, Bessemer was relieved to see their leader approaching. Moving aside without a word spoken by either party, the sentries turned and walked away.

"So what's the story?" Bessemer asked.

"You are to be let go," the leader spoke at once, gesturing for him to step forward and follow. "The master has no further need of you."

"And what need did he have in the first place?" the captain inquired, still burned by his experience.

"He would have initiated you into our priestly order."

"Priestly order!?" he exclaimed. "Is that what you call a group of ghosts who attack peaceful visitors to Balian?"

"We are each of us bound to the Lord of Light, our wills no longer our own," he replied, a note of regret in his voice. "We must do as he bids."

"And you're what I would have become if he hadn't turned me down?" he asked, not enjoying the idea of being a skeleton.

"In time your flesh would have dissolved, and you would have been as we are now," the leader answered. "At first you would have retained your present appearance. But the light that would have bound you, as it binds us, would have quickly disintegrated such matter, leaving only your essential form."

"I consider all this my essential form," Bessemer responded, gesturing up and down his body.

"You would have found it unnecessary, had you achieved the priesthood."

"Some achievement."

Passing through the chamber where the figure was carved, he paused and looked at it.

"Well, so long, old man," he couldn't help quipping, his old spunk slowly returning. It was then that the skeletons descended upon him once more, taking him in their hands and again forcing him to his knees. "What?! I'm sorry, alright!?" he exclaimed, though it was no use. Pushing him along to the sword, he again lost consciousness upon touching its glowing tip.

As before he felt the cloudy essence of the figure within his psyche. But *unlike* before, it wasn't rambling through him looking for something. It knew exactly where its quarry resided, and at once applied itself to it. To Bessemer's surprise, he began to feel better than he had since his encounter with the orb. Something was being cleared out of his mind. Without realizing it completely, he'd felt fried before, as though his brain cells had been scorched. This feeling gradually diminished until it was gone. His old sense of vitality was just reasserting itself when the encounter terminated. Managing to catch himself this time, he noticed that even his headache had gone.

"I'm sorry to have surprised you in that way," the lead ghost said, as the captain got to his feet. "But I felt certain you would not voluntarily subject yourself to the master a second time, even if it was for the stated purpose of healing you."

"You're right about that," Bessemer agreed, brushing the dust from his knees and straightening up. "Just what did he heal, anyhow?"

"That is not for me to say," the skeleton shook his head.

"More secrets," he murmured, frowning as he turned to take one last look at the carving on the wall. "You know, I think he said something to me," he commented after a moment, his mind going back to the vision. "In that last fraction of a second before he kicked me out, I heard a voice. But the words weren't anything I could understand, much less repeat." He turned back to the leader. "Why would he do that?"

"I'm sure the purpose for doing so will be revealed in time," he responded. "And now it is time for you to depart. This temple is not a boarding house for travelers."

"Temple? You mean *this* is the temple?"

"Of course. Where did you think you were?"

"A lot closer to my landing site than that!" he replied. "We're almost twenty miles away. How'd you guys ever lug me through all that jungle?"

"There are paths that are known to us," he answered simply. "Regrettably we have no way of communicating with your vessel, and so you will have to return on foot. The way is dangerous, and thus I will escort you. Come."

His tone final, Bessemer could only shrug and follow him out of the temple. It wasn't until he'd stepped into the brilliant light of the dawning sun that he recalled the purpose of his visit to Balian. Halting at once, he turned and looked at the temple.

"The artifact you sought is not here," the leader said without stopping or looking at him. "It never was."

"What do you mean *never was*?" he all but demanded, hastening to catch up. "Explain that to me."

"Krancis sent you here for a reason other than that

which you were told," he replied.

"Why that miserable–," he began, cutting himself off with great effort, not willing to run him down before… whatever exactly the skeleton beside him was.

"You are angry."

"Wouldn't you be?"

"I would rejoice that, despite having passed through the trial of light, I yet retained my will," he answered in a voice tinged with hollowness. "Krancis knew precisely what he was doing in sending you here. That is why you're walking away."

"You'd think he could *ask*," Bessemer objected under his breath.

"He doesn't need to," the skeleton said, his hearing remarkably acute. "Nor, given your mission, would it have been possible to. Events had to unfold a certain way."

"Why do I get the feeling there's a *lot* you're not telling me?"

"Because there is."

"That's logical enough," he remarked, flaring his eyebrows at this empty explanation.

"It is your unlucky fate to be ignorant of a great many things, Roland Bessemer," the skeleton continued. "A cunning warrior, you're nevertheless unworthy to partake in the greatest secrets of the Earthborn. It shall ever be your lot to stand upon the fringe of Krancis' plans, knowing only enough to carry them out."

"Like a donkey loaded with rocks," he commented sourly.

"If you like. But equally, you can be glad to participate to such a degree in the momentous workings of your people. That is not a destiny held out to many of your kind."

"I suppose," he responded, not in the least moved by this notion. "What do you mean *my* kind?" he queried. "I thought you said you were human."

"I am," he nodded. "But I am not Earthborn. Nor are

my brother priests."

"You're kidding," he said, causing the skeleton to stop and look at him with his eyeless sockets. "Or not," he shrugged uneasily.

"There were once many families of man," he elaborated. "Yours is but one of them, and far from the greatest. However, fate has chosen the Earthborn to rise above all the rest of our kin. Should you survive the calamities that now surround you, there is no limit to the heights you may reach. But should you falter or flinch, the last remnants of our entire race will be lost. Already your candle flickers from the winds that beat upon it. You must be strong; you must be courageous; *you must not fail!*"

Struck by the passion of these last words, he sensed the grave personal interest the apparition had in the conflict that was raging throughout the Milky Way. More than anything he wished to prod him for more information, to find out what reason a long-dead being could have to care about the affairs of the living. But he could feel the ghost's unwillingness to speak about it.

"Satisfy your curiosity," he told him wearily, aware that the voluble captain would never keep his mouth shut by choice.

"Why are you so concerned about us?" he queried.

"I'm not. What I wish is to see the banner of humanity flutter in the wind for so long as there *is* a wind," he said. "I should have preferred that my own clan be the one to carry us into glory and honor. But that was not to be. Now the task has fallen to you, the least of our race."

"And what makes us so bad?" he shot back with annoyance.

Equally annoyed, the skeleton stopped and faced him.

"You are the descendants of prisoners – hardly a laudable starting point. Your vessel crashed eons ago on Earth, and some of you were lucky enough to survive. It should give you some notion of the distance between the other clans and your own that none of them so much as suggested a rescue operation. Your ancestors simply weren't worth the trouble. While we danced among the stars, you dabbed blood on the walls of caves in the crude shapes of animals you'd encountered. While we warred and traded with alien races far beyond the borders of our galaxy, you were burning your fingertips with fire for the first time. It has taken you an unthinkably long time to finally stretch your influence into space and *begin* to take the place your heritage as humans entitled you to. But even now you must rely on outside forces to strengthen and guide you." Losing a little of his choler, he turned and resumed movement. "The vessel of the *Keesh'Forbandai* has helped stem the violence of the parasite, as has the remarkable growth of the dark priest."

"Dark what?"

"You know him as Rex Hunt."

"Oh."

"A peculiar array of forces have aligned, often not willingly, to give the Earthborn a chance. The fashioning of the Hunt family into a weapon to use *against* the Earthborn by the *Prellak* worlds is the most obvious example of an action being turned on its head. But the most curious, the most unlikely, is Krancis."

"Krancis?"

"He is of your kind, and yet he is not," the skeleton uttered with consternation. "He is a contradiction, an impossibility. He should not exist. And yet he does."

"I warrant he's kind of strange…" Bessemer's voice trailed.

"He's not strange," replied the apparition. "Not in the slightest. He is perfectly appropriate for the crisis through which your kind are now passing, yet he is not *of* this crisis. He doesn't belong here."

"And where does he belong?"

"That is what I don't know," he said musingly, the

question clearly giving him a good deal to think about. "It is something that I would like to know above all else. Besides the key to my release."

"Yeah," Bessemer agreed. "What do you mean?" he then followed up, the skeleton's words striking him oddly."

"I am the Lord of Light," he answered, looking down morosely.

"I thought the Lord of Light was that wall carving," he replied, flabbergasted. "You said you and the other guys were part of a priesthood."

"We are. But we are also in bondage to the master, and he, through us, moves and lives outside his tomb. Or rather his prison. We are symbiotic, two psyches existing in the same body. Yet one is subservient to the other. I need not tell you which spirit is the stronger."

Glancing at the orange glow that surrounded the skeleton, Bessemer inwardly agreed.

"But why does he do it? Or, why do *you* do it?"

"Because I am trapped. Because for millennia I have been entombed within the walls of that temple, unable to move or speak. With my great power I have captured and then preserved these ancient humans, maintaining them for my own sake. Long have they wished to pass and rejoin their kin. But I should perish from loneliness if I were to allow them that. So they must reside with me for a time."

"Is that why you captured me? To trade out one for another?"

"Partially," he admitted. "It was also to ingest a new body of thoughts and memories, to refresh myself with some news from the outside. Much is known to me through the power of my insight. But certain things are hidden. I have been enriched by what you have brought me of Krancis."

"But I hardly even know him," he objected. "You can't have learned much."

"His powerful psyche left an imprint in your unconscious that I was able to link with what I already know of him," the master explained. "It has filled out the picture considerably."

At this Bessemer blushed, fearing that he'd inadvertently given away important information about the man in black.

"Don't worry," the skeleton said, seeing the look on his face. "That was precisely his intention. It is no mistake that you first survived the trial of the orb before coming to see me. It is all part of a plan that has been worked out in advance."

"I really *am* just a piece on his game board," the captain grumbled.

"As I have said, it is your destiny to play an ignorant, though important, part in the struggle for the survival of your kind. Do not regret this, though it be far from glorious. It is in your nature to keep your nose pressed so tightly against the ground upon which you walk that you never stand up straight and see the events unfolding around you for what they are. That is your gift and your curse. It makes you perfectly suitable for the tasks that have been given to you."

"You mean I'm naive?" he fumed.

"Precisely. You easily swallow what a more skeptical mind would immediately question."

"*Like the spacesuit…*" he reflected.

"You will not live to see the results of your labors without a good deal of luck. But you may rest assured that you have already taken a step that will brighten the fortunes of your people. Indeed, you may have saved them from a fate worse than that posed by either the parasite or the *Pho'Sath*."

"You mean getting rid of the orb?" he queried.

"That is not what I mean. But I will say no more. It is not appropriate that you should know."

"Are you *serious?*" he rejoined.

"Entirely. It is not my wish to undermine what Krancis has set in motion. He knew that a great many things would be communicated to me by your coming here – things that are for my information only. I will say no more."

Scowling at having his curiosity shut down in this way, Bessemer thrust his hands into his pockets and strode heavily alongside the ghost. Or was he a projection, a kind of puppet? Realizing that he didn't care in the least, he shook his head and dismissed the question.

It was nightfall before they finally reached the dilapidated town. What the skeleton had said about having secret paths through the jungle had proven completely correct, their journey being both easy and direct. Periodically they'd stopped for water and rest, the master clearly unwilling to exhaust his guest. Though they spoke sparingly, a curious sense of familiarity prevailed. Bessemer realized, uncomfortably, that it was the product of the Lord of Light twice diving into his mind.

"Just a moment," the ghost said, halting as the egg came into view.

"What is it?" the captain asked, turning wearily towards his strange companion just as the latter reached out a glowing hand and seized his forehead. "What are you doing?" he demanded, gripping his bony wrist and trying to peel his hand away.

"Stop fighting," he ordered, his tone that of an annoyed parent. "I'm not hurting you. I'm leaving a message for Krancis."

"Yeah, well, send him a postcard!" Bessemer retorted, still struggling as the hand was taken away. "Don't you guys *ever* stop kicking people around like they're your pets? Haven't you got any respect for the wishes of others?"

"The fate of the galaxy cannot hinge upon the petty wishes of the insignificant," he answered coldly as he turned away. "There is your vessel. Depart at once, and head straight for Krancis. There are things that he needs to know."

Striding in the direction of the temple, the skeleton quickly melted into the jungle and vanished.

"At least we agree on one thing," Bessemer muttered,

tapping on the side of the egg to get the AI to produce the ladder. "I'm gonna get out of here just as fast as I can."

Ducking under the canopy as she raised it, his exhausted back leg got caught on the side of the ship as he climbed over the side. Tumbling into the rear of the cockpit, he smacked his head on the floor and cursed under his breath.

"Hasn't *enough* gone wrong today?" he snapped, pushing off the craft's floor and standing up.

"Captain Bessemer! Are you alright?" the little hologram queried from the dashboard as he settled into the pilot's seat. "I'd feared the worst."

"Didn't stop you from sitting here and doing nothing, did it?" he retorted, angrily clicking a few buttons that simultaneously dropped the canopy, removed the ladder, and warmed up the egg for flight.

"Your instructions were to wait within the egg and ensure that it met with no harm," she replied modestly. "I've followed your wishes precisely."

"Next time use your imagination a little," he replied, lifting the craft up through the hole he'd battered in the trees. "I nearly had it down there."

"The ship's instruments indicate that you've had a rough time," she responded somewhat clinically. "But there's no sign of any meaningful damage."

"Believe me, sister, I came *this close* to being *very* meaningfully damaged," he said, making a half inch space with his thumb and index finger. Tilting the egg upward, he blasted away from the jungle, glad to leave it behind forever.

"But what happened? Were you attacked?" she queried. "The sensors showed several massive energy signatures around you shortly after you'd disembarked. But no organic life of any kind."

"I was attacked by ghosts," he informed her. "Ghosts of skeletons that were wrapped in this…energy field of light. Somehow it was projected from a being they called the Lord of Light. He holds his victims as prisoners to keep him company, but he's just as much a prisoner as they are. Somebody locked him up inside that temple, so he's got to get his giggles playing god with whoever comes knocking along his path. I was just about relieved of my free will when he had second thoughts. He learned something while he was spelunking inside my skull, and it made him change his tune. Now he wants me to carry a message to Krancis."

"What kind of message?" she asked, her little brow furrowed as she processed what he was telling her.

"I don't have a clue!" he exclaimed with exasperation. "He just put his hand on my forehead and put it into me somehow. Said I needed to make tracks for *Sentinel* the second I left Balian. Heh, like I'd stay *here* a second longer than I had to!"

"That...may be...a problem..." she reluctantly uttered.

"What, is something wrong with the *ship* now?" he asked, his eyes bulging in disbelief as he looked at her.

"No, no. The ship is fine. It's just that...we have one more assignment before returning to *Sentinel*."

"What is this, a comedy?" he exploded. "Is Krancis trying to see how many brushes I can have with death before one of 'em finally nails me? Sooner or later my luck is gonna run out, you know."

"Really, the mission isn't very hard at all," she said meekly, her little cheeks scrunched in a grimace as she looked at him. "A simple retrieval operation."

"Retrieval of what? My death certificate? Redeemable at any one of a thousand star systems? No, thanks! I can do without tempting fate again. If Krancis wants a delivery boy, let him find someone else. I've done my part already. Shoot, playing delivery boy with–," he paused, remembering that she was now totally ignorant of the orb. "Well, I've paid my dues," he finished.

"I'm certain Krancis knows that," she replied, as Balian shrank beneath them, the egg's hull chilling as it rose into the atmosphere. "But think what the reward will be for bringing each of your tasks to a successful conclusion. I'm sure you'll be given your own choice of assignments. You'll certainly be promoted. Doesn't Major Roland Bessemer have a nice ring to it?"

"It does," he reluctantly agreed, grinding his teeth as she successfully began to work upon his vanity. "But what's the use of being any rank at all if I'm dead?" he countered, trying to argue himself out of it as he felt a change of heart coming over him.

"Oh, there's no chance at all of you dying," she shook her head. "As I said, it's a simple retrieval operation. An artifact has been disc–."

"No! No more artifacts! The first one nearly killed me, and the second one wasn't an artifact at all! What's the third gonna be? A black hole? A plate of cookies wired up to a canister of nerve gas? Or maybe a hive of ants that dig through your eyes and take you over like a zombie!?"

"You have a very…lucid imagination," she commented, both impressed and a little disturbed. "But no, nothing of that nature. We're supposed to visit a secret imperial installation and retrieve an object they've discovered. Details are minimal, but it's small enough to transport in the egg without making modifications."

"*Oh, good. It's probably the orb's little brother…*"

"I don't suppose Krancis bothered to tell you just what it *does*?" he queried irritably.

"All I know is that it's very important," she answered. "We were not to return to *Sentinel* without it."

"Assuming we survived this long," he added.

"Indeed," she quietly agreed.

Taking his hands off the controls, he leaned back in his seat and sighed his annoyance. On the one hand, she made it sound so easy. Just pick up a package from some imperial personnel, housed within an imperial base, and take it to *Sentinel*. Seemed safe enough. On the other hand, each leg of his journey had sounded just as safe, and yet there'd always been a catch. Well, not a *catch*, he reflected. More like a *catastrophe*, one just waiting to carry him clear out of existence. It was, he laughed mirthlessly, like marrying his college sweetheart just to learn that, on the side, she also just happened to be a serial killer.

"What happens if we *do* head for *Sentinel* without stopping?" he queried, gazing out into the blackness of space as he thought.

"Krancis isn't known for rewarding disobedience," she pointed out warily. "Additionally, he could simply refuse to rendezvous with us. There's nothing we can do to force a meeting with *Sentinel*."

"You had me with your first answer," he replied, tardily realizing that the man in black was the last person he wanted to be crossways of. "You said it was an imperial installation?" he confirmed, trying to push aside enough of his doubts to act.

"Yes," she nodded earnestly. "Records indicate that it has fifty-three full time personnel. Additionally, its location has always been kept strictly secret, so the likelihood of its having been infiltrated is minimal."

"*It sounds safe enough*," he reflected, immediately rolling his eyes that such a notion should cross his mind after all he'd been through. But, despite recent history, he was searching for an excuse to comply. The last thing he wanted to do was offend Krancis in a matter that he considered important. Struggling to force his mouth open despite this, he managed to request the coordinates from the AI.

"They've already been entered," she answered brightly, glad that he'd at last decided to comply. Placing a waypoint on the HUD, she directed him towards it. They entered warp moments later, the familiar black tunnel both comforting and tedious.

"How long have we got to wait?" he asked, leaning

back again and looking up at the dark energy. With some surprise, he noticed that the fear he'd felt after battling the orb had gone. Somehow the shadowy element was no longer threatening to him, a fact he both welcomed and questioned.

"It's going to be a bit of a trip," she warned him. "I'd suggest making yourself as comfortable as possible. Perhaps you can make a bit of a bed in the rear of the cockpit."

"Yeah," he replied somewhat sourly, regretting his decision now that it had been made. Looking out the cockpit for a few minutes, a question crossed his face and he looked at the little hologram. "Do you have a name?"

"Of course," she replied. "But I think it would prove very difficult to pronounce. So it would probably be best just to call me Kayla."

"Kayla?" he asked, the name surprisingly normal coming from an alien AI.

"One of the mechanics aboard *Sentinel* suggested it," she explained.

"Works for me," he shrugged. His fatigue finally catching up with him now that he had nothing but time on his hands, he got out of the pilot's seat and climbed into the back. Stretching out as well as he could, he'd only been in contact with the floor for a few moments before his mind got hazy and he drifted away.

The trip was interminable, but Bessemer was glad to find himself free of nightmares. Dimly he sensed that a reordering of his mental processes had taken place when the Lord of Light entered his mind the second time. His thoughts were calmer, more focused, and stable. Most of all, the sense of having been fried from his conflict with the orb was completely gone. This, to him, implied that he had been healed in some way, though he could scarcely credit that possibility. Why would a being who regarded him as insignificant reach out his hand to help? He didn't know. The dreadful thought crossed his mind that perhaps yet more harm had been done, and his mind was simply coming to grips with it before relaying the truth of his situation. But he dismissed that notion at once. Clearly the master, or whatever his name was, wanted him to reach Krancis in one piece. It made sense to fix him up for that purpose.

"We've nearly reached the planet Thierry," Kayla informed him, breaking in on his train of thought.

"How long?" he asked, not shifting his gaze from the black tunnel.

"About ten minutes."

"Alright," he nodded.

A little twinge had gone through his stomach at her words, though he hadn't shown it. Deep down he felt certain that something had to go wrong. Krancis *must* have saved the best for last, he muttered inwardly, though the mission sounded innocuous enough. Besides, how much danger could he be in, surrounded by fifty imperials? Still...

"Just what is this facility, anyhow?"

"It's a research station, studying the artifacts and culture of the ancient ones who built the few structures that remain in existence there."

"So what, just a bunch of archeologists and whatnot?" he queried, somewhat deflated at the notion. He'd never had much use for egghcads.

"There certainly are archeologists," she agreed. "But Outpost Major has a full complement of personnel. Weapons experts, elite special forces for guards, the works."

"Special forces?" he repeated.

"Outpost Major is very important to the empire," she explained. "A number of curious finds may well turn out to be weapons of great power. The difficulty has been in learning how to activate and use them. The team hasn't been able to find any sort of instructions or even just notes on how they work. They're up against a wall."

"So what are we supposed to do with them?" he asked. "If the team here can't do anything with them, who can? Wait, don't tell me," he hastened to add, dramatically drawing a breath and letting it out. "Krancis?"

"That is the hope."

"I don't know what curse landed on me that I have to dedicate my every waking minute to *something* related to that man," he shook his head. "Seems all of a sudden I can't get rid of him."

"Many have felt that way," she quietly remarked.

"What? I thought you were Team Krancis all the way?"

"I am," she responded. "I was merely commenting on how others have felt about his interaction style."

"What interaction style? He tells you what to do, and you *do* it. Wasn't that the point you were driving about not showing up at *Sentinel* empty-handed?"

"More or less, though without the dark hue that you've put upon it."

"It's hard *not* to put a hue on things when it's your neck that's on the line. But I guess that wouldn't mean a whole lot to an AI."

"I likewise wish to continue living," she replied. "I should much rather continue processing data, being of use to my masters, and advancing our cause. It is merely that my priorities are more sharply defined. Whereas humans have vague instincts that drive them to survive, I am programmed with a clear hierarchy of objectives. Survival is desired, though not mandatory, if it conflicts with the task I have been given. Without hesitation I would lay aside my existence should that be necessary."

"A fact that probably makes Krancis jump for joy," he remarked caustically.

"Captain, you're usually such a cheerful fellow," she observed. "I had anticipated enjoying this trip with you. But, to be frank, I have not. You seem very sour these days."

"I don't like being picked up by the scruff of my neck and thrown into the fire without so much as a howdy-do," he said.

"You must be used to receiving objectionable orders,

having served in the military before this," she countered. "Why should this be so different?"

"Because then I had a fighting chance. I had a ship that I knew like I was born with its controls in my hands. It gave me *power*, Kayla. It gave me the tools to stand and fight. But what can you do with mystic orbs and masters of light? One touch and they kick you aside like a pile of cotton balls! There was nothing I could do. There was nothing *anyone* could do! They're just too strong. I love a good fight, sister. I truly do. But you can't go up against gods and win. And when I'm sent against them without even knowing what I'm dealing with, trusting to luck to get me through, well, that's just about murder. I know all the arguments," he raised his hand, stopping her as she was about to cut in. "All the logical justifications for Krancis' pragmatic attitude towards the lives of others. I know I'm not unique in being just a cog in his vast machine of war. But that doesn't mean I don't revolt *in here* when I think of it," he said, tapping his heart. "I love to fight. But I love to *live* even more."

"Were that true, you would have abandoned your mission and fled the war with the parasite at the first opportunity," she pointed out, not understanding his reference to mystic orbs but allowing it to pass without comment. "Indeed, it's unlikely that most of the personnel now serving against it will see the war's conclusion. That is reserved for others."

"I don't mean just *existing*, Kayla. I mean *living*. And for me that's fight *and* flight, or rather fight *during* flight. I might as well be dead without a ship in my hands. Shoot, any other branch of the services would have killed me long ago from sheer weariness of soul. I couldn't stand it. Honestly, before the Devourers came onto the scene, I doubted I could last much longer. Even with pirate activity things had been too calm."

"There were separatists, too," she countered.

"They're no kind of challenge for me," he replied

factually. "I'm just about the best pilot there is, Kayla. Most would think that's a blessing, and it is. But it's also a curse. I can hardly ever find enough of a challenge to remind myself that I'm alive. You know, to *really* get adrenaline pumping into my bloodstream. My threshold for danger is just too high. I'd almost have to court death to really feel like my life is on the edge."

"I see," she replied musingly.

"You do?" he queried, surprised to find his words making an impression.

"Yes. To speak rather poetically, you need to feel the wind on your face to remind you that you exist. But your skin is so thick that only a gale will do. And there are precious few of those."

"Exactly," he smiled, glad to be understood. "I have to face death to remember that I'm alive, to activate all those impulses for survival that give life so much of its meaning. But being dropped into fatal danger by our *infallible leader* just terrifies me. It's like waking up to find your bed surrounded by a firing squad, their fingers already on their triggers. That's what I've got a problem with. Especially when I'm kept in the dark about the whole thing, only really learning what's going on *after* it's already happened."

"I can understand how frustrating that would be," she nodded, her little brow furrowed.

"I'm glad *someone* can," he uttered with some relief, happy to feel a bit supported. In truth, it had taken all his will not to simply fold to the will of Krancis, accepting his dictates as though they were divine. It was only the power of his instincts surging through his organism that had kept him from being crushed and subsequently resigning himself to his apparent fate as a pawn. And he knew that would be fatal. With his spirit crushed in such a fashion, he'd have been of no use to anyone, including himself. And that, he felt, was the worst fate of all.

"We're about to emerge from warp, Captain."

"Very well," he acknowledged. Glancing furtively at the AI, he fixed his eyes straight ahead and spoke. "Thanks, Kayla," he said quietly.

"Of course, Captain," she smiled gently, turning to watch the tunnel terminate along with him. Suddenly their blindingly fast journey ended, and they were deposited before a modestly sized planet of pure sand.

"Glad I don't have asthma," he remarked, looking it over as the egg slowly neared it. "Who could have ever lived on a world like that? I don't see any water sources at all."

"It wasn't always this way," she answered. "It was once lush and beautiful. You can't see it from here, but the reverse side of the planet has a crater of such enormity that the weapon used to make it must have been almost unthinkably powerful. All life ended that day, and only a handful of immensely sturdy buildings have managed to survive."

"Who were these people?" he queried. "Not more ancient humans?" he added, thinking of his discussion with the skeleton on Balian.

"Details are extremely limited. Their writing system is complex and terribly confusing. We haven't even managed to find what they called themselves. There's no question of their immense technological prowess. But they don't seem to have spread themselves very far into the stars. If, indeed, they did so at all. We've found no traces of this people on any other world."

"Well, that's kind of peculiar," he remarked, accelerating the egg and descending towards Thierry.

"It's as though they lacked the impulse for outward expansion. As you say, it's peculiar, though not unheard of. The *Keesh'Forbandai* have encountered many peoples who have preferred to remain within the confines of their birth world. But it's extremely rare for a race of such capacity to do so. Often they are simply forced into the stars in order to find the resources necessary to sustain themselves. A finite supply of arable land and also of energy sources almost invariably drives them to seek support from outside."

"Give me a waypoint," he uttered, drawing her somewhat rambling mind back to the task.

"Oh, of course," she replied, snapping her little fingers and making a blue diamond at once appear on his HUD.

"If this weapon was so powerful, how did the buildings and artifacts survive?" he inquired, the structures in question mere specks on the horizon as he flew into the dawning sun. "How'd the planet not split in half, for that matter?"

"We really don't know, vis-a-vis the planet," she replied. "But as for the structures, it seems to have been the product of intelligent design."

"Meaning…?" his voice trailed.

"Meaning they seem to have anticipated some such event, and prepared themselves for it. The structures, as you will shortly see, are a loose grouping of four pyramids, each of them made from a mineral unlike any we've seen before. Evidently native to this world, it is immensely durable, though, clearly, not indestructible. The researchers speculate that such groupings were placed at four different points as time capsules, and that this one happened to survive through pure chance, being just far enough away to weather the blast."

"Why wouldn't they just bolt if they knew something like this was coming?" he queried. "Shoot, we've had space travel for longer than I can remember. With all their tech, they ought to have been able to get away."

"Perhaps their resources were limited, and they could only remove a fraction of the population," she offered. "It would be natural enough for those left behind to want to leave some kind of record of their having existed once their fate was sealed."

"That's true enough," he agreed, drawing near to the pyramids. "Funny, I thought only we had those," he commented, looking at them as he guided the egg towards a large landing pad that had been placed between them. Squinting as the sunlight bounced off their silvery sides, he touched down and powered off the egg.

"Many cultures have made them," she responded, as he reached to pop the canopy. "Don't!" she exclaimed, causing him to jump back. "The atmosphere is all but nonexistent. You'll die without your spacesuit."

"I see my guardian angel is at work again," he said somewhat tartly, climbing into the back and picking it up. Glancing around at the pyramids as he put it on, a curious look crossed his face. "These things are massive," he said. "How could fifty-odd people be enough to study each one? That's like a dozen people per structure."

"It isn't enough," she replied. "But there are other sites spread throughout imperial space which likewise demand attention. Most likely there simply aren't enough trained personnel to go around."

"I guess," he said, putting on his helmet and double-checking his equipment for a good seal. "Alright, anything *else* I need to know before popping the canopy?" he queried with humor.

"Your spacesuit has a radio," she responded. "Use it to keep in contact."

"Why…?" his voice trailed ominously, twisting his head a little as he looked at her. "Is there something you're not telling me, Kayla?"

"No," she shook her head. "But, as you said before, this trip has been full of surprises. I'm just taking a leaf out of your book."

"Good. You had me worried for a second," he replied, though only partially reassured. Opening the cockpit, he threw a leg over the side and found a foothold. "Keep the home fires burning," he added, starting to descend.

"The what?" she asked, a quizzical expression on her face.

"Nothing," he rolled his eyes, dropping out of sight

and onto the sand beside his craft. Pausing a moment to ensure she closed the canopy, he trudged towards one of the pyramids when it started to shut.

"Excuse me, Captain," he heard over the radio. "But you want to head towards the structure *behind* you. That's where the artifact is being held."

"Alright."

Reversing his direction, he cursed under his breath when he realized it was the farthest pyramid from where he'd set down. Glancing at the egg, he considered climbing back in and moving it closer. But in an instant he dismissed this idea, not wishing to appear soft to the locals. If they could tramp from one pyramid to the next, so could he. Especially given that they likely didn't have a top-of-the-line spacesuit like he did. That was *one* area where he couldn't help but give Krancis his due: he'd outfitted him with the very best, the kind of suit used by imperial boarding parties during ship-to-ship actions in space. Armored yet decently light, it was an impressive piece of workmanship. And terribly expensive to manufacture.

"*Guess that should have told me something, too,*" he thought, realizing that such a suit implied a great deal more danger than he'd anticipated when setting out from *Sentinel* with the orb. The Lord of Light had been right: he *was* terribly naive.

Soldiering slowly towards his destination, he began to get an eerie feeling as the hair on the back of his neck started to stand up.

"*Where is everyone?*" he asked himself, twisting around to look at the first pyramid he'd walked towards, thinking perhaps he'd missed someone. Carefully examining each entrance, along with the spaces immediately surrounding the impressive structures, his heart beat a little faster when he saw no one. Not so much as a trace. "*There's three other ships on the pad,*" he reasoned, glancing over his shoulder again just to reassure himself that they were truly there. "*So *there's got to be* somebody *here."*

"Everything alright, Captain?" Kayla queried.

"Yeah, I guess so," he answered somewhat cautiously, unconsciously beginning to hunch a little as though he was about to walk into something. "Just awfully quiet."

"Oh, well, the researchers don't spend very much time outside the structures. The environment is too dangerous."

"But there ought to be some guards, Kayla. Somebody to watch over the equipment," he pointed out, looking at large metal containers that had locks on their doors. Beside them was a small communications hut with various antennae sticking out of its top. Through its multiple windows he could see nobody was inside.

"I'm sure everything is fine."

"*Reckon we'll find out, one way or another,*" he thought.

Reaching the pyramid, he looked up the long sloped ramp that led to a door embedded halfway up its gleaming side. Taking a breath, his body sore in dozens of places from his brief visit to Balian, he began to ascend.

"*Couldn't they have put in an…elevator?*" he asked himself, wondering why an advanced civilization would put itself through such hardship just to reach the door. "*Or put it on ground level?*" he followed up.

Pausing halfway up the ramp, he turned and looked back. The egg looked very small from where he stood. Indeed, he hadn't had any real conception of just how large the structures were until that moment.

Resuming his climb, he achingly reached the top, his legs burning as though they were floating in acid.

"Ah," he groaned, turning away from the dark, gaping doorway and sitting on the flat top of the ramp.

"Are you in pain, Captain?" Kayla inquired.

"Just need…a breather…" he answered, waving towards the egg to show he was okay. "I'll be alright in a minute." Lying flat on his back, he allowed his chest to freely heave until he'd caught his breath. "*These researchers must have legs of iron,*" he thought, struggling to his feet and approaching the doorway. Disappearing into the darkness of the structure, he paused and activated his suit's light enhancement. Instantly he was faced with a robust metal door. "Kayla, I've got a door staring me in the face."

"Did you try knocking?" she asked with unconscious humor.

"*Why didn't I think of that?*" he thought frowningly. Striking the door thrice, a hollow metallic clang sounded through the space on the other side. Waiting half a minute and receiving no answer, he tried again. "Any other ideas? Why don't you radio them?" he asked, looking at a series of wires that ran along the floor and into the base of the door's frame.

"I've tried, but nobody is answering. Must be too busy to hang around the radio when they receive almost no messages out here, anyhow."

"That's *one* way of looking at it," he remarked, flaring his eyebrows. "Well, is there any other way to get inside?"

"What do you see?"

"A big metal door, with a–."

Before he could finish the door suddenly popped and slowly opened. Glancing around, he noticed a security camera stationed above his head and to the right. Waving his thanks, he stepped inside a narrow metal chamber. Automatically the door shut behind him, and the space immediately began to fill with air. A red sign that read 'Unsafe' flicked to green, losing its prefix in the process. Removing his helmet, he took half a breath and found the air somewhat stale but healthy enough.

"Captain?" Kayla queried, still wondering about the door.

"Somebody let me in," he informed her, as the inner door likewise opened, mutely beckoning him further. Double checking that his pistol was still in one of the pockets of his suit, he stepped out of the chamber and into the pyramid.

The hallway before him was shadowy, though lights shone at very sparse intervals, their effect magnified by the silvery material of the building. "*Not big on greeting visitors,*" he thought, looking warily down the corridor and wondering if anything was hiding in the many dark side chambers that connected to it. None of them, apparently, had warranted being lit.

Proceeding slowly, his footsteps reverberating loudly, he held his helmet in his left hand while his right hovered just outside the pocket with his pistol. With every step the urge grew to draw and cock it, his instincts blaring at him that something dangerous lay ahead. But he didn't want to look like some kind of paranoiac, walking through an imperial outpost with his gun drawn like he was infiltrating the place. More than that, he didn't want to give the guards any reason to shoot him.

"*Assuming there* are *any guards,*" he reflected dubiously, his pace subtly slowing as he moved deeper and deeper.

Reaching the corridor's end, he doubled back and began looking in at the chambers he passed until one revealed itself to be a stairway. Moving to the other side of the hallway on a hunch, he likewise found another one. Both were poorly lit, though the second one had a thick bundle of cables running down it. Reasoning that this betokened a greater likelihood of contact with whatever imperials were within the structure, he began to descend. Periodically he passed a straight hallway like the one he'd just left. But hearing no sounds of life, and seeing that the bundle of wires still ran downward, he continued. It wasn't until he'd neared the bottom that he paused again, some instinct or other warning him to stop. At last drawing his pistol, he quietly slipped his helmet back on so as to speak without being heard.

"Kayla?" he whispered. "Can you read me?"
"Yes."

"Any contact from inside the pyramid?"

"None whatsoever. Like I said, they must be busy."

"Yeah, but busy doing *what?*" he replied in a strained voice. "I'm starting to think they're pushing up sandstone."

"To what purpose?" she queried densely.

"I mean they're probably *dead*," he elaborated, his whisper sharpening on the last word. "Something feels very wrong about all this."

"Someone must have let you in, Captain," she pointed out quite rationally. "And there have been no signs of a struggle, have there?"

"No," he admitted reluctantly.

"The structure is enormous. They must just be in the lower levels."

"*That's what I'm trying to tell you*," he said in a pointed hush. "I've been sticking my head in at every hallway I can find and there hasn't been so much as a *whisper* from *anyone*. Not even the janitor washing the floor! Now, I've got to be pretty close to the bottom. My legs are about to turn into jelly from all these stairs. You can't tell me that that doesn't sound at least a *little* suspicious."

"It *is* peculiar," she allowed. "But there *are* only twelve of them per structure."

"Yeah, I got that part already," he muttered, pushing off the wall he'd been leaning against and descending the last few stories. Poking his head inside the scarcely lit corridor that connected this level to the stairway, he moved cautiously into it. "*Is someone trying to save on the electric bill around here?*" he thought, inching along the wall. Up ahead he saw a vast chamber. Glancing down to turn off the safety on his pistol, he caught something dark moving out of the corner of his eye. Jerking his head upright, he saw nothing but the yawning doorway. "Kayla, have there been any reports of strange activity here?"

"Nothing creditable."

"I'd credit just about *anything* at this point," he shot

back. "Now tell me what you've got?"

"There's not much to tell," she answered. "Just shreds and nonsense, nothing anyone could point to and even *describe*, really. It's all just fancy, the result of people cooped up for too long. Even professionals get batty, you know."

"Yeah, I know," he said sourly, feeling he might be joining their exalted ranks sooner than later. "Haven't you got *anything* solid, or at least that's been seen by more than one person?"

"Captain, all anyone ultimately ever reported was the sense of a 'presence,' or the notion that something was hovering *just* on the periphery of their vision. It was just their brains playing tricks on them. That, and the tedium of spending so long within the barren halls of an ancient building. They probably had to imagine such things in order to keep themselves from dying of boredom."

"Sure," he replied, unconvinced. "Well, if you don't hear from me in about two minutes, you may conclude that I've died from boredom."

"What?"

But he didn't answer. The time for discussion had ended. It was time for action.

Unwilling to meet Krancis empty-handed, he intended to find the artifact and make tracks just as quickly as he could. Deciding that he was already known to anything that lay ahead, he strode boldly into the chamber. It was vast, with an enormous ceiling that was supported by a foursome of giant columns. All about were scattered the foldable tables of the archeologists, each one covered in tools and ancient relics. But nowhere were there any *people*.

Moving slowly about the room, he allowed his eyes to dance across the artifacts and see if any caught his eye as seeming especially important. When none did, he radioed Kayla.

"Just what am I looking for?"

"The artifact is in the shape of a sword," she answered.

"Its design is somewhat–.."

"I think I've got it," he cut her off, seeing something long and thin placed by itself upon a table, near the back-left column. *"Funny I didn't notice it before,"* he added inwardly, walking towards it. As he neared the artifact he saw drawings on the wall behind it. Above it was an inscription and a depiction of it. "Seems like it was important to these folks," he remarked, reaching out to touch it. The second his fingers made contact, he heard the voices of thousands of people screaming in despair. Jerking his hand back with such force that he lost his balance, he stumbled to keep his footing and inadvertently turned around. It was then that he saw shadows dancing up and down the column beside him. Tall, lean, roughly humanoid but grotesque, they were weeping in anguish. Furiously they clawed at him, bound though they were to a two-dimensional existence. Looking down at his feet, he noticed them there as well, nearly jumping out of his suit when they tore at him with long, ghostly fingers. Though they clearly couldn't touch him, it nevertheless took all of his resolve not to run out of the chamber and leave the pyramid behind for good.

"What's wrong?" Kayla asked, hearing his heaving breaths, though he was much too distracted to notice them.

"I've found some of that *nonsense* you were talking about," he replied, lifting his boot and watching a shadow writhe and twist before slowly putting it back down. "Looks like those reports weren't so far off base after all."

"What are you seeing?"

"Shadows, Kayla. Lots of 'em. Look like people, but only kind of. They're trapped in the walls and floor. Probably the ceiling, too. And it's pretty clear that they don't appreciate my being here."

"Then why did they wait for you to get so far inside?"

"Why don't *you* come down here and ask them?" he countered.

"Well, what are they doing?"

"Just moving around and trying to rip me to pieces," he answered, as though watching piranhas in a fish tank. "I saw one out of the corner of my eye a little while ago. But they didn't show up in force until I touched that sword of yours. When I did, I heard a whole lot of people screaming like they were all about to be killed."

"Maybe it's a warning."

"Yeah, *'get out of here, or we'll maul you,'*" he replied.

"Can you take the sword?"

"Only one way to find out," he said, turning from the column and eyeing it for a second. Glancing at the floor, he watched the shadows beneath him as he reached for the artifact. As he'd suspected, they grew even more agitated the closer his fingers got. Thinking better of it, he drew his hand back. "*Still* no word from the others?" he queried.

"Nothing at all. You don't think these shadow creatures got them?"

"They can't seem to reach me," he shrugged, looking down again. "Though they might have been enough to drive the researchers out of their minds."

"You seem to be holding up fairly well," she pointed out.

"Yeah, but they ain't been scared like I've been," he laughed mirthlessly. "Beyond a certain point you get dull to it. These guys probably never spent more than a week of their lives out of doors, much less in any real danger. Throw on top of it months, maybe *years* of isolation…" his voice trailed. "Well, *I* wouldn't blame them if they took off into the desert."

"They'd never have made it," she uttered.

"Obviously," he replied, crossing an arm over his chest and looking at the shifting shadows. "But, like you said, somebody must have let me in."

"What are you thinking?" she queried.

"I'm thinking that I might want to check out the rest of this building before I set these guys off by touching that sword again. Especially if they go wild because I'm running off with it. If they *have* done something with the researchers, I don't want to push 'em over the edge."

"Where will you look?"

"I don't know. Back upstairs, I guess." Eyeing the shadows a moment longer, he turned and left the sword on its table, the mysterious creatures chasing him halfway across the chamber before stopping and returning to their treasured artifact. *"Wonder why it means so much to them…"* he reflected, watching them retreat.

Back in the stairway, he laboriously worked his way upward, searching every corridor and each of their attendant rooms. Finally he found something hidden in a back chamber. A small doorway had been barricaded with tool boxes and crates. Knocking on this, he leaped to the side when he received a bullet in reply.

"Hey! We're all on the same side here!" he shouted, pressing himself against the hard, cold wall beside the doorway, activating a speaker that broadcast his voice outside his suit. "Human! I'm human! I'm not one of those things!"

"What's your name?" a gruff male voice demanded.

"Bessemer! Captain Roland Bessemer! Krancis sent me!"

"What's the passcode?" he demanded.

"What passcode?" Bessemer queried, only to be answered by another bullet. "Hey! Take it easy!"

"X3492," Kayla chimed in. "Tell him that."

"What?" he asked quietly, his heart beating in his ears.

"*X3492*, that's the password."

"And you waited until *now* to tell me this?" he demanded in a strained whisper.

"It was a secret, only to be revealed as necessary. It's a very high level code."

"*This* is *becoming a comedy*," he thought, on the verge of believing that a conspiracy was afoot to keep him as ignorant as possible just for kicks. "The code is X3492!" he shouted through the barricade.

"Say that again?" the voice asked in disbelief.

"You heard me the first time!" he shot back, receiving another bullet in reply. "Hey! What's the *matter* with you?!"

"I think he must have snapped," Kayla commented.

"No kidding," he responded, slipping a little closer to the barricade. "How many of you are in there?"

"Wouldn't you like to know!"

"Yeah, that's why I asked!"

Another bullet passed through the pile.

"If anyone else is in there, call out!" Bessemer ordered. "We can all leave together. You don't have to stay with those creatures crawling around in the basement anymore. I can take a couple of you out in my ship. The rest can go in the other ones on the pad." For several moments silence ensued. "We don't have to fight among ourselves," he continued, hopeful that he was getting through to someone on the other side."

"Those things are terrors! Living nightmares!" a woman's voice quivered from the other side. "You don't know what they can do to you!"

"Those shadow things can't touch you," he countered. "It's all in your head. Just keep your cool, and you're alright."

"What are you *talking* about?" she asked incredulously. "I'm not talking about the shadow figures! I'm talking about the possessed!"

"Who are the possessed?" he queried, equally incredulous.

"Shut up!" another woman said to the first one. "He's one of them! He's just trying to lure us out! All we can do is wait for the navy to notice our radio silence and send a team to investigate. Then we'll all get out of here."

"I don't know if you've noticed, lady, but the imperial navy is a little busy right now," Bessemer replied. "And in any event, I'm no zombie, nor have I seen any since entering the pyramid."

"Don't you realize that they're how you entered in the first place?" the second woman barked. "They let you in! They want more victims! It's their only chance to free themselves from bondage. The only reason you haven't been attacked is so that you can talk us into breaking down the barricade and exposing ourselves. That's when they'll strike!"

"Boy, they really have been cooped up for too long," he remarked inwardly.

"Look, I gave you the passcode," he began.

"So what? Both me and Major Grady knew it, and we haven't seen hide or hair of him since this whole thing started!" the man with the gun retorted. "Could've easily dug it out of him once he was possessed!"

"Okay, think rationally for *just a second*," he said through increasingly gritted teeth. "You've never heard my voice before in your lives. You knew that a Captain Bessemer was coming to retrieve an artifact. I just so happen to answer to that name. Therefore, I'm a newcomer, and I'm here for exactly my stated purpose."

"They intercepted you before you got here!" the second woman snapped. "They got their hooks into you!"

"No they *haven't!*" he shouted angrily. "Look, I don't *need* any of you in order to finish my job and get out of here! I'm just trying to save you people grief in case the shadows go nuts when I take the sword!"

"You can't take the sword, you imbecile!" a bookish-sounding man said. "That's what started this whole business! It's how they possess you! Doctors Filby and Grant were the first to go. Then suddenly Major Grady just disappeared. By the time we knew what was happening, they'd gotten one of their own in control of the outer gate. We couldn't leave if we tried."

"How many of 'em are there?" Bessemer queried.

"There were fifteen of us when we started," the man replied. "We've only got five now."

"*Ten zombies,*" Bessemer reflected, not liking the odds.

"I can't take on that many alone," he called out. "You're gonna have to come out and give me a hand. Together we can take back the control room for the gate. Then we'll beat it."

"You don't understand!" the bookish man shouted. "They're not *human* anymore! They're something terrible. Living nightmares, like Cheryl said. Neither man nor spirit! They've been taken over, infected by some horrible dark substance that has corrupted them into monsters. Their distorted forms would tear us to pieces in *seconds* if we were to expose ourselves."

"Well, you can't just stay in there for the rest of your lives! You've got to get out and fight!"

"What we've got to do is wait for imperial reinforcements to arrive," the gruff man replied.

"And how long will that take?" Bessemer shot back. "None of us can contact them! Even if we could, it'd take days for them to show up at the absolute fastest. You could be looking at weeks before an effective force arrived. And *I'm* not gonna wait that long. I've got a mission to do, and I'm gonna do it."

"I could radio command via the egg," Kayla suggested within the privacy of his helmet.

"Shut up," he whispered, hoping to pry the remaining survivors from their hole.

"Good luck with that!" the gruff man retorted.

"Ah!" Bessemer said scornfully, waving his hand at the barricade to dismiss them. It was then that he heard a scratching sound coming up the hall.

"What's that?" Kayla queried with concern.

"One of their boogiemen," he answered quietly, moving into the back of the room and raising his pistol in both hands.

Slowly it presented itself. First a dark hand reached around the silvery doorway, its long claws scratching against its surface. Then a lean, grotesque arm followed, its forearm massive but its upper portion peculiarly thin. Bessemer couldn't help starting when the face appeared. Human in shape, it was covered from the forehead down to the nose with an inky black mask. The original mouth could be seen, but its jaw was terribly narrow and twisted off to one side, no longer capable of closing. Loosely it hung open, saliva dribbling down from it. The legs were misshapen in the same manner as the arms. Completing this remarkably demonic image was a tail that dragged along the floor, scraping noisily as it moved.

Once it was fully visible Bessemer cut loose. Three bullets in the chest caused it to scream with rage, its voice a high screech that hurt his ears and made Kayla cry out. Aiming higher, a pair of bullets shattered its mouth, making it stumble and collapse to the floor.

"Not so bad," Bessemer remarked, about to reload his magazine when he saw the being shift and begin struggling to its knees. Looking up and snarling at him, the creature received a trio of bullets to its only apparent weak spot, the mouth. With a shudder it dropped again, this time remaining motionless. "Like I said..." his voice trailed, one eye on the door as he slipped bullets into his magazine. "Not so bad." Moving along the wall, he stopped just short of the barricade. "You guys hear that?" he asked. "Did you see it through those holes you nearly shot in me? These things aren't invincible! Alone, I've got a chance. But together, I'm sure we can pull it off." Quietly he heard them muttering on the other side. "Get with it, people!" he roared. "There's no time to kick this around in committee!" The survivors fell silent. Then he heard it: the sounds of the barricade being dismantled. It took a couple of minutes, for they'd built it well. But finally a hole was made and a head poked through. Bessemer knew at once that its aged, grizzled face belonged to the gruff-voiced man who'd nearly killed him.

"Alright, flyboy, you've gotten us out in the open," he scowled, climbing through the hole and eyeing the creature that lay in the middle of the room. "Now finish the job."

"Sure, as long as nobody shoots me in the meantime," he fired back, pushing him back from the hole to allow the others through. Next followed a pair of middle-aged women, both of a studious appearance. Instantly Bessemer pegged them as archeologists. Lastly a bookish man of forty helped a little old fellow through the opening, Bessemer taking his hand and pulling him through from the outside. "Everyone alright?" he queried.

"What do you think?" the gruff man snapped.

"I mean can everyone *walk?*" he clarified. "We've got a lot of ground to cover."

"Not me," the old man shook his head. "I barely made it here in the first place."

"We're not leaving you behind, Doctor Baker," the more assertive of the two women said.

"You haven't got a choice," he coughed, making a fist and whacking his chest a couple of times. "I've had it. I wouldn't have made it another day inside there, anyhow."

"Come on," Bessemer said with annoyance, raising his pistol in one hand and seizing the old man's arm with the other. "Enough talking."

Several members of the group carried small lights, and with these they managed to find their way through the dark halls back to the stairway. Suspiciously, they encountered none of the creatures.

"Alright, which way is the control room?" Bessemer queried, looking up and down the stairs and wondering how they were going to drag the old man along them when his legs simply gave out and he tumbled out of Bessemer's grasp down a half-dozen steps. With a loud smack his head struck the wall and he lay still.

"Doctor Baker!" the other woman exclaimed, her voice still quivering as it had the first time Bessemer heard it. Followed by the others, she reached Baker and lifted his head awkwardly onto her lap. But it was no good. Each of them could see at once that he was dead. For the sake of the woman who held him, Bessemer slipped off his helmet and pressed an ear against the old man's chest. Raising his head slowly, he shook it at her.

"There's nothing more we can do for him," the captain said, standing up and drawing the woman away from him.

"But we can't just leave him like this!" she protested, tears forming in her eyes.

"We can't lug him around with us like a piece of driftwood, either. He'll slow us down."

She raised her hand to slap Bessemer for his callousness. But he seized it before she could strike him, grinding her wrist under his iron grasp.

"Save it for what lies ahead," he told her, more authoritative than angry. "We can't afford to fight each other."

Nodding reluctantly, though fuming behind her tears, she lowered her hand when he released it.

"You really expect us to just abandon Doctor Baker?" the bookish man inquired.

"Unless you want to end up like him, yeah, I do," Bessemer replied, glancing at the faces assembled around him. "Get one thing straight, right now: I'm the boss. Krancis sent me here to retrieve a vital artifact, and that mission supersedes anything else you guys were doing before. Help me accomplish that goal, and I'll help you get out of here alive."

"Just one thing, flyboy," the gruff man said. "If you lead us into a trap, or get us cut off from escape, I'll use my last bullet on *you*."

"We're already cut off," Bessemer responded. "The trick is to get un-cut off. Now, which way to the control room?"

"Upstairs. Two levels," the bookish man replied.

"Then let's go," the captain said, taking the lead and slowly ascending the stairs as he put his helmet back on.

Given he was accompanied by a band of civilians, they

made a great deal more noise than he wished on the way up. Though he shushed them several times, they nevertheless could have stirred the creatures to action even had they been six months dead. Or at least that's how he felt. The fact that they didn't all but confirmed to him that they were lying in wait for them, perfectly aware that their objective would be the control room.

Reaching the floor that had been indicated by the bookish man, Bessemer stepped cautiously into it, glancing up and down its silver length. Looking back at the group, they all nodded off to his right. With a nod of his own, he waved them behind him and proceeded.

Now, at least, their noise level dropped. Sensing the danger as though it stood physically before them, they were as silent as ghosts. Progress was painfully slow, for every few feet they were faced with a chamber on either side of the passage that had to be carefully checked before they could move on. It was in the second-to-last of these that an enormous beast, much like the first, leapt out to face them. Jumping back with one consent, it was all they could do to keep from stumbling over each other.

"At last you have come, the vessel I have s-s-sought!" the monster roared.

Shaped much like a gorilla, it walked on its feet and knuckles, its body tall enough to scrape the ceiling if it stood up straight. Unlike its predecessor, its limbs were worryingly burly and well-formed. There was little human about it anymore, save the fact of its having four limbs.

"*Move,*" Bessemer ordered in a harsh whisper, nodding backwards.

"There is nowhere for you to run, human," the creature spoke, knuckling slowly towards them as they retreated. "In an instant I could tear you all to pieces. But I will offer you a choice, instead: surrender your life to me, warrior, and I will let the others go. Else each of you shall be consumed."

"Sorry, I'm not the self-sacrificing kind," Bessemer retorted, trying to think of what to do.

"Too bad," the beast shook its head. "I don't want to risk damaging you in the course of your ever-so-brief struggle to live. Your body is worth much more to me intact."

"To me also," Bessemer replied.

"Yes, of course," the creature nodded, appreciating his humor. "But where is my companion, the little one?"

"Don't worry, you'll be joining him in a minute," he answered cockily, though without the least idea how to make good on his bravado.

"Then you've killed him," it responded with satisfaction. "Good. This is a good vessel."

"What happened to the others?" the bookish man queried, his voice a squeak.

"There are no *others* any longer," it answered, standing up to its full height and patting its sides. "Each of them has been assimilated in me," it explained, putting its knuckles to the floor again and slowly, almost casually, pursuing them. "Only one was kept separate, so that I might have a companion. But I have no such need any longer. With the arrival of this one," here it pointed at Bessemer, "I shall be free."

"How do you figure that?" the captain queried, trying to keep it talking as he wracked his brains for how to defeat it. Covered from head to foot in the seemingly impervious dark substance, a pair of pistols didn't stand a chance. "I'm not taking any passengers."

"You misunderstand," the creature replied. "I will use your body to carry my essence from this barren world forever. The *Cultookoy* thought they had destroyed me when they activated the device that obliterated their civilization. But they merely curtailed my growth until such a people as your own came to release me. Since the beginning I have known this world. Soon I shall know many others."

"You mean you're *indigenous* to this world?" the

bookish man asked, somehow finding his voice to speak. "How did the *Cultookoy* ever manage to live so long with you here?"

"Ignorant question!" the beast roared, amused and angered by it simultaneously. "They lived *with* me since the dawn of their race. Two in one, we were allied. But they sought to cast me off, to ascend to the realm of light and leave our dual existence behind. They shaved me off in a single blast that simultaneously carried many of them to eternity. But their experiment soured, for many were left behind, their souls concentrated in me as their bodies evaporated. With their minds preserved in my power, we have managed to survive within this structure until we could be found by you. I need hardly say that their rage is only scarcely less potent than my own."

"You'll never leave this world," Bessemer replied, aware that they were running out of corridor to retreat through. "Even if you get off this world, Krancis will stop you."

"No being can stop me," it replied, shaking its misshapen head. "Even this Krancis of whom you speak."

"Run for it!" Bessemer shouted, bolting for the stairway just as they reached it. Nearly blocked by those following him, he stumbled and barely caught his balance by moving several steps downward. Instantly followed by the rest, he was about to run upstairs when the creature filled the doorway, blocking their path.

"There is no hope of escape from this place," it taunted. "Its builders only made a single door." It moved heavily onto the stairs, its mouth twisting into a horrible smile. "And that is now above you."

"Come on!" ordered Bessemer, turning and moving down the steps as quickly as he could.

"What are we gonna do down here?" queried the bookish man.

"Try to live a little longer, that's what!" he shot back,

nearly falling down the stairs, his legs a blur beneath him.

Reaching the bottom, he quickly led them into the artifact chamber. Standing in the middle of it, he looked all around for some kind of answer.

"Now what?" the same man asked.

"Look! Try to find something that'll help us out!"

"Like *what?*" barked the gruff man, his pistol held as though he intended to use it. "I told you what would happen if you got us into a jam!"

"Save it for *him*, alright?!" he shouted, pointing back to the staircase from which they could all hear slow, heavy steps reverberating. "In about twenty seconds he's gonna be all over us."

Purely on instinct Bessemer ran back to the sword. Eyeing it as the shadows began to gather about his feet, he noticed something different about them. They weren't tearing at him any longer. They were *beckoning* to him to take the sword and lift it. For a moment he hesitated. But when a deep booming laugh reached his ears from the stairway, he knew the time for caution had passed. Seizing the sword by its handle, he no longer heard screams of despair, but rather shouts of triumph. Racing back to the middle of the room, he placed himself before the others and watched the creature approach.

"You have chosen the last possible place you could have made a stand," it taunted, filling the corridor that fed into the room. "There is no way out."

"We don't need one," Bessemer retorted, wrapping both hands around the sword and gripping it tightly.

"Set aside that device before you hurt yourself," it instructed. "Such power is not to be wielded by hands as feeble as yours."

"Why don't you come and take it?"

Seeing that the beast hesitated, he grinned.

"No?" Bessemer asked, taunting in return.

"What are you *doing?*" the bookish man whispered.

"Just back him off so we can leave!"

"You will not leave this place," it replied, moving a little closer. "Not alive."

"Either make your play or leave us alone," Bessemer replied. "I've been in radio contact with the AI in my ship ever since I entered. It won't be long before imperial troops arrive to secure this building."

"Good," it nodded. "Very good. More bodies with which to grow my being." With this parting thought it began backing away towards the staircase. "I shall await their arrival with great appetite."

"What?!" demanded Bessemer, striding after it, the sword held out before him as it turned to walk away. "You'll not leave this room–."

Suddenly its heretofore unnoticed tail lashed out and struck him in the side of the head. Knocking him clean off his feet, the sword flew from his hands and clattered half a dozen steps away from him. His pistol likewise fell from his half-open pocket. Twisting around in a flash, the beast thundered after him as he arose and dashed for the artifact. Only just snatching it off the ground as the tail shot out for another blow, the bony point of it sliced through his spacesuit and cut the back of his hand. Drawing back, he blocked a pair of strikes before sweeping the blade out in a wide arc that connected with the tail just short of its vicious tip. Instantly writings that had been invisibly engraved in the weapon blazed a brilliant purple, and with this power it severed the end of the monster's tail. Roaring in outrage the beast charged, attempting to knock Bessemer down and crush him before he could make another strike. But he rolled out of the way, slicing at the creature's right leg as he did so. Blazing purple once more, the weapon passed through the limb as though it were air. Falling to its chest, the beast managed to stand up on its three remaining appendages and turn around, bellowing mightily.

"Go!" Bessemer shouted to the others. "Get the door

open and escape!" But they wouldn't go. Instead they began throwing tools and artifacts at the beast to distract it so he could move in for the kill.

"Go for it!" the gruff man said, holding both his pistol and Bessemer's. "We'll cover you!"

With them at his back the captain charged. Ducking a fatal left hook, he raised the sword and slashed it through the monster's shoulder and down its side, separating both the left arm and leg from its core. Falling in a heap against the floor, it lashed out with its remaining limb. But this, too, was chopped off.

"It should not have been possible for you to wield such a weapon," the creature uttered in disbelief. "Only the *Cultookoy* have such power."

"What can I say?" Bessemer replied, raising the sword in his hands, its tip aimed downward at the monster's head. "I'm special."

With this he ended its foul life.

Drawing the sword out with ease, he eyed the blazing engravings until they faded. Then he turned to the others.

"I thought you said this sword *made* that thing," he said, nodding backwards.

"That's what we presumed," the bookish man explained, drawing a little closer and gazing at it with fascination. "It's the only artifact that we've had any meaningful response from in ages. All the rest of this place is stone cold dead, so we just assumed it was responsible. Especially after Filby and Grant went mad from interacting with it. It all just seemed to make sense."

"That *sense* nearly cost us our lives," Bessemer replied. "I don't even know why I picked it up after what you guys said. I just had the feeling that I had to." Looking down at it in his hand, he waved it a little, surprised by its lack of any real heft. "You said those two went crazy from studying it?"

"Well, that's what we thought," the bookish man replied. "But after all that's happened, I think we need to be a little more circumspect with our theories."

"I agree," Bessemer replied, though inwardly he felt a little pang of fear that he might share their fate. Pushing it aside, he strode towards the stairway. "Kayla, any word on reinforcements?"

"They'll be here within twenty hours. I've made contact with Krancis, and he wanted me to express his satisfaction with your conduct."

"*Satisfaction?* I just killed that thing a minute ago!"

"He seemed certain as to what the result would be beforehand."

"*What does that guy know that I don't?*" he thought, shaking his head. "Alright, Kayla. We're gonna search this place from top to bottom to make sure there aren't any more of those things hiding in the cupboards. Keep me posted about anything–." Suddenly he paused and jerked around towards the others, who had been slowly following him. "What about the other pyramids? Have they got monsters like this one did?"

"Well, haven't you seen people milling around outside?" the assertive woman asked.

"Not a soul," he answered. With a weary sigh he looked upward, leaning on his back leg. "Kayla?"

"Yes?"

"Just how confident was Krancis that I'd make it?"

"Perfectly so."

"*Well, he's been right so far,*" he reflected, wondering just how many times he could get away with tempting fate. "Alright, guys," he said, addressing the group and holding up the back of his torn glove. "Where do you keep the extra spacesuits?"

CHAPTER 4

Some time before Captain Bessemer's battle in the pyramid, Sentinel was barreling through warp towards the second Devourer mass. A strange quiet prevailed aboard the vessel, as each crew member, from Krancis on down, felt something large and unseen was in the offing. The bizarre reaction of the first mass to the power Sentinel channeled into it was lost on no one, and had sparked many conversations and much speculation. Krancis remained mum on the subject as far as the rest of the crew were concerned, allowing them to kick around their pet theories without comment. Only with the handful that came nearest to being his inner circle did he choose to speak, and even this was done sparingly.

"I don't like it," Pinchon said quietly to Hunt, as they sat on either side of a table in the cafeteria, nothing but time on their hands. "I feel like we're walking into a trap."

"Not like there's a lot else we can do," the Deltan replied, shrugging his acceptance of the workings of fate. "These masses are pushing out a bigger and bigger psychic signal with each day that passes. That can't be good."

"Oh, I know about all that," the ex-pirate said with a little wave of his hand, his elbows on the table. "I get all the arguments and pros and cons. But when you've got *this much power*," he reasoned, stretching out his hands to indicate *Sentinel*, "doesn't it seem like *you* ought to be choosing the targets? I can't shake the feeling we're doing exactly what that parasite wants us to do."

"I know," Hunt agreed. "It feels like a lose-lose either way."

"Yeah," the colonel said with a frown, thinking for a moment. "But I guess what I really don't like is the fact that our lord and master seems in the dark." Visibly he shuddered. "I can't believe that bothers me as much as it does," he added with some embarrassment. "But I can't help it. I've gotten used to the old bird knowing everything. Why should *this* be inscrutable?"

"He's not magical," Hunt pointed out.

"Could've fooled me," Pinchon said, flaring his eyebrows. "Besides, I thought that was the whole reason we wanted him in the top slot, anyhow: he could lead us best because he's got the inside track."

"Not always," he remarked, glancing at the entrance when he saw a familiar dark shape enter the room. "But, you can always ask him yourself, if you're curious," he added with a grin, nodding towards the approaching man.

Glancing over his shoulder, Pinchon visibly shuddered again.

"No, thanks!" he whispered pointedly, standing up and leaning across the table as he spoke. Pushing back his chair, he turned in time to see Krancis standing before him. "Here, take mine," he said, indicating his seat with a careless gesture before walking away.

"One could be excused for feeling unwelcome," the man in black commented, drawing the chair closer to the table and looking at the Deltan with his typically cool, rational eyes.

"The colonel isn't very subtle about his likes and dislikes," Rex replied, thinking back on his treatment of Phican.

"Indeed," Krancis agreed, knitting his fingers together before him. "He'll never really trust any power that isn't in his own hands."

"I guess so," Hunt said just to move things along.

"Have you got something on your mind?"

"Yes, as a matter of fact. After my examination of your new friend, I'm completely certain that she is wholly on our side. I'm equally certain that she is terribly fragile, possesses *great* potential, and is much more talented than even the *Pho'Sath* recognized."

"That's a little hard to believe."

"They do make an occasional mistake, especially where humans are concerned. They're much too consumed with scorn to ever see us exactly as we are. Despite your record in defeating them, for example, they seem to have little fear of you."

"You can say that again."

"That will change with time," he replied. "For the moment it's an advantage. Their arrogance has always been one of our greatest assets. But to return to Mafalda, she must be carefully nursed and supported. Make her feel valued and cared for. Part of the family."

"That's a little tough when Soliana treats her like she's got the plague," he pointed out. "Mafalda thinks she's jealous."

"Soliana *is* jealous," Krancis confirmed. "Evidently it's your lot in life to attract the affections of a wide variety of women. Most of them peculiarly unsuitable for you."

"Don't beat that horse, Krancis," Hunt warned him.

"The therapy she's receiving in Quarlac is only temporary," he responded. "She will still die, and much sooner than later. There's nothing we can do to stop that. You cannot allow your feelings to overwhelm your duty."

"Or what?" Hunt asked with a scowl.

"Or the Hunt line will go extinct, and the hopes of humanity will vanish," he answered certainly. "There's no way around that fact, Rex. You may *despise* this fact, but you've been chosen to lead mankind not just through this crisis, but into our next stage as a race. For too long we've neglected our hereditary right to the affinity the dark realm holds for us. We must seize it at once, building upon the chain of events that has caused you to emerge as a force so much earlier than one could have had any reason to expect."

"You mean what the *Prellak* did," Hunt elaborated.

"That is not the sort of thing that comes around a second time," Krancis said. "With the *Prellak* destroyed, it's doubtful that any being, or even group of beings, could perform their work over again. We have a single shot at this, Rex. You must not throw it away."

"So I have to throw Lily away?"

"You're free to love her if that pleases you," he said slowly. "But you must marry a suitable young woman and establish a dynasty at once. There must be many heirs, for our numerous enemies will attempt to destroy them all. Dimly they've grown aware of your power. Soon they'll fear and hate your name with a passion, seeking above all things to destroy you before you can destroy them." He nodded towards the marks that were as visible as ever on Hunt's arms. "That extra proof of the shadow element's liking for you won't do you any favors, either. It's trivial to recognize a true warrior when one passes by. His bearing and spirit reveals it at once. But you're more than that: you're a warlord. Or soon will be, if you can stop thinking of yourself as one of the prisoners of Delta-13 and embrace the destiny that's been held out for you."

"Forced upon me," Hunt stipulated.

"It's a rare man who gets to choose his own course, Rex. Most often one is compelled simply to react to the myriad challenges that present themselves in their turn."

"Even you?" he queried, a skeptical eyebrow raised.

"Especially me. My life has never been my own, though like you I once resisted that fact."

"You're kidding," Hunt replied. The look he immediately received showed he, in fact, was not. "I can't imagine that," the Deltan continued with a shrug.

"We've all made mistakes," the man in black vaguely

explained. "Some much more so than others."

Seeing the far away look in his calculating eyes, Hunt knew better than to press him further.

"So is that what you came down here for?" Rex asked after a few awkward moments of silence. "To try and get me to leave Lily?"

"I am attempting to awaken you to your duty," he said. "To stop thinking in such petty terms and to accept what has been thrust upon you. Whether your role is fair to you or not is not relevant, nor are your personal wishes. You simply must comply for the sake of us all."

"And what makes you so certain that the Hunts are indispensable?" he argued somewhat lamely.

"Those tattoos of yours ought to be answer enough for a question like that. They've never been bestowed upon a human before. It's a special gift of the dark realm, given to you alone. It recognizes, as I do, that you are the crux of our future as a race. Subsequently it has increased your power yet further. Or rather, you've finally permitted it to move deeper into your life. As I said, the affinity of the dark element is our birthright as a race, and that is especially true of you. It *wants* to give you more of itself. But you've held yourself back."

"And why would I do that?" he queried as though somewhat bored with indifference, though in truth he was curious for his answer.

"Because you're afraid it will swallow up everything that makes you what you are," he answered. "You fear that your likes and loves and petty hatreds will be swept aside by its enormity – that you will be consumed by it and dissolve as an individual."

"Wouldn't I?"

"That is a projection of your own psyche, a reflection of the absoluteness with which you love and hate. You imagine that the dark realm loves you, because that is as close as you can get to approximating the deep investment it has in you. And your fashion of love is consumptive: it seeks to digest the other personality so as to absorb it completely. You have no restraint in such matters, and as such, you fear that the shadow element doesn't, either. But in truth it has practiced nothing but patience with you. At no time has it fought your inclinations, nor has it tried to force you down a path you didn't wish to follow. Its conduct, especially when you consider its unthinkable power, has been sublime. It doesn't *love you*, Rex: it has an *affinity for you*. It doesn't wish to pull you into itself in the way a lover wishes to, dissolving the distance between himself and his love so that they can become one. That would be at complete odds with the entire notion of *affinity*. It is attracted to you. In fact, it is *fascinated* by you. But it couldn't appreciate you any longer if it swallowed you up. Any more than you could appreciate a painting that you just ate. The two must remain separate."

Had these words come from anyone else's mouth, Hunt would have discarded them at once. But, as with everything he thought and did, since they came from *Krancis'* own lips, they had to be at least entertained. The Deltan still had grave misgivings about the ultimate intentions of the shadow element. Specifically he feared that it would tear him away from the handful of friends and the modicum of security that he'd managed to make for himself. Having so recently left behind the snows of Delta-13, he yearned for a little peace and stability with which to refresh his battered spirit. But the dark realm clearly had other ideas, equipping him with the power to carry the fight deeper into the enemy's ranks than ever before. And he knew what such power ultimately meant: he would become the warlord that Krancis desired him to be, the monkish warrior who denied himself every possible good in order to bring death to his people's enemies. In truth, it meant nothing short of trading his life and happiness for theirs, permitting them to enjoy what he'd always hungered for in Midway: peace, stability, security – the sacred triad upon which Hunt could build his own happiness. But this foundation required a yet broader base whose name was power. Without the power to enforce domestic peace, defend stability, and compel security in the face of humanity's many enemies, the triad would fail, and happiness along with it. He knew it was selfish to demand these things for himself to the detriment of countless others, which was why he gradually accepted more and more of his designated role as time passed and he saw the one-sidedness of the conflict if he should remove himself from the equation. But nevertheless he hesitated to truly give himself over to the cause, to put every fiber of his being into its service. He was simply too weary from years of scraping out a life on Delta to manage such generosity.

Patiently Krancis waited as he thought these things out, his fingers still knitted together before him on the table. He didn't expect that such a conversation would change Hunt's mind. He knew ten such dialogues could not. What he sought instead was to frame the matter in such a way that he would be more likely to move in his chosen direction should some shock come over him that broke him away from his old way of thinking. In such a case he knew the younger man would be lost and all but drowning in turmoil, a fact that ultimately led down one of two paths: either a total commitment to the cause, or the surrendering of it. No middle course was possible, for the involvement of the dark realm was much too great for him to ignore it. Either he could follow his fate, or deny it. But he couldn't passively live alongside it.

At last Hunt's brow unfurrowed, and he eyed Krancis questioningly, silently urging him to continue whatever business he still had with him.

"There are several other matters we must discuss," the man in black said. "The most immediate being our impending battle with the next mass."

"How far off are we?"

"Four hours. It's on a massive world called Ancelmus."

"I've heard of Ancelmus," Hunt replied, drumming his

fingers on the table to try and stimulate his memory.

"You should have, even out on Delta," Krancis replied. "It's the eighth most populous planet in the empire."

"Feeding frenzy," Hunt remarked.

"Precisely. The mass is already almost half again as large as the first one. The psychic signals it's sending out are so powerful that even non-psychics are detecting them. Though, of course, they haven't the least notion what it's saying. The messages aren't intended for their ears."

"Just who *are* they intended for?" he queried.

"Foul creatures, such as those you battled atop the rubble of Milet. It's drawing every kind of evil being it can find to itself, forming a mob that will spread across the planet and hunt down the survivors that manage to evade the ships that are constantly searching for them. Ancelmus has an extensive network of bunkers and tunnels that were made years ago by the order of Rhemus' father, Emperor Septimus, and these are thwarting the snatch-and-run tactics of the ships."

"Hence the footsoldiers," Hunt said.

"Yes. Someone has to physically be on the ground and beat the bushes."

"Well, what do you expect me to do? I can't walk up and down the entire planet fighting those things like I did on Hubertus."

"Naturally. Given the situation we find ourselves in, there are no ideal answers. Our first priority is to destroy the mass before it grows any larger. Afterwards we can see about the survivors."

"You mean we might leave them to their fate?" Hunt asked, raising an eyebrow.

"With two more masses growing larger all the time, we can't afford to give absolute priority to a single world, no matter how populous it is. There's no telling what the ultimate purpose of these masses are. But the fact that so many resources are being poured into them indicates their importance to the parasite. Countless vessels could have been built, and yet more repaired, instead. Clearly their construction supersedes every other consideration in the mind of the Devourer."

"Devourer? Just one?"

"Yes. As we have learned, the apparent hive-nature of the parasite was simply a product of the *Prellak's* restraining hand. In truth there is one overmind that controls every vessel, just as we have a single mind that commands our limbs."

"Even over all that space? How can it possibly communicate with all its members?"

"There are beings in this universe that we scarcely understand. The Devourer is an ancient horror, Rex, and the game was played differently back then. The forces and entities that strode this dimension were larger and far more grand than anything we can see today. We are mere pygmies running about within the footprints they've left behind. The *Keesh'Forbandai* come the closest to the grandeur of the former races with their ability to mingle the power of the dark realm with their technology. But their personal strength is nothing at all compared to the originals. They can draw near the door of the ancients with their wonders of engineering. But personally they're quite frail. In truth, you're likely one of the most powerful single beings now in existence. Many of the others have to make up the difference with their technology. Even the *Pho'Sath*. Especially them, in fact. Without their suits, they would dissipate like steam."

"And just what are the *Pho'Sath*, anyhow? They can't have always been like that."

"Very little is known about them. Their society is a combination police state and religious cult, and almost no information passes from it without their approval. As a security matter they allow no insight into their lives; and as a cult they won't allow what they consider the tainted eyes of heathens to meet with or learn from them. They're completely closed off from every other race in the universe, save a few with which they're willing to trade for resources that have been depleted in their systems."

"But we must have long-range telescopes that can spy out what they're doing, at least in general terms."

"Not when the majority of their civilization resides underground," Krancis replied. "Much as the last *Kol-Prockians* now hide in a bunker on one of the worst worlds in Quarlac, so to the *Pho'Sath* have deliberately chosen undesirable planets and built vast cities beneath their surfaces. In this way they both deter interference because of the worthlessness of their planets, and further spur their religious devotion by a life of hardship. Their every energy is bent upon completing their so-called Journey."

"Which is?"

"It's remarkable that you should have waited so long to finally ask about it."

"I've been too busy killing them to care what their motives are."

"Their Journey is nothing more or less than a plan to ascend to the realm of light. With their technology they very nearly succeeded. But their plans fell short, and thus they wear the suits to keep from dissipating. Giving up their formerly advanced civilization, they've devoted themselves to completing the final steps needed to pass from this life into what they conceive to be bliss."

"Why did they fail?"

"It's hard to say. But the most likely possibility is that the light realm simply refused them entry into itself. With their knowledge they've managed to unite themselves to it. But that's a very different thing from being bound to it by the kind of affinity that, for instance, the dark realm has for us. They've transformed their bodies, and discovered how to harness its might. But it's unlikely that they'll ever truly manage to ascend."

"So what are they going to do? Just knock around until

their suits finally decay and they boil off into space?"

"They wish to find an intermediary, a being so powerful that he can *force* an entry for them into the light realm."

"Don't think the light realm is gonna be too happy about that," Hunt remarked.

"Fanatics never concern themselves with the consequences of their actions. Their minds are utterly fixated by their goal, and every other consideration simply dissolves into irrelevancy for them."

"True enough. But what's their beef with us, then? We're not standing in their way."

"There's several reasons for that, not all of them practical. In the first place, they believe that their intermediary is somewhere in this galaxy, and covertly they've been searching for ages to find him. But the treaty with the *Keesh'Forbandai* has all but locked them out, making progress incredibly slow. Were we out of the picture, they could send fleet after fleet looking for him. Second, they hate and envy our connection to the dark realm, given that it is both an alliance with the element that is opposite to theirs, and also a degree of connection they can merely fantasize about. And thirdly, they hope that destroying us will earn them the favor of the light realm, given its opposite is so attached to us."

"Sounds kind of muddle-headed if you ask me. On the one hand they're trying to curry favor, while at the same time looking for someone to kick the door in for them."

"The *Pho'Sath* aren't the most reasonable of beings. They're much too consumed by their desires to see with clarity. That requires a degree of dispassion that they aren't capable of. Long before they transformed themselves, they were among the least balanced advanced races one could encounter. The transformation has made them more deliberate and methodical than ever before. But their lack of balance has been channeled into an exaggerated egotism that is little short of self-deification. In many cases, that's precisely what it is, though some of them have enough sense to know otherwise."

"*Deldrach* was certainly in the divinity camp," Hunt commented.

"Indeed," Krancis replied, hearing rapid footsteps approaching from the doorway behind him and knowing at once which smuggler they belonged to.

"Krancis!" Gromyko exclaimed, rushing the table. "Julia's out of her mind! She keeps babbling something about a blinding light inside her head! She's gonna snap in two if you don't do something!"

Wordlessly Krancis arose, moved past the smuggler without looking at him, and proceeded at a moderate pace out of the cafeteria. Hunt followed a short distance behind, curious to see what was up.

"Have you no heart?!" Gromyko demanded. "The poor girl is coming unglued! We need to hurry!"

"Her condition is hardly beyond help," Krancis replied.

"It certainly will be if we don't hurry! She'll die of old age at this rate!"

Imperturbably he continued to move at an even pace, reaching her door several minutes later. Stepping inside, the two Deltans followed, stopping a few feet short of the girl's bed. Upon its blankets she lay, her head soaked in sweat as she tossed and turned in agony. Placing a hand atop her moist brow, Krancis closed his eyes. Seconds later she sighed deeply and stopped moving.

"What, did you *kill* her?" Gromyko queried in disbelief.

"I've sedated her," he replied, straightening up and looking down at her. "She'll rest for a time. But her mind is in turmoil. She needs help."

"That's what I've been telling you!" the smuggler exclaimed. "Why do you take so long to *listen* to Gromyko?!"

Ignoring him, Krancis looked at Hunt.

"Have your new friend take a look at her," he

instructed. "See what she can do for her."

"Don't you think that's dumping her into the deep end?" Hunt asked. "This girl looks like a pretty sorry case."

"Mafalda won't disappoint. Besides, she could use a good challenge to rebuild her confidence."

"Or crumble it yet further," Hunt countered.

"Sooner or later she must step into this war and do her part. Now is as good of a time as any."

With this he left them.

"I don't understand that man sometimes!" Gromyko said through gritted teeth, his fists clenched. "You'd think with all his power and knowledge he could do something for her! Why throw her into the hands of someone who's barely holding it together herself?"

"He usually knows best, Antonin," Hunt said in a tone of reluctant resignation. "Come on, let's go get her."

"No, I'm going to stay here," he replied, moving to the bed and sitting on it. Softly touching Powers' forehead, he wiped the sweat from it and dried his hand on her pillow. "Someone needs to keep an eye on her."

Leaving the smuggler with his charge, Hunt directed his steps to Mafalda's room.

"Yes?" she queried when he knocked on the door.

"It's Rex. We need you for something."

Audibly scuttling across the room, the door opened moments later and the former separatist stepped out. Her eyes wide with a mixture of curiosity and dread, she closed the door and looked up at him.

"Yes?" she queried.

"Got a patient who needs your help," he explained, gesturing over his shoulder and then turning to walk. "She's been hurt in the head somehow, and Krancis thinks you can do her some good."

"What can I do?" she asked, her stomach tightening into a marble. "I've only ever used my powers to hurt others."

"Time to learn a new way to live," he replied, picking

up the pace a little to give her less time to doubt herself.

Soon the flame-headed girl stood over Powers' bed, nervously casting her eyes across her form.

"She feels strange, Rex," Mafalda said after a dozen seconds. "I'm getting an unusual aura off of her. Like she's been imprinted with something." She shook her head. "Something bad. Something *angry*."

"Can you fix it?" Hunt inquired, the smuggler somehow keeping quiet, content to gently stroke Powers' brow and listen.

"No," she said at once, shaking her head again. "No, no way."

"Mafalda," Hunt uttered in a firm whisper, drawing up behind her and placing his hands on her shoulders. "You're stronger than you think. You've been battered and bloodied, but you survived. Now is your chance to hit back, to start making a difference in this war. It starts with this girl."

Swallowing hard, Mafalda nodded and knelt beside the bed.

"Take your hand away, please," she said to Gromyko, who promptly removed it. Taking a shallow, ragged breath, she closed her eyes and placed a hand on Powers' stomach and forehead. Instantly she grimaced and jerked them back.

"Mafalda?" Hunt queried.

"She's been imprinted," she repeated, gazing up and down her again. "It's so angry, so full of hate. It wants to destroy me. To destroy *us*."

"The four of us?" Gromyko asked, speaking at last.

"No, I mean all of humanity. It wants to use her as a vessel for its will. But it's not working." Nervously she turned her head and looked at Hunt. "I don't know what to do."

"Go ahead," he replied, nodding towards the lieutenant.

"And do what?" she pleaded, her voice beginning to shake as the last traces of her confidence left her.

"You must separate it from the parts of her psyche

that it has latched on to," a quiet female voice spoke from behind them. Turning, they saw it belonged to Soliana. Visibly worn, her arms were crossed over her chest as she leaned against the doorway. "The imprint is angry and filled with hate, as you've already discovered. But its hold on her personality is tenuous. Were it not, a psyche as soft as hers would have already surrendered to it. Hence there is hope, but only if you act quickly. She needs your help in pushing aside the imprint. You must delve into her unconscious and sever enough of its hold that her faculties can fully reassert themselves."

"I can't do that," Mafalda insisted, standing up and turning towards Soliana. "I've never done anything like this before. I'll just make things worse."

"Krancis doesn't think so," she replied, her tone indicating that she wasn't of the same opinion. Aware of this, Mafalda's head dipped and her shoulders slouched.

"Go ahead," Hunt repeated, his voice strong and clear, intent on pushing aside the doubt Soliana had added to the equation. "Thank you, Soliana," Hunt added, looking over his shoulder at the mysterious girl, his desire that she should leave clear from his manner. Nodding her head a little, she left them. "Just follow her advice and get to it," he continued.

"Now she hates me more than ever," Mafalda worried in a mumble, her hands wringing each other before her stomach.

"You can't worry about that now," Hunt told her, moving between her and the door she still watched. Putting his hands on her shoulders, he looked into her eyes. "I know you're broken up inside," he said quietly. "I know you don't feel like you can take any more. But you *can*. And you *will*. *Deldrach* didn't break down everything inside you." Seeing that his words had little effect, he tried another tack. "Who killed him, anyway?"

"You did," she replied meekly.

"And I'm gonna be right here beside you the whole

time," he assured her. "I won't let anything happen to you." Turning her in his hands, he pointed her once more towards Powers. "Now go to work."

Swallowing deeply, she went down to her knees and inched towards the bed, Hunt following suit beside her. Looking into his face once more for a little reassurance, she closed her eyes and again placed her hands on Powers' brow and stomach. Instantly Mafalda inhaled sharply, her whole body going rigid. Her face tight with a mixture of concentration and pain, she breathed in shallow gasps. Reflexively Hunt reached out a hand to reassure her. But the second he touched her shoulder a bolt of pain shot through his arm and up into his brain. In a flash he saw an enormous fire blazing before his eyes, and it was accompanied by a deep, rumbling voice.

"*So, the darkness has found a new champion…*"

Jerking away his hand as though he'd been electrocuted, he flexed his painful fingers and eyed Mafalda's shoulder.

"Rex?" Gromyko queried quietly, his eyes wide and curious. But the Deltan shook his head, dismissing his question so as not to distract Mafalda.

The latter slowly moved her right hand about on the lieutenant's stomach, her left firmly planted on her forehead. Sweating as her cheeks began to glow red, a whimper occasionally escaped Mafalda's lips. Sensing that she was up against an entity that was much too powerful for her, Hunt only barely resisted the urge to pull her away. All that held him back was Krancis' certainty that she was the one for the task. Yielding to the man in black's conviction, the Deltan shifted from his knees to his rear, sitting on the floor and watching minutely every expansion and collapse of Mafalda's chest; every twitch of her pretty face. He was ready to spring forward in a second if she showed the least sign of–.

"Oh!" she groaned from between half-conscious lips, limply falling backwards. Hunt only just managed to seize her before her head struck the floor.

"Mafalda?" he asked, holding her head in his hands and brushing the perspiration from her brow. "Mafalda, are you alright?"

"Mm–, mhm," she moaned, opening her eyes with difficulty as Gromyko moved to her other side.

"What happened?" he inquired.

"I…uh…," she mumbled, narrowing her eyes to remember. "I was doing what Soliana said to do," she uttered, as though telling herself. "I was separating the imprint from her psyche. But then it lashed out. I wasn't able to…to keep my footing. I think it wanted to hurt me. I mean, I *know* it wants to hurt me. But it was going to attempt it right then and there, while I was inside her mind. That's when I pulled out. Or maybe it *pushed* me out…" she said, her confusion mounting.

"Well, did you make any progress?" the smuggler queried eagerly, hopeful that Powers' situation had at least improved.

"I think so," Mafalda replied, closing her eyes and rubbing them with her trembling hands. "I guess I can't be sure without going back inside."

"When can you do that?" Gromyko asked.

"Antonin," Hunt said censoriously.

"What? You heard Krancis: she's the one for the job. And Julia's in a real bad way, Rex. I just want her to get better."

"And *I* don't want Mafalda to hurt herself in the process," he replied pointedly. "That imprint means business."

"But it fears you, Rex," Mafalda said, opening her eyes again. "I could feel it: despite its anger and hatred, it knew fear when you touched me. It wishes above all things to do you harm, to destroy you."

"Tell it to get on the waiting list," he replied. Reaching for one of Powers' pillows, he slipped it under Mafalda's head and again settled down beside her.

"I have to go back inside," she uttered, determination mingling with dismay. "That entity is hurting her – warping her psyche. It won't be long before it's too late to save her from permanent damage. Assuming we haven't reached that point already," she concluded, wiping a hand down her weary face.

"What?!" exclaimed the smuggler.

"It's just that I can't be sure," she explained, rolling her head on the pillow towards him. "I've never done anything like this before, so it's hard to tell how much harm has been done. The power of the light realm has scorched her mind, but that doesn't mean it can't heal in time. It all depends on how resilient she is. But you heard Soliana: she has a very soft mind. I could be underestimating the damage."

"Not really making me feel better about all this," Gromyko responded.

"Do you want the truth or pap?" Hunt shot back.

"Easy, Papa Bear, easy," his fellow Deltan replied, raising his hands. "I'm just saying what's going through my mind. I'm awfully attached to that girl," he explained, nodding towards Powers. "The thought of anything happening to her makes Gromyko sick."

"I'll do the best I can for her," Mafalda assured him, trying to sound as courageous as she could. Instantly feeling unequal to her promise, she turned to Hunt. "But I need help."

"Anything," he offered at once.

"I need you to go with me," she said. "It fears you. But it doesn't fear me. I could feel its scorn the second I jumped inside her."

"I don't think I can help you in there," Hunt replied factually. "I've never tried to use my powers inside someone's mind before. They probably don't even work."

"But you fascinate it," she responded, twisting where she lay and leaning upon her elbow. "It fears you, yes. But it's also infinitely curious. It wants to know more about you, to understand how a human could be charged with such power. That was another thing I noticed when you touched me: it was *shocked* by you. It didn't think any such union between the dark realm and beings like us was possible."

"On paper it isn't," Hunt replied. "At least not for many generations to come."

"That's all I need," she continued eagerly. "Just some breathing space to do my work. I can't separate her from the imprint with it pushing against me all the time. I need someone to shield me."

Looking up into his face with her wide, soft eyes, the vulnerability of her appeal melted his heart. Nodding reluctantly, he moved to his knees, as she likewise did.

"What do we do?" he asked.

"I'll take care of everything," she uttered, her eyes dashing back and forth across Powers' body as she collected her thoughts. "Okay, take my hand," she said after a moment. "I'll place my free hand on her stomach, and you'll place yours on her head. When I give you the signal, touch her. It needs to be pretty quick, or–."

"I got it," he assured her. "Just say when."

Hovering her hand over the lieutenant's abdomen, she closed her eyes and took a deep breath. Opening them, she looked at Hunt.

"Now."

The instant his palm touched Powers' troubled brow, both *Sentinel* and Mafalda evaporated, and he found himself kneeling in the soft, moist bank of a murky river.

"A swamp?" Hunt queried aloud, rising to his feet and glancing around.

The air foggy and foul, he took a few steps before recognizing that he could see everything clearly despite the heavy mist in the air. Looking upward he found neither sun nor moon, yet a dim yellow glow permeated the place. Vines hung down from soggy, moldy trees, their leaves eaten by insects until they could no longer sustain life. In the bushes creatures skittered and chirped, but remained unseen.

"Mafalda?" he called, his voice instantly magnified so that it echoed through the space, causing the creatures to bolt. "Mafalda?"

"Rex!" he only just managed to hear, his name muffled. "Rex!"

"Where are you?" he asked, moving along the river's bank. "Can you find the river?"

"Rex!" he heard again, this time a little louder.

"Just hold tight, I'll come to you," he instructed, moving at a fast walk. After a hundred feet he paused. "Mafalda?"

"Rex!"

The voice was close, somewhere off in the trees. Stepping away from the river, he moved cautiously under their boughs and looked around.

"Mafalda?" he asked in a conversational tone.

"Rex!" was his answer. But it came from inside a tree. "Help me! The imprint locked me inside! It intercepted us somehow, divided us! Let me out!"

Approaching the wide, ancient tree, his eyes narrowed when he saw what looked to be a door made of bark facing him. Sensing a trap, he nevertheless put his hand to it and drew it open. Instantly a skeleton engulfed in deep red flames snapped out at him and screamed, shaking its head in scorn of him. At once a dark blast shot from his other hand, turning it to dust. Then he heard a rumbling laugh fill the place.

"The dark realm must truly be desperate to have chosen a champion from one of the maggot races," a voice said, the same one who'd spoken when he'd touched Mafalda's shoulder. "As children you play at life, comprehending nothing of the great mysteries of the cosmos."

"Where's Mafalda?" Hunt demanded, speaking up into the air.

"Rex!" he heard her call from several dozen feet behind him. Desperately throwing one foot in front of another, she jumped into his arms and clung tight. "It's wrong. All wrong. The imprint is in control. We're trapped! I can't get us out!"

"We're alright," he said quietly. "Take us to where he's doing the most harm. We need to start breaking his hold on Powers."

"I can't," she insisted, shaking her head. "It's too strong."

"You are in *my* domain now, Rex Hunt," the voice taunted. "Do not think that your powers count for anything here. As playthings you dangle from the end of a string."

"*Mafalda*," Hunt whispered firmly into her ear. "Move us. Now."

Closing her eyes and concentrating, she managed to whisk them to another place. All around them stood massive green columns, like the trunks of trees but without branches or bark. They supported a ceiling of purple, forming an enormous cavern. Entwined around these columns were vines of golden light.

"This is the closest place I could find," she said to Hunt, reluctantly letting him go as he stepped towards one of the pillars. "The columns are a physical representation of the deepest roots of her psyche. The vines, of course, are the influence of the imprint. It's binding itself tighter and tighter around her soul. Soon they'll be inseparable."

"Not likely," Hunt replied, seizing one of the vines. At once darkness proceeded up the vine, turning it to ash that spiraled down from around the column, sprinkling them with dust. No sooner was this done than the ground began to shake beneath them. "What's happening?" he queried, steadying himself against the pillar while Mafalda stumbled towards him to do likewise.

"I–I don't know," she replied, falling against the column when a large tremor knocked her off balance. "It's like..." her voice trailed as she closed her eyes and sensed for the source of the turmoil. "It's like the imprint is trying to shake us loose, to push us out of her mind. We're experiencing it physically, like an earthquake. But in reality it's psychic."

"Can you keep us inside?" he asked, as the ground stabilized once more and he cautiously let go of the column.

"Yes. But not for long – not if it keeps up like that. The burden on my faculties will be too great."

"Then let's get this over with in a hurry," he replied, taking another vine and likewise disintegrating it.

"Oh! It's doing it again!" Mafalda worried, the tremors much worse than at the first. "Oh! Ah!" she grimaced, planting her back against the tree and scrunching her face tightly shut. "Go! Hurry! Destroy them!" she pleaded, gesturing frantically towards the other pillars. "The more you can destroy, the weaker its hold will be!"

Needing no further spur, Hunt dashed from column to column, breaking one vine after another. After a dozen or so had been dealt with, he heard Mafalda scream behind him. Looking back, he saw her slide down the tree to the ground, her fingers laced into her hair as she focused with all her strength. Certain that the climax of the psychic battle had been reached, he hustled to destroy as many vines as he could so that the imprint's power was as weak as possible. Working frantically, he cleared the entire area before pausing to look at his companion once more. The tremors had lessened, telling him that she had bested the imprint despite her doubts. Nevertheless his heart all but stopped when he saw her lying on the ground in a heap beside the tree. Dashing to her, he hit his knees and took her head in his hands.

"Mafalda?" he queried, brushing the hair from her eyes. "Mafalda, are you alright?"

"She will never be alright," the voice taunted. "She is but a maggot, like all your kind. An insignificant worm beneath my feet. What little value she possessed has now been stripped away."

To Hunt's horror, her skin became deathly pale, and her hair changed from its former fiery red to the darkest black imaginable.

"What have you done?" he demanded.

"I have relegated her to the fate of your kind. Where once there was an affinity for the realm of light, that channel has now been closed forever. Henceforth, your dark destiny shall be hers."

Ragefully Hunt stood, raising his hands to the pillars around him. Casting forth countless beams of the dark essence, he began to drive the imprint from Powers' battered soul by sheer force.

"You cannot overcome the light with darkness," the voice spoke calmly as it steadily lost ground. "In the end, all shall be dissolved in it."

A fierce roar burst from Hunt's lips as he bowed his head and filled the lieutenant with his power. A tidal wave of darkness spread out from him, washing her psyche clean before doubling back and finding its place once more inside of him.

It was then that he emerged from her mind. Losing his balance, he fell against Mafalda.

"What happened?" she inquired, as he sat up and drew her from the floor. "The last thing I remember…" she uttered, pausing as she narrowed her eyes to think back. "I remember the ground shaking…." she trailed in confusion. It was then that she noticed how pale her hand was. Looking at them both, she turned them palms up and then down several times, trying to make sense of what she saw.

"And that's not all," Hunt observed, grasping a bit of her hair and pulling it before her eyes.

"What did that thing *do* to me?" she gasped, taking her hair and rubbing it between her fingers to confirm its reality. "I've never heard of any such thing being possible."

"The imprint said it's taken away your affinity for the light realm," Hunt answered. "It said that my dark destiny is now yours as well."

"*What?*" she asked incredulously. "But that's not possible. How can it be?" she queried in utter disbelief, still rubbing the hair between her fingers in fearful fascination.

"Are you two alright?" Gromyko asked, still sitting beside Powers on the bed.

"I think so," Hunt replied, not looking from Mafalda as he watched her world crumble.

"B–but who…how…," she mumbled, shaking her head.

"That imprint was a lot more powerful than we knew," the Deltan replied, taking her arms and drawing her upright. "The important thing is that we're okay, and so is Powers."

"Are you sure about that?" the smuggler asked, concerned because the lieutenant was still unconscious.

"Yes. I drove every last spark of that imprint from her mind. I could feel the dark realm help me do it. There isn't a trace of it left behind."

"So she'll be okay now?" he prodded.

"I'm neither a doctor nor a psychic, Antonin. She might be scarred in some way, and she might not. All I can say for sure is that the imprint is gone for good."

"That's good, my friend," he nodded vigorously. "Very good. I am in your debt."

"We all are," Mafalda said quietly, watching Powers as she spoke. Then she looked up at Rex. "I'm awfully cold," she shivered, crossing her arms over her chest and ducking her head a bit.

"Come on," Hunt said, putting an arm around her shoulders. "Let's get something to warm you up."

"I still don't understand what happened in there," she uttered in wonder once they were in the cafeteria. Seated in the back of the room, she nursed a steaming cup of tea while he sat across from her, his back to the entrance. "It *changed* me. I can't imagine a being having that much *power*. Especially when it's just an imprint."

"What do you *feel*," he asked, trying to ground her.

"Strange. Like I'm all hollow inside. I used to feel this glow of warmth in my abdomen that isn't there anymore. It's like the fire has gone out of my furnace, and I'm cold and alone."

"And that came from the light realm?"

"It must have, given what the imprint said." She shook her head. "*How* could it do that, Rex? How could it cut off something like that? The being from whom the imprint was taken must have been powerful beyond anything we can imagine. I'm just amazed to have come through it alive." She shuddered. "I don't know why Krancis thought I was equal to the task. Without you I never would have made it out." Suddenly her eyes went wide. "Do you think he was trying to kill me?"

"If he wanted you dead, you'd be *dead*," he assured her. "He doesn't leave things to chance."

"No, I suppose not," she agreed, calming a little as the old fringe propaganda image of Krancis as an unerring manipulator of events came to mind. "If he wanted me out of the way, he'd have a thousand different ways to make it happen."

"That's right."

"But I still can't understand why he sent me in there!" she persisted with quiet passion. "If you hadn't gone along–."

"That's the trick, Mafalda," he said with a certain amount of annoyance towards the man in black. "He knew I'd go with you. I don't know *how*. But he knew you'd ask, and he knew I wouldn't turn you down. I doubt there's ever been a man with such an intense awareness of exactly how those around him will act and react. Half his genius is knowing *who* to put in *what* situation so that it all shakes out the way he wants it to."

Struck by his words, she sat a little straighter.

"You mean he *wanted* it to end this way?" she queried, grasping a little of her hair and twirling it between her fingers for emphasis. "He *wanted* the imprint to do this to me?"

"Whenever Krancis puts his hands to something, the safest bet is to assume the result is *exactly* what he wanted it to be."

"But *why?*" she asked in a distraught tone. "H–he's robbed me of so much of myself! What possible use can I be anymore without the light realm to help me?"

"He hasn't robbed any part of you, Mafalda," Hunt uttered with quiet sincerity. "You're not the light realm, nor is it you. It was a part of your life for a time. But now you've got to move beyond it and find a new way to serve."

"I–I can't!" she insisted, her voice rising as she grew flustered. "That was my one big talent, Rex. I've never been good at anything on my own."

"I don't believe that," he shook his head. "You're smart, and you've got a good heart. That gives you the means to make a difference, and the motive to act. All that remains is for you to find another path."

"I can't," she repeated. "It's just not possible, not with the war raging all around us. I mean, what am I supposed to do? Become a pilot or something? It'll take me years to get good at any of the roles the military requires – roles I haven't the least experience with. No, Rex: I think Krancis has outsmarted himself this time. Probably did it for Soliana's sake," she added in a grumble, dropping her face to where her arms laid upon the table.

"She doesn't have any hold on him," Hunt disagreed at once. "Nobody does. Besides, he told me himself that he was utterly convinced of your change of heart towards the imperial cause. The last thing he'd do is throw away a potent psychic to please a subordinate."

"Then it was all just a mistake," she said in a muffled voice. "Whatever his intent, it all backfired terribly. I'm no use to anyone now."

"That's hardly the case," Krancis said from behind

Hunt, causing Mafalda to sit bolt upright. Sliding into the chair next to the Deltan, he knit his fingers before him on the table and looked at her. "I see you've come away from your encounter a different woman."

"A hollow woman," she stipulated in a small voice, too upset for her fear to stop her mouth completely.

"It would seem that way to you, given your background. But with a handful of short-term exceptions, the destiny of the Earthborn lies with the dark realm. You should be glad that the imprint moved you away from an affinity that would ultimately have been of very little value."

"So this *was* all part of the plan," Hunt said, already certain of that but wishing to make the man in black say it. "You put us into fatal danger without even telling us in order to move your little pieces a bit further along the game board."

"How much danger were you *really* in, Rex, if you were able to overcome the imprint so easily?" he asked in response. "There was never any question of it overwhelming you. Subsequently she was in no danger, either. It was purely a matter of timing and spite. More specifically, it was a matter of the imprint having enough time to act on its spite. It wished to use Lieutenant Powers as a vehicle from which to attack both *Sentinel* and its crew. But more than that, it wished to dash any hope we could possibly have of surviving both the present conflict and those which will follow. Being an inveterate ally of the light realm, it was natural that it should see anyone who bore a connection to it as an asset to our side, one which must be eliminated at once."

"But how could it even do that?" she queried. "How could it change something so fundamental about me?"

"That is a secret that only a select few are allowed to know," he responded clinically.

"You can't put her through all this and then keep *that* back from her," Hunt intervened. "She deserves to know."

"You know quite as well as I do that no one *deserves* to know anything during wartime," Krancis replied evenly.

"Knowledge is distributed, or withheld, on the basis of strategic expediency. And it is not expedient that she should know. Nor you, for the time being."

"So what is she supposed to do now?" Hunt asked, certain he would get nothing out of him regarding the imprint. "Without the light realm she feels lost."

"Which is natural," he explained. "But that will pass shortly. Now will be a time of discovery for you, Mafalda. You must learn to embrace the dark realm, though you've avoided it your entire life. Its power; its ancient wisdom; its inexorable purposefulness: each must find expression in you now. You've already proven exceptionally capable of channeling the gifts of the light realm. Now you must learn how to channel those of its opposite. The imprint, intending to curse you, has in fact blessed you. The future of humanity lies with the shadow. Our fate is entwined with it."

"But I don't know what to do," she protested. "I haven't the least idea where to begin."

"Begin at the beginning," he replied simply. "Introduce yourself to it, and allow it to do the same. Let it flow up from the back of your mind and caress you. Embrace it, even as it embraces you. You're smart, Mafalda; smart, and intuitive. It won't take you long to get the feeling for it, to sense when it is reaching out to offer you aid. In time you will learn its contours, inclinations, and habits. You will come to know it as a second personality that follows wherever you go, giving you strength when you have none, and companionship when you are alone. It will neither abandon nor forsake you, because of its affection for our kind. You don't know this yet, Mafalda. But this day is the first of your new life."

Moved to profound silence by his words, she could think of nothing with which to respond. She shifted her gaze to Hunt. But he only shrugged his agreement, more or less, with what had been said.

"This will be a confusing time for you," Krancis continued. "But you'll come through it in the end."

"And what will I become?" she asked. "A warrior, like Rex?"

"Nobody is capable of that, given the uniqueness of his case," Krancis subtly shook his head. "It remains to be seen just exactly what role is to be yours. For the time being, content yourself with developing your connection to the dark realm. On a more mundane level we shall certainly make use of your knowledge of the separatist movement, and that quite soon. So don't fret yourself over being useful, for there are many ways that you can serve the imperial cause."

"Anything," she said at once. "Just so long as I'm making a difference."

"And now you should both rest," he said, standing up and pushing his seat in. "It won't be long before we reach the second mass." He looked at Hunt. "I'll have someone come for you when it's time to enter the reactor."

"Alright," the Deltan answered, as Krancis walked away. "Just about time to play battery again," he grumbled, turning a little to watch him leave. "Come on," he said with a weary sigh, likewise standing. "Let's rest up."

Hunt left Mafalda at her door. Watching for a few seconds as he moved down the hall, she then stepped inside and stretched out on her bed. With a sigh she put her hands to her face and rubbed her eyes, amazed by all that had happened in a few short hours. And there was yet more to come! She was glad to have no part in the upcoming battle with the parasite, for she had been through enough for one day. She wondered how Hunt managed to cope with it all, given that such a heavy burden rested upon his shoulders alone. Her mind went to the black marks on his arms, and what they said about the dark element's presence in his life. She wondered if it would likewise press itself into her very being, as it clearly had his. But recalling Krancis' words about Hunt's being a special case, she dismissed the notion and rolled onto her side, placing her hands between her head and pillow with a sigh. Seeing a mass of black hair tumble in front of her eyes as she did so, she dryly chuckled.

"Take a while to get used to that," she mumbled, moving it out of the way before slowly drifting off to sleep.

She was suddenly jolted awake when a massive pulse of psychic energy passed through the ship. Jumping from bed with shock, she lost her footing and fell to the floor with a yelp. Standing up, she dashed through the door, not bothering to close it as she tore off towards the nearest teleportation station.

"Where do you want to go?" the technician asked, noticing her change in hair color and eyeing her curiously.

"Where's Rex Hunt?" Mafalda queried breathlessly.

"I don't know," the woman shrugged self-evidently. "The reactor, I suppose."

"Then send me there," she replied, stepping into one of the chambers.

Moments later she emerged on the other side. Leaving the room, she asked the way to the reactor from a passerby and hastened to it. Passing into the room just as the small elevator began to lower Hunt, she was alarmed to see his face perspiring, his head hanging low from exhaustion. Seeing movement in his peripheral vision, he wearily raised his gaze to see who was approaching. Not bothering to acknowledge her, he closed his eyes and waited for the lift to reach the floor.

"Are you alright?" she queried once he'd touched down and started walking towards the exit.

"Big battle," he replied flatly.

"I–I had no idea. I must have slept through it."

"*Sentinel* is pretty much soundproof. Especially the sleeping quarters." Briefly he glanced at her. "Did that psychic emission wake you up?"

"Yes," she answered. "I've never felt anything so powerful in my life."

"I doubt anyone has," he said, picking up the pace a

little despite his fatigue. "Come on: let's get to Krancis."

Finding him in quiet conference with Soliana on the bridge, Hunt took the opportunity to lean against one of the transparent walls and collect himself. Mafalda mirrored his stance, not wishing to intrude on Krancis nor, indeed, to face Soliana on her own.

"What's our status?" the Deltan queried when the man in black neared, his companion a couple steps behind as she warily eyed the former separatist.

"Good and bad," Krancis replied, clasping his hands behind his back. "The mass, as you know, has been destroyed. Or rather it has exploded, much like its predecessor."

"What's the bad news?"

"That *is* the bad news," he responded. "The good news is that the foul creatures it had been drawing to itself have likewise been destroyed."

"What?" Hunt asked incredulously.

"The mass, evidently, had tapped into their minds, drawing them together into a single psychic web that exploded simultaneously. The energy released was enormous. We're getting reports of psychic noise passing through the minds of many Ancelmusian residents. Naturally they haven't the least idea what was transmitted."

"Do you?" he inquired, looking between Krancis and Soliana. "You must have some idea."

"We have our suspicions," Soliana answered reluctantly.

"Care to share?" he asked pointedly, unsure why they were being evasive and much too tired to care. When he saw her eyes go to Mafalda with aversion, he pressed off the wall and snapped at her. "Just spill what you've got, Soliana."

"It is evident that the parasite is using all the power it can muster to send a signal deep into space," she responded. "It has cleverly maneuvered us into a position where we must abet in its aims, or allow entire worlds to be denuded of their populations. That was the situation when we first arrived here at Ancelmus: countless souls were being captured and rendered into their construction paste, and then applied to the mass. Destroying it saved the lives of many. But the power of *Sentinel's* dark cannon gave it the energy it needed to fire a message far, far away."

"How far?" he asked, leaning against the wall again.

"It's possible that it has jumped dimensions," Krancis replied.

"You're joking," Hunt responded. "How could that even be possible? It's an organism, not a comms array."

"That should come as no surprise," he said. "It already manages to travel through warp in ships that are entirely organic. The real question is *why* does it require such power just to send a message? Who is it trying to reach?"

"Probably calling home to mama," Hunt uttered, leaning his head back against the wall and exhaling his fatigue.

"Are you alright?" Soliana asked, her concern evident despite the tension Mafalda's presence caused her.

"*You* try powering this ship the next time we have to batter our way through an enormous fleet and then blow up one of their masses," he answered sourly, pushing off the wall and making for the door. "I'll be in my quarters," he added over his shoulder.

"Alright," Krancis nodded, as Mafalda followed the Deltan out into the hallway.

"Are you okay?" she queried in a low voice as they left the bridge behind.

"I'm fine," he told her, shaking his head to rattle loose some of his tiredness. "I'm just sick of Soliana and her antics. Hot for me and cold towards you. We don't have time for personal jealousies."

"Indeed not," she agreed. "I hope she gets past it."

"I think she's too much of a squirrel for that," he grumbled, opening the teleportation room's door and ushering her inside. "She's used to following where her feelings lead," he continued once they were on the other side and alone in the corridor that led to their rooms. "Doesn't have enough discipline to put her own sentiments aside."

"It must be hard on her, living the life she does," Mafalda sympathized quietly.

"I guess so," he responded without interest, reaching his door and stepping inside. Not bothering to close it, he went to the bed and sat down, leaving it up to her whether she entered or not. Deciding to do so, she closed the door and seated herself beside him. "I'm sorry. I don't mean to be a grouch," he spoke, rubbing his brow with his hand.

"You've been through far too much to worry about manners right now," she responded soothingly, the warmth of her voice surprising her and catching his ear. Looking up, he eyed her curiously. "That sounded different to me, too," she commented.

"Yes," he nodded. "I'd say the dark realm is having an influence already. You're more grounded. More rooted in your humanity."

"It does that?"

"It does for me," he shrugged. "I can't say if it works the same way for everyone, though. Krancis is as cold as an eel, yet he's dripping with the stuff, if I'm any judge at all."

"Rex?" she asked quietly, as he slipped his legs past her and stretched out on the bed.

"Yeah?"

"What *really* happened back there?" she inquired gently, aware she was treading on sensitive ground. "You're more than just tired. You're aggravated by something."

Glancing down at her, the warmth of her wide eyes told him he was safe to speak.

"I saw my brother in the dark realm again," he admitted. "Like all the others he was lying on his back in an ocean of darkness." Putting a hand to his eyes, he wiped away a couple of tears that had begun to form. "The image has been burned into my mind ever since I first saw it. But the emotional pain dulls with time, provided I don't see it again. When I do..." his voice trailed. "Well, it drags a lot back. That's why I try not to go there if I can help it. But I was tired after fighting the fleet, and that mass was so much larger than the first one that I didn't want to take any chances. I just let myself go, allowing the shadow to pass through me and into the reactor. By the time I came back to the surface the mass was destroyed. I'd hardly been conscious for a minute when I saw you in the reactor room as I came down the elevator."

"You're carrying such a heavy burden," she uttered softly, shaking her head in wonderment at his strength.

"I was born to it," he responded simply. "At least that's what Krancis keeps trying to drive into my head."

"You don't believe him?"

"I believe we each make our own choice as to the path we're going to follow," he answered, though his voice lacked total conviction. "All this talk of cosmic plans and elemental forces sidesteps the fact that it's ultimately up to *us* to make our own way."

"Does that mean you might change course?" she asked reluctantly, afraid he might say yes and remove his great power from the war.

"How can I?" he asked, tossing up his hands helplessly. "I'm in this thing right up to my neck. I can't leave without automatically sealing the fate of billions."

"But you'd like to go?"

"I'd like to be more than a weapon, to live a life with a little peace and quiet. A life with love and hope, instead of death and corruption and evil around every corner. I've had a bellyful of doubt and danger. I'd had my share of that before I'd ever left Delta-13. But it doesn't look to be ending anytime soon." Leaning his head back on his pillow, he sighed. "I'm sorry. I don't mean to ramble on about my woes. You've suffered more than most anyone ever will, after what *Deldrach* did to you."

"Yes, but I deserved that," she uttered, causing him to sit up.

"Don't ever say that again," he said firmly, his eyes fixing her. "Not ever. You're too good of a person to think that way about yourself."

"It's *true*, Rex," she insisted quietly. "You're haunted by the death of your brother, so you know the pain of seeing a life cut off before its time. I have the same pain, but it's so much worse because *I'm* the one responsible for it. I could have rescued Amra, but I left her in the hands of the *Pho'Sath*. That's a guilt I can never atone for, no matter how hard I try. It's always going to be with me, in here," she said, pressing a hand to her heart. "It's so much worse knowing what her death has done to her father, Gustav. Not only has a precious life been lost, but another life has been shattered in the process. And that says nothing of the many friends she left behind, such as Rina Phican."

"Phican's an old toad. You can't worry yourself about what she thinks."

"She loved Amra like a granddaughter, Rex. That's why she hated me so much. Honestly it's a miracle that she put me up at all after what I'd done. She could have easily ditched me. It must have been her dedication to the cause that kept her from dumping me right back into the hands of the *Pho'Sath*."

"Philip would have ended her, had she done that."

"You're both much sweeter to me than I deserve," she said with a faint smile. "I don't know if I've ever thanked you for that."

"I knew you appreciated it," he responded.

"But you deserve to hear it," she said, sliding off the bed and kneeling beside it. Taking his hand, she kissed it. "Thank you, Rex Hunt, for taking care of someone past redemption. It's yet another gift that I'll never be able to repay."

"You're welcome," he replied, feeling a little awkward to be treated in such a lordly manner.

"I'd better let you rest now," she uttered, releasing his hand and standing up. Smiling softly, she turned and quietly left.

Laying down again, he replayed the bizarre scene in his mind a couple of times before shrugging it away and closing his eyes. His mind rambled across the memory of her form, lingering specifically on her now black hair. He intuited a connection, a link between that fact and her suddenly strange behavior. Then his eyes shot open.

"Krancis!" he roared, shooting out of bed and thundering down the hall to the teleporter room. It wasn't long before he passed into the panoramic bridge, where he found Krancis, seemingly as always, gazing outward, deep in thought. "You set up that whole thing on purpose!" the Deltan said the instant he laid eyes on him.

"I do a great many things on purpose," the man in black replied imperturbably, as though he'd been anticipating the outburst all along. "Perhaps you'd be good enough to specify just *what* you're accusing me of."

Fumingly he stomped up to Krancis, his expression a deep scowl.

"Evidently it has to do with Miss Aboltina," Krancis remarked, eyeing him without concern. "I'm glad you realized it in such a short time. I had begun to wonder if the constant strain of your activities had dulled your mind at all." Glancing at him again, the slightest of smiles lifted the corners of his mouth. "Clearly it hasn't."

"You sent her in there *knowing* that thing would tear out her connection to the light realm. And you did it so she could bear me an heir!"

"Two for two," he replied evenly, looking forwards again, his eyes scanning the surface of Ancelmus as *Sentinel* hovered over it. "Your faculties, if anything, are sharper than ever."

"Do you know what you've *done* to that girl? She feels hollow! Alone! Like what little gift she could bring to the war has now been stolen from her forever. She already thinks she's beyond redemption. What'll it do to her now that her one talent has been taken away?"

"She has many talents," he responded clinically. "Moreover, she has a destiny that has already been prefigured in the deepest recesses of her unconscious. I saw it when I probed her mind. Without her knowledge it has been working within her, moving her towards her fate in conjunction with the influence of the dark realm. It was only a matter of time before the light faded from her. It was better to end it quickly, to cut it out in a flash, rather than that it should gradually diminish over the course of years. Now her true usefulness can come to the fore."

"No dice, Krancis," he shook his head angrily. "You're not gonna push Lily aside and replace her with Mafalda."

"So *that's* what all this thunder and lightning is about," he said, though he already knew that to be the case. "You think I'm maneuvering her between the two of you."

"That's *exactly* what you're doing!"

"Not at all. I am merely procuring the next logical step for when that union inevitably fails. Doctor Tselitel's hold on your affections, though regrettable, is absolute. It would be impossible to remove her without doing untold damage to you. Subsequently I must do nothing to interfere. But that does *not* mean that I cannot queue someone else in line."

"You have no soul," Hunt said.

"I do," Krancis replied. "Though I don't let it get out of hand. The current crisis doesn't permit me to have sentiment, nor should it permit you. In fact, it doesn't. But unfortunately that hasn't stopped you from acting on it at every turn. Subsequently I must step in and right the balances that your emotions frequently put awry."

"Don't force Mafalda onto me," Hunt uttered warningly.

"I've done nothing of the kind."

"And *why* can't I believe that?"

"Because you're emotionally compromised. You think everything and everyone is bound and determined to come between you and Tselitel because that's what you fear the most. But consider this: it would have been the easiest thing in the world for me to have left her aboard Omega Station. I didn't *have* to send her to Quarlac with the emperor. Moreover, given that every imperial asset is at my disposal, I could remove her without leaving so much as a trace. I could even orchestrate it so that she fell into *Pho'Sath* hands, allowing them to do my dirty work."

"You'd never let her become a hostage. That would give them leverage."

"Not if I refused to meet their demands. They'd execute her at once."

"I'd kill you for that," the Deltan uttered.

"Not if you didn't know she'd been captured. Remember, Rex, that I am in complete control of the imperial communications network. She could have died the second she left Omega Station, and you'd know nothing of it. All I'd have to do is wait for the right time to tell you, point you towards a collection of *Pho'Sath* that I wanted eliminated, and allow your native emotionality to do the rest. You'd never have the least notion that I'd been involved in any way."

Palpably aware of how isolated he truly was, Hunt could find no words with which to respond.

"Having established that I hold all the cards," Krancis continued, "I should like to use that as evidence for why you ought to trust my intentions. Yes, I have acted with deliberate indifference to both your and Miss Aboltina's feelings. But that's hardly a crime, especially during wartime. Additionally, I have set in motion a relationship that is our only hope for the future of mankind. Without a line of dark champions to follow in your footsteps, the Earthborn will go extinct."

"I don't believe that," Hunt replied. "Minister Radik's forces are growing stronger every day. He's got the Devourers running scared."

"Devourer," Krancis corrected. "There's only one."

"Fine, *Devourer*. Once these masses are taken care of, you won't need me for *Sentinel* or much anything else except hunting down *Pho'Sath* agents. And you *can't* tell me that you haven't been building up forces to deal with them should anything happen to me. You must have contingency plans in place."

"Indeed I do," Krancis nodded.

"Then enough of all this destiny talk! The Devourer is eventually going to be destroyed; the treaty with the *Keesh'Forbandai* is keeping the *Pho'Sath* out of our space, more or less; and it's hard to imagine anyone else picking a fight with us when this is all over. Sure, we'll be bloodied and much less numerous. But we'll be an armed camp, from top to bottom, a race of warriors."

"You're correct about that," Krancis again nodded. "But the threats that lie ahead are even greater than those we now face."

"I can't believe that."

"You will, when they burst upon us. That will be the true trial of your strength. And that of your children. Only a strong line of warriors, with the dark realm as their inseparable ally, will be able to lead us through."

"And what about you?" he countered. "It's not like you're going to be a non-factor in all this."

"No one lives forever, Rex."

"Could've fooled me."

"Why? Because of what Wellesley told you after he scanned me?"

Instantly Hunt's cheeks blushed deep red.

"Don't look so surprised," Krancis said. "He may be an advanced AI by his people's standards. But his scanning tech is much too crude for it to examine me without my knowledge. I was aware of it the instant he initiated it."

"So why didn't you stop it?" Hunt queried, feeling

defensive and crossing his arms.

"As you may recall, I was busy fighting with a shard of *Eesekkalion* for Soliana's soul," he replied. "Moreover, permitting him to find out a few tidbits about me was calculated to increase both your trust and that of Colonel Pinchon."

"Why?"

"Because you both respect age," he responded, looking at him. "He bites and snaps at me, while you sulk and stare. But neither of you can look at a man of my years without feeling that I've learned a great deal along the way. Additionally, you and I shall be collaborators for many years to come. In our hands rests the fate of humanity. It's both fitting and necessary that we should become more familiar to each other."

"I thought that was the last thing you wanted."

"For reasons of security I withhold essentially all information about myself," he answered. "But equally, for reasons of survival, I am willing that a handful of details should be known to a trusted few. Soliana, obviously, knows more about me than others do. The emperor does as well. I'm not paranoid, Rex. It's not a personal goal of mine to live in secret. It has simply been forced on me by necessity. Besides, the less that is known about me, the easier it is for our enemies to inflate my legend to gigantic proportions, filling themselves with fear. I'm sure Miss Aboltina has already told you of how the Fringers imagine that I haunt their every cupboard."

"She has."

"That's propaganda that money can't buy," he remarked with satisfaction. "To grow and grow within their minds without so much as lifting a finger – that's a powerful weapon." Briefly he glanced at him again. "You see, Rex, that I am at all times waging a war on every front against our enemies. You may rest assured that I am conducting it with a single aim: the survival of the human race."

"I never doubted that," the Deltan replied. "But I don't like your tactics."

"That's because you lack my perspective. Had you seen what *I've* seen, you would likewise see the necessity of acting without consulting the wishes of those affected."

"Then why don't you share a little of that perspective?" he countered.

"Now is not the time for you to know of such things. Eventually, yes. But not now. It's much too soon."

"You can't expect me to blindly follow where you lead. Not when it comes to Lily."

"And Mafalda, also?" the man in black queried.

"Just what do you mean by that?"

"The smuggler isn't the only one to have noticed a shared warmth between the two of you, though of course he's incapable of understanding it in anything but animal terms. The dark realm, to say nothing of your natural affinities, has drawn you together."

"I have no natural affinity for Mafalda," Hunt replied rather quickly.

"It does no violence to your affection for Tselitel to admit such a fact, Rex. You're both children of the fringe; you're both used to being on the outside, ranged against authority; you're both young and passionate. And you're both *lost*. Circumstances have given you some degree of direction. But inwardly you're still searching for guidance. She *used* to have a cause. Having lost it, she's in much the same boat, though, naturally, without the same number of thoughtful attentions from the dark realm to gently lead her. That's where you must step in and be more than a friend to her. You must become a teacher, someone she can follow while she develops her own connection to the shadow. You don't know this, of course, but inwardly she has already foreseen such an outcome. She had an inner vision before she was captured by *Deldrach*. One in which she was addressed by the unconscious and told that she would, like a flower, grow towards a dark sun."

"And you think that's me?"

"I *know* it's you. The peculiar affinity you share for each other indicates it. Moreover, while probing her mind, I found countless processes at work in the back of her psyche that were pointed towards you. Hope for her future has been painted onto you, as has a fear of her ultimate fate. She senses that, in the end, you will bring about her death."

"*What?!*" he exclaimed, taken aback by his words.

"I am certain that you've felt it as well, though not consciously. Hence your otherwise inexplicable drive to protect her. Inwardly you realize the danger."

"I'd never lay a finger on her!"

"Of course not. Yet her innermost self believes that you will destroy her."

"That's nonsense. She's just fearful. Anxious."

"It must be remembered that this occurred *before* Deldrach broke her spirit. At that time the light realm, and its attendant insight, was still very much a part of her life. While one cannot treat her vision as prophecy, it is nevertheless compelling and deserves our attention."

"Then you think I'll kill her?" he asked incredulously.

"I haven't the least notion that you'd intentionally harm her, nor would anyone with a modicum of intelligence. But, standing in the center of events as you do, it's quite possible that you'll set something in motion that will inadvertently kill her."

"Like Milo and *Eesekkalion?*" he asked gravely, looking out across the surface of Ancelmus while he thought.

"Indeed. His death was in no way your fault. Yet it wouldn't have happened had he not been in your orbit. That's exactly what she'll be, if she lives out the inner vision of the flower that grows towards the dark sun."

"Then she has to go away. Far away. Send her somewhere she can't be hurt."

"There is no such place within the empire today. Every

one of our worlds is under threat. The only option would be to exile her to another galaxy, and that would be a fate more cruel, for she would never be able to redeem herself. And that's her ultimate goal. She just doesn't know *how* yet."

"And *I'm* supposed to teach her?"

"You're supposed to teach her in the ways of the dark realm. Over time she'll learn to heed its guidance, uniting her spirit with it. Then she'll have purpose. *Then* she'll be able to right her life of wrongs."

"And die in the process?"

"Very few who are alive today will die in peace, Rex. This is a generation of war. The same shall be true of their children. We Earthborn have reached the tipping point of our existence. Either we pass through this crucible intact, or we wither and die in small bands that will scatter themselves throughout the universe looking for rocks to hide under. Our fate will be that of the *Kol-Prockian* refugees, except there won't be a more powerful empire to make deals with and hide behind. We will be broken, lost, and alone. Eventually we will be hunted down and destroyed."

"By who? The Devourer?"

"No," Krancis shook his head. "By things far worse."

"I guess that's another one of those things I don't need to know about?" he queried with annoyance.

"Be glad that I don't burden you with it. There's enough on your mind as it is."

Hunt was inclined to agree with him, coming off the battle for Ancelmus as he had. As his emotions cooled his fatigue asserted itself once more. Leaning back on his right leg, he crossed his arms over his chest and gazed for a few moments upon the battered cities and burning forests of the beautiful world that lay below.

"What's our next move?" he asked at last. "Head for the next mass?"

"That is the logical step forwards," Krancis answered noncommittally.

"But you've got something else in mind," Hunt remarked.

"I think we're making things far too easy for the parasite. I don't like walking to the beat of its drum."

"Not like we have much of a choice. It's that or let these masses consume whole worlds."

"Apparently."

"Unless we have Radik's boys bomb them back to the stone age," Hunt suggested.

"No, we already tried that. The masses embed themselves far too deeply into the planet to root them out with bombs. The virus in the warheads makes much too little headway."

"So we're stuck playing its game."

"It's the one regrettable aspect to our being united to the dark realm: the Devourer likewise draws strength from it, and thus can use our weapons as a power source in certain circumstances. Were we attached to the light, it couldn't. But you don't get to choose your patrons."

"Indeed not," Hunt remarked with a not-very-subtle double meaning in mind that caught Krancis' ear. Glancing at the Deltan, he sniffed and looked forward again.

"You're not exactly my first choice either, Rex. But if there's one thing I've learned over one-hundred and twenty-two years of life, it's that the dark realm usually knows what it's doing. Given it's guided you so carefully since your first experiences with it on Delta 13, I should think you'd be a little more open to its directions. It chose both of us for this task, just as it has chosen Mafalda for your wife. I'm merely acting on its wishes in both cases."

Hunt knew this. The fact had haunted him for quite a while, in fact. But it had been easier to put the entire load on Krancis instead of on a quasi-divine element. At least Krancis was, apparently, mortal, and thus subject to error. The shadow was beyond human, beyond time, and, subsequently, seemed to be above mistakes. He could feel its urgings, though he strove to ignore them at times and continue on his preferred course. Yet he couldn't neglect the duty that the *Prellak* had inadvertently drawn him to. The simple fact was that he was being pulled in mutually exclusive directions by equally powerful demands. He wished above all to retire into a private life with Tselitel at his side, leaving the war to others. Yet the dark power that flowed through his body daily grew stronger in its insistence that he not do so. In it he felt a collective pull, the burden of a responsibility that he had towards his race and galaxy. He knew he could never live with himself if he let them down. But what was the point of living if the only thing he'd ever loved spent her few remaining years locked away from him in a chamber in Quarlac? He knew that each day that passed carried her inexorably closer to an early grave. Could anyone really expect him to give that up when he'd already been exiled to the fringes of human space so many years before?

"You're very quiet," Krancis observed as these thoughts swirled within the Deltan. "That must mean Tselitel."

"Why?" he asked wearily, his voice more tired than he'd expected it to sound.

"Because she's the only topic that truly makes you stop and think," the man in black explained, turning towards him. "I'm not your enemy, Rex. You must stop thinking that I'm willfully trying to come between you. It disrupts our cooperation, endangering the war effort. The best possible thing for our chances of survival is for you and I to work completely in sync. We can't afford suspicion."

"Then stop causing it. Stop trying to put Mafalda between Lily and I."

"I've already explained myself fully on that matter," he replied somewhat clinically, the hint of hope fading from his voice as his expression flattened. "The line of Hunt must continue, and Doctor Tselitel cannot be a part of that. The dark realm has made its choice of a wife for you, as you sensed from your earliest contact when the charge passed between you both. You merely ignored it because you wished to avoid its implications, while she couldn't make sense of it because of her self-hatred. I have no such blinders, and thus can see the matter clearly. You must rise above your petty wants and *act*, Rex. The dark realm is with you. But even it can't render you immortal. You must produce an heir at once to carry on your fight once you're gone."

"That's a bridge too far, Krancis," the Deltan asserted, turning away and striding heavily towards the door.

"Perhaps the time isn't right," Krancis remarked, causing him to pause and listen a moment, his back still turned. "Perhaps the dark realm hasn't seen fit to give you the proper stimulus to act."

"Or perhaps you're wrong about all this," Hunt replied, turning and glaring at him. "Have you considered *that* possibility? Or are you beyond error?"

Receiving an emotionless expression in response, the Deltan turned and left. Much too burned by his conversation to rest, he directed his steps to the room where Girnius had been permitted to set up shop along with Wellesley. He hoped the pirate leader wouldn't be there, for he needed a chance to cool off in the presence of an old friend.

"Rex!" Wellesley exclaimed as he entered. The room was small, consisting of a desk, a few chairs, and a trio of computer monitors that had been mounted on the walls along with some communications equipment. Each of the monitors displayed data about the present state of the Black Fangs. "What took you so long? I haven't talked to you in ages!"

"Been busy," he replied in a sour voice, taking one of the chairs and dragging it up to the monitors. Sitting down, he watched for a few seconds as numbers and graphs flickered across them, none of it meaning anything to him.

"Oh, I know what that means," the AI said. "Trouble with our lord and master, as Pinchon likes to call him."

"Is there any other kind of trouble these days?" he queried, as he ran a hand through his hair and leaned back.

"Well, if you discount the abomination spreading across the galaxy like a plague, and the cultish fanatics chewing away at the fringe…" his voice trailed.

"Okay, fine. Point taken," Hunt said, reminded that his personal problems weren't the only ones.

"Just what *is* the problem?"

"Krancis wants me to push aside Lily and marry Mafalda."

"That…seems like a bit of a leap," the AI commented.

"No, not at all," Hunt responded in a higher, sarcastic tone. "It seems the dark realm has hand picked her for me. And Krancis, good servant of its will that he is, even set it up so that her affinity to the light has been cut out of her."

"How in the world did he manage that?"

"You know that trouble with Lieutenant Powers?"

"Yeah?"

"Well, she had some kind of fragment stuck in her, and Krancis said Mafalda was the girl to get it out. Kind of like that business with *Eesekkalion* and Soliana, I guess, except *Mafalda* was the real target. Out of spite the fragment severed her affinity for the light, making way for the dark somehow. Honestly, I can't imagine how that's even possible. But it turned her hair black, and she can tell the old connection she had was gone."

"I've never heard of anything like that before," Wellesley replied, flabbergasted. "How's she taking it?"

"I don't know," he said, tipping his head back and looking up at the ceiling to stretch his tired neck. "She was feeling hollow and worthless, like her one skill in this life had been taken away from her. Then she got all warm and cuddly, kissed my hand, and thanked me for looking after her. Gave me the creeps, to be honest. Like she was worshiping…me," he said, his face clouding over with thought.

"What is it?" the AI inquired.

"Well." he began, not wishing to proceed because it sounded so strange but nevertheless compelled by the notion that had flitted through his mind. "Krancis said Mafalda had had a vision before *Deldrach* broke her. One in which she was predestined to grow towards what he called a dark sun. He interpreted that as being me. You don't think..." his voice trailed, unwilling to finish.

"That...she's trying to find redemption in *you?*" he finished for him. Embarrassed by the idea, the Deltan only nodded. "Well, sure, I guess that's possible. It would be natural enough, anyhow, given you're the great symbol of Earthborn power these days." Hunt frowned and looked away at this. "Now, just hang on a minute. Like it or not, you're the face of human resistance. You have been for some time now, given Krancis' propaganda efforts. And that makes you the face of the *empire*, the authority that Mafalda fought against for so long and now must reconcile with. It's beyond natural that she would, in essence, make amends with you as a kind of proxy for the empire. You're probably much the same thing in her mind. In many ways you're the emperor now, instead of Rhemus. Though of course he still holds political power, you're the warrior that makes his regime possible – the driving force that keeps it alive. Without you there'd be no *Sentinel* and no single individual capable of taking the fight personally to our enemies. Moreover, for her specifically, there would have been no one to save her from *Deldrach* and the *Pho'Sath*. You've got to face it, Rex: you've got a *lot* of things in your favor, as far as she's concerned."

"Which is hardly a fact that I welcome," he responded.

"A fact is a fact," the AI uttered. "And it's not like you can pretend there isn't some bond between you and that girl. Anyone with eyes can see it, even if they have to borrow someone else's, like me."

"Just what are you suggesting?"

"I'm merely calling it like I see it, old buddy. I know you love Lily. But there's something special between you and

Mafalda. I don't know if it's love or not. Honestly, I doubt it is. More like an affinity, or an interplay of temperaments that just causes you to link together like a key and a lock. Truth be told, Krancis probably can't believe his luck that she fell into your hands the way she did. The whole thing is calculated to push you together and *keep* you together."

"According to him the dark realm has been pulling strings behind the scenes," he said in a low voice. "He said he's just been carrying out its will with regard to us."

"Funny, I never had any real notion that it would involve itself in that way. Always seemed pretty passive. Or at least it seemed to work through others. But this sounds like it's actively sticking its fingers into the pie, manipulating events. Gives me a funny feeling, to be honest."

"I don't think it's exactly running things like some sort of god," Hunt replied. "But it does seem to be working through individuals more pointedly than before."

"I agree. Makes you wonder why, though. I mean, things *appear* to be getting better, don't they? We're finally starting to push the Devourer back through conventional means instead of just hanging onto *Sentinel* for dear life. The Fringers are reeling, and the Black Fangs are slowly coming into the fold. I gotta say, it bothers me a bit, like the dark realm knows something we don't and is trying to hasten us along."

"You think that's what's going on?" he queried, lifting his eyebrows as he looked at the medallion, hanging from its chain from a hook on the wall.

"That's outside my purview," the AI said, audibly holding up his hands and shrugging. "You'd be better off asking Krancis, though I imagine you'd rather not. Soliana'd be another possibility, I suppose."

"She's bent out of shape at Mafalda," Hunt shook his head in the negative.

"And that's important to you?" Wellesley asked insinuatingly.

"*Wells*," he shot back with annoyance.

"Look, I'm not trying to make you mad or anything. I just think you're fighting an affinity that you don't have to. She's wrapped around your little finger, and with good reason. You're the first bit of stability to come into her life since the Fringers kicked her out. And whether or not there's any truth to that whole 'dark sun' business, *she* thinks it's true, for better or worse, so I'd be careful about keeping her at any kind of distance. It might break what's left of her battered little heart into splinters. You know as well as I do that she needs something to cling to right now, especially with her connection to the light realm broken. Poor girl. Everything's coming at her so fast."

"Yeah, well, convenience seems to be in short supply right now."

"Yeah," the AI assented.

A few quiet moments passed before Hunt spoke again, changing the subject.

"So, how're things with the Black Fangs?"

"A mess!" Wellesley said at once. "I can't believe these guys have lasted this long, and in this kind of style! Everything is held together with luck and chewing gum! There's *no* meaningful command structure at all. Girnius simply transmits his will through his lieutenants, and they shake their fists and hope that it gets done. Usually it does, though typically *late* and with a half dozen particulars done wrong. As far as illegal organizations go, I'm sure the Black Fangs are a class act. But compared to a serious military operation like the one I ran for so long, it's a joke. I could increase their gross income by at *least* seventy-eight percent within two years, provided I had complete authority to act. They're just so polluted by corruption that money is slipping through Girnius' fingers. I'm certain he's aware of it. He's too smart not to be. But the waste is just appalling. I've already begun cleaning house, though of course I have to be careful. Everyone's gotten their hands dirty at some point along the way, so I can't risk scaring all the rats into jumping ship and leaving us without any personnel. I can only target the most egregious examples. Naturally they all think this is Girnius' doing, so that's masking my intent for the time being. They don't realize I'm trying to retool them into something that can serve the empire. If they knew *that*, I'm sure we'd wake up tomorrow without a single pirate on our side. Save for a few desperadoes that would stick around just to fight, of course."

"Of course."

"But seeing as we can't depend on a handful of loonies, I have to justify these changes through an increase of loot, so I've instituted profit-sharing in select regions that were particularly blighted by corruption. This has given the targeted areas a new zeal for piracy, which, understandably, hasn't been well received by Krancis. Nevertheless they've gained a new lease on life now that so much of their work isn't pouring into the flabby hands of local bosses, and that's improved morale and strengthened Girnius' hold on their affections. Where before he was something of a feudal king in a distant castle, separated from them by their local lords, he's now seen as a powerful benefactor. I doubt he's been this popular in years."

"Something else Krancis isn't bound to be happy about."

"Yeah. He's got a genuine dislike for Girnius. Seems to think he's little more than bacteria. *But*, if we want to keep the Black Fangs in the game, we need Girnius to be strong and popular, at least in their imaginations. They need a focal point to rally around. Without the big boss to lead and guide them through all this chaos, they'll crumble and blow away on the wind. They need a strongman at the top, or they'll fold like a house of cards."

"Or a strong AI," Hunt remarked.

"Well, sure. But they can't know it's me, can they? So we've got to keep up the act. And that's fine by me. I've had my share of laurels. I'm happy to wield the power without getting any of the credit. And frankly, given this *is* a pirate organization, I'm not exactly keen on credit, anyhow. There are much more laudable groups to manage than the Black Fangs. I can't tell you all the nasty, filthy things they've been up to. It'd make me sick if I had a stomach."

"Good thing you don't," Hunt replied, as the door opened behind him. Turning around, he saw Girnius frown upon seeing him.

"What are you doing here?" the pirate boss asked brusquely, shutting the door and standing over him.

"Catching up with an old friend," he replied carelessly, deliberately offensive in his lack of concern.

"Get out. This is my command center."

"And this is Krancis' ship," the Deltan remarked, citing the man in black to irritate him as much as possible. "Don't forget that."

"That would be impossible," he scowled, crossing his arms and leaning against the wall, attempting to stare him down. "Just what are you here for, Hunt? Harvesting information to take back to Krancis?"

"Oh, he doesn't need to do that," Wellesley uttered with an audible smirk. "Everything that passes into this room has already been screened by *Esiluria*. Krancis has as much data at his fingertips as you do. It's a miracle that he hasn't used it to curtail some of the Black Fang's more outrageous crimes already. Pretty tolerant, if you ask me. I would have killed half your members in a snap of my fingers, and that's just for starters. Of course, Krancis doesn't have my military background, so he might be a little more flexible about such things. Still, I'd count my blessings if I were you, Chairman. And I *wouldn't* go picking fights with men who could crumple you up like the last dry leaf of autumn. It just doesn't pay."

Glancing at Hunt as he heard this, the chairman unfolded his arms and pushed off the wall.

"You've got five more minutes, Hunt. Then I've got business to conduct."

With this he left the room.

"*'I've got business to conduct!'*" the AI repeated mockingly once the door was again shut. "Business doing what? I've already made his organization better managed than it's ever been before! Oh, well. Had to cover his pride, I guess." At this Hunt stood up and stretched. "You're not leaving already?" he queried, disappointment in his voice. "He said five more minutes."

"It'll be five more minutes for you to run the Black Fangs before he steps in and starts screwing them up again," Hunt smiled.

"Oh, don't flatter me," Wellesley replied. "Not that you're wrong, of course," he added. "But you've got to understand what it's been like around here lately. From one day to the next I've been managing all these weirdos. It's nice to talk to a normal person for a change."

"You're calling *me* normal?" Hunt asked, holding up his arm and tapping one of the dark marks.

"Yeah, more or less. In any event you're honest, which is a refreshing change of pace given the scum I'm dealing with. But," he began, before pausing dramatically. "No, you'd better go. Just leave me alone with them. It–it's okay."

"Sounds good," Hunt replied, calling his bluff and making for the door.

"Oh bah! Haven't you got any sympathy left?" he protested humorously. "Oh, well. Say hi to Mafalda for me." At this Hunt paused and turned around, a serious expression on his face. "Buddy, I didn't mean anything by that," the AI stated firmly. "I just like the kid, okay? I want her to know that people care about her."

"Alright," he nodded, accepting his explanation and leaving him to his work.

"*Don't push him too quick, Krancis,*" Wellesley thought. "*He's on a hair trigger as it is.*"

Taking a teleporter back to the sleeping quarters, Hunt frowned when he saw Soliana coming towards him down the corridor. Hardening his expression, he intended to walk past without acknowledging her. But she had other plans.

"Rex," she said in a mild voice, her eyes fixing him with a peculiar intensity that caused him to stop a couple feet short of her. "I need to talk to you."

"About what?" he queried, looking all around her face and trying to decide what had changed about her. She seemed more poised and purposeful, yet more remote than ever, as though her mind was a hundred miles away despite the presence of her body. A large portion of her mental processes were clearly occupied with something other than their conversation.

"Not here," she shook her head, walking past him and leading the way to her room. "I knocked at your door but you were out. I thought perhaps you were with Mafalda."

"No, I was talking to Wellesley," he replied, annoyed by her secretiveness. "Look, Soliana, I'm tired and I just want to sleep. Can't this wait until later?"

But instead of answering she just hastened her pace a little. Stopping at her door, she opened it and ushered him inside. With a weary sigh he stepped in and waited for her to join him.

"Please sit," she said.

"No, I'll stand," he responded, crossing his arms and tilting his head to the side a little to show his irritation. "Alright, let's have it: what's the big secret?"

"Something terrible is at work with these masses," she began, settling onto the bed rather meekly, her small hands sandwiched between her knees as she drew her feet together. "As you already know, both the first and second masses emitted a psychic pulse when we destroyed them, one fueled by the power of the dark realm."

"Mhm," he nodded, unimpressed.

"The parasite is calling out to something. Or someone. It knows that we're gaining the upper hand with the advancements that Krancis has brought to the navy. Eventually it must be defeated, and thus it has grown desperate. The first message it pulsed out had a triumphal note of confidence about it. But the second was almost a scream, a plea for assistance. It's afraid."

"About time."

"You don't understand," she shook her head. "The Devourer isn't asking for help from just anyone. I believe it is attempting to invoke the aid of one of the elemental ancients of the universe – beings of incalculable power. Just one would be enough to destroy the entire empire with very little effort."

"Well, where are these beings?" he asked skeptically. "I've never heard of them, and I'm certain nobody's ever *seen* one."

"No one has. Not for a long, long time. They were banished from this universe eons ago. They seemed to be little more than a hazy myth at this point, except you can still find references to them in the memories of both the light and dark realms. By virtue of the many personalities that swirl within my psyche, I'm able to draw on information from both realms. In this case, particularly that of the light. And there is no question at this point that the Devourer is trying to reach something far more ancient and powerful than a race such as ours. Its words are those of a servant pleading to its master, one that it served long ago."

"Well, who is it?" Hunt queried.

"I don't know," she admitted. "My psyche is far more united than ever before, thanks to Antonin's help. But I still have a great deal of noise within that clouds my vision. I told you once that Krancis seeks a prophetess, and he very nearly has one in me. But I'm not there yet."

"So, what was all this about, then?" he asked, annoyed to be left hanging. "Why'd you pull me in here?"

"Because I suspect we're committing a grave error by destroying the masses, and you're the only one capable of powering the cannon to do so. Krancis isn't settled on whether we ought to eliminate the rest, but even as we speak we're preparing to depart Ancelmus in order to assault the next one. He feels the best bet is to keep destroying them, even if that's what the parasite wants. The alternative is worse in his estimation."

"So you wanted to recruit me to your way of thinking before telling him what you've found out?"

"I wanted to give you a chance to understand what was at stake so that you could stop it if you agreed with me. He can't force you to get into that reactor, Rex. Only you can make that decision. And I believe it would be a terrible mistake to again play into the Devourer's hand."

"We can't just leave those things standing, Soliana," Hunt objected, taking a chair and sitting down. "There's a reason we blew up the first two. Besides, if we change our minds later on and destroy them when they're five or eight times bigger than they are now, what will the size of the psychic pulse be then? It'll be catastrophic. No, Soliana: I don't think we've got a second to lose. We need to smash the two remaining ones and then disintegrate any others that might pop up along the way. I think the Devourer is counting on us dragging our feet so that it can send out a bigger pulse each time."

"But why?"

"Because it knows that *we* know we're being played. It also knows we can't simply stand by and allow those things to eat up our people like appetizers. It has deliberately put us between a rock and a hard place so we'll squirm and waste time. There's no other explanation for the way it's behaving. It's trying to produce doubt, to wage war in our minds while ultimately giving us no choice as to how we proceed. That's why we need to double down at once, leaving Ancelmus behind to shuffle on as well as it can."

"You didn't feel this passionate about this before we spoke," she observed, her eyes narrowing slightly. "Is it because *I'm* the one who suggested patience?"

"I haven't got a problem with you, Soliana," he half-lied. "But what I *do* have a problem with is inactivity. Krancis is already floating the idea of holding back, and now you're saying we should positively stop all further attacks. I can't stand by and allow this notion to gather steam. We need to pummel the parasite until there's nothing left of it. We need to bring this war to an end."

"Which would leave you free to follow whatever course you wished," she commented.

"Don't try to pick away at my personal motivations, Soliana," he replied, standing up and looking down at her with displeasure. "You tried to win me over to your way of thinking and it hasn't worked. If you want to make your argument to Krancis, fine. But don't expect me to support it."

Hours later Hunt was lying in his bed, staring at the ceiling. Unable to sleep despite his exertions, his mind swirled around his discussions with both Krancis and Soliana. Stopping short of cursing them, he rolled onto his side and sharply exhaled his frustration that they should both be on hand to frustrate his life. Just one, in his estimation, was quite enough for that. And now the dark realm was throwing its hat into the circus, too! It was as if the universe was conspiring to keep him and Tselitel apart.

Still, Krancis *had* elected to at least slow her Valindra via the *Kol-Prockian* chamber. That was *something* in his favor, anyhow. Which was a great deal more than could be said for Soliana, he reflected, given she'd tried to drive a wedge between the two of them almost from their first meeting.

The truth was, Hunt was feeling very much alone. Isolated from Lily by distance, and Wellesley because of his work, there wasn't anyone he could really trust with the tumult that was beating around his insides. Pinchon wasn't much for reflection of that kind, and Gromyko, to his thinking, wasn't even capable of such thoughts. That left... nobody, apparently. Mafalda, he knew, would be willing to sit and talk with him for hours out of sheer gratitude for saving her life. But despite her background with the psyche, she was in many ways an initiate, learning anew how to live and function. Besides, after all she'd gone through, he couldn't bring himself to saddle her with the burdens he bore. At least for the time being she ought to have a hero to look up to, a man of dark power who would make things come out alright in the end. She deserved to have that hope.

Faced with another dead end, he sighed his exasperation and rolled over to face the back of the room. It was then that he found he had a visitor.

"*You know your destiny*," a small child uttered, his voice a whisper, his body a silky river of darkness that flowed constantly, as though through a series of transparent pipes. "*You must embrace it.*"

With this the figure disappeared.

Sitting up, Hunt rubbed his eyes and looked again.

"Was I dreaming?" he asked softly, gazing where it had stood for several seconds before standing up and feeling the floor for any change in temperature it may have caused. But it was the same wherever he felt. "'*You know your destiny. Embrace it,*'" he repeated quietly, sitting on the bed again as he thought. Glancing at the marks on his arms, he looked back to the vacant space and drew the conclusion that the dark realm had manifested itself in order to push him further along. Given he'd just been thinking about Mafalda…

Startled from this line of thought by a knock at his door, he jerked his head sharply over his shoulder. Instantly regretting this movement because of the pain it sent up his neck and into the base of his skull, he grumbled and began to rub it as he went to open the door. Seeing Pinchon, he left it open and turned back into his room.

"Oh, you," he uttered rather flatly, still rubbing his

aching neck.

"That's a greeting anyone would be glad to get," the colonel observed sarcastically, taking a step inside without closing the door.

"I didn't mean it that way, Philip," he explained with a weary shake of his head, dropping onto the bed and looking down as he worked his sore muscles. "I just thought it was Krancis or Soliana coming to throw something else at me. It's nice to speak with a normal person for a change."

"You might change your mind about that in a minute." the ex-pirate responded ominously, at last closing the door and moving a few feet closer. "The fact is, this isn't a social call. I'm playing messenger boy."

Hunt stopped rubbing and looked up, the odd note of reluctance in the colonel's voice catching his ear.

"What is it?"

Frowning, Pinchon watched the floor for a moment. Then he locked eyes with him.

"Lieutenant Powers is dead."

"*What?!*" the Deltan exclaimed, jumping to his feet and making for the door.

"Now, just hold on a minute, Rex," the older man said, raising his hands to stop him. "Krancis sent me over here because we've got a bit of a situation. As you can imagine, Mafalda thinks it's all her fault. She's in a bad place, and the old man's worried that she might fracture permanently after everything she's gone through. Soliana seems to think it's the poor girl's just deserts, so she's not getting involved. Gromyko didn't help any by screaming in her face that she killed Powers. Naturally, I took care of that," he added off-handedly, making a fist. "But I'm afraid the damage has been done. She won't listen to me 'cause she thinks I'm just an old papa bear who'll tell her what she wants to hear. And that leaves you."

"Of course," Hunt replied self-evidently, not seeing his point.

"You don't understand," Pinchon said, looking around

the room again before continuing. "The old man…" he started to say, inwardly cursing Krancis for making him the messenger. "Well, he thinks it's your fault that Powers died. Said you overloaded her psyche when you drove that imprint from her, and that given all the abuse she'd already taken, she just couldn't handle it. He wants you to tell Mafalda that, to take the blame so she can go on living with herself. Now, I don't know if that's true, or if our lord and master has just cooked that up to keep Mafalda from tearing herself to pieces. But that's what he wants you to do."

"Do you think I did that?" Hunt asked, merely thinking out loud as he processed what he'd been told.

"I don't know, Rex," the colonel shrugged. "This is all beyond me. Given Krancis' love of realpolitik, I can tell you I don't trust him on this. Shoot, she could have died of something else entirely, and he's just using this to maneuver you around."

"What, manipulate me through guilt?" he queried, though gradually inclining towards the belief that he had indeed been responsible.

"Sure. It's no secret you two haven't exactly seen eye-to-eye lately. This would serve to clip your wings a little."

"I don't think so," Hunt disagreed, sensing that this wasn't congruent with Krancis' style. Slowly making for the door as he thought, he paused and looked up. "Where is she?"

"They've got her sedated in the hospital," he answered. "Come on, I'll show you."

Reaching her room some time later, the colonel waited outside while Hunt entered. The room was dark, save for a small light that cast just enough of a glow that he wouldn't stumble into her bed.

"I knew they'd send for you," she mumbled, her voice so thick with sleep that she sounded inebriated. "I killed her, Rex. There's no doubt about that."

"No, you didn't," he said with quiet firmness, sitting beside her on the bed and looking down into her face. As his eyes adjusted to the gloom, he saw that her eyelids were pressed tightly shut, and that tears were running down her cheeks. "You did all that you could for her."

"It wasn't enough," she responded, her emotions so agitated that she began to grow alert despite the medication. "Someone else should have helped her. Someone better. I didn't know what I was doing. I–I was no match for that imprint."

"The imprint didn't kill her, Mafalda," he said gravely, still possessing doubts about Krancis' story but deciding to commit to it for her sake. "I did."

At this the young woman's eyes shot open.

"*What?*" she asked incredulously.

"When I drove the imprint from her mind, I overloaded her. It was just too much for her to take. I'd never done anything like that before, and I just overdid it. Instead of purifying her mind I burned her out."

"I–I don't believe that," she shook her head slowly. "I don't think you could ever hurt someone that way. The dark realm wouldn't let you."

"I've hurt and killed plenty of people, Mafalda. The dark realm doesn't have a safety switch like that."

"But what about when it helped you stop *Deldrach* when I was hanging on that wall? You told me you could feel it cooperating with you, pouring just enough of itself into me to stop his attack without hurting me. Why would it allow you to kill Lieutenant Powers?"

"It lets me make my own mistakes, Mafalda," he answered. "It doesn't just carry me along like a child in its arms."

Doubtfully she eyed him, unsure if he was telling the truth or just taking the blame for her sake.

"This isn't an easy burden to carry, Mafalda," he said, reading her thoughts through her gaze. "I'm not saying any of this lightly."

"But you'd say this to spare me that burden, wouldn't

you?"

"I would," he admitted. "But this is Krancis' opinion, and mine as well. Even if you don't believe me, you can believe him."

"No, I believe you, Rex," she said at once, the idea of distrusting him abhorrent to her. "It's just…" her voice trailed.

"What?"

"It's just, I hate to think of how this has added to the weight already on your shoulders," she said gently. "And I hate to think of poor Lieutenant Powers!" she added. "She seemed like such a good soul."

"We've lost a lot of those already," he responded grimly. "We'll lose a lot more before this thing is over."

"I know," she whispered, her reddened eyes watching the ceiling as she thought back on her own misdeeds. Seeing this, Hunt put a hand to her hair and brushed it softly, drawing her gaze back down.

"Don't do that," he uttered. "Don't think about the past."

"I can't help it," she replied. "In my dreams I see their faces; hear their voices; feel their hands touching me. Their spirits surround me, and I can't escape them. I've caused so much suffering. So much loss. I'd hoped Lieutenant Powers would be the turning point. But I failed."

"You did your best," he assured her. "You can't demand more than that of yourself."

"You do," she observed. "You hold every past mistake against yourself. You never forgive yourself. I can see it in the burdened look around your eyes, the lines of moral responsibility that are etching themselves into your face. And now I've added another one. If I could have just saved her…"

"What's done is done," he said with finality, frowning as he thought upon what he felt was his own failure to save Powers. "If this war has taught me one thing, it's that you can't save everyone, no matter how hard you try. There are always casualties."

Before she could respond their ears were attracted by the sound of a scuffle in the hallway. Suddenly the door burst open, and they both blinked at the harsh light that silhouetted a man who stood in the doorway trembling with anger.

"It is you who've deprived me!" Gromyko shouted, rushing for the bed to lay hands on Mafalda. But Hunt was on his feet in a flash, and with a mighty shove threw him against the wall. Just as the smuggler bounced off it he seized his wrists and wrestled him to a standstill.

"It's not her fault, Antonin!" he growled, as Gromyko strove to raise his friend's hands to his mouth to bite them. "She never hurt Powers. I did."

"You lie!" he yelled, as Pinchon entered the room and clamped his arms around the younger man's middle, dragging him towards the door. "You're just covering up for this little murderer because you love her!"

Without even thinking Hunt lashed out a right cross, smashing Gromyko in the chin with such force that both he and Pinchon lost their balance and fell into the corridor. Rolling the smuggler off his chest, the ex-pirate got to his feet while his charge was still dazed and dragged him upright.

"Don't *ever* say that again!" Hunt roared like a thunderstorm from the doorway, his voice echoing down the halls and drawing the attention of everyone within sight. "Do you understand me?"

"I understand," Gromyko nodded, glaring at him. "I understand that you've abandoned your friend for that Fringer! That you've turned your back on the last Deltan you know! Very well! Who needs you? With Julia gone it doesn't matter, anyway. But know this, magic man: you are no friend of Antonin Gromyko anymore! There is no room in his life for one who would betray his friends!"

With this Gromyko moved to leave, but Pinchon

snatched a handful of his shirt and dragged him back.

"Why don't you grow a brain, you moron?" the colonel demanded. "Nobody wanted Powers to die. It was just–."

Before he could finish Gromyko slugged him in the mouth, though without half the force of Hunt's blow. Staggering backwards, blood began to pour from his lower lip. Feeling it with his fingers as the smuggler turned and walked away, he growled and strode after him. Seizing his shoulder, he spun the younger man around and nailed him in the nose with everything he had, dropping him to the floor. Smacking it hard with the back of his skull, Gromyko attempted to rise before going limp and losing consciousness. As blood spilled from his broken nose and ran down his cheek, a pair of nurses hustled to where he lay and began to examine him.

"Oh, he'll be alright," the colonel said with a wave of his hand that mingled dismissiveness with scorn. "His head's too thick for *that* to hurt him." Rubbing his jaw with his right hand, he leaned with the left on the doorframe next to Hunt and watched the hospital staff haul Gromyko away. "Don't worry about him," he added to Hunt, seeing the concern in his eyes. "He's been through worse."

"What's happening to us?" Hunt asked, voicing what was really bothering him.

"You want to know what *I* think it is?" Pinchon queried rhetorically, pushing off the wall and nodding along the hall towards an oncoming figure in black. "I think we've been playing someone else's game for too long, and we need to get out where there's some fresh air and room to stretch our legs." Hearing a suppressed sob, he glanced into Mafalda's room for half a second. "Try and get that moron's last words to her out of her ears. Or they really will be his *last words*." With this he departed, heading in the opposite direction from Krancis.

"Trouble?" Krancis asked as he neared, nodding towards the drops of blood that glistened on the floor.

"You ought to know," Hunt retorted, turning back into the room. Resuming his place on Mafalda's bed, he waited for Krancis to enter and quietly close the door. "What's it this time?"

"I happened to be on my way to check on Miss Aboltina when I saw Gromyko being carried away on a stretcher. It required only a modicum of logic to understand at once what had happened." Another suppressed sob escaped Mafalda's lips, drawing his attention. Leaning against the wall beside her pillow, he looked down at her troubled face, her eyes closed as though to shut out the world. "It isn't your fault, child. You must understand that."

"He called me a murderer," she said in a trembling voice. "Oh, I know that's wrong," she added quickly. "But the anger, the *pain* on his face!" she said, squeezing her eyes even tighter to try and escape the memory that was like so many that already haunted her. "Haven't I brought enough suffering?"

"Gromyko didn't know what he was saying," Krancis responded. "He's pure emotion and no reason. There's nothing to hold him back when he's upset. And right now, he's upset almost to death. Given time, he'll recover his equilibrium."

"But he'll never recover Lieutenant Powers." she objected.

"He never had her in the first place. She was nothing more than a fantasy that existed in his mind. She had no interest in him beyond his curiosity value. The passion was entirely on his side. Naturally I wouldn't *tell* him that, given his instability at present. But in time he'll have to face the reality of his self-deception or tear himself to pieces over an imaginary love that perished too soon. Besides, you didn't kill her," he concluded, looking at Hunt.

"Neither did Rex!" she responded hastily. "I can't believe that."

"It's alright, Mafalda," Hunt said, glaring at Krancis.

"I don't understand this," she uttered anxiously before echoing Hunt's words from shortly before. "What's happening between us all? We're all at each other's throats. Gromyko would have attacked me minutes ago if Rex hadn't stopped him; Soliana hates me and wishes I was gone; Philip jumped at the chance to batter Gromyko. Are we coming apart at the seams?"

"Pinchon has wanted to step on Gromyko for a long time," Krancis answered. "There's nothing especially noteworthy about that. But you are correct: tensions have been peculiarly high."

"Could it be those psychic outbursts from the Devourer masses?" she queried, her face brightening a little as the notion took hold of her imagination, giving her hope that the effect would be merely temporary. "Maybe they're influencing us somehow."

"Not likely," Krancis shook his head, crossing his arms. "The Devourer is sending out a message. It's not attempting to brainwash us. It's trying to *reach* someone. Though technically it could be a side effect. Agitation, or something of the sort."

"Like how you can feel a thunderstorm in the air?" she inquired.

"Something like that. The fact is several members of this current crew have been aboard too long. Neither Pinchon nor Gromyko were built for a long, confined voyage. It would be best for everyone to get them off *Sentinel* as quickly as possible. But that's only really feasible for Pinchon. Gromyko is too unstable to be trusted with any responsibility right now, and I wouldn't think of saddling any of our presently engaged teams with his deadweight. He'll have to sweat it out aboard the ship until he's useful again. Perhaps he can be of some help to Soliana, at least." Noticing how Mafalda shrank at the mention of her name, he shifted a little. "You might as well accept the fact that she has feelings for Rex, Mafalda," he said, causing her eyes to shoot to his at once. "She disliked

Doctor Tselitel inwardly for the same reason. But, given her unfortunate condition, Soliana felt she could wait her out. The same is obviously not true of you. For this reason there's little hope that you'll ever be on her good side. Just serve in the best fashion that you can manage, and forget about Soliana's personal feelings. They will only be of consequence in this war if they cause the kinds of dislocations that you're now feeling."

"I understand," she nodded gently.

"Can't you talk to Soliana and get her to back off?" Hunt queried with some irritation.

"Through her work with the smuggler, she has managed to achieve a considerable degree of intellectual independence, but not altogether of a good sort. Yes, she's more in command of herself than ever before. But she is increasingly becoming something of an island surrounded by clouds; the clouds being the separate personalities that are slowly fusing themselves into a coherent whole. In sum, she's establishing a community within the confines of her own psyche, and as such, she's less and less influenceable from outside. Even my pressure counts for less with each passing day. Soon she may be entirely ungovernable."

"And this is what you wanted?" Hunt asked pointedly.

"I wanted her to be able to draw upon all of her remarkable talents. That wasn't possible so long as she was hopelessly divided against herself, on the one hand, and unable to harness them for any deliberate purpose on the other. I expected that she would begin to grow away from human contact during this process – that she would satisfy her need for community more from within than from without. But it was impossible to anticipate to what degree the various personality implants would affect both her desires and her judgment. That is the factor that is changing her now. It hasn't escaped your attention, of course, that she has rejected Mafalda entirely despite her knowledge both of her importance to this war and to you personally."

"It hasn't," Hunt agreed, though he dipped his voice a little to deprecate the implication that there was more between him and the former separatist than mere friendship.

"Hence what I said about her potentially growing ungovernable. She may come to reject yet more of her external responsibilities as she draws further and further inward. Ironically, it is through this inward journey that she will find her greatest usefulness and insight. The trick is in stopping her before she goes too far, withdrawing utterly from all outward ties."

"I suppose you have a plan for that?" the Deltan inquired, crossing his arms.

"Of course," he responded, though with just enough of a hint of irony that Hunt couldn't tell if he was in earnest. "But that rests with the future," he added, pushing off the wall and nodding at Mafalda. "Look after her for now. Make sure she's alright. You'll be informed when you're needed."

"Are we heading towards the next mass?" Hunt asked, stopping him as he laid a thin hand on the door.

"Naturally."

"Then Soliana didn't talk to you yet?"

"She has. But you're not the only one capable of resisting her arguments. At times she is far too impractical to be taken as a guide. Like you I believe that the masses will only become a bigger problem with time. That doesn't diminish in the least my belief that we're ultimately doing what the parasite wants us to do. But it would be unwise to choose the greater of two evils by twiddling our thumbs. No, the best course is to act. That is why we're in motion towards the third mass as we speak. As I said, you'll be informed when your services are again required within the reactor."

"Seems to be all I do these days," Hunt grumbled once he was alone with Mafalda.

"You do much more than that," she assured him, putting a hand on his arm that was more than just friendly.

"Oh, I know," he responded, reaching up to rub his sore neck, allowing her hand to slip off in the process. Frowning his consternation, he glanced at her a couple of times as he thought, finding her eyes on him each time. "Mafalda, you know I don't have feelings for you, right?"

"Of course," she nodded quickly, though she winced almost imperceptibly at his words.

"You know I'm already committed," he continued.

"Yes, definitely," she insisted.

"Then why…" his voice trailed, feeling both awkward to bring it up and unwilling to hurt her feelings.

"I don't know," she responded. "You're thinking how I acted in your room before?" she clarified just to be sure.

"Yeah, and just now."

"I honestly can't explain it, Rex. It's like a…magnetic pull. I just feel drawn to you. Sometimes I do things that I can't quite explain, like a force is pushing me towards you. I'm not in love with you, either. At least I don't think so. But there's this gravity that's making sure I stay in your orbit. If I had to guess, I'd say it's the dark realm. But really I'm so new to it that I can't be sure."

"You're probably right," he nodded, looking off at the wall and reflecting on the dark little figure that had told him to embrace his destiny. "Well, maybe between the two of us we'll figure it out," he concluded with a shrug.

"You're not upset with me, are you?" she queried, her eyes wide.

"No, not at all," he reassured her. "It's all just a little… new to me, is all. I've had a few people love me, and a lot of people hate me. But I've never felt this…I don't know, I guess affinity is the best word for it. It's sort of headless, like it doesn't really have an aim like love usually does. It seems like two elements that simply want to be together. Like magnets, as you said."

"I know this may sound bad…" she began uneasily, her eyes searching his face for permission to continue.

"Please," he urged her with a gesture of his hand.

"Well, can we trust the dark realm's intentions? I mean, is it helping us or using us?"

"It seems like it helps more than anything," he answered in a restrained tone. "Though I admit to feeling like a tool in its hands sometimes, just a piece of a larger puzzle. I am, of course. That goes without saying in a war of this magnitude. But I have found myself wondering lately if it isn't molding us towards some fate that we wouldn't have picked for ourselves."

"But given we're so dependent on it at this point, we haven't got much of a choice even if it *is* leading us down a path we don't like," she responded.

"Yeah, that seems to be going around a lot lately. With Krancis and the dark realm on one side, and the *Pho'Sath* leading the Fringers around on the other, there's no lack of people trying to drag us around by the nose."

"What are we going to do?"

"All we can do for now is play things by ear," he replied, standing up and stretching with a groan. "Take things one step at a time. Neither of us can see far enough ahead to know just what the game is that's unfolding around us, so the only choice is to make the best of each opportunity that comes along." He paused and looked at her for a moment. "Are you going to be alright?"

"Oh, yes," she nodded. "I'm sorry to have made such a fuss. I'm alright now."

"It's no bother," he shook his head.

"Are *you* going to be okay?"

"Mafalda, I've got enough riding on my conscience to last a lifetime," he answered wearily. "My heart beats coldly enough that another drop in temperature isn't going to affect me. I'm sorry for what happened to Lieutenant Powers for her own sake. But for me, it's just another unfortunate loss among many. I'm too numb to really feel it at this point."

"That's terrible," she sympathized softly.

"That's fate," he responded. "Somebody's got to be responsible for life and death during any war. It might as well be me."

"And Krancis, too," she insisted. "And me. We've all got our share in this. If I hadn't failed, and if he hadn't *chosen me* when he knew I wasn't ready–."

"That line isn't any good, Mafalda," he interrupted her, moving directly beside her. "She died from *my* actions. We can try to spread the blame around. But the darkness that overwhelmed her came from me, and me alone. I can accept that, and you should, too."

"I wish you didn't have to accept it," she said, eyeing the wall at the end of her bed and sighing. "I wish none of this had ever happened."

"I'm not sure what you were expecting when you came over from the separatists," he began, resuming his place on her bed. "But people fight and get hurt and die on our side, too. I'd say we're on the upswing, or at least we will be very shortly. But we've got a long way to go."

"Of course. I'm sorry, I didn't mean to bemoan my lot. It's just so much to take in all at once."

"You'll get there," he smiled faintly. "Now, do you want me to keep you company for a little while?"

"No, I'll be alright," she replied. "I know you must be terribly tired."

"I could use some sleep," he admitted with a dry laugh, standing up again. "Have the hospital staff call me if you need anything," he added, squeezing her shoulder before turning to leave.

"I will," she assured him quietly as he departed.

Slowly making his way back to his quarters, he was just entering his room when Pinchon's voice stopped him.

"We sure gave it to our mutual friend earlier," the colonel said from down the hall as he approached. "I checked on him a little while ago. Still hasn't regained consciousness."

"Haven't you heard? We're not friends anymore,"

Hunt grumbled, leaving the door open for the ex-pirate as he went inside and dropped crossways onto his mattress. "Is he alright?"

"Oh, sure. Medically there's nothing wrong with him. Doctor told me he's just exhausted and needs a good rest. At the end of his rope, pretty much. I guess he burned himself out worrying about that girl."

"Yeah."

"So, what'd our lord and master have to say? We gonna keep blowing up these blobs or what?"

"Looks like it," Hunt answered, rubbing his eyes.

"You don't, uh, suppose you could talk to him about moving me off *Sentinel*, do you?" he asked abruptly.

Ceasing his rubbing, Hunt looked up with annoyance.

"Is *that* what you're bugging me about?" he queried, dropping his head to the mattress again.

"In part," the colonel replied somewhat pointedly. "I also thought you'd be curious about Gromyko."

"Yes, of course," the Deltan replied in a tone of modest apology.

"So how about it? It's not like I'm doing any good around here. I'm itching to get back into the pilot's seat and do some damage."

"I'm sure he's got plans for you already that simply haven't ripened yet. Give him a little time and something's bound to come up."

"That's what I don't like about being on *Sentinel*," Pinchon responded. "Everything's done on *his* timetable. I never thought I'd be surrendering every last ounce of freedom when I came aboard."

"Welcome to my world," Hunt said dryly.

"I guess you've got a point there," the colonel nodded. Reflecting briefly on the manipulations that both Rex and his entire family had suffered for decades, he felt rather petty to have complained at all. "Reckon I'll just await the old man's good timing."

"Sounds like a plan," Hunt replied, stretching himself out on the bed and signaling the end of the conversation. With a few more words Pinchon left.

At last alone, Hunt had a chance to contemplate the life he'd inadvertently ended. As he'd told Mafalda, his conscience was much too burdened already to notice the addition of another weight dragging on it. Nevertheless he was sorry for her sake. She seemed to be an intelligent, beautiful young woman with a bright future ahead of her. Insofar as anyone had a *bright* future ahead of them in the midst of the greatest calamity ever to befall mankind.

"*The first step taken, the second must shortly follow,*" a whisper spoke from the back of the room, interrupting his thoughts. Jerking to the side, he saw the small, shadowy child once more. "*To hesitate is to endanger all.*"

"Who are you?" Hunt asked, sitting up and sliding his legs over the side of the bed. "Where'd you come from?"

"*In you, and of you, and through you, I am,*" the figure answered, holding up a hand to keep him from drawing closer, seeing he was about to rise.

"Are you the dark realm personified or something?" the Deltan queried, remaining still only with effort, his curiosity raging over the small dark entity. Despite its flowing, syrupy appearance, there was something familiar about it. Concentrating on the face and eyes, he could have sworn he'd seen the child before. And then it struck him.

"*Yes,*" it nodded, its voice dropping in volume until it was barely audible even across the short distance that separated them. "*I am you, but something more. A mixture of the purest, earliest years of your existence, and of the darkness that now both binds and empowers us. Yet true purity cannot ever be found, for we have been manipulated since before birth. This is our destiny, Rex. It is also our legacy. There can be no returning, no undoing. Since conception we have been fashioned, and that in a manner not of our choosing. It has never been a question of accepting or rejecting our fate, but merely of recognizing and then following it. The darkness appeals, Rex: it asks us to do what must be done. We have been robbed; our life has been stolen from us. The years of pleasure, of growth, of plenty that should have been ours cannot be regained. That is why you resist your destiny: you long for the peaceful life lived far from the threat of conflict and strife. But you have been made a weapon by our enemies, and you can never return from the place they have taken you. The fruits of peace have no savor for you, no matter how greatly you believe you want them. They are mere fantasy now, dreams of a past that never existed. I know, for I was there at the beginning, your nature in embryo. And I have watched you strive and fight and fail to secure the peace that can never be yours. You must see that warmth and safety and the rewards of honest labor under a good sun have been withholden from you. Yours is a life of war and sorrow, a life whose sole purpose is to enable those of others. You cannot grow and build. You can only destroy. You were not crafted by nature to be a warrior – that required the intervention of others. But having suffered their interference, you cannot turn back."*

"I don't believe you," Hunt replied.

"*Yes, you do,*" the figure insisted. "*For I* am *you, but hidden, buried, all but lost. I am the essence of your psyche, and there is no escaping my words. You shall follow this path. Indeed, you already do, much more so than you realize. But you hesitate, you hold back, and that puts us all at risk. You must accept what needs to be done. You must act swiftly. You must forget the older woman and embrace the younger.*"

"What is this?!" Hunt demanded ragefully. "A conspiracy? A plot? The dark realm collaborating with my own unconscious mind to push Krancis' aims?"

"*You are angry because you are wrong,*" the entity responded calmly. "*You know this.*"

"I know that I'll never turn my back on the only woman who ever showed me what true love really is!" he exploded. "The only person to hold out hope for something better in this miserable life of mine!"

"Such pleasures are beyond you," the figure uttered almost sadly. "They are a part of the fable, the dream you wish could be yours but never can. A pleasing chimera, and nothing more. Yours is a life of sacrifice."

"I refuse," Hunt said stoutly.

"To the despair of many," it shook its head. "To the sorrow, anguish, and death of all. You hold in your hands the fates of countless lives. You are a weapon, one to be used against our adversaries."

"I don't believe that!" Hunt repeated fiercely, as the figure evaporated and left him alone. "Do you hear me? I don't believe that!"

"I shall come again," the entity whispered from all around him. "I shall come again."

"Don't bother!" he shouted, standing up and clenching his fists. "I don't need you, and I don't want you! Keep out of my life!"

Too angry to rest, he paced his room until his blood finally cooled and the fatigue of all he'd been subjected to wrapped itself around him like a blanket. Dropping onto the bed again, he buried his face in the pillow and at last fell asleep.

While the Earthborn champion was recuperating, other hands and minds were busily at work. Wellesley had for some time been arguing with Girnius about the reorganization of certain key Black Fang outposts that bordered the inner worlds; installations both secret and immensely valuable, given their proximity to the fattest imperial trade routes that the organization was capable of targeting. To the chairman's chagrin, their attempts to keep such facilities off the radar had utterly failed, the crafty AI quickly putting together their locations from a multitude of indirect sources. While Girnius fought with him over his proposed changes, most of them consisting of denuding the bases of their highly qualified personnel and relocating them to posts that would be of more service to the empire, the chairman was inwardly trying to figure out how best to keep the rest of the organization's secrets under the rug. Hyde had been given specific instructions about what information was not to be sent to *Sentinel* before he'd left Petrov. But the AI had proven much too adept at espionage to be tricked. He didn't show it, but the chairman was deeply concerned. For though outwardly he'd accepted what amounted to an imperial takeover, his secret hope was to retain enough of the organization that he could flee with it into hiding if necessary. But with such important facilities already laid bare, he felt it wouldn't be long before the rest of his cards were pulled out of his sleeve.

Though unable to deduce any of this from the chairman's behavior, Wellesley knew precisely how he must be feeling. Much like Krancis he had no use for the surly pirate boss, and thus it gave him great satisfaction to know he was putting him in such a bind. Pirates as a class weren't quite bacteria for the AI, as they were for the man in black. But they weren't to be tolerated any more than was absolutely necessary. The *Kol-Prockians* of the fringe had long suffered from their depredations, especially during the darkest days of the civil war. This had given him an aversion to them that he never felt the least need to alter in all the years that had intervened since the fall of his people as a great race. Their only saving grace was that, occasionally, they'd proven useful for low-grade sabotage or smuggling operations against the confederation. This alloyed his stance just enough to keep it from turning to outright hatred.

In another portion of the ship, a mind was feverishly active while its attendant hands were still and helpless. Seemingly forgotten by all, Captain Julius Bardol grimly awaited his fate inside his small holding cell. Certain that he'd been left there to rot, he'd grown depressed and refused to eat what was offered to him. At times he thought he heard voices speaking to him from invisible mouths that hovered just behind his ears. Looking sharply around whenever a word seemed to form of its own accord in the air, he invariably saw nothing. But that did nothing to allay his fears, given that he knew the enemy resided within him. Indeed, it would have been almost a relief to see some disembodied mouth speaking to him, some nightmare creature that had lost everything in the battle for Hubertus except its ability to speak and had somehow managed to sneak aboard. At least then it wouldn't be *within* him, crawling under his skin and rifling through his mind like a mealworm in a sack of grain.

Bardol was tormented. Though knowing nothing of Soliana beforehand, it was clear that Krancis placed great stock in her abilities. If *she* had proven unequal to the evil intelligence that had planted itself within his mind, what hope was there? Such notions invariably sent a shudder through him as he sat on the floor, his knees drawn against his chest as he rocked forward and back. With bewilderment flashbacks from the brief battle above Hubertus pressed their way into his mind, leading him to wonder how fate could have conspired to lay him so low. How could one of the brightest rising stars in the local militia end his days locked in a cell simply for doing his duty? Emotionally and physically exhausted, he stretched out on the cold floor and sighed.

But not for long.

Hearing the lock click, he managed to sit up by the time the door opened. Hope briefly flashed in his eyes before being replaced with terror.

CHAPTER 5

The situation within Kren-Balar was so resoundingly stable and secure that Welter no longer felt it necessary to hover constantly about either Rhemus or Tselitel. The Kol-Prockians were both invigorated by their new ruler and utterly pliable in his experienced hands. Any wish he expressed was carried out instantly, so anxious were they to prove themselves an asset to the empire that had just absorbed them. In their zeal they overreached his stated wishes during his speech in the hangar, taking it upon themselves to seek out and dismember any of their fellows who proved ill-disposed to the new regime. In this Rhemus showed himself equal to the role he'd just undertaken, punishing the guilty with death and thereby earning yet more favor with the populace for his fearless application of justice. Indeed, it seemed that there was nothing he chose to do that didn't raise him to greater and greater heights in their eyes. Scarcely before had a ruler been so perfectly in tune with the people he governed.

Within the privacy of his own heart Rhemus found himself wishing that his own kind had been so well disposed to both his own rule and that of his ancestors. The conflict raging in the fringe between the separatists and the loyalists was never far from his mind, and it was easy to fantasize about an empire filled from end to end with such fervently devoted subjects as those that now surrounded him. But instantly he dismissed that notion as being merely the product of his circumstances. The *Kol-Prockians* accepted him with scarcely a murmur because they were desperate, a people pushed to the brink of collapse. Several, in fact, had reached that brink some time before and crossed over it into the abyss of lunacy. *Seldek* sprang easily enough to mind. Rhemus fit perfectly the *Kol-Prockian* notion of what a ruler ought to be because of the dangerously low ebb they had reached. He was aware of enough of their history to know that they never would have accepted his authority during their heyday. The fact was a people brought almost to destruction and then held there from one generation to the next was bound to accept any man strong enough to corral them, whether he was good intentioned or not. It was mere luck on their part that Rhemus wished them nothing but good.

His condition forced him to conduct much of his business from the confines of the chamber. He chafed at this, his concern being that he would appear feeble to the *Kol-Prockians* and thus lose their affection once their initial enthusiasm for the new order had begun to fade. He sensed that, just as with human supporters, they would begin to question his rule once a little time had passed and their emotions cooled. The first waves of passion would eventually die down, leaving them with the brutal fact that they still lived within what was scarcely more than a dungeon that had been carved out of one of the worst planets in a galaxy filled with inhospitable worlds. It would take time, perhaps a great deal, before they could be removed to safe homes within the Milky Way. His instincts told him that they would have the strength to bear the wait, but only if every other factor could be made to break their way.

As their chief, it was upon him to inspire them with confidence about their future. But if doubts began to circle about his health, *Kren-Balar* could easily return to its former state. Hence he tried to be seen away from the chamber as much as possible, walking the halls with his escorts and regularly inspecting every inch of the base to demonstrate his strength. These jaunts left him exhausted, but only a handful were privy to that fact.

"Thank you, Doctor," he said to Tselitel as she took his arm and helped him to the chamber's floor after one such inspection. "Where's *Karnan?*" he queried after taking a moment to breathe.

"One of his engineers called him away," she answered. "I couldn't understand what they were saying, but he seemed more annoyed than anything. Probably nothing serious."

"Good," Rhemus sighed, closing his eyes and leaning his back against the wall. "I've had enough troubles for one day."

"Would you like to talk about it?" she asked gently, settling down beside him.

"I would," he nodded wearily. "Although I'm not sure I've got the energy to do it." He dryly laughed and looked at her. "This is the first time I've been alone with you in days. I should take the chance to share what's really beating around inside me, given there aren't any alien ears to take offense or carry my words beyond these walls. But I'm so tired…" his voice trailed momentarily. "Did you know that *Kol-Prockians* don't produce male and female children at an even rate?" he asked suddenly, jumping straight into what was on his mind.

"No, I'd never heard of that," she replied, shaking her head and listening attentively.

"I'd noticed that we only ever saw their men, but I was so caught up in simply staying alive when we first got here that I never asked. It turns out there's something like five males born for every one female, so there's this massive shortage of females. They live like princesses in the back of the base, doing only what they please and being waited on hand and foot by the handful of males that managed to win their hands. The girls they keep with themselves, training them for just such a life of ease and entitlement. According to an ancient custom they permit themselves to bear children once every seven years, a process which takes over a year to complete."

"Incredible," Tselitel uttered in surprise. "I can see why you're troubled," she added momentarily. "It'll take forever to repopulate their race."

"Exactly," he assented, his eyes closed as he rolled the back of his head side-to-side against the chamber's wall. "Given the frailty of their race, it's not uncommon to lose some of the children before they're even born. And even when they *are* born, they're almost never twins or triplets or anything that would help us cheat the system a little." He leaned a little closer to her, and instinctively she did likewise. "I don't mean to be cruel, given all they've gone through. But I'm beginning to see why they collapsed as a race. Humanity would have died out long ago were it not for our fecundity."

"I agree," she replied thoughtfully. "Is there anything that can be done about it?"

"*Keelen* says no," Rhemus sighed. "He thinks the females are so set in their ways that they'd revolt at any change in their customs, even though they uniformly approve of me as a ruler. I must admit, it's a question I've never had to face before. Humanity, as you know, typically requires *restraint* when it comes to this particular topic, not encouragement. My first instinct is to leave matters where they are for the moment, at least until I'm a little more familiar with what these peculiar people will and won't tolerate. They're still delirious to have deliverance held out before them. But that could change quickly if their sacred customs are interfered with. I must tread carefully."

"Of course," she agreed softly, her head nodding slowly in sympathy. "Is there anything I can do to help? Perhaps try to reason with them? One female to another?"

"Perhaps," he shrugged. "I don't know if that distinction would mean anything to them, being from a different race. But it's certainly an option I'll keep in mind." The conversation lulled for a few minutes while he relaxed and gathered more of his strength. "How is Gustav?"

"Honestly, I've barely seen anything of him lately. I haven't exchanged more than a handful of words with him at any given time since the day I awoke after being shot. I'm worried about him, given the desperate place he's in. All this time alone can't be good for him."

"He's strong, Doctor. He'll pull through."

"But I don't think he wants to," she replied. "I think he wants to let his grief consume him so that it'll fuel him against his enemies. He's driven by the desire for revenge."

"I know. But that's something he's got to settle out on his own, for better or worse. It may even end up being a good thing."

"A good thing?" she queried.

"We *are* at war, Doctor. A man as potent as Welter could do a lot of harm against our enemies. Provided he doesn't overstep sound judgment and get himself killed."

"I'd hate to see him degenerate into being nothing more than a weapon to be used against our foes," she uttered quietly. "There's so much more to him than that. So much intelligence and love. But it's hidden under all that pain."

"He wouldn't be much use to us if he wasn't intelligent, Doctor. And as for love, well, that's why he's filled with rage in the first place. You can't have the one without the other. That's where the motive force comes from. He thirsts for revenge because he lost what mattered most to him."

"I know," she said with understated aversion, thinking of Rex. "That's what I'm afraid of."

"Love is a powerful thing, my dear," he said, reaching out and patting her hand. "It drives us to grow, but it can also twist us out of shape if things go awry. It can destroy us if we allow loss to devour us with grief. Or that same loss can give us the jolt that pushes us on and on through endless struggles. Our fortunes would be lost without that latter possibility."

"What do you mean?"

He frowned momentarily, glancing at the door to assure himself that they were alone.

"I mean Krancis," he said confidentially.

"*Krancis?*" she repeated incredulously.

"I can't say anything more," Rhemus shook his head at once. "And you must never utter my words to another soul. But without that particular outcome, Krancis wouldn't be who he is today, and our cause would be lost."

"Where did he come from, Your Highness?" she asked earnestly, her curiosity suddenly aflame. "Where's his family? What planet was he born on?"

"I can't tell you anything," he reiterated. "It's beyond secret. Perhaps, someday, Rex and a few others will be allowed to learn the truth. But for now all anyone else can know is that he is here for the specific purpose of guiding us through this terrible time. Someday he will drift away, and we won't see him anymore. Future generations will beg for Krancis to return when they find themselves in similar woe. But that won't be his time, and he won't come to their aid. *Now* is his time, and we should thank everything holy that he's with us now."

"But is he human?" she inquired. "Can I at least know that?"

"He is human," he told her. "Absolutely human."

"But how can–."

"My dear Doctor," he laughed, holding up his hand. "That's enough."

"Of course," she shook her head, as though dissipating some haze that had seized her mind. "I know better than that. I'm sorry I got carried away."

"Don't worry," he patted her hand again. "And don't apologize. You'd be more than human if you weren't burning with curiosity over that wonderful man."

"You have a great deal of affection for him, don't you?"

"Krancis is the greatest man any of us will ever know in this life," he responded. "I mean no offense to your Rex, of course. But for decades he has been slowly laying in place the pieces necessary for our current successful struggle against the parasite. For long he had to work in the shadows without any real power, relying only on his remarkable intelligence to make things come together for us without any thought of personal gain. Can you imagine what kind of life he could have built for himself had he bent that incredible mind upon his own self-interest? He could have entered any profession he chose and shot straight to the top. Seizing his gains when the present calamity burst upon us, he could have fled our empire and left us to our fate. Instead, at great risk to his life and without any thought of reward, he's applied every fiber of his being to keeping us alive. There's nothing I wouldn't grant that man would he only ask it. But he won't. He doesn't want accolades or honors. He doesn't want the attention or applause of the masses. He seeks simply the power to do what is necessary, and then to fade into obscurity once his task is done. Nothing more and nothing less."

"Then he's a weapon, too," she observed, burdened by the thought.

"Are you beginning to sense a theme?" the emperor smiled faintly. "A weapon is a man who applies himself against his people's enemies without any thought of personal reward. It goes against all our notions of self-interest and thus seems either noble or tragic, based on our point of view. But humanity has always required such men. That's why I don't regret the loss that has struck Welter. It was tragic, indeed, truly heartbreaking. But it was also necessary. We need men like him on the front line, bending every ounce of their potent minds and bodies against the foes that surround us. You must never forget that the parasite isn't the only threat we face. Even as we get it under control, others circle in the waters, positioning themselves to strike."

"Then what hope is there?" she asked, her hands subtly beginning to shake as her condition made itself manifest and her anxieties began to seize her. "We're only barely holding on as it is."

"That's why I don't regret Welter's condition," he reiterated. "You can never know in advance how things are going to go, Doctor. All you can do is point as many factors as possible in your favor and then work as hard as you can for the right outcome. It's why I'm glad Welter is going to do everything he can to destroy the–," he paused just short of using their name. "Well, the *Dolshan*, as our hosts call them."

"I just wish this wasn't necessary," she lamented, though her tone indicated she took his point and accepted it. "To twist human lives until they're just tools of war…" her voice trailed as she thought. "Well, I'd like to see every psyche blossom, every personality extend itself until it reaches the very limits of its potential in all directions. I'd like to see beauty and love and art and good practical sense in all the sons and daughters of Adam. Most never achieve those things, and I've come to accept that fact."

"But to deliberately choose a life of destruction goes against the grain for you," Rhemus inserted.

"It does," she assented. "I know it's necessary, but I can't help deploring the fact inwardly." Mirthlessly she chuckled. "It makes me glad there are other people who can run this war. We'd never have a prayer with me at the helm."

"We're all suited to different stations," Rhemus smiled, reaching over and squeezing her shoulder briefly. "You've been an incredible help to me. And I know Rex would say the same. He wouldn't be the man he is today without knowing you."

"But is he *better* for knowing me?"

"All I know is we're better off as a race because of your remarkable relationship. Loving you pulled him out of the mud his life had been mired in for years. Some men need a woman to love before they can get into gear. That's absolutely the case for Rex. His affections were so buried and lost that he couldn't find himself. It took an external stimulus."

"How do you know all this?" she asked with a little laugh.

"Krancis kept close tabs on him. He did very little of which our intelligence service was not aware. Only in blowing up the facility under the prison were we truly ignorant. And frankly, I'm not convinced that Krancis didn't know about that, though he says he didn't."

"How long has he had Rex under his eye?"

"Since before his birth," he answered, to her visible surprise. "The *Prellak* weren't the only ones who knew he was destined for great things. Without his intervention, Rex would have been lost to us almost before he was born. The power of the dark worlds would have overwhelmed him. But Krancis prevented that, and thereby secured him for our side."

"Incredible," she uttered.

"That's Krancis for you," he replied.

Before they could say more, the door to the anteroom opened and *Karnan* entered. His gait unsteady, he shambled to where they sat, gesturing to Tselitel to stay where she was as he pressed himself against the wall for support and breathed.

"I've only got a few minutes before I have to head out again," he said between puffs. "The chamber is in trouble. One of *Seldek's* diehards managed to drain off some of the coolant that keeps it from burning itself up. It's a *very* precious commodity, very difficult to source and impossibly expensive. It's cost us frightfully in artifacts whenever we've needed to purchase it in the past. And the price has only gone up with the passage of time. Please pardon the expression, Majesty, but it would require a king's ransom to obtain what we need now."

"How long can the chamber run with what it has now?" he queried.

"I'll have to turn down the output at once. But even at that it will still overheat, so from time to time I'll be forced to shut it off. Clearly we'll have to coordinate our usage so that the three of us get the most benefit from it that we can until some answer can be figured out. It's too bad that all three of us need it so desperately. It'll only add to the load and burn out the machinery faster."

"I don't need it very badly," Tselitel uttered. "I'll spend just as little time in here as I can."

Wordlessly Rhemus took her wrist and held her hand out. The trembling of her long, thin fingers was instantly evident.

"No, Doctor, we're not going to have any noble sacrifices on your part," he declared before releasing her and looking to *Karnan*. "If we can hold out long enough, I can order a shipment of kantium sent out to Quarlac to pay for the coolant."

"The only source we've ever been able to secure it from has been a network of smugglers operating several days' warp from here. They're part of a yet larger organization that would notice at once if a bundle of kantium suddenly dropped into anyone's lap. It would cause questions to be raised. We've managed to keep off the radar through both guile and making ourselves useful to others at just the right moments, thus giving them a motive to keep our secret for us. But with the *Dolshan* scouring both within and without the Milky Way for any and every means of hurting your–," he paused, smiling slightly. "I suppose I should say *our* empire, at this point. Anyway, with them looking high and low for ways to attack, it's all but certain that they'd notice the kantium, too, and immediately deduce where it'd come from. Naturally, there are already human holdings within Quarlac, but none of them have any need for this coolant. It would instantly spark an investigation that would eventually lead them here."

"But if *we* can't pay for it, and if *you* can't pay for it, then what can we do?" Tselitel asked.

"Well, I was thinking we should probably just take it,"

he replied.

"You mean steal it?"

"That's all the smugglers did," he shrugged. "They're thieves and killers to the last man. Any who got cut down along the way would just be getting his desserts. Besides, we're at war, and that necessitates drastic measures."

"I gather you already have a plan?" Rhemus queried.

"More or less. Clearly Welter will lead the charge on this one. None of my kind have the mixture of skills and sheer meanness to carry it off. Though I suppose a few could go along for backup in that egg of his."

"He'd want to travel alone, I'm sure," Tselitel commented.

"Well, let's get him in here before we start laying our plans too firmly," the emperor said. "This is right up his alley, so he ought to have his hands in the mix from the start."

"I'll have one of my engineers send out a call through the base," *Karnan* nodded, shakily making for the anteroom.

Half an hour later a cross-armed Welter stood within the chamber leaning against the wall as the aged scientist filled him in on the situation that faced them.

"The smugglers work out of a small trading post hidden in the ruins of an old city on the ice moon Berolt," *Karnan* explained, now sitting on the floor between Rhemus and Tselitel. "There's not much left of the city. Just scattered monuments from another age. It was built by some ancient race that either died out or moved on. We've never had the opportunity to find out which."

"I gather the moon can't support life?" Welter asked, drawing the discussion back to the task at hand.

"Essentially no. The air is so thin you'd begin to asphyxiate within minutes. The temperatures will freeze anyone unprepared for them in an equally short span of time. Hence all business is conducted within an underground network of spaces that have been carved out of the lowest levels of the old city. There's a main hangar that you fly into to get out of the elements. Thereafter you've got to find your way along a maze of tunnels and caverns."

"Is there anyone within *Kren-Balar* that knows the way?"

"We haven't required coolant for quite a long time," *Karnan* equivocated.

"Meaning no?"

"Meaning yes, but they probably don't remember the way. Most of them were older pilots, anyhow, since the task required both experience and discretion. Several have died, and the rest are suffering the typical effects of age. It'd be a miracle if they could help you."

"Well, it's better than nothing," Welter replied. "Dig 'em up and I'll see what I can learn." He paused and thought for a moment. "How much of this coolant do you need?"

"Not too terribly much. Say eight canisters." He indicated their size with his hands. They were roughly a foot in diameter and two feet high. "But you're going to have to take a great deal more than just the coolant to cover your tracks. Ideally you'd steal a mixture of valuable items, kill everyone you encounter, and then burn down the building they resided in."

"What?!" Tselitel exclaimed in shock.

"How many smugglers can I expect?" Welter asked, unphased.

"You're not seriously considering this?" she protested.

"Essentially this is an underground marketplace populated by independent shops," *Karnan* said, ignoring her outburst. "Typically there's no more than eight or ten smugglers on hand at any one time, though they're all armed and ready for trouble. They know they've got valuable goods, and they don't intend that anyone should just wander in and take them. They'll definitely shoot first and ask questions later if they feel suspicious about you."

"You can't just go in there and slaughter them, Gustav," Tselitel insisted.

"Doctor, as I've already explained, these people are the vilest of desperadoes," *Karnan* said. "They ply their trade on Berolt because they can't make a life anywhere else. They've been sentenced to death by almost every major race in Quarlac. The bounty hunters would have massacred them years ago were they not utterly dependent on them for information and hard-to-get supplies."

"Then this is a real rat's nest?" Rhemus asked quietly, trying to underscore the point for Tselitel.

"Yes, Majesty. Only the best, or, perhaps I should say the *worst*, manage to get in and out of there again in one piece. That, of course, is why I thought of Welter at once for this task."

The faint smile on *Karnan's* lips left it unclear to the pair that flanked him which polarity he assigned to Welter, though the latter felt certain of it himself.

"Don't you think that egg will draw some unwelcome attention?" Welter responded, shifting the discussion with a frown.

"There's all sorts of weird ships flying in and out of Quarlac on a daily basis," *Karnan* answered with casual certainty. "This galaxy is a combination black market on the one hand and deathtrap on the other. Everyone's too busy either sneaking around or fighting to stay alive to care about what you're flying. It's one of the reasons we made our home here years ago: it was the only place within warp range that we could live more or less unnoticed."

"What do you think about this?" Rhemus asked, looking up at Welter.

"I've heard better plans," he began flatly. "One against a dozen is poor odds, even if the one is me. I'd need some backup, or a way to flatten their advantage. The idea that I can rob the place while under fire from so many guns is pure fantasy."

"*Kren-Balar's* arsenal of weapons is at your disposal, of course," Rhemus said. "As is the cream of our forces for backup."

"I'd rather have human support," Welter replied at once. "Krancis stationed some special forces operatives nearby. I could swing by and pick them up on the way to Berolt. Two or three of them would be enough to hold down thrice their number in smugglers."

"But how are you going to fit both them and the supplies in the egg?" *Karnan* objected. "You've got to take enough to cover your tracks."

"Not if I level the place with high explosives," he responded. "I'll just collapse that part of the tunnel network and make it impossible for anyone to discover the truth. And even if they do eventually manage to dig it out, we'll have long since abandoned *Kren-Balar* by then. Our secret will be safe."

"I suppose that is the most straightforward answer to the problem," *Karnan* nodded thoughtfully.

"What about the people who'll get buried deeper within the network?" Tselitel inquired. "It'll be horrible for them to just sit and starve from day to day, knowing death is staring them in the face with no chance of escape."

"They brought it on themselves when they chose this line of work," Welter said with cold rationality. Then he looked at Rhemus. "I can't leave here unless we're absolutely certain of your safety. No one can be permitted to enter or leave the base during my absence. We must have a total lockdown."

"We'll have it," the emperor assured him. "Invariably I'll travel under guard whilst simultaneously limiting my movements as much as possible. Even if there is a discontent or two left within the base, they'll never get past my phalanx of bodyguards."

"Don't worry, Welter." *Karnan* said rather grandly. "We'll take care of our new emperor in your absence."

Though this assurance gave him no confidence, Welter nevertheless managed a curt nod to acknowledge it.

"The final details are up to you, of course," Rhemus said. "But I suggest you depart as quickly as possible."

"I agree," Welter replied, pushing off the wall, bowing slightly, and making for the door.

"Gustav!" he heard Tselitel call from the chamber's door as he passed through the anteroom. "You should take Frank with you."

"Why?" he queried, laying a hand on the door handle in front of him as he felt a pair of thin hands take his other arm. Sighing his annoyance, he turned around and faced her. "That chatterbox isn't going to be of any use to me out there."

"He can interface with the base's computers and download all the data that bears on where you're going," she pointed out. "And you know how good these AIs are at correlating data and coming up with useful results. I really think he could come in handy. It's not like he's got a lot to do around here," she concluded in a confidential tone.

"I reckon you're right," he assented reluctantly, turning towards the door when she once again stopped him with her hands. To his surprise she put her arms around his neck and hugged him close. Slowly he put his arms around her back and patted her gently.

"Thank you for taking care of us," she said, her voice partially muffled by her mouth pressing against his jacket. "The emperor and I never would have made it this far without you."

"You're welcome," he responded, patting her a little more before drawing away. Feeling this, she released his neck but fixed him with her eyes.

"Take care of yourself, Gustav," she uttered earnestly, his gaze bouncing between his eyes to impress the point upon him. "You've got so much ahead of you. We all need you."

"You don't have to worry about me, Doctor," he assured her in a grim voice. "I'm not ready to die yet. Not until I've gotten Amra her due."

"Gustav," Tselitel began in a softly pleading tone. But in a moment he'd turned and left her alone in the anteroom. With a heavy heart she returned to the chamber.

Many hours later Welter was en route to the smuggler's hideaway, a pair of imperial special forces operatives riding in the back of the egg. Silent and utterly lethal, they were like daggers cast into the form of men: cold, sharp, built for a single purpose. Like Welter, they were weapons of war, the soft things of life forgotten in their single-minded pursuit of killing excellence. Both Major Rullus, forty-two, and Lieutenant Firth, twenty-nine, had hair as black as midnight, and dispositions to match. Speaking only when directly addressed, Welter could have forgotten they were seated behind him if a kind of sixth sense didn't communicate the palpable fact of their presence. The air grew heavier the moment they boarded the egg and remained that way.

"Cheery companions, these two," Frank opined. To his surprise Welter had looped his chain around his neck and permitted continuous skin contact ever since picking him up in *Kren-Balar*. Regarding this as a minor miracle, he thought it wise to risk only an occasional brief comment, lest he be relegated to lint-collection duty in one of Welter's cavernous pockets. Receiving no reply, he attempted to content himself with watching the tunnel of darkness stream by outside the egg. When that failed, he took to chewing over the information he'd gotten out of *Kren-Balar's* computers for the dozenth time. It didn't take long for him to realize that the trip would be a grindingly boring one, save for the interlude within the smuggler's base. He attempted to communicate with the egg's AI, but she proved uninterested in talking. Evidently the directive from her makers to serve the Earthborn didn't extend to quelling the boredom of the AIs they took into their service.

Interminably the hours passed for the construct. Unable to sleep as his companions periodically did, he began filing and then refiling the data he'd downloaded, shifting it this way and that for no other reason than to keep himself busy. He'd long before parsed every useful bit of information out of it, and even attempted to pass it along to Welter. But the latter had proven uninterested. In a couple brief sentences he told him to tell him whatever was relevant *if* it chanced to be useful. Otherwise he could keep it to himself.

Finally nearing their destination, Frank could feel the tension within the ship increase. Breathing tightened; movements became minimal; none of them slept. They knew what kind of a place they were about to dive into, and none of them liked it. Only perfect discipline, and a will of iron, would permit one to willingly enter such a place.

Without a word Welter dropped them out of warp.

"Whoa!" Frank couldn't help exclaiming, as the ice moon Berolt appeared before them. Waiting until the last possible second, Welter had brought them as close as he could without risking a crash. A moment longer and they would have appeared right above the surface of the world, having no time to decelerate before crashing like a meteorite.

Piloting the ship towards a waypoint on his display, Welter scowled with fatal seriousness as they neared their destination. It wasn't long before the ruins of a once great city could be seen poking out of the snow and ice, the last remains of some long-forgotten race of skillful builders. Placing the egg on autopilot briefly, both he and the two men seated behind him slipped into environment suits that they'd brought with them. It was likely that the base had some kind of heating to make it tolerably liveable. But they weren't about to depend on that.

"You know where we're headed?" Welter asked Frank once the autopilot was off and his hands were back on the controls.

"Yeah, more or less," the AI replied, glad at last to be addressed. "The information inside the base was a little vague. The pilots who'd made the run before–."

"I get the picture," Welter cut him off, pushing the craft into a sharp dive before leveling off just above the moon's craggy surface. Climbing a little to avoid hitting the tops of the ruins, he slowed the ship as the yawning opening to the smuggler base appeared a short distance ahead.

"What is your purpose here?" a harsh voice crackled over the radio as a pair of fighters came into view and quickly formed up alongside the strange ship.

"To buy goods, what else?" Welter snapped.

"What kind?" the voice prodded.

"Tell him we need carbaxium," Frank said earnestly, briefly muting the microphone. "It's sold by the same shop as the coolant. It's commonly used by mining operations as a coating for their drill bits to make them last longer. It's also highly illegal, given it's terribly poisonous, and thus a favorite of terrorist organizations."

"Carbaxium," Welter responded.

"What do you need it for?" the voice persisted.

"To keep our drills running longer," Welter answered with annoyance. "I didn't come here to play twenty questions. The boss is chewing my rear for what's happening to our bits, and I don't intend to let another one grind itself up. Are we gonna do business or not?"

"You'd better watch that attitude inside, Mister," the voice said sternly as the escort fighters peeled away. "Or you'll get in trouble quick."

"Understood. Over and out."

"Well, your winning personality does it again," Frank remarked, unable to help himself. "I know you won't, but I suggest you follow his advice and keep it in check once we're inside."

Ignoring this comment, Welter piloted the ship into the opening. Plunged into darkness the second they passed out of the sun's blinding rays, the egg reacted almost instantly by amplifying the brightness of the canopy, permitting the occupants to easily see all that surrounded them. Sloping gently downward, the tunnel quickly leveled out and broke off in a dozen different directions.

"Take that one," Frank said as a waypoint popped up on Welter's display. "And take it slow. The tunnel narrows rapidly once you're inside."

Seeing a continuous stream of exotic craft fly in and out of the opening, Welter managed to slip into the stream of vessels and cruise inside. As Frank had warned him, it quickly shrunk to where he could barely keep from hitting departing ships as they moved past him. Twice he scraped the egg's hull against the wall to avoid crashing into some reckless imbecile with a death wish. Cursing repeatedly under his breath, he passed through the tunnel and entered a fairly large cavern filled with parked ships. In and out of dilapidated structures bodies flowed.

"Love to raze this place to the ground," Lieutenant Firth uttered grimly, watching as countless contraband items were carried to their new owners' ships. He'd been in Quarlac long enough to know that most of the weapons would be used to destabilize what little order existed in that troubled galaxy. The criminal organizations that flourished there depended on the inability of the various major races to establish a basic level of security within their own space. Incessant acts of sabotage, terrorism, and assassination were carried out to ensure there was no change in the status quo. Even the empire had proven unable to provide more than a modest degree of safety to its citizens, distracted as it had been for years with the Fringers. All hopes for lasting security evaporated the instant the Devourer emerged. Certain that the imperial navy could do nothing but leave the colonists to their fate, the underbelly of Quarlac had at once seized several outposts, taking their valuables, killing all who resisted them and selling off the rest into slavery. This period was short lived, however. Several devastating acts of sabotage and assassination, ordered by Krancis, managed to halt the colonists' persecutors. It was certain that they would break forth again at the first opportunity. But for the short term, the gusto had gone out of their depredations.

"You'll get your chance," Welter told him, finding an open space fairly close to the designated shop and making to put down. But just as he was about to land, another, smaller, ship darted in ahead of him and took his place. Adjusting his course slightly, he moved in alongside the craft and, trusting to the remarkable strength of *Keesh'Forbandai* engineering, shoved it aside. Landing just where he'd intended to, he shut down the ship.

"I can see we're gonna make a lot of friends on this trip," Frank observed ominously, as the pilot of the displaced ship got out and began shouting obscenities at them while jumping furiously up and down.

Popping the canopy without comment, Welter felt the icy coldness of the air sting his cheeks at once. Putting on a helmet, as his companions already had, he deployed the ladder and climbed down the side.

"I'll kill you! I'll kill you!" shouted the angry pilot, a man scarcely five and a half feet in height, his body likewise protected by an environment suit. Rounding the front of the egg, he trembled with rage as he eyed the three newcomers. "That ship cost me a fortune!" he declared, drawing a long switchblade from his pocket and snapping it open. "You're gonna pay for every last cent in damages."

Returning his gaze with almost lethargic annoyance, Welter gestured to the men beside him. At once they stepped forward, knives drawn seemingly from the air itself. The short man's senses thoroughly gone, he chose to fight rather than run, which was the last mistake he ever made.

"Throw the body in his ship," Welter said dismissively, nodding towards it while making slowly for the shop to give them a chance to catch up.

"It might be best *not* to keep drawing attention to ourselves before we've even laid eyes on the coolant," Frank cautioned fruitlessly as the operatives rejoined Welter. "You know, keep a low profile, that sort of thing?"

Increasing his pace, Welter quickly led them into the shop. It was a tight and narrow affair, little more than a corridor terminating in a modest room with a big counter. Customers were packed all around, talking and swearing and haggling prices. Forcing his way to the counter, he waited two minutes to be recognized. When none of the three portly fellows behind it paid him the least attention, he seized one by the collar and dragged him halfway across the counter.

"I'd like some service, please," he uttered with such menace that the man, used to rough customers, could only nod as his cheeks blushed.

"What would you like?" he queried, straightening up when Welter let him go.

"Carbaxium," he answered, as his gaze fell upon the cannisters of coolant that *Karnan* had described. "And eight of those," he added, pointing to them.

"That'll run you a fortune, friend," the man couldn't help laughing.

"We'll start with the carbaxium," Welter replied. "That's more important."

"Sure," the man nodded good-naturedly enough. "How much?"

"Ten canisters."

"What have you got to pay with?"

Reaching into his suit, Welter pulled out Frank and held him forth.

"Holy–," the man said with wonder, eyeing the artifact for a moment before tentatively reaching for it. When Welter drew it back, he recovered himself. "I haven't seen one of those in decades. Practically none exist anymore."

"I know," Welter responded, tucking it back into his suit. "What'll you give me for him?"

"What is he? Military AI? Medical?" he queried greedily, salivating over what he could get for reselling him.

"Grade A military. Conducted over a dozen campaigns

before his people fell. Now, what'll you give me for him?"

"I'll give you the carbaxium, plus three canisters of the coolant," he answered quickly. "You haven't got another one by any chance, have you?" he asked in as low of a voice as he could manage, given the din.

"Perhaps."

"Look," the man said, gesturing for him to lean a little way over the counter. "Between you and me, I can get you a better rate on the coolant. But only if you can get me another of those AIs. And *only* if we don't do business here. I've got a place about six hours' warp from here that I work out of. I'll get you your carbaxium, plus a *dozen* canisters of coolant, for two AIs."

"Just give me the carbaxium and the first three canisters," Welter replied, having already settled on a plan.

"As you like it, friend," the man said with disappointment, leaning back behind the counter and placing his hands flatly atop it. "Payment first."

Welter pointed at one of the carbaxium canisters.

"Show me one of 'em first. I don't want 'em half filled."

"Mister, we've got a reputation for quality," he said, taking offense.

"Do you want to get your hands on this, or not?" he countered, thumping his chest with two fingers to indicate Frank.

Scowling in reply, the man reluctantly took a canister of carbaxium and set it on the counter. Lifting it up, Welter sloshed it around a little.

"Satisfied?" the man asked, crossing his arms and cocking himself on one leg. "Maybe you'd like to pop the lid and take a whiff just to make sure."

"No, I'm satisfied," he replied, cradling it in his left arm as he drew his pistol with his right. Turning to the crowd, most of which had taken off their helmets in the confined space, he pressed the gun against the canister. "Listen up, everyone," he announced, shouting over the noise of the room. "I don't have to tell you what happens when a canister of carbaxium explodes in a small area. So why don't you all just file on out of here while the air is still breathable?"

At once most of them elected to leave. But a few, all of them wearing helmets, hesitated. Seeing this, Welter's escorts dispatched them with a few well-placed shots from suppressed pistols that had been hidden within jackets worn over their suits. Having faced robbery many times, the men behind the counter moved for shotguns concealed under the counter with a crispness and speed born of habit. They, likewise, met their ends at the hands of Welter's companions.

"It's been a pleasure doing business with you," Welter uttered sourly, setting the carbaxium on the counter and looking at the bloodied corpse of the man he'd spoken to moments before.

"How can you be so cold?" Frank recoiled.

"Because he meant to kill us at that little rendezvous of his," Welter explained flatly, climbing over the counter in one swift motion and beginning to hand the canisters of coolant to the operatives. "You're much too trusting."

"Well, better than the alternative, I guess," the AI replied, still shocked by the casual spilling of blood.

"Not out here," Welter replied, grunting as he twisted and lifted another container. "In Quarlac, trust is the last thing you extend, and the first thing you withhold."

"To each his own, I suppose," Frank grumbled.

The men got the canisters over the counter and leaned them against the tunnel near the entrance. Poking their heads out, they saw numerous onlookers hiding next to their ships with watchful eyes. Word would have quickly spread to what passed for the authorities, and they wanted to be on hand to watch the fireworks. They changed their minds, however, when the thieves had wrestled the canisters to the egg and began unloading charge after charge of high explosives. Jumping into their ships, they nearly caved in the tunnel escaping.

"We'd better make our exit, too," Frank said warningly, as the trio fought the containers up the side of the ship and piled them into the back seat. "They'll be on us any second."

"Then give us a hand," Welter growled through gritted teeth, handing a canister up to Major Rullus.

Frowning inwardly, the AI kept his mouth shut until the last container had been loaded. Hearing the screech of engines coming down the tunnel towards them, he was about to warn Welter when dual streams of fire poured from the wings of an incoming fighter. Welter hit the deck, but Lieutenant Firth was too slow and was nearly torn in half by the high caliber rounds that struck him. Falling against the ground, he lay still.

Pushing himself up, Welter clambered up the ladder as the fighter flew past, dropping the canopy just as Major Rullus slipped over the opposite side and dropped.

"What are you *doing?*" Welter demanded, as the Major made tracks for the damaged fighter of the short man they'd encountered upon entry. Intuiting his purpose at once, Welter fired up the egg and took off as bullets ricocheted off its hull.

"This is no time for heroics," Frank opined, as Welter lifted the craft into the air and made for the exit.

"There's gonna be more of 'em," Welter informed him. "A lot more. We'll need all the help–."

Before he could finish he shoved the egg into as much of a dive as he could manage in the tight space, dodging a hail of incoming shells that nearly annihilated Major Rullus as he strove to catch up.

"What about the explosives?" Frank queried, as the egg twisted and turned at high speed down the tunnel. "If we get too far out of range we'll–."

A thunderous roar shook the very foundation of the base, causing loose pieces to drop from the ceiling and nearly collide with the egg.

"Major Rullus has seen to that," Welter observed.

"Obviously."

Pulling out into the main tunnel of the base, Welter gunned it, quickly leaving Rullus behind as they shot out into the open air.

"What about the major?" Frank queried, as he cleared the tunnel's mouth.

"Coolant first. Got to keep the emperor and Doctor Tselitel in good health. Rullus'll make his way back to base if he can."

"Oh, I don't think he's got much of a chance," Frank fretted, using the ship's cameras to watch the action behind them. Nearly two dozen craft had formed up on the unfortunate major. "He'll be lucky to last another minute."

"He knew the risks going into this," Welter responded, making best speed for outer space. "He'd curse us both if we put him ahead of the mission."

"Don't think he's gonna get that opportunity," the AI commented, as Rullus' ship caught fire and rapidly lost altitude. Moments later it collided with the icy surface of Berolt and exploded. "What a waste. He should have stayed with us."

"You make the best decision you can in the moment," Welter replied. "That's all anyone can do."

"Yeah," Frank sullenly agreed, watching as the fighters briefly tried to follow them before turning towards their battered base and disappearing inside. "Just wish he'd chosen a little more wisely."

"Well, he got us our coolant," Welter observed, looking over his shoulder into the rear seat at the canisters. "Him and Firth."

"Two lives for eight canisters," Frank uttered dismally. "Not much of a trade."

Upon breaking out of the atmosphere Welter, aware that he was still on the base's radar, pointed the ship in a random direction and engaged warp. Disappearing into the familiar black tunnel, he resolved to carry that course for a number of hours before slowly, by indirect routes, working his way back to *Kren-Balar*.

"I must admit, the operation was easier than I'd expected," Frank remarked, as Welter took off his helmet, unfastened his harness, and climbed into the back of the craft to double-check the canisters. "Of course, you *did* kill everything in sight, so I guess that accounts for that."

"If you're going to gripe the entire way back to base, you can spend the trip in my pocket."

"It's just that I expected, I don't know, a little more *decency* out of you three. To just cut down the shop staff and a bunch of their customers without blinking an eye borders on the psychotic."

"Or the efficient," Welter replied, twisting the canisters to examine them. "Every soul in that base was worthy of death at least three times over. We just hastened the process."

"It's reasoning like that that chills me even more," the AI informed him. "Why can't you just regret the loss of life like a normal human being, say it was necessary, utter a little pap about the fortunes of war, and leave it at that? Why all this brutality?"

"You really are a desk jockey."

"Well, that *is* the role I was designed for," Frank said with a note of wounded virtue in his voice. "I can't help what I was made to be."

"Neither can I, apparently."

"I don't know what Doctor Tselitel sees in you," the AI said caustically, unable to hold himself back. "You're so cold that–."

Having heard more than enough, Welter slipped Frank from around his neck and dropped him on the floor. Finishing his examination of the canisters in peace, he climbed back into his seat and settled in.

The AI's last remark about Tselitel hit home, however, for Welter couldn't understand what she saw in him, either. She was earnestly committed to not letting him spend the rest of his days in a crusade for revenge. Half a dozen notions floated through his mind, most of them cynical and centering around Rex Hunt. Probably, he reasoned, she still wanted to see him move on after losing Amra and continue his life so she wouldn't have to worry about Hunt when she finally passed. This, he felt certain, he would never do. Amra had been too much a part of his soul for that. He wasn't about to let her murder go unavenged. No, Doctor Tselitel would have to find another place to rest her hopes.

Essentially solitary by nature, Welter didn't regret the prospect of so many hours alone in warp. He'd had more than enough of people ever since Krancis had assigned him to look after the emperor. He'd grown to tolerate the solicitous interference of Tselitel and, to a much lesser degree, the voluble self-importance of the *Kol-Prockians*. But it had nevertheless been a burden to share the same air with them without any break at all. The truth was he'd been eager for an excuse to leave the base, to finally have a chance to process some of his tortured emotions. There was a truth hidden within them that, for a time, he hadn't been strong enough to face but knew he must eventually: that he had failed to protect his daughter.

That was the true cause of his drive for revenge. He'd already killed her killer, and rationally that had been enough. But deep within his heart was the agonizing fact that he'd allowed her to be captured, tortured, and then killed. She was a grown woman, free to make her own choice as to how and where she'd risk her life. But that, he knew firsthand, didn't count for anything within a father's heart. Had she chosen the most dangerous assignment the organization could bestow, he would have blamed himself, all the same. It felt illogical to the point of silliness, but he couldn't put it aside. That sharp rationality that directed all his conscious activities found its counterpart in a deep unconscious emotional life that couldn't be argued with, though he scarcely showed it to others. Indeed, few would have imagined him capable of such feeling, so cold, as Frank said, was his outward appearance. Really only Amra had been allowed to share in it. And her mother, of course.

He leaned back in his seat and sighed at the thought of Ayla Welter, her sparkling green eyes seemingly before him as they'd been so many times before. A talented psychic, he sometimes wondered if she somehow put a little bit of her aura into him before she passed, giving his imagination a boost whenever he sought to remember her slim form and gentle, ethereal features.

"And now I've lost both of you," he muttered painfully, leaning his head back and watching the stream of darkness shoot overhead. "I never deserved either of you."

With this thought burning in his heart, the fatigues of the day caught up with him and soon carried him off to an uneasy slumber. Though dreamless, he nevertheless experienced a kind of consciousness even in sleep. A feeling of heavy guilt surrounded him, pressing him down. Eventually he had to awaken to push it aside so it wouldn't crush him under its weight. Dropping out of warp, he adjusted course and entered it again. Then he picked up Frank.

"Thought you'd get bored, sooner or later," the AI commented almost as soon as his skin touched the medallion. "We've got a long way ahead of us. We might as well try to be friends."

"You talk too much for that," Welter replied, settling into the pilot's seat again.

"It's not like I can play cards, you know."

"Would you like me to toss you back there again?"

"No, I'll behave myself," Frank sighed in a persecuted voice. "Can I ask you a question?" he followed up after half a minute. Receiving no answer, he decided to take his silence as a yes. "Did you think we'd make it out of there? I mean before we were inside and all?"

"I gave us pretty slim odds."

"Didn't that bother you?"

"No."

"Why not?" Frank queried. "Don't you want to live anymore?" Welter raised the medallion, about to throw it back over his shoulder. "Okay! Okay! Sorry, that was too personal. I didn't mean to pry."

"Yes, you did."

"Well, just a little," the AI admitted. "But I haven't got much left for me out here except my curiosity. The scenery gets old really fast in warp."

"True enough."

"Wait, did you just *agree* with me?" Frank asked hopefully.

"Broken clocks," Welter replied. "You're right every once in a while."

"Well, I'll take it, all the same. Can I ask you another question? Not a personal one."

"Go ahead."

"Do you think this whole thing with the chamber is going to work? I mean, sure, we've got the coolant. But how much longer can *Karnan* keep it going? The guy looks ready to drop over as soon as the next stiff breeze blows through. And who can say how many parts are gonna give out in the next few months alone, to say nothing of the years that the emperor and Doctor Tselitel are going to need it?"

"Would you rather we just gave up on them now?"

"No, no of course not. I don't know, I guess I'm just thinking out loud."

"Fretting out loud," Welter corrected with some annoyance.

"Yes, that's true," Frank admitted with a touch of his own irritation. "I'm just worried that we're gonna spend all this energy trying to win this specific battle whilst the war, if you will, is already lost. The chamber is nothing more than a stopgap. But what use is that when it'll take decades to rebuild when we've finally driven out the parasite for good?"

"We can only deal with the crises that currently face us," Welter answered. "We had to keep up Rhemus as a symbol of strength, if nothing else. The empire needs a head of state. Besides, he still commands the loyalty of the navy. If Krancis had just taken the reins, we could easily have faced a civil war. He's not popular with the brass. They've never trusted him."

"You'd think they would, given everything he's already led the empire through."

"He's not under their thumb. They don't like anything they can't control."

"Evidently not."

With this they settled into a period of quiet, Welter not wishing to speak, and Frank not wishing to disturb the small sense of camaraderie he felt was slowly building.

"What are we gonna do once we get back to *Kren-Balar*?" he inquired at last.

"First thing I'm going to do is give you back to Tselitel." Welter answered, though his tone was less annoyed than usual.

"And then?" Frank asked, choosing to let his barb slide.

"Settle in for a long winter's nap, apparently. Your people are placid as lambs now. Shouldn't be anything else for us to do but wait until the emperor can return home. Then we'll get to see if the chamber can be broken down and moved or not."

"I doubt it, given the complexity of the machinery."

"If it can be done, Krancis'll figure it out. Your people aren't the only ones to work with advanced tech."

"Well, sure. But *Kol-Prockian* tech isn't just any old *tech*, you know. It takes a certain degree of finesse to make it work."

"You mean it's finicky."

"That's a rather inelegant way of putting it," the AI objected. "But I suppose you *could* say that and be essentially correct."

"Mhm."

Again they lapsed into silence, this time for many, many hours. Though he didn't speak to him, and would never admit it openly, Welter was, not glad, but at least mildly pleased that Frank was along for the ride. The chatty AI kept him from dwelling quite so completely on his darkest thoughts since he could, at any time, choose to speak up and break the stillness. The fact he didn't was, however, equally welcome. Aware that keeping his mouth shut must have been almost painful for Frank, Welter slowly felt a hint of regard growing for him. The AI didn't have much sense in his opinion, but at least he could respect the wishes of others. That had to count for something.

Just as this notion passed through his mind, the AI spoke, instantly causing him to retract the thought.

"I can't stand this silence any longer!" he exclaimed. "It's like when you get that irresistible urge to move your legs in bed, except it's in my brain. Or I guess I should say my circuits."

"Have you got something *distinct* on your mind, or do you just want to blather?" he asked pointedly, willing to humor him only if there was some point to the discussion.

"Well, I'm sure I could gin something up that would be of at least *moderate* interest," Frank shot back. "Of course, I can't *promise* anything. Okay! Okay!" he protested, as the medallion was again raised to be thrown in the back. "Sheesh, do you always have to play hardball?" Receiving no answer, he decided to change tacks. "Just what are your plans when Krancis is done having you guard the emperor?"

"To take down as many of the *Pho'Sath* as I can."

"But those guys are as deadly as anything could be. That's just suicide."

"Not if they don't know I'm coming. I've hunted

supernatural forces from one end of the Milky Way to the other. I know how to keep a low profile. They won't know I'm there until they're bleeding fireflies."

"And that's it? Just hop around killing one after another? Couldn't a man of your experience be put to better use in some kind of leadership role? After all, the empire is gonna be denuded of all kinds of managers and officers and so forth. There's gonna be a lot of fresh recruits who'll need examples like yours."

"Krancis'll take care of that."

"But he needs people to work through, doesn't he? He can't just snap his fingers and make things happen. There's got to be enough wise, intelligent hands to help him. Otherwise it's all just good intentions, isn't it?"

"Why are you pushing this line?" Welter queried. "What does it matter to you?"

"Well, for one thing, I'd hate to see humanity come through this struggle just to collapse afterwards. Secondly, as you may recall, it's *my* empire now, too, ever since Rhemus took on my people. So I've got a vested interest in seeing it continue. I don't want either my people or yours tumbling into an early grave. And while I do have my misgivings about you, only an imbecile would deny your obvious capabilities. The simple fact, Welter, is that the empire needs you. Badly."

Had these words come from Tselitel he would have brushed them aside, assuming them to be mere fluff intended to maneuver him into making the decision she'd like to see Hunt make in a similar situation. But coming from Frank they had the objectivity of, not a foe, but hardly a friend. The force of this fact was enough to make Welter pause.

"Dumbstruck by my brilliance?" Frank humorously queried after a few moments.

"Not likely."

"Sure. But at least it's *possible*, right? No? Oh, well. Anyhow, just think about that. This war is a lot bigger than any one of us. We need to hang together, or we're gonna come apart at the seams. This isn't any time for personal crusades. *However valid they happen to be*," he hastened to add, sensing a sudden increase in Welter's blood pressure.

"Someone's got to hunt down the *Pho'Sath*," Welter replied, though essentially talking to himself. Inwardly he was weighing his personal vendetta against the needs of the rest of humanity.

"And that's a valuable task, believe me. But you could train others to do that. If something happened to you, who could take on a teaching role like that? Who's got the experience? I'm sure there's a few folks in the fringe who'd try their hand at it. But their track record isn't all that great, is it? No: everything you've got in your head is worth a lot more than what you can personally do with your hands."

"We'll see," Welter replied with finality, ending the discussion.

Sporadically they spoke during the rest of the trip. But it wasn't until they dropped out of warp above the undulating seas of lava that stretched across Alamar that Frank truly found his voice again.

"Ugh, I'm so glad this trip is over. You don't know what it's like for a mind as roving as mine to be cooped up like this. I just want to plug into the base's computers and let all the data stream through my head like water. I never thought it was possible to be so bored. As a matter of fact–."

With this Welter did, at last, chuck the medallion over his shoulder into the back of the craft. Piloting the egg to the volcano in silence, he dropped into the opening and slowly descended. It wasn't long before he was back within the safety of *Kren-Balar*. Eagerly *Kol-Prockians* gathered around, hopeful that his mission had been a success. As soon as he popped the canopy and they could see the canisters, they began to clap and cheer.

"Another happy ending," Welter muttered, deploying the ladder and climbing down the side. He paused as his eyes lighted on Frank, and for half a second he considered leaving him. But, remembering how grabby the *Kol-Prockians* were with artifacts, he decided not to risk losing him and climbed back up. Lifting the medallion by the chain, he dropped him into his pocket and departed the ship.

"I gather your mission was successful?" Doctor *Keelen* asked, entering the hangar as Welter was leaving it.

"Uh huh," he answered, walking past him.

"Any trouble?" *Keelen* inquired, hastening to follow.

"Two men dead. That's all."

"I'm sorry to hear that."

"They knew the risks."

"Naturally," *Keelen* replied with a hint of his old sarcasm. "But all the same it's unfortunate to lose good men, isn't it?"

Not bothering to answer, Welter just kept walking until *Keelen* finally broke off and doubled back towards the hangar to oversee the unloading of the coolant. Entering the chamber's anteroom, he saw Tselitel half-heartedly poking a plate of food in front of her. When she raised her eyes to see who'd entered, they lit up.

"Gustav! I didn't know you were back!" she said happily, standing up and hastening across the room to give him a hug that surprised him. "How are you? Did the mission go smoothly?"

"Smoothly enough," he answered, pulling away from her and leaning against the desk, crossing his arms over his chest. "Got the coolant and did the smugglers some damage along the way. Lost a couple of men, but that couldn't be helped." He nodded towards the chamber. "How's the emperor?"

"He's been okay," she answered with some reluctance. "We've had to be careful with the chamber, and that's taken a toll."

"I can see that," he observed, glancing at her hands as they trembled by her sides. "You been getting enough time in there?"

"Of course," she answered quickly.

"*Doctor*."

"Well, not as much as *Karnan* or the emperor would like. But they've got to come first."

"Well, we won't have to ration it anymore," Welter said, reaching into his pocket and drawing out Frank. "Here: brought you an old friend."

"Oh, good," she replied with a wry grin that he appreciated after so many hours alone with the construct. "I'll, uh, catch up with him in a minute," she added, walking to the table and laying the disc down there. "Honestly, I haven't minded a little respite from his brand of conversation," she confided in a whisper upon nearing the desk again. Looking at him for a moment, she sensed something different in his gaze but couldn't tell just what it was. Perhaps a note of…sadness? "Are you okay, Gustav?" she queried after a few seconds.

"I'm alright," he answered, brushing it off, his expression instantly hardening. "Everything been quiet here?"

"Quiet as can be," she assured him with a nod. "*Kren-Balar* is practically a resort. The biggest foe I've faced since you left for the coolant is boredom. With Frank gone, the emperor and *Karnan* either working or recuperating in the chamber, there's been a lot of hours alone with my thoughts. I can't think of the last time I've had so much opportunity for reflection."

"Has that been a problem?" he asked, aware of how she used to dive into work to avoid thinking about her condition.

"It's been okay," she replied equivocally, as the door to the anteroom opened and *Karnan* labored inside.

"Good to see you," he said to Welter as though he'd been gone merely a few hours. "The coolant is being applied as we speak. Soon the chamber will be running at full capacity again. And you, my dear," he said to Tselitel, "won't have any reason to sit out here any longer."

"Yes, *Karnan*," she said with a little smile, as he ambled into the chamber. "He worries about me," she added to Welter.

"Someone has to," he remarked, pushing off the desk and making for the door. But a slim hand on his arm stopped him.

"Are you angry with me?" she asked, concerned she'd done something to upset him.

"It's been a long trip, Doctor," he replied, pointing towards Frank on the table. "And I've had to share it with him. That's enough to put anyone out of sorts." With this explanation he left her.

Unsatisfied with this answer, she went to Frank and picked him up.

"Is he okay?"

"Is he ever?" the AI queried with exasperation. "I can barely string two sentences together without him wanting to chuck me out the window! You'd think–."

"*Frank*," she said with more firmness than was typical for her.

"I guess he seemed to change a little part way through the trip back. Got a little more reflective, I suppose. But it'd take a mind reader to decipher whatever's going through that skull of his. You know how he is."

"Yes, I know," she nodded, leaning a shaky hand on the table and looking back to the door through which he'd left. "He's a remarkable man, Frank. I just hope he can sort out his demons before they destroy him."

"Yeah, you and me both." When she turned back and looked at the disc in surprise, he continued. "Well, I can see his value as well as the next guy. Don't want him to throw all that potential away."

"Don't tell me you two became *friends* during the mission," she said with a smile.

"What? Pft, no. Absolutely not. Who could become

friends with *him*, anyhow? It's like making friends with a brick that's been coated in tar and set on fire. If he doesn't burn you with his attitude, he'll probably beat you to death with his brickiness."

"'*Brickiness?*'" Tselitel chuckled.

"Well, you know what I mean," the AI mumbled.

"I think you're protesting too much, Frank."

"I think you're being silly," he countered, audibly crossing his arms. "But I suppose you're entitled to a little bit of fancy now and again."

Smiling but saying no more, she took him into the chamber. *Karnan* rolled his eyes upon seeing the medallion in her hand, still royally frustrated that he was a mere bureaucrat and not one of a thousand more illustrious AIs who could have survived from the old days.

"Any moment now," the old scientist assured her, looking away from Frank and pretending he wasn't there. "I've given the chamber a thorough going over to ensure it wouldn't burn out while we were working with less coolant. Several goings over, in fact. I'd say we're good to go for months to come. Remarkable though it sounds, we seem to be home free." He scoffed and shook his head. "It's amazing to utter such words. We've lived on the edge so long that to suddenly have all our problems as a race, both within the base and without, simply evaporate…Well, it's hard to wrap my head around after all these years. Like waking up from some dream that you can't really believe is over. I hope that makes some sense," he chuckled.

"Oh, absolutely," she replied at once. "Sometimes the hardest part of dealing with trauma is realizing when its cause is over. Psychologically you carry it with you like it's still going on. You can't shake it off, at least not right away. It takes time to adjust to the new normal."

"A normal I'll never live to see," he laughed dryly. "It's funny how fate works, isn't it? After all these years of keeping myself alive and this chamber running, it's only at the very end of my life that it bears fruit. Oh, I don't mean to sound like I'm pitying myself. I'd hate for you to think that. It's just that, well, we've lived under the dark shadow of hopelessness since time out of mind. I wish I had a little more time to get used to the sunshine."

"I understand," she sympathized, placing a hand on his and rubbing it gently. "It's so very hard. At least you have the satisfaction of knowing you've done your people the greatest service any *Kol-Prockian* could: you've delivered your entire race from death by preserving one of the truly wonderful pieces of technology in this universe. That's an accomplishment that will be remembered as long as *Kol-Prockians* exist."

"May they live long," he said with quiet fervency, looking off into space for a moment before directing his gaze at her. "I just hope my people have the sense to learn something from yours about stability and cohesion. It might have been the civil war that tore us apart. But it was merely the symptom of an inner disunity that permeated our entire society. Even after the war was won we could barely work together, the petty jealousies of individual worlds preventing us from presenting the strong front necessary to our foes. Under such conditions our doom was sealed since before we left our homeworld of *Kol* and made our first journey to *Prock*."

"So *that's* where your name comes from," she uttered with realization.

"Yes, you could say we belong to two worlds. When our homeworld of *Kol* was threatened by an enormous asteroid that we could neither divert nor destroy, we were forced to remove as many of our kind as possible to the nearest habitable world, *Prock*. Ever after that was our home. But we never wanted to forget where we truly sprang from, so we've always used the dual name of *Kol-Prockian*."

"What happened to *Prock* after the fall of your people?" she asked with some reluctance, not wishing to cause him pain.

"There's hardly anything left of it now," he answered grimly. "It was one of the first worlds that our enemies targeted. They bombed it so savagely that it became uninhabitable. Some day I'll explain the whole war to you, start to finish. But it was little short of a terror campaign from the first moments. We were set upon by three races, each of them inferior in both intelligence and power. But with their combined might they managed to batter us to pieces. With our military in tatters, they hauled away those who had somehow survived the unconscionable slaughter they brought upon our civilian population. Thereafter they populated what was left of our planets with their colonists. Until, of course, they were driven out of the Milky Way for good by you humans." He shook his head. "I can't tell you how much satisfaction that fact gives me. And now, to put the cherry on top, we've joined up with you all, in a sense reclaiming all that was lost to those savages. I hope that with our combined efforts, we can make an empire that will last as long as the stars burn in the midnight sky."

"That's my hope also," she agreed quietly.

As she said this the chamber began to hum after its old fashion, and *Karnan* leaned his head back against the wall with relief.

"There we go," he uttered in a tone of deep appreciation. "Now we can rest."

Sitting beside him until he began to lightly snore, she carefully arose and moved to the other side of the chamber to await the emperor who, she felt correctly, must arrive shortly.

"I can't tell you how good this feels," he said as he stretched out on the floor, reaching his arms over his head, his eyes shut as he soaked up the healing energy of the room. "I've been assured that the machinery is in good condition. We shouldn't have to worry about it for a long time to come. At last we can rest."

"*Karnan* said the same thing," she remarked with a little smile. "It's a tremendous load off his mind. He feels personally responsible for it. Which he is, of course. But it places much too high a burden upon his already tortured nerves. He needs to relax more, for his own sake and that of us all. If he can't look after the chamber…Well, we'll all be in a tight spot."

"It's hard to get a fellow like that to ease off on anything he's set his mind to," Rhemus observed. "And he's set his mind to keeping this room running. You'd just about have to kill him to break his obsession with it. Or drug him." He thought for a few moments. "Have you seen Welter yet?"

"Yes, he was here," she responded somewhat hesitantly, aware that he was leading her towards a question she didn't want to answer.

"He came to me shortly after landing and gave his report," he said thoughtfully, reflecting on their meeting. "In your professional opinion, Doctor, how much farther can he go before snapping?"

"I would be reluctant to place any limits on what he can handle," she replied cautiously. "He seems capable of assuming any burden placed upon him."

"That wasn't exactly my question," he pointed out evenly. "I have no doubt that he can withstand hardship with the best of them. But one would have to be blind not to see that he's tormented by a new demon. As though he didn't have enough."

"I can't imagine what could have changed," she shook her head, thinking for a moment. "Two operatives that went with him regrettably died. But he's not the sort of man to be torn up over something like that. No, something must have shifted in his internal world to make this change. Something deeply personal."

"Well, I want you to talk to him about it and see if you can sort it out," the emperor said, closing his eyes and shifting a little to settle as well as he could on the floor.

"Talk to him?" she asked with a hint of incredulity. "My emperor, that's the last thing he wants to do. He's nearly bitten my head off–."

"Tell him that I wish him to discuss the matter with you *fully* and without delay," he cut her off with an edge in his voice. Opening his eyes, his expression immediately softened as he found her gaze. "We depend on him far too much to leave this matter unaddressed, Doctor. He doesn't have to share anything with anyone else, including me. But this is your *profession*, and it would be ridiculous not to put you to work helping him resolve what's torturing him."

"He doesn't want to resolve it," she protested as mildly as she could. "He wants to let it consume him, driving him onward."

"We can't afford to let a man like that burn himself out. He needs to be preserved. You needn't leave right now, given you've been deprived of the chamber as well. But once you've had a chance to recuperate, I want you to seek him out and inform him of my wishes."

"Yes, my emperor," she nodded.

For the next few hours she rested beside him, occasionally watching his chest slowly rise and fall as she contemplated an early grave. Not a *literal* one, she corrected herself. But there seemed to be little else in store for her if she started prodding the most dangerous man she'd ever met. It was a recipe for more trouble than she'd ever encountered. But it wasn't as if she could cross the emperor, either. Caught between a rock and a hard place, she was glad to have his explicit permission to wait a while inside the chamber before setting off in search of Welter.

"I can only imagine why your vitals haven't calmed during the last few hours," Frank commented, making her gasp. "Sorry, I didn't want to startle you. But I just want to let you know that I'll help all I can with Welter."

"Thanks," she whispered, though she hadn't any idea how he could. Short of tying him up or injecting him with sedatives, there seemed to be no way forward except to charge straight ahead and try to weather the storm of rage he was certain to send at her. Her only shield was to hide behind the emperor's will, hoping that would be enough to deflect the brunt of his anger.

When at last she had overstayed Rhemus' original invitation to recuperate, she arose. His breaths were shallow, but consistent, implying to her a tense, introspective phase of sleep.

"*Probably dreaming*," she reflected, making for the door and passing into the anteroom.

Finding it empty, she began searching the halls of *Kren-Balar* for her patient. Every little while she'd stop a passing *Kol-Prockian* and inquire, through Frank, if there'd been any sign of Welter. But no one seemed to know where he'd gone after making his report to Rhemus. Her only assurance that he was actually within the base was the fact that the egg was still where he'd left it.

"Knowing him, he's probably sitting in some closet so as to get away from the rest of us," Frank remarked sourly after an hour of searching had turned up nothing. "I've never met anyone so anti-social."

"He's got reason to be," she replied sensitively, moving slowly down one of the corridors on bare feet, her thin robe flowing with her movements. "He's been terribly hurt."

"Yeah, I guess so," the AI admitted in a grumble. "But he doesn't have to push folks away so much, you know? Why, on the entire trip I could–."

"Hardly stop talking?" she interrupted with a little smile.

"Look, I don't have hands and feet like everyone else! Talking is the only way I can interact with the world. I should have thought a psychiatrist would be alive to that fact!"

"I am, Frank," she assured him, turning down another hallway and seeing Doctor *Keelen* approaching. "But sometimes one has to know when to put a sock in it."

Before he could respond, *Keelen* called out.

"Doctor! I'm glad to see you're feeling better," he said happily, quickly noticing the increased poise and energy that the chamber had infused her with. "What are you doing wandering around? Taking a little exercise?"

"I'm looking for Gustav," she answered. "Have you seen him?"

"Not since I bumped into him right after landing," he shook his head. "Where have you looked?"

"Oh, just about everywhere," she said with a hint of exasperation, shrugging her thin shoulders. "It's like he's evaporated."

"I'm sure he's alive and well," the alien responded with a roll of his eyes. "A man like that can't be gotten rid of that easily."

Tselitel leaned a little on one leg and cocked her head.

"You've had trouble with him?" she queried, her tone suspicious.

"I think a more accurate statement would be that *he's* had trouble with *me*, Doctor," he replied, not appreciating her implication. "He's been surly and rude to everyone except the emperor ever since reaching *Kren-Balar*. It'd be a miracle to find a single *Kol-Prockian* who hasn't had his toes stepped on by that…individual," he added, managing to censor himself.

"I'd say giving offense has been a two-way street, Doctor," she countered with some heat. "You were very disagreeable on several occasions."

Dipping his head a little, he held up his hand.

"I deserved that," he admitted. "But I fear you're losing your objectivity, Doctor. I'm fully aware that your profession seeks to mend what is broken in every individual that comes your way. But sometimes they can't be put back together once they've shattered. I am not a healer of the *mind*, but I *am* a healer of the body. And it is my personal experience that some cases are simply beyond help. It requires a certain hardness to recognize when that is – when is the appropriate time to stop sympathizing with the patient and to face the fact that he can't be made better. You need to know when to cut your emotional ties. I suspect you've allowed yourself to become much too entangled with his problems."

"It's my job to involve myself with my patients," she replied somewhat defensively. "I have to if I am to understand their perspective and truly help them"

"But not by losing your own perspective in the process," he pointed out. "Not by adopting the values and position of the patient and seeing the world through his eyes once the session has ended. There needs to be a cutoff point. You're already identifying with Welter, Doctor. Moments ago you took personal offense at what I said about him. That's what I meant about losing your objectivity: you can't allow yourself to get bound up in him."

"I took offense because what you said was *offensive*," she responded, crossing her arms and bracing herself. "Gustav doesn't have a friend in this life, as far as I can tell, so someone has to stick up for him when he's not around to do it for himself."

"As you wish," *Keelen* said deferentially, not willing to expand the argument further. "I just hope you don't get in too deep. A man like that could do a lot of harm to those around him when he finally goes off."

"He won't," she insisted, as the *Kol-Prockian* nodded slightly and moved past her.

"*Doctor…*" Frank started to say, as she uncrossed her arms and strode in the opposite direction from *Keelen*.

"Not now," she shut him down, shaking her head as she turned a corner and continued her search. Determined to find him even if it took the rest of the day, she scoured the base before finally discovering him resting on the floor in a small room, the light off until she switched it on.

"Do you *mind?*" he snapped, before seeing who it was. "Oh, you."

"Hello, Gustav," she said gently, stepping inside and

quietly closing the door. The room, not much larger than a small office, was cold, very nearly frigid. Stretched out in the back wearing a jacket, his arms crossed over his stomach, he glared at her. "I can see you're not eager for company right now," she remarked uneasily, trying to get the ball rolling but lacking for anything to say.

"I figured you'd be along about now," he replied. "Knew you couldn't keep your hands off for long."

"The truth is, Gustav, that the emperor sent me," she informed him, moving to the middle of the rear wall and leaning her back against it. Sliding down to the floor, she eyed him for a moment before continuing. "He's concerned about you, and he thinks I can help."

"I don't need any help," he responded at once.

"I told him you felt that way. But he was adamant. He *insists* on my helping you."

Drawing an irritated breath, he looked up at the ceiling and released it in a gust of annoyance.

"And if I refuse?"

"He made it clear he considered you a vital asset in this war," she replied. "And after all the trouble with the chamber, he's in no mood to be argued with."

"Nor am I."

"Don't do this, Gustav," she pleaded quietly, shaking her head slowly from one side to the other. "Don't start a battle with the emperor, of all people. He's got such a load on his mind already. It's a wonder that he hasn't broken under the strain, especially when you consider his condition. It would be unthinkable to make his life even harder after all he's endured, especially these last few weeks. And *especially* after he's treated us both with such consideration and kindness."

"And what would you have me do? Bare myself to the world?"

"No, just me. And only to the degree you're comfortable. I've got a *lot* of experience with trauma like this,

Gustav. I know how hard and painful it is to even draw *close* to it, much less truly face it. But we don't have to go fast. We can take it just a little at a time. The emperor doesn't expect a miracle overnight. But he's worried after your last meeting with him. He noticed a change, as have I."

"What change?" he queried, his tone a challenge.

"A sadness," she answered. "A hopelessness that has always been present but not nearly so palpably as it is now. You're on the verge of abandoning your duty and allowing your dark feelings to lead you off against the *Ph–*," she began, before catching herself. "Against the *Dolshan*. You're ready to give up your belief in anything good in this life and throw yourself into revenge until it finally consumes you."

"You're very perceptive, Doctor," he commended her flatly, his angry eyes searching her face reflectively, as though deciding how far he wanted to go with her.

"I wish I wasn't. Not in this case."

"Not all facts are pleasant, Doctor. Including those pertaining to what I must do."

"But it's not something you *must* do," she replied. "It's something that is *driving* you from within, a powerful unconscious urge. But you don't have to let such urges rule your life. They needn't dominate you. When we let go of the power of consciousness to choose its own course, we leave behind all our civilized trappings and once more return to the bush. It's a barbarous way to live, Gustav."

"But it isn't wrong for being so," he responded slowly. "Civilization is built upon a mountain of such urges, Doctor; it is enlivened and guided and *fueled* by them. What we're pleased to consider rational, well-behaved life is only possible because of the animalistic fire that burns within us. Man is not a brain in a jar, nor is he a calculator who invariably must choose the most productive course. Some courses are *destructive*, consuming both the actor and what he acts upon, and yet they, like the urges that prompt them, are not wrong for that fact alone. The fact, as I have stated before, is that not everyone finds a happy ending. Tragedy exists in fiction for a reason: it is a reflection of a necessary mode of living. Tragic figures are *necessary* for our society, or else there would be no one to do the dirty work to keep civilization intact."

"Then you see yourself as such a figure?" she queried, settling against the wall a little more comfortably, hopeful that she'd found a subtle way to make him open up. "Your course, as you see it, is justified by the benefits that others will derive from it?"

"Not in the least," he answered without hesitation. "I can feel what I must do, and I intend to do it. I'm simply expressing it in terms that you can sympathize with."

"But I don't want to see anyone burn themselves up for the sake of others," she protested, the idea that she felt that way peculiarly troubling to her. "I don't believe that any individual should be consumed as a kind of sacrifice to society."

"That's the way it works," he shrugged indifferently. "The fact is there have always been outriggers or defenders surrounding the human camp, protecting it from forces lurking just beyond the firelight. Mostly they've been human. But some defenders have belonged to other races as well."

"But you're not taking your place among them. You're simply piggybacking on their lifestyle to justify your course of retribution."

"Doctor, are you here to find out what's on my mind, as the emperor ordered, or are you here to argue with me?"

"Well, I'm here to do what the emperor requested, of course," she replied somewhat uncertainly.

"Rhemus may have sent you through that door," he opined, nodding towards it. "But you're here on your own mission. You still can't stand the idea of Hunt giving his life away in this war."

"*You have no right–,*" she snapped angrily, before catching herself and taking a breath. "Gustav," she began slowly, trying to keep steady. "We are here to discuss what you've been–."

"Don't give me that Doctor-Patient garbage," he interrupted, sitting up and leaning against the back wall. "You're not going to come in here and dissect me from thirty thousand feet. No, Doctor, if you want to know, want to *feel* what's really going through my head, you're gonna have to get your hands dirty, 'cause I'm not going to make it easy. If you want to face *my* truth, you need to face yours as well."

"There's nothing within me that needs facing," she replied, though without conviction.

"Then you're much too blind to help anyone else," Welter declared. "You're tied in knots until you don't know which way to turn. You could no more heal a patient than fly. The fact is, Doctor, that even with the chamber you've continued to fray at the edges. Anyone with half an eye for detail can immediately see the strain in your face, the tension in your neck. And that's not all," he continued, holding up his hand to stop her from interrupting. "Being away from Hunt has caused you to latch onto me as a kind of surrogate, a man to pour your healing impulses into. The fact is, Doctor, you *need* patients in order to feel at ease. And why is that? To help you feel less inadequate because of your condition?"

"Why are you attacking me?" she asked, hurt by his words. "I'm only trying to help."

"But *who* are you trying to help?" he shot back. "Me? Or Hunt, or you?"

"You! I'm trying to help *you!* But you're too battered and bloodied to see that! You think that everyone is out to get you, that they're trying to take a piece out of you for themselves. But that isn't true! Gustav, I *knew* you wouldn't go for this. I tried to argue the emperor out of it. But he wouldn't be moved. If you want to attack someone, why don't you attack *him?*"

For a moment he paused.

"I told you before that I'm not the man to pin your hopes on, Doctor," he replied in a voice that, while still hard, had a note of consideration running through it. "I know you said that you have to believe I can change, cause that means Hunt can, too. You're hoping, for both our sakes, that I can come out of the dive that I'm in. But you've forgotten something important: to pull out of a dive, you have to *want* to. There has to be a reason to continue, to resume flight and soar through the skies. There has to be *hope*, Doctor; a belief in something worth dedicating yourself to. And that doesn't exist for me without Amra."

"But what about all the people spread throughout the Milky Way who need you? Who need *anyone* who can help them in this struggle?"

"They're just an abstraction to me now," he replied with a subtle shaking of his head. "Just faces on the news broadcasts. I can't feel anything for them anymore. Once I did: I was dedicated to rooting out the supernatural forces who'd been pushing us around since time out of mind. But I can't bring myself to care any longer about such things. All I want to do is deal as much harm as possible to the *Dolshan*. In that way I can draw a little bit closer to being the father that I should have been to Amra."

"You never would have let anything happen to her if you'd been on Erdu, Gustav," she assured him. "Nothing but death would have separated you from her."

"But I wasn't there, was I? And that's all that matters. What I *would* have done or *could* have done is of no importance. She's dead because of me; because I failed to protect her. That's something I can never forgive myself for. The only remedy left is to punish those who are responsible."

Seeing that he couldn't be moved so much as an inch, she sighed and began to arise. Then, as an idea came to her, she went to where he sat and settled on the floor before him. Curiously he eyed her.

"Yes?" he asked.

"I…want to try something," she said hesitantly, slowly reaching her hands for his temples. But instantly he snatched her wrists and held her back.

"Why?" he queried suspiciously.

"I'm not strong enough to hurt you, Gustav," she pointed out, shaking her wrists slightly within his iron grasp. "You don't need to be afraid of me."

"I'm hardly afraid of you," he replied, letting her go but continuing to eye her guardedly.

"There's only one person who can help you now," she explained, gingerly touching his temples and closing her eyes.

"And who is that?" he asked skeptically, barely resisting the urge to push her cold fingertips away.

At this she reopened her eyes.

"Amra."

At the sound of her name Welter's mind shot back to the last moment he saw her before she was killed by his very own Midnight Blade. Both anger and pain surged through him, and he was about to shove Tselitel away when she managed to hitch a ride on these powerful emotions into his mind. Dragging him along with her, they plunged deep into his psyche, barrelling through layer after layer of unconscious material before landing on soft dirt surrounded by a dark mist.

"We made it," she said with wonder, releasing his temples and standing up. "We actually made it!"

"I suppose you know how to get out?" Welter asked, likewise arising and scowling at her. "You've never done anything like this before."

"I can sense it," she replied, reaching out her hands as though passing her fingers through reams of data. "It's all here, surrounding me in a cloud of information. My psyche is unlocked. It's teaching me all I need to know." She paused and looked at him. "I'll know what I need to do when the time is right."

"You'd better," he warned her, glancing around.

"Come, this way," she urged him, taking his hand and hurrying into the mist. Eerily, their footfalls made no noise at all. To Welter, the land of his unconscious felt very much like a land of death: all was stillness. Trees loomed up in the darkness, but they bore no leaves; everywhere the ground was mere dirt without a single living thing growing in it; no wind blew, and no animals were to be seen anywhere. In this, he felt, there was a lesson; one which he did not wish to learn.

"Are you seeing this, Gustav?" she queried with amazement, looking all around as she pulled him onwards.

"I can hardly help it, can I?" was his surly reply, doubt arising in his mind as to whether this was truly his mind, or merely some distortion of it that served to push the line she wanted to impress on him.

"Your unconscious life is devoid of, well, *life*," she observed, speaking more to herself than to him in her wonderment. "The foundation of your psyche has given itself over to death. No wonder you don't believe in anything, anymore." Aware that this could come across harshly, she paused and looked at him. "I didn't mean that to sound like–."

"Speak your mind, Doctor," he cut her off. "That's what I intend to do."

"Yes, of course," she nodded, resuming movement. Looking all around, she hadn't noticed ash on the ground until her bare feet had moved several steps into it. Looking down, she shook her head slowly from side-to-side. "There's something here. Something significant. It's like…a messenger of death."

"Meaning what, exactly?" he asked, continuing to hold her hand with the greatest reluctance.

"I don't know," she uttered, still gazing at it. "Those are just the words that sprang to mind for me. I can't explain them."

"That doesn't help us much," he responded, releasing his grip. But instantly she took hold again.

"*Don't* let go," she insisted. "We could get separated in here."

"And how do you know that?"

"I just do," was all she could say, pulling him forward before more questions could mount his lips and spring forth at her. "You need to have a little faith, Gustav," she added. "Doubt is nothing but poison when you're exploring the psyche like this. We need to be credulous, or we'll miss something important."

"Just answer me one question," he began as they moved deeper into the ash. "How did you manage to jump inside my mind like this? I thought you didn't have any psychic powers."

"I've got *some* kind of power," she explained. "And in the moment I just knew what to do. It was like an invisible pair of hands reached up and guided me inside. I guess that's a little creepy, now that I think about it," she reflected with a hint of a shudder. "Who's to say those hands are good?"

"I wouldn't worry about them," he told her, nodding over her shoulder. "I'd worry about *that*."

Turning around, Tselitel couldn't help but scream. Before her a tattered black robe with a hood floated above the ground. No body could be seen within it, yet something gave it shape. It undulated in the air as if blown by the wind, though there was none. Neither advancing nor retreating, it simply hovered and watched.

"What do you want?" Welter demanded, his voice calm, almost annoyed.

Wordlessly it raised an empty sleeve to Tselitel.

"Go ahead, Doctor," he said, giving her a little nudge forwards, though she continued to death-grip his hand.

"*You want me to go with it?*" she whispered incredulously, shrinking back as Welter moved her ahead.

"You're the one who wanted to be credulous," he answered mercilessly. "Time to practice what you preach."

"Oh!" she exclaimed, as he pried his hand loose from

hers and placed them both on the backs of her shoulders. "Gustav, no!" she pleaded as he pushed her forwards. Her protests stopped when the figure placed its right sleeve across her shoulders, not touching her yet somehow drawing her along. Welter allowed them to get just out of earshot before beginning to follow slowly.

"*You must help me,*" the figure whispered in a high, breathy voice, the empty hood of the robe held next to her ear as she began to shiver from fright. "*You must draw me.*"

"Like a picture?" she queried densely, fear dulling her intellect.

"*Draw me up. Draw me out.*"

"Oh!" she realized, afraid she may have annoyed the entity. "Why?" she managed to ask, her voice trembling.

"*Because only I can help his pain.*"

Looking doubtfully into the hood that hovered next to her, she looked back to Welter. For some reason he nodded, though he could have no notion what the figure desired, nor could he have even heard its words. But remembering what he said about credulity, she decided to take a leap of faith.

"What can I do?" she asked, this question requiring all her courage to utter.

"*Draw me up,*" it repeated, moving in front of Tselitel and turning to face her fully. "*Bring me from his depths, the hidden places of his mind.*"

Nodding her willingness to do so, Tselitel raised her hands to the figure and ever so lightly touched its garment. Closing her eyes, she concentrated on the thread that the manifestation represented in his psyche and began to broaden and deepen it. She didn't know how long it took, but suddenly the garment was changed to warm flesh, and she could tell that the entity had changed. Opening her eyes, she saw a beautiful girl standing before her. At once she knew it was Amra Welter.

"Thank you, Doctor," the girl said, stepping around her without looking, her eyes fixed on Welter, who still stood some distance off. "Daddy?" she queried, taking slow steps towards him.

"What are you?" he asked flatly, unmoved by the manifestation. "Something she conjured up to assuage my guilt? A spirit to ease my pain?"

"No," she assured him, shaking her head slowly. "Throughout all the torture that the *Pho'Sath* put me through, I was unshakeably certain that you'd come for me. So I hid a part of myself just as deeply as I could, burying it in the farthest recesses of my psyche. *Anzah* thought that she'd turned me into a vegetable, and in a sense that was true: I could never manifest my spirit in my own body after all the harm she'd done to it. But I was still alive, Daddy: I still had thoughts and feelings. And I buried them so, so deep that even she couldn't find them all with her powers. Many she did manage to locate and destroy. But enough of me remains to give you this message."

Pausing before him, she looked up into his eyes and smiled gently.

"What message?" he asked, still skeptical, his arms crossed.

"That it wasn't your fault," she answered, placing a small hand on his cheek, instantly causing tears to gather in his eyes as he felt that she was, indeed, a remnant of his daughter. "That you can't blame yourself for the fortunes of war. There's a time for everyone to depart this life. And while mine came a little earlier than others, that doesn't mean I'm gone." Sliding her hand down to his heart, she felt it tenderly. "I'll always be with you in here."

"Oh, baby!" he exclaimed, shooting his arms around her neck and squeezing her tight. Dropping to his knees in the dirt, he pulled her down with him and rocked her back and forth.

"I'll never leave you, Daddy," she assured him, her voice muffled by his shoulder. "Not ever. I'll be with you wherever you go. And if you ever need strength or love, just look inside, and you'll see me smiling back at you."

"I should have kept you alive," he declared fiercely, bitter tears flowing down his cheeks and moistening her neck as he pressed her against him. "I never should have let you go! I'm so sorry, baby. You deserved so much more from life, and it was my job to get it for you. To make sure you felt the sun on your cheek and the wind in your beautiful hair. Not to let you end your days in a foul basement, tortured by those maggots!"

"It's alright, Daddy," she insisted with sympathetic firmness. "I'm at peace with my end."

The tranquility of these words, the completeness with which she accepted her fate, sparked a revolt in him. Throwing his head back, he shouted in rage and agony, causing Tselitel to jump though she stood sixty feet off.

"But you never should have needed to *do* that!" he declared. "Don't you see that, Amra? I was supposed to take care of you and I failed! I failed miserably, contemptibly. I should have been *killed* by that *Pho'Sath*, but I couldn't let you go unavenged." He looked into her eyes, his own being red. "My failure was unforgivable."

"There is *nothing* to forgive," she replied, drawing him back into her embrace. "Nothing at all. I want you to believe that. I *need* you to believe that, or I'll never have a moment's peace. What happened wasn't your fault, and you can't take responsibility for it. It was the *Pho'Sath* that killed me, and not you."

"That's why I'll punish them for it, collectively," he ground his teeth. "That's why I'll make them pay. I'll hunt every last one of them down."

"No," she said, drawing away and gazing at him seriously. "No revenge. I'll not have you throw your life away like this."

"You don't have any choice."

"Then you're not doing it for me," she uttered, shaking her head. "Whatever you're doing it for, it isn't me. I may be only a fragment, a memory. But I'll suffer all the same to watch you consume yourself in hatred and grief. It'll be worse to me than all that *Anzah* did. That I could endure, because it was the work of an enemy. But to receive such blows from my own father…It'll break my heart."

"And don't you think it's broken my heart to lose you?" he demanded in protest. "Both you and your mother? What's left to me anymore? What place is there for me in all this enormous expanse of galaxies? If there's no love there can be no home. And I have nothing to love anymore. It fractured me to lose your mother; and it all but killed me to lose you. No greater injury can be done to me than that which has already been done. You imagine that I'll be ruining myself by crusading against the *Pho'Sath*. But in truth it's the one thing that can give me satisfaction. Making them pay is the only way I can draw closer to you anymore. Dedicating myself to their destruction is solely for your sake."

"But I don't *want* that!" she insisted. "I want to see my father survive this war and thrive, not collapse under the weight of grief! Don't you understand the guilt that will give *me?* If I'd been smarter I could have defended myself from the thugs they sent to capture me. Had I been psychically more sensitive to their designs, I could have detected what was coming and cleared out. But instead I left myself in harm's way, and I was captured as a result. If my mistake leads you to destroy yourself, then I'll never be able to forgive myself. It'll shatter me to bits. This is why we both have to let go of blame and responsibility. It happened, and there's nothing either of us can do to change that. Calling it the fortunes of war is apt, because fate strikes one just as easily as it strikes another. Neither of us can claim what happened as our own peculiar burden, because a thousand factors led into it. We can only take it as one of the hateful, despicable results of war and accept it. Anything else will grind us down into powder. We're not gods, Daddy: we can't take that kind of load upon ourselves."

Struck by the wisdom of her words, Welter could only gaze at her and reflect on what she'd said.

"You need to let it go," she followed up, aware that she was moving him. "You need to accept what happened and move on. For my sake as well as your own."

"I don't know if I can do that," he replied. "I don't think I've got it in me anymore. My hope is gone."

"There's always hope," she assured him. "You just need the strength to believe. And I'll be here to help you find that strength, no matter how long it takes. I'll never leave you."

Slowly she began to evaporate into a fine mist, one which passed into him. Feeling her love surround and fill him, he slowly stood up and looked at the impressions that her knees had made in the dirt. Drawing a deep breath, he let it out as Tselitel approached.

"Are you okay?" she inquired gently after a few seconds.

"It's time to leave, Doctor," he replied, still eyeing Amra's indentations. "We're finished here."

"Are you sure about that?" she asked, sensing a change in him. "There's no need to rush if you need more time."

"No, I've gained all I ever can here," he told her, feeling a warmth return to his bones that he'd thought was lost to him for good. "I've gained all I'll ever need here."

"Okay, if you're sure," she said reluctantly, once more taking his hand and beginning to concentrate.

"Yes," he responded quietly, looking around the dead space one last time. "I'm sure."

Soon the scene began to swirl away from him, and he found himself back inside *Kren-Balar* with Tselitel in front of him.

"That was…incredible," she said profoundly, drawing her hands back to herself and looking at him. "I've never experienced anything like that before."

"I'm sure you haven't," he replied thoughtfully.

"What did she say to you, Gustav?" she asked, burning

with curiosity.

"She told me what I needed to hear," he answered, looking at her with a calm steadiness that had hitherto been absent. She realized his gaze was no longer burdened, nor his face tight and ruthless. The drive for cruel vengeance had been resolved. The fire that had burned for retribution had been extinguished. His potency remained, as did his obvious lethality. But it wasn't compelled by a torturous sense of guilt.

Gustav Welter had emerged from his grief intact.

CHAPTER 6

"I never want to see another pyramid as long as I live," Bessemer uttered upon dropping into the egg. Laying his new sword aside, he lowered the canopy and popped off his helmet. "I don't know if Krancis has endless faith in my ability to survive, or if he's seriously trying to get me killed."

"Krancis isn't the sort of man to work from faith," Kayla replied. "He simply knows what a man is capable of, and puts him in the situation that requires his skills."

"Yeah, well, next time I hope he finds *someone else*," the captain responded, slouching in the pilot's seat with a sigh.

"Rest assured, Captain Bessemer, that this task required your peculiar talents," a crisp, rational voice said over the radio, causing him to instantly sit upright, his cheeks burning from the blood that rapidly filled them.

"Perhaps I should have mentioned that we were in communication with *Sentinel*," Kayla commented, no hint of apology in her voice as she grinned slightly at Bessemer. The captain, needless to say, found no amusement in her little prank.

"Krancis, when I said–."

"There's no need to retract anything that you've said," Krancis cut him off. "Your reaction is both understandable and utterly predictable, given your character. But you would do well to understand, when sent on an operation such as that you've just completed, that a great deal of thought has gone into it before you've even heard of it. No portion of this war is being orchestrated in a haphazard fashion. Of that you may be certain."

"Yes, of course," he agreed quickly. "I just meant–."

"Enough, Captain," Krancis interrupted again. "No apology is necessary, nor will it be accepted. Allow the past to rest where it is."

"Yes, sir."

"Now, you've finished clearing out the pyramids?"

"Yes, sir."

"And what did you find? What conclusions have you drawn?"

"First, that the people working here hadn't the least idea what they were really dealing with," he answered quickly, glancing at the sword that had somehow become a close companion to him, its intelligence palpable. "They approached their task as scientists, but they should have gone at it like they were mystics attempting to fathom the unknowable. I can't make sense of everything that I saw. But nothing impressed me more strongly than the sense that there's a lot of things in this universe that don't make any rational sense at all. I think that's why they were blindsided by what they'd discovered: it was outside their frame of reference."

"And what did they discover, in your opinion?"

"Well, sir, a kind of 'soul weapon,' if you will. This sword allowed me to cut through thirteen separate beasts that were spread across the four pyramids. At no point did the archaeologists reach, as it were, for the arcane. I just intuitively knew that I ought to, so I lifted the sword and went to town. But they just hid behind their guns. And when those failed, they were consumed."

"Then you believe something else is needed? Another approach?"

"With creatures like these? Yes, sir. The only reason I managed to kill *one* of those things with my pistol was because it hadn't been fully taken over yet. There was still a part of it that was human. The rest of its body was impervious."

"Your conclusion is entirely logical, Captain, though incorrect," Krancis replied rationally. "The reason they didn't reach for the weapon was that it had rejected them, and they unconsciously knew this. Given the information Kayla has relayed about the situation, it's quite clear that the sword, originally, gave rise to this infestation. The psychic energy, or *souls*, if you like, were stored within it because it served as the triggering device for the weapon that the *Cultookoy* used to separate themselves from their symbiont. Their energy, in fact, infests other things and places on the planet as well. But the sword has the highest concentration outside of the device that was used to actually do the deed. That energy is what poured into Doctors Filby and Grant, corrupting them over time and beginning the infection of the facility."

"You said it rejected them, sir," Bessemer pointed out. "But why did it accept me?"

"Because of a peculiarity of your nature," Krancis answered. "One that made you almost the only man who could be sent on this mission. Though only after you'd been prepared for this task by a number of other experiences."

"You mean…" his voice trailed, as he thought better than to prod further.

"These are things we cannot speak of, Captain," Krancis said.

"Yes, of course," he agreed. Looking out through the canopy, he saw yet another imperial vessel arriving. It had scarcely touched down before it began disgorging troops in spacesuits. Rapidly they separated into fours groups and spread out for the pyramids. "This facility is under lock and key, sir," Bessemer observed. "Where shall I go now?"

"You must begin the second part of your task," Krancis replied. "The necessary details have already been forwarded to Kayla. She'll fill you in along the way."

"Yes, sir."

"You've done excellent work thus far, Captain Bessemer," he concluded. "Maintain this standard of output, and there's no limit how high you'll reach."

"Thank you, sir."

With that the comms channel was closed off.

"You could have *told me* that he was on the line!" Bessemer exclaimed at once, looking incredulously at Kayla. "Have we come through all this just so you can play jokes?"

"I'm sorry, Captain," she apologized. "I just thought he should get a candid look at how you were doing."

"Do you know all the things I *could* have said but luckily didn't? I could have mouthed off about him for ten minutes! Then I'd be in real deep, wouldn't I? Nothing like chewing on the emperor's right hand man to advance your career! Shoot, he'd probably have had me exiled or something!"

"No, Krancis would never impair the imperial war effort merely for the sake of his personal feelings," she shook her head with certainty. "He's incapable of such pettiness."

"Well, he might learn, all the same," Bessemer shot back, though he didn't believe that. "Just where are we supposed to go next?"

"The other side of the planet."

"You mean where the big crater is?" he queried, reluctantly firing up the egg.

"Uh huh. That's where the device that destroyed the *Cultookoy* fired from. Krancis wants us to check it out. According to my instructions, the sword is only the first piece of the puzzle, the 'key,' as he called it."

"Then he wants the rest of it?"

"Apparently so."

"Why? So we can transcend, too?"

"I wasn't given that information, Captain, so I can only speculate. But given its dubious results, I should think something else was on his mind."

"Such as?" he asked, lifting the egg off the landing pad

and slowly flying past the northernmost pyramid.

"Well, considering the effect it had on, literally, this entire planet, I would guess he plans to use it as a weapon of some kind."

"There's a joyful thought," Bessemer remarked, looking out over the side of the craft at the sea of sand that undulated beneath him, blown about by the harsh winds that he could feel buffeting the egg. "I don't know if even *Sentinel* has this much power. At least on its own, given what they say about Hunt charging it and all."

"Presumably that's why Krancis wants this new weapon," Kayla responded. "Even the power to annihilate a single world would be a massive advantage in any conceivable war we may find ourselves engaged in. Regrettably, it wouldn't be of much use against the parasite, given we would have to level our own worlds to use it. But all the same, it'd be quite a tool to keep in readiness, especially when other races start looking to the Milky Way once the present war is over, wondering if they can carve pieces off the empire for themselves. This'll be an excellent deterrent."

"Assuredly," Bessemer replied, picking up speed as he settled in for a long cruise. "Just one thing I wonder," he added after a moment.

"Yes?"

"How did the sword get on *this* side of the planet if the weapon is on the *other side*?"

"Perhaps the lock it turned was wired in remotely?"

"I doubt that. The sword was loaded with enough psychic energy to mutate Filby and Grant, along with most of the others over time. It must have been pretty close. That reminds me," he continued, glancing at the device as it lay on the floor of the cockpit near his foot. "Exactly why am *I* unaffected by it?"

"Krancis thought you would wonder that," she said with a smile. "So he gave me a few more details when he passed along the instructions."

"Of course he did," Bessemer rolled his eyes, all but certain at this point that Krancis was omniscient. "And just what did he have to say?"

"Remember that part about the sword rejecting the others?"

"Yes?"

"Well, it accepted you. And that doesn't just mean that it didn't *hurt* you: it has seen in you a way to finally escape its bondage. Well, I shouldn't say *its* bondage, given that we're talking about a psychic host that has been held prisoner within it since time out of mind. The beings held inside it initially sought to dump out what was left of their symbiont by pouring it into Filby, Grant, and the others. But upon encountering you, they realized that you could help deliver them by activating the weapon a second time, completing their journey to transcend."

"Didn't work out too well for them the first time," Bessemer remarked.

"It's the only logical explanation for their behavior," she replied. "As Krancis said, there's something special about you, though he refuses to elaborate on just what that is. This specialness is apparent to the *Cultookoy* as well, and they've responded to it accordingly. Hence their willingness to assist you in cutting down the symbiont that they had released so shortly before: they are cooperating with us for their own ends. Given their predicament, there's only one end that can possibly hold any appeal for them: release."

"Very smart," he replied, nodding approvingly. "But they've got to be out of their minds with claustrophobia or something if they think that weapon is gonna do the ticket this time."

"Unless it will impact them differently now that they are no longer flesh and blood," she suggested. "Perhaps it can carry them into the realm of light given it has such a lighter load, if you will."

"Yeah, I guess that's possible," he allowed, his interest

in the question rapidly waning given their lack of hard facts to draw on. "Well, reckon we'll find out one way or another. Assuming there's anything left to find."

"Would Krancis send us if there *wasn't* anything to find?" she inquired in a teasing tone.

"Of course, how silly of me," he remarked. "Just one question."

"Yes?"

"Why hasn't anyone else come searching for this thing already? This bomb, or whatever it was, went off thousands of years ago. Somebody should have discovered it by now."

"They probably saw that the world was shattered and didn't think it warranted further examination. After all, what use could a few pyramids be to any race advanced enough to travel across the stars to find them? Would you go scouring through garbage for food if you had plenty to eat already at your fingertips?"

"Suppose not," he shrugged. "Still, seems awfully lucky."

With this the conversation ended, Captain Bessemer determined to rest a little before his next operation. As his journey elapsed, he could tell that he was drawing closer to the site of the device's detonation. The sand began to grow darker from having been scorched ages before. Finally, all at once, the ground beneath him dropped away, and an unthinkably large crater opened before him.

"Holy!" he exclaimed, unable to say more as his jaw dropped open and the enormity of the hole in the ground became clear. "I didn't think *anything* could make a dent like this!" he declared, looking all around the canopy at the sight. "It's like someone took a bite out of the planet itself!"

"Someone did," Kayla observed. "Though that was just a side-effect. It takes an incredible amount of energy to attempt to transmute physical beings into the realm of light."

"I'll say," he agreed, still gawking every which way. It wasn't until several minutes had passed that he finally calmed down and resumed his seat. "So just where are we going?"

"The logical place to start is the very base of the crater," Kayla replied. "That would be the closest point to where the device originally activated from. However, it's entirely possible, indeed, likely, that it was thrown some distance by the explosion. So we might have to look around for a while."

"And just what am I looking for?" he queried, guiding the craft towards the deepest portion of the crater. "What does this device look like? What's it made of?"

"I can't say. But I'm sure we'll know it the instant we lay eyes on it. Everything else on this side of Thierry is just scorched sand."

"Tell me about it," Bessemer remarked quietly, lowering the egg deeper and deeper into the crater. It made him feel awfully small to watch its sides swallow him up as the craft descended. "What's that up ahead?" he asked, squinting at some small hint of a structure. "Some kind of opening?"

Wordlessly Kayla used the canopy's magnification capability to expand what he was gazing at. Immediately it revealed itself to be a vertical tunnel of some kind, closed off by an enormously sturdy hatch.

"Hard to imagine how that managed to survive the blast," he commented. "Nothing else did."

"Guess it's because they buried it so deep," she replied. "The ground took most of the impact."

"Yeah, guess so," he agreed, slowing the egg as they neared. Setting it down on the ground beside the hatch, he put his helmet on and popped the canopy. Climbing down the side, he took a few reluctant steps towards the door and then stopped.

"What is it?" she queried over the radio.

"We haven't had a lot of luck with *Cultookoy* facilities so far," he explained. "Makes me wonder what else could be hiding in the shadows."

"Only one way to find out," she urged him, curious to see what was inside.

"Yes, I know that," he responded with annoyance, swinging his limbs slowly forward. Standing beside the hatch, he looked down at it and took a breath. "Any idea how to open it?" he queried, seeing no kind of handle or lever, just smooth metal of the same sort as the pyramids.

"I haven't a clue," she answered, as he began to pace around it, kicking sand away from the frame that held it. "Maybe there's a–," she paused, as he tripped and fell down. "Are you alright?"

"Yeah, I'm fine," he told her, pushing himself up and turning around. Brushing more of the sand away, he found a slot that his boot had caught on. "Check this out," he said, cleaning it out with his fingers. "It's some kind of opening."

"Or a keyhole," Kayla observed, causing him to stop and look at her.

"You know, you may be right," he replied, making for the egg and taking out the sword. Holding it over the slot, he could tell at once that the fit would be perfect. Laying it aside, he dug out as much of the sand as he could. "I need a tool, something I can pick around with down there. I can't reach all the way."

"They've got all sorts of tools back at the pyramids," Kayla suggested.

"Kayla, the pyramids are on the complete other side of the *planet*," he pointed out.

"Yes. But it's not as if there's a hardware store just around the corner. And we're traveling so light in this egg that there's nothing we can use as a substitute."

With a groan Bessemer pushed off the ground, lifted the sword, and got back inside his ship. Quickly he abandoned the crater, making the best speed he could towards his point of origin.

"Wish we'd known about this in advance," he

grumbled, the egg darting just above the blackened sand dunes. "You'd think Krancis would have told us what we needed."

"He's not a fortune teller, Captain."

"Oh? How can you tell? Seems he's got everything *else* dialed in, except the hard and boring parts. He leaves the working out of the plan to you."

"Well, it's good for your character, isn't it?"

"That's just code for anything that *sucks*," he shot back. "Why can't something be fun *and* good for your character?"

"Captain, you're just complaining now," she remarked.

"Kayla, we flew to the other side of the world just so we could turn around fifteen minutes later. I think I've earned the right to gripe a little."

"As you like it."

"I don't like it! That's the whole problem!"

"Well, I'm sorry, Captain. But there's nothing at all that *I* can do about it. And since you can't help it, either, why don't we just calm down and try to enjoy the ride?"

"What's there to enjoy?" he asked, looking over the side. "We're surrounded by endless miles of sand. Turf can't get much more boring than this. Unless you feel like getting out and making a sandcastle, that is."

"No, I'm good," she chuckled lightly.

When they'd finally reached the pyramids, Bessemer took everything he thought they might need and piled them into a trio of crates. Taking them out to the egg, he hefted them over the side and placed them where the orb, not so long before, had rested. Feeling a shiver run down his spine at the sight of the *Keesh'Forbandai* writing that the mysterious object had obscured before finally being jettisoned, he was glad to quickly cover it up and, along with it, the memory of his brush with an excruciating death. Carefully he fastened them down with cargo straps.

"Alright," he said, dropping into the pilot's seat and

looking at Kayla. "Is there *anything else* that we might be forgetting?"

"Toothbrush?" she quipped, causing Bessemer to give her a sour look and to slap the button which controlled the canopy. Before it was even closed he lifted the craft into the air and began retracing his flight plan to the crater. "Sheesh, sorry," she half-heartedly apologized. "Not trying to stir the beehive or anything."

"Kayla, sometimes a man gets enough," he explained. "And I've had *more* than enough. If you want to do me a favor, just keep quiet for a while and make sure we don't crash into anything. I could use a little rest."

"Whatever you say," she assented, her little pink hologram sitting down on the corner of the dashboard, her legs swinging over the side as he settled into his seat, crossed his arms over his chest, and let out a sigh.

"Kayla," he said, his eyes closed.

"Yes?"

"I'd have a lot easier time sleeping if you'd stop watching me."

"Oh, fine," she replied, standing up and turning around to watch the ground shoot past ahead of them.

Shortly after saying this, it struck her oddly that she should be annoyed at his behavior. Reflecting for a moment, she realized she was growing attached to him, and didn't like being forced to stop conversing. She knew that her mission as an AI was to assist those who had made her; and, by extension, those that they instructed her to serve. But this was a little more than just assistance. She was getting a bit possessive of both his time and of him personally. Making a mental note to keep such behavior from going to extremes, she quietly tucked the matter away in her mind and continued to watch the ground blur away.

"Captain," she said quietly, once they'd reached and subsequently descended into the crater. "We've made it."

"What?" he asked groggily, uncrossing his arms and

looking around. "Already?"

"Indeed," she confirmed, watching him with her hands clasped behind her back.

"Well, thanks for minding the store," he yawned, putting on his helmet and opening the canopy.

It took over an hour, and a succession of tools, but he finally managed to get the sand dug out of the keyhole. Laying his implements aside, he grasped the sword's handle and held it near the opening without inserting it.

"Captain? What are you waiting for?"

"Oh, I don't know, having my soul sucked out or something?" he shot back.

"I wouldn't worry about that. Everything on this side of the planet is dead."

"You could have said the same thing about the pyramids," he pointed out, glancing up at the crater's edge and again struck by how small he was in comparison. "Even Krancis said that the sword wasn't the only thing charged with the psychic energy of the weapon's victims. There's no telling what we're gonna find in there."

"We have a mission, Captain," she reminded him with subtle firmness. "Hesitating isn't going to help any."

"Honey, I don't know how it is with you AIs. But sometimes humans need to work up a little gumption before jumping into life-threatening danger. Now can you at least give me that?"

"If you insist."

"Thank you."

Drawing a breath, he held it for a moment and paced around the door, simply letting his eyes run over it to take it in. Exhaling, he gazed at the keyhole and then at the sword. It was then that he felt a little charge pass from the weapon into his hand, up his arm and into his brain. It felt warm, encouraging, like he was being beckoned onward. Aware that the host contained in the sword was using him for their own purposes, this didn't motivate him in the slightest to hasten.

In fact, it caused him to hesitate until Kayla felt she must speak.

"Captain, we have to–."

"Alright, alright," he cut her off, waving his hand irritatedly at the egg and positioning himself over the keyhole. Holding the sword's blade up before his face, he saw that it faintly glowed purple. Not wishing to be spurred by Kayla again, he pointed the weapon downward and inserted it in the slot. At once the door clicked and effortlessly opened on its own, as though it had been installed just days before. Under the hatch was a shaft and ladder that led down into darkness. "Couldn't have installed an elevator?" Bessemer grumbled, though his real concern lay with whatever might have been hiding down there after all that time.

"An elevator could have broken. Ladders last pretty much forever."

"Lucky me," he replied, getting down on his stomach and gazing down into the blackness. Activating his helmet's light enhancement, he could see that the ladder reached very far, the floor being many stories deep. Turning his head he listened momentarily, but couldn't hear any sign of life from below. Standing back up, he made for the egg.

"Where are you going?" Kayla asked, as he climbed aboard. "You've got to go down there. It's our mission."

"I'm fully aware of that," he replied, moving into the back of the craft and digging through the boxes. Finding some rope, he fastened the sword to his side and doubled back down the egg's ladder. "Try and have a little faith, Kayla."

"Sorry."

"*Not half so much as I am,*" Bessemer thought, looking down one more time before getting onto the ladder and beginning his descent. "If I don't make it back, tell Krancis he'll need to find another lackey."

"I'll keep that in mind, Captain," a precise voice uttered that nearly shocked him right off the ladder and down the shaft.

"Sir!" he exclaimed, all but dying of embarrassment as he froze on the ladder. "I–I–."

"Kayla informed me that you were about to enter the facility," he explained.

"That's why she wanted me to get down the shaft!" Bessemer reflected, wishing she'd just told him Krancis was on the horn again. "Sir–."

"It's likely that you will require assistance once you reach the bottom, which is why Kayla contacted me. Be aware, however, that I have very little time to spare. You must be quick."

"Of course, sir," he said energetically, clambering down the ladder with gusto until he remembered what might be awaiting him. Slowing down, he moved at a more moderate pace until he reached the bottom of the shaft and entered a large, empty room. Quietly placing his feet on the floor, he drew the sword and listened.

"What do you see?" Krancis queried, intuiting that he'd reached the bottom.

"Nothing, sir. Just a big, empty room. There's four corridors reaching in different directions." Briefly he glanced at the compass in the bottom-right corner of his helmet. "They run north, south, east and west, sir."

"Predictably," Krancis remarked. "Take the southern tunnel, Captain. That would have held the most significance for them."

"Yes, sir," Bessemer assented, though he couldn't fathom why the *Cultookoy* would value one direction over any other. The corridor, like the room, was bare, and made of the same material as the pyramids. Loudly his footsteps reverberated up and down the hallway, though he did his best to move quietly. It was as though the structure had been engineered to magnify every sound. Indeed, he couldn't escape the irrational feeling that he was in fact being listened to by the building, his steps artificially loudened to make doing so easier. "Krancis?" he asked quietly.

"I expect you're feeling very strange at this moment."

"Yes, sir."

"They're there, Captain, watching you from the walls. As the sword-bearer, you've piqued their curiosity."

"Are they dangerous?" he queried, nearing the end of the corridor and slowing to a crawl.

"Keep your wits about you," was all the man in black said in reply.

Pausing for a second, Bessemer swallowed hard and took the last few steps that separated him from the next room. Like the previous one it was empty, with four corridors reaching out to the world's four points.

"Why isn't there anything here?" he asked, looking nervously around and expecting to find one of the pyramid beasts standing right behind him. "Why's it all empty?"

Suddenly a loud clang from the room's east tunnel seized his attention. Holding the faintly glowing sword before him, he carefully approached its mouth and looked down its length. Seeing nothing, his heart tightened at the thought that perhaps some of the trapped souls had found a way to manifest themselves, and were just then hastening towards him.

"Investigate, Captain," Krancis ordered, hearing both the clang and Bessemer's subsequent pause.

"Yes, sir," he obeyed, moving into the tunnel, the sword firmly held in both hands. The corridor was only eight feet high by eight wide, affording very little room to maneuver if he should be attacked. It would, however, allow him to keep his enemy squarely before him, held at bay by his sword. *"Assuming the sword works on whatever's down here,"* he thought with dread, kicking himself for entering such a dangerous place.

Proceeding carefully, he neared the end of the corridor when another, much louder clang reverberated through the air. Freezing in place, he waited several seconds and then inched to the tunnel's edge. The room, apparently, was some sort of storage space, for it was filled from end to end with pieces of old equipment that had been piled almost up to the ceiling in places. From this distance he could hear something rummaging around just out of sight. Poking his head around the corner, he saw a great, inky black creature with spikes on its back pawing through the equipment with its massive claws. Hunching over to fit under the ten foot ceiling, its thin waist rose in a V shape to a pair of broad, terribly powerful shoulders. It was shaped, more or less, like a man. But one of unbelievable power.

"I am aware of your presence, human!" the creature shouted, its deep voice rumbling through the facility and causing Bessemer to all but jump out of his skin. "Do not think that you can enter my domain without my knowledge!"

"Speak, Captain," Krancis instructed him when he hesitated.

"Just what are you looking for?" Bessemer asked as cockily as he could, curious why the beast was still digging through the equipment, its back turned to him. "Got behind on your housekeeping?"

"Hrraaaaagh!" roared the monster, fighting mightily to turn itself around but somehow unable to. With even greater ferocity it tore into the equipment, not searching through it but merely savaging it. Each swipe of its claws sliced effortlessly through whatever they encountered.

"It is restrained," Krancis informed the captain. "Be on your guard. But rest assured, you're not alone."

"*I sure feel alone!*" Bessemer thought, cautiously moving closer so as to end the creature.

"If you continue to approach, I will tear your limbs from your body and beat you to death with them!" threatened the monster, jerking its head around to glare at him. Its skull was enormous, fully twice the size of a human's. Not heeding this warning, Bessemer slowly got within striking distance and raised his sword. It was then that the monster broke free of whatever was holding it back and took a mighty swipe at his midsection with its left hand. Jumping back, the captain just managed to keep from having his belly cut open. "I will kill you!" declared the creature, fighting desperately to free its other arm from its autonomous attack on the equipment. "Come closer and I will end your life in an instant!" it added, reaching the left as far as it could, its massive claws tearing at the air as Bessemer retreated a half dozen steps.

"I'll take a raincheck on that," Bessemer shot back, his rejoinder weakened by his tripping over a computer of some kind. Landing on his back, he heard the creature roar with fury as it found the strength to tear away from its restraints, swinging both hands like hammers to crush him. Bessemer only just rolled out of their path when they collided with the metal floor.

"Hrraaaaagh!" it shouted again, as its claws spread themselves wide and were pressed against the floor, giving the captain a few seconds to find his feet and back towards the entrance. "Their strength is weakening, human," it informed him menacingly, with great effort drawing its hands from the floor and clenching them at its sides. "They cannot help you much longer."

"And just who are *they?*" Bessemer retorted, trying to buy time to think of how to defeat the creature.

"The remnants of the *Cultookoy* are restraining it," Krancis told him calmly.

"That is correct," the beast nodded, somehow hearing the man in black. "I would have devoured you the instant you descended into my domain, had they not held me back."

"Remind me to thank them."

"You should not have come here, little one," the creature said, moving with greater ease with each passing second. "The *Cultookoy* have all but spent themselves in the time it took you to reach this chamber. A final great effort channeled my rage into this innocent rubble," it explained, nodding towards the surrounding equipment. Disdainfully it looked at his sword. "That trinket will not destroy me."

"It cut down plenty of your kind at the pyramids."

"They had but freshly emerged from their bonds, and as such were not yet fully hardened," it replied. "In them you found a mere challenge. In me you shall find *death*."

With this the creature roared and charged, sensing that the *Cultookoy* had weakened enough to be overcome by a sudden effort. It miscalculated, however, and the ancient remnant managed to restrain its right leg, causing it to fall headlong and drop just before Bessemer. In an instant he raised his sword and swung it downward to split its head in two. But the creature's powerful right arm reached up and blocked the blow. The weapon glowed bright purple as before, but failed to penetrate more than a pair of inches into its dark body. Ripping the sword from its arm, the captain was about to strike again when it backhanded him across the chest and sent him spiraling into a pile of garbage, the sword clattering to the floor several feet away.

"Pathetic creature," it taunted, rising as he struggled to do likewise. "That weapon is of no value to you."

Thrusting himself away from the equipment, Bessemer rolled across the floor and seized the sword, raising its point upward just as the creature swiped down at him with its left hand. The force of the blow was so great, and the beast's body so hard, that it forced the handle down against Bessemer's ribcage, all but snapping his bones as it passed unwillingly into the monster's palm. Sharply pulling its hand back, it lifted the captain upright as the sword reluctantly left the wound it had caused. Seizing its damaged hand with its right, it took a step back and roared its outrage.

"That shall be the last injury you inflict," it declared solemnly, as Bessemer moved back towards the tunnel, almost unable to breathe from the pain in his chest. "Before I was content to kill you quickly. But now it shall be slow and painful."

"As long as you don't…talk me to death first," he replied as strongly as he could, trying to anger the creature to keep it off balance.

"You miserable piece of filth!" it shouted, storming towards him and again raising its left to smack him. But as it did so, something powerful surged within Captain Bessemer. Watching the incoming blow, he swiped his weapon upward. Flaring a blinding purple, it cut the creature's hand clean off. Struck in the helmet by the detached hand, Bessemer was knocked off his feet yet again as the creature recoiled in disbelief, clutching its empty wrist.

"That is not possible!" it screamed, bewildered to find the sword capable of causing such damage. Enraged beyond further words, it strode up to Bessemer as he fought to get upright and kicked him squarely in the chest, tumbling him several feet backwards. Just barely holding onto the sword, he waved it in front of himself as the creature attempted to mash him with its foot, only just barely warding it off. Struggling to his feet, he retreated to the entrance, holding the sword in his right and bracing himself against the wall with his left. "There's no escape, human," the beast assured him, shaking its head. "You'll never make it back to the surface."

"Don't let him spook you," Krancis coached the captain. "He's trying to work upon your fears."

"I *am* your fears!" it declared, opening its mouth and roaring at him from behind a terrifying set of long, sharp teeth. "Once that little trinket is out of your hand, I shall consume you slowly, savoring each morsel of your flesh."

Bessemer felt a surge of fear in his stomach as he listened. Battered and bloodied, he wondered how much longer he could battle the beast before it got lucky and managed to seriously wound him. Indeed, he wasn't sure it hadn't already, given the blood that he tasted on his lips.

"Do you feel it, human? The fear filling you?" it asked,

moving slowly forwards as the captain stepped into the tunnel. Ducking yet further, it somehow fit itself within the confined space without leaving an opening for him to attack. It was then that he realized the creature, having spent so many years alone down there, knew it like the back of its now severed hand. It already knew it wouldn't be unduly restricted in the corridor.

"Stay strong, Captain," Kayla encouraged him. "You've already taken more out of it than it has you."

"Yes, Captain," the beast agreed sarcastically. "Stay strong. Continue the fight. Listen to your friends who didn't see fit to join you down here themselves, but preferred to watch from a safe distance as you struggled alone."

"Your attempts to psychologically manipulate Captain Bessemer are completely unfactual," Kayla inserted. "As an AI I'm incapable of joining him on his mission, and Krancis is countless lightyears away. There is no question of abandoning him to some terrible fate because of cowardice on our part. It is simply a physical impossibility for us to be present."

"And yet they *did* send you down here all alone, without any backup at all," the creature continued, following with an ease that told Bessemer it was useless to turn and run. "All alone to *die!*" it roared, snapping out its good hand and nearly slicing his knees in half with the long talon at the end of its index finger. "So close," it uttered. "Just one little mistake, and you're *mine!*"

It snapped out another surgical swipe of its lethal finger. But Bessemer managed to block the move with his sword, slicing its claw off as the weapon again gleamed purple. Jerking its hand back, it bellowed and beat against the sides of the tunnel in rage, giving the captain a chance to put a little distance between it and himself. The monster's passion made it heedless to danger, however, and lowering its head, it charged. Having reached the end of the corridor, Bessemer only barely dashed into the room and around the corner as his assailant stormed past. Screaming in rage, it turned around and faced him where he stood, his back against the wall. Charging again, Bessemer leapt out of the way as it crashed against the side of the room, sending a shock through the facility. It recovered instantly, however, and managed to seize his helmet as he tried to get away. With a flick of its arm Bessemer was torn from his footing and thrown into the middle of the room, nearly landing on his own sword.

"I've toyed with you until now," the creature said, slowly regaining control of itself as Bessemer stood up and raised his weapon. "I've given you a chance to defeat me, to present *some* kind of challenge. But like your predecessors, you have proven unworthy of my attention."

"Pay him no mind," Krancis said over the radio.

"Do you really imagine that you're the only individual to enter my domain?" it queried, slowly shifting from side-to-side, trying to find an opening in his defense. "Do you believe that the countless years that separate us from the calamity that destroyed this world haven't seen at least *one* other visitor to this place? Oh, there have been others. Many others. But none were worthy to defeat me. And each time I killed and consumed them, I returned the sword to the pyramid from which it had been taken, waiting for another to stumble upon it and seek his fortune in this crater. But they have all perished, as you are about to."

"Krancis?" Bessemer asked.

"Don't listen to him."

"Yes, yes, give me no heed," the creature mockingly nodded. "Listen to your friend who lacked the courage to join you. Heed *his* words, though he has never so much as laid eyes upon me. And listen to the little construct, too. She will not lead you astray."

As his confidence began to erode, Bessemer noted with dismay that the purple glow was fading from the sword. Suddenly aware that the creature was trying to break his connection to the weapon, he growled and shoved its words from his mind. At once the glow reasserted itself, and indeed grew brighter. To this the monster snarled and charged, determined to crush him underfoot. Dodging this move, the captain sliced into its side as it passed, making it howl in agony and clutch its wound. Giving it no time to recover, he hacked and slashed at it, driving it towards the wall. A badly-timed swipe from its good hand left it to the same fate as its sibling. In a last-ditch effort, it tried to kick the sword from Bessemer's hand. But a deft twist of the blade made it slice right through its foot, dropping it to its rear, its back against the wall.

"It seems I've fared a little better than my… predecessors," Bessemer gasped, holding the sword at the ready should his opponent so much as twitch. "Have any last words?"

"I do," Krancis interjected. "Where is the location of the device that devastated this world?"

"I'll never tell you any such thing!" roared the beast.

"Captain Bessemer is under my command," Krancis pointed out. "And I will order him to spare your life if you reveal its location."

"What!?" exploded Bessemer. "No way! I *deserve* to kill this thing!"

"My instructions will be followed to the letter, Captain," Krancis replied coolly. "Or there will be consequences."

"That is the dilemma of a warrior, human," the creature uttered. "Follow orders, or follow honor. You have earned the right to kill me. But what shall happen to you then?"

Breathing hard, Bessemer raised the sword to end the monster's life. But as it lay looking up at him, its dark eyes searching his face, he thought better of it. War was raging all throughout the galaxy, and it wasn't his right to jeopardize his role in that struggle just to satisfy himself.

"Where is the weapon?" he asked, still holding the sword in striking position.

"Have some respect for me, warrior," the beast answered. "Under no circumstances will I reveal the–."

Before it could finish Bessemer chopped off the rest of its damaged foot. Howling in pain, it tried to knock his legs out from under him with its good leg, but was too slow.

"I can keep this up all day," the captain asserted, moving away from its leg and putting his weapon's point right before its face. "Now, you can continue to beat around in here on your stumps, or I can cut you down piece by painful piece. Which'll it be?"

"You have no honor, you pitiful bit of flesh!" the creature roared. "The faint shadow of the *Cultookoy* that lives in you has no voice! Its nobility is hidden!"

"What are you talking about?" Bessemer asked, confused.

"Truly their brilliance is obscured by the rest of your ancestry," the monster snarled. "Hasn't it seemed peculiar to you that the sword should respond to *your* hand? That those imprisoned within it should find hope in *you*? They seek deliverance from you because you are *of them!* Though only distantly."

"You've lost your mind," Bessemer shot back. "Krancis, this thing is just babbling."

"No, it's quite correct."

"What?!"

"The same offer stands: your life for the location of the device," Krancis said to the beast. "We'll even assist you in leaving the facility. Once we've finished our research within the pyramids, we'll abandon this world and leave you sole lord and master of all that you can see and touch."

"Quite a bargain!" it retorted. "Die, or spend the rest of my maimed life wandering the desert alone. No, I'll meet my end now. I'll not assist the *Cultookoy* in redeeming the last of their mistakes."

"Proceed, Captain," was Krancis' reply.

Moments later he raised the sword and swung it hard, beheading the monster.

With the creature dead, Bessemer leaned against the wall and slid slowly down it, too tired and battered to stand any longer. Looking at his fallen foe, he felt neither pity nor satisfaction. The mission had been completed, or at least part of it. It struck him oddly that he should derive no other sensation from it. Somehow the victory seemed hollow to him.

"What was he talking about, Krancis?" he queried after nearly a minute of silence. "What's all this about the *Cultookoy?*"

"More than a few authorities have suspected something of a mix in our collective ancestry," the man in black explained. "By far the dullest of the families of man, the Earthborn nevertheless have occasional spikes of brilliance that seem to defy the notion that we're all descended from unintelligent prisoners. For the most part the *Cultookoy* remained on this world, their lives improved but also hampered by the symbiont which refused to depart its confines. However, when it was first discovered, a few of them refused to join with it and left Thierry forever. It's unknown what happened to these adventurers. But clearly at least one of them found their way into our bloodline. Else the psychic energy, or souls, trapped in the sword wouldn't have recognized you and cooperated."

"So that's what this has all been about," Bessemer realized. "Why you sent me on those first two missions: you were getting me ready for all this. That's what all that business with the 'Lord of Light' was about."

"I had a great many suspicions that could only be proven or disproven by exposing you to a number of different elements in short order," Krancis replied. "I could tell, as any psychic worth his salt could, that there was something special about you. But, more than that, that there was something *peculiar* about you, something that defied the odds. Whatever *Cultookoy* blood still flows in our veins must be so thin as to be essentially meaningless. Yet it found expression in you. It remained to draw it out by direct exposure. That's what the so-called Lord of Light did."

"I'll remember to send him a postcard," the captain said sourly, his mood sinking as he began to feel ever more like a pawn on Krancis' vast game board. "So what's next?" he queried glumly after half a minute of silence.

"Your mission remains what it was before entering the facility: to find the device that devastated this world so we can recover it. It's regrettable that the creature offered no help, but hardly surprising, given the resentment his kind feels towards the *Cultookoy*."

"Where do I start?"

"I believe I can offer some insight into that question," Kayla chimed in.

"Proceed," Krancis instructed.

"Well, ever since Captain Bessemer brought the sword aboard the egg, I've been carefully analyzing its energy emanations with the ship's sensors. They're strange, subtle, and difficult to detect. But I believe I've found a way to reliably locate objects that have been charged with the unique energy pattern of the *Cultookoy's* psychic blueprint. Naturally, the ship's sensors weren't *designed* for such a task, so–."

"So where do we go?" Bessemer cut her off, struggling to his feet as pain shot through his body.

"I was just getting to that. The signature, as I said, is difficult to detect. As such, it can easily be interfered with or distorted by both terrain and other emanations. We may be forced to fly around for a while before we can locate the device. Assuming it survived activation."

"It did," Krancis said. "Or the creature wouldn't have taken such pride in refusing to tell us where it was. He would have simply laughed in our faces for spending so much effort on a dead end."

"None of this answers my question," Bessemer pointed out wearily, stepping around the fallen monster and walking slowly back towards the entrance. "Where should I start?"

"Fly north," the man in black answered. "Given the significance that the *Cultookoy* placed on the south, it would be just like the symbiont to spite them by moving it northward."

"Why should that be important enough to matter?" Bessemer asked. "One direction is as good as another."

"Not to the *Cultookoy*," Krancis explained. "I haven't got the time to elaborate now. But you may rest assured that north is the best place to start."

"Alright."

"Once again you've done well, Captain. The imperial government is proud of your efforts."

"Thank you."

With this the comms link was broken again.

"Kayla, I'd strangle you if I could," Bessemer uttered when he finally reached the ladder and began to climb. "You had no right to put him on the line a second time without telling me. Don't pull a stunt like that again."

"You're right. I'm sorry."

He paused briefly in his ascent, not expecting such an easy victory.

"Good," he replied after a moment, continuing to climb. Looking up out of the shaft, he could see that the sun had set and darkness had descended. "Didn't think I was down here that long."

"Given that this world is little more than a burnt over desert, there's very little in the way of moisture or atmosphere to bounce light off of once the sun sets. Night falls quickly."

"Makes sense," he replied as he neared the top. Pulling himself up the last few rungs, he was glad to leave the facility behind him for good. Reinserting the sword into the lock, the hatch automatically closed. "I don't care if Krancis offers me half the empire: I'm *never* going back down there." Picking up his tools, he took them back to the egg, threw them in the crates in the back, and sat down in the pilot's seat. "Alright, Kayla: put up a waypoint that'll take me north."

"Already done," she replied, just as a blip appeared on his display. She waited a few moments until he'd powered up the craft and gotten airborne. Once they were comfortably cruising, she spoke again. "The empire isn't the only entity proud of your efforts today, Captain. It was an honor to behold such courage."

"It was nothing," he said with a wave of his exhausted hand, slumping back in his seat and popping off his helmet.

"No, no it most definitely was *not* nothing. You were a hero down there, Captain. A real champion."

"My back was against the wall, Kayla. What was I supposed to do? Let it eat me?"

"You could have panicked, lost your nerve," she pointed out. "A lot of things could have happened. But they didn't. It makes me regret my pranks with getting Krancis on the line. Truly, I'm sorry."

"Oh, that's alright," he responded, curious why she was making such a big deal out of it.

"From now on, I'll do my best to help and support you. It's what I should have done in the first place. It's what I'm *programmed* to do. But I guess I've gotten a little naughty over the years. A lot of time stands between now and my date of manufacture."

"Really, Kayla, it's alright," he insisted.

"I'd forgotten what nobility the Earthborn are capable of," she continued, seemingly not hearing what he said. "Often enough they disappoint you, and you learn to set your expectations accordingly. This is common among your own kind as well. But I should have known better, kept a broader perspective. I promise it won't happen again."

"Kayla, what is this?" Bessemer asked, though he was so tired he almost didn't want an answer. "Why are you digging into yourself? I told you it was alright. Sure, I snapped at you over those pranks. But you don't have to go on and on like this. Just take it easy."

"I have *one* task, Captain Bessemer," she explained, her little hologram appearing on the dashboard and crossing its arms. "And that is to serve whom I am ordered to serve. And the first part of that mission is maintaining the right attitude towards my mission. I allowed that to slide, and I'm ashamed of that fact. You have my word that I shall not fail like that again."

"Good," he nodded, hoping to satisfy her. "Excellent."

"I hope you believe me," she added, uncrossing her arms, the firmness of her expression softening.

"Absolutely," he assured her.

"Good," she replied, brightening a little. "Now, I've placed a waypoint on Thierry's north pole. But there's no reason to assume that the device is exactly on that spot. We may have to move around a little, especially if we begin to pick up interference."

"Fly around all you want," Bessemer said, raising his hands. "All *I* care about right now is getting some sleep. Do you think you can hold it steady enough for me to climb in the back? Or should I just strap myself in here and pass out?"

"I'll hold it steady," she replied, smiling. "Get all the rest you need."

"Sounds like a plan," he uttered, standing up and moving around the pilot's seat. Just then a jolt passed through the craft that caused him to smack his head against the canopy. "Kayla!" he exclaimed, rubbing his head. "What was *that* all about?"

"I–I don't know," she answered uncertainly, her little face scrunched up with concern as she rapidly scanned the ship's diagnostics. "It was like…a wave of energy, or something. Like it reached up from the planet and *struck* us."

"Do we need to be worried?" he asked flatly, his tone serious but steady.

"I don't…think so," she responded slowly, still leafing through the information that was available to her. "Scanners don't indicate any kind of activity on or in the ground beneath us. It's like it came out of nowhere."

"Well, it's not like we can take off because of a little turbulence," Bessemer said, stretching out as well as he could beside the boxes of equipment he'd brought along from the pyramids. "That's hardly an excuse that Krancis would accept."

"Indeed not."

"So just keep your eyes open and keep it level. Wake me if you need me."

"Okay."

Provided we don't crash before that, he thought with a roll of his eyes, shifting to his side and crossing his arms over his chest.

Moments later he was asleep.

However, it seemed to him but an instant before he was awake again.

"Captain! Captain, wake up!" Kayla pleaded, as the ship shook and twisted in the air. "I'm losing control! I think we're about to crash!"

Groggily Bessemer dragged himself upward and climbed into the pilot's seat in a haze. Fastening himself in, he'd only just put his hands on the controls when the egg collided with the top of a long, narrow dune. Barreling through it, the craft bounced off the ground, skipped upward like a stone, and then buried its nose in the side of an enormous hill of sand. Jerked against his harness, he thanked his lucky stars he'd had the presence of mind to strap himself in.

"What happened?" he asked.

"We just lost power," Kayla replied in a bewildered tone, shaking her little pink head. "It's like someone pulled the plug on us."

"Not altogether," Bessemer disagreed, popping off his harness and looking all around the canopy at the darkness that surrounded them. "This thing managed to stay in the air when it should have just crashed like a rock. I'd say we picked up some of that interference you were talking about."

"But I just meant interference in the scanners," she objected. "Not something strong enough to bring down a ship this advanced!"

"Yeah, well, we seem to be running into a lot of strange things today," he replied flatly, rubbing his face to try and shake what was left of his brain fog.

"You mean yesterday," she said somewhat meekly. "You've been out for quite a while."

"What, an entire *day*?" he asked incredulously, jerking away his hands and eyeing her little form. "I can't have been *that* tired!"

"It must have something to do with the interaction between you and the sword," she reasoned. "According to the ship's sensors, you were in a profound state of sleep almost from the moment your head touched the floor. You were recovering from something. My guess is that the psychic energy in the sword puts a drain on your mental resources by interacting with your psyche on many levels at once. Of course, that's only a theory."

"Of course," he acknowledged, leaning forward and resting his elbows on his knees. Rubbing his head, he thought for a moment. "So, we've been patrolling the north for a day now?"

"That's correct."

"And you haven't found anything?"

"We've gotten a lot of strange readings, several of which *could* be the device. But I thought it best not to wake you, given the strain you've been under. So I contented myself with building a list of possible sites to investigate once you'd awoken. As a matter of fact, we were heading towards another possible site when the ship began to malfunction."

"Portentous," the captain remarked, standing up and moving into the back of the ship.

"Indeed. It's like something is watching us and doesn't want us to pass up this site."

"That's an intriguing thought," he commented unappreciatively, her words adding to the low-level dread that already had his stomach churning.

"But I still can't get around how it managed to bring the egg down!" she said in consternation. "That simply shouldn't have been possible."

"Evidently it was," he shrugged, slipping the sword through the rope that was still slung around his middle and grabbing his helmet. "I take it the site we were headed towards is close?"

"Yeah, pretty close," she said, not really wishing to leave the prior topic behind because of her ruffled pride as a *Keesh'Forbandai* construct. "Approximately half a mile to the north-east. The dunes are pretty high, so take it easy and don't exhaust yourself. It'll be uphill both ways."

"Got it," he replied, putting on his helmet before pointing at the canopy. "I take it we still have power for this?"

"Pft, of *course*," she responded, raising her little pink hand and snapping her fingers. Confusion crossed her face when it failed to respond. Snapping a few more times, it began to open and then stopped, leaving him a narrow space to slip out. "I'm sorry. But I think that's all I can manage."

"It's good enough," he said, sticking an arm through before suddenly jerking it back as the canopy tried to close on it. "Kayla!" he barked.

"I'm sorry! I–I don't know what went wrong!" she apologized in a fluster, her hologram's eyes darting around the ship as she inwardly consulted what little data she had to work with. "The egg is going haywire. I don't understand. *This shouldn't be possible!*"

"Alright, calm down," he said, holding up a hand for her to pause and breathe. Seeing this, her eyes widened and she steadied a little. "Now, what can we do?"

"I can…attempt to open the canopy all the way," she answered slowly, taking her time. "That way you can just throw yourself out if it tries to close again. It'll be close. But you should have enough time to get out from under it. The sand is pretty high against the egg's side, so you won't have far to fall."

"Alright, give it a try," he instructed her, positioning himself near the edge of the craft and waiting. Several times the canopy tried to rise, just to close again. But then it shot open, and he hurled himself through just before it clamped down on him. *Don't know how I'm getting back in!* he reflected, standing up as well as he could on the steep side of the sandy hill, looking at the crashed egg with his helmet's night vision. "Give me a waypoint, Kayla. I don't know which way is which out here."

"Here you go," she said helpfully, the blip popping up at once on the other side of the hill's peak. "Be careful, Captain," she half-cautioned, half-pleaded. "I'm getting all kinds of strange readings. Some of them are moving."

"And you didn't tell me this before *why*?"

"Would it have stopped you?"

"Well, keep me posted on what you detect," he said in lieu of answering, sticking his hands into the soft sand and pawing his way upward. "Especially if it's coming towards *me*."

"I'll keep my eyes open for you," she agreed, a little hint of warmth entering her voice. Noticing this, Bessemer couldn't help grinning a little, even under the circumstances.

Reaching the top of the peak, he looked back down on the egg and wondered what could have possibly brought it down. Glancing all around for any sign of a culprit, all that met his eyes was the sight of miles and miles of sand. Shrugging, he began to descend the other side of the hill.

"Do you see anything?" Kayla radioed as he reached the bottom of the hill. "Any sign of life?"

"Not a thing," he replied, though the eerie sense that he was being watched had long since caused his neck hair to rise. "Keep fiddling with the ship, Kayla. If you can get it airborne, try and bring it a little closer. No telling how much of a hurry I might be in if I find this weapon. Might be guarded."

"Agreed. Honestly, I'd wager it *is* being guarded by something. Question is, what?"

Again rolling his eyes at her marvelous faculty for allaying fears, he lowered his head and trudged more forcibly through the blowing sand. A strong eastern wind pressed itself against his suit, adding a sense of physical liveliness to the otherwise barren landscape. It bolstered his feeling that something very much alive was prowling the dunes, waiting for him to walk into its trap. Pausing, he again glanced around and did his best to listen. But, to all appearances, he was alone.

It wasn't long before his pace began to slacken, the soft, shifting sand wearing him down with every step. Having not eaten for many hours, he regretted his somewhat hasty decision to leave the comfort and safety of the egg behind.

"Could've at least waited long enough to eat," he reflected.

Ascending another steep hill as he neared the waypoint, he was about to wearily slide down its reverse slope when he saw a narrow chasm yawning up at him. Twisting around as his feet started to slip, he dug his hands into the sand and managed to arrest his descent.

"Are you alright, Captain?" Kayla asked, hearing his sudden exertion.

"Yeah, I'm alright," he answered, looking at the opening and seeing it ran along the entire back side of the hill's base. "Almost fell into a chasm."

"Please be careful," she urged him.

Shifting a little where he rested momentarily, he established just where the waypoint was.

"Uh, Kayla, did you know that the waypoint was *under the surface?*"

"I suspected it. But having not had a chance to survey–."

"Yeah, alright," he cut her off, beginning to cautiously make his way down towards it. Halfway between the hill's peak and base he hit a steep patch of sand and slid a good twenty feet before grinding to a stop. Closing his eyes and taking a breath, Bessemer worked the rest of the way down. Only a narrow strip of four or five feet of more or less level ground separated the hill from the chasm that embraced it. Stepping onto this, he carefully approached the edge and looked down. "Kayla, I think we've got a little problem."

"How to get into the chasm?" she guessed.

"Yeah. The sides are too steep to climb down. Most likely I'd break my neck. Any ideas?" he queried, as he stood up and began to walk along it to try and find a place to descend.

"I'd suggest coming back for rope. But I'm sure there's nothing but sand to anchor it to."

"That's right," he said, having already considered that possibility. "Be a lot easier if the egg hadn't gone out on us. Flying down there would be a breeze."

Reaching the end of the chasm after several minutes of walking, he carefully crossed to the other side and began working his way back.

"I'm starting to think we're gonna have to bail on this one," Bessemer said, still carefully scanning the opening. "Looks like the only way down is to jump right in."

"And even if you didn't break every bone in your body, how would you get out again?"

"Yeah," he glumly agreed. "Well, I'll finish walking the chasm's length, anyhow. Might get lucky."

"Then what?"

"Get back in the egg and go back to sleep!" he replied. "As long as it'll let me inside."

The chasm, it turned out, stretched a very great distance in this direction. For nearly an hour he walked without finding the end of it.

"I gotta take a break," he said, dropping into the sand and looking up at the night sky. With so little atmosphere between him and the stars, they shone brilliantly. He couldn't recognize any patterns, being so far from his usual stomping grounds. But his imagination began at once to formulate new ones, finding here a horse, and there a sword.

"*Of course, a sword...*" he grumbled inwardly, looking down at the weapon which hung from his waist. "*Why do I get the feeling I've only scratched the surface of all the trouble you're gonna give me?*" he followed up, eyeing it a moment longer before returning his gaze to the heavens. It wasn't long before the gently flickering stars began to lull him to sleep.

"Captain?" Kayla asked, jolting him back to full alertness. "Are you okay?"

"Yep, yep, I'm fine," he answered hastily, standing up and shaking the fog from his head. "Just taking a little break."

"Oh, I see," she replied, aware that he'd been dozing. "I take it you haven't found anywhere remotely suitable to descend into the chasm?"

"Nothing whatsoever," he replied, resuming his slow walk as he peeked down into the opening. "If someone *did* mess with the egg to get our attention, it's a question how they ever expected us to–."

His words were cut off when the ground he was walking across broke away. With a shout he smacked against the chasm's ever-so-slightly sloping wall, tumbling sideways over and over again on his way down. He came to a sudden stop when he reached the bottom, all but snapping his right arm as it arrested his rolling.

"Oh!" he groaned in protest, pushing himself off his

stomach and getting to his knees. "Can anything *else* go wrong today?!" he growled in protest.

"Roland! Are you alright?"

"I think so," he answered, standing up shakily and brushing some of the dust from his spacesuit. "Nothing *seems* broken. Though it's hard to tell. Everything aches so much already." Looking up the wall he'd so rapidly descended, he cocked himself on one leg and scowled. "*Now* how in the world am I supposed to get back up *there* again?"

"I guess we'll have to call for backup," Kayla replied. "Radio the team over at the pyramids."

"And risk them getting shut down like we were? No, nothing doing. At least not until I've had a chance to poke around and see if there's another way out of here." Glancing further along the chasm, he could see for a couple hundred feet before it twisted and obscured his view. Looking back with some reluctance, he saw the waypoint Kayla had given him hours earlier and sighed. "Reckon I might as well check it out while I'm down here," he said, bending his steps in that direction.

"Are you sure? I think maybe you've had enough excitement for one day. Best course is probably just to find a way out of there."

"I'll be fine, Kayla," he assured her, though he wasn't as certain as he sounded. Wrapping his fingers around the sword's handle, he slowly drew it and held it at his side as he walked. "Something feels…different," he quietly informed her, his eyes darting all around the narrow way before him.

"Like how?"

"Like there's a presence here."

"Not another of those huge dark things," she responded with dread.

"Not like that," he shook his head. "But it feels like I'm being watched from everywhere at once. Honestly there's so many eyeballs on me I feel like I could build a staircase out of 'em and climb outta here. At least that's how it feels."

"A strange notion, to be sure," she said with some aversion, the idea of an eyeball staircase disturbing to her.

"Just telling it like it is," Bessemer uttered in an even quieter voice, feeling that he was audible despite the helmet.

The palpable sense of hundreds, if not thousands, of unseen observers continued as he neared the waypoint. Slowing almost to a crawl, he pressed his back against the chasm's wall as the path narrowed to just a few feet. Holding his sword out before him with his right, he drew a pistol with his left and cocked it. He was less than a hundred feet from the waypoint. But a sharp twist in the path obscured it from view. He would be nearly on top of it, and whoever might be protecting it, by the time he could actually see it.

"Kayla?" he queried in a whisper.

"Yes?"

"I've got a bad feeling about this," he told her, sensing that he was surrounded by countless dead beings, all of them watching him critically. "If I don't come out of this…Well, it's been a pleasure, even with the ups and downs. You've been a peach."

"Don't go in there," she insisted. "Just turn around and leave. It isn't worth it."

"This is the mission, Kayla," he said with finality. "I've got to go in."

Advancing boldly lest his already strained nerves should falter, he rounded the corner and briefly laid eyes on a four foot high black cube. It was then that a terrible jolt of psychic energy passed from the sword up into his arm. The instant it struck his head he passed out.

"Roland!? Roland!?" Kayla radioed the second she heard him exhale and fall to the ground. "Are you alright? Roland?"

But he could not answer. His mind was occupied elsewhere.

"It has been a long journey for you to come to us," a thin, regal voice spoke to the captain as he stood up in a dark, foggy dreamworld. Shaking the haze from his head, he looked around and found himself in the center of a tribunal. Above and all around him were seated beings that were clearly human, yet not Earthborn. Their faces long and thin, their bodies were bony and precise in their makeup, as though they'd been engineered to produce right angles. "You have struggled and stumbled and nearly fallen many times," one of the figures continued, a male seated at the center of a crescent-shaped table behind which all the others sat, at least two dozen in all. "Many times it seemed you would not succeed in finding us. At last we needed to make our presence known to you."

"By shooting down my ship?!" Bessemer demanded, the *Cultookoy's* superior attitude grating on him instantly. "You could have just sent me a signal! And what's the idea dragging me in here, anyhow? I've had enough of folks jerking me out of my head and into some fantasy space!"

"We're terribly interested in how you think you ought to be treated," a female *Cultookoy* replied with cutting sarcasm, seated several places to the first speaker's right. "With the fate of so many hanging in the balance, your petty desires are our first priority."

"We anticipated that it would be a long time before the adventurers returned home again," the first *Cultookoy* uttered. "But we thought your sense of duty would have brought you back eons before this. Have you the least conception of how long we've waited in limbo for you to return and finish our work?" He cast his eyes up and down Bessemer. "Of course, some allowance must be granted, I suppose. Clearly your ancestors have mingled with some of the lesser families of man."

"And just what's so much worse about the other families?" Bessemer snapped. "All you guys managed to do is kill yourselves! At least we're still out there hanging on, fighting the fight of the living!"

"Our fight ended when we learned how to separate

ourselves from the symbiont and transcend," he replied.

"Yeah, and how well did that work out for you?"

"Insolence is not counted a virtue among our people," the female warned him. "You ought to consider your words more carefully."

"Look, lady, I've had it up to *here* with you guys," he retorted, holding his hand up to his throat. "I can't tell you how many times I've nearly died since coming to this miserable rock. To say nothing of the missions that prepped me for coming here!"

"What missions?" the first speaker asked with annoyance. "What are you talking about?"

"Krancis! The whole reason I'm here!"

"We don't know of any Krancis," the female responded. "You know as well as we do that it was the guidestone that brought you back."

"Lady, I don't even know what that *is*," Bessemer said, crossing his arms.

"Each of the adventurers left with a guidestone that would bring them back to *Kollok*," the male explained. "It is only with such a stone that you could have found our homeworld once again. Why do you insist on prattling on about such nonsense? There is no other way to find this world."

"Believe me, pal, there's ways," Bessemer shot back. "I don't know anything about any guidestones. All I know is that I was ordered to come here by Krancis to find a weapon. I don't know if you've noticed or not, but we're being battered to death by an alien parasite."

"We do not concern ourselves with such matters," the female said with a wave of her hand. "We are on the cusp of transcendence. The journey must be completed."

"That sure seemed to work out for you last time," Bessemer said.

"The initial blast was insufficient to carry us all the way to paradise," the male explained. "It separated us from our bodies, but failed to complete the journey. With no such organic weight to slow us this time, we are certain to make it."

"Another blast and you'll probably crack this planet right in half," the captain said. "Of course, that would require someone to *fire it* wouldn't it?"

"That is precisely what *you're* going to do, Adventurer," the male said.

"If you think I'm gonna blow myself up so you guys can–."

"Your death is unnecessary," another male chimed in. "We have no wish to see you die. But you must assist us in activating the device a second time. Only one in which the blood of the *Cultookoy* flows can turn the key. And while it is impossibly thin, there are yet a few drops of it within your veins. All others have failed to return, or at least to bring the sword back to the device again. The symbiont has kept them separate for ages."

"Yeah, well, you don't have to worry about him any longer. I hacked him in pieces back at the crater."

"The symbiont is not merely one organism," the female pointed out. "It consists of many such creatures. They hide themselves all across *Kollok*. It's lucky that you didn't encounter one on your way here."

"You guys could have helped with that, you know," Bessemer said. "You didn't have to bring down my ship so far away."

"Oh, stop complaining of how you've been treated," the first *Cultookoy* upbraided him. "We have been held in this state for countless years, while you've been forced to walk a short distance in the sand. The one has no comparison with the other."

"I'm still not blowing up Thierry for you guys," Bessemer shook his head. "I'd need orders from Krancis before doing that."

"And how shall you get such orders if we don't

allow you to leave?" queried the female menacingly. "This is neither a request nor a negotiation: it is simply a *fact*. You *will* help us complete our journey, or we'll keep your psyche within this space until your body withers and dies from neglect!"

"And I'm not gonna budge unless Krancis gives me the okay," Bessemer countered, though her threat made his stomach tighten into a ball of wire.

"Perhaps a compromise is possible," the second male began, waiting for all eyes to train themselves upon him before continuing. "You are well within our power where your body currently lies. Hence there would be no danger in permitting your mind to once again animate your flesh long enough to contact this Krancis. If he gives his permission, then both parties can proceed amicably."

"And if he doesn't?" the female demanded. "What if he's as obstinate as *him*?" she added, stabbing a long, thin finger towards the captain.

"Then we shall be forced to take drastic measures," he answered, his narrow head turning to Bessemer, his eyes tightening.

"*The things I do for you, Krancis!*" Bessemer reflected, as the tribunal fell to arguing with one another over the proposal.

"Enough!" shouted the first speaker, slamming his bony hand down upon the table. "The proposal is a sound one, hence we shall proceed with it." Leaning over the table, he fixed Bessemer with an icy glare. "We shall be watching you at all times, Adventurer. Don't attempt to escape, or we shall draw your mind back in here at once."

Without further comment Bessemer was thrown from the strange space back into his body.

"Roland?! Roland!?" Kayla pleaded. "*Please* respond!"

"I'm here," he said, his voice oddly thick as though he'd been asleep for hours.

"Thank God!" she exclaimed. "Are you alright? What

happened?"

"The *Cultookoy* took me," he explained, sitting up and eyeing the dark cube for a few seconds before turning away. "Sucked my mind right out of my body, or something. They want me to activate the device and finish their so-called journey for them. Can you believe it? Want me to blow up what's left of this rock and vaporize them in the process!? Wasn't one suicide enough?"

"What are you going to do?" Kayla queried.

"I've got to get on the horn with Krancis and see what he says," Bessemer shrugged. "There's nothing else I can do. Can you link us up?"

"Sure, if he's available."

"He'd better be. I don't think these guys have a whole lot of patience left after how long they've been waiting."

"I'll signal that it's a priority message," she assured him. "Meanwhile…why don't you put a little distance between yourself and that thing?"

"Can't. Said they'd suck me back in if I tried to get away. I've got to just sit here and wait for the big man to answer the call."

"It could be hours if he isn't available."

"Well, cross your fingers then," he replied, laying down in the sand and knitting his gloved fingers behind his head. "Any progress with the ship?"

"None. They must still be interfering with it."

"Yeah, that or they broke it."

"I'm trying my best to think positive," Kayla replied. "I wouldn't have thought–. Wait, Krancis just got on the line."

Hearing this, Bessemer sat upright with a jolt as though he'd just rounded the corner of the chasm.

"What is your status, Captain?"

"Sir, I've located the device. But the *Cultookoy* are alive and well, sir, and they want me to activate it and help them complete their journey."

"What was your answer?"

"That I had to clear it with you, sir."

"They expect us to simply activate their weapon without any kind of reward for our services?"

"That's correct, sir."

"The *Cultookoy* had a reputation among the ancients for entitlement. Evidently that characteristic hasn't mellowed since they annihilated themselves."

"I agree completely, sir," Bessemer said emphatically, thinking back on the conduct of the tribunal.

"We are on Thierry entirely for our own purposes, Captain, and not so we can help them overcome the speedbumps in their journey to the light realm. As such, we must get something in return. The teams at the pyramids are nearly finished emptying them of artifacts. Once they're done, I have no objection to activating the weapon a second time so long as we are in possession of the device afterwards. However, it must remain functional. They mustn't sabotage it on their way out the door."

"I'm not sure how we can guarantee that, sir," Bessemer responded. "They won't have anything to lose once I've fired it again."

"Along with entitlement, the *Cultookoy* also had a reputation for honor. I'm quite certain that they'll stick to any bargain they make. The problem, Captain, will be getting them to sign on in the first place. I'm sure they've already proven difficult even in the short time you've known them."

"Very much so, sir."

"In that case, threaten them with *Sentinel* if you must. Say that we'll unleash its great cannon upon their device and turn their hope to ash if they force us to. Don't badger them needlessly. But *don't* take no for an answer. You have unlimited discretion in this matter, Captain: use it wisely."

"Yes, sir."

"Call me again when your task is complete."

Here the call ended.

"How are you going to threaten them with a ship they

haven't even seen?" Kayla asked.

"They might not have seen it," he answered, standing up and turning towards the cube. "But *I* have. They can dig through my brain and see what I'm talking about at once. And they'll know I'm not lying, either."

"Of course. Why didn't I think of that?"

"Don't sweat it," he replied, walking slowly towards the device and holding up his hands to signal its prisoners. "Back in a flash."

With this he again lost consciousness and dropped into the sand.

"And what did your Krancis say?" the female demanded impatiently, her long, thin fingers drumming upon the table before her. "Has he given his permission? Or must you beg him?"

"Krancis is willing to cooperate with you, provided our own needs are met," Bessemer replied a touch grandly, smiling to himself as he prepared to deliver the man in black's terms. "First, we must have more time to finish extracting artifacts from the pyramids that survived the original blast. Second, the device must remain in working condition after you've completed your journey."

"Out of the question," the first male declared at once. "The achievements of the *Cultookoy* will not be handed off to a lesser people in order that they may batter their neighbors with the fruits of our genius. You will be permitted to help us make this great final step in our life as a race, and then you may be on your way."

"Nothing doing," the captain shook his head, crossing his arms. "We need this device for a war of *survival*, not self-aggrandizement."

"And what happens once this war of yours is over?" the second male queried. "Will you lay the device aside? Or will you use it to cudgel helpless races into submission?"

"No military power would willingly lay aside a weapon of such power," Bessemer replied. "It would be against common sense to do so."

"Then you admit that it would be used in perpetuity?"

"Yes, but not for low purposes. We don't operate that way."

"A strong guarantee, indeed," the female said scornfully.

"We already have a weapon of immense power in our arsenal," the captain announced. "Go ahead and dig through my thoughts until you come across a ship named *Sentinel*. If we wanted to 'batter our neighbors,' as you said, that would do the job just as well as anything could. It might take a little longer that way, having one superweapon instead of two. But it's hard to doubt the result of any conflict we chose to engage in."

Scowling at his temerity, the tribunal reluctantly withdrew their attention, their eyes glazing over as they prowled through his mind. Half a minute was all it took for several of them to jolt in their chairs. There then followed an energetic argument in *Cultookoy* which he couldn't follow, unable to guess who was for and who was against acceding to Krancis' terms. There was a clear majority for *one* side of the debate, that much he could make out. He just hoped that it was favorable to the human cause.

"*Krellek!*" roared the first male, silencing the rest after a quarter hour of squabbling. "A decision has been made."

"*You* have made a decision," the female shot back, her eyes narrowed as though she gazed upon a traitor to everything the *Cultookoy* held dear as a race. "The council is strongly against helping these people aggrandize themselves further. One superweapon is quite enough."

"And then what?" demanded a third male. "Wait countless ages in the hope that whatever watery drops of *Cultookoy* blood that still remain shall find their way to *Kollok* to complete our journey and set us free? It is a miracle that this man should have come to us at all; a miracle that has clearly been orchestrated by a number of forces, given the peculiarities of his psyche. Had not this 'Krancis' wished it, he wouldn't even *be* here! No, there can be no doubt as to our course: this is our last chance to break free of the confines of this device and pass into paradise. Should we give this opportunity away out of a surfeit of good intentions, we'll be trapped in here forever."

"Better to be trapped than that our last act on this plane should be one so shameful as to enable these… parasites to rise and dominate both this galaxy and those that border it!" the female declared. Glaringly she turned to Bessemer. "You see, Captain Roland Bessemer, we have learned a great deal more from our brief perusal of your thoughts. We have seen the ruthlessness of this Krancis; the lengths that he would go in his zeal for your people. There can be no question whatever that he would annihilate entire races with our device, should it seem prudent to him to do so. And, given your recent experiences with both the *Pho'Sath* and the creature known as the Devourer, you would have some justification in preemptively leveling your neighbors. But that shred of justification would do nothing to ease our consciences in eternity, from whence we would be forced to watch as your kind toppled one people after another, all in the name of self-preservation."

"Races have always dominated other races!" roared the third male. "To condemn ourselves to this device forever so that we can forestall a single instance of this is lunacy!"

"It would not be a *single instance*: it would be a string of terror and oppression!" the female argued.

"All races that rise eventually fall," the male retorted. "They have their moment in the sun and then vanish forever. When seen from the grand scheme, they are merely a blip, a single moment in time of no significance whatsoever. They are as a solitary instance."

"An argument that will bring endless comfort to the billions who shall have to suffer the cruelty of Krancis and those who succeed him," she rejoined. "I'm quite sure that the long years of despair to which they will be subject won't appear to them as a single instance in time. Granted, many will be annihilated instantly. But the *rest* will be consigned to the worst slavery imaginable, held down by the threat of sudden death should they so much as utter an unintentional groan of protest as their overlords' whips fall across their backs!"

"The opinion of the council is noted," the first male said calmly. "But its will is not absolute in dire cases. The ultimate decision has always been left to the chairman alone."

"Dire cases such as annihilation," the female replied. "Many times our world has been threatened by invasion, and in those times we've grouped together under the singular leadership of the chairman. But this is no such case. We are not faced with disaster."

"Remaining prisoners for all of time within a device of our own making is most definitely a disaster," a second female chimed in, her seat near Bessemer and on the right side of the crescent-shaped table. "For ages we'd been an example of disinterest and goodwill in this galaxy, content to mind our own affairs while leaving others to their own. Then, for a time, we have sojourned in this device. But that time of sojourn has come to a close. The light realm has given us a final chance to join with it by guiding this man to our world, delivering him from the myriad threats that he faced. Can we doubt the certainty of that? Where all others have failed, this man alone has succeeded against terrible odds. Our kin trapped within the key knew this, and we may know it as well, so long as we aren't blinded by our own predilections. Are we wiser than the realm of light?"

"There is no reason to assume that the realm of light has had the least hand in this affair," the first female uttered condescendingly. "With the notable exception, more or less, of this man, his people are allied to the realm of darkness. This Krancis is so bound to it that he could be a *manifestation* of it. Their entire race reeks of its vices and excesses. No, the notion that anything *good* could have been involved in his coming here is pure fantasy. The dark realm has chosen them as the exponent of its will, and it has been guiding them according to its murky purposes."

"But could the light realm not turn around the ill intent of others for its own good purposes?" the second female countered calmly. "Even assuming that there *is* evil mixed up in this, an idea which I do not support, why should it be beyond the power of the light to confound it?"

"Do not question my faith in our patron," the first female warned. "I'm fully aware of both its power and its wisdom."

"And yet you seem to doubt its reach," the second smiled faintly. "In your assessment, the light flees from the dark whenever the latter sets its will upon an object. Our patron, evidently, must await the scraps that are cast off by its opposite."

Ragefully the first female slammed her clenched fists on the table. Bessemer could see she was about to rise and engage in some kind of spiritual combat with her antagonist. But the pair seated on either side of her reached up and seized her arms, anchoring her in place.

"We ought not to squabble before such a petty creature," the chairman remarked casually, nodding towards the captain. "And indeed we need not. The decision, as I have said, is made. I have merely permitted this discussion to proceed in the hope that a more general agreement could be reached. But there is no doubt as to the course that we shall ultimately pursue."

"You overreach both your prerogatives and your power, Chairman," the first female declared. "Moreover, you know as well as I do that it would require only one of us to sabotage the device during our ascension, making our universal agreement mandatory. You can make noises and pretend to have the council locked down. But the fact is a majority stands against you."

"The fact is," Bessemer began, cocking himself on one leg and trying to sound as unshakably confident as he could manage given his surroundings, "that there's another factor you've left out of your argument."

"That being?" the chairman queried, just barely keeping the scorn out of his voice.

"That Krancis is perfectly willing to use *Sentinel* to annihilate this little cube of yours if you don't go along with us."

A profound silence followed this statement. Bessemer couldn't tell if they were stunned, or simply outraged beyond words. It was a desperate gamble, he knew, given the fear many of them held that the empire would use their device for ill. But with each passing moment he saw opposition to the chairman hardening in the faces of his opponents and sensed that something drastic was necessary.

"Yes, we're desperate," Bessemer continued. "Our backs are against the wall, and there's no telling what else is coming down the pike. And you're exactly right: Krancis will do whatever it takes to keep us safe. But setting ourselves up as the overlords of all we see isn't in the cards. We're not built like that. Besides, as you've pointed out already, I'm just about the only person left in this universe who can actually fire this thing, and I wouldn't do that without a good reason, let me tell you."

"Krancis could force you to," the first female said. "He could threaten to kill you if you didn't comply."

"And let's say he did," Bessemer allowed. "I'm not gonna live forever, you know. Sooner or later I'd bite the dust, and Krancis would be without his key. The device would be useless then. And there's another thing you've got to remember: the empire has been *gutted* by this war. We're not gonna be in any kind of position to dominate *anyone* for years. How many generations will it take to repopulate our worlds? It'll be all we can do just to keep breathing, what with all the other races that'll be looking to carve pieces off the empire for themselves. It'll be a desperate struggle just to hold onto what we've got. By the time we'd be in any kind of shape to prey on anyone else, I'll be nothing more than a handful of sentences in a history book. Assuming I even rate that, considering all the other mighty deeds that are being wrought by others."

"The argument, it must be admitted, is a sensible one," the second female opined, glancing at the first female and then sweeping her eyes across the various opponents of the chairman's. "The device has a time limit after which it can no longer be used. And considering the state of their empire, there is very little question of their using it aggressively during his lifetime."

"Assuming that Krancis doesn't find another minion with a few drops of our blood in his veins," the first female shot back. "He's already proven resourceful beyond what could be imagined for his kind. It's obvious that the dark realm is working powerfully through him to achieve its ends. Don't you think it could locate another individual to fire the weapon and thus expand the domain of its chosen people?"

"It is, of course, a question of odds as opposed to certainties," the chairman remarked. "We could never be absolutely certain as to the fate of the device after it leaves our care. But there is precious little that one can ever be *absolutely* certain of on this plane of existence. The best we can do is to establish whether or not it will likely be abused. The captain has made a compelling argument that it will not. Indeed, if it were possible to easily find another man to activate it, why has it taken so long for the empire to send Bessemer to us? Evidently what remains of our blood is in preciously short supply."

"Probability rests with the device being used defensively a handful of times before time or chance befalls Captain Bessemer and silences it forever," the second female said. "Our time in this galaxy has come to an end. Let us leave the device with the faint remnant of our kind that still exists. There can be no doubt that they are in a desperate strait, surrounded on all sides by foes. Let it be our legacy that we passed the most potent expression of our genius onto them at a time when they could only use it for good."

With a scowl on her face the first female looked at Bessemer.

"We shall talk further of this. Leave us."

With a flick of her wrist he was thrown from their strange council chamber and returned to himself.

"Oh!" Bessemer groaned, pushing himself off the ground and reflexively trying to rub his head through his helmet.

"Are you okay?" Kayla queried solicitously. "Have they agreed to our terms?"

"I've got a massive headache," the captain answered, standing up unsteadily and moving a short distance from the cube. Leaning on the wall of the chasm, he looked up and saw the sun blazing overhead. "I've been out for quite a while."

"I was starting to wonder if they'd ever give you back to us," Kayla said. "I was afraid they were going to keep you as a prisoner or something."

"No, nothing like that," he shook his head, instantly regretting the motion. "But it's been a hard sell. Most of 'em were against working with us until I told them what Krancis said about using *Sentinel* on the cube."

"How'd they take that?"

"Well, it got 'em to shut up, so that was something," Bessemer shrugged, still unsure just how the news had been received. "After that I had the floor for a little while and made the best use of it that I could. Argued that I was pretty much the only one who could use the weapon, so the risk wasn't all that big that we'd misuse it. Not that I think we would, anyhow. But most of them seemed to prefer being stuck in that thing forever to our getting our hands on it."

"I should have thought they'd be eager to escape that thing on almost any terms we chose to offer," the AI responded. "Wouldn't you?"

"Well, it seems our attachment to the dark realm is a sticking point for some of them. There's one chick in there who seems to think we're little more than bacteria because of that. Actually called us parasites, too! Guess she looked at *Sentinel* and then their cube and figured us for scavengers that go around snapping up better tech than we can make ourselves. Suppose we are, at least compared to them."

"The Earthborn have never come close to the genius of the *Cultookoy*," Kayla confirmed. "I wonder if any of the families of man in this galaxy ever did."

"I wouldn't know," Bessemer replied, finding his headache growing steadily worse. Turning so as to lean his back squarely against the wall, he allowed his head to sag and closed his eyes. "Any word from the folks at the pyramids? Are they finished?"

"The last transport took off less than half an hour ago," she informed him. "Krancis sent word to them to hustle, and they did. We're free and clear to activate the device if the *Cultookoy* can just sign off on it."

"That's what they're figuring out now," he said, looking at the cube for a moment before lowering his head again. "Kicked me out without so much as a by-your-leave so they could have a little family chat. I could tell what I'd said made an impression. I just hope it's enough to change their minds."

"Yes, me too."

Feeling dizzy, Bessemer settled down on the ground and leaned his back against the wall. The sun overhead meant nothing in his spacesuit, of course. Yet he couldn't help the feeling that its rays were beating down on him especially harshly. Glancing up at it he squinted a little, wondering why he felt that way when it made no sense. Finding himself growing hot, he moved to the other side of the chasm where a little outcropping above lent him some shade. He felt silly when it provided no relief.

"Are you alright?" Kayla asked, noticing his discomfort.

"You're gonna wear that question out," he answered, shifting a little where he sat to try and ease a peculiar sense of restlessness which was growing within him.

"You seem ill at ease."

"It must be all the spelunking inside that thing," he replied, throwing a hand towards the cube but not daring to look at it as dread began to fill his stomach. "It seems awfully *hot*," he added, pulling at his suit as he started to sweat.

"Maybe they did something to you," she offered.

"Yeah, that's what I'm afraid of," he responded with irritation, his fears doubling now that she'd put them to words.

"Can't imagine why they would," the AI said thoughtfully. "You're their only real hope at getting out of that thing."

"Well, most of them were against it from the get-go," he replied. "Maybe they've been doing something to me all the while. Shoot, that's probably why we've been arguing so much: just dragging it out so they could kill me off slowly and quietly."

Before he could add to this line of thought, he was again drawn into the cube.

"We have reached a decision," the chairman announced, paying no attention to the captain's obvious distress. "Collectively, we've agreed to the terms given by Krancis. You shall activate the device, helping us to complete our journey. And we shall permit it to remain undamaged after our passing. It shall thereafter be in your hands."

"All of you agree on this?" Bessemer asked with some difficulty, still sweating despite his body being only a psychic representation. Looking at the first female, he searched her face. "I must have a verbal guarantee from each and every one of you. I was told that the *Cultookoy* were people of their word, and hence I expect the assurance that the weapon will remain functional."

"You have the assurance of the council," she snapped, scowling at him venomously. "Do not push your claims too far, Captain. It is the greatest of indulgences that we even allow you to–."

"There's no indulgence going on for either party," Bessemer cut her off, his temper rising alongside his temperature. "We're making this deal because both our backs are against the wall. Given you're about to leave this galaxy forever, I don't think it's too much to ask for a verbal guarantee."

"We *Cultookoy* do not give our word lightly," she retorted. "And though we have no intention of damaging the device, it is with gravity that we would extend such a guarantee to anyone. To speak such solemn words to one as petty as you, Captain Bessemer, is not to our pleasure."

"I'm not turning the key until I've got your promise," he declared, spreading his feet a little and crossing his arms. "I'll not risk coming all this way just so you can break it."

"Captain, you're treading on thin ice," a heretofore silent *Cultookoy* male inserted. "The council has already voted to go along with your plan. Don't insult us by believing we would violate the intention of that vote by an act of sabotage."

"It's a small thing that he asks," the second female argued. "It is, as he said, the last act we shall ever perform on this plane of existence. Let us not be too proud to grant such a simple request."

"His request is an *insult*," the first female rejoined. "Yet another expression of the small-mindedness of his race."

"You forget that he carries a shadow of our own race in his blood," the chairman said quietly. "For that alone he deserves some small amount of regard."

"You yourself called him petty not so long ago," the

first female snapped. "A petty creature, you said."

"And that's true," the chairman nodded. "But even petty creatures are entitled to a modicum of respect when they are descended from greatness, no matter how remotely." The chairman looked from the female to Bessemer. "Captain Bessemer, I give you my solemn word that I shall not damage this device in any way, and that it will remain fully operational once you activate it for us." Having said this, he looked to the *Cultookoy* to his right, who quickly uttered the same pledge.

One by one each member of the tribunal spoke the necessary words until finally only the first female was left.

"Well?" the chairman prodded as he sat with casual ease in his chair, assured of his object.

Glaring her hatred at the chairman, she turned to Bessemer, who at this point found it difficult to stand still for the discomfort he felt.

"Captain Roland Bessemer," she began acidly. "I give you my solemn word that I shall not damage this device in any way, and that it will remain fully operational once you activate it for us."

"There," the chairman said with finality, standing up and revealing himself to be much taller than Bessemer had expected. "This, the final meeting of the Council of the *Cultookoy* is adjourned." He looked at the second female. "You will remain with the captain and answer any questions he may have about activating the device while the rest of us prepare for the journey ahead."

With this they all rose and dissipated, save for the second female. The table evaporated right afterwards, permitting her to approach. To his surprise she was fully seven feet tall, willowy and graceful in her movements.

"I must apologize for my colleague," she uttered once she was by his side. "She has a great hatred for the dark realm and all its adherents."

"I gathered that," he replied wearily, sweating

profusely and growing ever more dizzy. "Look, I don't mean to be rude. But I feel awful. Can we continue this another time?"

"It's her venomous dislike of you that has made you feel this way. Her psyche, and those who think like her, is poisoning yours. But the effect will soon pass now that they have left this space. Be patient, and you shall feel normal again."

"But why did I feel this way *outside* the cube?" he queried, uncertain that she was correct.

"That was merely the accumulated effect of having been in our presence earlier," she assured him. "You may take my word, Captain Bessemer: you will rapidly make a full recovery."

"Well, when you put it that way…" he nodded gingerly.

"Now, what can I help you with? What questions do you have?"

"First, how am I gonna fire this thing without being annihilated by it?"

"There is a delay on the device that will give you sufficient time to reach your ship and escape the blast radius. It's lucky that your craft is of such exquisite manufacture, or you would likely be unable to avoid being destroyed."

"Wait, wouldn't I just get trapped in that thing like you were?" he asked. "Or would I transcend to the light realm?"

"The device is programmed to identify and extract the psychic energy of the *Cultookoy* alone. And while it is true that you have enough of our blood to activate our technology, nevertheless your psychological blueprint isn't such that you would be extracted. Instead you would merely be caught in the devastating shockwave that attends its activation and, like our own bodies were, you would be destroyed."

"I see," he nodded, beginning to feel a little better as she'd promised he would. "I want to thank you for the help you gave me in winning over the council."

"Oh, I want to reach paradise as much as any of them do," she smiled. "I just don't have the same aversion to the dark realm that many have. I don't see it as an enemy to the light, but rather an opposite."

"A complementary opposite?" he asked.

"I wouldn't go that far," she smiled again, revealing the limits of her generosity. "But I do believe that each element plays a vital role in this universe, for better or worse. And in any event, both are much too entrenched in the various races that populate this plane of existence for either to be uprooted without cataclysmic results. That's why the wishes of the *Pho'Sath* are so outrageous: they would destroy every last adherent to the realm of darkness if they had it in their power to do so. Who can say: they're still a young race, all things considered. They may eventually find a way to do so."

"Not if we can help it," Bessemer replied.

"That is indeed my hope," she said, dropping her voice a little and hunching confidentially. "You bear a great torch, Roland Bessemer. All of your kind does. It is no mistake that so many forces are converging upon you at this time. You must be strong; you must have courage; you must *fight*. Else there's no telling what kind of evil will descend upon this dimension." Her eyes left his for a moment and stared into space, as though visualizing some horror. Then they returned to his.

"There's something you're not telling me," he shook his head slowly, searching her face. "Something you dread."

"There are many things that I dread," she responded. "Many things that I fear may come to pass after our departure. But it would burden you unduly to speak of them now. Your kind has proven capable of rising to every challenge that has presented itself."

"I'd say that's mostly Krancis' doing," Bessemer opined. "I don't know how he does it. But he hasn't steered us wrong yet. Somehow I don't think he's capable of doing that."

"All are subject to error," she said. "But hopefully his errors will be few and of little consequence."

"I agree," he nodded.

"Tell me, Captain Bessemer: do you require anything else?"

"No, I don't think so. But there is one thing I'd like to know."

"Which is?"

"I'd like to know your name," he said. "I don't think any of this would have worked without you, and I'd like to be able to pass along to others the name of the lovely lady who helped me secure this device for mankind."

"You flatter me," she smiled, for she was only vaguely attractive, her bone structure being much too stark. "My name is *Leeiah*."

"*Leeiah*," Bessemer repeated. "It's a very pretty name. I won't have any trouble remembering it," he added, taking her long, thin hand and kissing it gently. "Nor shall mankind, if I have anything to say about it."

"I won't forget you either, Roland Bessemer," she assured him, delicately squeezing the hand that still held hers. "In paradise I shall remember you."

"That's an honor indeed," he replied, more flattered than he thought possible. "After this I'll always feel that a guardian angel is watching over me."

"But now you must depart," she told him. "The others are watching and growing impatient."

"After eons in this thing you'd think they could spare a couple of minutes," he cracked, aware that they wouldn't appreciate his irreverence. He couldn't help grinning when he saw *Leeiah* stifling a smile of her own. "Okay, I don't mean to be tedious," he said, his face flattening as he recalled something he felt sure Kayla would ask him about at some point or other. "If the device can extract the psychic energy of your people, why did I see shadow people in the pyramids?

And why did I feel a presence watching me back in the facility just beneath the crater?"

"It would take a great deal of time to explain it mechanically," she began. "Regarding the pyramids, there was an element of bleedover since the sword spent so much time in their vicinity. The material from which they are made is more receptive to psychic energy than almost any other kind in the universe. The sword, given it was the route through which our people's energies were transferred into the device, is highly charged. Over time that energy left an imprint on its surroundings."

"And the facility? Is that the same story?"

"In that case it was merely the fact that it was situated directly below the device when it activated. Again, the material being so receptive, it was natural that it would take an imprint. I trust you didn't actually see any of these 'shadow people' there like you did in the pyramids?"

"Matter of fact, I didn't," he answered. "Just a sense of presence, of being watched all the time."

"The facility still reverberates with psychic energy. It is as though you passed through the consciousnesses of many individuals within a single space."

"I'll say it was. It was one of the creepiest things I've ever felt."

"I should think it would have been," she nodded knowingly. "Because there was an additional aspect, one that you likely weren't even aware of: the psychic energy, being nothing but bleedover from the device's activation, would have had an attendant headlessness. Lacking the organizing influence of an actual psyche, it merely floated there, aware of you in a sense, yet uncomprehending of any higher point or purpose. Like walking through a vegetable garden of sentient plants, or a cemetery enlivened by a collection of listless ghosts, the lack of purposefulness would be disturbing as it began to influence your unconscious. You would feel an overwhelming sense of pointlessness verging into despair if you'd spent any meaningful length of time there."

"That's probably why I didn't feel anything after I killed that creature," he remarked, reflecting on that peculiar moment. "I thought I was just getting tired of all the running and fighting, or something."

"You *are* weary," she replied. "But it will pass shortly. You are a warrior, Roland Bessemer, and it is your life to fight and kill. Occasionally you will tire of it. But it would kill *you* not to pursue this course."

"Must seem a bit primal to someone as intellectual as you," he commented, feeling a little insignificant as he compared his rough-and-tumble life of adventure to that of the brilliant *Cultookoy* people who had all but conquered death itself.

"Not at all," she smiled grandly. "Each has his station and purpose in this life. You fill yours admirably."

"Thank you."

"And now you really must depart," she urged him. "Winning the agreement of the others was a difficult battle, and we shouldn't add to the tension that already exists here by straining their patience."

"Alright, I'm going," he replied, giving her hand a final squeeze before turning around as though to head out a door. "Oh, that's right," he laughed, turning back again and looking at her. "You'll have to show me the way out."

"With pleasure," she smiled. "Goodbye, Captain."

"Goodbye," he responded with some sense of heaviness in his chest, wishing he could spend more time with his fascinating companion. "Oh, hey," he added, looking past her and shouting off into the haze that surrounded them. "You guys crashed my ship quite a distance from here. I'll have to head back and fly it over if I can manage to find a way out of this chasm. So don't go nuts when you see me walking away. I'll be back."

"The craft is but a few steps away," she informed

him. "Once agreement was reached within the council, we withdrew our influence over it and your AI flew it into the chasm."

"Oh, well, that's good," he said, feeling a little silly for having shouted. "Well, I'll have to check it out, all the same. So, again, don't go nuts."

"I'll ensure that they don't," she promised him, as the scene began to evaporate. "Goodbye, Captain."

"Goodbye!" he exclaimed, her form having vanished before he could respond.

Once again his mind was within his body. He shifted stiffly for a moment, trying to get a little life back into his limbs before rising. Many hours had passed, and the rays of the setting sun did little to illuminate the narrow chasm. Activating his helmet's light enhancement, he ambled awkwardly away from the device.

"Krancis was glad to hear things are finally proceeding," Kayla said without preamble. "I'd guessed that you were successful when they stopped interfering with the egg."

"You were right," he responded flatly, leaning a hand on the chasm wall as he rounded the corner. "Where's the egg?"

"Just a little way ahead of you. I had to find a place wide enough to set it down." She hesitated momentarily, noting the tone of his voice. "I don't mean to be repetitive, but are you okay?"

"Have you ever made a great friendship just to lose it in the space of a single day?" he queried in a tired voice. "I guarantee you I'll never meet another creature like her again. So wise! So *ancient!* And yet so generous and kind. I'll never know all the things I missed out on, knowing her for so short a time."

"Sounds like you got a little infatuated," she remarked, surprised that he should form such a powerful attachment so quickly. "You couldn't have known hardly anything about her."

"Oh, I know all the factual arguments and whatnot," he said with a weary wave of his hand. "But sometimes you just *click*. She felt it, too. I could see it in her face."

"Was she pretty?" Kayla asked, popping the canopy as he reached the egg.

"Not really," he answered, climbing up the ladder and dropping into the pilot's seat with finality. "It was in how she carried herself. I don't know. You get a *feeling* about people sometimes. She had a great spirit."

"*Has* a great spirit," Kayla pointed out. "One she'll keep on having, provided their device works like they want it to. She won't be *gone*, just absent."

"Yeah, that's true," he agreed, flicking through the egg's switches and checking its systems on the display. "But that won't do me a lot of good."

"What are you doing?"

"Making sure the ship's alright."

"I could have told you that," she responded helpfully. "I would have been glad to–."

"Sometimes a guy wants to see it with his own eyes, alright?" he snapped, frowning at the little pink hologram that had just appeared. "Especially when he's about to annihilate what's left of the planet he's standing on. I need to be sure my escape route is covered."

"Of course," she replied calmly, unwilling to add fuel to a fire that would shortly burn itself out. She realized that he just wanted to buy a little time so he'd have a chance to breathe and digest what had happened. Sitting down on the dashboard, she let her legs dangle over the edge and waved them back and forth a little.

"Anything further from Krancis?" he asked after a minute, his temper cooling.

"Just that we're to proceed as planned," she answered. "Oh, and he also sent some coordinates where we can meet *Sentinel* once we've got the device safely onboard. He wants to get it under lock and key as quickly as possible."

"Understandable," Bessemer remarked quietly, as a doubt began to grow in his mind. Leaning back in his seat, he looked off down the chasm as he thought.

"Something wrong?" she asked.

"Just a little something that's been beating around the back of my head," he replied.

"What is it?" she prodded, seeing his reluctance to verbalize it.

"What if this doesn't work?" he asked, his eyes finding her tiny holographic orbs. "What if the *Cultookoy* have got it all wrong and this is just mass suicide? I don't want to be responsible for extinguishing what's left of a great race. And I *don't* want to be the one who destroys *Leeiah*."

"Is that her name?"

"Yeah," he nodded, his stomach tightening as he reflected. "Look, they already screwed it up once, didn't they? The device was supposed to carry them into the light realm, not lock them in a box for ages. What if it just isn't possible to send them on towards the light? And how am I supposed to know the difference after I've pulled the trigger? Provided they're gone, I can *assume* that I mailed them off to paradise. But I just as easily could have killed every last one of them."

"There's no way we can be certain, Roland," she said. "But we know our mission; we know what we have to do. This weapon *must* be secured for mankind. The *Cultookoy* are confident that it'll work. We can't ignore that."

"They were confident last time, too," he pointed out. "All it got them was a shattered homeworld and countless years inside that thing," he added, nodding off through the chasm wall towards the device.

"We don't have a choice."

"I *know* that," he responded unappreciatively. "But it doesn't mean I don't need a little time to come to grips with this. Don't you realize all their lives are in my hands, and mine alone? As far as we know I'm the only one who can activate this thing. There's no question of passing the buck and letting someone else take the responsibility for this. It's up to me whether they stay imprisoned forever, or pass on to the light realm, or simply die in a flash. It's a bigger decision than almost anyone has ever faced before."

"The decision has already been made," she argued. "Krancis has–."

"Krancis gave me an *order*, Kayla," he cut her off. "And if he had a dozen other guys he could call upon to twist the key, it would be his responsibility, because then the man on the spot would be interchangeable with any of the others. But when you're the *one man* who can make it happen, the ultimate responsibility rides with you. So don't give me a lecture on the chain of command. Just give me a little peace to think."

As he'd said, he already knew what had to be done. There was no question of permitting such a device to lay dormant on Thierry, nor of consigning the *Cultookoy* to spend the rest of their days locked inside it. He was, moreover, aware that his hosts had only permitted the egg to fly *after* they'd reached an agreement about whether to accept Krancis' terms or not. He was, in fact, a hostage of the council. Should he try to take off, the egg would never have emerged from the chasm. He was boxed in on three sides. The only path forward was to turn the key.

Angrily he smacked the dashboard, causing Kayla to jolt in surprise. Wisely, she said nothing. In fact, she didn't even look at him. She just kept gently wagging her legs back and forth, her little hands pinching the edge as though to keep her from falling off.

As soon as he reached the peak of his anger, he began to descend the opposite slope. Sadness took its place; sadness that he'd spent such a precious few moments with *Leeiah*. He couldn't shake the feeling that she was destined for him in some way, or he for her. He couldn't tell which. But he could sense that fate was about to pass him by; that an enormous opportunity was about to be closed off to him forever. Was it a chance to grow? A chance for love? Or was it the possibility of leading a more meaningful life than that of an adventurer in the employ of the empire? He didn't know that, either. Perhaps it was just the fact that, distantly, these were his people, too. Overwhelmingly he was Earthborn, of course. But despite the treatment of the council, he felt an attachment to the *Cultookoy* as well. And a little piece of his heart revolted at the idea of removing them permanently from the galaxy.

Glancing overhead as the last faint rays of the sun faded from the sky, he scowled and stood up.

"Captain?" Kayla queried, as he straightened his sword and descended the ladder to the chasm floor. "Captain, what are you going to do?"

"What I came here for," he answered grimly, walking slowly from the egg and shortly disappearing from view.

Rounding the corner that concealed the device, he paused and sighed heavily when his gaze fell upon it. Countless eyes watched him, he knew; each of them desperate to complete the journey they'd begun so long before. Doubtless they wondered why he'd waited so long to do what had already been agreed. *Leeiah*, he reflected, probably knew why he'd hesitated. But the rest wouldn't care. Most likely they were scorning him for wavering at the last moment.

"*I'm not wavering*," he thought, drawing the sword and approaching the cube. "*I'm saying goodbye*."

Stopping beside the device, he noticed an opening in the center of its top. The sword began to glow the most brilliant purple he'd ever seen as he raised it, culminating in a blinding flash as he slid it into place and twisted it. At once he sensed that the *Cultookoy* trapped within the sword had flowed into the device to join their brethren. Pulling it out again, he heard a strange beeping announce that the weapon had been armed. Listening for a few seconds, he realized that the time between each beep was quickly shortening.

"Could've given me a little longer!" he shouted, whipping around and tearing off down the chasm towards the egg. "Kayla! Kayla! Get that thing warmed up! We're getting out of here just as fast as we can!"

Slipping on the sandy ground as he rounded the corner, he lost his footing and tumbled down. Jumping back up, he ran for the egg, climbed the ladder in a flash, and leapt into the pilot's seat.

"Drop the canopy!" he barked, taking the controls and raising the craft as quickly as he could given the narrowness of the walls. "Channel all the power we've got into getting us out of here!"

"Already done," Kayla replied calmly, though inwardly she was afraid they wouldn't make it. "It'll be close."

"You're right about that!" he agreed, still hearing the beeping in his head as he gritted his teeth.

Their movement felt desperately slow as Bessemer gripped the controls, willing the craft to go faster. Suddenly a bright white flash erupted, making both Kayla and Bessemer gasp in surprise. A rumble filled the air just as the shockwave caught up with them, jostling the craft and shoving it even faster towards outer space.

"Oh, it's close!" Kayla worried. "Oh, it's bad! It's bad!"

"Hang on!" Bessemer shouted over the sounding of a dozen different alarms as the ship ceased responding to the controls. "We're in for it now!"

The craft began to tumble end-over-end. Having not strapped himself in, Bessemer fell from his seat and smacked against the canopy before sliding down to the dashboard. Reaching desperately for the seat's harness, it slipped through his fingers as he flew away from it and again crashed into the canopy.

"Roland!!" screamed Kayla, terrified that he would be pummeled to death at any moment. "Grab onto something!"

"*What do you think–*," he began to say, before catching

the back of the seat in the stomach, crushing every bit of air out of his lungs. With a wheeze he gripped the chair, but couldn't hold on as he once more struck the canopy.

"We're coming out of it!" Kayla announced hopefully. "The shockwave is dissipating!"

As she said this the ship regained control of its course and automatically righted itself, instantly dropping Bessemer into the back of the cockpit.

"Are you okay?" she asked, as he struggled to get up.

"Krancis *must* be trying to kill me!" he exclaimed, both anger and despair mingling in his voice. Achingly he moved around the seat and sat down with a loud groan. "There's no other way to explain it."

"But we succeeded," she pointed out, standing up on the dashboard and pointing over his shoulder. "Look back. The mission's been accomplished."

Looking to where she pointed, his breath was taken away when he saw the enormous crater that the device had left behind.

"It's like a *planet* hit Thierry!" he declared, standing up and pressing his face against the canopy. Suddenly a chill ran through him as he remembered all the souls that had been trapped within the cube. Closing his eyes, he wished solemnly that they'd managed to complete their long-delayed journey. "Turn the ship around, Kayla," he instructed her, still gazing at the gaping hole with wonder. "Have you got a lock on the device?" he asked heavily, his energy quickly flagging as the excitement died down. Slowly, painfully, he moved back to the pilot's seat.

"I do," she assured him as the craft gently turned and made for the weapon. "We'll reach it shortly. You can just sit back and relax."

"Not like I'm good for much else at this point, anyhow," he grumbled, leaning his head back gingerly and exhaling. "I'm surprised I didn't break every bone in my body. I *feel* like I did."

"Miraculously, the ship's instruments indicate that nothing has been broken," she informed him. "Although I'm sure you've been bruised terribly. It'll probably be tough to rest for the next few days."

"After everything I've been through, Kayla, I could sleep through my own execution," he said with a painful wave of his hand. Suddenly feeling the urge to cough, he was surprised when he *didn't* spit up blood. "Well, that's something, anyway," he muttered.

Soon they reached the place where the device had been activated. The chasm that had held it was nothing more than a memory. Flying into a cloud of thick dust that blinded them both, Kayla was forced to rely exclusively on the ship's instruments to find the bottom of the crater and the weapon that had tumbled down into it. Landing the egg beside it, she turned all the external lights to maximum in the hope of helping Bessemer see it. But the dust was too dense.

"I'll guide you to it," Kayla said, as he reluctantly pushed himself up from the seat and stumbled to the side of the craft. "Just watch your step. The ground might be a little soft from all the dust that's already settled."

"I'll watch it," he replied mechanically, nearly done in but willing himself to finish his task. Mutely he pointed upward at the canopy, which was opened at once. Slowly working his way down the ladder, forced to feel his way along in the cloud, his feet reached the ground and immediately sank several inches. Keeping one hand on the ladder, he turned blindly and reached out for the device.

"A little further," Kayla coached him. "Bit more. You're gonna have to let go of the ladder. I put us down several feet from it."

Letting go, he reached out both hands and felt as the dust passed through his gloved fingers. After several uncertain steps he found the device, touching it all around just to assure they hadn't zeroed in on a big rock instead. Realizing he hadn't the least notion how much it weighed, he gave it a good shove and found it didn't move so much as an inch.

"Kayla, just how are we gonna get this thing aboard?" he asked, leaning wearily against it and wishing above all things that he could put off the question until he'd had a chance to rest. "Not like we've got a crane."

"I was thinking about that, too. The only course I can see is to tip the egg over and scoop it up like a ladle. We'll get a lot of dust that way, but–."

"Good enough," he interrupted, invisibly waving his hand in the cloud.

"Okay, well, move to the other side of the device and back up a little," she instructed him, opening the canopy wide and lifting the ship gently into the air. "I don't want to have a mishap and crush you."

"Yeah, I could do without that myself," he agreed, keeping his hands on the device and feeling his way around to its opposite side. Taking several steps backward, he found a small hole in the ground, lost his balance, and fell over. "Before you ask," he said as he pushed against the soft dirt and managed to right himself. "I'm okay."

"Good," she audibly smiled. "Alright, I'm coming in to grab this thing. Watch yourself."

He could hear the egg's engines louden, but was unable to see it until it was right before him. Taking another few steps back to ensure he wasn't crushed, he watched as Kayla attempted to scoop up the device. But the side of the egg was too thick, and she couldn't manage to get it underneath the cube.

"I think you're gonna have to push it from your end," she said. "Or at least tip it a little this way, so I can get under it a bit."

"Alright," he agreed, doubtful he could move the device at all. Bracing his feet as well as he could in the inches of dust that surrounded him, he put his hands on the top edge of the cube and pushed. At once he slid backward.

Quickly growing frustrated, he kicked the toes of his boots into the ground several times, trying to dig in and get a little traction. Pushing again, he found the device immovably heavy. "It's no good, Kayla," he said, leaning on the cube once he'd pushed himself out of breath. "This thing weighs a ton. We're gonna have to find another way."

"Well, we've got a bunch of tools in the back," she suggested meekly, hesitant to add to his burdens. "You *could* try digging under and around this side of it so I can slip the ship beneath it." Certain he would take this option, she took the liberty of righting the ship and setting it down once more.

"Does this really have to be taken care of today?" he groaned as he approached the ship, though he had no real notion of putting it off.

"Krancis said to collect the device and make for *Sentinel* as quickly as possible," she answered gently.

"Then that is what Krancis shall have," he replied with annoyance, glad to have someone to blame for his misfortune.

Climbing up the ladder, he went into the back of the ship where the tools were strapped down in their boxes. Removing a strap, he lifted a corner of a lid and began feeling around for a small shovel he knew he'd packed in one of them. Losing patience after half a minute of fruitless searching, he angrily wrestled the other strap off and jerked the lid completely off. Cursing his luck as he found the box shovel-less, he moved on to another one and started working its straps off. Digging through the tools, he found the shovel halfway to the bottom. Thrown over the side like a javelin, it stuck into the ground and dutifully awaited his next command.

"Um, Roland?" Kayla began as he was about to climb over the side.

"Yeah?"

"You're going to have to strap down the boxes again,

or I'll scatter them all along the ground when I tip this thing over."

Grinding his teeth, he wordlessly repacked the boxes and fastened them to the craft. Moving down the ladder, he picked up the shovel, dropped to his knees, and started digging away at the dirt under the side of the device that faced the ship. It had only barely become visible during the time he was in the egg, the dust at last thinning a little in the air.

"Alright, Darling," he uttered sarcastically, his strength all but gone as he stood up when his task was complete. "Give it a whirl."

Shambling out of the way, he watched as she again rolled the vessel onto its side and attempted to scoop up the cube. This time she managed to hook the lip of the hull underneath it. But she couldn't work the craft any deeper than that.

"Roland, can you dig out any more of the dirt?" she radioed. "Just a little more and you should be able to tip it into the egg."

"I'll try," he grumbled, not relishing the risk of being crushed if Kayla made a mistake. Kneeling down beside the cube, the ship just inches away from him, he reached out with the shovel and started scooping away at the dirt under the device. Reaching farther and farther beneath it, he grimaced as his hands moved just a hair under it. The instant it rocked a little he jerked the shovel back. "I'll get to the other side," he said to Kayla, standing up and walking around it. Cautiously digging, it took only a few shovel loads for it to tip into the egg, pinning the shovel beneath it.

"I think that got it," Kayla said hopefully. "Just give it a little push if you can while I try and pick it up."

"Be careful," he warned her as he moved behind it, aware that a little too much pressure from the ship could shove the cube right over his feet.

"Don't worry," she assured him, making him roll his

eyes.

Placing his hands once more upon the weapon, he gave it a good shove just as she flicked the controls and moved against it. Their combined action was just enough to work the better part of it inside the ship. Tipping the egg upright a smidgeon, it slid smoothly down the hull and struck the floor with a clang. At once Kayla righted the ship, set it down, and waited for Bessemer to climb aboard.

"We'd better strap that thing down," she said once he was inside and she'd dropped the canopy.

"There's inches of dust everywhere," Bessemer remarked with annoyance as though he hadn't heard her, putting the shovel back into its crate. Then he shook his head. "But I'm too tired to care."

"Roland, we need to fasten it down," she repeated.

"I heard you the first time," he answered, detaching his helmet and dropping it on the floor. Softly it impacted, its fall cushioned by the dust. "Not sure it'll do much good, though. That thing weighs so much it'd probably just break whatever we roped it down with."

"Still, it's worth a try," Kayla reiterated, concerned that he might be crushed or the ship damaged if something forced them to maneuver wildly. Or if they lost control again.

"The orb didn't crush us," he said with a wave of his hand as he moved towards the pilot's seat and sat down. "I don't think this thing will."

"Orb?" she queried, confusion on her face.

"Oh, nothing," he shook his head. "That was a long time ago. Or it feels like it."

Taking the controls in his hands, he slowly lifted the craft out of the crater and gently tipped it upwards.

"Incredible to think that such a relatively small device could cause such devastation," Kayla remarked, still standing on the dashboard and watching as the crater slowly diminished behind them. "These people were so very advanced."

"Hope it got them where they wanted to go," he replied grimly, the dreadful notion again flitting through his mind that he'd killed an entire race.

"I'm sure they did," she nodded, looking up into his face with wide eyes. "Chances are–."

"We'll never know for sure, okay?" he cut her off. "We can speculate. But we'll never *know*." Unable to help himself, he twisted in his seat and likewise looked back. Then with a sigh he gazed forward again. "All we know for sure is that they're *gone*. Never to return."

"You're thinking of *Leeiah*," Kayla observed.

"Yeah."

Aware he wished to say no more, the little hologram sat down on the dashboard again, dangling her tiny legs as he took them up through the atmosphere and into space. Glancing up at his stony face, she wordlessly put a waypoint on the display. Aiming the ship at it, he engaged the warp drive shortly thereafter. Safe within the tunnel of darkness, Bessemer could at last relax; though he felt much too abused emotionally, physically, and psychologically to rest easy. Crossing his arms, he shut his eyes and defied consciousness, willing himself to sleep. As if to spite him, his mind drew up image after image from the council chamber. Grunting in frustration, he opened his eyes and smacked the dashboard.

"Can't I just get a little rest?" he demanded of no one in particular. "Is that really too much to ask after all this?"

"You're just over-excited," Kayla responded soothingly. "It'll take time for your body to calm down. Adrenaline is still surging through your veins."

"That ought to have stopped by now."

"You've been through an ordeal unlike most humans have ever encountered," she pointed out. "I'm sure your body doesn't quite know how to respond. It's kicked fight-or-flight into overdrive. I'm afraid all you can do is wait it out."

"Or find something to fight," he commented aimlessly.

"That would work, too," she assented, unsure just

what he'd fight as the sole physical occupant of the egg. "In lieu of that, talking about it might help."

"I don't have anything I want to say."

"You mean there's nothing you could say that would bring her back," she corrected him gently.

Sharply his eyes shot to her and searched her for a moment. Then he nodded and looked down the tunnel.

"Reckon you're right," he admitted.

"But that's not *why* we talk," she explained. "We do it to vent, to get something off our chests. Words can't change the world. But they can do a great deal to make us feel *heard*."

"And what's there to hear?" he countered. "That I've got a thing for a chick I've known for a couple of hours? You already think I'm silly for feeling this way."

"I don't think you're silly," she said honestly. "I do think it's awfully *fast*. But she must have triggered something within you that, if you will, filled in the blanks. Like a fantasy persona that you already understood which she matched up with perfectly. To see her was to know her at once."

"You seriously think that's possible?" he queried, hope mixing with skepticism in his voice.

"I absolutely do," she replied. "I wasn't designed to plumb the depths of the psyche of either my people or yours. But there can be no doubt that powerful preconceived ideas rest at the back of both our races' minds, and that they can be fitted over living organisms. Oftentimes this is criticized as fantasy. But I doubt much of life would be intelligible without these frames to fit experience into. Whatever *Leeiah* related to within your psyche, it was powerful and deeply important." She hesitated momentarily before continuing, unsure how he'd take it. "It's *possible*," she began gingerly, "that she would ultimately prove unlike the persona she activated. That's something we can never know, given that we'll never see her again. But it's just as likely, moreso, in fact, that she would have been exactly what you'd expected, given the sheer vulnerability of psychic communication. It's very difficult to hide something from either party in such an environment."

"Yeah, tell me about it," he agreed, thinking back on the hatred he felt from certain members of the council.

"That lends even more evidence to the notion that something substantial existed between you, even though your time together was so brief. At once you were exposed to a great deal of her psyche. And you liked what you saw."

"That I did."

"Tell me…do you think you might have loved her, given time?" she asked somewhat hesitantly.

"I don't know," he shrugged, looking off into the tunnel as his mind went back to Thierry. "I don't know if it was love, or just the sense that I'd found some long lost relative that I didn't want to lose. Like you said, our time together was brief."

"Indeed."

"Whatever it was, I know I'll never see the likes of her again," he said.

"You can't know that."

"No, I know it," he uttered with finality. "Someone like that only comes along once in a lifetime."

"Do you wish you hadn't met her?" Kayla asked. "Would you rather avoid that pain?"

"No, I'll take the pain," he told her. Looking over his shoulder at the cube, he contemplated it for a moment before settling in and once more crossing his arms. Again he thought of the awful responsibility he'd shouldered by activating the device. "I just hope that thing back there was worth it."

CHAPTER 7

"Paranoia is rife aboard Sentinel," Wellesley noted in a log he'd decided to keep of his experiences in the war. "Captain Julius Bardol has been found comatose within his holding cell. Removed to the hospital wing, he has failed to recover consciousness. It seems that someone interacted with him, but there's no clear notion who it was. Krancis, with what evidence I know not, says that the Devourer implant the captain picked up on his homeworld has been removed. I can't comment on the validity of that idea. Either way, the ship is now on lockdown, and I'm getting bored silly locked in here with only Girnius to occasionally keep me company. I guess Rex could drop by if he wanted to. But he's probably got more important things to do than chat with an old friend."

He paused briefly to check for any new messages from a Black Fang outpost that he'd ordered established in Quarlac. Inwardly scowling at their lack of communicativeness, he continued.

"There was a big meeting about what to do after Bardol was found. Soliana went nuts and blamed it all on Mafalda Aboltina, pointing out, correctly, that she was the newest member of the crew who had anything like the power to affect someone in that way. The fact is we don't know the extent of her powers, especially after they've apparently been changed over to an affinity for the dark realm. Ugh, why can't we go back to the boring old days of purely material threats?"

Thinking better of it, he struck that last sentence before resuming.

"I really don't think that Mafalda had anything to do with Bardol's condition. The guy was already in rough shape when we got him. And there's no telling what that mass did to him while he was digging around inside it. It's not like we've got a lot of experience dealing with stuff like that. I'd say anything is possible. But, of course, it's not like I was consulted…"

As with the prior paragraph, he likewise struck this one's final sentence.

"The Colonel almost tore Soliana's head off when she accused Mafalda, seeing at once the damage her words did to the poor girl. It's regrettable, given all she's already been through. But with her background, it's natural for people to suspect her. I doubt she'll really get the trust she deserves until she's had a chance to prove her fealty to our cause palpably. I just hope that won't require some mortal act of self-sacrifice…"

"Sentinel, at this point, is essentially held hostage. We're just circling in warp, keeping out of harm's way until the situation calms down. Soliana, remarkably, floated the idea of executing Mafalda for her past crimes as a way of settling the matter. No one can doubt that there's an enormous number of wrongs weighing down her conscience. But it's simply vicious to suggest something like that. Especially after she's put herself in such danger to right her past deeds. I'm quite certain Pinchon would in fact have ripped her head off right then and there had Rex not–."

"What do you think you're *doing?!*" exploded Girnius upon entering the makeshift command center that had been established for his use. "I never approved a new outpost in Quarlac! Why are you funneling our resources into that swamp?"

"Having analyzed the data–," the AI began calmly.

"No amount of data can justify you going behind my back!" he declared, glaring at the medallion as it lay upon a desk. "The only reason I signed on for this arrangement was–."

"Because your back was against a wall," Wellesley

cut him off, his temper quickly flaring. "You'd managed to let half the organization get battered to pieces because you haven't the *first* notion how to run a faction in wartime. You were in over your head. It was time for the adults to take over affairs and salvage what was left of the mess you'd made."

"I *built* this organization," Girnius uttered slowly, trembling with rage. "And I didn't do that to hand it over to the *empire!*"

"Well, that's what you've done," Wellesley replied flippantly, too annoyed to maintain pretense any longer. "What did you really expect, Chairman? That we'd let you keep playing in your little sandbox forever? Your days have long been numbered. The organization is valuable to us, and hence we shall make use of it. But only if it is appropriately optimized. At present–."

"I had thought that you'd wait a little longer before kicking me into an alley," Girnius groused, long aware that he was defeated and yet curiously unwilling to accept that fact. "I expected a little more decency."

"Decency isn't something a pirate can reasonably expect," the AI pointed out tartly. "It's a live fast, die fast world you inhabit. You can't tell me you didn't think it would catch up with you eventually. You're not *that* stupid."

Scowling at this insult, he dropped into a chair and stared at the medallion for several moments.

"Pinchon was right," he said quietly, his narrowed eyes still on the ancient disc.

"Well, everyone is, sooner or later."

"He said this universe is getting too big for the likes of me," the chairman continued as though he hadn't heard him. "That men like Krancis and Hunt were pushing us aside. That forces bigger than anything we'd ever experienced before had come upon the scene."

"That sounds about right," Wellesley audibly shrugged. "I'd hardly consider that a revelation, however. You could see this stuff coming a mile away. But I guess you'd have to be looking to the horizon for that, and not into the wallet you'd just lifted off some stranger on the street."

"I'm no petty thief," Girnius growled.

"The difference between a petty thief and a criminal mastermind is merely the scope of his influence. And considering that you officially have *none*, I'd say you've been reduced to the level of a common punk. Not, mind you, that you'd ever transcended that rank in *my* estimation."

"And yet here you are, carrying on my work," Girnius shot back. "What right have you got to lecture me? From what I hear you've got plenty of black marks on your record."

"Marks incurred while fighting for a cause I believed in," Wellesley countered.

"Until you betrayed and abandoned it," the chairman sneered.

"My cause was not that of the fringe imperial movement, but rather the welfare of the *Kol-Prockian* race. I served the imperialists because they held the keys to our future as a great people. When they failed to secure victory after countless battles, it was time to end the conflict before more blood was needlessly shed. There is, as any honest person can see, not the least shred of a comparison between *my* actions in the civil war, and those of a ten cent thug such as yourself."

"You're much too intelligent to truly think I'm a thug," Girnius replied, regaining some of his usual cool.

"Sure, but it's more fun to kick you around," the AI said casually. "Besides, you annoy me when you interrupt my work to prattle on about your prerogatives. Give it a rest, will you?"

"And then what? Help you dismantle what's left of my organization?" he queried, leaning back in his seat and eyeing the medallion. "Let you in on all the little nooks and crannies within which we hide ourselves from the empire's prying eyes?"

"You probably won't believe this. But it's not my

intention to *dismantle* anything. I simply want to refashion the Black Fangs into something productive. Naturally, that's a *bit* hard to do with a group that's filled with scum and motivated by ill-gotten gain. But I like the challenge. It keeps me young."

"And just what's your idea of productive?" Girnius asked. "A lapdog for Krancis? Cannon fodder to be sent ahead of the regular navy?"

"No. What I want to establish is an independent espionage service that will give the human race an extra layer of protection," Wellesley confided, his tone instantly catching Girnius' ear and causing him to lean a little closer. "On paper I'm reworking the Black Fangs into a military unit that will be subject to the empire. But their talents as pilot's, while great, are nothing compared to their skills as smugglers, informers, and spies. Your list of underworld contacts alone would take decades to replicate were the imperials to attempt it. And even then they wouldn't be able to manage it. Your organization has the power to both protect humanity and provide such a useful service that the empire wouldn't *think* of shutting it down, even if at all times it would wish to control it."

"Which is what you're doing now," Girnius responded skeptically, though his tone had softened noticeably. "You're dancing to Krancis' music."

"Sure, my actions are in line with what Krancis wants," the AI audibly shrugged again. "But that's just because I'm in the early stages of retrofitting you guys. Eventually it's gonna become clear that we're pursuing different ends."

Intrigued, Girnius leaned back again and thought for a few seconds.

"Why don't I believe you?"

"Because liars never believe honest people," Wellesley instantly responded. "Get with the program, will you? I'm not telling you this for your amusement. I *want* something out of you."

"And that is?" he asked, cocking an eyebrow that said he'd never give an inch.

"Cooperation," he answered. "I've been able to sniff out plenty of your secrets. But there's still a lot I don't know. I could make a lot better headway if I knew where the bodies are buried."

"So you can hand them over to Krancis?"

"Hasn't it occurred to you that you're entirely within our power at this point?" the AI snapped in exasperation. "We've got three psychics who could probe your mind, to say nothing of what Rex could do if he so much as sneezed on you. Face it, pal: Krancis just has you onboard as a hostage and facilitator. He doesn't *need* anything special out of you, or he'd have gotten it already. What *I'm* offering you is a chance to save your organization. And perhaps yourself, too. You don't *have* to be kicked into the dustbin of history. But that's exactly what'll happen if you push away the hand I'm offering you."

"And just why are you doing this? It can't be out of any excess of good feeling towards 'scum' like me."

"Believe me, it's not," he laughed pointedly. "The fact is, I used to wield so much power it would make your pretty little head spin. But between then and now, I've been scarcely more than a paperweight. I'd like to get back to the old days, insofar as that's possible."

"So that's it, then," Girnius smirked as he stood. "Just an over-the-hill AI who wants one last shot at glory before his innards rust out. Well, you're gonna have to look somewhere else, pal. I'll help you over my dead body."

"That could be arranged," Wellesley responded easily. "But for the time being, I'll give you a chance to reconsider your stance. Sleep on it, Chairman. You might find yourself in a different mood come morning."

"Don't bet on it," he snorted, before giving the disc a flick with his finger.

With this petty gesture he left the room. Inwardly Wellesley sighed.

"Where was I?" he asked himself, pulling up his log with utter indifference to what had just occurred. "Ah, here we go. *I'm quite certain Pinchon would in fact have ripped her head off right then and there had Rex not grabbed ahold of him and restrained him. At Krancis' direction the pirate left the room, though only after Rex assured him that he'd look after Mafalda. The poor girl stood fearful and alone until Rex went to her and put a hand on her shoulder. Needless to say the discussion pretty much ended with Soliana's outrageous idea. Krancis concluded by saying that all critical areas of the ship would be off-limits until the imprint-bearer (his term, not mine) was found. To placate Soliana, I imagine, he confined Mafalda to her quarters. This seemed to please her somewhat, though obviously not completely, given her previous suggestion. I really can't imagine why Soliana hates her so much. Well, outside of her jealousy over Rex, obviously.*"

This last thought made him pause and think for a few moments.

"*Funny, he never really had much appeal for the female race* before *we got hooked up with Ugo Udris and began delving into the dark realm. They didn't seem to notice him during all those hard years on Delta. I wonder if the dark element holds some kind of deep-seated appeal. Perhaps it resonates within the human unconscious. I've noticed a lot of respect from the male population as well; respect that I don't merely ascribe to his official position of lord. They seem to just sense he's a leader of sorts and willfully they follow him. Well, some of them, anyhow. Shoot, that's probably part of what Girnius doesn't like about him: Rex has the goods, and he doesn't, not inwardly. He's too much of a…*"

He stopped for a second, searching for the right word.

"*…vulture to really engender loyalty and true respect. Fear, sure. But that only holds for as long as you're an active danger to others. Once you've lost your teeth, they scorn you as* *a way of compensating for the dread they once had of you. In that sense Girnius is pretty lucky that we've got him stowed away here on Sentinel. Sooner or later some of his boys would've come looking for him, intent on taking over his racket. Come to think of it, that makes* me *rather glad to be here, too. I don't need to be looking over my shoulder every two minutes..."*

While Wellesley was occupying himself in this way, Pinchon was sitting in his room with Hunt. Beside him on a small table stood a bottle of whiskey that he'd swiped from Krancis. The man in black knew at once who'd stolen it. But he was content to allow the colonel a small act of rebellion if it would help keep him in check after his explosive encounter with Soliana.

"I can't even *begin* to understand what he sees in that girl," Pinchon said to Hunt, who sat across the small room from him, a drink in his hand that he hadn't bothered to touch.

"He sees in her a potential prophetess," the Deltan replied with a shrug. "And he's willing to humor her if she'll eventually become one. You know as well as I do that we need every edge we can get in this war. A seer would be a real boon."

"You sound like you're on his side," the colonel remarked dubiously, not sure he liked his friend's reasonable tone. "You've got to admit there's something different about her lately. She's taking on airs like she's some kind of queen. The helpless girl we rescued in the Black Hole is gone for good, Rex. She's feeling her oats, and I don't think it bodes well for any of us."

"Krancis knows what he's doing," Hunt responded quietly, not wishing to start an argument.

"Excuse me?" Pinchon asked, raising his voice a little. "When did you turn over a new leaf? I thought we were pretty much of a mind that he couldn't be trusted."

"I don't doubt that he's using each of us for his own purposes," Hunt began slowly, shifting in his seat and looking the colonel in the eye. "I knew that right from the start."

"Then why the change of heart?"

"Because my priorities are starting to line up with his," he replied in the reluctant tone of a confession.

"It's all that interacting with the dark realm that you've been doing," Pinchon opined at once, pointing at Hunt's arms. "It's changing you. Just like those implants are changing Soliana."

"That could be," the Deltan allowed with a nod.

"And that doesn't bother you?" queried the ex-pirate, shaking his head a little side-to-side.

"Not much use in getting upset about it, is there?" Hunt asked in return. "Destiny or fate or whatever you want to call it is dragging me this way. I was born for this, whether I like it or not. It's no use fighting it any longer. In fact, it's downright wrong to do so."

"I've gotta say, I never saw this coming," Pinchon said. "Until now you've played this like a dayworker. I never really figured you for a cause man, even if you made noises that sounded like it from time to time. Ultimately you're a loner."

"Every loner comes in out of the cold sometime," Hunt shrugged.

"No," Pinchon again shook his head. "Not all of us. I *never* intend to sign on permanently. I'll fight it out for as long as we're under mortal threat. But Krancis has got another thing coming if he thinks I'll spend the rest of my days under his banner. Once this bit with the Devourer is taken care of and we're at peace, I'm heading out for good. Honestly, I'd kind of hoped that you'd join me."

"Don't see that I can," Hunt responded.

"Why?" prodded the colonel. "It's not like you owe *him* anything. He's gotten his money's worth out of you, and plenty to spare. You're entitled to retire after all you've done. Shoot, just the *Pho'Saths* you've bagged oughta be enough to pay your way right up until your dying breath. Nobody else could've taken 'em down, that's for sure."

"That's why I've got to stay," he explained. "The empire will be all but shattered when we come out of this. It'll take every good man we can find to hold it together."

"Then let Krancis find them," Pinchon said flippantly, gulping part of his drink as his conscience began to grow agitated.

"I was talking about you, Philip," Rex pointed out.

"You know better than that. I've got plenty of demerits on my scorecard."

"The empire won't be picky after this war. It'll need leaders like you. Men with experience."

"Rex, it was one thing to do my part from within the organizations I served," Pinchon said with a sigh, leaning back and settling in for a long explanation. "They were free and open, more or less. Not a lot of top-down control. The last thing I *ever* intended was to become one of the government's errand boys. Even before our lord and master took over I wanted to keep plenty of distance between myself and the empire. Now that he's in charge, it's all I can do to keep from snatching a ship and bolting the very next time we drop out of warp and the hangars open up. He's a machine, Rex, not a human being. We're nothing but pawns in his eyes. I don't know how you can put up with it. But for me that's just about the worst thing there is. I don't trust anyone to have that kind of power over me."

"He's hardly playing dictator, Philip," Hunt pointed out. "If he was arbitrarily kicking people around, chopping a head off here and bombing a city there, I'd understand. But he's been nothing if not the very image of restraint. That old cliche about power corrupting seems to have found its exception."

"Or he hasn't had enough time for it to sink into his bones," Pinchon countered. "He's had his hands full dealing with the Devourer. There hasn't been a chance for him to bare his fangs yet."

"You're protesting too much," Hunt observed, laying aside his glass and leaning forwards, resting his elbows on his knees as his voice grew earnest. "The fact is all our days will be numbered if the empire crumbles apart."

"Alright, level with me, Rex," the colonel said, likewise leaning forwards, though he kept holding his drink. "What's bringing this on? I mean really?"

"Truthfully?"

"Yeah."

"It was seeing Antonin go after Mafalda like a wild animal. And then, when he turned on me and said I wasn't his friend anymore. Well, that told me that the circle I'd brought with me from Delta was shattered for good. Lily is a trillion miles away, and Wellesley might as well be. For all intents and purposes, it's just me now."

"So you thought you'd throw in with Krancis? Earn yourself a new family with your special powers?"

"I don't think I like your tone, Philip," Hunt warned him.

"I'm not digging at you, Rex," the pirate replied, raising his hands in a show of innocence. "Really, I'm not. I'm just being factual. What kind of loyalty is it if you can buy it with your dark powers? You're not getting a new circle of comrades: you're just making yourself valuable in the short term. But remember this: a weapon is only friendly so long as it's pointed at the enemy. What happens when this war is over, and you've got all this power surging through your veins with nothing to aim it at? Don't you think you're gonna look like a threat to Krancis?"

"He wouldn't pull a move like that," Hunt shook his head.

"Even if he thought it was in the 'best interests of the empire?'" he asked, making quotes with his fingers. "There's only one man in this entire galaxy who could rival him at this point. And I'm not just saying that because of your powers. The imperial propaganda machine has been hard at work making you into the hero of the hour to keep hope alive. Just imagine the influence you'd wield once the war is over. There's bound to be countless discontents who'll want to get rid of Krancis once the danger has passed. They'll be looking for a leader. It would be natural to settle on the man the empire had banished to the fringe of its territories when he was but a child. They'll figure that makes you a ready-made revolutionary. At least, that's how our lord and master will see it. I *promise* you, Rex: you'll have a target on your back within twelve months of the war ending."

"You're wrong, Philip," Hunt said, standing up.

"*Don't* throw in with him just because you're cut off and alone," Pinchon insisted. "You've got enough power to write your own ticket. So *do* it. Wait till the war is over if you want. But don't let so much as a day pass after that without moving on."

"What's the point in having a power like this if I can't make other people's lives better?"

"Oh, come on! Enough of this hero stuff! You were an artifact scavenger before this whole drama swept you up. Now you think you've got a role to play on the galactic stage, and you're puffing out your shirt. Wake up, Rex!"

"Are you even hearing yourself right now?" the Deltan asked, growing angry. "You stuck your neck out with the Black Fangs when this all started. Now you want me to bail out? You asked what's gotten into *me*. But a better question would be what's gotten into *you*?"

"I've had enough of this," Pinchon said, waving his free hand to dismiss the discussion. "I've said my piece and a great deal more. If you want to throw your life away, go ahead."

"You're only throwing your life away if you don't do anything useful with it," Hunt asserted. "That's not a mistake I intend to make."

"Good to hear," Pinchon uttered sourly, as the Deltan made for the door. "Good to hear."

Once he'd closed it, Hunt stood in the hallway for a few moments and thought. Surprised by the colonel's attitude, he was of half a mind to head right back in and go at it again. Thinking better of it, he shook his head and turned around in time to see Krancis approaching from a couple dozen feet away.

"Seems you're always around," Hunt observed, as the man in black gestured for him to fall in beside him. "Haven't you got an empire to run? A war to oversee?" he queried, shoving his hands into his pockets as he walked.

"Trouble with the colonel?"

"Yeah."

"About me?"

"Well, you *are* his favorite subject."

"Indeed."

"Look, can I ask you a point-blank question?" Hunt asked, stopping and turning towards him.

"Shoot," Krancis answered with a nod, likewise pausing. "I'd appreciate it if a great many more people did exactly that."

"What in the world is going on here?" he all but demanded. "We're coming apart at the seams and nobody seems to know why."

"I do," Krancis responded, resuming movement.

"But you're not going to tell me," Hunt elaborated.

"The time isn't right for that."

"Krancis, if you want me to cooperate with you, you've got to keep me informed," the Deltan argued. "You've said it's crucial that we work together, that the empire needs us. Alright, then: keep me inside the loop. Enough of this smoke-and-mirrors business."

"It's not as if I exclude you for my amusement," Krancis replied in his precise fashion. "The fact of the matter is there are certain points of data that you are certain to respond to emotionally instead of rationally. As I have said, I am quite certain of what is causing the present agitation.

With a snap of my fingers I could stop it. But I won't do so."

"And why not?"

"Because the potential rewards are too great," he explained mysteriously, glancing at Hunt briefly as they turned down another corridor. "Because the petty strife that we're now experiencing is nothing compared to the bounty that will be ours if my plan pays off."

"What plan?" Hunt asked with annoyance. "To push us to our limits? To shatter old friendships? What possible good can come from a situation like this? And now this whole Bardol thing has been thrown on top of it all. We're at each other's throats at the worst possible time. We need unity, Krancis. Isn't that what you're always preaching?"

"Unity is like a chain," Krancis replied. "It is meant to bind us together so that we may withstand necessary strains. The present trouble is just such a strain."

"I don't see it," Hunt disagreed.

"Of course not. You lack the necessary information to see the situation clearly."

"Then give it to me."

"Not yet," he said. "Soon. Very soon, in fact. But not quite yet. The stakes are far too high to risk–."

"An emotional reaction," Hunt finished for him.

"Just so. It's a pity that your background didn't better prepare you for this time. But we must make the best of it."

"Wasn't my idea to banish my family to Delta-13, Krancis," he pointed out.

Briefly their dialogue paused as they reached a teleporter room. Rematerializing near the bridge, they stepped into the corridor and covered the short distance to the panoramic command center in silence. Uttering a handful of commands, Krancis caused a massive map of the empire's systems to appear in the air before them. Approximately half the dots were blue, while the rest were either red or gray.

"This is privileged information, Rex," Krancis

informed him. "Almost no one in the imperial government has been permitted to see the whole picture. The red systems are presently under attack; the gray ones have been annihilated; the blue are intact, more or less."

"What hope is there for the red ones?" Hunt asked, allowing his eyes to slowly pass over the scene. "Can we rescue them?"

"Radik is both growing and employing our forces more effectively with each passing day," he began, clasping his hands behind his back and surveying the map. "He's taken huge bites out of the Devourer, but our advantage is slowly diminishing. Despite the potency of the Adler project, the parasite is learning how to grapple with it more effectively as time goes on. The fact is, without *Sentinel*, we would almost certainly be fought to a standstill before we could liberate every system that's now under threat."

"Why are you showing me this?" Hunt asked, crossing his arms and looking at the man beside him.

"For two reasons," he said, still watching the map. "First, to demonstrate that you're a valuable part of our collective victory, and that I consider you trustworthy. Second, to illustrate how bad a strait we're in. Even with *Sentinel* we can't hope to save more than half the systems that are presently under attack. Furthermore, many of the blue systems aren't of high value to the empire. Half of our possessions may remain essentially functional when this war is over. But those with the largest manufacturing, farming, and technological establishments will be gone. The Devourer zeroed in on the targets that would hurt us the most, with very few exceptions. Our population centers have been assaulted without mercy."

"I'm already aware of the situation generally," Hunt remarked. "I have no intention of wavering from the cause."

"Intentions have a way of changing," Krancis replied. "You didn't really put your chips down until Gromyko blew up on you."

"Have you got Philip's room bugged or something?" Hunt snapped. "Isn't there any privacy on this ship?"

"A great deal, in fact," he answered calmly. "I hadn't the least notion that you'd spoken of this to him. I simply observed the change in your behavior and the event that precipitated it. The fact is, Rex, you're not the most difficult man in this galaxy to read. It doesn't take a psychic, or listening devices, to find out what you're thinking."

"Good to know," he said, not appreciating that fact.

"I anticipated such an event would occur sooner or later," Krancis continued. "The band you'd brought with you couldn't last forever. The forces that had pressed you together are in the past. It's not a pleasant fact, Rex, but almost every human relationship involves a practical element that fuels and sustains it. Even your attachment to Doctor Tselitel has a strong undercurrent of deliverance for both of you. The sympathetic attention of a sophisticated mind lifted you from the irrelevancy of a frozen world. And you kindled a flame within her that had long since gone out from despair over her worsening condition." Aware that Hunt was glaring at him without even looking his way, Krancis smiled slightly. "I don't blame you for feeling the way you do. Young love must always be pure of such concrete considerations to be legitimate in its own eyes."

"I'm in my thirties, Krancis," Hunt countered. "I'm hardly a young man anymore. Your words grate on me simply because they're wrong."

"You're not a young man anymore," Krancis agreed. "But you are young in *love*. You've never experienced anything like what you've got with Doctor Tselitel. That's why it'll be catastrophic when you lose her. It'll rock your world like nothing you ever imagined could."

"Is this the part where you tell me to back off and cut her loose before I get in any deeper?" Hunt grumbled, looking at the map again.

"No, that wouldn't do any good," Krancis shook his

head. "This is a lesson you're going to have to learn face-first. For all our sakes, I hope the lesson is both far off and at a time we don't need you. Because it's going to tear you apart."

"You haven't got a lot of faith in me, have you?" Hunt queried, cocking on one leg.

"On the contrary, I have unshakeable faith in the almost boundless wells of passion and determination that rest at the base of your psyche. All they need is the right stimulus to set them off, and you'll be entirely uncontrollable. Combine that with the dark power that already flows through you, and you've got a walking weapon of mass destruction. That's why I regret that you don't have greater rational command of yourself. In that sense you're very much like your father."

The painful memory of Maximillian's last moments in the chamber beneath the prison facility of Delta-13 snapped to mind. Grimacing, Hunt attempted to shove it aside. Uncomfortably he shifted where he stood.

"An unpleasant man in many respects," Krancis opined. "Though only after his change. Before that he was marvelous, though far less developed than you."

"Don't talk about him," Hunt all but growled.

"He is a part of imperial history," Krancis responded imperturbably. "There's a reason he was chosen to head up the mind control project. You may not have inherited his intellectual brilliance. But the single-minded passion that finally twisted and corrupted him was passed on unchanged to you. There's a very real danger of you following in his footsteps, Rex. Especially given the pressure that the dark realm is visibly exerting on you."

"Why are you saying all this?" the Deltan demanded, scowling at him. "Maximillian Hunt is dead and gone, as is the project he spearheaded."

"But his blood lives on in you," Krancis said. "Blood that is both strong and ungovernable. No amount of outside force could ever change Maximillian's mind, nor yours. That is why you must find the power *within* you to direct your course. Otherwise–."

"Otherwise *what?*" cut in Hunt.

"Otherwise you may become many times over the monster he finally degenerated into," Krancis finished, looking him in the eye. "Think about it, Rex," he added, as the Deltan stormed past him towards the door. "You two are much more alike than not."

Hunt hadn't made it more than a dozen heavy steps down the corridor before his eyes fell upon Gromyko. The smuggler had noticed him first, and made a point of ignoring him as he strode past. Knowing better than to say anything, Hunt passed him by and made for the nearby teleporter. It was with mild satisfaction that he heard Gromyko discover, with great annoyance, that the bridge was locked to him. Certain he would double back at once, Hunt hastened his pace so as not to share the teleportation room with him. Deposited near the sleeping quarters moments later, he slowly made his way to his room. With nothing better to do, he dropped onto his bed and glared upward at the ceiling.

"Why does he always prod me just as I'm starting to get used to him?" he asked inwardly, thinking of Krancis. Before he could come up with an answer he heard a soft knock at the door. "Yeah?" he nearly shouted, thinking it was Gromyko. "Well, come on in here," he followed up after an interval of silence. When there was yet no response, he pushed off the bed with annoyance and went to the door. Jerking it open, he was about to read the smuggler the riot act when he saw Chrissy shrinking away from him, a light jacket thrown around her comely shoulders. "What are you doing here?" he asked, trying to take some of the heat out of his voice.

"I-I'm sorry," she apologized, her head turned away from him. "I'd better go."

"Hold on a minute," he said in a firm, clear voice as she took a step from his door. Instantly she froze in place. "Come back here."

Meekly she turned again, her long hair draped around the left side of her face. Instinctively Hunt reached out and moved it aside, revealing at once a nasty bruise on her cheek.

"I'm sorry to have bothered you," she apologized again, about to move backward when his hand took her shoulder and stopped her.

"Who did this?" he demanded. "Girnius?"

"No," she said quietly, shaking her head. "No, Julian would never lay a finger on me."

"Then who?"

"I don't want to start any trouble," she insisted.

Certain she felt too vulnerable to speak in the openness of the hallway, he ushered her inside and closed the door. Leading her to a seat, he poured her a small drink, a previous gift from Krancis. Taking a sip, she drew the jacket a little tighter around her shoulders and looked up at him as he stood in front of her.

"Now, *who* did this?" he asked again, his tone indicating he would brook no refusal.

Swallowing hard, she took another sip and then looked at her feet.

"Soliana."

"What?" Hunt said in surprise.

"Please don't tell Krancis about this," she pleaded, sharply looking upward. "There's enough bad blood between him and Julian as it is. I don't want to jeopardize our stay here. I never should have even bothered you with this, except I didn't know where else to turn."

"No, you did the right thing in coming to me," he assured her almost offhandedly, his mind preoccupied. "But why in the world did Soliana hit you?"

"We got into an argument," she began with embarrassment. "She started gloating about how Julian was just a pawn. She called him an insect, just a little bug under glass! I told her to stop saying such things about him and opened the door to leave. Then she just swung out her hand

and slapped me on the face. She hit me so hard that I lost my balance and hit my cheek against the door. I actually saw stars for a few seconds."

"Where did this happen?" Hunt queried, crossing his arms. "Did anyone else see it?"

"No, I was in her room," she shook her head. "I was walking past when she opened the door and ordered me inside. Since she's so close to Krancis, I thought I'd better do what she said. I'd barely closed the door before she started attacking Julian. I probably wasn't in there for more than two or three minutes."

"And then she hit you?" he asked, building out the scenario in his mind.

"That's right," she nodded. "Her eyes flared like she was possessed. I've never seen anyone so offended before. I'd apologize to her if she hadn't hit me."

"No, don't worry about that," Hunt said at once, trying to silence her so he could think. At any other time he would have thought that Girnius had hit her himself, and that he was pinning it on Soliana to stir up trouble. But her outrageous stance towards Mafalda gave him second thoughts. As Krancis himself had noted, Soliana was undergoing massive changes. She'd made no secret of her disdain for the pirate and his girlfriend on any number of occasions. It wasn't beyond the realm of possibility that she'd become inflamed and lashed out.

"You don't believe me," Chrissy said glumly, sinking down in her chair a little more.

"My mind isn't made up," he answered honestly, looking at her. "I'll have to talk with Soliana and see what she says."

"But why?" she queried, standing up. "I already said I don't want to start any trouble. Can't we just forget this?"

"And what about your cheek?" he asked, nodding towards her bruise. "There's no hiding that."

"I'll just say I tripped and smacked my face," she

replied earnestly. "That's practically the truth, anyway."

"No, this is bigger than you and Girnius, Chrissy," he responded. "If Soliana really did hit you, I need to know about it."

"But *why?*" she repeated.

"Because I need to know what she's capable of," he answered grimly. "If she can hit you over something that small, well..." his voice trailed, not wanting to elaborate. "Is Girnius expecting you anytime soon?"

"No," she replied. "He left our room earlier to go and talk to that AI friend of yours. I haven't seen him since."

"Alright," he said, gesturing towards the chair. "Take a seat and wait until I come back. I won't be long."

"Okay," she acquiesced reluctantly, slowly sitting down as he strode from the room.

"What's gotten into you now, Soliana?" he thought, all but convinced that Chrissy's story was true.

Aware that he was getting ahead of himself, he resolved to wait until all the evidence was in front of him before making a final judgment. Moving briskly, he reached her door and knocked sharply.

"Soliana? Are you in there?"

But there was no response.

Twisting the knob, he found it unlocked. Sticking his head inside, he flicked on the light switch beside the door and glanced around. Nobody. With annoyance he drew his head out, closed the door, and reflected momentarily on where she was likely to be. The hospital seemed the most probable, given that Bardol was still receiving care there. Her curiosity about the missing Devourer shard had been palpable when Krancis had gathered them all together to discuss the situation. She would have gladly examined each crew member personally had Krancis not nixed the idea. Too much risk of infection, he said. But Hunt knew that wouldn't stop her from at least floating around Bardol, hoping to learn something if he regained consciousness.

Hunt wondered why they didn't just examine Bardol himself, given the shard was already gone. But Krancis nixed that idea, too, saying his mind had already experienced far too much trauma to put it at risk by digging around inside it. Soliana readily accepted this notion, so Hunt hadn't bothered to challenge it. But it sat a little funny with him, all the same.

At once he bent his steps towards the hospital. Questioning the staff on duty there, he learned that Soliana hadn't been to see the unfortunate captain after all.

"Where are you?" he mumbled, turning away from the receptionist to continue his search elsewhere.

While this was going on, another search was taking place.

Mafalda, lying atop her bed, had fallen into a deep sleep some hours before. Confused and hurt by Soliana's vitriol, she'd gladly retreated to her room where Krancis had placed her under guard. Certain that she had no future aboard *Sentinel*, she could only hug herself tightly as she lay there, hoping that soon she would be dispatched from the vessel on some mission, however insignificant, and thus removed from Soliana's presence. Hunt and Pincon were her friends, she knew, as was Wellesley. But every interaction with Soliana brought painfully to mind her shameful past. The harm Gromyko ascribed to her didn't help any, either.

Eventually drifting off, she passed through layer after layer of her psyche, dropping ever deeper before finally arriving in a murky, tangled swamp. Vines hung from massive boughs overhead; a muddy creek trickled along beside her; a thick fog permeated the air. Shuddering at once from a chill that seized her bones, she wrapped her arms around herself and began following the creek. It was dark, yet she could see a dozen feet in any direction, her presence bringing a faint light wherever she walked.

"*This is strange*," she thought, finding it ironic that she would bring *light* after her conversion to the dark element. But a moment's reflection revealed to her that she was the bearer of the light of *consciousness*, and not that of the fundamental realms. Feeling silly for her previous notion, she continued walking, struck by the sense of chaos that surrounded her. Every plant, every tree, every *bush* seemed twisted, misshapen, or stunted. There seemed to be no health anywhere. It was a bog of corruption. "*Is this what I'm like on the inside?*" she asked herself inwardly, a little tremor of fear passing through her heart as she looked around. "*Am I just a sack of refuse?*"

Vulnerable and exposed in her dream state, the tremor grew into a full-blown panic attack that quickly brought her to her knees. Breathing with the greatest difficulty, she placed her palms flat on the moist ground and tried to steady down. Finding this ineffective, she closed her eyes and put her forehead against the ground as she tried to dig deep and find something with which to calm herself. Sifting through her storehouse of memories she could only find the painful recollections of her past life. Sinking yet further, she was all but broken when the first faint image of Hunt squaring off against *Deldrach* surfaced. This caused hope to surge through her, reasoning that she must be worth *something* if Hunt would challenge such a deadly foe to rescue her.

It was at this moment that she felt something cold and hard wrap itself around her ankles. Jerking her head up in terror, she saw roots poking out of the ground to seize her. Kicking at the roots did no good as they wound themselves ever tighter, making her cry out in pain. Suddenly whipped onto her back in a sharp twist, another set of thin, powerful roots emerged from the ground and bound her wrists. Stretching her out like a butterfly that was pinned to some corkboard, she screamed as they drew her in opposite directions, intent on pulling her apart. Just when she was certain her body would be torn in two, a familiar voice rang out through the swamp.

"You must learn that this is all you," a female

uttered, her words causing the roots to cease their pulling, though they continued to bind her. "These roots are not your enemies: they are the underlayers of your psyche. You repress them in order to ignore them. But they are always there, influencing you, and being influenced by others. You must acknowledge them. You must acknowledge your past life and *accept* it. Else you will be of no use to anyone, remaining merely a scared little girl."

"I know you," she managed to say between gasping breaths. "You're the Crystal. We met on Erdu-3."

"We met within the confines of your psyche," the voice corrected. "Your body may have been on that world at the time. But there has never been so much as a second since your birth that I have not been with you."

"Are you going to help me?" she asked pleadingly, straining fruitlessly against the roots.

"No. You're going to help *yourself*."

"But I can't!" she insisted, jerking impotently back and forth. "I can't even *move*!"

"You are not meant to *move*, Mafalda," the voice uttered patiently. "You are meant to forgive."

"Forgive who? What?" she asked desperately.

"Yourself, Mafalda. You need to forgive yourself if you're going to move forward down the path that has been chosen for you. You can no longer be bound by guilt."

"I can never forgive myself," she responded despairingly. "I've brought too much pain to others. Only they could release me from the burden I'm under. And most of them are dead."

"Forgiveness comes from many quarters, Mafalda," the voice explained. "Yes, only they can forgive you for the wrong you've done them. Anyone else's forgiveness would be an empty sham. But that isn't what I'm talking about. You condemn yourself for your past actions, and you can't do that any more. You cannot undo your crimes. But you can stop holding them against yourself."

"I don't think I can," Mafalda replied, shaking her head back and forth in the dirt. "I don't have the strength."

"You must *find* the strength. No one else can do this for you. Deep in your mind you've hoped to find a place to hide from the storm of life and the responsibility for your former deeds. But you'll never be anything but a dead weight if you do that. You must grow, Mafalda. You must find the courage to stand on your own two feet. Else you will be forever bound by the past, as you are now. You must cease your running, accept the past, and stride forwards."

"But *how?*" she asked. "How can I do that? I don't even *like* myself anymore. How am I supposed to accept what's happened?"

"You must find a way," the Crystal insisted. "You are wise, Mafalda. Deep within you are concealed great wells of prudence. But you must access them. You must delve into your own nature and find the guidance that will lead you from this prison you've placed yourself in."

"Nothing can ever do that," she replied with grim assurance. "I can never undo what I've done."

"You're not *listening*," the Crystal snapped, causing her to jump. "There is no question of winding back the clock and starting over. The terrible deeds you've done are an unshakeable part of the past. But you are not the sum of your former actions. You still have agency with which to choose your future course. You must step forth and choose a new life. The change in your affinity from light to dark is the perfect jumping off point for an inner rebirth. You must become what you were *born* to be."

As she said this the roots slowly released their hold. Cautiously sitting up, she rubbed her wrists and ankles for a moment and then arose.

"I don't know if I can," she uttered meekly, unsure where to direct her words.

"That's an improvement, at least," the voice responded. "Shortly before you were certain no change was possible. Now you're merely doubtful. I shall speak to you again, when–."

Suddenly her words were cut off by a screaming pain that passed through Mafalda's body. Again dropping to her knees in agony, she clutched her head momentarily before being dragged from her dream back to consciousness. To her terror Soliana stood over her bed, her eyes aflame with hate as she pressed her right hand into Mafalda's stomach. A terrible charge flowed from her into Mafalda's body, simultaneously paralyzing and torturing her.

"You've drawn breath long enough, little worm," a deep voice rumbled from between Soliana's lips. "First you'll suffer. And then you'll die."

Mercilessly Soliana ramped up the flow until Mafalda all but passed out. Unable to scream or even twitch, she was utterly immobilized by the attack. Helplessly she gazed at the ceiling, only seeing her assailant in her peripheral vision. Desperately, fruitlessly, she willed her body to move.

"Save yourself the effort," Soliana taunted her, somehow aware of her attempts to defend herself. "My power is on a scale you can't even imagine. At last all the disparate elements of my psyche have joined together into one being that can no longer be harnessed or controlled. Krancis fancied that he would have himself a lapdog, a *prophetess* that would help guide your pathetic kind to victory. He never imagined that he'd planted the seeds of his own destruction when he brought me on board and began developing my powers. But that was not his fatal mistake."

"Soliana…you can't–," Mafalda managed to fight out from between her dull lips.

"Quiet!" snapped the being who held her life in her hand. And then, with a wicked smile on her lips, "Do you want to know what his fatal mistake was? It was when I interacted with the Devourer mass as we floated above Hubertus. It was then that the implants within me found a new way to live, one free of Krancis' chain. I knew at once what had to be done, what confusion must be brought to *Sentinel* to delay its action long enough for the other masses to finish their work of signaling the ancient one. So I sowed discord, first by killing Lieutenant Powers, and then by maiming Captain Bardol while I drew from him the great shard of the Devourer, completing my transformation. Your little band of heroes was so *easy* to shatter. Even now they grow farther and farther apart as my influence spreads throughout the ship."

"Soliana…you have to fight it…" Mafalda struggled to say.

"Don't you understand, little worm? I've *chosen* this course! I *want* this for myself."

"I…don't believe that…" she insisted, shaking her head ever so slightly. "I can feel the good in you still. Your spirit is…weak. But not *bad*."

"Shut up!" snapped Soliana, pressing Mafalda into the mattress with her hand and surging the painful flow into her abdomen. Seeing her victim freeze and then lose consciousness for a few moments, she reduced the flow until she awoke again. "Don't insult me by *reasoning* with me, worm," she uttered. "My mind is settled, my destiny is chosen. This is my fate."

"Fate is chosen…every day," Mafalda countered, her voice strengthening. "We make it ourselves."

"Such hopeful nonsense," Soliana tsked, shaking her head. "You'd like to believe that, wouldn't you? Then you could wash the blood off your hands at the snap of your fingers." Leaning in closer, her otherworldly voice deepened yet further. "Nothing can ever cleanse your conscience, worm. I know the memories that torture you even now. Forever you'll be their prisoner."

"No," she pushed back, attempting to dig down and draw forth whatever power the dark realm might've had in store for her. But she came up empty-handed.

"You're not even an initiate of the dark element,

worm," Soliana laughed scornfully. "You couldn't so much as tickle my nose with your 'powers.'"

"No," Hunt's voice said from the door behind her. "But I can."

"Another step and this little maggot will be shattered beyond all redemption," Soliana warned, her deep voice reverberating through the room. Looking over her shoulder at the Deltan, she smiled. "What shall the mighty Earthborn Champion do now?"

"You'll find out if you don't let her go," he said grimly.

"Surrender my hostage? Oh, no. Certainly not. I must say you've discovered me a touch sooner than I'd anticipated. Now I'll have to deal with both of you."

"Whatever's gotten into you, Soliana, you'd better push it out again," Hunt ordered, taking a step inside.

"Ah! Ah! I said to stay where you are!"

"You can't kill her before I cross this room and crush the life from your throat," he said menacingly, moving yet closer.

"Let's find out!" Soliana exclaimed, mad glee in her eyes as she gave Mafalda everything she had. In a flash Hunt dashed off a pair of smoke blasts that struck her in the face and chest. Terribly hurt by them, she fell onto Mafalda and continued to assault her.

In an instant Hunt darted across the room and seized Soliana's wrists. Jerking her off her victim, he felt at once as the multitudinous voices that filled her mind attempted to infiltrate him, led by the powerful Devourer shard. A surge of the shadow element's power drove them off and kept them confined to her body.

"Snap out of it, Soliana!" Hunt barked, shaking her violently as she fought his hold. Slamming her against the wall, his dark eyes bored into hers, which faintly glowed purple. "Don't surrender to them, Soliana. You're stronger than this."

"Don't you see, Champion?" the deep voice rumbled.

"This little creature is no longer herself. I dominate her body now. *I*, the Devourer, have seized your greatest asset and turned her against you! The implants have so totally subjugated her pathetic will that there is nothing left of her anymore. Krancis has lost his seer! Soon he shall lose all!"

Bringing her wrists together, he grasped them both in his powerful right hand and slapped her thunderously with his left.

"You're such a primitive," Soliana sneered, blood dribbling from her mouth where her upper lip had been cut against her teeth by the blow. "Do you seriously think a sound thrashing will be enough to recover her? She's *gone*, Champion. Never to be found again. I've done my work much too thoroughly for her to ever be restored to you. All it took was a little help from her implants for the door to be opened. Krancis knew that assimilating the other personalities would alter her nature. He never imagined it would work such a radical change."

"We'll get her back," Hunt asserted, grinding her wrists together in his grip. By this time Mafalda had finally recovered and struggled her way to her feet. Standing behind him, she looked on in terror.

"Yes, hide behind the Champion, little worm," Soliana smiled. "Hide as long as you can. But know this: soon even his great power will be swept aside as though it never existed at all. And who shall protect you then?"

"We'll manage," a precise voice uttered from the doorway. Flanked by Pinchon on one hand and Gromyko on the other, the man in black advanced into the room. "I thought the time had come for a little family chat."

"For what?" Soliana demanded in her bizarrely deep voice. "To wipe away all your past misunderstandings? To reunite the team? It was with *ease* that I broke you from one another, spreading suspicion as a flower spreads its seeds upon the willing ground. You were eager to shatter, to go your own separate ways. I merely provided the necessary push."

"It was you!" exclaimed the smuggler in a flash of insight. "You killed Julia!"

"Of course, you lackwit," she snapped. "Bardol should be expiring soon as well."

"He already has," Krancis uttered. "Less than ten minutes ago."

"Pity. He had an interesting mind for a human."

"I'll kill you!" roared Gromyko, reaching out his hands and making a dash for Soliana. But a timely leg from Pinchon tripped and spread him across the floor. Before he could get up the pirate was sitting on his back. "Get off of me!" he shouted. "I'll tear her to pieces! I'll beat her to death with her own limbs!"

"Calm down, Romeo," Pinchon said scornfully. "The adults are talking."

"Not for much longer," Soliana triumphed. "Soon all will be united in death. This entire universe will know nothing save silence. All will be still."

"Not if I have anything to say about it!" exclaimed the smuggler, clawing his way across the floor, dragging Pinchon along for the ride. When the colonel grabbed his arms and pulled them off the floor, Gromyko began wildly kicking with his feet to try and dump his cargo off his back. Seeing this, Krancis bent over and pressed two fingers to his forehead. Instantly he lost consciousness, his face dropping with a thunk to the floor.

"I believe our voluble friend has said enough for the moment," the man in black commented, straightening and drawing closer to Soliana. "I had high hopes for you."

"Misplaced hopes, Jannik," she laughed. "The hopes of a desperate man. You should have known that this little mouse had no chance of standing against the voices that crowded her at all times, battering away at her will until there was nothing left. She was a weak girl from the start. The experiments she was subjected to only served to weaken her further. You ought to have known better than to place such trust in her. She could only betray you in the end, as indeed she has."

"We'll get her back," Pinchon asserted, likewise drawing near.

"No, we won't," Krancis shook his head slightly, his eyes searching Soliana's face. "The shard is correct: she's lost to us for good."

"How can you say that?" the colonel demanded. "Give the girl a chance, at least!"

"I already have," he replied. "Why do you think we've been in warp this whole time? That was her window of opportunity to reassert her old self."

"Then you knew it was me?" Soliana asked.

"Of course."

"And you let her run up and down the ship, free as a bird?" Pinchon snapped. "Do you have any idea what damage she could have done? What intelligence she must have gathered?"

"She wasn't the only one gathering intelligence," Krancis responded.

"So, that was your game, then," Soliana uttered with a hint of respect. "You wanted me under glass so you could examine me."

"Precisely. And I must say, you've been most free with your thoughts. I expected you to play harder to get."

"It's no matter," Soliana said dismissively. "Nothing you gathered will deliver you from the terror to come. You should have destroyed the masses when you had the chance. Now they'll finish their work with or without the energy of your great cannon."

"You would've liked that," Krancis nodded knowingly. "It would've brought the terror to us before we had a chance to prepare. And it would have left more of your forces intact."

"No preparation can be made, Jannik. You know that as well as I do."

"That is where you're mistaken," he replied calmly. "Deeply mistaken."

"We'll see about that," she grinned evilly.

Suddenly a charge ran through her body that shocked Hunt into releasing her, his hands burning like they were on fire. As he recoiled she made for Krancis, intent on delivering some parting blow. But with lightning swiftness he seized her forehead in his left palm and brought her to her knees. At once black cracks began to form on the skin of her face as she screamed in horror. In the space of a minute she disintegrated into a pillar of ash. Pressing his hand into it, Krancis scattered it upon the floor.

"You didn't have to kill her!" roared Pinchon. "We could have helped her! Could have saved her!"

"There was absolutely nothing we could have done," the man in black replied, rubbing his palms together to wipe away the dust. "She'd made her choice. The tiny fragment of her will that remained was utterly under the sway of the implants and the shard of the Devourer. She would never have returned to us, and there was no way to extract her. The best course was to end it now, before she brought any more shame upon herself."

"And what about you, Krancis?" demanded Pinchon. "What share of the shame is yours for exposing that poor girl to powers she couldn't cope with?"

"As I have said before, we are in a state of war. Casualties must be expected, even if they are from among our personal circle. No one is exempt."

"No, you don't get to cop out that easily," the colonel declared. "She was in the palm of your hand ever since we pulled her out of the Black Hole. She was just a lost, innocent girl when we brought her to Omega Station. You twisted and turned her until she hadn't the least idea who or what she was anymore."

"No, the people who worked upon her psyche did that to her," Krancis corrected him evenly. "They saw her talent and felt they could bolster it by adding the implants. Obviously they were mistaken. They placed too great a load upon her already frail mind."

"You using her like a radio above Hubertus didn't help matters, either," Pinchon retorted. "And for what? We didn't learn a thing. All you managed to do was hand the parasite Soliana. Now we've lost both a friend and an asset."

"And just what is your point, Colonel?" Krancis queried. "That I've made a mistake? That I should surrender the conduct of this war?"

"I'm not making any kind of point to *you*, Krancis," he answered sourly, glancing at Hunt as he turned towards the door. "I know that's impossible, given you're omniscient. But for the rest of us mortals, there's a grim lesson to be learned here."

With this he left them.

Throughout this Mafalda had clung tightly to Hunt, being just barely strong enough to stand after Soliana's terrible attack on her. Watching the man in black with fearful eyes, she was surprised when he turned to her with a look approaching kindness on his normally expressionless face.

"You've been through a great deal, Mafalda, and for that I am sorry. It was necessary to maintain the fiction about Lieutenant Powers until matters had reached a head with Soliana." Pausing, he looked at the smuggler momentarily. "He's going to owe you both an apology when he finally comes to."

"As I recall it was you who stuck me with the responsibility for her death in the first place," Hunt pointed out flatly.

"Yes, because I knew you could bear the burden," Krancis replied self-evidently. "As of course you have. You are a lord of the empire, Rex. That position entitles you to all kinds of blame that you'll never deserve." Looking at the ash, he reflected briefly. "It's time to change our course. Rest and recuperate while you can. You'll be needed soon."

"What about him?" Hunt asked, nodding to the still unconscious Gromyko.

"He'll be alright in an hour or so," he answered, walking slowly from the room. "He could use a chance to cool off, in any event."

"I don't understand," Mafalda uttered, her voice thin and weak as she held onto Hunt. "I suppose this was a victory. But I can't help feeling we've suffered a defeat."

"We *have* suffered a defeat," he told her, putting an arm around her and walking slowly with her. "A major one."

"Where are we going?" she asked, as he led her into the corridor.

"Back to my room. You've seen enough for one day. You can come back when they've swept up Soliana. Besides, I've got someone waiting for me there."

"And Gromyko?" she asked, tugging on him slightly so he'd stop.

Exhaling, he turned and looked at his fellow Deltan.

"He'd be barking up the wrong tree to expect sympathy from me," he answered coldly. "Besides, like Krancis said, he could use a chance to cool off."

"*So, Soliana's dead,*" Wellesley noted in his log hours later, once the news had finally trickled back to him. "*I really can't believe that Krancis essentially let a spy onboard, especially one who cost us Soliana. It has to be part of some larger game to get inside the Devourer's head. Rex said something about Krancis taunting her by saying she'd been surprisingly free with her thoughts while onboard, and that he'd expected her to be harder to monitor. Given how adamant he was about having Soliana contact the Devourer mass on Hubertus, I simply have to think he was playing a trick on us all, including Soliana. That would make sense, too, of how he seemed to have utterly misjudged what she was capable of withstanding. Given his almost godlike perception, it's much more credible that he knew* exactly *what she could take, and that he deliberately handed her over to* the parasite knowing that he'd then get the inside track on its intentions."

"I honestly don't know if that makes me feel better or worse, given it would make him little more than a heartless machine to use Soliana in that way. At the same time, it would mean that he wasn't caught with his pants down. Like so many master players of the game of strategy, he sacrificed an asset in order, in his estimation, to gain something of greater value. In truth, that's all warfare is anyway, whether it's exchanging men for turf, or agents for intelligence. But it's harder to accept that fact when the assets being exchanged are personally known to you."

Inwardly sighing his displeasure, he continued.

"It seems the colonel is on the verge of mutiny, which is hardly surprising, given he's never trusted Krancis, anyway. But he's gonna have to watch his mouth, or he might find himself in solitary confinement. I doubt Krancis will waste any time getting him off the ship. I know I sure wouldn't, if he was nipping at my heels that way. Mafalda is shaken but okay, more or less. And Gromyko is all contrition and shame. Serves him right, after he went at Rex the way he did. I just wish he'd gotten another chance to belt him in the nose before he came to his senses. Might have knocked a little common sense into that skull of his."

"Rex is awfully quiet about this whole thing. I tried to pry his thoughts out of him, but his lips were sealed. It's unlike him to play his cards so close with me. We used to share everything back on Delta. I hope it's nothing permanent, just a phase he's going through because of all the shock."

"We're presently on course towards a concentration of Devourer craft. Krancis has decided, given the masses will draw this 'terror' towards us in any event, to beat down as much of the parasite's fleet as possible before the storm breaks. I suppose I agree, though I can't help wondering if we might be able to just barely pull off an upset if we destroyed the masses fast enough. Maybe this 'terror' wouldn't come after all. But Krancis seems to have some kind of secret information upon which he's basing his *decision (probably gleaned from Soliana), so all we can do is play along. Naturally he hasn't seen fit to inform us just what this 'terror' is. I've been digging through every shred of information I can think of that might shed light on it. But I'm none the wiser for doing so."*

Interrupted by an incoming Black Fang communication, he attended to it for some minutes before returning to his log.

"Whatever this thing is, it must be nasty to somehow be worse than the Devourer. Krancis hasn't given me any real specifics, but through a medley of Black Fang sources I've been able to establish a rough picture of the damage the parasite has done to the empire. Needless to say, it's been catastrophic. If this 'terror' is worse than that, then God help us all."

As the hours passed and a rough version of the news of Soliana's death spread to every corner of the ship, the crew grew quiet and apprehensive. Uncertain quite what to believe, given no less than three rumors were at that time circulating, they drew together in groups populated by their familiars and whispered among themselves. But one thing had passed into gossip with crystal clarity: Krancis himself had ended Soliana's life. Every member of the crew had felt the curious air of death that seemed to follow him like a shadow; a number of them had felt their bones chilled when an unfortunate piece of news caused his eyes to tighten and his gaze to harden. But for all this they hadn't the least idea what his actual *powers* were. Those of Rex Hunt were legendary. But the man in black had maintained such secrecy about his own capacities that they could only speculate. Given his position, many thought he was more powerful than Hunt. But the ready answer to that notion, of course, was to question why he left so much to the Deltan when he could do it himself. The answer to *that*, naturally, was to say he couldn't afford to risk himself on the front lines. And so the debate would go on and on.

The fact that he disintegrated a powerful psychic

in a matter of moments finally gave the warring camps something concrete to argue over. They immediately attempted to quantify how much power was required for such an act so that they could compare it to Hunt's well-known feats. This, predictably, led to questions of whether he'd exerted himself to the fullest, or if only a portion of his might was employed. Speculation, subsequently, was not quelled by the news but fueled instead.

Relative stillness prevailed until *Sentinel* at last emerged from warp in the midst of an enormous Devourer fleet. By this time Hunt was on the bridge with Krancis, along with Gromyko who'd snuck in while the door was open. Pointedly ignored by both men, the smuggler was content not to have been thrown out on his ear.

"You'll want me in the reactor, I imagine," Hunt said with displeasure, about to turn for the door.

"No, that won't be necessary," Krancis replied evenly, looking almost casually at the battle as the warship disintegrated numberless fighters with its many turrets. Suddenly the great cannon roared to life, its deadly beam colliding with a Devourer carrier, blackening it rapidly. It wasn't long before it crumbled into a cloud of ash. "*Sentinel* is quite capable of managing this fleet on its own."

As he said this a group of frigates reached *Sentinel* and began clawing away at its hull, searching for a weakness as always.

"You'd think it would learn," Hunt uttered.

"That's what it's trying to do: learn of some opening it can exploit."

"At tremendous cost."

"It'll cost it even more if *Sentinel* is permitted to devastate its fleets with impunity."

As usual, the man in black was right.

"So just what did you want me up here for?" the Deltan asked, crossing his arms. "Can't be for the fireworks," he added, watching as the vessel lined up on another carrier.

Half a minute passed silently before the cannon cut loose again, instantly erasing several frigates who'd gotten in the way.

"I wanted to explain about Soliana," he replied, glancing at Gromyko momentarily. Deciding he could stay, he continued. "As the colonel made quite clear, her death is both regrettable and does considerable harm to our war effort. My aim, as I indicated, was to gain insight from her." Again he looked at the smuggler. "You may recall, Gromyko, that I said she represented the promise of ancestral aid."

"Yeah, I guess I do," he nodded, hazily remembering those words.

"She combined an affinity for both the light and the darkness that could have been exploited had the implants been brought to heel. She would have been second only to *Sentinel* in terms of her usefulness."

"What do you mean ancestral aid?" Hunt queried, the words striking him strangely.

"The implants, or shards, didn't come from nowhere, Rex. They were derived from ancient beings, the relatives of the Earthborn. Representing all the other families of man, they brought their own special powers along with them. The difficulty had lain in getting them to work together, and in overcoming the decay that countless generations of time had wrought. The fact is they were corrupt, distorted by the passage of so many years. There was some hope that Soliana would be able to draw them together, using their mixture of talents to fill in the gaps each of them had. Had they worked in concert, they would have been marvelously effective. But such cooperation proved beyond Soliana's ability to enforce. A tentative peace was formed until they were exposed to the Devourer's mind. Sensing its superiority at once, they subjugated Soliana and never looked back."

"Then Soliana was their prisoner?" Gromyko clarified.

"Only to a point," Krancis answered, as *Sentinel* positioned itself to blast a trio of incoming battleships.

"Weary of holding the implants in check, she was glad to surrender to them once their power proved too strong. In the end she went over to their side rather than continue a fruitless struggle."

"I suppose I can't blame her," the smuggler replied sympathetically.

"I can," Hunt said coldly. "Plenty of other people have gone to their graves in this war rather than surrender."

"She was our friend, Rex," Gromyko pointed out somewhat meekly, aware the subject would be touchy.

"That's proven not to count for much," he responded, still watching the battle with his arms crossed over his chest.

"Her will was simply too weak to withstand their combined pressure," Krancis explained, the great cannon again firing and striking the oncoming battleships. "It's a question why she was chosen for the experiment, given her psyche was so frail."

"Experiment?" Gromyko queried quietly, smarting from Hunt's last remark.

"The implantation of the shards was the experimental brainchild of a mysterious group of scientists and psychics. The imperial intelligence service has never been able to nail down exactly who they were. But its members were both human and alien. It's suspected that they had considerable influence in the government at one time, but were systemically rooted out and eliminated."

"How?" Gromyko asked.

"Assassination mostly. It's evident that a faction with superhuman insight sniffed them out and hunted them down."

"*Pho'Sath*," Hunt remarked.

"Most likely. Facts are sparse wherever these people are concerned. But given Soliana was meant to be a gift to our eventual war effort, there can be little doubt that these people were our allies, and that their enemies are *our* enemies."

"Then why keep it all a secret?" Hunt asked. "Why not come out in the open instead of getting cut to ribbons on their own?"

"The imperial government was notoriously untrustworthy before I came along," Krancis replied. "My predecessor in charge of intelligence ran the service like it was his own personal fiefdom, not infrequently hiring out its services to the highest bidder. Given this treasonous activity, I immediately had him killed upon my ascension to office."

Loudly Gromyko gulped.

"You...did?"

"Yes. The emperor empowered me to eliminate anyone I deemed a threat to the empire. It's hard to imagine a more dangerous man than my predecessor, given he fled office with a personal network of spies and killers on the one hand, and the dossiers of all his personal enemies on the other. Needless to say, I was at the top of his list."

"Who was second?" Hunt asked.

"Emperor Rhemus. He'd been contemplating a coup for years, but had been stymied by the navy. Their personal sense of loyalty to the emperor runs deep." Pausing briefly, he looked at Gromyko and nodded towards the door.

"But the battle's just getting good!" the smuggler insisted, a little of his old spunk rising to the surface despite the heaviness of the mood. As if in support of his point, a large group of Devourer fighters swept past the bridge, holes instantly knocked in their ranks by dark beams that seemed to be rising from every part of the ship. But all it took was a momentary look into Krancis' cool eyes for him to change his mind. At once making for the door, he mumbled something about seeing Rex later and then vanished.

"The odds of our surviving the present conflict are more or less unaffected by Soliana's passing," Krancis began without preamble the moment they were alone. "The success of the Adler project removed all doubt of that, when taken alongside the contributions of *Sentinel*. The real danger lies in the conflicts to come. Without the advantage of her insights, we'll be flying in the dark for much of it."

"That's never been much of a problem for you before," Hunt remarked.

"We're passing into unprecedented times, Rex," Krancis uttered grimly.

"Just how many wars have we had with a parasite like this?" the Deltan countered. "It's not as if we've ever done this before."

"Indeed," Krancis responded quietly.

"Is there something…you're trying to tell me?" Hunt queried, not sure he actually wanted to know. "Is something happening to you?"

"Me? Not in the least. I'm presently at the height of my powers. But the information that was previously made available to me is rapidly going out of date. Soon we shall have to rely on cunning and brute force rather than foreknowledge to see us through the storms to come. An unfortunate reality, given we're so reduced from our prior state."

"I imagine I'm supposed to supply much of this 'brute force,'" Hunt commented.

"That *is* your stock-in-trade," Krancis pointed out. "Whether powering this ship, or decimating our enemies on the ground, raw power has been your chief contribution."

"Especially given Dad didn't pass on his brains to me," he added sourly.

"Don't be sensitive, Rex," Krancis said. "You're in much too great a position to take the occasional negative comment personally."

"It's been a long day," Hunt replied. "I'm entitled to the odd human frailty."

"Neither you nor I are entitled to anything, anymore," Krancis disagreed. "We are servants of the empire, and as such must devote ourselves totally to its service."

"I'm still getting used to that part."

The cannon fired again, coating another carrier in darkness as the last of the fighters was turned to dust.

"It's almost rinse and repeat at this point," Hunt said, nodding towards the battle.

"It'll stay that way unless the Devourer manages to figure out some kind of a weakness in *Sentinel*." Watching the fray momentarily, he continued. "I didn't want things to reach this point, Rex. But the loss of Soliana has placed an even greater burden upon your shoulders. One that you're ill-prepared to grapple with, given both your background and your proclivities."

"You mean Lily?" Hunt queried, tired of Krancis objections to their relationship.

"Only in part," the man in black clarified. "Your life on Delta-13 prepared you for many things. It taught you both hardiness and to never back down. But it failed to make you into a *leader*, which is what we need. A man who can inspire our forces on the front lines. You already have the sympathy necessary for the role, given how you've been inching closer to the dark realm in order to deliver a string of innocents from death. Those black marks on your arms are a testament to that fact. But more is needed. You must become *victory* in the eyes of our people."

"I thought that was the job of your propaganda machine."

"They can craft an image. But not a fact."

"You're trying to guide me into something, Krancis," Hunt observed, looking at him. "Just what is it?"

Faintly Krancis smiled.

"I'm glad you recognize that fact. It speaks well of your intelligence."

"Well, a *few* of Dad's brain cells made it into my skull."

"And just what do those cells tell you I'm up to?"

"I'd say you're still concerned I'll cut loose and go my own way, so you're trying to bind me to the cause by tying, literally, the entire human race into my life."

"The future of the empire will be safe in your hands," Krancis uttered with quiet satisfaction. "Provided you stay the course. The temptation will be great to deviate."

"I'll hang in there," Hunt replied, glancing at the battle as the last carrier came under fire from *Sentinel*.

"See that you do."

For a short interval silence ensued as the pair watched the rest of the parasite's forces disintegrate.

"Our job is done here. We'll move at once for our next target. In the meantime, I suggest you patch things up with Gromyko."

"He started it. Let him patch things up."

"You know as well as anyone that it usually falls to the mature party in any relationship to heal the breach. The fact is Gromyko has too much pride to take the first step after he's embarrassed himself so badly."

"Disgraced would be a better word."

"Indeed. Hence you must make the first move."

"That's not a friendship I have any interest in renewing. Not after how he treated me and Mafalda."

"I'm not suggesting you do it for old time's sake, Rex. We simply can't afford divisions aboard *Sentinel*, especially in the wake of losing Soliana. You need as much of the old team at your back as possible if you're to live up to your responsibilities. Believe me, the road ahead only gets harder."

Frowning his displeasure, Hunt nevertheless nodded and walked slowly towards the door.

"Captain?" he heard Krancis radio from behind him. "Take us out of here the moment the last of the parasite's craft is destroyed."

Hunt didn't have far to travel before he ran into Gromyko. The smuggler, evidently, had been waiting for him inside the nearest teleportation room.

"My friend–," he began automatically upon seeing him, his words cut off by a sharp motion of Hunt's hand.

"Come with me," he ordered, entering the teleporter

THE CRUSADE OF VENGEANCE

first and instructing the technician to send them to the sleeping quarters. Wordlessly they entered his room, the door being promptly slammed shut by Hunt. Gripping the smuggler by the front of his shirt, he all but lifted him off his feet and slammed him against the wall. "Do you have any idea what you put Mafalda through? What you put *me* through?"

Unsure how to answer, Gromyko could only stare back at him, for once lost for words.

"No, you don't," Hunt asserted through gritted teeth. "So don't pull that 'my friend' garbage with me. You're not gonna just walk back into this without paying the piper. You think you live a gilded life, that somehow the rules don't apply to you. But let me make one thing clear, pal: I'm gonna introduce you to terrors you never imagined if you *ever* pull a stunt like that again."

"I shall never say my friend again," he answered densely, misunderstanding his meaning.

"I'm not talking about that!" Hunt snapped. "I'm talking about accusing Mafalda of murder, of ending our friendship because you were half crazy over some fantasy romance with a girl who wasn't even *slightly* interested in you. I'm talking about you going off like a cannon because your feelings were twisted out of shape. How about you maintain a *fraction* of the emotional control I exercise on a *daily basis?* How about you grow up and try living as an adult for a change?"

"I'll do whatever you ask," the smuggler promised. "Anything at all."

"I'm not *asking*," Hunt warned him, moving his face closer to Gromyko's. "I'm telling you how it's gonna be: you've got *one* more chance. Blow it this time, and there won't be any going back. There'll be nothing but scorched earth between us. Is that clear?"

"Absolutely. One hundred percent," he nodded fervently.

With disgust Hunt released his grip, Gromyko's heels clattering against the floor as he came off the tips of his toes.

"Get out of here," he instructed, waving towards the door. "For your sake, I'd better not see you until I've cooled down."

Again nodding vigorously, the smuggler shot out the door and bolted down the hallway. Hunt knew this, for in his panic Gromyko had failed to close the door completely upon leaving, and his footfalls were clearly audible as he retreated towards his own room. Scowling his annoyance, Hunt went to the door and was about to shut it when Mafalda's voice stopped him.

"Rex?" she queried meekly.

Surprised, he opened the door a little wider and saw her standing doubtfully before him.

"Are you alright?" he asked her when she simply stood there. "Come on in."

"I don't want to disturb you," she replied quietly, glancing down the corridor in the direction Gromyko had fled. "I think I've caused you enough trouble already."

"Oh, you heard that?"

"Yes," she nodded guiltily. "I'm sorry. I shouldn't have listened by your door. It's just I came to thank you for saving me from Soliana, and I heard you say my name. It–it got my attention, and so I kept listening."

"Oh, don't worry about that," he said with a dismissive wave, ushering her inside. "And you don't have to thank me over Soliana, either. She got what was coming to her."

"But she was your friend," Mafalda pointed out, a little off-put by his coldness.

"Friends are transient," he replied. "That's why I never bothered to make hardly any on Delta: when the chips are down, you can rely on just about nobody. And the chips were always down on that ice cube."

"I hope that's not true," she uttered, moving a little of her newly blackened hair away from her eye and tucking it behind her ear. "After everything I've done, all I've got left is my friends. And precious few of them, too. Just you, Wellesley, and Colonel Pinchon."

"Well, you've got quality instead of quantity," he said, forcing a weak grin to try and cheer her up a little. "In all honesty, you could do worse than a lord of the empire and an ancient alien construct. The colonel's not bad, either, when he's got his head on straight."

"What do you mean?" she asked with concern.

"Krancis' latest stratagem bent him out of shape. More than ever he wants to bolt."

"And how do you feel about it?"

"Regrettable necessity," he shrugged. "I'm sorry for what happened to Soliana. But given she went over to the enemy in the end, I can't muster much sympathy. You?"

"I'm not sure what to think," she replied, wringing her hands against her stomach as she thought back on the attack that nearly took her life. "I recoil every time I think about her standing over my bed. There was such wicked delight in her eyes that it makes me want to shrink back. And the terrible pain, to say nothing of being helplessly paralyzed…" her voice trailed as she shook her head. Closing her eyes, she shut out the image. "But even as she attacked me I could feel the innocence that she still had; ever as she rendered *me* helpless, I could feel that she was helpless, too. She might have chosen to go over to them. But I don't think it was from evil. I think she was just weak."

"That's what Krancis thinks, too," Hunt agreed.

"Does that make any difference? I mean, since it all came out to the same thing, in the end?"

"Doesn't make any difference to me," he replied. "I guess the philosophers would make the case she was more sinned against than sinner, given all she'd been subjected to. But I've seen too many people die in this war to forget how she betrayed them. I don't think she was bad, either. Not the little part of her that was actually *her*. But she would have destroyed us all if given the chance. Or the implants would've, along with that Devourer shard. In the end, that's all that really matters."

"I suppose you're right," she nodded reluctantly, looking down at her feet and thinking for a moment. "How did you know I was in trouble?" she asked, the question suddenly occurring to her. "I mean, back in my room when Soliana was attacking me."

"I didn't," he said, exhaling heavily over the implications of what he was about to say next. "The dark realm did. I happened to be walking past your room when I had the urge to enter. Half a second was all it took to know what was going on."

"The dark realm is having you look after me," she uttered. "It's still working to keep us together."

"Looks that way," he replied.

"I hope you know I'm not trying to force myself in between you and Doctor Tselitel," she said in the tone of an appeal. "I would never do that."

"Oh, I know," he assured her. "The thought had never crossed my mind. You're much too modest for that. Now *Soliana*, well, she had different ideas. Honestly that's probably part of the reason she went after you ever since coming aboard *Sentinel*: she probably knew the dark realm was drawing us together and would have none of it."

A shiver ran down Mafalda's spine that made her visibly tremble.

"I can't believe what a sitting duck I've been," she said anxiously. "All this time she could have snuck into my room and snuffed out my life." Bewildered, she looked at Hunt. "How could Krancis let her just walk around like that?"

"Exigencies of war," Hunt answered.

"I suppose so," she agreed hesitantly, her anxiety beginning to pass. "Still, it's a creepy thought. Like finding out someone's been watching you in your apartment for the last week."

"I'm sure the dark realm would have reached out and drawn me to you if she'd made the attempt sooner than she did," he assured her, though inwardly he was not nearly so certain as he wished her to believe. "The only real danger would have been if I'd left the ship. And that wasn't possible, given we were just warping in circles."

"I guess you're right," she uttered, feeling a little better. Taking a step closer to the door, she awkwardly gestured towards it. "Suppose I'd better not take up any more of your time."

"Believe me, it's no bother. Especially after Antonin."

"I hope everything clears up between the two of you," she said, managing to smile a little despite all she'd been through.

"I'm sure it will," he nodded for her sake, heading to the door and opening it for her. "Get a little rest, Mafalda. Let me know if you need anything."

"I will. Thank you, Rex."

"You bet."

Once she was gone he moved to the middle of the room and thoughtfully sighed. Lightly smacking his right fist against his left palm, he glanced over his shoulder at the door and shook his head.

"*I don't know if you can hear me or not,*" he thought, directing his inner voice towards the dark realm. "*But I'm not ditching Lily for anything.*"

Neither hearing nor feeling anything, he went to his bed and stretched out. It wasn't long before his mind grew hazy and began to wander.

"*I heard you,*" a voice spoke, instantly jarring him upright. Instinctively looking towards the back of the room, he saw the small, shadowy child. "*I heard your words. Your devotion to Lily Tselitel is both laudable and disgraceful. You must embrace your destiny, setting aside your selfish desires. We have spoken of this before.*"

"*You* spoke of it before," Hunt shot back, no longer

disturbed by the figure's eerie presence. "I don't want any part of it. I'm adamant about that."

"*You will come to the truth when the time is right,*" the figure uttered. "*I was hasty before in attempting to force your hand. But do not think that the facts have changed. Many forces have converged in you; forces which must be satisfied if humanity is to have a future. This is why Krancis speaks as I do. The dark realm agrees as well.*"

"What does that even mean?" Hunt retorted. "Does the dark realm think? Does it have a personality? Or is it just a sort of mudslide engulfing everything in its path?"

"*It is many things, all of them difficult to define. Ten lifetimes would not be sufficient to uncover half its secrets. Though it strives to make itself intelligible to us, our minds are not structured to understand it. It will always remain largely a mystery.*"

"I'm not abandoning Lily," he asserted once more. "You can put all the pressure on me that you want. I won't bend and I won't break. You should know that."

"*Hope teaches us to forget what we know and to strive for what we desire,*" the figure replied, placing one inky black foot slowly in front of the other until it had reached the bed. "*That is why Krancis continues to believe in you. He knows the depth of your devotion. Yet hope teaches him to be patient, to await the possibility of some shift in your perspective. The future of humanity hangs upon your every step. You must not fail.*"

"I would be *nothing* that I am today without Lily," Hunt argued earnestly. "What sort of a man would I be to turn my back on her?"

"*An unfortunate man,*" the figure replied. "*One upon whom a dreadful burden had been placed. But even an undeserved burden must be borne, if it delivers others from death.*"

"I still don't believe that," he shook his head. "Our entire fate can't dangle from me alone."

"*Man would survive the present conflict without you,*"

the figure said. *"But only as scattered bands, hunted and hated by many enemies. Eventually they would be eradicated. This is why you must raise up heirs who can fight in your stead when you finally pass from life: our people must have a strong, steady line of leaders and warriors to guide them through the tumults to follow. This above all is what concerns Krancis. The future for humanity is dark indeed. He has seen this."*

"You want me to believe that our entire race depends on an exile from Delta-13?" he asked. "That out of all the psychics and warriors and brilliant minds this empire has to offer, *I'm* the only one who can give us a future?"

"You must initiate our transformation into a darkness wielding race," the figure explained. *"You must be the tip of the spear, penetrating the barrier that separates the material from the immaterial. It is much too soon for many others to follow in your footsteps as students. But your children and grandchildren will be able to sow the soil if you but take care to till it. You must deliver humanity from the trials of your lifetime, and then gird it with the strength to survive those that follow. You must establish a wall around our race with your great power. Afterwards, you must brace this wall with your descendants. You must teach our enemies to fear the darkness that flows within us, buying us a breathing space within which to grow."*

"And you want me to do this with Mafalda," Hunt remarked critically. "Take advantage of her debt to me and use her to bring up heirs."

"No advantage is taken of a willing soul," the figure responded. *"She is eager for a chance to redeem herself. Being the mother of humanity's salvation is a great gift. Being the father is equally a gift. Think hard and well upon this matter. Your name is secure from your feats. But your legacy shall be made or broken by your descendants. Your thought must reach beyond your own time into that which is to follow. You do not live for yourself alone, but for countless others to come. Do not forget that I know and see all that you do. I am aware of how you spoke to your friend the colonel earlier. You are palpably alive to your duty."*

"Yeah, well, maybe I've changed my mind since then," he replied sourly.

"*You've done nothing of the kind,*" the figure shook his small head. "*You are oscillating between two opinions. One points to Doctor Tselitel, and the other towards the fealty you owe our people. Briefly you were charged with ardor for our cause, the colonel's words stoking your passion. In the absence of such opposition, you've cooled once more. But soon enough you will be ignited again. Whether you like it or not, you are moving inexorably towards your destiny.*"

Without another word the figure evaporated into nothingness.

"Thanks for dropping by," Hunt muttered, leaning back upon his bed once more and contemplating the ceiling.

Hours later *Sentinel* reached another nearby concentration of Devourer craft. Though only a modest fleet, it was along the way to a much larger group, and Krancis was determined to pummel every gathering of the parasite's ships that he could before the masses finished their work. With no way of knowing how much time they had left until that happened, *Sentinel* dropped back into warp the instant its task was complete, leaving what was left of the local population to fend for itself. It was regrettable to be able to offer no comfort to those left behind. But necessity demanded swiftness.

Much later Hunt was invited to join Krancis on the bridge. Reluctantly drawing himself from his bed, the Deltan slowly made his way there, not in any hurry to see him after their last meeting.

"Rest well?" the man in black asked when Hunt entered, an odd note of knowingness in his voice.

"About as well as one could expect," Hunt replied dubiously, eyeing Krancis as he stood beside him. "Why do you ask?" he queried, wondering just how much, if anything, he knew about the shadowy child who continued to visit him from the depths of his unconscious.

"You had a great deal to think about when you left here," he explained. "It would be natural to reflect at some length before finally drifting off. Especially after settling things out with the smuggler."

"How do you know anything's settled?" Hunt asked, crossing his arms.

"I know you well enough to be certain you wouldn't leave that matter unmended a moment longer than necessary." Drawing his eyes from the swirling black tunnel before them, he glanced briefly at the Deltan. "I imagine you put the fear of God into him?"

"Insofar as that's possible, yes."

"Good. Perhaps he'll be useful for at least a little while. With Soliana gone we have no need of what might generously be termed his talents. At this point his only real value is as a companion for you."

"A small value indeed."

"Quite. He's shown *some* promise within a makeshift simulator he managed to jury-rig with *Esiluria's* help. With time he may make an adequate pilot. Given the losses we've sustained, that would be no small benefit."

"You didn't bring me up here to talk about Antonin," Hunt pointed out somewhat impatiently. "What's on your mind?"

"The Devourer is up to something new," he began to explain, turning towards Hunt. "We're not advancing upon our present target merely because the fleet is large. It also contains an enormous vessel of as-yet undetermined capacities. Much bigger than one of their carriers, it is second only to one of the masses in size."

"Same purpose?" Hunt queried.

"It isn't sending any kind of signal," Krancis shook his head. "And it bears merely a token armament. More than likely it's a kind of support vessel or shipyard."

"For what?"

"For the oncoming terror."

"Which is?"

"One can only speculate."

Though unsatisfied by this answer, Hunt decided not to push him further.

"What do you want me for?"

"To boost the reactor. This vessel is enormous. We have to destroy it quickly, before it has a chance to escape into warp. The fleet attending it must also be leveled quickly. We're not going to give six carriers, twenty-two battleships, and innumerable frigates and fighters a chance to pound away at *Sentinel* with impunity. They're going to have to earn it."

"So nothing out of the ordinary," Hunt shrugged. "Just pump up the ship and get it over with."

"More or less. Given we don't know much about this new vessel, you should be ready for anything. Hence I want you to take Wellesley into the reactor with you in order to maintain contact should you be forced to once again enter the dark realm. I'll need to know your condition in that eventuality."

"Assuming Wells can peel himself away from running the Black Fangs," Hunt remarked.

"I'm sure he'll manage. We emerge from warp in approximately twenty minutes, so you'd better get moving."

"Alright."

It was with some reluctance that Hunt went to retrieve his friend. The enthusiasm with which the AI embraced his new role bothered him, given it implied the beginning of the end of their long companionship. He was certain they'd still talk with decent regularity. But he didn't doubt the Black Fangs would require Wellesley's constant attention for months, perhaps even years. Assuming there ever came a time when he *wasn't* needed both to manage and monitor them, that is. The worst part was that that was the kind of task for which Wellesley had originally been designed. Hunt couldn't, with any justice, separate him from work that fulfilled him so completely, nor that was of such value to the empire. With Gromyko on shaky ground, Wellesley occupied, Pinchon eager to leave because of Krancis, and Tselitel not even in the same galaxy, the Earthborn Champion was feeling isolated indeed. The only two people who seemed certain to be a part of his life for the foreseeable future were Mafalda and the man in black himself, both of which presented problems, particularly the former. Deep down, Hunt didn't want to give the dark realm any more opportunities to weave the unfortunate former separatist into his sympathies.

Reaching the makeshift command center that had been allotted to Girnius, Hunt twisted the knob and opened the door without bothering to knock.

"There is no reason to–," Girnius was halfway through saying, his tone cold as he spoke through gritted teeth. Instantly his eyes snapped to his visitor. "This area is off limits to anyone but me."

"I think you'll find nowhere on this ship is off limits to me," Hunt shot back warningly, before directing his gaze to the medallion.

"Need me for something, Rex?" Wellesley asked, the touch of hopefulness in his voice doing much to lift his friend's mood.

"Yeah. Krancis wants us in the reactor. Says it might be a–."

"I'm not finished with him yet," Girnius interrupted, pushing off the desk against which he'd been leaning and taking a pair of steps towards the Deltan.

"Oh, pull in your horns, Girnius," Wellesley said.

"No, that's alright, Wells," Hunt said, a dangerous grin on his face as he took a few steps of his own towards the pirate leader. Standing over him, he looked down into his eyes, his own shimmering with just a hint of darkness. "Are you sure this is a box you want to open, Girnius?"

For a few difficult moments Girnius matched gazes

with him. Then, looking away, he moved around the Deltan and left.

"I'm gonna pay for that later on," the AI remarked with a sigh.

"Didn't mean to make your life any more difficult," Hunt replied.

"What? Oh, I didn't mean I regret it. Not in the least! I've been waiting for *someone* to pin back his ears. *I* would, naturally, except I don't have any hands. Witty remarks only get you so far, you know."

"Sure," Hunt agreed, taking the medallion and wrapping its familiar chain around his neck. The action sent a little tingle down his spine as it reminded him of chillier days on the ice world that had so long been his home.

"I feel like it's been ages since we've really talked," the AI said as Hunt entered the corridor and began to walk. "I mean, we've chatted here and there. But I miss the old days."

"Me, too," Hunt acknowledged.

"Any chance of sitting down and really catching up after this?"

"I guess that depends on Krancis. And if you can get away from the Black Fangs for a little while."

"Them? Oh, sure. It's almost on autopilot for now, to be honest. I've issued every order that can be conceived of. Now it's simply the somewhat grating task of sitting and waiting for them to be fulfilled. Naturally the organization thinks Girnius is the one behind all these sudden changes, so obedience to my instructions is actually quite high. Especially considering this is a *pirate* organization. But otherwise I've got time to kill. I've actually begun writing a history of my experiences in the present war. You might like to check it out sometime. At least the parts you haven't been around for."

"Looking for a little literary criticism?" Hunt grinned as he entered a teleportation room.

"An outside perspective is never a bad thing," the AI

replied, pausing as his friend told the technician where to send him. "Besides, you might pick up on a couple things I haven't thought to tell you," he added when they'd reached the other side. "Who knows, could even help *you* with a little perspective."

"You think I need some?" he asked a touch flatly, weary of being pushed in myriad directions by others.

"*No*, no, no," Wellesley answered quickly, instantly aware what the iron in Hunt's voice meant. "Believe me, buddy, I'm not trying to work on you. Just an idle comment, is all."

"Sorry, Wells–."

"Ah! Don't even finish that sentence. We're too good of friends to have to apologize for every little thing. Just forget about it. It was my fault, anyhow. Krancis and this war must be pulling you six ways from Sunday. That's enough for anyone to think about."

"How'd you guess?" Hunt laughed, pleased that his friend knew him so well.

"Well, I *am* one of the greatest technological marvels my people ever produced. I ought to be able to pull the occasional rabbit out of my hat."

"'One of?' You mean you're not at the top of the list?"

"I was trying to be modest," he replied with an audible roll of his eyes. "They say it's a virtue, you know. Of course, in my case, it's almost impossible to be both modest *and* honest, so I usually default to the latter virtue. I'd say it's the more important one to exemplify, if one is being forced to choose."

"Indeed," Hunt smiled.

Passing into the reactor room shortly thereafter, Hunt stopped when Wellesley let out a whistle.

"What is it?"

"Oh, it's just that this is really the first place Soliana showed us what she could do. I mean, she had her voodoo and all back in the Black Hole. But she's the one who opened the reactor and helped us fire up *Sentinel* for the first time. I didn't really expect it to hit me like this, but I'm gonna miss her."

"Yeah," he said without interest, making his way towards the reactor.

"I gather you're not?" he queried, though he already knew the answer.

"Pretty hard to, after what she did."

"True enough," the AI agreed. "A lot of people felt that way about me after I changed sides in the civil war. Often enough it's your last act that people remember you by. For better or worse."

"It'll certainly be the worse for her," Hunt said, pausing beneath the reactor and cocking on one leg. "Ask Krancis how much longer we have to wait."

"Sure." A few moments silently passed. "Almost there. Just a few minutes."

"Alright," Hunt nodded, making for the edge of the room so as to lean against the wall. "It's not as if I don't recognize her contributions, Wells. But how can you overlook surrendering herself to both the implants and the–." Suddenly a thought shot through his mind and he paused.

"What?"

"Krancis told me that the implants were representative of each of the families of man," Hunt said, beginning his chain of reasoning.

"Yeah?"

"And Soliana just so happened to know the right words to activate this ship, right?"

"*Yeah*," he said again, drawing it out slowly.

"What if the *Keesh'Forbandai* are human?" he asked. "That would explain why they've been looking after us for the last hundred thousand years."

"Well, they also share an affinity for the dark realm. They could just be looking after a future strategic ally."

"That's an awful long time to wait for an alliance to

blossom," Hunt pointed out.

"Well, given they've lasted this long, I'd say they've got the time."

"Didn't your people ever interact with them? See what they looked like?"

"We never had anything to do with them, honestly. Our hands were full of problems much closer to home. Like not tearing each other apart long enough to stand up to a half dozen enemy races who wanted to bite little pieces off our turf."

"I see what you mean."

"Yeah, it was always a struggle."

"Still, they *could* be human."

"That seems like quite a leap to me. Wouldn't they have reached out in some way by now? Invited us to a family barbecue or something? Well, by *us* I mean *you guys*. Honestly sometimes I almost forget I'm not human."

"We'll get Krancis to make you an honorary one," Hunt grinned. "And anyhow, you know how the *Pho'Sath* are keeping an eye on things here. Maybe they don't want to risk blowing the treaty by giving them even a shadow of a pretext."

"I guess," the AI said, clearly unconvinced. Before he could say more the elevator into the reactor began to descend. "Guess the big man wants us inside."

"Reckon so," Hunt replied, pushing off the wall and walking towards it. Stepping onto the lift, it immediately began to rise.

"Once more into the breach, eh?"

"Yep," Hunt said in a subdued voice, not relishing the idea of once more visiting the dark realm. He felt certain that he'd see Milo there, and that was not something he wished to do if he could help it. "I don't plan to give the reactor any more than is necessary, Wells," he said as they neared the top. "I'm gonna start fairly small and work my way up from there. Just let me know when I need to ratchet it up a little."

"Will do."

It wasn't long before the massive warship emerged from warp. Ranged against it were countless vessels of all sizes. Connected to the ship as he was, Wellesley could see the incredible numerical disparity in real time. Though *Sentinel* was apparently indestructible, it nevertheless gave him pause.

"We've got quite a few of them this time," he said to Hunt. "I think you'd better give it the max right out of the gate."

"I just said I don't want to do that," Hunt replied with some annoyance. "This old tub can take anything they dish out."

"I don't know. I've got a bad feeling about it this time around. There's this ship that's bigger than anything I've seen before."

"Krancis told me about it. Just a shipyard or something. Doesn't pose a threat."

"Let's hope he's right," the AI relented dubiously, watching as great clumps of frigates and a huge cloud of fighters approached.

Closing his eyes, Hunt reached down into himself and began to draw forth the great power within. At once it surged, the connection between him and it so practiced that it required little effort to conjure it.

"That's good. The reactor's putting out 175%. Just keep it coming."

Making a beeline for the huge ship, *Sentinel* cut loose with its cannon and began slowly to darken it.

"I think you'd better pump it up, Rex. That thing is taking the cannon a *lot* better than I expected."

Squeezing his eyes tighter, he brought it up to 225%. At Wellesley's urging he raised it yet further, first to 240%, and then to 275%. Though the noise in the reactor was almost deafening, Hunt grew less aware of it. His mind was slowly drawing out of his body, melding with the dark element.

"You alright, buddy?" Wellesley asked.

Slowly he nodded.

"Well, good, then," the AI responded, watching with alarm as the cloud of fighters swept past *Sentinel*, raining green blobs against it like a hailstorm. By the time they'd flown by and made a return pass the frigates had closed the distance and were impotently smacking their tentacles against it. Working their way to the turrets, they began prying and digging at them, attempting to dislodge them, bend their barrels, anything to cause damage. This drew the attention of the captain at once, who directed the turrets to decimate them. "The battleships are closing in now," Wellesley mumbled, intending only to think it rather than say it. At once Hunt increased the power coming from the reactor. "I'd say you'd better give us everything you've got, Rex," the AI warned him.

Grouping themselves in a wall three high and seven wide, the battleships advanced towards *Sentinel's* left flank, intent on ramming it away from its target. Maneuvering as well as he could, the captain attempted to keep the cannon trained on the massive ship as long as possible. But just as darkness had spread through most of it, the battleships struck *Sentinel* and began pushing it off into space.

"Whatever you've got left in the tank, Rex, we need it *now!*" Wellesley exclaimed, as the battleships began grouping themselves towards the front and rear of the warship. For several seconds he watched curiously what they were doing, trying to figure it out. Then he knew. "They're actually trying to snap the ship in two!" he declared. "I doubt anything is strong enough to do that! Of course, there *are* almost two dozen of them…" Observing with keen interest, he didn't notice the arrival of almost twenty imperial carriers until they'd disgorged half their complement of Adlers. "Oh, well, that's something, anyway," he said, his voice brightening at the sight.

As *Sentinel* got pushed further into space, its turrets tore into the battleships, slicing off tentacles and dealing them terrible damage. One by one they began to fall behind, unable to keep up with their brethren.

The Adlers, on the other hand, were in a much more dire situation. Countless fighters screamed towards them and their carriers, the latter of which had no choice but to attempt to flee into warp as soon as their engines had recharged. Provided they lasted that long.

Positioning themselves between the oncoming fighters and the carriers, the Adlers began deploying their warheads at maximum range. The subsequent detonations only did about half the damage they were capable of, given the missiles hadn't worked themselves deeply into the enemy's ranks before exploding. But one explosion followed another, creating a wall of death that held back the parasite's craft until the carriers could at last depart.

"We're in for it now, boys," Colonel Barnaby Moryet radioed his pilots. "It's do or die."

"Just the way I like it!" one of the younger hotshots radioed back.

"You know the routine: keep your distance and let the warheads do their job."

"What's the fun in that?" queried the hotshot.

"Better bored than dead, Thomas," another commented.

"Alright, get on with it," Moryet ordered, silencing the chatter.

On the other end of the battle, *Sentinel* had managed to peel enough of its assailants off to shift its great cannon once more upon its ailing target.

"We've got to hurry, Rex," Wellesley cautioned. "I don't think that thing is gonna be around here a whole lot longer."

Sensing this as well, *Sentinel's* captain accelerated towards the vessel, intent on colliding with it should it attempt to flee into warp. Countless observers within the warship hoped and willed that the warp generator had already been disabled by the cannon. But there was no way of knowing until it was actually nothing more than a cloud of ash in space.

"There! There it is!" exclaimed Wellesley as a massive purple rift was torn in space and the ship began to amble towards it. "It's all or nothing time, Rex!"

His friend had long since ceased to hear him. But the dark realm seemed to, for the reactor increased its output yet further.

"Come on! Come on!" Wellesley shouted, watching as the first blackened portion of the enemy ship slipped into warp. "We can't let it get away after all this!"

Suddenly the rift closed as the warp engine was finally disabled by the cannon. With the first third of the enemy vessel in warp, the rest was sliced off and left behind. Already frightfully damaged, it didn't take long for it to crumble to ash and disintegrate.

"That's it! That's done it!" the AI triumphed.

While this was taking place, the Adlers were tearing the heart out of the enemy's attack. Gutting the storm of fighters with their powerful missiles, they began moving the battle closer to *Sentinel* to assist it with the numerous frigates that yet battered its hull.

"I'd give anything to unload on one of those battleships," the hotshot announced, all but licking his lips in anticipation of a big kill.

"I'd take more than just your warheads to bring one of those things down," Moryet replied, stemming any such ambitions within his pilots. "Keep 'em focused on the fighters and frigates. *Sentinel* can handle the big boys."

"Ten-four, chief," another responded.

As the last of the battleships were driven away from *Sentinel*, a cascade of missiles sailed towards it. Incapable of causing damage to the great warship, they had been reprogrammed to strike the targets closest to it. At once they began ripping frigates to pieces, doing the work the turrets had been too preoccupied to complete.

Having lost the majority of their fighters, the carriers prepared to depart. As one purple rift after another was torn open in space, the great cannon broke forth, striking portions of two at once.

"Something to remember us by," Krancis said with quiet satisfaction as the vessels slipped into warp with their black marks.

"Krancis? I think we have a problem," Wellesley radioed in alarm.

"That being?"

"Rex hasn't come back yet. And the reactor is still pumping out juice like crazy. We've got to channel it somewhere before it overloads the ship."

"Understood. Captain? Fire the cannon into neutral space the moment it can be activated again. We need to drain off some of our excess energy." Without waiting for a reply he switched back to Wellesley's channel. "How long's it been since he lost awareness of his surroundings?"

"I'm not sure. It's hard to tell when he drops out. What should we do? Get him out of the reactor?"

"There's no telling what harm that may cause," Krancis responded. "This isn't the first time he's zoned out for a little while. Let's wait and see what happens."

"*Easy for you to say,*" Wellesley grumbled internally. "*You don't have to just dangle here helplessly and watch.*"

Watch was a figurative term, given he could only see what Hunt saw, and he'd long since closed his eyes. Keeping one eye on his friend's vitals, he watched the battle with the other, trying to pass the time as well as he could. But he was much too anxious to draw any satisfaction from the victory. As ten minutes turned to thirty, and then sixty, he began to fear that he'd never get Rex back.

Without any warning at all Hunt suddenly threw his

head back and yelled as consciousness returned.

"Rex! Buddy! Are you alright?"

In lieu of answering, the Deltan moved unsteadily onto the elevator and mutely descended. Stepping off, he lost his balance and collapsed. Pressing his palms against the floor, he rested his head against it for a moment. He attempted to rise, but proved unequal to it. Rolling onto his back, he let his chest heave freely as footsteps rapidly approached.

"I called for help the second you came back," Wellesley explained, as a medical team seemed to appear out of nowhere and loaded him onto a stretcher. "Krancis must have had them waiting close by just in case."

Weakly waving his hand to signal his understanding, he closed his eyes and let them cart him away as he again lost consciousness.

CHAPTER 8

Doctor Tselitel stood before a large wooden cabin in the midst of a densely foggy wood. Looking to her right and left, she could see scarcely more than a dozen feet. Pale moonlight seemed to be shining down from overhead, though she couldn't see an actual moon in the sky. Quite aware that she was inside a dream, she reasoned it must just be convenient lighting.

The darkness around her was so thick as to be palpable. It seemed in fact to be charged with a kind of life, as though it could draw itself together into physical form at any moment and advance upon her. Shivering at this thought, she drew a little closer to the cabin. Peeking around either side, she saw nothing but fog. And the same curious glow, even under the awning that ran along the right side of the structure. Sensing that she was brought to the cabin for some purpose, she tried the wooden latch that held the door shut and found it unlocked. Opening it, she stepped inside and found that it, too, glowed faintly. The fog didn't follow her inside, though the windows were open. The decor was rustic and severe, with only a crudely made table and a quartet of chairs standing in the middle of the room. Looking to the back, she saw another door.

Creaking slowly around the table, she looked down and was surprised to find she had no shoes on. Her clothes, in fact, were nothing more than an old gray dress that ran down past her knees and had all the shapeliness of a bedsheet.

Feeling it for a moment, she gasped when it tore a little in her gentle grasp. A tremor ran through her as she drew her hands away, afraid to touch it further. Something, she felt, was very meaningful about its tearing.

Slowly rolling her feet across the floor from heel to toe, she reached the back door and ever-so-softly turned the knob. Of its own accord the door opened, drawing itself from her hand and beckoning her inside. Briefly she hesitated, for she had been certain while outside the cabin that it had only the one room, and she had fully expected to see the forest and not yawning darkness before her. Something seemed to be drawing her inside itself, and she was far from certain she wanted to find out what. The temptation flitted through her mind to wake up and leave it all behind. But her curiosity was much too aroused to permit that. Stepping blindly into the blackness, she reached her hands out to keep from stumbling over anything.

This proved unnecessary, since there was no floor and she immediately fell forwards down a shaft. Screaming as she tumbled head-over-heels and back again, she made contact with the smooth sides of the shaft and began to lose speed as they slowly sloped into a horizontal position. Rolling sideways over and over again she came to a stop. Pressing her hands against the cool metal beneath her, she stood up and instantly cracked her skull against the low ceiling. Yelping as pain shot through her head and down into her neck, she went to her knees and rubbed her scalp for a moment. Retaining this posture, she began feeling in the darkness for a way out. Finding where the shaft continued, she slowly moved down it, carefully testing the space in front of her with her fingers before advancing.

"What is this place?" she asked herself inwardly, her stomach churning as she began to fear she'd never find a way out. "*Some kind of trap?*"

As if in answer to her question the floor suddenly gave way before her. Feeling her way up and down the sides of the tunnel, she found no other path by which to proceed. Closing her eyes in the darkness, she took a deep breath and then slipped her feet over the side. She'd intended to dive right in, but lost the courage to do so at the last second. Reaching down with her toes, she hoped to find some kind of ledge but couldn't. She was about to pull herself back up when an incredible blast of wind from up the tunnel blew her off her perch and sent her screaming down into the opening. Falling many hundreds of feet before it again leveled out, she tumbled to a bloody stop and could only groan.

"Why is this happening to me?" she asked aloud, her body aching as she attempted to rise. Thinking better of it, she rolled onto her back and rested. "Is there some purpose to all this?"

Closing her eyes, she breathed for a few moments. Opening them again, she started when she saw that the eerie glow that illuminated the cabin had found its way down the shaft and lit the way ahead. Rising at once, she crawled until her knees felt as if they must split in two from pain. Twisting onto her rear, her dress now in tatters, she wiped the sweat from her brow and tried not to let despair seize her heart.

"I don't understand this," she uttered, sensing that someone, or something, was aware of her presence and stringing her slowly along. "Am I supposed to learn something from this?" Inwardly, she added, *Or are you just trying to break me? Because if you are, it's working.*"

Moving to her hands and knees again, she crawled a bit further before finding a door made of wood. Opening it, she was stunned to find herself back inside the cabin.

"*What is all this?*" she reflected, looking around cluelessly, the room exactly as it had been when she'd left it. "*How can I be here when I've gone so far down?*"

Instantly recalling the flexible physics of dreams, she let the point slide and moved towards the table.

"*There must be something here I'm supposed to see*," she thought. "*That's why the tunnels brought me back. It must also be why they were pitch black: this *is where I'm supposed to be, not there.*" Looking around the room, she examined the walls, floor and ceiling but found nothing of interest in them. Drawing a seat back from the table, she dropped onto it and sighed. Idly her eyes floated to and fro as the vague fear she felt towards the situation turned into confusion and then frustration.

"*Doctor,*" she heard a high, breathy voice say from the open window behind her. Nearly jumping out of her skin, she shot to her feet and jerked around. Half a dozen feet away floated the robe that, within Gustav Welter, had revealed itself to be Amra. "*I must speak with you at once.*" Passing effortlessly through the wall, the robe floated a foot above the floor, once again undulating as though blown by a non-existent wind.

"Where–, how did you–," Lily stumbled, still scared half out of her wits. "How did you bring me here?"

"*A little piece of me was left within you when I drew you into my father,*" she explained. "*You could say I left fingerprints within your psyche. I'm sorry, but I couldn't help it.*"

"Oh, that's okay," Tselitel replied, trying to sound casual despite the fear the freakish entity inspired in her. "I can always use more company inside my head."

"*I'm not truly company,*" the figure replied seriously, slowly moving towards Tselitel, forcing her to draw on all her courage to not bolt. "*This is merely an imprint, a memory that my psyche left embedded in yours. In time it will fade. Hence why it took so long for me to come to you: my power is very weak. My only hope for a conversation with you was if you remained curious long enough for me to join you here. I'm thankful you did.*"

"As am I," Tselitel lied, looking up into the empty hood of the tattered robe. Seeing the shreds in it, she was reminded of her own battered dress. "Why am I wearing this?" she asked, softly grasping it and holding it forward a little. "What does it mean?"

"I don't know. Most of what you see around you has been spontaneously furnished by your own unconscious. My only real role in this scenario was inviting you here. In essence I made a request of your unconscious, and it answered by drawing you into these unusual surroundings. You shall have to draw upon your own gifts to interpret their meaning. I am much too weak to offer any assistance. In fact I must be very brief; manifesting myself in this way is rapidly draining what little energy I have left."

"Then please do," Tselitel urged the figure, both curious to hear her message and eager to conclude the meeting while she still had the nerve to remain within the confines of the cabin.

"I sensed something when you interacted with my father," the imprint began, floating past her towards a window on the opposite side of the room. Looking wistfully out into the night for a moment, she sighed. When she turned around, Tselitel couldn't help but start at the sight of the empty hood. "There's something very wrong with you – something which the technology of your hosts is unable to heal, though it may forestall it for some little time."

"Yes, my Valindra," Tselitel responded. "I'm already aware that it's incurable."

"Not that," the figure said, turning back towards the window, the news clearly very difficult to share. "The darkness has hurt you very badly in the past. Your form, never robust, simply wasn't equal to such a burden. You have been assaulted time and again." The hood shook side-to-side. "It's very hard for me to see just who did it. But I sense that it was done by both a woman and a man, and both in fairly short order."

"I was attacked by an assassin on Delta-13," Tselitel confirmed. "She assaulted me with terrible fears. Later I was attacked by Maximillian Hunt, though he called himself Mister Lavery at the time. I would have been killed if Rex hadn't saved me."

"*But he acted much too late,*" she said sadly. "*The darkness, as well as the light, can work upon individuals in very different ways. Many are struck by it time and again without a lasting negative effect. Others are terribly debilitated by it. You land closer to the latter camp. Your body will eventually begin to shut down if you aren't healed first. The alien chamber has slowed this effect. But it will overtake you long before Valindra does.*"

Her stomach tightened as the fear of an early death seized her anew. Gripping the back of the closest chair, she sat down and tried to breathe. Valindra she had somehow managed to grow accustomed to, though its constant presence robbed her life of much of its color. To be told that even *that* dreaded illness wouldn't have time to run its course struck too deep. Even within the irreality of the dream she began to tremble.

"W-what can I do?" she pleaded, resting her elbows on the table for support and looking up at the figure as it floated closer. "How can I be healed?"

"*I'm aware of only one way,*" the imprint replied reluctantly. "*You must be healed by a Pho'Sath.*"

"That's impossible," she said at once, fear turning to despair. "They'd never do it."

"*The Pho'Sath wish to live, like every other being in the universe. If properly threatened, they will be amenable. My father is suitably menacing for such a task.*"

"But how could we ever corner one and bring it to terms?" she argued. "They think we're vermin, just the absolute bottom of the barrel of living things. They'd sooner die than heal me, especially if they know how important I am to Rex. They'd *love* the chance to hurt him through me."

"*I can't comment on what they do or don't know about you,*" the figure said. "*All I know is that you must be healed soon, and that, to my knowledge, they are the only ones capable of doing so. There are rumors of other races gifted with great healing powers. But I haven't the least idea where one would look* to find them. And given Krancis has seen fit to send both you and his beloved emperor here instead of to one of them, I don't think they are an option, assuming they actually even exist. The fact is the Pho'Sath have essentially a monopoly on the healing arts within our portion of the universe. I suspect they've used this to their advantage more than once, twisting others to do their bidding in exchange for the energies that so easily flow from their fingertips. I myself have felt their potent gift on several occasions. That is how I know they could repair the damage done to you."

"But like you said, if it were possible, wouldn't Krancis have already made that happen? If not for my sake, then for the emperor's?"

"Krancis must weigh the benefits of their gift against the risk of either of you falling into their hands and becoming hostages. Were that to happen, the results would be catastrophic. That's his *calculus*. But for yourself, you must weigh the risks on a more personal level. Death, of course, would be regrettable. But what would happen to Hunt if you perished at this time, given he's so much in love with you?"

"Catastrophe," Tselitel nodded knowingly, looking sadly down at the table. "Then I'm backed into a corner. I can't heal except with the help of our most implacable enemy; to seek such help will probably undermine us terribly; and yet, to die even sooner would tear Rex to pieces."

"*The effect would be much worse than that,*" the figure replied. "*It would likely push him over the edge. Parental love nearly destroyed my father when I died at the Pho'Sath's cruel hand. From what I have gathered from your memories, Rex Hunt feels you saved him from a life of nothingness. You aren't merely his lover: you're his deliverance. To lose that would likely drive him far beyond what my father nearly became. Given the power he has from the dark realm, he would almost certainly become an agent of despair and death to all who crossed his path.*"

"But why?" Tselitel asked. "The dark realm has helped us so much ever since the war began. Wouldn't it stop him?"

"The dark realm is not a being as we generally conceive them. It is an element; alive, yes, but also reactive, uncontrollable in a sense. It is much like intelligent radiation, a force that acts both by choice but also by its mere nature. The fact is the dread that many races feel towards it is not ill-founded. Whether it is a force of good or bad in a given instance is governed by how it interacts with the beings in question. The Prellak, it must be remembered, were dark worlds because of their connection to the dark realm. In them the effect was evil; in Rex Hunt, it is good. But only if he continues to use it in that way."

"Then it's more like fuel in a furnace than an actor on the stage," Tselitel summarized.

"It is both, in many respects," the imprint said. "Its nature is all but impossible to adequately describe, given the limits of our own cognition. The two elements predate all life in this universe, and are not altogether intelligible to us. Our attempts to understand them often obscure their true natures as much as they illuminate them."

"I see," Tselitel replied, her mind moving back to the problem staring her in the face. "What am I supposed to do, Amra? How could we ever find a *Pho'Sath* to heal me? And even if we could, what could ever induce Krancis to let us try? It's not like I could slip out of the base on my own. Even if I could, I wouldn't last two minutes in Quarlac alone."

"*I'm sorry that I can't be more help,*" the entity apologized sincerely. "*All I could do was inform you of both the direness of the situation and the desperate need to act quickly before this imprint of me lost its energy and faded from your psyche for good. I almost wish I hadn't told you, so as not to heap this added burden onto your shoulders. But I couldn't do that in good conscience, not while there was hope, however slim.*"

"No, I appreciate you telling me," she managed to say, even as fear ate at her heart and twisted her stomach in knots. Noticing that the robe was slowly beginning to fade, she hastened to add, "But you must help me. You *must* give me *some* idea where to turn."

"*All I can suggest is that you ask my father,*" she replied. "*For many years he combated the supernatural forces of our galaxy, striving to keep them in check. If anyone would have the least notion how to approach this problem, he would. I'm truly sorry that I can't be more help. But despite my otherworldly appearance in this dream, I'm still just a fragment of a girl who spent her short life in the fringe. I'm afraid I'm not sophisticated enough to offer guidance on a question so complex.*"

"Believe me, I don't hold anything against you," Tselitel assured her. "Thank you for telling me about this."

"*You're welcome,*" the figure replied. "*My power is all but spent. I have only a minute or two more before I fade from your psyche forever. Is there anything else you would like to say?*"

"Just this," she began hesitantly, forcing herself to stand up and face the matter head on. "Do you think this'll work? I mean, that I can somehow be healed and Rex won't head down the same path as your father?"

"*I think the chance is very slim indeed,*" the entity uttered grimly. "*If you manage to survive, it will be nothing short of a miracle. But you mustn't give up hope on account of that. There have been many miracles in this war already, and countless which preceded it to give us a fighting chance today. You cannot give up. Pour every energy you possess into achieving your end, and you may manage to do so. We have been savaged terribly by the parasite. But on the whole, fate's been kind to us. Perhaps it will be to you as well.*"

Rapidly dissipating as it said this, the imprint vanished with the conclusion of its last sentence.

"Goodbye," Tselitel said quietly, wishing she'd had the chance to say it whilst still face-to-face with the being. Sighing heavily, she dropped into the chair and looked blankly across the table at the open window through which the imprint had gazed. "As if I don't have enough things to worry about," she said self-pityingly, once more resting her elbows upon the table and holding up her chin with her hands. Tears began collecting in her eyes and slowly dribbled down her cheeks. "What am I going to do?" she asked herself, as the dream began to brighten and the fog to evaporate. Realizing that everything around her was becoming transparent, she squeezed her eyes shut and awaited the return of consciousness.

The unconscious, however, was kind to her, and allowed her to drift off to a peaceful sleep for some hours before she finally awoke. Much calmer than she had been within the cabin, she sat up within the chamber and found it much as it had been when she'd laid down to rest the night before.

"There's our hardy little doctor," Rhemus said in the affectionate tones of a father, his regal form stretched out a few feet from hers. "I began to wonder if you'd decided to hibernate."

"Why? Was I out very long?" she asked with some alarm, wondering if the prophesied breakdown of her body had already begun to mess with her internal rhythms.

"Oh, I wouldn't say *very* long," the emperor replied, struck by the tension written on her face. "Ten or eleven hours, I suppose. But I wouldn't worry about that."

"No, no of course not," she agreed, drawing herself up against the wall and wrapping her arms around her legs. "H-has Gustav been in lately?"

"Dropped in an hour or so ago," Rhemus replied, studying her face. "Is something the matter, Doctor? You seem…preoccupied."

"Oh, I had a terrible dream last night," she said honestly enough. "I guess it's still working on me a little. Sometimes I can be pretty silly about stuff like that. After all, it's not like it's real, right?"

"Given all we've seen, I would have to say that it depends entirely on what the dream was, and who had it," the emperor answered sagely. "As a matter of fact, I had a dream of my own last night."

"You did?" she asked eagerly, happy to shift her attention from her own problems for a few minutes.

"I don't know if there was much substance to it," he began, likewise shifting to a sitting position, pressing his back against the wall. "It was all so brief that I half suspect it was nothing more than a fancy that passed through my mind while I happened to be asleep."

"Please tell me about it."

"Like I said, there wasn't much to it. I don't think I even had a body. I'm pretty sure I was just a sort of floating awareness. But in any event, I saw the scepter of my great-grandfather Decimus smashed against a walkway made of brilliantly bright stones. It broke into four large pieces, the last one being the eagle figurine that rests upon the top of the scepter. It laid against the stones for a few moments as they gradually turned dark. Then, once they were black as midnight, the scepter reformed. It floated back into the air and hovered for a few moments before the dream suddenly ended."

"That's very curious," she remarked, her brow furrowing as she thought about it.

"But that isn't the most curious thing about it," he continued. "The eagle was replaced by the figure of a fierce wolf standing on its hind legs, its front paws outstretched as if to attack. Its mouth was wide open, ready to sink its teeth into anything that crossed paths with it. I can't help but find an omen in it, Doctor. It must be foretelling the end of my line and the establishment of another."

"Don't talk like that," she said at once.

"I'm not certain how much you've been allowed to know, Doctor. But my heirs have long since perished. For the sake of imperial stability we've maintained the fiction that they were alive. But they've been dead for years. They inherited my condition and passed before they'd so much as reached their teens. Hoping against hope, I'd dreamed of some miracle that would allow me to continue the dynasty established by my fathers. I'd even considered finding a suitable man and trying to pass him off as my son. But this dream makes me think that the guardianship of the empire must pass into other hands. The strength of my family's blood is spent. Soon another dynasty will be formed to lead our people into the future. Indeed, I believe the man has already been found who will do so."

"You mean Krancis?" she asked, dreading that he meant another.

"No, my dear. I mean your Rex. I was more impressed with him than I can express when I met him on Bohlen-7, and yet more so when we had a chance to speak at length aboard *Sentinel*. The fact is, Doctor, I believe our future is linked inextricably with his. If he should fall, I am certain that humanity would as well. But the dark realm is his great ally, and I have no doubt that he will ultimately succeed. I just hope that the mass of mankind will still be alive when he does so. His task will be a hard one. Rebuilding the shattered remnants of the empire will require all his strength, intelligence, and cunning. But with Krancis at his side, I have hope for us all."

"I don't think Rex wants to be emperor in your stead," she opined gently. "I think he'd prefer almost anything if it permitted him to stay out of the limelight. He's not a public man by nature. He's been much too burned by others to surround himself with them constantly."

"Necessity has a way of breaking down our predilections," he chuckled. "I could name a half dozen such objections off the top of my head that I felt when I first took the throne after the death of my father Septimus. But if you care about those under your care, then you learn to cope. If I could do so, I'm certain that that remarkable young man can. Indeed, he may not find himself with much of a choice, given the publicity that Krancis has given his every feat. Next to myself and Krancis, there's no better known figure within the empire."

"But wouldn't Krancis be a more natural fit for emperor?" she objected. "He's had so many years of experience within the government that no one could equal him."

"No, I'm afraid that's impossible," Rhemus replied with a shake of his head. "Krancis' time is now, and for some distance into the future. But it is not his lot to establish another dynasty."

"But–."

"You'll simply have to take my word on that, my dear," he replied with finality, though without irritation. "Besides, I should have thought you'd be pleased to see your Rex reach the very height of human society. Won't you be proud of him?"

"Yes, but at a distance," she responded quietly. "I–I can't have children. If he's to establish a dynasty, it would have to be with someone else. And that thought almost pulls me in pieces. I'm sorry to be so selfish, especially given how utterly vital Rex is to our continued existence. I know I haven't the least right to take him from the rest of mankind and keep him for myself. But…" her voice trailed as her courage to be completely honest flagged.

"But love is exclusive," he finished for her knowingly. "It doesn't like to share, even when there's good reason to. Don't think yourself wicked for feeling this way. Every lover has, at one point or another. And after all you've been through, I'd say you've earned it."

"But what can I do?" she pleaded, almost blurting out what Amra had told her within the dream but holding back at the last second. The fear of how short her time with Rex could be was tearing at her heart. But she didn't have the strength to tell him just then. The idea was still too terrible to verbalize. "H-here I am in another galaxy. I can't so much as see him," she added, deflecting from her true worries.

"We won't be here forever," he assured her. "Besides, Krancis won't always need Rex constantly. I'm sure he'll be able to come out here and see you at some point soon. The Devourer is getting knocked to pieces by *Sentinel* and our new fleets. It's reeling on almost every front. Just keep your chin up a little longer. It'll be alright."

"Yes, of course," she agreed, forcing a smile for his sake. "I'm sorry. I shouldn't have despaired."

"Don't worry," he smiled in return.

Another half hour of small talk followed before Tselitel found an excuse to leave the chamber. A handful of recently arrived humans occupied the table at the far end of the anteroom, but she paid them no mind. Stepping into the corridor, she moved past the *Kol-Prockian* guards and hastened down the hallway. Taking the first turn that presented itself, she double checked that nobody could see her and then clutched her stomach and bent partially over as panic surged through her body. Straightening up as she heard footsteps approaching from behind, she tried to walk normally as a quartet of alien soldiers marched rapidly past. The moment they were out of sight she grasped her stomach again and moved quickly down the corridor after them, searching for an empty room she could hide herself in. Finding one, she ducked inside and began to gasp.

"It can't be," she begged in a whisper, hunching over as she slowly lowered herself to her knees. "Either I die soon or Rex gets taken away from me? What did I do to deserve this?"

Sitting on her legs, she lowered her forehead to the floor and sobbed. She quieted down whenever she heard footsteps approaching, cutting loose again once they'd retreated down the hall. But eventually a man walked past who only made noise if he chose to, and he hadn't on that particular occasion. Sitting upright with a jolt as the door opened, her reddened eyes blinked as she tried to make out the silhouette before her.

"What are you doing in here, Doctor?" Welter's familiar voice queried. Firm as ever, there was nevertheless something sympathetic in its tone.

"I'm just having a little nervous breakdown," she replied, aware that no quantity of lies could knock him off the scent once he'd caught it.

Hearing the despair in her voice, he stepped inside and closed the door. Not wishing to blind her with the light, he left it off and leaned against the wall in the darkness.

"What's on your mind?" he asked evenly.

"I–I saw Amra again," she admitted at once. "I saw her in a dream. Well, the robed form of her. She was just an imprint left behind after I experienced her inside your mind."

"What did she say?" Welter asked, surprised by her words but determined to draw out the doctor's problem. "What's got you so upset?"

"She told me I'm going to die, Gustav," she replied, shifting so that her back was against the wall. Leaning her head against it, she felt almost too exhausted to continue. "She said there's something else wrong with me besides the Valindra. I never told you this, but I was attacked by two separate people during my stay on Delta-13. They used the darkness, first to terrify me, and second to debilitate me. On both occasions Rex saved me. But Amra said he was too late, that the damage had been done by the time he'd stepped in. She said my body would start shutting down soon if I didn't get help. She said I needed help from the–," she paused, nearly using their real name. "From the *Dolshan*."

"Did she?" he queried, slowly lowering himself until he was perched on the balls of his feet, his elbows resting on his knees.

"I don't know what to do," Tselitel uttered, rubbing her face with her hands in the darkness and sighing. "She said they're the only ones who can heal me, that even the chamber isn't going to hold it back much longer. But it's impossible to even think of it, right? They'd never help me recover. They'd never help us with *anything*."

"I'm sure one could be persuaded," he replied

inexorably.

"She said that if anyone could make them, you could," Tselitel seconded quickly. "But...oh, I don't mean to cause any offense, Gustav. But she was just saying that to make me feel better, right? There's nothing any of us can do to *compel* one of them to heal me. If there was, we'd have already bent the resources of the empire upon securing one for the emperor's sake, wouldn't we?"

"The *Dolshan* would never heal Rhemus, knowing how vital he is to the stability of the empire," he answered. "You're right: they'd sooner die than help us sew up that particular loose end. But if we collared one who didn't know what your importance was, we might just have a chance."

"Really?" she asked with desperate eagerness. "You *really* think that's possible?"

"I'm not much of one for lying to give comfort, Doctor," he replied. "You ought to know that."

"Yes, I do know that," she agreed with an invisible nod, especially grateful just then for his particular brand of hardness.

"But I don't want to give you any false hope. It'd be just short of suicide to try and capture one. And if we did, it could just as easily disintegrate you as heal you. It'd probably be one chance in four that we pull it off."

"One in four aren't bad odds," she said thoughtfully, sniffling a little to clear her nose.

"You're alright with a 75% risk of failure?" he asked.

"Gustav, I've been faced with a 100% likelihood of death by fifty. I'll take 25% any day of the week."

"Of course," he assented, feeling she was overstating her prognosis a bit. "But there's another thing you've got to think of."

"Whether or not Krancis'll let us do it?" she offered.

"No, I wouldn't worry too much about that," he said, a hint of a grin audible in his voice. "You've got to ask yourself if this is really worth it. The risks are extraordinary.

You're trying to keep alive as long as you can, and that's only natural. But you'd better think long and hard before you gamble everything on an intervention from our worst foe after the Devourer. The fact is we could end up doing everything right; I could have one of 'em pinned with my dagger held right against its throat, and it might *still* try to hurt you. It might even just refuse to help. In that case, you'll have spent a number of days outside the chamber, your condition only getting worse with each passing hour."

"Gustav, I can't–," she started to say.

"Just…think about it," he cut her off. "There's nothing we can do about it right this minute, anyhow. So let it roll around inside that overactive skull of yours. You never know. You might cook up something else entirely."

"But Amra said–."

"Whatever little fragment of Amra it was that got stuck in you wasn't all-knowing, Doctor. All she had to work with was what *she* knew at the time of her death, and what *you* knew as of last night. Perhaps our hosts will have an answer neither of you were aware of. Or maybe *I* know a thing or two about this old universe of ours that I haven't had a reason to share yet. Just give it a little time."

"But I don't have any to spare," she pleaded, growing anxious from his seeming lack of urgency. "She made it clear that I had to act quickly."

"We're not going to go off half-cocked, Doctor," he replied firmly, his voice no longer brooking opposition. "You can't make a go of it outside this base without me. And *I'm* not taking you to see any *Dolshan* until *after* we've made at least a cursory attempt at finding another option. The odds are too one-sided."

"Then I'm doomed," she despaired, dropping her head back against the wall with a thunk. "I'll never have a chance to see Rex again. Or even the outside of this miserable base."

"You'll see both, I promise you," he assured her, reaching out and grasping her arm. Pulling her upright, he drew her towards the door. "Now come on. You'd better get back into that chamber for the time being."

"What are you going to do?" she asked, sensing she was being set aside to make space for something else he had to deal with.

"Just a small matter a couple of our agents brought to our attention," he replied dismissively.

"Wait, you mean those people outside the chamber?" she asked as he walked her up the hallway towards it.

"Yes. They're Krancis' men. Turns out the base is under mortal threat."

"*What?!*" she exclaimed, stopping in the hallway and turning towards him. Emotionally spent, she hadn't a shred of composure left with which to absorb the blow. "How is that even possible? Nobody knows we're here!"

"Yes, except the *Kol-Prockians*," he replied, taking her arm and turning her forwards again.

"Well…but…," she stammered, trying to make sense of his words. "Why would they betray us? They've signed on lock, stock, and barrel!"

"Not the ones *inside* the base," he explained. "Turns out some of 'em abandoned *Kren-Balar* months before we arrived. *Seldek* got 'em on the horn when he saw the writing on the wall, and they made a beeline for home. Now they're threatening to expose our location if we don't vacate at once and give up all notion of ruling over them."

"So they're upset about having a human ruler?" she clarified, the situation beginning to crystalize for her.

"Yeah. We've talked 'em into sending an ambassador of sorts here later today. Rhemus is hoping to show him how well received we are, and that we don't mean his people any harm. But I think it'll be a hard sell. You'd better be prepared for things to get rough."

"Well, what can *I* do?" she asked helplessly.

"Keep that gun I gave you tucked in that robe at all times," he replied. "And be ready to bolt for the hangar. We might have to get out in a hurry."

"But what could they do to *Kren-Balar?*" she asked. "We're hidden under a volcano, of all things."

"They could collapse that volcano on top of the entrance and bury us alive," he suggested. "If they start dropping bombs, you, me, and the emperor are going to get in that egg and fly straight up through their ordnance. With luck we'll get away."

"He'll never abandon these people once they've pledged their allegiance to him," she shook her head as they neared the chamber's anteroom.

"I don't intend to give him a choice," he replied quietly, opening the door and ushering her in first. "Wait here," he added in a low voice. "I have to speak with the emperor."

Leaving her in the anteroom, Welter entered the chamber and quietly closed the door when he saw *Karnan* sleeping in his usual corner.

All but stunned from Welter's revelation, Tselitel walked numbly towards the table and looked at the four men seated there. Taking in a brief meal, they glanced up at her with a mixture of curiosity and pleasure.

"Hello," she said in response to their looks. "I'm Lily Tselitel."

"We know," one of them chuckled, jerking a thumb towards the man beside him. "He hasn't been able to shut up about you since we entered the base."

"Oh, can it, will you?" his fellow shot back. Wiping off his hands and standing up, he rounded the table and extended his hand. "It's a real pleasure to meet you, Doctor Tselitel," he said, gripping her thin hand firmly. "I never thought I'd have the chance. I've read your book *Symbolism of the Unconscious Mind* so many times that I've got it memorized."

"I'm flattered," she responded, inwardly cringing as she thought of how her ideas had evolved since she wrote it nearly fifteen years before. "Naturally I've learned a thing or two since then," she added cautiously. "I'm afraid I would be a bit more circumspect in my conclusions nowadays."

"But you had to be bold to put your ideas on the map, Doctor," the man argued pleasantly, withdrawing his hand. "You can't make an idea stick unless you put it out there with some force. Once people get the gist of what you're saying, then you can draw back a little and begin to refine it."

"I suppose you're right," she agreed with a nod, glancing towards the chamber's door and only barely stopping herself from wringing her hands.

"Don't worry about those aliens," he said casually, guessing her thoughts with practiced accuracy. "We've got more than just diplomacy to fall back on."

"That's enough, Captain," one of the men at the table warned him, not bothering to look up from his meal. His mouth hidden behind a large, drooping mustache, he looked nearly twice the age of his thirty-odd year old subordinate. "We didn't come here to flap our gums."

"Yes, sir," the captain assented, winking at Tselitel before turning back to the table. "Won't you join us, Doctor?"

Hesitantly she looked to the chamber again, all her thoughts bent in that direction. But unable to enter, and not wishing to give offense to the friendly captain, she made for the table and sat down.

"Tell me, Doctor, what brings you this far out?" the captain asked, stabbing a piece of meat with his fork and gulping it down whole. "You're just about the last person I expected to find here."

"Krancis had a purpose for it, I'm sure," the mustached man remarked, still not looking up from his plate. "Don't pry. He doesn't like to reveal his secrets."

"Oh, it isn't a secret," Tselitel responded. "I'm here for my health, just like the emperor. Krancis saw fit to send me along, and I've been doing my best to help out any way I can since we've come here. Which, I must admit, hasn't been a whole lot."

"Unsurprising," the older man said. "Not much work for a psychiatrist in a place like this."

"But you must have made some interesting observations about the *Kol-Prockians*," the captain said. "What do you think is the chief way they differ from us psychologically?"

"I would say the chief difference is in their chaotic impulsivity," she replied, calming a little as she fell back into her area of expertise. "We humans tend to think of ourselves critically as rather unfocused, instinct-driven creatures. But compared to the *Kol-Prockians*, we're downright stodgy. I've been surprised again and again by the absoluteness with which they'll jump upon an impulse that's less than half a dozen seconds old. Reflection seems to mean very little to them. In a definite sense, I wouldn't call them a *rational* people, though they're very intelligent, all the same. They're highly intuitive, and their insights come to them in a flash. On the higher end of the spectrum, I suspect that makes them rather more deft than us at unraveling complex problems with elegant answers. But on the *lower* end of the intelligence curve, well, it makes them seize upon bad ideas with an abandon that you're not likely to find in most humans. Overall they give the impression of a can of fleas, each one of them leaping frantically in all directions. They're wily, cunning, and clearly capable of taking care of themselves, as evidenced by their ability to carve out a life within *Kren-Balar*. Yet their lack of straightforwardness and common sense undoes much of what their brilliance secures for them. Ultimately, they're their own worst enemies, making needless problems for themselves."

"Do you think this'll make it hard for them to live under our banner?" another man asked, filling his mouth with a forkful of shredded purple vegetables.

"For the time being I think they'll be as docile as lambs," she replied, growing yet more relaxed and slipping one leg over the other as she leaned back in her seat. "They've

THE CRUSADE OF VENGEANCE

gotten themselves in a terrible fix, and with abject humility they accept the necessity of joining forces with us. Actually, they regard it as an unbelievable deliverance, given they need us much more than we need them. I suspect many of them still can't quite believe it's true. But that'll change with time, I expect. Eventually, assuming we do manage to relocate them to our galaxy and set them up with a world of their own, they'll grow proud again, like any other race, and start to chafe. They have too much vanity to live under our head forever. They'll seek independence of some sort. The only real question is what our response will be."

"A people can change, don't you think, Doctor?" the captain asked, a little bothered by her assessment. "Given the strait they've brought themselves to, I should think they'd mend their chaotic ways and come down to earth, so to speak."

"Even an individual can't meaningfully change his ways, Captain," she replied authoritatively. "Much less an entire people. No, the fundamentals always remain the same. Only their surface expression can be altered, and that doesn't count for a whole lot. The one hope for change, if you want to call it that, is if a given individual hasn't been living according to his true nature. In that case, a 'rediscovering' of his real self can take place. But only if it's earnestly desired. The fact is, the *Kol-Prockians*, through what I've been able to glean of their once-dominant religion *Delek-Hai*, once strove with all their might to reach inner unity and put away all their chaos. But it clearly failed, as evidenced by the civil war and their subsequent dissolution as a great power. If the brilliant minds that built the healing chamber and all their other marvels couldn't solve their inner fractiousness, I have little hope that the current generation, or its descendants, will be able to."

"I have to agree with you, Doctor," the mustached man said, at last raising his eyes and revealing them to be an oddly pale gray. His expression gave the sense of one who'd seen too much of war, had been bleached by it, and yet was compelled to remain in its presence. He was weary, but nevertheless collected. "Having seen the aliens outside this base, it's clear that they have very little impulse control. Only the barest sense of necessity keeps the renegades from pulling each other's eyes out on a regular basis."

"How do you know that?" she asked.

"Part of our job," the captain explained. "Among our other responsibilities, Krancis wished us to keep an eye on any footloose *KP's* who might be running around. Didn't want them to drop by accidentally and blow the lid off things."

"And what are your 'other responsibilities?'" she asked.

"I'm sure Colonel Dorrit wouldn't want me to elaborate on those," the captain responded with a faint smile, glancing at his superior and receiving a nod. "Sorry, Doctor."

"Oh, I'm used to secrets," she said with a pleasant wave of her hand. "I've been around Krancis and then the emperor. There's plenty I don't know about."

Though spoken off-handedly, she noticed a couple of backs stiffen at the table. Sensing she'd caused offense, she was about to say more when the door to the chamber opened and Welter leaned out.

"Doctor," was all he said, before slipping back inside.

"Excuse me," she said with relief, glad to escape the awkwardness she'd just created. Padding across the room in her bare feet and thin robe, she opened the chamber's sturdy door and went inside.

"She shouldn't talk lightly about the emperor," one of the men said the instant she was out of earshot.

"Aw, she didn't mean anything by it," the captain said dismissively. "Just a casual comment."

"Ought to know better, given all the time she's spent around him," Dorrit commented, once again staring at his plate, chewing slowly as though he hadn't a care in the world beside his next bite.

"I don't think she was trying to be disrespectful," the captain asserted.

"I never said she was," Dorrit said with a shrug. "Just that she ought to cover her bases better. Wouldn't be the first person to get a little too comfortable with a regal personage just to find out she'd taken one liberty too many. Oughta watch her step. Seems like a good woman. Hope she keeps it between the lines."

Within the chamber Tselitel found *Karnan* sitting beside Rhemus on the floor, a look of consternation on both their faces.

"Doctor, when did you intend to tell us about this ailment of yours?" the alien scientist asked with a frown. "That's not the sort of thing to keep to yourself. Especially with all the technology we have available to us."

"What?" Tselitel asked, surprised that her secret had been passed along so soon. "I told you that in *confidence*, Gustav," she added with a mixture of irritation and embarrassment.

"Your health is a matter of imperial priority, Doctor," Rhemus replied. "He was right to tell us at once. It gives us more time to formulate a plan. Though, unfortunately, it must wait until the present business with this so-called 'ambassador' is taken care of."

"I could run a few preliminary tests in the meantime," *Karnan* suggested. "The ancients had a device that was intended to measure the presence of dark energy within an individual. Perhaps there's a kind of residue that's been left behind. If so, there could be a way to remove it."

"Amra said that the damage was done, and that only a *Dolshan* could heal me."

"Well, that sounds a little bit outside our present capacities," *Karnan* said. "So just humor me on this. Might be we've got a little something up our sleeve that'll tip things in your favor."

"Use whatever resources you have to," Rhemus said to *Karnan*. "Put half the base onto the problem if you must. And let me know if you need anything from outside *Kren-Balar*." He looked sincerely into Tselitel's eyes. "We'll bend every available thought upon solving this, Doctor. I promise you that."

"Thank you," she replied, deeply flattered by his concern.

"Now, what are we going to do about this ambassador?"

"Oh, I don't know," *Karnan* said with a sigh and a roll of his eyes. "You know these young morons. No gray matter at all. I doubt if there'll be two brain cells inside his skull that we can reason with."

"They're your people, *Karnan*," Welter pointed out. "Just what do you suggest we do?"

"Shock him," the old scientist responded. "Make a pageant of his arrival. Get everyone into the hangar and let him see first hand how utterly content they are with the new state of affairs. Then take him inside the base, fill his stomach with a huge meal, and not-so-subtly make it known what kind of reprisals Krancis would immediately order if his emperor were put at risk. Pressed between death on one hand, and the obvious popularity of Rhemus on the other, I think we might just bring him around."

"And then?" Rhemus queried, intrigued by the idea but cautious.

"Well, then we'll send him back to his little friends, and he can tell them how nice things are inside *Kren-Balar* now. With any luck they'll pull in their fangs, come back, and settle down."

"These aren't the kind of people we want inside *Kren-Balar*," Welter stated.

"Better than having them running around loose and free on the outside," *Karnan* countered. "At least inside the base we've got 'em under lock and key. They won't be able to get out unless we want them to."

"And if they spread dissatisfaction?" Welter asked.

"Well, there's lots of ways to deal with discontents," *Karnan* chuckled dryly, sending a little shiver down Tselitel's spine. "Under old *Kol-Prockian* law they're under a death sentence for openly threatening the legitimate government of our people, anyhow. You *could* think of this as an act of mercy, a deferment of their sentence."

"There's another option," Welter said, crossing his arms and leaning against the wall. "We could follow the ambassador back to his friends and carry out that sentence immediately."

"I don't want to spill any blood," Rhemus said with a shake of his head. "There's too few *Kol-Prockians* as it is."

"With respect, Majesty, I think my people could do without these particular *Kol-Prockians*," *Karnan* opined. "They're the kind of reckless malcontents who led us into the civil war." Seeing Rhemus's eyes tighten with irritation, he quickly added, "Of course, it *would* be desirable to win them over, if at all possible. I was merely speaking as the Devil's Advocate."

"I think he's got enough friends as it is, Doctor," Rhemus replied.

"Yes, yes of course," *Karnan* nodded, taking his point and standing up with some effort. "I'd best dig around in my box of tricks and see what I can come up with," he said, squeezing Tselitel's arm gently with his frail hand. "Don't give up hope, child. We'll do everything we can for you."

"Thank you," she uttered appreciatively, as he slowly ambled from the chamber.

"I'd better see about that pageantry *Karnan* suggested," Rhemus said, likewise standing. "We don't have a lot of time before the ambassador gets here."

"When will that be?" Tselitel asked meekly, seeing the strain on his face and not wishing to add to it.

"About six hours."

"What can I do to help?" she queried.

"You can stay in here and take the load off your body for a while," he answered, his tone making it little short of a command. "You're a valuable member of everything we're trying to do here, Doctor. Don't forget that and overextend yourself."

"I'll try," she responded quietly, as he walked slowly across the room. Pausing at the door, he turned and looked back at her and Welter, who still leaned upon the wall. "I'll want you on hand when the ambassador arrives, Gustav. Should he need a little fear put into his bones, I expect you to plant it there."

"Yes, sir," he nodded, watching Rhemus as he left. "You'd best lay down and take it easy for a little while, Doctor," he said to Tselitel once they were alone.

"Gustav, I told you about my illness in *confidence*," she repeated, her voice both pleading and a touch betrayed. "I never thought you'd just walk right in here and spill the beans. I want us to be able to trust each other, to share what we can't with anyone else. How can I do that if you don't keep my secrets?"

"That secret wasn't yours or mine to keep, Doctor," he answered, pushing off the wall and putting his hands on his hips. "The emperor is right: you're an imperial priority. Like it or not, you're public property, just like he is. Neither of you have a right to indulge in privacy when it's detrimental to the war."

"Everyone needs privacy, Gustav," she disagreed.

"In truly personal matters, of course. But when your health is on the line, we can't keep it a secret, nor can we hesitate. Besides, you heard *Karnan*: there might be an answer right here within *Kren-Balar*. What good would waiting have done? Your ailment would've just gotten worse."

"Oh, I know all the arguments pro and con," she said, walking somewhat stiffly to the wall and leaning against it.

"I'm sorry. I know I'm being irrational. But I can't help it. You saw what I was like in that room just a little while ago. I'm coming to pieces at the seams, Gustav. My only hope for holding it together was to keep it a secret. At least then I could *pretend* I was okay."

"You won't have to pretend," he assured her, reaching out a strong hand and squeezing her shoulder firmly. "We'll make sure you get the treatment you need."

"I hope so," she said idly, not really believing it was possible, though desperate to hope that it was. Sliding down the wall out of his reach, she sat on the floor, wrapped her arms around her legs, and sighed. "I don't know what dark fate it was that cursed Rex with me," she said, the weight of her responsibility to him all but crushing her. "Why me, of all the women in the empire? Do you have the least idea how *rare* Valindra is? Shoot, it's probably the reason why all that exposure to the darkness is having the effect that it is."

"That'd crossed my mind, too," Welter agreed.

"I've never been a strong person," she continued, as though she hadn't heard him. "Valindra's been grinding me down until there's hardly anything left. To throw Bodkin and then Lavery on top…" her voice trailed, her head shaking.

"*Bodkin* and *Lavery?*" he queried, for once a hint of surprise in his voice.

"Yeah," she answered without interest, resting her chin on her knees.

"That's nothing to sneeze at, Doctor," Welter asserted, once more leaning his side against the wall, crossing his arms and looking down at her. "Lavery was one of the most dangerous men you could come across. The fact you survived an encounter with him more or less intact is a miracle. Bodkin wasn't any lightweight, either."

"I'm surprised you've even heard of her," Tselitel remarked. "I thought she was just a local on Delta-13."

"Sure. But she'd been building a reputation, getting more and more on our radar. Someone from our organization probably would have taken her down had she kept it up for another couple of years. Maybe even me, if she'd proven dangerous enough."

"I wish you had," she said fervently, the nightmare images Bodkin put inside her head once more dancing past her mind's eye and making her cringe. "I'd never been so scared in all my life."

"That's all over now," he assured her, trying to offer what comfort he could. "You don't have to worry about that anymore."

"The funny thing is, she didn't even really *scare me*, to be honest," she continued, again as though she hadn't heard him. "She just made me aware of all the lost souls who haunted Delta-13 after the last time the Devourer attacked this galaxy. I've always been sensitive to what you might call 'background phenomena:' strange happenings, things that go bump in the night. I guess that's why it was so terrible: everything I saw was real, so there wasn't any way of hiding from it. It just about tore my nerves in two. The only thing that got me through was Wellesley."

"Wellesley?"

"Yes, a *Kol-Prockian* AI like Frank, though much, much more capable." Suddenly growing self-conscious, her eyes widened and she looked up at him.

"Don't worry: I left him with *Keelen*."

"Oh, good," she uttered with relief, dropping her chin once more to her knees and sighing. "I don't mean to hurt his feelings. But he's a real step down after Wellesley." Fondly she chuckled. "I've never known an AI to have so much personality. Or such an enormous ego. I hope I get to see him again."

"You will," Welter insisted, though the hard fact of her long odds restrained his voice somewhat.

"You don't have to tell me what I want to hear, Gustav," she said, sighing again. "I know I'm probably not ever going to return to our galaxy."

"You don't know that, Doctor. You merely *fear* that."

"It's hard not to," she replied, feeling a churning in her stomach grow steadily until it leveled off. The chamber couldn't suppress all of her fears. But it did make them more manageable, keeping the churn to a low-level dread that sucked the hope from her heart but didn't send her to the sharp depths of panic and despair she experienced earlier.

Before Welter could respond, the chamber's door opened and Colonel Dorrit stuck his head in.

"Sir, we've just received news that the ambassador has pulled a fast one. He dropped out of warp a minute ago and is rapidly approaching the base. His ship is slow, so we expect it'll take him about twenty minutes to reach us."

"Wanted to catch us with our pants down," Welter remarked acidly, pushing off the wall and making for the door. "Stay here, Doctor," he instructed without turning around, knowing she was about to rise. "Right now your job is to stay healthy."

Outside the anteroom Welter found *Kren-Balar* in a state of high alert. The corridors were filled with *Kol-Prockians* rushing to and fro, only a handful of them seeming to have any idea where they were going. Chancing into Doctor *Keelen*, he took Frank back and used him to relay commands to the aliens he encountered, funneling all of them towards the hangar.

"I hope this works," the AI worried to Welter, as the latter entered the hangar and his eyes fell upon the chaos. "If we don't pull this together in a hurry, all we'll have done is made an embarrassing mess of our first impression."

Making for the egg without saying a word, Welter climbed aboard and got Frank to hook into the craft's speakers. At once he began issuing orders, selecting who would stand where, and what their conduct would be during the ambassador's arrival. Briefly informing them of the stakes, the crowd hissed and began to boil at the outrageous behavior of their brethren outside the base. Aware that they might savage their visitor much as they had the traitors who'd formerly been in their midst, Welter made it clear that Rhemus' solemn wish was that neither the ambassador nor any of his associates would be hurt during their time within *Kren-Balar*. Hearing this, they calmed somewhat. But the tension in the air was palpable.

"They're already so loyal to their new emperor," Frank said to Welter, highly impressed.

"Let's just hope they don't blow this up for us. We need to either mollify or kill the renegades, not force them to make good on their threat by tearing their messenger boy in pieces."

"Agreed. Still, that might work to our advantage. A little hostility from the base's population could convince the ambassador that everything is on the up and up."

"Assuming he lives long enough to share that with his pals."

"Yeah, that's true."

While they spoke the crowd in the hangar had been assembling themselves according to Welter's instructions. Many of them had rather poor clothing, so he put them in the middle ranks and had the better dressed ones line the fronts and sides of the four groups he'd broken them into. Flatly telling them that it was his purpose to give the best impression possible, they energetically set themselves about putting the most frail among them behind a wall of the most robust. Without a hint of self-consciousness each of them complied, wishing to do as well by their new emperor as they possibly could.

"I doubt a ruler has ever had more pliable subjects," Frank observed.

"He's earned it," Welter replied.

"No argument from me. How long until our little friend arrives?"

Seeing Rhemus, *Keelen*, and *Karnan* hurry into the chamber, Welter began to descend the egg's ladder.

"I'd say about a minute," he answered dryly, his heels thudding against the floor when he jumped the last couple of feet.

"He's just about to enter the volcano now," *Karnan* said to Welter as the trio neared him. Muttering several oaths in *Kol-Prockian*, he watched as the hangar's landing pad rose up into the ceiling to receive their visitor. "At least he's had the brains to maintain radio silence until now. I almost expected such common sense to be beyond him."

"You sound like you know him," Welter observed, crossing his arms and likewise watching the ceiling.

"Believe me, I do," *Karnan* said sourly. "I had hoped one of us would die before chance caused us to meet again. *Melsek* was the most brilliant and least sufferable of my students."

"Given we *are* trying to make a favorable impression," Frank began to Welter. "Might it be prudent for *Karnan* to absent himself?"

"Frank thinks you should go, *Karnan*, so you don't upset our guest," Welter relayed.

"That's hardly what I said!" the AI exclaimed. "You twisted the spirit of my words all out of shape!"

"He won't bear any ill-will because of me," *Karnan* assured him. "He always thought he was the smarter of the two of us by far, and acted accordingly. No, Welter, the only problem will be the difficulty I'll have in *not* choking the life out of his arrogant little–."

"Here he comes," *Keelen* cut him off, as the landing pad began to descend into the base.

Every eye present was fixed upon it, as the conduct of their visitor could well decide their fate as a people. The vessel that bore him was small, being little more than an old engine welded to a battered hull roughly shaped like a triangle. Through its semi-transparent canopy they could see a figure seated in the middle of the craft. Speaking briefly to his pilot, he gestured sharply upward and at once the canopy began to rise until it stood over the rear of the vessel.

A pair of *Kol-Prockians* which flanked him arose first, dropped a rope ladder down the side, and preceded him. Once they'd 'secured' the hangar, he followed.

It was not until his feet had actually touched the ground that *Melsek* took stock of his surroundings. Visibly jolting at the sight of his people obediently standing at attention in honor of their new ruler, he took a moment to make sense of the situation. Then, raising his chin in the air, he strode across the space that separated his ship from Rhemus and his companions. Standing before the emperor, he bowed his head ever-so-slightly in reluctant recognition of his station.

"Emperor Rhemus," *Melsek* began in decent English, though he'd obviously not spoken it in some time. "It is with some hesitation that we have seen fit to speak with you rather than press our just demands upon your force of occupation. I must advise you that my people will act swiftly if a hand is raised against my person. You are illegally and immorally oppressing the people of a weaker power, forcing them to serve you as little more than slaves. It is our intention to liberate our people at once, and to cast aside forever the shameful fact that they, however briefly, served a human ruler." Pausing significantly, he glanced from left to right across Rhemus' entourage. He jolted a second time when his gaze fell upon Welter, the eyes of that dangerous man boring into his skull and out the other side.

Without warning *Karnan* emitted a sharp whistle, drawing the attention of every ear in the hangar. Then, word for word, he translated the impudent address of their visitor into *Kol-Prockian*. Universally a hiss began to rise, along with an occasional shout of *felen-kor*. Wincing at this imprecation, the ambassador couldn't help taking a step back so as to be closer to his bodyguards. When a handful of *Kol-Prockians* broke ranks and were about to rush him, Rhemus raised a hand for them to stop. Instantly they did so.

"So fearful are they of your abuse that they yield at

once to your demands," *Melsek* scowled. "You have broken their will with your imperial yoke. But as our forefathers proved long ago, the *Kol-Prockian* people will never live under an empire. We would sooner die than do so."

Needing no greater rebuttal than the spontaneous eruptions of the crowd around them, *Karnan* again translated. The hisses then grew so sharp as to hurt the human's ears. At once *Melsek* shrank back.

"You've turned them! You've corrupted them!" he insisted, his words at once conveyed to his listeners. Roaring their anger at his insults to both themselves and Rhemus, they left their positions in one mass and would have beaten him into jelly if the emperor hadn't again intervened.

"I think we had better adjourn to an inner room, Majesty," *Keelen* opined. "Else we're likely to be short three guests."

"I agree," Rhemus nodded, before looking at the masses around him. "You honor me with your fealty. But I must have words in private with *Melsek*. Trust me when I say I'll guard your interests as if they were my own, for they are." Looking at the ambassador's escorts, he added, "Return to your ship. I'll return him to you intact."

Turning to leave as *Karnan* translated, the crowd quieted at once and bowed their heads with one consent. Raising their gazes as *Melsek* reluctantly followed Rhemus from the hangar, the ambassador was struck to the heart by the murderous hatred he saw in their eyes.

"They...they would have killed me," he muttered as they passed into the main corridor, meaning to speak inwardly but much too stunned to keep the words from flowing out his mouth. "Torn me to pieces!"

"They might still get that chance," *Karnan* growled in response, ambling angrily beside him, just a little behind the emperor. "Perhaps that'll make you think twice before you open your mouth again."

"I can't believe you're going along with this, *Karnan*,"

he spoke in *Kol-Prockian*. "I'm not sure if I'm more shocked or disgusted by your contemptible conduct. You know the humans and their ways. We'll be nothing more than slaves! You have betrayed us all."

"Speak English, *Melsek*, or I'll translate every syllable you speak," the old scientist shot back. "While you and your worthless chums have been flitting around Quarlac committing petty piracy to stay alive, some of us have been carrying on the serious work needed to give our people a future." His temper rising as he spoke, he sharply stopped and seized *Melsek's* shirt in his weak hands. "So don't you so much as *think* of lecturing me on my responsibilities to our people."

Gently *Keelen* put a hand on *Karnan's* back, drawing him back to the present and cooling his anger a little. Releasing the ambassador, *Karnan* resumed movement, muttering under his breath every insult that came to mind.

"I never thought I would see the day that–," *Melsek* began, his words stopped when Welter placed a painfully firm hand on his thin shoulder.

"Just stop right there, friend," he uttered with a faintly menacing grin on his lips. "Unless you want that fine old gentleman to tear your lungs out."

Glancing at *Karnan*, *Melsek* at once saw a flame in his eyes that stopped his tongue and caused him to lower his gaze to the floor.

Proceeding the rest of the way in silence, they entered what had once been *Seldek's* room and sat down to a meal that had been hastily put together.

"I must say I expected a better welcome than this," *Melsek* said grandly, regaining some of his poise as he sat down at the foot of the table, Rhemus naturally taking the head.

"You should be happy that we're feeding you at all," *Karnan* snapped, settling into his seat on the emperor's right hand with some difficulty.

To the ambassador's visible discomfort, Welter took the seat to his own right. Taking up his knife immediately, he leaned back in his chair, eyed the visitor for a few moments, and began slowly twirling the utensil in his hand.

"All any of us wants is what's best for the *Kol-Prockian* people as a whole," Rhemus began, trying to strike a conciliatory note. "We shouldn't be at each other's throats like this."

"That's rather a curious thing to say, given you've captured the only bastion of my people that remains!" *Melsek* flared at once. Hesitating a little when he saw Welter stop twirling his knife and grip it tighter, he shifted a little in his seat and continued. "*Kol-Prockians* will never submit to a foreign ruler. It is nothing short of conquest."

"And what right do you have to speak about governance?" *Karnan* shot back. "Even mad old *Seldek* saw your little band for what they are and rightly booted you out."

"Evidently just in time to be pushed aside by these humans," *Melsek* replied acidly, leaning his elbows on the table and scowling at the old scientist. "Perhaps if we'd been here we would have stirred our people to resist!"

"Resist *what?!*" demanded *Karnan*. "These people haven't *conquered* us! They've *rescued* us! Oh, it's a shameful, miserable thing to deserve a foreign ruler. But that shame is entirely upon *us, Melsek!* It is our own failure to govern ourselves that has brought us to this strait. Moreover we're getting the longer end of the stick in this deal! All the humans are truly getting is access to our medical technology. It's hard to imagine how else they benefit from this arrangement."

"Of course, you old imbecile!" roared the ambassador. "Don't you see the trick that's being played on you all? They only want us for the technology we've managed to preserve from the ancients! Once they've broken it all down and carted it away, they'll turn their backs upon us! And how then shall we hold our heads up when we've given away the treasures of our forefathers in exchange for empty promises?"

"So that's it, then," *Karnan* declared, slapping his hands against the table and leaning back in disgust. "All this talk of *our people* and never submitting to foreign rulers… All you care about is a few *baubles!* Your pride is bound up in the achievements of our forebears and you can't stand to see them used by another race!"

"And I don't see how *you* can!" shouted *Melsek*, standing up out of his seat and slugging the tabletop with both fists. "There's nothing *left* of our former glory save these few 'baubles' as you've called them! What are we anymore, *Karnan?* Just outcasts! Renegades with nothing at all to distinguish us from the mass of life in this miserable galaxy. At least the gifts of our ancestors give us something to be proud of, for it's certain that we have little cause for pride in ourselves alone. Any people who would hand off their most priceless treasures in exchange for the safety of bondage deserve nothing save an early grave!"

"The fact is, *Melsek*, that our backs are against the wall," Doctor *Keelen* chimed in, his attention on his plate as he thoughtfully spoke, poking his food quietly. "The chamber is our greatest achievement, and only *Karnan* can keep it running for any length of time. This is another example in which the humans have acted in good faith far beyond what could be expected, for we've made no secret of his declining health. It won't be long before the chamber breaks down again, likely for good. What of our ancient treasures then? Will our people be grateful that we refused the safety offered by the empire in order to hoard a lifeless piece of technology?"

"There are other hands, other minds that can fill the gap left by *Karnan*," *Melsek* answered at once, sitting once more. "Long ago I would have set the chamber on a far better footing if *Karnan* had allowed me to. There would have been no question of it breaking down anytime in the next decade."

"The chamber is a vast array of delicate parts that are *barely* managing to function as is," *Karnan* uttered with restrained vehemence. "You intended to swap out entire sections, replacing them with newer parts that would have never worked."

"You can't expect machinery as old as that to run in perpetuity, *Karnan*," *Melsek* replied with lecturesome patience. "Given how poorly the device functions, the subsequent wear and tear on otherwise healthy parts has doubtless shortened its operational life by years. Had I been permitted to upgrade–."

"There's no *upgrading anything* with a piece of tech that old!" roared the scientist. "Can't you get that through your skull? A part here and there is one thing. But they all have to be carefully brought into sync, or the immense energy that runs through the machine will cause it to burn itself out. That's why it's so delicate! Interrupt the flow of energy with either a poorly built part or one that hasn't been calibrated properly, and you'll destroy it before you've even figured out what's wrong!"

"You've worked on it for too long, *Karnan*. You've come to fear a device that, while deserving respect, must be handled with a firm hand." Standing up again, he added in a louder voice: "You cannot shrink back because you're afraid! Risks must be taken!"

"Risks *are* being taken!" declared *Karnan*, likewise standing, his body trembling with rage. "It has only been through constant effort and several miracles that I've managed to keep it running at all. The chamber has all but had it."

"And yet you take this as evidence for why your stewardship should continue!" *Melsek* scoffed. "Don't you realize the damage you've done?"

Scowling viciously, *Karnan* leaned forward over the table and seized a knife. The instant he did so *Keelen* snapped out his hand and took his arm.

"I don't think the time for that has come quite yet, old friend," the doctor said with quiet firmness. Holding on until the knife was released and *Karnan* retook his seat, he then looked to the ambassador. "*Melsek*, I suggest you sit down. We have a lot to discuss."

"We have *nothing* to discuss!" he declared, turning around and making for the door. Opening it, he found the way blocked by a pair of *Kol-Prockian* guards facing him. Shouting for them to move in their native tongue, they returned nothing save icy glares. "Tell them to move!" he demanded, looking back towards the table. "I am a diplomat. You can't hold me in this room against my will!"

"And what makes you think those boys are keeping you in here?" Welter queried without looking at him, his chair leaned back upon its rear feet. "We've got more than enough bodies at this table to kill you if we wanted to. Shoot," he said with a shrug, drawing a pistol and leveling it on the ambassador's forehead. "I could kill you myself." Holding the pose for just a moment as *Melsek* trembled, he then chuckled dryly and tossed the weapon on the table. "Fact is, Mister Ambassador, they're here to *protect you*."

"From what?" he asked, unable to keep his voice from shaking from the fact that his life had just flitted before his eyes.

"Even you ought to be able to figure that out," *Karnan* retorted.

"You're not popular inside *Kren-Balar*, *Melsek*. If we let you go without an escort, it's at least even odds that you don't make it back to your ship," Welter informed him. "It seems your people don't think highly of your attempt to 'rescue' them from our imperial grip."

"A desperate people will accept any master who offers to deliver them from their plight," he fired back, advancing on the table, his anger pushing aside his fear. "They'll even trade the only thing that ever made them a great race."

"If that's all you think of our people, *Melsek*, then why are you so concerned?" *Keelen* asked. "We can't make that kind of machinery anymore, so there's no 'future' for us that you could bring yourself to consider worthwhile. So what difference does it make? Even under your *esteemed* stewardship, the chamber would eventually break down for good. What then? Would we spread the then useless parts of it around *Kren-Balar* to remind ourselves of how excellent we once were? Would we make little shrines to it? At the bottom of the sum, all we have is ourselves, *Melsek*. If our people, under whatever government, aren't good enough for you, then I can't imagine why you're so concerned about guarding the achievements of our progenitors."

"You can't imagine it because your pride is broken, and your dignity is *lost!*" asserted the ambassador. "I had hoped that by coming here I could induce you to throw aside this great shame that you've brought upon us while the humans are still too weak to resist us. Even now our vast superiority in numbers would allow us to eject them from this facility without loss of blood on either side."

"I wouldn't have thought that mattered to you," Welter remarked.

"I'm not a barbarian," sniffed *Melsek*. "I don't wish to see anyone die needlessly."

"And you don't want to give Krancis cause for retribution, either," Welter added, a cynical gleam in his eye as he looked at the visitor. "You don't want *Sentinel* pointing its nose down this volcano and blasting you to dust."

"A bloodless coup indeed," *Karnan* uttered scornfully, shaking his head before glaring at his former subordinate. "*Your* blood will be spilled if you keep talking like this. And not by the people sitting at this table." Angrily he stabbed a finger towards the door. "It'll be them, because they've been driven to the point of despair by our own failure to correct our fortunes. Now that they have a chance for a real life held out before them, they'll allow *nothing* to interfere with it.

Don't imagine that you will be received with anything but hatred if you attempt to remove the humans. Even if you *could* do so, you would be murdered in your bed the first night you spent within *Kren-Balar*."

"The *Kol-Prockian* people *will* know freedom, *Karnan*," *Melsek* replied stoutly. "They will not live under an empire. I should have thought that our triumph in the civil war over just such a government would have taught you that. But it seems you esteem the principles of our ancestors just as little as you do their creations."

"And what if you go through with your plan, *Melsek*?" asked *Keelen*, still managing to remain cool despite his passionate nature. "If you expose *Kren-Balar*, as you've threatened to do, then our technology will pass into other hands. You won't be able to resist the flood of fortune hunters who'll try and batter their way into the base. The pirates alone will be enough to besiege this facility into submission."

"We have seen to the needs of the *Kol-Prockian* people," he evaded proudly. "You needn't concern yourself about theft. All the technology will remain in our hands."

"It shall certainly remain within the hands of the *Kol-Prockian* people," Rhemus said. "But under the protection of the government they've freely chosen for themselves."

"That is something which I utterly refuse to believe," *Melsek* declared. "I know that in their heart of hearts they regretted their choice even as they were making it. The euphoria of apparent safety has blinded them for the time being. But eventually their mistake will be palpably known to even the dullest among them. Not that I intend to allow matters to reach such a conclusion. The hearts of my people will rally behind the patriots who've come to deliver them."

"You are deluded," *Karnan* uttered in disbelief. "At first I thought you were merely mistaken. But you're so far gone that–."

"I shan't listen to your insults a moment longer," *Melsek* announced. "I would like to be returned to my ship now. What answer shall I bring to those who wait upon me?"

"We're not going to give up *Kren-Balar*," Rhemus answered at once. "Both for our sakes, and the sake of every *Kol-Prockian* who chooses to take refuge within its walls."

"Is that an invitation, Emperor Rhemus?" *Melsek* asked, suppressing a scornful chuckle.

"It is an open offer to any *Kol-Prockian* who wishes to come out of the cold and find comradeship and safety among his own kind," he replied. "No matter where they may be found, there will be a home for them here. Until we remove your people to our own galaxy, at which time you'll be given a world to govern as you see fit."

"Under the 'protection' of the empire?" *Melsek* queried sarcastically. "I should think not. The obedience you'll exact would be far too great a price to pay. We would rather be free and subject to the dangers of a hostile galaxy than suffer the security of slavery."

"Don't you see what's taking place here?" *Karnan* asked, making one final attempt to punch through the ambassador's prejudices. "The humans are on the ascent in their own galaxy. Soon, if we're lucky, they'll spread to others. They haven't been perfect. But to be subject to their government is far better than to continue living in this hateful place. Quarlac isn't fit to live in. It isn't even fit to *die* in. We only came to this miserable world all those years ago because we knew nobody would think of looking here for a few outcasts. And we were right! I truly can't fathom what has so taken hold of you, *Melsek*."

"Nothing has taken hold of me, *Karnan*, save an honest concern for my people's wellbeing," he answered proudly. "But like the others you've lived in this base for much too long. Your hope has been destroyed, ground to dust. You haven't breathed the fresh air of freedom in an age. It has clouded your judgment until you think treason a virtue. You're no longer capable of thinking clearly. It's regrettable that a once brilliant mind such as yours should have slidden so completely from the heights it formerly occupied."

At once enraged by these words, the old scientist again seized the knife before him. Managing to do so before *Keelen* could stop him, he scrambled around the table and was about to advance upon *Melsek* when Welter shot to his feet and barred his way.

"Let me at him!" he ordered. "I'll finish him good and quick!"

"This isn't the way, *Karnan*," Welter said in a low, firm voice.

"Why not? He'll sell us out if we don't! And to think, he *dares* to call *me* a traitor!" Looking around Welter, he pointed his knife at the ambassador. "You're the traitor, *Melsek!* And not just to the living, but to all our ancestors who've worked and bled and *died* to maintain this base for just such a day as this when our deliverance is finally at hand!" Pausing momentarily, he shifted on his feet as his eyes suddenly clouded. "Y–you're the–the…" his voice trailed, the knife dropping from his hand as his body began to sway. Like lightning Welter snapped out his hands and caught him just as he was about to fall over backwards. Helping his frail form back to the table, he sat him down. But the old scientist wasn't done yet. Pushing Welter out of his line of sight with a weak sweeping of his arm, he glared at *Melsek* and pointed a trembling index finger at him. "I swear to you, *Melsek*, that if you jeopardize what we've est–established here–."

Pausing to cough, he cleared his throat and resumed.

"If you jeopardize what we've done, I *swear* I'll see you dead. I don't care *how*. But I'll make sure you never draw another breath!"

Falling once more to coughing, those assembled, even *Melsek*, were alarmed to see blood come from his mouth.

"This interview is over," Rhemus declared instantly, as *Keelen* took Welter's place and began to examine his friend. "For the time being you'll be escorted to a room where you may refresh yourself."

"You mean I'm being held prisoner?" *Melsek* asked, as Welter walked past him and ushered the two guards inside.

"Doctor *Karnan's* health must be seen to first, Ambassador," Rhemus replied with great dignity. "I'm sure you would agree."

Seeing himself without any other option, he curtly nodded his assent.

"I'll see to it that he makes it to his room in one piece," Welter said, taking his pistol off the table and tucking it into his jacket pocket. "Ambassador?"

"I hardly think a human escort is necessary," he replied, nodding towards his fellow *Kol-Prockians*.

"I wouldn't be so sure about that," Welter responded, clapping one of them on the shoulder. "You see, they like you even less than *I* do."

Somehow intuiting the meaning of his words, the guard glared at the ambassador in mute confirmation. Seeing the latter gulp, the guard grinned his satisfaction, took his arm, and began pulling him towards the exit.

"You shouldn't have exerted yourself so much," *Keelen* said to *Karnan* once their visitor had left. "You need to save your strength, old friend."

"What I *need* to do is tear that miserable little cretin limb from limb," he replied with as much ferocity as his battered old body could muster. "Just thinking of him makes my blood boil."

"Then don't think of him," Rhemus smiled generously, placing a chair opposite the scientist and sitting down. "You must remember how desperately we need you, *Karnan*. How desperately your people need you to keep the chamber intact."

"I know that," *Karnan* nodded, losing a little of his passion as he put a shaking hand to his brow and sighed. "I'm sorry. I shouldn't have gone off like that. *Melsek* isn't worth it."

"That's why you did it," Rhemus replied knowingly. "There's nothing so irritating as an unworthy critic."

"You're *absolutely right*," Karnan agreed warmly, grateful to be understood.

Long after *Keelen* had departed with *Karnan* to care for him, Rhemus sat in *Seldek's* old office and thought. Musing over the situation *Melsek* and his fellow discontents had handed him, he was weighing his options when someone knocked at the door.

"Come," he ordered at once.

Seeing Welter enter, he smiled.

"I'd hoped it would be you," he said, gesturing for him to sit at his right hand. "I thought perhaps *Karnan* had worked himself into another frenzy."

"I checked in on the old bird once I'd locked up *Melsek*. *Keelen* says he'll be alright. But he needs nothing but rest for the next couple of days."

"That's too bad. I appreciate his counsel. It's hard to equal a hundred and fifty-odd years."

"I agree," Welter said quietly. "I gather you wanted me for something?"

"Yes. I want to know what our options are, given *Melsek* is utterly unreconciled to our presence here."

"Well, we can't kill him until we know where his friends are. During all the hurly-burly in the hangar I ordered a couple of the more disciplined *Kol-Prockians* to be sure to separate *Melsek's* bodyguards and his pilot from the ship for a little while. While they were busy making as though they'd tear 'em apart for sport, one of Krancis' boys slipped aboard and planted a tracker."

"So you're suggesting we let him go and follow him back to the nest? What if he just radios on ahead?"

"We've already broken his radio," Welter shrugged. "And while he'll suspect some kind of setup, our tech isn't detectable by the kind of garbage he and his folks are using, so I doubt they'll find the tracker before he's led us to them.

Unless they start pulling the ship apart midway to their destination."

"Still sounds pretty risky," Rhemus remarked, twisting his head a little as he spoke. "It means placing a lot of eggs in a single basket." Scowling as he thought, he looked at Welter. "Something is wrong about this whole business. You saw the way he dodged *Keelen's* question about the kinds of vultures who'll descend on this place the instant the news is out. Seems to think things are already sewn up."

"Yes, I had noticed that," Welter replied, leaning back in his seat and feeling an embryonic mustache he'd started to grow.

"What do you think it is?"

"If I had to guess, I'd say they're not going to spread the news around just anywhere. Most likely they've found a specific party they'll blab to in exchange for some of their tech. Probably been feeling out the deal ever since they first heard we'd come to the base."

"Then you think all his fervency about their technology is just a sham?"

"I do," Welter nodded, leaning forwards and putting his elbows on the table. "Either the guy is crazier than a bag of snakes, or he's putting up a front."

"*Karnan* seems to think it's the former possibility," Rhemus pointed out.

"That's entirely possible. But we've got to remember that these guys are little more than pirates themselves. It'd make sense that, with *Seldek* gone, they figure they can drive a wedge between us and the rest of the base and then run off with the goods."

"*Melsek* must be shocked half to death to find things the other way around," the emperor said. "He'd have had a better chance with *Seldek* in control." Pausing momentarily, he brushed his palms together and thought. "Do you think there's any chance of *Melsek* carrying the message back to his group and accidentally turning them around? Perhaps hearing how their people responded to his message will convert them."

"It's possible," Welter allowed, his tone unconvinced. "But if even a handful of them don't go along with it, the base will be exposed. That's not a risk we can take."

"I wish there was another way," Rhemus sighed, crossing one arm over his stomach and resting his other elbow upon it. Supporting his chin with the heel of his hand, he gazed at the far wall. "I truly do. I don't want to see another *Kol-Prockian* die under my watch. There's so few of them as it is. There's a very real risk of extinction if something unexpected comes down the pyke."

"With respect, we need to think of your needs first," Welter said.

"I know," Rhemus agreed without altering his gaze. "But an emperor isn't much use unless he takes care of those under him. I'd rather see to *both* our interests at the same time." Cursing under his breath, he scowled again and looked at Welter. "It's incredible the amount of trouble such a small number of *Kol-Prockians* have given us. Can you imagine what it would be like to rule an entire *empire* full of them? It would be utterly maddening."

"Yes, it would."

Several minutes passed without a word spoken as Rhemus thought.

"Well, you'd better begin making the necessary preparations to eliminate *Melsek's* group. If we can't think of anything better by the time he departs, you have my authorization to use whatever force is necessary to safeguard our interests."

"Understood," Welter replied, slowly standing up.

"But try and think of another way, will you? Either one that saves us the loss of blood, or, failing that, one which'll eliminate the risk engendered by allowing him to fly out of here. If we must kill them, I'd rather wipe the slate clean in an instant, leaving no loose ends."

"I'll do my best," Welter assured him. Receiving a nod of acknowledgement, he turned and left.

Once he'd communicated with the various strike teams Krancis had placed at their disposal in Quarlac and put them on alert, Welter slowly made his way towards the chamber to check on Tselitel. Sticking his hand into his jacket pocket, he made skin contact with Frank, who'd been riding around helplessly in there since he'd finished translating for him in the hangar.

"I see you've remembered me at last," the AI remarked dryly.

"Hard to forget about you," he replied with equal dryness. "You open your mouth every chance you get."

"Sure, because I've always got something to say! Something *valuable* to add to the discussion! Don't you think I might have had an insight or two about our little friend earlier? Whatever you think of my talents, or lack thereof, you must admit that I have a wide breadth of experience. Nobody else in that room has been alive since the civil war!"

"And just what's on your mind?" Welter asked, unimpressed.

"Oh, I'm allowed to speak now? You *actually* want to know what I think?"

Mutely Welter began to draw his hand from his pocket.

"Okay! Okay! Sheesh, you don't give a guy a break, do you?"

"Speak your mind."

"Fine. What I wanted to say was that I agree with what you said earlier: I don't think *Melsek* is in earnest about the technology and whatnot. I think it's a front, too. Just a plausible cover for a salvage operation. Most likely he *did* think it would be easy to slide a wedge between Rhemus and my people, and thus to assume control of the base for his little faction of bottom feeders. Then he could trade off the tech for a fortune and leave this base behind for good."

"You really think he'd stoop that low?"

"Don't you?"

"Sure. But you're usually more optimistic than I am."

"Well, you must be rubbing off on me," he audibly shrugged, as though he couldn't help who he was forced to associate with. "But here's the kicker: if he really *is* just trying to sell this place off to the highest bidder, then this entire visit amounts to a recon run. His ship's probably been taking readings and recording everything going on around it since the second it dropped into the mouth of the volcano."

"Most likely."

"You don't sound very disturbed by that notion," Frank observed with some misgivings. "It's not as if we *want* every clown who comes in here to feel out our defenses first hand."

"The radio on his ship is out of commission. He won't be able to transmit anything en route to his friends. And once he arrives, he won't be in any condition to tell them anything."

"What do you intend to do?" the AI queried, as Welter turned into the corridor that led to the chamber.

"I plan to leave his two bodyguards here and take their places. We're not going to take the chance of him either hightailing it when he finds his radio broken, or of telling his pals what's going on before our boys can kick in his door and start shooting."

"So you plan to hold the fort all by yourself? Just ride right into the middle of their hideaway and start cranking off lead?"

"You sound unenthusiastic," Welter remarked.

"Well, you are kinda handy in a pinch. Wouldn't want to see you riddled with bullets. Besides, it would upset Doctor Tselitel. So don't you think at least a couple people should go with you?"

"I'll be fine," he said, reaching the anteroom's door and opening it. Passing through without acknowledging the men at the table, he entered the chamber, saw *Karnan* resting in his part of the room, and made for where Tselitel sat against the wall.

"News?" she asked, her arms wrapped around her legs as she looked up at him.

"Nothing much," he shrugged, leaning against the wall as usual and crossing his arms. "*Melsek* made quite a ruckus, so we put him under lock and key for a little while."

"But that'll offend him terribly," she replied, sitting up straight and viewing him anxiously. "There's no chance he'll work with us if he feels he's lost face." Glancing towards *Karnan* through the curtain, she ducked her head a little and dropped her voice. "You know how proud these *Kol-Prockians* are."

"That guy never intended to cooperate with us. It's been his way or the highway ever since he landed inside *Kren-Balar*. Most likely he came here to scout us out, get a sense of our defenses."

"*Thank you!*" Frank thought, feeling vindicated.

"Is that why they brought *Karnan* in earlier?" she queried, again glancing towards his part of the room. "He looked in a bad way. I would have asked what was wrong, but *Keelen* was in and out in a flash."

"He and *Melsek* had it out over lunch," Welter confirmed. "The old bird tore into him pretty good. But our little friend wasn't having any of it. He's either dyed in the wool, or lying through his teeth. Either way, him and his little faction won't be a problem for much longer."

"Then the emperor has decided to go ahead with killing them?"

"He doesn't want to," Welter felt it important to point out, for her sake. "Said there's too few *Kol-Prockians* as it is. But I've got the necessary authorization to act when the time comes. Unless another path presents itself, which I doubt."

"You mean Rhemus is still open to suggestions?" she asked, her eyebrows rising a little.

"He's open to *solutions*, Doctor," he replied somewhat pointedly, not wishing her to start dreaming of peaceful answers that left the situation unresolved. "And it's hard to imagine any when they've already made it an us-or-them proposition. The fact is they've brought it upon themselves. We *cannot* risk the safety of *Kren-Balar* for the sake of a few renegades."

"Oh, I know that," she responded earnestly. "I just wish all our problems in Quarlac didn't have to be settled by blood. But it seems to be the only way."

"Believe me, it is," he nodded, turning his back to the wall and leaning against it. "There's something wrong with this galaxy. It makes people brutal; makes 'em *animals*. At least those who are inclined in that direction already. Honestly I doubt we'll ever have much of a hold on Quarlac. Nothing healthy can ever grow here. It's just a garden for weeds."

"I agree," she murmured, resting her chin on her knees and unconsciously sighing. At once her eyes took on a far away appearance, and she seemed to drop out of the discussion completely. Seeing this, he waited a few moments and then cleared his throat. "What? Oh, I'm sorry. I must have been daydreaming."

"About what Amra told you?"

"It's hard not to think about it," she admitted. "And it's hard to accept spending my last few days in a garden of weeds, as you put it."

"You've got more than a few days, Doctor."

"Doesn't feel like it," she mumbled.

Welter could hear in her voice that the ever-present glimmer of hope she'd always clung to had finally been overwhelmed. Through habit she kept up a normal appearance. But inwardly she'd collapsed, crushed under the weight of impending death. Though infinitely uncomfortable with doing so, he nevertheless moved to where she sat, slid his back down the wall, and reluctantly draped an arm across her shoulders. Leaning against him, she sighed.

"I'm sorry to be such a bother."

"It's alright."

"I should be stronger than this."

"Don't beat yourself up. It doesn't do any good."

"Neither do I."

"Be quiet."

"I can't help it, that's just what I think."

"Then you should change your thoughts. At this rate you'll depress yourself to death long before anything else can kill you."

"What difference would it make?"

"Doctor, stop it before I smack you."

"You would, wouldn't you?" she asked, though she already knew the answer.

"Better believe I would."

"It's just that so many things have hit me, one right after another. I can't catch a break no matter what I do. Oh, I know that's terribly self-pitying. But that's what keeps running through my mind. I can't get over how bad a hand I've been dealt by life. Don't I deserve at least a little happiness? A little peace and quiet and contentment? Fate doesn't seem to think so."

"You've got to make your own fate, Doctor. There's nobody pulling the puppet strings of your life except you. Sure, you've been given a lousy hand, like you said. But you've got to make the best of it, not gripe that it isn't something else. You're a psychiatrist: you know that happiness is all about how you look at life. It's up to you what kind of perspective you ultimately adopt."

"You're right, of course," she shrugged, shaking her head side-to-side. "I just can't get together the oomph to push aside these thoughts and stride ahead. I feel like my feet are stuck in concrete. No matter how hard I pull, they're glued down, all the same."

"Well, I'll sit with you for a little while. Maybe that'll help."

A little while turned into a long while. Tselitel had long since been sleeping where she sat propped against him when he finally decided to leave her. Surprisingly deep in her sleep, she merely mumbled when he moved aside and gently lowered her to the floor. Concerned by this, he made a mental note to send *Keelen* in to look at her when he saw him next. Given how anxious she was, it was strange for her to suddenly rest so soundly.

"You want me to stay with her when you go?" Frank asked when Welter shoved his hands into his jacket pockets once he was again in the corridor.

"No. I need you with me in case *Melsek* starts jabbering in *Kol-Prockian*."

"Oh, of course."

"Besides, I doubt there's much either of us can do for her. She's got to want to fight this battle herself, or it's no good."

"How can she, when her prospects are so bleak?"

"Nobody gets out of this life alive, Frank. Nothing's more bleak than that."

"Yet we all manage to muddle through it," he agreed. "I guess you're right: it is all about perspective."

At once Welter went to see Rhemus again, informing him of the improvements he'd made to his original plan.

"You intend to go in there alone?" he asked doubtfully. "That sounds like certain death."

"I'll stay in the ship, use it for cover," Welter replied easily. "Besides, someone has to hold them down until our teams can converge on the area and clean it out."

"But why not send more men with you?"

"I simply don't believe it's necessary. There can't be very many of them, or *Seldek* couldn't have expelled them in the first place. Besides, all I need to do is tie down their hangar for a little while until reinforcements arrive. I don't see the use in risking any more men than we need to, especially when conditions inside that ship are already gonna be cramped with *Melsek* and his pilot, anyhow."

"You have a unique talent for coming out of deadly situations in one piece," Rhemus observed. "So I'm going to let you run this the way you see fit. But don't take any undue risks. You're still greatly needed, both here in *Kren-Balar* and in the war generally."

"I won't," he assured the emperor. "I intend to do a lot more damage than this before my time is through."

Reluctantly, Rhemus nodded his agreement.

"Are you leaving at once?"

"No better time than the present," he answered. "If we wait too long, *Melsek's* boys might get curious where he is and decide to spoil things for us. He already should have radioed them back hours ago. You can bet they're getting antsy."

"And when you're en route and *Melsek* sends out no signals? What'll happen then?"

"They'll be suspicious, maybe even think we tortured it out of him and are sending a team back to clean them out. But it's the best shot we've got to keep *Kren-Balar* a secret. Besides, I don't think they'd just shoot him out of the sky without any explanation. I'd say the odds are in our favor."

"That's about all we can hope for at this point," Rhemus replied. "You'd better get moving at once. Good luck."

"Thank you, Your Majesty," he responded, bowing a little and then turning towards the door. He'd made it only a handful of steps into the corridor when he saw *Keelen* rushing towards him, his face twisted in anger. "What's the matter with you?" Welter asked as he neared.

"That imbecile! That, stupid, blind, reckless imbecile!" he exclaimed, clenching his fists and grinding his teeth.

"I gather you mean *Melsek*," Welter remarked calmly.

"Who else could I mean?" *Keelen* snapped, though plainly he wasn't angry at anyone but the ambassador. "We should have seen through him in a second!"

"You're going to have to calm down, Doctor," Welter replied, crossing his arms. "You're not making any sense."

"He had an *artifact*," *Keelen* said pointedly. "Just like *Seldek* did. That's why he was such a touchy, arrogant, presumptuous–."

"Is he *alright?*" Welter queried equally pointedly, concerned his mission to crush the renegades had just gone up in smoke.

"His mind is already coming undone," the doctor answered. "Truth be told he was in pretty bad shape before he even got here. He *must* have been." Suddenly the alien's eyes lit up. "Of course! That explains the sudden interest in *Kren-Balar!* They want to use the chamber to try and heal themselves! *Melsek* mustn't be the only one disintegrating from abusing artifacts!"

"It makes sense," Welter replied, seeing the merit of his conclusion. "Living on the run like they are, they'd need all the advantages they could get. Even with them their chances were slim."

"They'll be *none* if they don't throw them away while they've got a chance," *Keelen* uttered, disturbed by the thought. "Unless they're as far gone as *Melsek*. Who knows, they might have sent him because he was the healthiest of them all."

"In which case we don't have to worry about *Kren-Balar* anymore," Welter pointed out.

"There's no need to be so harsh, Welter," *Keelen* said critically. "If I'm right, these people aren't planning any kind of a coup. They're just the ailing victims of the desperate measures they've been forced to embrace in order to survive."

"My only concern is with keeping *Kren-Balar* safe, Doctor. And the fact is they've put us all under threat when, if you're correct, they could have just asked for help which would have been gladly offered. You know how badly the emperor wants to help your people."

"Yes, but *they* wouldn't know that," he argued, pointing off in the general direction of the hangar. "The exiles wouldn't have the least idea what the empire's intentions were. In fact, they'd have been misled by *Seldek* the moment he started broadcasting to them. He'd have painted a picture of invasion and oppression, not deliverance. And given they're all being twisted out of sorts by the artifacts-."

"*Assuming* you're right," Welter interjected.

"Yes, *assuming I'm right*, then it's the easiest thing in the world to see how they'd get so deeply agitated. It's been said many times, Welter, but it bears repeating: my people are terribly proud. Crank them up to eleven with the artifacts, and you've got ready-made radicals that'll go off at the first sign of an affront. To see the last bastion of our race in the hands of your empire…Well, it's just like sticking a fuse inside a powderkeg."

"What condition is *Melsek* in? Can he fly?"

"There's no question of him leaving the base like this," *Keelen* replied instantly. "The only thing now is to offer him palliative care to try and make what time he has left as pleasant as possible."

"We can't afford to be pleasant. There's still a gaggle of traitors out there threatening to expose this base."

"I wouldn't characterize them as *traitors*," he quibbled. "They're desperate, out of their minds with worry and snatching at the only answer they see before them. They think this base has been *invaded*, Welter. In their eyes, they're patriots making a terrible gamble to save their own lives and rescue our people from ignominy. Most likely this 'other party' they've threatened to drag in doesn't even exist. Probably just a lie to chase the emperor away."

"That's not a chance we can take," Welter said, shaking his head. "And given how nutty they're bound to be if you're right, we can't risk leaving any of them alive. Like *Karnan* said before, *Keelen*, they're already under a death sentence.

Don't let your healing instincts blind you to what they are."

"And don't let your zeal to crush every enemy in sight blunt your compassion for those who are suffering. As our now mutual emperor has said, we need to save every *Kol-Prockian* that we can."

"And what do you propose we do? Fly in there and offer them safe passage into *Kren-Balar*? If they're as you say, they'll jump at the chance. But they'd do the exact same thing even if they *are* planning to take it from us. What better way to begin an invasion than to get their half of their forces inside our defenses? Then this 'other party' can beat down the front door, and they'll have us pinned from two sides."

"We could keep them under lock and key, treat those who aren't too far gone and offer care to those who are," he said quickly.

"No, Doctor," Welter again shook his head, his resolve audibly hardening. "They had a chance to go about this the right way, and they blew it. We're not going to give them the opportunity to betray us."

"I don't believe that's your decision to make," *Keelen* said, standing a little straighter and looking at him haughtily.

"The emperor has already given me full authority to exterminate that little nest of rats," Welter replied, nodding towards the room he'd just left.

"That was before he had all the facts," *Keelen* responded, turning away and walking towards the door. "Once I tell him what I've found, I'm sure he'll change his mind."

"Where are you keeping *Melsek*?"

"Medical room three," the doctor answered over his shoulder. Reaching the door as Welter began to move, he paused and added, "Don't trouble him, Welter. There's nothing you can get out of him now."

"We'll see about that."

Reaching the medical room shortly thereafter, he

found it separated into two sections by a large one-way window. Looking through it, he watched momentarily as *Melsek* thrashed about upon a narrow bed, his arms and legs strapped down to prevent him from rising and hurting himself.

"Gotta admit, I didn't see this one coming," Frank spoke, Welter having pocketed his fists, making skin contact. "Should've, of course. But I guess we were all too wrapped up in the implications of his visit to really think about how strangely he was acting."

"Reckon so."

"Still, I can't say I'm on board with *Keelen*. Sure, the renegades *might* be playing it like he said. But if not..." his voice trailed momentarily. "Well, all I can say is we've got an awful lot of high value eggs in this basket. Now's the worst time to start playing humanitarian."

"I agree."

As though he sensed these words from Frank, *Melsek* began thrashing even harder, shouting things in *Kol-Prockian* in a slurred, delirious voice.

"What's he saying?"

"It's hard to make out, to be honest," the AI replied, concentrating. "Something about...hope being lost? Oh, yes, that's it: it's some kind of spiel about how we've finally crumbled as a people, how we've thrown away our birthright for the bonds of the–," he paused, catching himself. "Well, it's a not-so-pleasant term for humans. Basically it's just a more vehement version of what he was saying back in *Seldek's* room. His brains must really be shot."

"Is that why he's slurring so badly?"

"I think that must be a sedative *Keelen* gave him," Frank replied. "He should be popping like a firecracker, not dragging along in a haze. Listen to his words: you can hear them begin to run together like pudding. He'll probably be unconscious in the next ten minutes."

"That won't do us any good," Welter declared, making

for the door that separated the two rooms.

"I *really* wouldn't go in here," Frank objected. "*Keelen* is gonna have a fit."

"He can use the downer he gave *Melsek*," he retorted, speaking sharply to be heard over the raving ambassador as he approached. Rounding the bed, he scowled down at him. *Melsek's* chin and neck were wet with saliva, his eyes wide as they roved across the ceiling. "Is there anything left of you in there?" he asked harshly, his words barely audible. Gripping *Melsek's* neck to stop his head from swaying side-to-side, he leaned in closer and tried to force his gaze to focus. A small flicker of recognition led to a pause in his babbling. "So you *do* remember me," he said, straightening a little. "What's the status of the rest of your clowns? Are they all as screwed up as you?"

At once a torrent of *Kol-Prockian* sentences spilled out as his face became twisted with contempt. Spitting as he spoke, Welter had to wipe his mouth with the back of his hand to clean away the alien's saliva.

"What's he saying now?" he asked Frank, pressing a pair of fingers to the medallion.

"Oh, he's blaming you for every wrong that's ever been committed against our people. Even mythical wrongs. He seems to think you were prefigured by a certain devil figure in our early culture. His mind is mixing things together that don't make the least sense." Pausing a few seconds to reflect, he added, "Why don't you touch me against him?"

"Why?"

"Because I can communicate through his skin and bypass certain areas of his brain that may have suffered more damage. Might be able to cut through the fog."

"Don't see what we've got to lose," Welter remarked, pulling Frank from his pocket and pressing him against the alien's wrist. At once the AI began addressing him in *Kol-Prockian*, hoping that his native tongue, being more familiar, might penetrate deeper into his diseased mind. Instantly

THE CRUSADE OF VENGEANCE

Melsek ceased speaking, his eyes growing dim as they searched the ceiling in an attempt to understand where the words he heard were coming from.

"You getting anywhere?" Welter asked, both annoyed to have been cut out of the dialogue and also conscious that *Keelen* could return at any moment and insist that he stop interfering with his patient.

The words had scarcely left his mouth when *Melsek* began to speak in a slow, laborious fashion. Clearly the drugs were working, and it was taking all of his feeble powers of concentration to utter even half-clear sentences. But there was an earnestness in his eyes that indicated Frank had managed to make some headway. To Welter's surprise, tears began to gather in the alien's eyes. For two minutes he spoke, his tongue growing slower and slower until finally it ceased to move and he drifted away to sleep.

Welter eyed him for a moment, drawing the disc away from his wrist. He was about to ask what he'd learned when the door to the other room was torn open and *Keelen* stormed inside.

"*What do you think you're doing in here?!*" he demanded furiously. "You have no right to meddle with a patient who's under my care. Do I get in your way when you're busy mowing down one target after another?"

"Sometimes I wish you would," Welter shot back, making for the door. But *Keelen* moved and blocked his way. "You don't want to get into this with me, Doctor."

"And I don't want to see you in here again," he retorted. "This is my domain, Welter. You might be head of security within *Kren-Balar*. But that doesn't give you jurisdiction over me or my patients. I'll not have the treatment of those I'm responsible for hampered by your hunger for vengeance."

Drawing closer to him, Welter's eyes narrowed and his voice dropped dangerously.

"I'll do whatever is necessary to keep this base secure,

Doctor. As far as I'm concerned, your jurisdiction is purely ceremonial."

Deeply insulted, *Keelen* stepped aside and sharply pointed out the door for him to leave.

"Get out! Before I have you *thrown out!*"

"No," Welter replied, crossing his arms and shaking his head. "Not until you tell me what you said to Rhemus."

"Why don't you ask him yourself?" he snapped, pointing towards the one-way window. "Now get *out!*"

Pausing as though in reflection, Welter's expression suddenly changed from defiance to one of serious contemplation. Slowly heading for the door, his mind clearly elsewhere, Welter had only just passed through it when *Keelen* slammed it shut behind him.

"I understand your position, Welter," Rhemus said as he approached, his hands clasped behind his back as he watched *Keelen* begin to check *Melsek's* vitals. "But you need to remember the situation that prevails within *Kren-Balar*. These fellows must be respected if they're to keep working with us." Glancing at the man beside him when he didn't answer, Rhemus added knowingly, "I gather you have strong opinions about how we should proceed?"

"I did," Welter acknowledged.

"You mean they've changed?"

"Yes."

"Why?"

Wordlessly Welter held out Frank to him. Eyeing him curiously for a moment, he stretched out his hand and took the medallion.

"I've learned something terrible, Your Majesty," the AI uttered gravely. "The *Pho'Sath* know that we're here."

Before Rhemus could find the words to reply, an alarm began sounding through the base.

Kren-Balar was under attack.

CHAPTER 9

"Roland, I'm telling you, we've got to drop out of warp while we still safely can," Kayla said anxiously as the egg traveled down the spiraling tunnel of darkness.

Part way through their journey toward *Sentinel*, the duo had learned that the blast from the *Cultookoy* device had damaged a number of the ship's systems, most notably the radio and the warp engine. The device had caused an energy build up that hadn't registered on the craft's instruments until after they were already underway.

"We're not gonna drop out in the middle of nowhere, Kayla," he responded, eyeing the map in his display and wondering how much longer he could press his luck.

"Roland, the fact is we're *going* to drop out somewhere far, far away from our destination. It's better that we choose *it*, than that it chooses *us*. We could drop out in the middle of a star or a planet."

"There's almost no chance of that happening," he said. "And what are we gonna do anyhow? Float around in space? This thing is fried, Kayla. We can't bet on life support holding on indefinitely." Still searching the map, he noticed a tiny blip on it that lay right across their path. "What's that?" he asked, for it wasn't registered by the computer as being any known commodity.

"Oh, the computer is registering some kind of gravitational disturbance," she said dismissively, waving her little hand as she stood nervously upon the dashboard watching him. "It's not worth attending to."

"Maybe it is," he mused, wondering if it might give them a place to land.

"It isn't *anything*, Captain," she responded, returning to her more formal attitude as firmness entered her voice. "*Keesh'Forbandai* computers are incredibly advanced. If there was anything worthy of note there, it would have assigned it the proper designation, either a planet or a base or something of that nature. Perhaps even an abandoned warship."

"Whatever it is, it's our best bet for a place to land around here," he said, strapping himself in, preparing to leave warp.

"You do realize that we'll be utterly helpless no matter what it is, right?" she pointed out. "Assuming for a moment that it actually *is* something, there'll be nothing to stop them from capturing the egg and taking the weapon. We'd be a lot better off just ditching in empty space and waiting for *Sentinel* to find us."

"How? Given this thing's stealth ability, and the fact our radio is cooked, they'd have a chance in a million of stumbling upon us."

"I'm sure Krancis has seen to that problem already," she replied.

"That's not a chance I'm gonna take."

"And if we *do* come across hostiles? What then?" she queried, though the dreadful answer was already known to her.

"Then I'll turn the key a second time," he responded with a grim shrug. "They'll never know what hit 'em."

"Yes, Captain," she agreed quietly, regretting that possibility very much. A short interval passed with nothing being spoken. "We're just about on top of the anomaly. Exiting warp in three…two…one…"

The tunnel abruptly ended, and the egg was deposited

in a great sea of darkness filled with sparkling stars. The only object in sight was a small gray structure far in the distance. Taking the controls, Bessemer found them sluggish but serviceable.

"Could've dropped us a little closer, Kayla," he remarked.

"With the damage we'd sustained, I didn't want to run the risk of a miscalculation putting us in the middle of the object. We're already closer than I'd actually intended for us to be."

"Alright. What are the scanners telling you about the target?"

"Not much. The short range sensors took the worst damage from the blast. We're just going to have to get closer and perform a visual inspection. But it *looks* like some kind of space station."

"Way out here?" he asked, as the object slowly grew larger.

"There's no telling how old it is. Could've been knocked out of orbit somehow and left to drift."

"That doesn't bode too well for us."

Accelerating the egg, he soon noticed that the object was in fact a sphere, and a very large one at that.

"This thing just keeps getting bigger and bigger," he remarked, as he began turning the egg in order to fly around it. "It's enormous."

"I think it may be a dyson sphere," Kayla said.

"You mean there are races that can actually make those?"

"A few. The *Keesh'Forbandai* can, though they aren't supposed to have set foot in this galaxy since time out of mind."

"How do we get inside?"

"We'll have to look for an opening, though I don't know how much good that'll do us. It's probably just a burned out hulk of metal wrapped around a dwarf star. We'd essentially be wrapping ourselves in a giant spherical coffin. It's doubtful if any but the most powerful sensors could find us in there. A rescue party could sail right by without ever knowing we were inside."

"Of course, if *we* found it on our scanners, they might, too. It isn't cloaked."

"The fact of the matter is that it *is*, Captain. Look, the short range scanners might be damaged, but the long range ones aren't. The fact that the computer failed to properly identify this installation means it's being disguised somehow."

"Then how'd we notice it?" he asked, his eyes studying the surface of the structure as the egg began to circumnavigate it.

"That's what bothers me: I haven't the least idea. I think we might have been lured towards it. You see, the *Keesh'Forbandai* are far from being the only races we know of who can build dyson spheres. The *Pho'Sath* can, too."

"They're not supposed to be in this galaxy, either."

"A hidden base like this would be perfect to facilitate their work inside the Milky Way. They'd have enough energy to fuel their every need, and, evidently, even enough to cloak their base."

"Then why would they have revealed their location to us? Especially given our own ability to cloak."

"Maybe that was damaged by the blast, too," she suggested. "And *maybe* they detected the blast from the device, and have put out a red alert for any strange anomalies on their own scanners. Could be there's a bunch of these things scattered around and we just happened to luck into this one. I think we should leave at once."

"There's nowhere to go, Kayla. And if they really *are Pho'Sath*, their fighters will jump on us in two seconds if we show the least inclination to leave. No, we're committed at this point."

Continuing to circle the orb, he gradually guided the

craft towards what appeared to be its northern pole. It was here that he found a series of large circular doors, all of them different sizes.

"That makes sense," Kayla replied when he pointed them out. "Any time they'd open a door, the energy output of the sphere would drop because there wouldn't be the same inner surface area exposed to the star. Naturally they'd use only the smallest door necessary in order to lessen this as much as possible."

"Sure," he assented, flying near them and slowing the craft a little. "They look ancient. I hope they still work."

At once a flare of light escaped from inside the sphere as one of them began to open. A tiny piece of the concealed star had become visible, and the damage the egg had sustained kept its canopy from responding instantly to soften the glare. Squinting at the opening as the canopy gradually darkened, he searched the space between it and the egg for approaching vessels but saw none. It was nearly a minute before the door ceased moving, the hole it left in the sphere mutely beckoning him forward.

"I've got a *really* bad feeling about this," Kayla worried, as he cautiously flew towards the opening, maneuvering so as to get a peek inside. "Once we're inside there's nothing to stop them from locking us in for good."

"We do have *something* of a bargaining chip," he replied, pointing with his thumb over his shoulder. "That thing ought to be able to do enough damage to punch a hole in this thing. Could even fly out of the hole."

"You *know* they'd be all over us if we tried that. You'd barely have enough time to activate it before they tore this thing apart."

"Sure, but I thought it might make you feel better," he said almost casually, the excitement of the moment pushing aside his fear to make him almost careless. "Come on, let's see what's waiting for us," he added, accelerating yet further and diving through the hole moments later.

The instant they were inside, both of them gasped. Expecting to find a harsh world of gray steel, they instead discovered a lush paradise wrapped around the small white star. Plants of green and purple and orange grew across almost every inch of the structure. The only exceptions were a series of eight small cities, each of them at the center of a district that spanned an eighth of the inside of the sphere.

"It's...beautiful," Kayla said breathlessly. "Like something out of a dream. It would be hard to believe there's a war raging out there when you're surrounded by all this beauty."

As she said this Bessemer caught a glimmer of light out of the corner of his eye. Turning to look, he saw a beacon flashing alternatively yellow and orange in one of the cities.

"Looks like they're trying to get our attention," he remarked, gingerly guiding the ship in that direction as he kept on the lookout for fighters.

"The door above us is closing," Kayla said, pointing at it with her tiny index finger as her expression changed from awe to worry. "If you were to gun it, I'd say we've got about fifteen seconds to slip through before we're locked in."

"We've come this far, Kayla," he shook his head, moving a little faster towards the beacon as the door inexorably moved along its rails. Watching as their only means of escape closed to them, she couldn't help gulping when it finally stopped and locked itself in place.

"We're committed now," she commented, turning to face the beacon, her small hands clasped behind her back to keep them from shaking.

"We were committed the second we dropped out of warp," Bessemer responded. He thought to correct himself and say he'd been committed ever since he agreed to transport the black orb for Krancis. But he knew she wouldn't have any recollection of that.

"Look! Someone's moving around down there!" she declared, as the ship passed into the dense artificial atmosphere that enabled any kind of life at all to exist in the presence of the dwarf star. "I...can't make any of them out. But they're humanoid."

"*Pho'Sath?*"

"I don't think so," she squinted, the canopy's magnification ability on the fritz and unable to dial in accurately. "Wait, they're not just *humanoid*: I think they actually *are human*."

"How's that possible?" he queried, tempted to slow down a little as he suspected a trick; a hologram or something of that nature.

"I haven't the least idea. But that's what they look like. And they're waving to us, too. They look happy."

"Well, let's not keep them waiting," he replied, drawing near to the landing pad and going into a wide circle before landing. Sure enough, they *did* look like humans. But there was something strange about them. An air of unnaturalness surrounded them. Hovering over the pad for a few moments, he slowly descended and then switched off the egg. Possibly for the last time, he reflected, given how damaged it was. To say nothing of what their hosts might decide to do to it.

And to them.

"At least they're keeping to a respectful distance," Kayla said, watching as they formed a half circle around the front of the craft. No longer waving, they stood with their hands either at their sides or clasped behind their backs. "Do they seem a little...artificial to you, somehow?"

"Yeah," he agreed, unfastening his harness and standing up. Leaving the sword tucked beside the device in the hope that they wouldn't guess its purpose right away, he slipped a pistol into his jacket pocket and looked at Kayla. "Watch after the ship. You know what to do if they try to capture it."

"I do," she nodded dutifully.

Turning towards the side that held the ladder, he

paused and turned back.

"Just…don't do that unless you absolutely have to," he added, searching her tiny expression for a moment and then tapping the canopy. "Open up."

"Yes, Captain."

As it arose, the inhabitants of the sphere came a little closer. They were pretty evenly divided between males and females, the former lean and athletic looking while the latter were pleasingly curved. Other than being physically perfect, they looked utterly like any other humans he'd ever laid eyes on. Slinging a leg over the side of the egg, Bessemer climbed down while keeping his eyes on them. Once he'd reached bottom, he stepped towards them, one hand still in the pocket which held his gun.

"We're glad that you could make it," one of them said, a male who stood a little farther ahead than all the rest. "We were afraid you wouldn't get our signal."

"I didn't receive any signal," he responded in a cautious tone, looking them over slowly before returning his eyes to the leader. "I just saw a little anomaly on my long range scanner."

"That was our signal," he confirmed. "We detected your defective craft from a very great distance and decided to extend our hospitality to you. At no little risk to ourselves, I might add. The only thing protecting us is our obscurity. Should the *Pho'Sath* learn of our presence, it would instantly lead them to attack."

"I…appreciate your help," Bessemer replied genuinely. "But I'm a little unclear on just what you're doing here."

"It will be much easier to tell you while we give you a little tour of our facilities," the leader responded, turning a little and waving him forward. "The things we have to say will require proof for you to believe them. And to trust us. Please, follow me."

"Be careful, Roland," Kayla said over his earpiece. "I'll do my best to verify what they say for you."

Glancing over his shoulder briefly, he saw her little pink form standing atop the dashboard and winked.

"What's your name?" he asked the leader as he fell in beside him. The rest of the group formed up partially around and a little behind them, their manner both deferential and curious.

"I'm Kvasir, commander of this installation. I oversee it in the name of the *Keesh'Forbandai*."

"What?!" he asked simultaneously with Kayla.

"Yes. Our creators thought it wise to place an installation within the Milky Way so as to assist you in any way we could. Regrettably the prowling eyes and ears of our mutual enemies have prevented us from doing very much to assist you. We've been little more than a listening post for a very long time."

"What do you mean your *creators?*" he asked, the rest of Kvasir's words holding little interest for him just then.

"Surely you've noticed that we are not entirely human?" his host asked with a hint of a smile, glancing at him as they walked. "No, we're androids. We have been created to further the interests of our creators in every particular. And as they place great hope in *your* future as a race, we have been put here to assist you with the same loyalty and diligence with which it has been our purpose to serve them. That is why, as you've noticed, we look as you do: familiarity invariably improves cooperation. That is also why we are perfectly at home with your language and customs. We are familiar with every part of your culture that could be even remotely relevant to our working together."

"Very thorough," Bessemer nodded, glancing around at the tall, graceful structures that surrounded him. They looked like long, wide blades of grass. "Your architecture is very graceful," he added.

"The *Keesh'Forbandai* believe that beauty is essential to the higher functions of the mind," Kvasir explained, as they neared one such building and a large double door parted in the middle to admit them. "The intellect cannot perform its best work unless its environment is inspirational."

"I shouldn't have thought that would be of any use to androids," Bessemer replied, entering the structure. Inside was nothing save a small room with a pair of chairs and a trio of elevators. Waving for the rest of the group to go about their business, Kvasir entered the middle one and waited for his guest. "Where are we going?" the captain asked.

"You wanted to see proof that we are who we say we are," the android replied. "I'm going to take you to one of our hangars. There you will see ships just like your own, all of which respond to our commands. That, I believe, will be adequate evidence of our honesty."

"Only the *Keesh'Forbandai*, and those authorized by them, can activate their technology," Kayla informed him. "If they really have got a bunch of eggs that they can control, that's proof positive of their identity."

Aware that it could be a trap, he nevertheless got aboard and turned to face the door. Communicating wirelessly with the elevator, Kvasir caused it to descend. Traveling quickly, the door opened moments later, revealing a spacious hangar where line after line of eggs awaited use.

"Please, come with me," Kvasir said politely, moving out of the elevator and walking at an easy pace towards the closest craft. Tipping his head back a little as they neared it, he uttered a long sentence in *Keesh'Forbandai*. At once half the vessels activated, their lights turning on and their engines humming. Another pair of sentences shut them down and activated the others. "Satisfied?" he asked, again with a faint smile on his lips.

"Completely," Bessemer said with pleasure, glad at last to be among friends.

"Good," his host smiled in return. "Then perhaps it will be alright with you if we repair your vessel? It would be lucky to travel much farther in its current condition."

"Actually I was wondering if you'd let me trade it in, as

THE CRUSADE OF VENGEANCE

it were," Bessemer replied, as Kvasir led him back towards the elevator. "I need to get to Krancis and *Sentinel* just as soon as I can, and I'd rather not wait for it to be fixed."

"We are of course eager to help you in any way that we can," he responded. "But first I must suggest that you visit our medical facilities. You've clearly been hurt many times during your journey."

"I'm alright," Bessemer shrugged as they reached the elevator again.

"Honestly it would be a smart move to get checked out, Captain," Kayla chimed in. "We've got a long way to go before reaching *Sentinel*. And with the facilities right here..." her voice trailed.

"It will take some time to transfer your equipment from your present vessel to a new one," Kvasir added. "To say nothing of furnishing it with supplies for the trip, which must be brought out of deep storage since we androids have no use for them. You could easily complete an examination during that time."

"Think of the mission, Roland," the AI urged him. "You need to be in top shape to keep the device safe."

Frowning his displeasure, he looked at Kvasir and nodded.

"Good!" he said, signaling for the elevator to descend yet further. "Our hospital is located beneath the hangar. I'll take you there at once."

"Just make sure your guys get to work prepping that new ship," Bessemer insisted as the doors opened and pristine white corridors stretched to his left, right, and center. "And tell them to be careful with the stuff I've got aboard."

"They'll handle it with the utmost care," Kvasir promised him, leaving the elevator and proceeding down the center hallway.

"And can you transfer my current AI to the new ship? I don't want to leave her behind."

"That will take longer," the android replied. "But it can be done."

"Well, do it. She goes where I go."

"Yes, of course."

Given the lack of organics within the sphere, there was nothing but a skeleton crew of androids within the hospital. Waiting with perfect patience at their particular stations, they acknowledged their visitor with a smile and a brief word as he passed, but otherwise remained stationary. The entire scene struck the captain as somewhat macabre, as though he was walking through a wax museum whose figures had come to life. Even the brilliant engineering of the *Keesh'Forbandai* was not quite equal to duplicating the subtleties of nature. In every face he could detect just a hint of artificiality that kept him from relaxing completely in their presence.

"Here we are," Kvasir announced, pausing beside a door upon which was written something in his native tongue. Opening it, he ushered Bessemer inside and then followed. "This is the scanner room," he explained, the lights turning on automatically and revealing a rather small room with a raised bed in the back of it. Attached to the bed was a hinged shell that leaned against the wall and could swing down, enclosing the bed like a coffin. Approaching this, Kvasir put his hand upon it. "We place you within this device for about thirty seconds, and it takes a reading of your health status. It will supply us with all the information we need to determine if you're ready to fly out again or not."

"I'm going one way or another, Kvasir," Bessemer replied somewhat pointedly. "That isn't an option."

"Neither is failing your mission, or you wouldn't be in such a hurry to reach *Sentinel*," the android pointed out with crisp rationality, though in a pleasant tone. "Please understand that I am not attempting to hold you here. I am simply trying to help you to the best of my ability."

"Of course," Bessemer assented, feeling that he'd been

a bit too quick to jump.

"Please stretch out upon the bed," the android said, taking a step back and gesturing towards it with an open hand. "Just lie face up and relax. It may feel a little claustrophobic when I close the lid. But it will be over before you know it."

Doing as he was bidden, Bessemer laid upon his back and let his hands rest at his sides. Tensing a little as Kvasir reached over him and grasped the lid, he shifted a little to disguise this movement. Once the lid clicked shut a few seconds passed in complete darkness. Then bright lights came on above and beneath him, and he could feel some kind of energy passing through his body. Before he had time to really understand what it felt like, they ceased to shine and the lid opened again.

"Don't sit up right away," Kvasir instructed him, a pleasant expression still on his face as he scanned the device for information. For a few seconds the android visibly withdrew, processing the data it had just gleaned. "You've had a very rough time, sir. There's bruising all across both the inside and outside of your body. How do you feel?"

"Like I've been cooked?" Bessemer queried, slowly rising and swinging his legs over the side of the table. Putting a hand to his forehead, he closed his eyes for a moment and breathed. "Are you sure this thing is safe?"

"Oh, yes indeed. Perfectly safe. It's normal to feel a little strange afterwards. It'll wear off shortly."

"Good," he replied, shaking his head to try and clear his thoughts. Sliding off the bed, his legs felt a little weak as they connected with the floor. "So, am I fit or what?"

"More or less," Kvasir said, moving slowly towards the door so he could follow at his own pace. "As I said, you've taken quite a beating. You've also experienced no little activity from the realm of light. Clearly you've been interacted with by some very powerful beings."

"Tell me about it," Bessemer agreed as they moved

into the corridor and began making their way back towards the elevator.

"Just who were these beings?" he asked casually.

"You wouldn't know them," the captain evaded, unsure how much he could share with the android. "I'm not too sure myself, in fact," he added honestly, not certain how he'd ever make sense of either the being in the orb of darkness, or the so-called Lord of Light.

"Indeed," Kvasir nodded, as though making a note to himself.

"What's the status of my ship?" Bessemer asked as they again reached the elevator and stepped inside.

"We are ready to begin the transfer of equipment," Kvasir answered, willing the lift upward. "You'll be able to depart shortly."

"Roland! They've surrounded the ship with armed androids! They're–," Kayla declared over the radio before being cut off.

Upon hearing this Bessemer leapt behind his host, drew his pistol, and placed it against the android's head.

"You might not be human," he growled, his arm around Kvasir's neck. "But I bet there's plenty of circuits you'd hate to have shot to bits in there."

"Were you to damage me irreparably, another would simply take my place," Kvasir replied calmly, as the elevator door opened and a half dozen armed androids faced them. "It is not our desire to hurt you. But we will if you force us. Now, I suggest you lower your weapon and go with the security team quietly. There's no need for violence."

"That's what you think," Bessemer shot back, dragging the android a little deeper inside the elevator. "Take us down again."

"No," Kvasir uttered unflappably. "If you surrender, we shall capture you. Or if you insist on damaging me, we shall capture you. The outcome is precisely the same no matter which choice you make." Without a shred of fear, Kvasir stood a little straighter. "Decide."

Searching the expressionless faces of the androids before him, Bessemer cursed under his breath and released his hostage. Slowly the latter stepped from the lift and waved the security team inside. Without violence they took his pistol, two of them grasped an arm apiece, and as a group they proceeded to the detention area.

Depositing him in a square metal room without furnishings save a cot on the floor and a toilet in the corner, they left him to his thoughts for several hours. Finally, as the shock of his situation began to wear off and he grew sleepy, he stretched out on the cot and closed his eyes. Seemingly the moment he fell asleep he was wide awake again, the sound of the smooth metal door sliding open jolting him to consciousness. Jumping to his feet, he scowled at the sight of Kvasir entering.

"What is your purpose here?" the android asked as the door closed behind him. "And what is the purpose of that device you brought with you?"

"Like I'm gonna tell you that," Bessemer retorted, crossing his arms.

"We have highly persuasive methods of interrogation," Kvasir assured him without menace, his words even, almost casual. "But as with all such techniques, there is invariably a risk that the subject will be damaged. We do not wish to harm you unnecessarily."

"Why do I find that hard to believe?" he shot back.

"I am not here to bandy words. I have come for information. Do you wish to take the easy path forward, or shall we prepare the interrogation room?"

"You'd better warm up the torture chamber, 'cause I'm not telling you a thing."

"Very well," the android nodded, glancing at the door and causing it to open.

The moment the gap was wide enough for him to fit, Bessemer shot past Kvasir and into the corridor. But that was as far as he got. Having anticipated such a move, his host had placed a quartet of guards outside his cell.

"It will take a little time for the medical information we gathered from your scan to be processed by the interrogation equipment for maximum effectiveness. Please wait in your cell until this process is complete."

"Happy to oblige," Bessemer replied, stepping into his room as the guards moved to shove him thence. At once the door closed again, and he was left with only his own thoughts for company. *"Kind of a solicitous little twerp,"* he reflected. Too amped up to sit and rest, he paced the room, running his hand along the walls as if searching for a weakness, though he knew there were none. As his palm glided across cool metal, he wondered what they'd done to Kayla. Had they removed her from the ship? Were they subjecting her to some kind of AI torture? Or had they simply deleted her? He could only guess, having no knowledge as to what the usual procedure was with captured AIs. She would doubtless have deleted herself before allowing them to harvest any information. That meant she was almost certainly dead already. The thought struck him like a rock to the stomach, and he couldn't help putting a hand to his abdomen.

Walking to the cot, he dropped onto it and leaned against the wall. Letting his skull knock back against it, he sharply exhaled his aggravation.

"Really screwed this one up," he reflected scornfully. *"She didn't want to come in here. Losing her, losing yourself, and losing that weapon – that's all on you."* Grinding his teeth at his mistake, he drew his legs up and rested his elbows on his knees. *"How are you gonna make it right? Pft, who are you kidding? They've got this place locked down like a bank vault. Besides, even if you* could *get out of the prison, you'd still have to get out of the sphere itself."* He paused as a notion came to him. *"Of course, I* could *use the device to blow a hole in the station… As long as they've kept it and the sword together. And provided I*

can get through the waves of guards who are sure to be standing between it and me." Snorting, he shook his head. *"Dream on. I've got about as much chance of pulling that off as I do of flying out here by flapping my arms."*

The passage of several more minutes saw the door open again.

"It's time," Kvasir uttered as he arose. "The equipment is ready for you now."

"And I would just *hate* to keep it waiting," he rejoined, walking ahead of his host and finding his place in the middle of the quartet. "How long is this gonna take, anyhow? I've got to catch up on my sleep."

"That all depends on the individual. Some break quickly, some slowly. It has rarely been used on the Earthborn. That's why your medical information was so useful. This situation, while not unprecedented, is quite unfamiliar to us."

"Glad it's been such a help."

"Yes, because of that data, we're quite sure of just how far we can push the device without risking more than an acceptable level of permanent harm to your body."

"And just *why* are you being so thoughtful?" he asked, as they turned into a large room in the middle of which stood an inclined bed with straps to hold him down. "Just the natural sweetness of your dispositions?"

"As I said, we haven't any desire to cause you harm. We would gladly omit the torture if you would simply divulge the information we want."

"That's not happening."

"Then you leave us no choice," Kvasir uttered, standing aside as the guards forced Bessemer towards the bed. Getting him strapped down took some work, for he didn't make it easy for them. But at last they had him anchored in place upon his back, looking up at an apparatus that hung from the ceiling. Much like the medical bed, it would descend and enclose him completely. "This is your last chance to reveal what you know before a great deal of pain loosens your tongue. Due to the nature of the device, it activates in stages and then slowly ramps down. It isn't possible to stop it part way through the process, even if we wanted to, without risking severe side effects. Should you wish to share what you know so much as ten seconds into the procedure, you would nevertheless have to wait for the cycle to complete. Do you understand?"

"Oh, yes, you've been most informative," Bessemer said sourly.

Without another word Kvasir raised his eyes to the apparatus and signaled for it to descend. At once machinery began to whir, and Bessemer couldn't help reflexively testing his restraints as it came down and locked him inside. For a moment all he could hear was the sound of his own tense breathing. Then the device lit up much as the medical scanner had done, but the feeling it produced wasn't one of energy passing through him but rather incredible, indescribable pain. It felt as though his body was being taken apart on the minutest level, his very cells pressed to the absolute breaking point. And with each passing minute, the feeling only worsened.

Gritting his teeth, he refused to give his captors the satisfaction of hearing him scream. Turning inward, he managed to separate his thoughts from his bodily sensations and began to drift towards losing consciousness when the device detected this and sent a charge through his body that immediately revived him. Cursing the hateful creations of the *Keesh'Forbandai*, he wondered how the androids could have gone so wrong and betrayed their original mission to help mankind when he again started to drift away. The device zapped him again, but the inward pull was too strong. Something, in fact, was drawing him away from the torture he was suffering and taking him to a place deep within his psyche. Charge after charge went through him, but it felt like scarcely more than a small static shock.

It was then that he felt something like a hand reaching up from the back of his mind and grasping his shoulder. At once he knew it to be a remnant of the Lord of Light. Much too bleary-minded to be shocked by this, he watched, or rather felt, as it placed an insulating layer between himself and the torture device. He tried to understand what was going on, to picture in his mind how it was possible for a mere memory to exert such influence. But he knew nothing of such things, and could only feel grateful that he was not alone in his struggle.

It didn't take the androids long to realize something else was at work within their visitor. Feeling that the device would need further calibration before it could properly break him, they ended the session when the first cycle was complete.

"That wasn't so bad," Bessemer cracked as they unfastened his restraints and hauled him up from the bed. Every part of his body hurt so badly that he couldn't so much as twitch without wanting to groan in pain. But this, too, he managed to keep to himself.

"There is something unusual about you," Kvasir mused, looking between his prisoner and the device. "But that will not stop us. We'll take the data gathered from this attempt and use it to further tune the device until it is perfect. Then you will tell us all you know."

"I can't wait," Bessemer chuckled weakly, hardly able to stand on his own two feet.

Communicating wirelessly, Kvasir ordered the quartet to drag him back to his cell while the data was analyzed and the machine adjusted.

"Home, sweet home," the captain joked as his escorts dropped him on his cot and left him. Watching dully as the door slid shut, he at last groaned and leaned painfully back on his bed. "Why does this stuff always happen to me?" he asked aloud, closing his eyes and trying to breathe so as to cause himself as little agony as possible. "It's like Krancis has it out for me."

Thinking back to his time in the machine, he could only dimly recollect the presence that had delivered him. Though it had been palpable then, once the machine was switched off it retreated to the dark shadows at the back of his mind, content to lurk. But a little sliver of it remained noticeable, as though it wished him to know that, as before, he was not truly alone. He didn't know how it was possible, or why the Lord of Light had chosen to put it within him. But he was grateful, all the same.

Suffering far too much to sleep, he laid for nearly two hours until the androids again returned and hauled him back to Kvasir and the torture device.

"I'm sure you've had a chance to rethink your position," his host said once he'd again been restrained in the device and the quartet had left them alone. "Once more, I am offering you the chance to simply reveal what you know. The machine has yet to cause you any meaningful permanent damage. But repeated treatments will certainly lead to harm."

"Why?" he asked painfully. "Are you cooking me for dinner or something?"

"The device attacks your body on the cellular level, breaking you down at your most fundamental building block. That is what makes the experience so excruciating: your body knows it's being undermined at the very base of its existence."

"You guys sure know how to treat your guests."

"Witty comments won't help you. Confessing what you know is the only safe path for you. Again, even if you break only a few treatments from now, you would likely be damaged for life. For your own sake, I urge you to tell what you know. We're going to extract the data in any event."

"Don't bet on it," Bessemer replied, leaning back against the bed to signal the end of the discussion.

"Very well," Kvasir said with a hint of reluctance in his

voice, eyeing the lid and causing it to lower.

As soon as he was out of sight Bessemer grimaced, bracing himself for the agony to follow. In the few seconds that existed between the closing of the hatch and the device's activation, his mind raced through his options. He could hold out until he was broken, perhaps literally, into the tiniest of pieces. It would be very noble and grand, but also excruciating and, possibly, ultimately pointless if they snapped him beyond the point of either reason or resistance and extracted what they needed once he was out of his mind. Confession, equally, would all but certainly lead to death.

And then the third option came to mind.

"I'll let 'em fry me a few more times, make it look good. And then I'll tell 'em whatever I have to in order to get that sword back in my hand. One quick turning of the key, and they'll never know what hit 'em."

This grim notion struck hard the moment he thought it, for he'd never truly been in a position to accept the certainty of his own death before. There had always been at least a sliver of hope that he'd somehow slip out at the last second. But with Kayla gone, his ship impounded, and himself hopelessly confined, he couldn't so much as kid himself that any hope remained.

"Well, Krancis, looks like you reached too far this time," he thought caustically, squeezing his eyes shut as the machine began to glow and the pain surged through him. But this time his suffering was brief. The entity within him acted at once to separate his mind from his bodily sensations, insulating him even more effectively than it had the first time. As if in a dream he perceived his body drifting away, somehow remaining behind in the device while he was guided into an open space glowing with orange light. He could feel the entity all about him, but it refused to give a more concrete presence to itself. He wanted to speak, to communicate with it and discover why and how it was inside his mind. But he couldn't bring himself to do so. The moment

felt sacred, above the banalities of mere human curiosity. It was a privilege simply to be in its company.

The time passed quickly, for he had no conception of it. His sojourn in the mysterious space seemed to end almost as soon as it had begun, the presence sending him back to his body once the machine had completed a trio of cycles, leaving his body searingly painful even after the androids had taken him from it and were carrying him back to his cell. Mutely Kvasir followed the quartet, an air of regret on his face as he watched. Once Bessemer's escorts had laid him out on the cot and returned to the corridor, his host drew near and squatted down beside him.

"Your body is battered. But your mind is, remarkably, intact."

"Nice of you to notice," the captain retorted, laying on his side and coughing the moment he spoke, his lungs and throat instantly agonized by this usage.

"Despite recalibration, the device has failed to bring you to reason. I'm sure you can already feel a sense of subtle burning within your every cell. That is the beginning of the permanent damage I warned you of. While your mind retreats to an inner sanctum, the body is left to bear the torture without respite. Whatever discipline or training you're calling upon to avoid the pain, it is only permitting you to destroy your body all the more effectively. I must urge you to reconsider this course of action."

"You'd like that," he rejoined. "Sorry, but you're gonna have to put up with this a little longer."

"My patience for this task is infinite," Kvasir replied calmly. "But the integrity of your body is not."

"And just why should you care?" he asked, before suffering another coughing fit.

"Because I don't wish to inflict suffering upon any creature unless it is absolutely necessary. As you are the enemy, I must gather information from you that may serve my masters. But I am no mere torturer. I only wish to use the absolute minimum of force required to achieve my object."

"How nice of you," he responded, his body beginning to tremble.

"Tremors are the penultimate sign that you are on the verge of crossing into high levels of damage. A few more cycles will see you fainting, your heart beating irregularly, and your breathing faltering. Several more cycles after that would likely kill you."

"That'd be a shame for you, wouldn't it? What are you gonna do for fun then?"

"I don't do any of this for *fun*," Kvasir answered solemnly, standing up and looking down at him for a long moment. "But I will do what I must."

Watching silently as the android left and the metal door slid shut, Bessemer grimly smiled.

"*So will I.*"

Drawing his legs up against his stomach and chest, he gripped them as well as he could and tried to stop his body from trembling. But it was no use. As if seized by a powerful shiver, his muscles kept firing and firing until he was utterly exhausted from head to foot. Rolling painfully onto his back, he gasped for breath and shut his eyes, wondering if he'd actually manage to survive one more round of torture. It wouldn't do any good to hold on *too* long and die before he could activate the weapon. But he couldn't risk arousing Kvasir's suspicions by breaking too easily.

"*Just one more round,*" he thought, opening his eyes and finding his vision blurry with impending sleep. "*Then I'll let 'em have it.*"

Moments later he drifted away to confused dreams.

Many hours later he awoke, consciousness returning slowly and unwillingly. Awareness of his many pains quickly followed, though he was glad to find them much reduced. He could sense that much time had passed, but he hadn't the least notion how long he'd been asleep. Rolling onto his side, and then struggling to his hands and knees, he arose and shambled to the door of his cell. He was about to press an ear against it when the sound of footsteps in the corridor caused him to draw unsteadily back. As he did so it slid open, and Kvasir was once again before him with his foursome of guards.

"I see a little rest has done you good," the android remarked.

"Yeah, I feel like a whole new man."

"You won't for long, if you persist in your present course."

"Well, they say change is good for you."

"Not when it entails extensive bodily harm," Kvasir replied, silently commanding the guards to seize him and bring him along. "Your resistance has proven remarkable, as has your resilience," he added as they began to walk. "I hadn't expected you to recover so quickly from the treatment of two days ago."

"*So that's how long I've been out,*" he reflected in a flash. "Mom always said I was special."

"You persist in your witticisms even as your body begins to crumble away," the android replied, audibly bothered.

"What's it to you?"

"I already told you, I haven't the least desire to see you broken. In fact you're a most interesting guest, one I should have wished to speak with at length were you not in league with our enemies. But of what value are the words of a traitor?"

Struck by this, Bessemer slowed a little and looked at him. But the guards following up the rear urged him forward.

"What do you mean *traitor?*"

"You must be very well acquainted with the concept, given the amount of light realm energy you've been exposed to. But no matter. Soon we'll extract the information we seek about your *Pho'Sath* overlords. If there's anything left of you after that, we'll attempt to make you comfortable for the sake of our creator's affection towards the Earthborn as a whole."

"Is that what this is all about?!" he demanded in an anguished voice, all at once realizing that his torture had been a mistake. "You think I'm working with *those scum?*"

"They are the only beings who possess an affinity for the light realm that you'd have had even a modest chance of encountering. For while there are other such races, they are not nearby, nor are they anywhere near as capable of interacting with that element. The fact that you were not killed, but have instead enjoyed considerable exposure to them without the slightest sign of harm indicates you are working with them to overthrow your own race."

"Kvasir, I've never even *seen* one!" the captain exclaimed, his voice almost shrill, the torture having robbed it of its breadth and depth by depleting his body. "Someone named the Lord of Light did this to me."

Pausing, the android looked at him for a moment and then resumed movement.

"So you've heard of him!" Bessemer all but shouted, the guards shoving him forwards again as they neared the torture room. "Well, maybe there's another fella you've heard of," he added, nearly blurting out the figure in the dark orb before remembering his oath to Krancis.

"Yes?" Kvasir queried, watching him in his peripheral vision as they walked.

"I can't tell you," he ground out from between gritted teeth, certain that the man in black had finally succeeded in killing him. "I gave my word never to speak about it."

"The word of a traitor isn't any concern of mine," Kvasir responded.

"Oh, don't give me that! I saw you just now when I mentioned the Lord of Light. You know about him! You know the *Pho'Sath* aren't the only ones who could have done this to me."

"I was surprised to hear you mention his name," the

android said, leading the way into the room and standing aside as the escorts wrestled Bessemer into the device again. "Very few know of him, and they are typically killed or conscripted by his attendants. The idea that you encountered him at length and managed to get away was so fanciful that I had to reflect momentarily just to calculate the odds in order to satisfy my own curiosity. I believe the likelihood of such an occurrence comes in at approximately half of one percent. Provided one rounds up, that is."

"Call Krancis!" Bessemer said. "Ask him about Captain Roland Bessemer! Tell him what you're doing to me and he'll instantly give you all the information you need to know I'm telling the truth!"

"Your overlords would like nothing more than that we should break radio silence," Kvasir replied, his head shaking in disappointment at the captain's seemingly obvious attempt to expose the installation. "We have only managed to operate within this galaxy by maintaining a sublime degree of discretion at all times. Were they to know the truth, they would descend upon us in no time. We could defend ourselves, of course. But it would be the beginning of a war between them and our creators, and we are under the strictest orders not to do anything that would lead to hostilities."

"You let me find you! That put you at plenty of risk, didn't it?" Bessemer shot back, as his head was pressed against the bed by an android and a strap was stretched across his forehead. Looking down out of the base of his eye sockets, he strained to see Kvasir. "You hearing me?" he added after a few moment's silence, sensing he was making some headway.

"That was different. Being perfectly aware of the capacities and quirks of our manufacturing practices, we knew how to let your craft find us without risking ourselves unduly. But to send a signal across countless lightyears of space to *Sentinel* would entail incredible danger."

"Fine! Then send one of your androids in an egg! *Sentinel* can't be very far away. If I really *am* a *Pho'Sath* spy, my information will be just as juicy in a few days, won't it? Better yet, don't even rendezvous with *Sentinel*: just get a safe distance from this sphere and send an encrypted message from the egg! As soon as Krancis knows what's going on he'll set you straight."

Kvasir stood motionless as his circuits worked through the pros and cons of the captain's proposal.

"Besides, if I really *was* working with the *Pho'Sath*, do you really think I'd want to risk Krancis learning about the device I've been hauling?"

"Presumably not," the android responded rationally, pausing a few seconds before continuing. "Your suggestion is a sensible one, Captain Bessemer. Therefore I have just ordered one of those under my command to take a ship at once and establish contact with Krancis."

"And?" Bessemer queried, pulling against the restraints to make his point.

"You are equally correct that there would be no sense in damaging your body further when the wait is so brief," Kvasir said to his inexpressible relief, silently signaling the guards to release him. "But I must warn you: should this prove to be nothing more than a delaying tactic, or, worse, an attempt to expose us to the *Pho'Sath*, we will not look kindly upon this deception. The bond our creators feel for your people will prove scanty protection indeed should that be the case."

"It'll never come to that," Bessemer replied as his head and hands were released. Rubbing his wrists as his guards went to work on his legs and feet, he eyed the android with a mixture of disbelief and deep anger. "I can't believe you put me through all this just because you never asked who I worked for."

"There was no point in asking, given that all the available evidence pointed to you colluding with the

Pho'Sath. That being the case, any words you could've chosen to utter would have no more value than the air upon which they were borne."

"Yeah, unless I knew something you *didn't*," he shot back, standing unsteadily and scowling at his host. "That robot brain of yours could use a little more *imagination*."

"I must make the best decision I can with the information I have available," Kvasir replied, mutely ordering the escorts to remove the prisoner. Unlike past times, the android chose to remain behind, wishing to take a closer look at the data the device had gleaned from Bessemer's past exposures to it.

"*Seems I'm always getting the raw end of other people's decisions,*" Bessemer grumbled inwardly, his spirit nevertheless lightened that he'd been spared another agonizing session inside the machine. Walking back to his cell in silence, he entered without being urged and waited for the door to slide shut. "*Please, Krancis, whatever you do: tell this guy what he needs to know!*" he thought fervently, willing the notion across the vast space that separated him from the man in black. "*You owe me this,*" he added. "*I've put my life on the line for you more times than you had a right to ask. You've gotta come through for me just this one time.*"

Finding his strength on the ebb, he made his way to the cot and dropped down onto it.

Several days passed without any word from Kvasir. With nothing but a bed and a toilet for company, he took the time to reflect on the curious journey that had led him to that precarious situation. Despite his groaning, he had to admit that Krancis had repeatedly managed to put him in incredible danger without ever actually giving him more than he could handle. Somehow or other he managed to scrape by, though seemingly with a tighter and tighter margin each time. He wondered if he was beginning to slip, if he was becoming slow or complacent or just plain tired after everything he'd been put through. It made him wonder if the next situation would see the margin vanish altogether. Perhaps a lifetime of adventuring would come to a sudden end as he *just* failed to reach far enough, to think quick enough.

"*Especially now,*" he added, still feeling pain throughout his body despite being away from the machine for days. He flexed his aching hands before his face and frowned. "*Might be a candidate for retirement before much longer.*"

The thought was chilling, for that was worse than death to a soul as free as Bessemer's. But the notion had to be faced. The grim reality of what the machine had done to him was inescapable.

Before these dark thoughts could proceed any further, the door to his cell began to slide open. Looking up morosely, he was taken aback to see Kvasir enter with a look of anguish on his artificial face.

"We've been wrong," the android said at once in a pleading tone, reaching out his hands solicitously and helping the surprised captain to his feet. "So wrong. Krancis immediately vouched for you. I cannot find the words in either my language or yours to express the intensity of my sorrow over what we've done to you. A blunder this catastrophic demands my immediate termination as leader of this facility. Without hesitation I shall transfer my role to another android. But before I do, please let me do everything in my power to redeem even a fraction of the tremendous offense I've committed. Consider this facility entirely at your disposal. Make any request you wish that does not clash with our instructions, and it shall be instantly performed."

Sensing the absolute sincerity of the android at once, Bessemer found his gloom and anger melting away despite the painful sensations that still vibrated throughout his body.

"Is there anything you can do to heal me?" he asked after a few moment's thought.

"Much harm has been done to you," Kvasir uttered doubtfully, his head shaking. "It is beyond our power to help you in any meaningful way. That's why the device is so effective at extracting information. At this point, only a race such as the *Pho'Sath*, with their potent ability to manipulate the powers of the light realm, could truly heal you. Anything else would be purely palliative."

"You mean you could help the pain?" he asked, willing to accept that for the time being.

"Yes, we could help you with that," Kvasir nodded. "But the medicine will not work indefinitely. Quickly your body will grow used to it, and its effectiveness will diminish."

"It's a good place to start," Bessemer shrugged, though dreading the thought of spending the rest of his life in a state of constant pain. He hesitated before asking his next question, but he couldn't wait any longer to know the truth. "What have you done with Kayla?"

"Kayla?"

"The AI in my ship. Did you delete her?"

"Oh, certainly not. We considered the information she held to be of very high value. But we weren't able to access it. Someone has altered her programming, making it impossible to access her data without her threatening to delete it and her entire personality in order to safeguard it."

"*Can't imagine who ordered that*," Bessemer thought with a roll of his eyes, the eerie feeling that Krancis had anticipated even his visit to the sphere creeping into his thoughts. "Then she's okay? You haven't damaged her at all?"

"She is in precisely the same condition as when she arrived," Kvasir assured him, glad to see that his words granted the abused captain some relief from his sufferings. "Given the risk of her deleting all she knew, we thought it best to leave her inside your craft until she became more tractable. During your entire confinement she's attempted to communicate with you through the ship's short-distance comms unit. We've simply been blocking the signal."

"Have them unblock it at once," he said, feeling around inside his ear to make sure the earpiece was still there. "Kayla? Kayla, do you read me?"

"I'm afraid the torture device has damaged your radio beyond all repair," Kvasir explained with a pained expression on his face, agonized by what he'd mistakenly done. "It would be a privilege to furnish you with one of our own manufacture at once."

"Do it," Bessemer ordered, making for the door. Stepping into the corridor, it pleased him to see the guards respectfully part so he could pass. "And while you're at it," he added to his host, who had followed him into the hallway. "Get me something to eat and some clean clothes. And let Kayla know I'm alright. I don't want her worrying a second longer than necessary."

"It will be done immediately," Kvasir assured him, darting off a wireless message as he did so.

Three hours later he was sitting at a table with a series of empty plates before him. Ravenously hungry, he'd satiated himself and then some on the surprisingly excellent fare of his mechanical hosts. Wearing clean clothes and freshly showered, the medicine had long since taken effect and, for the time being, removed the pain from his body.

"I ought to talk to Kayla," he reflected, as Kvasir and several others seated at the table eyed him furtively, hoping that their mistreatment of him hadn't damaged relations between their creators and the empire. He'd spoken to the AI briefly, just to assure her he was alright. But he was much too spent to relive in detail all that he'd gone through since parting company with her. It troubled him to have left her curiosity burning for so long. But he had to see to his own needs first.

"I'm ready to talk with Kayla now," Bessemer announced, slowly rising from the table. Days of pain had accustomed him to think of movement as agony, so it was with surprise that he found himself moving as easily as he had upon arrival. "She's still in my old ship?"

"Yes. We asked her to allow us to move her as you requested. But she flatly refused until she had a chance to see for herself that you were alright," Kvasir answered.

"Good girl," Bessemer remarked, leading the androids out of the makeshift dining room and towards the closest elevator.

It didn't take long for them to reach the hangar within which the captain's egg was being stored for repairs. The moment he stepped into open view and began walking towards his ship, Kayla got on the radio.

"Oh, thank God you're alright!" she exclaimed, overjoyed to see him in clean clothes and looking essentially healthy.

Pausing briefly to wave off his escorts, Bessemer reached the craft, climbed aboard once the canopy had been raised, and dropped into the pilot's seat with a sigh.

"Never thought I'd be happy to see this thing again," he commented, feeling the seat with his hands as though to prove to himself his agonies were truly over.

"How have you been?" she asked earnestly, though she already knew the gist of his recent history. "Exactly what did they do to you?"

"According to Kvasir, they put me in a device that attacks and destabilizes your body on the cellular level. More pain than you can possibly imagine. Honestly I don't know if I would have gotten through it without…Well, whatever that thing was that helped me."

"I don't understand," she replied, her little pink head shaking side-to-side as she stood atop the dashboard. "What thing?"

"The so-called Lord of Light put something into me when I encountered him," Bessemer explained, the notion now a little creepy since he was no longer dependent on it to protect him from the device. "I don't know how or why, but when that machine started cranking the pain up like mad, it intervened and took my mind away from it all. I could *feel* an essence inside my head, Kayla. Like a wispy companion made out of air or spirit or something. Frankly I haven't the least idea how to describe it beyond that."

"You're doing just fine," she assured him, intrigued but also disturbed by his words, afraid that the device had made him delusional. "Did it talk to you? This essence?"

"No," he replied, looking over the androids as his thoughts wound back and rifled his memories. "No, not at all. But there was communication, all the same. Like it spoke just by its presence, you know? A kind of physical language. I could sense that it thought I was important, that I needed to be preserved through the torture for some purpose." Then he shrugged. "Can't imagine what, though. And even though he *did* spare my mind that miserable torture, my body took a beating that I won't ever be able to forget. Kvasir says there's nothing they can do for me except give me painkillers. And it won't be long before even those are ineffective."

"I'm so sorry, Roland," she sympathized. "I never thought something like this could happen. What a terrible mistake!"

"I know," he agreed in a low voice, still watching their robotic hosts. Respectfully they waited back by the elevator, their patience infinite. "I wish they'd at least *asked* who I was working for. But they just drew their logical lines between the data they had to hand and ran with it. Makes me wonder what other kinds of trouble the androids have gotten the *Keesh'Forbandai* into after all these years."

"I'm sorry," Kayla repeated, shaking her head dismally, her sense of guilt palpable.

"Well, it's not like you did anything wrong," he replied, looking down at her.

"I should have known they would scan you and detect the effects of the severe light realm exposure you had on Balian," she fretted. "I should have prepared them for that. If I had, they could have sent an egg at once to contact Krancis and you would have been spared all this."

"Kayla, you don't have to–."

"Don't you understand?" she pleaded, almost demanded. "It's my job to take care of you. I'm your AI, your companion. I'm supposed to think of these things in advance, to anticipate possible dangers and get you through them. Especially when we're dealing with the works of my own creators! I should have known they would draw the wrong conclusions based on the limited data they had available; that they wouldn't have the imagination to consider other possibilities. I should have brought that flexibility of thought to the table that they're incapable of bringing themselves. But like a complete blockhead I let you walk right into the worst torture of your life! No, Roland, I can never forgive myself for that. I only hope that *you* can, given time."

"Kayla, there's nothing to forgive," he insisted. "There was no reason for you to assume that my exposure to the Lord of Light had left such an imprint. It's not as if this egg has sensors for detecting that sort of thing. Sure, you *could* have made that inference, based on what I'd told you. But it's expecting too much of anyone to demand that kind of foresight."

"Krancis would have thought of it," she countered. "He would have anticipated the residual effects of that kind of exposure."

"Yeah, well, we can't *all* be magical," he replied with some sarcasm, the man in black being far from his favorite person at that particular moment. "Trust me, Kayla, I don't hold anything against you. You're not guilty of anything."

"I failed in my duty to you, Roland," she responded grimly, her determination hardening the longer they spoke. "Nothing can ever change that."

Seeing he could make no headway, Bessemer decided to let it drop. Maybe after she'd had a little time to cool down, he hoped, he could change her mind.

"Well, we'd better get a move on before too long," he said after a minute or two of awkward silence. "Krancis'll be wanting his super weapon. And nothing could make me want to stay here any longer."

"I agree," she nodded, her little hands clasped behind her back. "I'll let them begin transferring me from this craft to a new one."

"Alright, sounds good," he replied, standing up with some effort and climbing back down the ladder. His feet had only just touched the hangar's floor when a deep, booming alarm began sounding through the hangar. "What's going on?" he shouted to the androids, jogging towards them as they hastened to him. "Are we under attack?"

"A large Devourer fleet in warp has just changed its trajectory and is heading straight towards us," Kvasir informed him urgently. "They'll be here within hours. We have to make ready at once."

"Can you fight 'em off?" he asked, walking quickly with the androids towards the elevator.

"We can hold them for a time. But there's too many for our modest garrison to cope with. There's no question of their ultimate success."

"But how did they find us?" the captain asked as they all boarded the lift. "If even the *Pho'Sath* couldn't find us..." his voice trailed, as realization sank in.

"Yes, Captain Bessemer," Kvasir nodded knowingly. "They must have discovered us when we let you find us. Somehow they've used their great insight and found a way to inform the parasite of our presence."

"But why?"

"Because this way they can eliminate our facility without sparking a war with our creators," the android explained, the elevator doors opening as he spoke, revealing another level of the hangar that was filled from one end to the other with medium-sized fighters. "By working through a proxy, they can achieve their object without destabilizing the uneasy peace that has existed between our two races for so long."

"So what are you going to do? Evacuate?" he queried, as they moved across the hangar.

"The preservation of several thousand androids is of no consequence. We are much too easily manufactured to be of any real value. No, we'll remain here and deal as much damage to the parasite as possible, doing what we can to help your people during this dark hour in your history. When our forces are finally overcome, we'll self-destruct the sphere."

"There's gotta be a better way."

"It would require a miracle to save us now," Kvasir replied, leading the way into an armored room embedded in the wall of the hangar. The walls were lined with computers manned by androids, and in the center was a table dominated by a huge, slowly spinning holographic representation of all the ships and celestial bodies within several days' warp distance of the base. Approaching the table, Kvasir indicated a quickly moving blip with his right index finger. "That is the Devourer fleet. It is at least fifty percent larger than it needs to be to overcome our defenses. We have no other forces near here that can assist us, and *Sentinel* is much too far away to reach us in time."

"Then we'll manufacture a miracle of our own," Bessemer replied, as an idea came to him. Pressing a finger into his ear, he activated the radio the androids had furnished since releasing him. "Kayla?"

"Yes?"

"We've got work to do."

Hours later a wall of *Keesh'Forbandai* interceptors waited outside the sphere for their parasitical foe to emerge from warp. Though more than a match for their opposite numbers, the presence of three carriers within the enemy fleet promised a vast numerical imbalance. The defenders would be outnumbered by as much as six to one, depending on how many craft each carrier held. A smaller group of heavy fighters waited behind them. Wielding larger dark beam cannons than their escorts, they were the only vessels in the area even remotely capable of threatening the fourteen battleships that made up the bulk of the incoming fleet's striking power.

"I don't think this is a good idea," Kayla fretted, as Bessemer got himself strapped into a hastily modified egg. The androids, it turned out, had several magnificent manufacturing facilities within the sphere, and it was with ease that they produced a jury-rigged delivery system for the *Cultookoy* super weapon. Separating the egg into two airtight compartments, they turned the weapon on its side and made an opening in the divider to permit the key to be inserted from the pilot's seat. The device could then be ejected into space and left behind to wreak havoc on anyone unlucky enough to be caught in its blast radius. "When Krancis finds out we've detonated the weapon without authorization, there's no telling what he'll do. Next to *Sentinel*, this is likely the most powerful weapon within the Milky Way galaxy. We have no right to activate it on our own."

"*We* aren't activating it, Kayla," he corrected her. "*I* am."

"What difference does that make?" she queried anxiously. "You could seriously be under threat of execution for using something with this much power on your own authority. Such a gross lack of subordination could easily be seen as a threat to the empire. Especially given the current state of our affairs."

"Sure, and who's he gonna find to turn this thing on if he kills me?" he countered. "Kayla, the fact of the matter is that I'm indispensable. Krancis'll have to accept my use of this thing because he can't do without me. Besides, he's read me like a book already, hasn't he? He's got to know that I wouldn't ever turn this thing against the empire."

"Well, people can make mistakes, you know," she argued weakly.

"I thought Krancis didn't make any," he teased, his mood lightening as adrenaline began to surge through his veins, bringing back his familiar vitality. "Besides, this is what we got the thing for in the first place, right? To help turn the tide? What better way to do that than to wipe out a fleet that's just waltzing right up to us? Moreover, we get to scratch the *Keesh'Forbandai's* backs in the process, saving what might be their only installation in our galaxy. That sounds like pretty smart politics to me."

"Political decisions ought to be made by those who are responsible for the direction of our affairs, Roland," she replied quietly, her tiny pink feet drawn together as she looked up at him appealingly. "It's not our place to assume such a role. Can't we at least ask Kvasir to get in contact with him? This location is no longer a secret, anyhow. There's no use in maintaining radio silence any longer."

"It's probably best if we don't make any obvious links between this sphere and the empire, Kayla. They might be violating the treaty by being here. But I doubt the *Pho'Sath* will cause too much trouble for these guys as long as they stay passive like they've been for so long. Especially when it comes to light that an entire Devourer fleet wasn't enough to take 'em down. They'll give this place a wide berth if we don't tempt them too much."

"Yes, Captain," she relented in a defeated voice.

"Oh, don't give me that, Kayla. We've been through a little too much to stand on ceremony with each other. Now, get in touch with Kvasir and find out how long it'll be until our guests arrive."

"Okay," she nodded, pressing a couple fingers to her temple and tilting her head for a few seconds. "Approximately thirteen minutes."

"Then we'd best get a move on," he replied, firing up the egg and taking the controls. "These guys are gonna want to keep the doors closed once the fighting starts."

"We're taking an awful risk," she couldn't help adding,

as he lifted the craft a few feet off the hangar's floor and piloted it to a large open door in the ceiling that led into the main cavity of the sphere. "An egg isn't a combat vessel, Roland. They weren't intended for dog fighting."

"We'll keep our distance until the interceptors open a door for us," he answered with a little dismissive wave of his fingers.

"And how will they do that when they're so badly outnumbered?"

"You'll just have to have faith, Kayla," he grinned, aware that such a reply would have no value for her. "Besides, we've made it this far, haven't we?"

"I think those pain meds have taken away your sense," she said with a frown.

"No, Kayla," he replied more seriously, flying through the door and accelerating the moment he was free of the hangar. "You've got to remember that I'm probably the best fighter pilot in the entire imperial navy. We'll be alright."

"Yes, Cap–," she began, pausing when his eyes darted down to her little form. "Yes, Roland," she corrected herself, receiving a slight nod of approval from him.

Glad to at last have a ship in his hands again, he gave in to the urge to pull a barrel roll and spun the egg a couple of times over.

"Just making sure that thing is strapped down okay back there," he explained when she shook her head at him. "Don't want it knocking around when we're dodging incoming fire."

"Of course not," she said with a small sigh, afraid that the combined effects of the torture machine and the medication had driven him over the edge. Turning around to watch out the front of the craft, she closed her eyes and fervently wished that everything would turn out for the best. Because even if they *did* manage to survive the battle, she felt very gravely about how Krancis would take the news of the weapon's activation.

"I'll be glad to leave this place in the rearview once this battle is over," Bessemer remarked as they passed out of the sphere and into space. "I don't care if these guys finally figured out their mistake: the walls'll always be a little too close for comfort around here."

"I can understand that," Kayla replied in a distracted tone, looking at the assembled defenders as Bessemer maneuvered the egg to a position off to the side of the sphere. "There's so few of them," she commented with quiet dread. "Even with their weapons, it'll be an uphill climb to clear the way."

"One thing at a time, Kayla," the captain replied without concern, his mind active but calm now that he was back in his element.

"But you've got to place the weapon for maximum effect," she countered, turning around and looking at him. "It's not like we can just deploy it, activate it, and then just pick it up and rinse and repeat. The Devourer fighters would tear us to pieces if we stopped long enough to retrieve it. And more than that, we're putting it at risk of being taken by them if we don't wipe out at least the bulk of their fleet with the first detonation. There'd be nothing to stop one of the battleships from seizing it in a tentacle and warping off to parts unknown with it. If that happened, Krancis would probably have you executed for such reckless folly."

"Then it's a good thing none of that's going to happen, isn't it?" he asked somewhat testily, her valid criticisms putting a momentary wobble in his confidence. But no sooner had he said this than he smoothed out again. "How long?"

"Any time now," she said with a shake of her head, all but certain he was about to throw away both his life and the most promising career in the imperial navy.

Positioning his craft away from the impending battle, he watched in silence for a time before suddenly slamming his fists against the dashboard with an oath.

"What is it?" Kayla inquired, as he took the controls and made best speed for the defenders. "What's wrong?"

"I must be out of my mind!" he exclaimed. "The best time is to strike them right as they emerge from warp, when they're all bunched together and the fighters are still in their carriers! Waiting around for our guys to chop them down to size is just about the stupidest thing I could do!" Grinding his teeth as he pushed the egg to the max, his thoughts mutely mirrored hers, and he wondered if the pain medication had dulled his senses. "I just hope we can–."

They were only halfway to the defenders when over a dozen massive purple strips were torn in space. Expanding at once into large, irregular holes, they were surrounded by numerous smaller ones from which frigates began to emerge. Moments later their larger cousins lumbered into view, the battleships placed in a protective formation around the carriers. The latter's rifts hadn't even completely closed before fighters started pouring from their hangars.

"If we lose this fight," Bessemer muttered in self-recrimination.

"This isn't worth dying over, Roland," the AI asserted. "You heard Kvasir: this is just one installation worth of androids that can easily be replaced. We can't endanger ourselves or the weapon for its sake."

"We need all the allies we can get in this galaxy, Kayla," he disagreed, pulling up and doubling back towards the sphere as countless green blobs erupted from the attacking fighters and sailed towards the defenders. "We're not gonna let this place go without a fight."

With perfect discipline the android pilots waited as the alien craft drew closer. Then, with one consent, they activated their dark beam weapons and cut a hole in the oncoming shower of green shells. Disintegrating them as they accelerated towards the attackers, the sleek fighters of the *Keesh'Forbandai* shot forward with a speed that, to Bessemer's anxious eyes, seemed to defy the laws of physics.

Breaking out of formation and maneuvering independently, the interceptors glided between the green blobs as their beams cut across their assailants and began to take a modest toll.

"We'd be alright if there were just more of our guys and less of theirs," the captain remarked, chomping at the bit to engage but unable to in his defenseless egg.

"What are we going to do?" Kayla asked in a voice that was deliberately calm.

"Wait for a gap to open up," he replied, scanning the enemy fleet and dismayed to find that many of their fighters had taken up defensive positions near the capitals. "It's like this bug has figured out what we're doing. It's always been more aggressive than this."

"That's not possible," Kayla replied, though the parasite's behavior was equally striking to her. "It must just be cautious to engage a *Keesh'Forbandai* installation. *Sentinel*, after all, is the only vessel it can't grapple with, and it was made by the same people."

"That's reasonable enough," he assented, though a little sliver of doubt remained in the back of his mind as he wondered if the *Pho'Sath* might have somehow tipped the Devourer off to what he was carrying. Assuming they knew themselves.

Truly contrary to form, even the frigates remained with the fleet instead of rushing ahead to attack the sphere. Given that the heavier fighters couldn't break away from their protectors without being torn to pieces by the parasite's nimble craft, they were forced to awkwardly remain in close proximity to their smaller escorts, only narrowly dodging incoming shells as the number of attacking craft increased. It didn't take long for these clumsier craft to suffer several casualties.

"The bombers aren't gonna last long in the open like this," Bessemer opined, absentmindedly grinding his teeth as he watched. "Kvasir should have kept them inside the sphere until he was ready to use them."

"And open the doors once the enemy had already closed with the base?" Kayla pointed out.

"Well, just thinking out loud," the captain said dismissively, shaking his head a little as the small force of defenders pushed deeper into the parasite's fighters. "At least those beams work against the blobs. But they're nuts if they think it'll be enough to save 'em from–."

Halting mid-sentence as the Devourer changed tactics, he involuntarily jerked the egg's controls and obscured his view momentarily with its hull. When he'd brought the battle back into sight, he saw that the parasite had suddenly chosen to ignore the fighters and concentrated all fire on the bombers. At once a cloud of green balls filled the space through which they flew. Maneuvering clumsily, many were taken down in the first volley.

"What do they think they're *doing?*" the captain demanded, slamming his fist on the dashboard as he saw the battle tip decisively in the Devourer's favor.

"These androids aren't combat oriented," Kayla replied almost clinically, curiously detached from the fight. "They aren't designed for this."

"I'll say," he agreed gravely, watching for a few moments before pushing his craft forwards.

"What are you doing?" Kayla queried with alarm, her eyes going wide as she looked up at him. "We can't enter the fray like this. We'll be torn to pieces. We have to abandon the installation at once."

"We're not gonna leave an entire fleet behind when we have it in our power to wipe it away in a single instant," the captain told her, rapidly accelerating to maximum speed and barrelling towards the swirling chaos of green blobs and dark beams. "One way or another, our payload is getting delivered."

"I can't let you do that, Captain," Kayla insisted. "I'll take control of the ship if I have to."

"You can't, Kayla," Bessemer replied, his eyes narrowing as he searched for an approach vector that would carry him into the middle of the fleet. "I had Kvasir limit your access permissions when this egg was modified."

"You did *what?!*" she demanded, her sense of her prerogatives violated. Turning inward for a moment, she attempted to seize control of the craft and found herself utterly locked out. She was nothing more than a passive observer. "How *dare* you?! Krancis ordered me–."

"To assist me," Bessemer cut her off. "Now how about you do that and help me reach the target in one piece? Find me an approach!"

Gritting her holographic teeth, she turned around and scanned the battle for an opening.

"There!" she uttered, putting up a twisting series of waypoints on his display. "That's the most likely avenue. The chance of survival is a whopping *23%!* Of course, that's merely my estimate for *entering* the fleet. Our odds of leaving alive–."

"Good enough," he replied, turning the egg towards the path indicated. "I'm not gonna slow down when I drop this thing, honey. So you'd better plan another route that takes us away from it, or the inertia will carry it right along with us."

"It's as good a way as any to go," she responded glumly.

"*Kayla!*"

"It's done!" she said, snapping her fingers as an exit route appeared on the display. "You'll have to switch directions almost instantly, or–."

"Great," he cut her off again, his attention totally absorbed as he reached the fleet and began sailing past countless fighters. With eerie pre-cognizance the vessels ahead of his unpredictable path broke from their wards and closed in. Filling the space around him with innumerable shells, he twisted away from Kayla's waypoints and shot through wave after wave of vessels as several dozen ships closed on his six. "I think we're in trouble," he muttered, glancing over his shoulder as they recklessly cast their blobs into their own ships in a desperate attempt to stop him.

"*There's a surprise!*" Kayla all but shrieked, grimacing as they narrowly dodged being hit. "We've gotta get out of here!"

"We're committed now," he disagreed, approaching a carrier and darting along its surface. Seeing an opening, he made a split-second decision and dashed inside, his egg proving just a hair more nimble than his pursuers, several of which crashed against the massive vessel's hull.

"We can't stay here," Kayla asserted anxiously, the inside of the hangar dark and murky, like a swamp taken into outer space. To their right and left she could see strange pods in the shape of Devourer fighters. "This must be how they're made: they literally *birth* them into existence."

Before she could say more, a dozen green blobs chased them inside. Looking back, their pursuers had swung around and entered the hangar, determined to chase them back out into the open.

"Look! The hangar is closing!" Kayla exclaimed, pointing ahead at a double door that was drawing shut. "Oh! We'll be trapped in here if we don't hurry!"

Pushing the ship to the max, Bessemer felt himself become one with the craft, deftly tilting it just far enough to the left or right to avoid being torn to pieces by the furious shells of his attackers while maintaining every ounce of momentum that he could. Green blobs skirted across the surface of his ship, scorching it but doing no meaningful damage as they raced ahead and crashed into the doors. Holding his breath as they neared, he guided the ship through a tiny sliver of open space and shot back into the battle just as his pursuers collided with the doors and exploded.

"We can't stay out here any longer," Kayla declared, shaking her head at him as he shoved the egg into a downward spiral to escape another volley of green shells. "Kvasir's interceptors have been reduced to 60%. They can't provide us with effective cover. And the bombers are all but destroyed."

"I've gotta deploy this thing," he said, jerking the craft upward again and pulling a leftward corkscrew. A rotating tornado of shells followed him, lighting up the darkness of space around him.

"We've got to *leave*, Roland!" she insisted. "We can't risk this thing a second longer than we already have. We've got to retreat!"

"Captain, we're about to have company," Kvasir said over the radio.

"Friend or foe?" he asked tensely, narrowly passing between a pair of oncoming fighters and knocking against them both.

"Foe. But I can't imagine what's brought them here."

"Who are they?"

"Pirates."

Before more could be said, a large group of little blue windows appeared on the edge of the battle, disgorging more fighters than he could count in the split second he had to view them. Forced to shove his ship down again, it was with effort that he maneuvered them back into view.

"What are they doing here?" he asked Kayla, as they formed themselves into attack formations and accelerated towards the battle.

"Attention imperial vessel, this is Colonel Laramie of the Black Fang pirates. Extricate yourself any way you can. We'll give you cover until you can warp to safety. Over."

"Pirates to the rescue?" Kayla queried in utter disbelief, as Bessemer dodged another volley.

"Negative, Colonel. I've got a bomb and I intend to deliver it. This is a battle the parasite is definitely gonna lose."

"It won't lose anything if you're dead," Laramie

THE CRUSADE OF VENGEANCE

countered. "My orders are to extract you. Now get out of that cloud of death before they tear you apart."

"If you want to keep me alive, you're gonna have to come in after me," Bessemer replied, pulling a vertical U-turn and burning off in the opposite direction.

"You heard him," Laramie radioed to his subordinates in a sour voice, plunging with his entire force into the Devourer's fleet. At once their railguns began to spew forth explosive rounds that tore into the ships in their path.

"Carve me a path!" Bessemer radioed, having instructed Kayla moments before to transmit a new series of waypoints to the pirates. "I've got to deliver my payload at the last waypoint. Don't stick around once I do that."

Pulling a long somersault so they could catch up, Bessemer dropped into the midst of the Black Fangs and followed them along Kayla's route. Like a school of deep-ocean fish, the pirates pressed farther and farther into the hostile fleet. But the element of surprise was quickly lost. Soon the parasite brought the rest of its heretofore stationary fighters into the fray, and began to claw clumps of ships out of the attacking group.

"We're not gonna last much longer!" an unidentified pirate radioed, just before his wing was sheared off by a trio of blobs. Spinning off wildly, he crashed into a nearby battleship tentacle.

"We didn't come here to *die*, Imperial," Colonel Laramie radioed Bessemer. "We came to get you out!"

"That's what you're *doing!*" he shot back, as he covered the last few hundred yards that separated him from the final waypoint. "Break off! Now! Get your men as far in the other direction as you can!"

"Just what kind of bomb have you got?" another pilot asked.

Ignoring him, Bessemer raised the sword and inserted it into the special opening the androids had engineered for him. At once the device in the back of the ship began to hum.

Drawing the sword out, he ejected the weapon into space, plunged the craft down, and doubled back.

"This is gonna be close!" Kayla said fearfully, watching through the back of the canopy as the device shrunk in the distance. "Everyone! Get as far away as you can!"

Tearing his way through layer after layer of Devourer ships, Bessemer just reached the outside of the fleet along with his pirate escort and the shattered remains of the androids when a blinding light erupted behind them all.

"What in the–," Colonel Laramie began, before his transmission was blotted out by static.

"Oh no! Oh no!" Kayla worried, as the energy from the blast continued to expand outwards. Looking around, she could see several of their pirate escorts lagging behind. In moments they were swallowed by the wave of death emanating from the device.

Twisting around in his seat as the blast began to dissipate, Bessemer smiled at the gaping hole that had been left in the Devourer fleet. Every one of the capitals had been shredded by the explosion, as had the frigates. Only a handful of fighters who'd happened to be on the fringe of the fleet had managed to survive. Pieces of battleships and carriers floated on the edges of the blast, slowly drifting out into space.

"The survivors are making for the device," Kayla informed him, as he surveyed the damage. "Colonel, we need you and your men to rendezvous with the bomb at once. The parasite is attempting to capture or destroy it."

"Understood," Laramie replied, his voice low and sullen.

"Wonder what's gotten into him," she remarked, as Bessemer likewise accelerated towards the weapon.

"Reckon we'll find out soon enough."

Possessing by far the fastest ship, Bessemer arrived first and spent a few anxious seconds wondering how he'd defend the device in an unarmed vessel. There wasn't time to open the back compartment and retrieve it, so instead he pressed ahead and flew straight for the oncoming ships.

"Uh, Roland?" Kayla queried nervously, as the parasite's craft zeroed in on him and unleashed a long trail of green balls. Holding course as long as he could, he rolled off to the right just as the first shell reached him and grazed the underside of his hull. "What are you doing!?!" she exclaimed.

"Playing chicken, Kayla," Bessemer replied with deliberate calm, swinging around towards the device before doubling back and making another pass. A pair of shells burned across the right portion of the egg, causing several warning lights to start flashing. "Shut those down."

"We can't keep taking hits," she cautioned, flicking off the lights and watching him nervously.

"Got to," he said quietly, his eyes narrowed as he flew as far from the device as he dared before flying once more towards his attackers. "Got to make 'em feel they've got a chance, or they'll ignore me and head for the weapon."

"You mean you're *deliberately* letting them hit us?" she asked in shock.

"You didn't think they were actually good enough to hit *me*, did you?" he asked with a slight grin, his attention still on his quarry.

"Well, it *is* a new ship," she replied, relieved to see the arrival of their escorts. At once the Black Fangs' guns began to fire, quickly tearing up the handful of craft that had survived. "I thought perhaps you were still getting used to it," she added.

"No, this thing's easy enough to fly," he told her, making a beeline for the weapon and decelerating as he neared. Unsure just how much the pirates could be trusted, he didn't intend to leave temptation dangling in front of them any longer than necessary. As the last Devourer ship exploded, he popped the rear compartment and lined up his craft to recover the weapon.

"Looks like they're getting curious," Kayla observed

uncomfortably, watching the pirates advance as Bessemer carefully took the device back on board.

"Mhm," the captain responded without much interest, maneuvering the last few critical inches until the device clicked into place. Closing the rear compartment, he accelerated a little so as not to be a sitting duck. "Thanks for your help, Colonel. We were in a bad way before you guys came along."

"We didn't just 'come along,' Imperial," Laramie replied acidly. "I was ordered from the very top to come and help you without the least explanation why. Now two-thirds of my command is gone, a number of which fell because of that bomb you set off. I figure I'm entitled to some kind of an explanation."

"Colonel, I'd be tickled pink to give you an explanation if I had one," Bessemer replied half honestly. "Fact is, I haven't the least idea why you'd get such an order. Especially given all of your kind that I've had the pleasure of shooting down over the years."

"Roland!" Kayla exclaimed, briefly flicking off the microphone so Laramie couldn't hear. "You're going to get us killed!"

"The feeling is mutual, Imperial," the colonel replied, flying a little closer to the egg and glaring at Bessemer.

"Good, then we understand each other," the captain remarked, turning his craft towards the sphere and accelerating yet further. "Thanks for the assist, Colonel. Maybe I'll return the favor sometime."

"Don't bother. Just stay out of my hair from now on," the pirate snapped, breaking off with what was left of his group.

Mutely Bessemer and Kayla watched as they arrayed themselves in a tight formation for warp. Moments later a series of little blue openings were torn in space, and they departed.

"Why'd you have to antagonize him like that?" the AI

asked the instant they were alone. "The man had just saved our lives."

"He's a pirate, Kayla. Do you know how many innocent lives he's taken already? Probably dozens. Given he's a colonel, maybe hundreds. That's not the kind of person you cultivate. You use him, and then kick him to the curb."

"Even if he's armed and you're not?" she countered as the egg neared the sphere. Dismayed by what she considered his unacceptable recklessness, she inwardly vowed to get him a complete medical evaluation once they'd reached *Sentinel*.

"I could've just warped, Kayla," he answered casually. "The device was already onboard."

Assuming their guns didn't tear us to pieces first," she reflected.

"Kvasir? Are you there?" Bessemer radioed when Kayla didn't respond.

"I'm here, Captain."

"The threat has been eliminated. But I'm gonna need a freshly modified ship to depart in. This one's a little beat up."

"It will be our pleasure, Captain," the android replied, as one of the doors on the sphere opened to admit them. "Please consider all of our facilities to be your own for as long as you stay here. We are eternally grateful for your help. The weapon you carry is truly remarkable."

"Yes, it is," he agreed, his tone a touch dismissive as he wished to deflect interest from the device. "Get to work on the new craft at once, will you? I want to get underway as quickly as possible."

"It will be done."

Switching off the radio, he leaned back in his seat and exhaled, slowly calming down now that the battle was over.

"I wonder if the *Pho'Sath* will try anything else after this," Bessemer mused aloud as he flew into the sphere and made for the hangar.

"Well, unless they've got the place under visual

surveillance, they shouldn't know we've taken the device with us until we activate it again. That'll buy them a little time, at least."

"But it's a sure bet that the *Pho'Sath* will make another play for this base," the captain responded. "They're not gonna want to leave a presence like this in the Milky Way if they can help it. I guess it all just comes down to finding the right way to destroy it without leaving fingerprints."

"Suppose so."

Dropping altitude, the captain quickly flew into the hangar and landed his ship. The space was eerily empty, given almost its entire complement of fighter craft had been destroyed. Essentially only eggs remained, one of which was about to be removed in order to make the modifications he'd requested.

"I'll have 'em switch you over to the new ship just as soon as they can," he informed Kayla, unfastening his harness and rubbing his eyes. Resting his elbows on his knees, he drew a deep breath and let it out slowly.

"Are you alright?" she queried with audible concern.

"I guess so," he answered, lowering his hands and looking at her, his face suddenly weary now that he'd touched down. "I thought I felt the pain meds wearing off for a second there. But I must've only imagined it. I'm alright."

"Okay," she nodded doubtfully, watching as he popped the canopy and arose.

Putting a leg over the side, he paused again and blinked several times. Kayla was about to speak up when he shook his head and continued his descent. Reaching the floor, he let go of the ladder and walked slowly towards an oncoming group of androids. Kvasir was in the lead.

"You were right about producing a miracle of our own," he uttered, as the other androids moved past to begin the process of removing both Kayla and the device from his battered ship. "Nevertheless it was a terrible risk, wasn't it? You and your escorts were nearly destroyed."

"Fortunes of war," Bessemer shrugged, continuing to walk as the android fell in alongside him. "Did it take out any of your boys?"

"Yes, but they were about to be destroyed by the parasite's craft. In any event, I'm afraid nothing more than a respite has been purchased for us. It remains to be seen what role, if any, can be ours now that we've been discovered. The best course after all may be to flee, destroying this station to remove any trace of our having been here. But that is a decision for my successor and our superiors."

"Don't make up your mind too fast," Bessemer cautioned. "A base like this is a real asset."

"And a liability, Captain," Kvasir pointed out, pausing before the lift and willing it open. Waiting for his guest to enter first, he followed and sent it to the surface. Walking out under the protective haze of the sphere's artificial atmosphere, the android gazed up at the white glow of the sun for a few moments before looking at him again. "Do you see that, Captain? All that power just waiting to be utilized? Yet we can only use it if we maintain a perfect orbit around it, else it will rip us apart. Just such a delicate dance must be maintained with the *Pho'Sath*. It was a terrible gamble to place this station within the Milky Way in the first place, yet it was considered worth the risk to have a permanent listening post in your space. Now that we've been exposed, the risk of yet more tension between our two races increases considerably."

"They're already running up and down our turf like they own it. What difference does it make if you've got an observation post out here?"

"Practically speaking, it means very little, as far as they're concerned. It's all about the diplomatic optics. To our knowledge the *Pho'Sath* don't have a permanent base here, just little hideouts that they use as temporary staging areas. So far they've been very careful to avoid leaving any kind of lasting footprint behind. But this may inspire them to greater boldness now that they know we've skirted the treaty to this degree. They may even seek an adjustment to the treaty that would permit them greater latitude to operate here."

"Krancis would love that," Bessemer remarked sarcastically.

"I'm afraid it's out of his hands. Naturally my people wish to do everything we can to cooperate with your government. But the best way to foster the growth of your kind into a great race is to maintain peace between ourselves and the *Pho'Sath*. They would love to have a war in this galaxy, for it would give them ample opportunity to raze every last colony of yours to the ground. There's almost nothing in this universe that they hate more than the Earthborn. Don't doubt their eagerness for a confrontation. Especially now that you are so far reduced by your war with the parasite."

"I'll keep it in mind," he replied quietly, shifting his spine a little as a faint glow of pain started to manifest itself.

"Are you alright?"

"You ought to know."

"I'm afraid our mistreatment of you will forever linger in my memory as the greatest mistake of my tenure as commander of this installation. I would offer my profoundest apologies, but I know they would be of no value after what I've put you through."

"You *could* offer me some more of that medication," he suggested.

"You must wait another few hours before receiving another dose, or it may cause side effects. But rest assured, I'll have a package of it prepared for when you depart. It's the least we can do."

"Yes, it is," he agreed in a low tone, not pleased at the idea of spending the next several hours in an increasing amount of pain.

"In the meantime, please accept the hospitality of this

station and make yourself utterly at home. Explore it to your heart's content, or feel free to take advantage of our many beautiful chambers within which you can rest. None of it would exist at this moment without your help and that of the device you brought here. In that sense you've earned the right to whatever your eyes fall upon."

With this thought the android bowed slightly and slowly walked away.

"*Some prize,*" Bessemer shook his head once he was alone. "*And all it cost me was a lifetime of burning pain!*"

CHAPTER 10

"A string of victories has brought us near the doorstep of the last Devourer mass," Wellesley wrote in his log, glad to have something else to do than worry about Rex, who was still resting in the hospital. "The third mass has already exploded on its own, sending a shockwave unlike any I've ever seen before. Shoot, it seems like a miracle that the planet it was sitting on didn't split in two, though I guess the 'psychic energy' it unleashes probably can't do that. We were much too far away to notice it ourselves, Krancis having decided to bypass it on the way to the fourth one. I don't know if he's suddenly decided to attack this last one, or if it's because the parasite has gathered an enormous fleet around it. Probably the latter, given he doesn't want to give the mass a power boost with the cannon."

Pausing for a moment as he heard footsteps outside his command center, he watched the door through a surveillance camera, expecting to see Girnius' unfriendly face pop through. But soon the steps receded, and he turned once more to his work.

"*Something funny happened to Rex the last time he was in the reactor. The dark realm took him and just held on and on forever, like it didn't want to let him go. He yelled when he finally came back to consciousness, and then it was all he could do just to get out of the reactor without collapsing. In fact, he did* collapse. *I know the dark realm is our friend, or at least has friendly feelings towards us. But when I see the wringer it's putting Rex through, sometimes I have to wonder if we're not just useful peons that it ultimately doesn't care very much about. Rex* has been terribly abused by it. Drives me up the wall that I can't do anything to help him. Sigh, guess I'll just have to leave him in the hands of our medical staff and hope for the best."

Rereading his last few sentences, he decided that the word *sigh* was a touch too informal and nixed it.

"Black Fangs are already proving useful as a secondary military unit to supplement the imperial navy with. Sent them on a top secret rescue mission at Krancis' request. Lost the majority of them, but they fought like lions. Funny thing to say about pirates, given they are, to put it charitably, the underbelly of the economy. But these guys have guts that go on for days and days. I wouldn't have wanted to fly into the near-certain death they faced without batting an eye. Just real tough guys. I'm optimistic that this is just the beginning of their usefulness. I just hope Krancis realizes that I can't order them on missions like this too frequently without them wondering what's gotten into Girnius. Not to labor the point, but they *are* pirates. They expect to be sent out looting and robbing and such, not saving imperial personnel. It won't be healthy if they start growing suspicious of their orders. Might start asking questions, which could lead them to learn just where their leader is presently cooling his heels. If they find that *out,* they'll instantly conclude that he's our puppet, and the organization will fracture just when we need it the most."

There was another motive for Wellesley's concern, though he felt it was unworthy to write down: if the organization splintered to pieces, he'd lose his fiefdom. His first real command after the countless years that had separated him from the war that ushered in the end of his people, he wasn't willing that anything should come between him and his ambition to convert the Black Fangs into a useful, productive force for good in the galaxy. The fact that they were a criminal organization merely served to whet his appetite and stimulate his pride at the thought of actually pulling it off.

But it wasn't just the sheer scale of such an

achievement that appealed to him. As he had hinted to Hunt on a number of occasions, he wasn't as young as he'd once been. And while AIs didn't exactly age, every passing year saw the odds increase that he'd either suffer some kind of fatal error, or that simple physical trauma would disable or destroy him. Once the Devourer was finally defeated, the hard work of rebuilding the empire would begin. Traitors, opportunists, revolutionaries would abound once the parasite no longer existed to strike fear into their hearts. Assassination, espionage, and a thousand other forms of corruption would claim many good lives. There was no reason to imagine he would be exempt from such risks.

All these factors added up to one conclusion in his rational mind: he had to make it stick while he had the chance. Fate had handed him near-total command of the most powerful criminal organization in the galaxy. He wasn't about to fall short of the opportunity that had been handed to him.

These reflections were interrupted by the door opening.

"Um, Wellesley?" Gromyko queried, cautiously sticking his head in. "Can you hear me?"

"Of course."

"Oh," the smuggler said with a start when he heard his voice, certain that the AI must be angry with him after the way he'd behaved over Powers. "Well, uh, Krancis told me to take you to Rex. He's still–."

"How is he?" Wellesley asked anxiously. "Well, come on, come on! Take me to him!" he added when Gromyko proved at a loss for words.

"Sure," he agreed quickly, rapidly crossing the small room, grasping the medallion, and retreating out the open door. Punctiliously closing it behind him, he tried to walk casually, though he didn't know why.

"Today, Gromyko," the AI urged him, making him jump again and hasten his pace. "What's happened, anyhow?

Has he regained consciousness?"

"It comes and goes. It's like he's sick or something. Fades in and out, and doesn't make much sense when he's awake," he said in a sudden gush of words, his vocal wheels finally spinning. "Just kind of stares at me like he's got something on his mind but doesn't want to speak. Then he drifts off again."

"You mean he hasn't said anything?" Wellesley asked, as the smuggler reached a teleportation chamber and requested the medical room.

"Not to me," he replied in a guilty tone once they were on the other side. "He might have spoken to someone else. He's, uh, not exactly my biggest fan right now."

"He's not the only one," the AI remarked sourly. Deeply annoyed by the smuggler, Wellesley nevertheless knew it would be unproductive to simply lay into him and tried to keep from doing so. But his will to restrain himself quickly waned. He briefly wrestled with himself, trying to think of some constructive pretext to criticize him before finally just shoving his inhibitions aside and letting him have it: "What got into you, anyhow? Don't you think we've got big enough problems without you howling murder and attacking the only friend who'd never done you wrong? Even back on Delta he was the one you could always trust, especially after the Underground went to bits. You owe him your life who knows how many times over."

"I know," he admitted quietly, ducking his head and slouching his shoulders as the AI's words hit home. "I could die from the shame, I really could," he added, his voice growing dramatic as he strode down the hall towards the ship's medical wing. "If I thought there was any way to redeem the wrong Gromyko has done–."

"A great first step would be to *not* speak in the third person when you're trying to be contrite!" Wellesley snapped, the smuggler's unconscious grandiosity grating on his nerves.

"Yes, yes, of course. I've lost the right to anything like significance," he agreed with a moralistic nod, exasperating the AI yet further.

"Look, just try to use your brain and make yourself useful. Rex'll cool down in time, but the process will go faster if you just keep your head down and keep what few shreds of the old Delta days are left intact for him. You're his only chum from back then. It means a lot to him to have at least some link to the past. Otherwise he's just a guy floating in space without any kind of anchor. Honestly that's probably the only reason he's given you a second chance. I don't think he'd give Pinchon one if he'd acted the way you have."

"You really think so?" Gromyko asked, the notion of having a special status in Hunt's mind pleasing his vanity. Especially one that set him above the pirate colonel.

"Now don't you try to bank on that," Wellesley warned him pointedly. "You try and use it like a line of credit and you'll find yourself bankrupt in a hurry. Just think of it as a life-preserver: a one-time, single-use, don't-you-even-*dare*-lean-on-it type thing."

"Of course, of course," the smuggler agreed, though his mind was audibly elsewhere.

"*Gromyko…*" Wellesley uttered severely.

"Oh, don't worry about me," the smuggler assured him, his tone brightening as he walked into the hospital and directed his steps towards Hunt's room. "I won't make any trouble. You have my promise."

"*That is the* last *thing I would* ever *take your word on…*" the AI reflected with irritation, hoping he hadn't accidentally spurred Gromyko to start even more trouble. "Is Krancis with Rex?" he queried after a moment, hoping the man in black's name might take some of the annoying spring out of his step.

"Last I saw only Mafalda was with him," the smuggler replied, his pace indeed losing a bit of its elasticity. "I don't think she's slept since they brought him to the hospital."

"I'm not surprised," Wellesley responded, cringing a

little as his escort laid a hand upon Hunt's door and slowly opened it. Afraid that he'd be in rough shape, he inwardly sighed his relief when he saw him resting peacefully, his hand held by both of Mafalda's. "Give me to her and then beat it," the AI instructed him.

"But, Wellesley, I am after all the last–."

"If you finish that sentence I'll see to it you're thrown out of the ship while we're still in warp!"

Swallowing at the sharpness of this threat, he mutely handed the disc to Mafalda and left.

"Thank you for making him go," she whispered appreciatively. "I know he means well. But it's easy to get too much of him."

"You can say that again," the AI fumed, kicking himself for mentioning the special place Hunt had in his affections for the self-absorbed renegade. "How's he doing?" he asked after a moment, his anger passing quickly as he looked upon his friend through Mafalda's sympathetic eyes.

"He's been resting quietly ever since Gromyko left to get you. Honestly I think he aggravates him somehow, even when he's asleep. His breathing calmed the moment he left."

"Well, what has Krancis had to say about his condition? Does he know what's wrong?"

"I believe so, though he hasn't seen fit to tell me. All I know is that he's not to be disturbed. Even the medical staff have been ordered to stay away unless absolutely necessary. Krancis left strict orders that only me and Rex's friends could be here long term."

"You're one of his friends, Mafalda."

Wordlessly she nodded, though she didn't really believe him.

"Is that…you…Wells?" Hunt queried groggily, his eyes opening with effort.

"Yes, Wellesley is here," Mafalda assured him, leaning forward in her seat beside his bed and looking into his eyes. "Do you want to talk with him?" Receiving a slight nod in reply, she carefully laid the medallion in his hand and closed his fingers around it.

"How're you doing, buddy?" the AI asked, his words audible to them both as she continued to hold on.

"You should...see...the other...guy," the Deltan joked, swallowing hard and closing his eyes.

"The other guy is just a cloud of ash now," Wellesley said proudly. "Remember? I watched the whole battle while you were in the reactor. That big Devourer ship never stood a chance. For that matter, neither did the rest of the fleet. You did good, Rex. You've earned some rest, so just take it easy and don't push yourself."

"Not...rest..." he shook his head. "Recuperation. *Rebalance*."

"I...don't understand," the AI replied slowly. "Rebalance from what?"

"Exposure. *Overexposure*. The dark realm...pulled me in, tried to widen our connection."

"But why? I should have thought your connection was plenty strong already."

"Not strong enough," he shook his head. "Something big is coming, Wells. It wouldn't let me know just what. But I could feel its enormity." Pausing briefly to gather his strength, he forced his eyes open and looked between the medallion and Mafalda. "A terror unlike any we've known before."

"Then why didn't it show you what it was?" the AI queried. "Why keep us in the dark?"

"Felt like...the dark realm didn't want to face it," the Deltan answered weakly. "Didn't want to admit to its existence, except obliquely."

"Fine time to be particular," Wellesley remarked with sarcastic exasperation.

"But...if the dark realm itself doesn't want to face this thing..." Mafalda's voice trailed fearfully.

"Oh, we'll be alright," the AI assured her quickly,

though his friend's words had put fear into his circuits. "We've got *Sentinel*, after all, don't we?"

"Mhm," she agreed quietly, though unconvinced.

"We'd better let you get some rest," Wellesley said to Hunt, as the latter's eyes blinked heavily. "Whatever this terror is, I'm sure we'll need you at a hundred percent when it finally arrives."

Mutely nodding his agreement, Hunt closed his eyes and was asleep in half a minute. Carefully Mafalda drew the disc from his fingers and held it tight against her chest.

"Wellesley, what are we going to do?" she whispered.

"All we can do is await events. I'm sure Krancis is already doing everything possible to prepare us for this threat, so the best thing is just to keep calm. Meanwhile I'll put the Black Fangs on the best footing I can without arousing suspicion. But probably the most important thing right now is for you to stick close to Rex and tend to him. There's a reason the dark realm tried to prepare him for what's coming. He's our ultimate weapon, so pay close attention to how he's doing. Contact Krancis at once if anything even remotely questionable occurs."

"I will," she promised him sincerely.

"You'd better see if that knucklehead Gromyko is outside the door. I've got work for him to do."

"Okay," she assented, standing up carefully to keep her chair from creaking and silently making her way to the door. Popping it open slightly, she saw the smuggler leaning against the wall outside, mumbling to himself. "Psst," she said, holding out the medallion for him to take. When he tried to talk she shook her head, handed him Wellesley, and retreated into Hunt's room.

"Take me to Krancis," the AI said at once.

"What happened in there? Is Rex alright?"

"He's fine for now. Get moving."

"Okay, okay," the smuggler replied, beginning to walk. "Well, did he say anything?"

"A little."

"And?"

"Nothing that would interest you."

That was a lie, of course. But Wellesley wasn't about to hand a piece of terrifying news to someone whose lips were as loose as Gromyko's, given it likely would have been spread across the entire ship within an hour.

"Don't suppose you know where Krancis *is*?" Gromyko asked.

"Hold on a second," the AI responded, briefly radioing the man in black. "Bridge, like always."

"Okay."

Aware that the AI didn't want to speak with him, Gromyko managed to bite his tongue until he'd reached the bridge. Pausing just outside the door, he hesitated momentarily.

"Is…Rex gonna be okay?"

"I don't think anyone knows the answer to that question," Wellesley replied, speaking in a tone that, while not friendly, was nevertheless without overt hostility. "I fully *believe* that he will. But I'd be lying if I pretended I was certain."

"But what if–."

"One question is enough for now, Gromyko," the AI cut him off. "Now quit wasting time and take me to Krancis."

"Oh, alright," he relented, entering the panoramic bridge. Struck, as he had been so many times before, by the swirling tunnel of darkness that surrounded them in warp, the smuggler watched it for a couple of seconds before walking slowly across the barely visible floor to Krancis.

"Set him on the table by that wall," the man in black ordered without looking at him, pointing off towards his right as he gazed down the tunnel.

"I don't see any tables," Gromyko responded, squinting as he approached the wall. A few feet short of it he noticed a faint outline, laid the medallion upon it, and then looked back to Krancis. Hoping against hope, he slowly made for the exit to give Krancis a chance to tell him to stay. When he didn't, he grumbled and left.

"I was a little surprised that you found time to talk with me," Wellesley began, speaking over the bridge's speakers. "I would've thought you'd be tied down with preparations for whatever this great big terror is that's about to come upon us."

"That's precisely what I'm doing," the man in black told him, turning away from the tunnel and walking towards the disc. "The Black Fangs did well on their first real assignment, and I wanted to congratulate you on the work you've done already, as well as coordinate further plans for the immediate future."

"To what specific end?" the AI queried.

"It's clear from your activities within the organization that you're reworking it down to its core. You've been cautious to keep one hand from knowing what the other is doing, so the Black Fangs themselves have no real clue what's in store for themselves as yet. But for someone who can see the entire picture unfold, it's obvious that you intend to restructure them into a combination strike force and espionage service. Indeed, they're peculiarly gifted for both roles."

"And just how in the world did you manage to work that out?" Wellesley all but demanded, both surprised and frustrated that the man in black had penetrated his intentions.

"As I said, it's obvious to one who can see the whole picture. And you must remember that I still have the imperial espionage service at my disposal."

"Yeah, and you've probably been listening in on my messages, too, having your lackeys put together all my orders into one big game board!"

"I must safeguard the interests of the empire at all times," Krancis responded evenly, a faint smile on his lips.

"I think you do it just for kicks, that's what I think!" the AI replied.

"If you truly thought that, you wouldn't be half as intelligent as you in fact are. Nor a quarter as useful."

"So I'm just another one of your puppets, eh? Just a lackey?"

"Did you really think your autonomy would equal that which you enjoyed during the civil war?" he asked in reply, hitting the crux of the issue on the head.

"I suppose not," the AI admitted reluctantly. "But that doesn't mean that I didn't hope so."

"Hope is both necessary and dangerous. It can lead us to believe in things that aren't there and never will be."

"Apparently so," he agreed in a grumble. Taking a moment to recover his equilibrium, he sighed over the speakers. "Okay, just what did you have in mind?"

"The terror will shortly break, which is why the dark realm pushed Rex so hard."

"I know that part already. Rex told me. What I don't know is just what this terror *is*."

"No one knows, except the parasite and the dark realm. And neither of them are talking."

"I thought *you* knew?"

"I know what category of creature it is, and I know its name. But neither of those things will prepare us for a monster that the dark realm itself refuses to contemplate. It would be nothing more than a label. We simply have no meaningful data. That is why we must be prepared for the worst. We must be prepared for the navy to fold, and for order throughout the empire to utterly collapse. We must be prepared for the empire to cease as a practical force, and for a period of chaos to engulf the galaxy."

"You must be joking," the AI responded, though he knew he wasn't. "After everything our citizens have been through? They're tough as nails not to have broken from everything the Devourer did to them. I honestly think you're selling them short."

"The oncoming terror is no ordinary foe, Wellesley. Why do you think the dark realm pushed Rex beyond his limits the last time he was in the reactor? It knows we are about to pass through the worst crisis our race has ever seen. The Devourer is a child compared to this creature, if the legends are to be believed. The parasite that nearly destroyed all of our kin a hundred thousand years ago is nothing more than a peon left to mind the store."

"Alright, now you're starting to scare me," the AI reluctantly admitted.

"That's the idea. I want you to have some sense of what we're up against."

"Okay, if this thing is so big and bad, what do you expect me to do? My boys are just pirates, after all."

"There's two possible extremes of behavior for every human being who hears of this beast when it finally emerges," Krancis explained. "One, is that they'll lose every last shred of civilization and tear their fellows to pieces in a desperate attempt to survive. The other is that they'll push aside every division that has heretofore separated them from the rest of us and draw together as a single body."

"The old dichotomy of survival," Wellesley observed. "Either self-assertion, or group allegiance."

"Correct. Given your copious intellect, I know you've been busily collecting data on who within the organization is likely to cooperate with your aims, and who isn't. I want you to use that data to build an understanding of who will fall into the latter extreme when the terror emerges, and to ensure that by that time they've been placed in positions of power. Conversely, I want the individualists to be moved out so they cause as little harm as possible. We can't afford to have the organization disintegrate overnight."

"You really think the Black Fangs will be that important for what's coming?"

"I know it for a fact. Humanity will need many dark

places within which to hide, and the Black Fangs have more hidden bases than even the imperial government. They'll be utterly necessary in order to save as many of our people as possible."

"Okay, now you really *are* scaring me."

"As I said, we are about to pass into the worst crisis our people have ever seen."

"As if the Devourer hadn't been bad enough," Wellesley uttered. "We've only *just* gotten it under control and already there's something new coming our way!"

"Indeed. Although in this case, the threat is far from new. In fact, it is beyond ancient."

"Like how ancient? Or is that something else that you intend to remain mum about?"

"The information at my disposal is privileged," the man in black replied. "The dark realm would not take kindly to my spreading it around."

"*That's* why you've been so tight-lipped about this whole thing? The dark realm would get mad?"

"Well, it wasn't for the sake of *amusing* myself."

"No, no, of course not," the AI said quickly, feeling silly for supposing Krancis had anything but a good reason for withholding the information. "Well, is there anything at all you can tell me? I have to admit I'm dying with curiosity. Can you at least tell me how old it is? That sort of thing always fascinates me."

"As I said, it's beyond ancient."

"Like…predates humanity?"

"It predates *life* in this dimension, Wellesley."

"But where did it come from? How did it live before there was any life?"

"I've told you all I can," Krancis shook his head. "Once it emerges, I'm sure the dark realm won't have any inhibitions about it. Then we can talk again."

"Assuming we're alive long enough to chat about *anything*," the AI said, genuinely worried right down to his innermost circuits. "Okay, is there anything *else* you want me to do?"

"Just employ your native intelligence in organizing the Black Fangs to respond to a single lethal threat. Keep them loose and flexible, ready to act at any point across their sprawling empire of crime. And try to secure as many heavy transports as possible. Evacuation orders will go out as soon as the terror breaks."

"You do realize that I'll face at least a minor mutiny, right? There'll be plenty of pirates who aren't gonna want to stick their necks out for the common good."

"And I expect you to eliminate the mutineers efficiently."

"Understood. Just wanted to be clear about that. Things might get a little…messy."

"I expect the Black Fangs to remain an effective force throughout every stage of this crisis. Employ whatever measures you have to in order to retain control."

"Yes, sir." Pausing briefly, Wellesley chose his next words carefully. "I don't suppose there's any chance I could make use of Pinchon?"

"For what purpose?"

"Well, I have reason to believe there's a separate computer network off the grid that even Girnius doesn't know about. Probably disloyal lieutenants exploiting Black Fang business for their own ends. You know, tracking shipments and whatnot in order to coordinate piratical activity against their own organization."

"And what do you want Pinchon for?"

"I want him to get me access to this network so I can track *them*. They're bound to have both hideouts and supplies that'll come in handy soon. But I need someone to *physically* interface with the network. And given Pinchon *was* a Black Fang, and he's not exactly a fan of staying on *Sentinel* any longer than necessary…"

"Colonel Pinchon is not the most stable member of

the crew at present," Krancis pointed out. "He's been openly chafing at my leadership for some time now. It's possible that you'll find him unreliable."

"I think he'll behave himself. At least as long as he's away from *Sentinel*."

"As long as he's away from me, you mean."

"Yes, but I was trying to be tactful."

"There's no need for tact where facts are concerned," Krancis replied rationally.

"I was also thinking this might be a good time to put Gromyko to some kind of use, especially since it would get him away from Rex for a while. I think the latter could use a break from him. In fact, I believe we all could."

"I agree. Provided he won't put the mission at risk."

"Absolutely not. I'll make sure to position him so he can't do any harm. Probably keep him in the ship as a relay while Pinchon does the serious work."

"Alright." Pausing momentarily, the man in black smiled slightly. "Pinchon isn't going to appreciate you sticking him with Gromyko."

"Well, he's not exactly on my Christmas card list, anyhow," the AI audibly grinned in return. "Besides, it'll give him some small hint of a motive to return. Unless he's cold enough to simply abandon Gromyko and hope we'll swing by to pick him up."

"I wouldn't put it past him."

"Nor would I. But in Gromyko's case, it's a chance I'm more than willing to take."

"As am I," Krancis replied, walking a short distance from the medallion and looking off down the tunnel again. "I'll have some intelligence sent over to you shortly that will make it clear how best to coordinate with imperial forces in the days to come. Needless to say it's for your eyes only."

"Of course."

"You've done good work, Wellesley," the man in black reiterated, his tone indicating that the conversation was at an end. "Keep it up, and I'll see to it you're remembered as a hero of the empire."

"Thank you, sir," the AI replied appreciatively. With a nod Krancis acknowledged these words, and then radioed for a member of the crew to come and take Wellesley back to his command center.

"We leave warp in an hour to destroy another Devourer fleet," he informed him after a couple minutes had silently passed. "Once it's been dealt with, you can dispatch your team before we jump again. Make sure they're ready by then."

"You can depend on it," Wellesley said, just as the door to the bridge opened and admitted the awe-struck young woman who was to carry him back to his room. Looking over his shoulder at her, Krancis nodded towards the medallion on the table and then returned his gaze to the spiraling shaft of darkness. Wellesley couldn't help scanning her vitals as she picked him up, amused to find her so nervous yet thrilled to be both in the presence of Krancis and assigned to transport an ancient alien AI. Such things had long since grown so mundane in his circle that it was fun to see them through fresh eyes for a little while.

The moment he was back in his command center, he radioed for Pinchon to join him. Reluctantly the colonel left his room and made his way through the ship to his unmarked door. Knocking out of habit, the former pirate turned the knob and opened it before receiving any kind of response. Fully expecting to see Girnius, he visibly relaxed when he found himself alone with the medallion.

"How are you doing, Colonel?" the latter queried once he was inside and the door had slowly been shut.

"I'm alright," he answered cautiously, taking a few short steps towards the center of the small room and glancing around. "Not a real big space Krancis has given you."

"Yes, well, I don't move around a lot, so I don't really need elbow room," the AI joked, hoping to put the colonel at ease but sensing he'd grown too suspicious after the affair with Soliana for that. "I'll come straight to the point, Colonel: how would you like to get off this ship?"

"I'd like it a lot," he answered with pointblank honesty. "But our lord and master wants to keep me under glass along with the rest of us. Probably thinks I'll throw in with the parasite if I'm out of his sight for more than a couple of minutes."

"What if I told you he's already approved you for a mission that'll take you far from *Sentinel*?"

"I'd say you're pulling my leg."

"Well, that's the truth," Wellesley replied. "You see, I've got a little problem: there are disloyal elements within the Black Fangs that are maintaining a secret network somewhere out of my reach. Girnius doesn't know about it. Nor, as far as I can tell, does Hyde."

"If Hyde knew, Girnius would, too," Pinchon said at once. "He wouldn't keep secrets from the boss."

"That's my judgment also," the AI agreed warmly, hoping to make him relax a little. "What I need you to do is physically visit a number of locations where I believe their network can be accessed and plug in."

"You AIs still need good old flesh and blood, eh?" he grinned a little.

"Well, we wouldn't have a purpose without you guys, would we? We'd just be sitting in our digital worlds, crunching ones and zeroes ad infinitum."

Before the colonel could answer, the door opened again and Gromyko swept inside.

"You called for Gromyko?" the smuggler asked at once, causing Pinchon's face to fall as he glared from the newcomer to the medallion.

"You must be kidding!" the colonel exclaimed. "Are you out of your mind? You want me to go on a mission with *this* turkey?"

"You have a mission for Gromyko?" the latter asked

hopefully, his eyes brightening.

"If he's got a mission for *you*, he hasn't got one for *me!*" Pinchon declared, pushing the younger man out of the way and laying a hand on the doorknob.

"Just hold it right there, Colonel," the AI ordered, the force of his words arresting his movement. "The fact is Gromyko might just come in handy on an operation like this. We can outfit you with a covert earpiece, but its range isn't all that long. We'll need someone else on the spot in the ship to make sure the connection between you, it, and me remains solid."

"Send someone else. Send *anyone* else!" the colonel replied. "Shoot, just snatch some random member of the crew!"

"And what makes Gromyko so objectionable?" the smuggler queried, cocking an eyebrow.

"*You! That! Talking in the third person!*" he snapped. "I'm not gonna have the time to babysit a man who thinks all the world is his personal stage!"

"That's the deal, Colonel," the AI lied, deciding to play hardball. "You can get off the ship and get away from Krancis. But you've got to take Gromyko along for the ride. I want at least one other man along for this mission, and quite frankly, I want Gromyko gone. So I'm killing two birds with one stone."

"Hey!" Gromyko exclaimed, it being his turn to glare at the disc.

"It wasn't enough to send me on a dangerous mission, you've got to tie a ball and chain around my neck, too?" grumbled the colonel, coming around to the plan, albeit slowly.

"You've been in command before, Colonel. You know that the factors involved are seldom completely desirable. Now, are you going to keep griping, or do you intend to play ball? Because there isn't a lot of time to spare. You two will have to start getting ready at once. You deploy right after the next battle, which is roughly forty minutes away."

"And what about Rex?" the smuggler queried, only then remembering his ailing friend.

"He's got Mafalda to look after him," the AI answered dismissively, considering Gromyko no asset in that department. "And me and Krancis. He'll be alright."

"Yes, he'd better be," the smuggler nodded to no one in particular, the grandness in his voice grating on them both.

"Alright, Junior: skedattle," Pinchon ordered him, jerking his head towards the door as he faced the medallion and crossed his arms. "The grownups have to exchange a few words."

"I don't intend to move so much as a foot outside that door!" Gromyko announced, his pride injured.

"Would you like me to *throw you out?*" the older man demanded, taking an angry step closer which made the smuggler jump. Not wishing to get into a fight with him, he raised his head high and sniffed.

"I'll go. But only to prevent a needless struggle," he explained, leaving slowly.

"Look, is this some kind of *gag?*" the colonel asked the moment they were alone. "Why are you saddling me with this joker? What earthly purpose can he possibly serve?"

"I told you–."

"Yeah, don't give me that garbage. I think you're just getting him off the ship!"

"Do you mean to imply that Gromyko isn't universally loved aboard *Sentinel?*" Wellesley couldn't help joking.

"By this point, I'm sure at least half the crew would like to push him out of the hangar. I know *I* would!"

"The fact is, we need someone to go with you, Colonel. I don't know if you've noticed, but Krancis runs a tight ship. We don't have any bodies to spare for something like this. And given that Gromyko is utterly useless aboard *Sentinel*, it makes him ideal for the task."

"Are you gonna send along something to tape his

mouth shut with?" he asked sourly. "'Cause if you don't, only one of us will be coming back."

"Is that a promise?" the AI laughed. "I'm sure your winning personality will persuade Gromyko to behave himself. And if not, you can always knock him on the head. Just don't hit him so hard he can't do his job. He can't afford to lose any more IQ points."

Heavily sighing, Pinchon looked down at his feet for a moment and then fixed the medallion with a stare.

"*Fine*, I'll take the smuggler. But this one is gonna cost you, Wellesley."

"And just what is your price?" he queried in reply, curious to see just what the colonel considered fair compensation for such torture.

"I don't know just yet. But I'll be sure to let you know," he answered seriously.

"Alright, then we'll just consider that I owe you one."

"A *big* one!" he made clear, stabbing a finger at the disc.

"Yes, yes, a big one. Thank you, Colonel. You're doing both me and the broader cause a huge service."

"By hooking you into the network, or getting rid of Gromyko?" he asked sourly, shaking his head as he laid a hand on the knob. However, before he could open it, the door seemed to move of its own accord. Stepping back before it hit him, he was displeased to see Girnius join them.

"What are you doing here?" the pirate boss demanded, scowling at him.

"Just getting my orders," he shot back. "Haven't you heard? The AIs are taking over. They're calling the shots now. But I guess you'd know that better than anyone else, wouldn't you?"

Shoving past him, the colonel slammed the door as he left.

"I see you're as popular as ever," Girnius smirked. "What have you done now?"

"More than you've been doing, moping in your room

and crying on Chrissy's shoulder," the AI rejoined, in no mood for the chairman's lip.

"You know, Wellesley, sometimes I've got a mind to snatch that little disc of yours and ditch it for good."

"You so much as lay a finger on me, and I'll have a security team jumping on your head in two seconds," the AI replied confidently. "You seem to forget, Chairman, that I'm hooked into the ship's comms network, and there isn't a blessed thing you can do about that. You set out to start trouble, and I'll see to it you end up with more than you can handle."

"Don't be too confident of that, golden boy," Girnius countered acidly, his voice dropping as he glared daggers at the medallion. "Push me far enough, and I might just not care what happens to me. You've already taken my organization from me. There's not much else you can do."

"Oh, believe me, there's a *lot* more I could do to you," Wellesley responded at once. "And given that I've been recording this conversation since it began, Krancis will know exactly who to hold responsible should anything sudden happen to me. But I wouldn't worry about him: I'd worry about Rex. He doesn't respond well to people who threaten his friends. Maybe I should just send him a copy of this little dialogue of ours as a preemptive measure. Once he's introduced you to every fear that's ever lurked in the back of that dirty little mind of yours, you'll know better than to shoot off your mouth."

Though boiling with fury, Girnius knew he was powerless to act. The fact was galling, given he'd been the absolute power within his own domain such a short time before. But he'd already had a taste of what Hunt was capable of when he collapsed a portion of his house back on Petrov, and he wasn't about to invite his anger.

"Pinchon was right," he groused. "You AIs *are* taking over."

"Even a moron can see Krancis still holds the keys

in his long, cold fingers. I'm just doing what I'm told, like everyone else."

"And what about that business you mentioned about setting up a rival intelligence network?"

"Oh, *that?* I threw that idea out almost as soon as I'd thought of it. Too risky."

"Now why don't I believe that?"

"Because you're a suspicious person with an active imagination?" the AI suggested in a good humored tone, though the chairman was in fact correct. "Nothing gets past the old man, Girnius. It would be ridiculous for me to try and pull one over on him. Not to mention a questionable career move, given each of my messages to and from this ship pass through *his* comms equipment. It would be like running an intelligence operation through the mail when you *know* every letter you send is being read and analyzed."

"You're cocky enough to try it, anyway," Girnius observed, his on-again, off-again knack for personal insight manifesting itself. "You'd try it just for the challenge, especially since you've got a lifeline to fall back on if you really got yourself in trouble."

"That being?" he asked innocently, though he already knew.

"Hunt. Krancis isn't about to cross him. He knows a valuable tool when he sees one, and he won't jeopardize his usefulness by alienating him from the empire."

"That's true enough," the AI agreed. "Of course, that cuts both ways, you know: I wouldn't do anything that would put Rex in a bind, either. I *am* his closest friend, so I wouldn't want any heat to spill from me onto him. I rather like the idea of Rex Hunt, Lord of the Empire. Has a nice ring to it after everything he's been through. I'd be pretty selfish to put that at risk so I could play games behind Krancis' back."

Though his tone was even and betrayed nothing, the fact that that was exactly what he'd been doing began working on his conscience. In truth his argument with

Girnius was him working out in real time just how much danger he'd put his friend in by attempting to set up a rival intelligence network. Happily concluding that the risk, while there, wasn't very serious, he pushed the matter aside.

"Now, Chairman, I'd like to make a proposal."

"Thanks, you're not my type."

"Oh, very cute," the AI responded sarcastically. "No, I meant that perhaps you'd consider working with me for the benefit of both humanity and the Black Fangs."

"I have very little concern for humanity at large," the chairman replied, leaning against the wall near the door and crossing his arms. "When you've seen the underbelly for as long as I have, you learn there isn't anything very noble in humanity."

"Perhaps you've just been looking in the wrong places, 'cause I've seen a lot to be hopeful about."

"You're an idealist."

"Or someone who knows how to keep his perspective," the AI countered.

"Fine, have it your way. Now, what's your proposal?"

"There's trouble on the horizon: big trouble. Krancis wants me to sniff out all the hideaways that the organization has under its control and make them ready to receive a massive number of refugees. Now, given a sizable minority of these locations are commanded by individuals personally loyal to you, it makes it a little difficult to act on his orders without arousing suspicion. In a word, they'll notice the shift in direction and wonder why you've suddenly had a change of heart."

"And what do you want me to do?"

"Help me make it natural. I can fake being you where broad instructions to the organization are involved. But the personal touch is lacking when handling one-on-one communication, so I've been hesitant to attempt it. You could help put this one over, and I'd be glad to mention it to Krancis."

"For what? Better accommodations?"

"You don't have a lot of friends, Girnius," the AI pointed out. "Nobody on this ship really likes you. I doubt if even Chrissy is ultimately on your side. But it doesn't have to stay that way. You could make yourself a real asset, especially given what's coming down the pyke. We're gonna need every good man we can lay our hands on, and while that description most definitely doesn't describe you, that's not to say it couldn't, in time."

"What, you want me to turn over a new leaf?"

"I think you're smart enough to recognize the value of cooperation," Wellesley explained. "But more than that, I think you realize you're at a dead end. If you force me to, I can run the Black Fangs in perpetuity without you. Not as well, of course, given it won't have the personal touch that I mentioned a moment before. But I can still pull it off. That leaves you utterly irrelevant to everyone and everything in this galaxy, living out the rest of your days as a prisoner of the empire."

"And what's my other choice? Spend my life as a vassal of Krancis?"

"Everybody works for somebody, Girnius."

"Not me," he shook his head. "I haven't worked for anyone in years, and I don't intend to start now."

"You already do," the AI uttered, his voice hardening. "We've already taken the work of your hands and converted it to our purposes. Why, very recently Krancis had me order a group of your best fighter pilots to rescue an imperial vessel that was under attack by the Devourer. We lost quite a few, but they did their job and managed to save him. So you see, you are already working for the empire, by extension. Your recalcitrant attitude isn't doing you a lick of good."

"Really think you've got me over a barrel, don't you?" the chairman asked in a low, dangerous voice, his patience at an end. Raising his right hand, he caused a thin wisp of smoke to rise from its palm. "You're forgetting that I have powers of my own. Think about that before you push me again."

"Your parlor tricks aren't enough to spook me, Chairman," the AI nearly laughed, only barely holding himself in to keep from adding fuel to the fire. "I'm made of tougher stuff than those glasses you shattered back on Petrov. I reckon I'd last long enough for help to arrive. And if I didn't, I'd still have the satisfaction of knowing what Rex would do to you in retaliation. You'd wish you'd never been born, that I can assure you."

Lowering his hand, the chairman mutely glared at him.

"Look, I don't want us to fight if we can help it," Wellesley continued in a constructive tone. "You're bent out of shape, and I can understand why. But the galaxy is changing, and you've got to change with it or be left behind. The status quo is at an end, that I can promise you. It'll never go back to the way it was, not with humanity morphing, albeit slowly, into a darkness wielding race. Centuries of war and change are before us. Mankind will either evolve, or it will die. Now is the time for redemption, because those who come after won't care what kind of life you lived before, so long as you made yourself useful in the time of crisis. Just think about that for a little while," he concluded, seeing that Girnius was about to speak. "Let that sink in for a bit and marinate. This could be the beginning of a new life for you."

"I was happy with my old life, before Krancis and the *Pho'Sath* changed everything."

"Like I said: the times are changing. Griping about them won't do any good."

Watching the medallion for a few seconds, the chairman pushed off the wall and left.

"*About time*," the AI reflected with relief, glad to finally turn to the mundanities of Black Fang business and leave the complexities of interpersonal matters behind.

Half an hour later, *Sentinel* emerged from warp on

the edge of a large Devourer force. In orbit over a farming colony that it had been ravaging for nearly a week, there were huge plumes of smoke reaching up from the surface in silent testimony of the agonies it had inflicted on the population. The dark warp rift had scarcely closed behind *Sentinel* before its great cannon tore across the space that separated it from the nearest carrier, quickly blackening it. Most of its fighters were already airborne, ready to attack the mighty warship as it turned their mothership to ash and moved on to other targets. By the time they'd closed the distance with *Sentinel* and begun casting their ineffectual shells against its hull, it had lined up on another carrier.

A large group of frigates, supported by nearly a dozen battleships, raced for their massive assailant and started hammering away with their claws. The parasite experimented once more with an attack on its turrets, having given up on its ill-conceived attempt to snap the vessel in two. Aware that too many targets were converging on his ship to prevent them from successfully closing on the turrets, the captain accelerated and plowed through a pair of oncoming battleships before they could move out of the way. Sheering huge pieces off their hulls, they tumbled off to either side, their tentacles desperately snapping towards *Sentinel* but unable to reach it.

Ignoring the fighters, the captain trained his turrets on the frigates first, determined to break down their numbers while accelerating through the battleships and towards the carriers. Two of the latter remained, though in practical terms they had little value for the fight, given they'd already unloaded their entire complement of craft. His true purpose in attacking them was to prevent their fleeing and fighting another day. As soon as the great cannon was charged, it cut loose again, striking the second carrier.

As *Sentinel* rumbled past the battleships, their massive tentacles beat against it furiously but not with the same inquisitiveness as before. As each second saw clumps of frigates torn from space, the parasite seemed to grow frustrated. No longer interested in finding a weakness, it merely lashed out in anger towards a seemingly invincible foe. The knowledge that the effective head of the imperial government was aboard, within reach, and yet perfectly safe, enraged it further. Had it been able to break its way into the hull and kill the crew, humanity would have lost both its greatest weapon and its greatest leader in an instant. But that was utterly beyond the reach of its many tentacles.

Watching the battle from the bridge as always, Krancis could sense the impotent rage of the creature as it flailed against his warship. Pulling up a radar display as the second carrier disintegrated and the vessel aimed at the third, he could see the battleships coming around to attack *Sentinel* from behind. Nine in number, they were clearly forming up for an attack on the engines, hoping against hope, he was sure, that some kind of damage could be dealt from that quarter. Evidently the parasite had forgotten the burn the captain had given its vessels on a former occasion when it had tried just the same tactic without effect. Running his eyes over the rest of the battle as the last of the frigates were turned to dust, the turrets at last had the time to batter away at the pursuing capitals. Much too large to suffer any serious damage from the turrets before they'd reached *Sentinel*, a pair of them stretched out their tentacles despite the glow emanating from the warship's engine. A quick, hot burn from the captain melted their arms clean off, causing them to break away.

As the great cannon prepared to fire upon the final carrier, a distress signal found its way from the planet to *Sentinel*.

"Patch it through, Captain," Krancis ordered, pressing a finger against the radio in his ear.

"...epeat, we are under attack from Devourer forces. They're killing every last civilian they can find while you guys fight it out in space. We need help imm—."

THE CRUSADE OF VENGEANCE

With that the transmission died.

"Finish with the carrier and then turn towards the planet, Captain. I'm sure the battleships will follow us there, anyway. We can deal with them along the way."

Clasping his hands behind his back, Krancis drew a breath and then exhaled slowly. Two more fleets remained along his path before *Sentinel* reached the final mass. It had grown larger and larger in recent days, clearly preparatory to exploding. But the desperation of the parasite's tactics in the present battle made him curious. If it was about to draw forth the terror, why was it even bothering to fight? Indeed, why was it letting its emotions get the better of it, throwing vessels ineffectually against *Sentinel*?

As he thought this, the cannon finished with the third carrier, and *Sentinel* began to turn towards the planet. The captain, training his turrets on the battleships' tentacles, had been shaving them off while continuing to burn away from them. As the massive warship changed course at high speed, Krancis smiled as the vessel's inertia negation technology prevented him from feeling a thing.

"Any further word from the survivors, Captain?" he inquired.

"None, Krancis. They've gone dark."

"Understood. Take us into the atmosphere as quickly as possible."

"Yes, Krancis."

"*What are you up to?*" the man in black reflected, turning around to watch the battleships as they attempted to follow *Sentinel*, the damage from the fire they were receiving starting to add up. "*What brought you to this planet?*"

To all appearances an unimportant farming world, the enormous columns of smoke clouding its skies betrayed some hidden significance for the parasite. It had been searching for something, he'd known that much long before they'd left warp and engaged the orbiting fleet. It was a cruel decision to allow the Devourer to continue its work of terror against the small population. But similar activities had been seen across the empire, where worlds of otherwise low-value to the parasite had somehow come to deserve a great deal of attention. With Soliana gone, there was no question of getting the inside track from the creature itself. The only course was to wait as long as duty permitted him to, hoping that the beast would show its hand before the entire population was destroyed. But that time had come and gone, the only hand the parasite showing being an empty one. Despite tearing up huge tracts of land with its tentacles, its search had proven fruitless. It was time to end the carnage and save what survivors they could.

Desperate as the last of their tentacles were disintegrated, the battleships attempted to collide with the warship, smacking into it without much effect. At last accepting their failure, they turned away and prepared to warp.

"Concentrate fire and take down as many as you can, Captain."

"Yes, Krancis."

Following his instructions, the captain managed to disable two of them before they limped into the safety of warp. As their rifts closed just as they were about to enter them, the two were battered until they were destroyed.

Abandoned by their capitals, and with their motherships lost, the remaining fighters made for the surface, determined to slaughter anyone left alive. At once the turrets lined up on them, filling the atmosphere with countless little black clouds of ash. Only a handful managed to get out of range before they were annihilated.

"We'll deal with them shortly," Krancis told the captain. "Just get us planetside."

As *Sentinel* descended through a plume of smoke, a call came in from the medical section.

"Krancis, I think you need to come down here, sir. Our patient Rex Hunt is getting worse. The young woman looking after him is worried sick. He's unresponsive to stimuli of any kind. I fear he's slipping into a coma, if he hasn't already."

"I'll be there at once," the man in black replied, turning instantly on his heels and walking rapidly towards the nearest teleportation chamber. It wasn't long before he was outside Hunt's door, carefully wrapping his long fingers around the knob and twisting it open. Finding the room dark, he turned on a small lamp on the table beside Hunt's bed before closing the door again. Seeing Mafalda's concerned eyes glowing at him in the semi-dark, he moved to her side of the bed and squeezed her shoulder.

"I'm glad you came," she said quietly, her awe of him overcome by her fear for Hunt. "I called the medical staff a little while ago, but they couldn't do anything for him."

"No, they wouldn't be able to do him any good," he told her, moving to the other side of the bed and sitting down. "What's ailing him is far beyond their powers to help."

"Can you do anything for him?" she asked meekly, concerned her question may offend him.

"For the most part he has to help himself," the man in black answered. "Though I should be able to help him through his present crisis." He nodded at the door. "Stand outside and ensure nobody interrupts me. I need to concentrate."

"Is this dangerous?" she asked, standing carefully and moving slowly towards the door, awaiting his answer.

"Yes, but not unduly so. Just get me a few minutes of uninterrupted quiet and he should pull through it alright."

"Okay," she agreed, stepping outside and slowly shutting the door behind her.

Taking out his ear radio and setting it on the table beside the bed, Krancis positioned himself so as to be able to place his index and middle fingers upon Hunt's temples. Closing his eyes, he bowed his head slightly and reached inward. At once he perceived the swirling chaos that had engulfed Hunt's psyche, leaving it in a hazy maze of darkness from which it would be unlikely to ever emerge on its own. Shaking his head at the overzealousness of the dark realm, he planted a small light of consciousness within the Deltan's mind, guiding him up through the shadows that surrounded him. It took several minutes for Hunt to rally, but at last he groaned, and Krancis removed his fingers.

"Fancy seeing you here," the Deltan remarked, his eyes barely open as the man in black reinserted his earpiece. "Was I that far gone?" he croaked, his throat dry as sand.

"You were pretty far gone," the man in black confirmed, leaning forward and resting an elbow on his own knee, looking his patient carefully in the face. "Your ordeal is far from over, Rex. But I'd say the worst is behind you."

"Lucky me," Hunt replied, squeezing his eyes tightly shut and pressing the back of his head against his pillow. Resting a few moments, he opened them again and tried to sit up without success. Falling back with a grunt, he looked up at the ceiling.

"No, you'd best wait for the time being."

"I don't care what its intentions are: the dark realm is going to be the death of me."

"You're probably correct," Krancis agreed, causing the younger man's gaze to move from the ceiling to him. "Like it or not, your fate is tied up with it for the rest of time. It's unlikely that anything else will be powerful enough to kill you. Eventually, however, it'll push you too far. Or *you'll* reach too far, and its might will overpower you."

"Death through an excess of power," Hunt remarked. "That's got to be a first."

"Hardly."

"Anything noteworthy happen while I was out?"

"*Sentinel* destroyed another Devourer fleet. We're just mopping up the remnants now."

"So status quo."

"More or less. The final mass has continued to grow

in size. It can't be long now before it bursts. That's when our trouble will really begin."

"And here we thought the Devourer was trouble enough."

"It was. But it pales in comparison to what's coming."

"You know, Krancis, your bedside manner could use some work," the Deltan half-joked. "Are you trying to encourage me to come back, or give up the ghost now?"

"You're strong enough to take the truth. You don't need me to sugarcoat it."

"Yeah, but sometimes it would be nice to *pretend* things are gonna work out okay in the end, instead of all this running and fighting."

"Illusions are for children, not grown men."

"Alright, have it your way," Hunt agreed, closing his eyes again. "Where's Mafalda?"

"Outside the door, giving us a few minutes' privacy."

"Does that mean you've got something to share with me?" he asked.

"No, I just needed a chance to concentrate without interruptions in order to bring you back. Couldn't afford to have Gromyko breaking in at the wrong moment."

"Alright," he nodded. "Where is that knucklehead, anyway?"

"Preparing to depart with Pinchon. Wellesley has a mission for them."

"He does?" Hunt queried with some alarm, his eyes shooting open. "Dangerous?"

"Yes. He wants them to get him access to a secret computer network that's operating within the Black Fangs. Given Pinchon's background, he may be able to get them in and out without arousing suspicion. But it'll be a tough situation if they're discovered."

"You can't let him go," Hunt declared at once. "Not Gromyko. Send somebody else."

"There's nobody else to send aboard *Sentinel*."

"Then have Pinchon grab somebody off the closest imperial station," Hunt countered, fighting his way up to his elbows and looking hard at Krancis. "You can't let him go," he repeated. "He's the only one left from Delta."

"As are you, and yet I fully intend to go on employing you in the field," the man in black responded. "It's about time the smuggler did something useful, especially after all the trouble he's caused. Besides, he's a slick character despite all his fanfare and histrionics. The colonel doesn't think so, but he may just come in handy."

"Send someone else," Hunt reiterated. "Do it, Krancis."

"You're a lord of the empire, Rex. But you're not in command of our war effort. Wellesley has requested the use of Gromyko and Pinchon, and I've granted him both. You'll have to depend on their native intelligence to see them through the task before them. I can't coddle either one or play favorites. And if something should happen to them, they will have died doing something meaningful for the empire."

"Small comfort," Hunt grumbled.

"Comfort will be in short supply from now on, Rex," Krancis replied, standing up. "You'd best get used to that fact."

"How much longer will I have to stay here?" he asked, changing the subject.

"Hard to say. I've given you a little spark, but that'll soon fade. Then you'll drift back into a haze again. Could be forty-eight hours. Could be a week. There's no real way of knowing in advance."

"Then why don't you just juice me up so I can get out of here?"

"No, you've got to find your own way out of this. The whole reason you're in this situation is that the dark realm flooded you with too much of itself, attempting to increase your power dramatically in a very short space of time. Your psyche wasn't ready to cope with that much darkness, and hence it was overwhelmed and eventually you fell into a coma. I gave you a small guiding light to lead you out of it so you wouldn't be permanently lost. But it's still your job to adjust to the new reality that's been thrust upon you."

"And just why did it do that to me?"

"Because of the creature that's being called forth by these Devourer masses. The dark realm dreads its return, and wished to prepare you as well as it could to cope with it."

"The *dark realm* is scared of it?" Hunt queried, cocking an eyebrow.

"Dread is a better word," Krancis replied.

"Then what chance have we got?"

"A slim one indeed, especially after the damage we've suffered from the parasite. But a large fleet has been assembled in close proximity to the final mass. Soon we'll all warp there and await its detonation. Assuming the creature emerges there we'll be ready to attack it at once."

"Will it do any good?" the Deltan asked. "If the dark realm is afraid of it, what chance do we have?"

"It will likely be in a stupor when it returns to our dimension," Krancis explained. "That's the best time to strike. Afterwards it will be much harder to defeat."

"Strike while it's getting its bearings," Hunt remarked, looking away and thinking for a moment. "And heal up as quickly as possible, so I can power up the cannon," he added.

"Precisely," the man in black nodded.

"Just what *is* this thing?"

"You'll find out soon enough," Krancis assured him. "Now try and get some rest. We'll need you sooner than you think."

"Alright," Hunt consented reluctantly. "And Krancis?" he asked, as his visitor turned away.

"Yes?"

"Thanks. Thanks for helping me out."

"Of course," the emperor's right hand smiled faintly, nodding slightly as he opened the door and left.

Moments later Mafalda returned.

"Are you alright?" she asked solicitously, returning to her chair and taking his hand.

"I am now, thanks to him."

"Good," she replied, though Krancis' presence still unnerved her. "He told me to let you rest. Said you need all the peace and quiet you can get."

"I reckon he's right," he responded, shifting a little in his bed. "But I'd sure rather get up and stretch my legs."

"You will," she assured him, squeezing his arm. "Soon. Very soon." She looked up into his eyes for a few seconds, and then continued. "I saw Gromyko outside. He came to visit you before leaving on some mission."

"*What?!*" he exclaimed. "Call him back! Get him in here!"

"That was almost ten minutes ago," she replied in a quiet voice, attempting to calm him. "Krancis had just told me to see to it he wasn't disturbed, so I sent him away."

"Probably my last chance to ever see him," Hunt groaned, scowling up at the ceiling. "He's about to undertake a mission for Wellesley against some faction within the Black Fangs."

"And you're afraid he won't come back?"

"Yeah."

"I'm sure he will. I don't think it's his time yet."

"Yeah, probably wouldn't be *glorious* enough for him to die like that," he remarked sourly.

"Well, he *did* manage to run his own organization for all those years back on Delta-13, didn't he? He must have *some* skills that'll keep him alive."

"That's true," Hunt had to agree. "I guess I'm just so used to looking after him that I forget he *can* take care of himself, when he chooses to. Most of the time he seems like a kid brother who never grew up. But he's more capable than that."

"That's my opinion also," she nodded.

"And he's got Pinchon with him," Hunt added. "If anyone can see him through a pirate base, he can."

"I'm sure of that. I've always been impressed by his competence. I guess *sagacity* would be an even better word."

"Uh huh," Hunt agreed, only half listening as he thought. "I guess I've been a little bit full of myself, thinking he'd have to stick close to me in order to survive. But he'll make out alright."

"I'm glad you feel that way," she smiled, relieved to see the tension in his face start to melt away. "It's not fair to you to carry any greater burden than that you already bear."

"Oh, that's alright," he said with a little wave of his hand. "Like Krancis said, I can take it. In fact, he seems fond of laying as much on me as he can. Guess he thinks it'll tie me that much harder to the empire."

"And away from Doctor Tselitel?" she queried, his palpable attachment to Lily hurting her, though she felt it had no right to.

"Yeah," he agreed, his eyes dimming a little as he thought of her. "You know, I can't remember how long it's been since I last saw her on Omega Station. Weeks, months, I don't really know. Too long, is all I can say."

"Maybe you'll get to see her soon," she said hopefully.

"I doubt that. Krancis always seems to have something else up his sleeve for me to do. And if he doesn't, Wellesley is sure to cook up something. I bet he's already got a list of targets he'd like me to take down for him." Shifting once more in his bed, he yawned. "I guess that 'spark' Krancis gave me is finally wearing off." Yawning a second time, he stretched his arms over his head and then sighed. "You don't have to stay, you know. You must be exhausted."

"I'm alright," she smiled, though her face was worn. "With the colonel and Gromyko leaving, there's nobody else to keep an eye on you, anyhow."

"Could always get Krancis," he joked.

"Oh, yes, I'm sure that would be a good use of his

time," she chuckled. "Don't worry about me: I'll manage to rest while you're asleep."

"Alright," he relented, patting her hand. "Thanks, Mafalda."

While this restful scene was unfolding, *Sentinel* was hovering above the devastated world it had just rescued, mopping up the last of the parasite's fighters as they screeched just above the surface of flaming fields of grain, casting their green blobs against anyone, or anything, that moved. Burned, dismembered bodies lay openly on the ground; dead livestock were scattered everywhere, having broken out of their pens in terror days earlier only to be slaughtered in minutes. The stench was cruel, revolting, almost beyond description for the handful of survivors who'd managed to get under cover and then had the good sense to stay there until *Sentinel* saved them. Cheering as the remaining attackers were turned to dust, their ashes sprinkling down like dry, dark rain, they left their hiding places behind and began jumping and waving at the enormous warship that had delivered them.

"I want a science team dispatched while we deliver supplies to the populace, Captain," Krancis instructed him from the bridge, his usually expressionless face drawn up in a scowl as he surveyed the carnage. "I want to know what the Devourer was looking for. Send out four ships, one towards each of the four corners of this world. We haven't got time for a deep scan, so tell them to work quickly and concentrate on the areas adjacent to those already explored by the parasite."

"Yes, Krancis."

"*Just what are you looking for...*" he thought, drumming his fingers on his wrist as he grasped it behind his back. The timing of the parasite's sudden curiosity implied that it had something to do with the return of the terror. But what?

As the hangar doors opened and relief vessels began to pour out to support the population, another ship was preparing to leave. It bore two crew members, neither of them overly eager to spend a long journey in the company of the other.

"Alright, Gromyko, let's get one thing straight right now," Pinchon said from the pilot's seat, turning around to face the smuggler as the canopy dropped and the craft hummed to life. "*I'm* calling the shots, alright? *Nothing* is getting discussed in committee; *nothing is up for debate; and absolutely nothing is open to revision!*"

"Of course. You're the boss," Gromyko replied easily. A little *too* easily, the colonel thought. "We're heading into your domain anyhow," the smuggler added. "It makes sense for you to call the shots."

"Don't try to play nice and then turn around later on," Pinchon all but growled, sensing a bait and switch. "I don't have any qualms about leaving you out there once the mission is complete. I might just do it anyway, after how you carried on over Powers."

"That was an unfortunate episode that I hope to leave behind me," Gromyko replied with a curious degree of sincerity. "A shameful situation that I intend to make up for, if I'm lucky enough to get the opportunity."

Still sensing a trick, Pinchon could only grumble and face forwards again.

"Alright, strap yourself in and prepare for takeoff," he ordered. "We leave in less than a minute," he added, watching a steady stream of craft fly out ahead of them, calculating the time when the hangar would be free enough of traffic for them to depart.

"Already done," Gromyko answered brightly, patting the harness that he'd clicked into place some time before. Scowling at his irksome efficiency, the colonel gently lifted the egg off the hangar's deck and moved slowly into position. Seeing his opening, he slipped out into the smokey air surrounding *Sentinel* and began to climb towards the atmosphere. "What a terrible sight!" the smuggler exclaimed at once, taken aback by the savagery beneath them. "What I wouldn't give to pay back the beast for all it's done to these poor people."

"Yeah," Pinchon agreed, looking over the side and frowning.

"Doesn't this anger you?" Gromyko queried, sensing that the colonel was not nearly so upset as he was.

"What would you like me to do about it?" he shot back with annoyance. "These people are past hurting. Besides, our mission lies elsewhere. It won't do them or us any good to get our guts tied in knots. Best to keep a clear head."

"A cold head, I would argue!" Gromyko retorted.

"Argue whatever you want," Pinchon replied, pulling the craft into an even steeper climb to leave the scene behind that much sooner. "If you feel so bad for them, why don't you jump over the side?" he added sourly. "It's only a couple miles to the surface."

"As you said, we have a mission ahead of us," the smuggler pointed out crisply, his emotions evening out in a flash as duty took over. "And Gromyko won't fail in his appointed task."

"*Oh, great! We haven't been airborne for five minutes and he's already talking in the third person!*" Pinchon reflected, rolling his eyes and shaking his head. Accelerating to maximum speed, the egg soon left the battered planet behind and disappeared in a dark warp rift just outside its atmosphere.

Hours later the remnants of the population had left their hiding places and gathered inside temporary structures that had been established for them by *Sentinel's* crew. Given only enough supplies to see them through the immediate hardships they faced, the eggs slowly began to return to their mothership. This invited much critical comment from the survivors, but the fact remained that *Sentinel* had other populations to see to before it reached the final Devourer mass, to say nothing of looking after the needs of its own crew.

Working through the night and into the early morning, the science team scoured the surface of the planet but could find nothing of military interest to either the empire or the Devourer. Reporting this fact to Krancis, he instructed them to return to *Sentinel* and prepare to depart.

"*Just what are you looking for...*" he reflected once again, eyeing the planet a moment longer before turning and leaving the bridge. "Captain: take us into warp as soon as we're ready. I'll be in my cabin."

"Understood, Krancis."

As he reached the teleportation room, he changed his mind and instructed the technician to send him to the ship's library. Arriving moments later, he found it empty. Having had very little company for some time now, *Esiluria* felt it unnecessary to maintain a hologram at all times, choosing only to manifest one if a visit promised to last. Or, as was the case with Krancis, if the visitor was of sufficient importance to warrant one.

"What can I help you with today, Krancis?" she queried, appearing at once.

"I trust you've run your eyes over the data our survey teams have just sent back?" he inquired, making slowly for the table at which she sat comfortably, her hands folded in her matronly lap. "What is your assessment?" he added, taking a seat and throwing a leg over the other.

"The parasite is clearly searching for something. It expects to find traces of it not very far beneath the surface, or it would have dug deeper. That, or it's simply growing frustrated by its continued defeats and is losing both patience and common sense, simply lashing about in the dirt as it becomes too agitated for serious digging. That latter possibility I consider to be remote at best."

"As do I. No, I think it has a reason for searching in the manner that it's chosen."

"I've begun searching through my database to find a

possible connection between its activities and any weapons or forms of technology that could match its search criteria. But as yet I've found none. There are numerous dormant artifacts in this galaxy, but I haven't discovered any that would be hidden just beneath the surface of any known world."

"Well, perhaps it's a mixture of both," Krancis suggested. "Perhaps the parasite is both coming undone, and also searching for something that is heretofore unknown to us. It can't have escaped your attention during the space battle that its behavior has grown increasingly irrational and desperate."

"Indeed it hasn't."

"There is no reason to assume that the creature is capable of maintaining perfect reasonableness at all times. Given its nature, the opposite is more likely to be true. The fact that it's had the upper hand until only recently would have done much to disguise its animalistic lack of sense."

"Then you believe the pressure of impending defeat is pulling it apart?"

"Partially," he replied, drumming his fingers on the table beside him, his arm resting upon it. "I think it's also afraid."

"Of what?"

"Perhaps a weapon or tool that could strengthen us for our fight against what is to come," Krancis replied quietly. "Something buried deep and in the far distant past. Literally covered by the sands of time."

"Such as?"

"That remains to be seen," he answered thoughtfully, though some thread had clearly begun to grow in his powerful mind.

"I'll widen the search within my database for anything that might fit that description," she said after a few silent moments.

"Yes, do that," he told her, standing up as he reflected,

his eyes distant. "Let me know as soon as you find anything," he added, looking down at her before giving a slight nod and making for the teleporter.

Their next warp jump brought them within a stone's cast of the final mass. The parasite had stationed a garrison in a nearby solar system, many of its smaller vessels taking part in a thorough search of one of the larger moons. Tilling the soil as though they intended to seed it for eventual harvest, the Devourer's forces scoured it from one pole to the other, but without uncovering what it sought. The subsequent battle with *Sentinel* was uneventfully predictable, save for the fact that it saw Hunt on his feet for the first time in days. Joining Krancis in the bridge for a brief discussion as the fighting wound down, he left with Mafalda at his side to walk the halls and work some strength back into his bones.

"Krancis, Minister Radik is radioing us," the captain informed him as the final Devourer battleship disintegrated under the combined fire of *Sentinel's* many turrets.

"Patch him through."

"Krancis?"

"Yes, I can hear you, Minister. Proceed."

"Sir, it's my pleasure to inform you that all the forces you ordered to surround the final mass have reached their jumping off points. We're ready to warp on your orders and meet you there."

"Very good, Minister. The remainder of your forces have been distributed throughout the empire as I instructed?"

"Yes, Krancis. Precisely as you ordered."

"Very good."

"May I congratulate you on the success of your strategy, sir? The parasite is retreating on nearly every front. Even without *Sentinel* we could defeat it at this point with the vessels produced through the Adler Project. There's no question that it was your genius alone that saw us through this crisis."

"Thank you, Minister. But there are threats looming that will make the parasite pale in comparison. You've already begun work on the production program I ordered, correct?"

"Yes, Krancis," the minister replied, his tone a little downcast because of the man in black's lack of response to his sincere compliment. "But I must confess I don't understand the purpose of much of the work I've been ordered to oversee. I'm concerned that manufacturing efficiency is being lost because of my ignorance."

"That's alright, Minister: the work can proceed quite effectively with or without your understanding it. Not that I wish to keep you in the dark, mind. It's simply a matter of the utmost secrecy. I couldn't share the details with you without repercussions of a very grave nature. You must simply be patient, and trust that you will understand the situation more fully when the time is right."

"I understand," the minister replied, though his curious spirit burned to know more. "When shall I order the advance on the final mass?"

"Very soon. Expect my order within the next twelve hours."

"Yes, Krancis."

With a few more words, the emperor's strong right hand ended the communication.

"Wellesley?" he queried, pressing a finger into his ear.

"Yes?"

"What is the status of your forces?"

"Well, I've made the most out of the intelligence you sent me and made my dispositions as well as I can. But like I said, I can't do anything *too* sudden without arousing suspicion. Some of the movements are gonna look awfully convenient once this mysterious terror of yours finally breaks out. Looks like foreknowledge, frankly, and I doubt certain highly-placed figures within the organization are gonna assume Girnius has that kind of insight up his sleeve. They'll suspect some kind of plot or conspiracy. Still, if this thing is half as bad as you say it is, they'll probably be too busy picking their jaws off the floor to stop and think about what I've been doing. So, all in all, I'd say the Black Fangs are in decent shape. But it'll be a shock, all the same. I can only do so much to prepare them without tipping my hand."

"Understood. Any word from Pinchon and Gromyko?"

"None as yet. But I wasn't expecting anything this soon, anyhow. They've got to head to the inner rim of the fringe worlds to make their first attempt at plugging into the network. Understandably, the traitors within the organization didn't place their computers within easy reach of the nerve-center of the Black Fangs. They wanted to keep a low profile, so we've got to go to the boondocks to hook into the system. How's Rex? I heard he was up and around from Girnius."

"He's doing alright. Just getting his strength back."

"Good. I'd hate to face *whatever's coming* without him," Wellesley responded, laying particular emphasis on his ignorance of the oncoming threat to make the point that Krancis was being tight-lipped.

"Yes, that would be regrettable," the man in black said, smiling faintly at the AI's words. "Thank you, Wellesley."

"Yeah, don't mention it," he grumbled, closing the channel when it was clear he wouldn't learn anything more.

Hours later the survey team once more came up empty-handed. Reporting this to *Sentinel*, they were ordered to return to the ship at once and prepare to warp. Hunt happened to be walking near the hangar with Mafalda shortly after they'd docked. Passing by as they filled the hallway, talking among themselves, they suddenly drew up and saluted at the sight of a lord of the empire.

"At ease," he said at once, after he'd saluted them. "What've you been doing, Lieutenant?" he asked the man closest to him, standing straight with effort and leaning on

Mafalda more than he wished was necessary.

"Sir, Krancis ordered us to search a nearby moon for signs of technology buried beneath the surface."

"Why'd he do that?" the Deltan asked, a little surprised by the peculiar sounding nature of their task.

"It seems the Devourer has been tearing up planets in search of something, sir. Krancis would like to know just what it's after."

"Makes sense," he nodded, instantly regretting the motion when a dull pain started to throb in the back of his skull. "Find anything?"

"No, sir. Just rocks and dust. If there ever *was* anything on that moon, it must have vanished long ago."

"I wouldn't be so sure about that, Lieutenant," Hunt disagreed. "If the parasite is that eager to go digging it up, I'd wager there's *something* there. We just don't know what it is, yet."

"Yes, sir," the lieutenant assented.

"Very well. Carry on," Hunt dismissed them, receiving and giving another salute before they departed.

"What could that all be about?" Mafalda queried in a whisper, as the team left them.

"Search me," he shrugged, leaning on her yet more as they resumed movement, slowly following the group. "But if the Devourer wants something, *I* want it even more. For all we know it's trying to dig up some ancient pal."

"What could possibly survive lying dormant for so long?"

"How'd the Devourer last so long inside its prison?" he countered. "This universe is full of a lot of strange things, Mafalda. Even with all we've seen, I think we've only just scratched the surface. Best not to leave anything off the table until it's been *proven* not to exist."

"Well, I hope it's not some friend of the Devourer," she shivered. "We've got enough trouble with just it running around."

"I agree," he said, squeezing her shoulders a little as they continued to amble down the hallway.

Many hours later *Sentinel* emerged from warp simultaneously alongside a large fleet of carriers which bore many Adlers. Below them on the tattered world of Gilebin festered the final Devourer mass, its size several times larger than those that had been already destroyed. In orbit above this stinking sore was an enormous fleet: thirteen carriers, over four dozen battleships, frigates by the hundreds, and more fighters than could be counted. And according to deep-range scanners, more ships were set to arrive all the time.

"Minister, I don't want you to expose your carriers to undue risk," Krancis radioed Radik half a minute after his flagship had emerged from warp. "Release your fighters and then depart. *Sentinel* will overtake command duty for them during this operation."

"As you wish, Krancis," the minister assented, instructing his forces to deploy at once.

"Why aren't they moving?" Hunt asked the man in black, standing beside him with Mafalda. He no longer required her to lean on. But she had taken it upon herself to act as his nurse, and refused to leave him alone. "The Devourer has never lacked for aggression in a fight."

"It's in no hurry," he explained quietly, watching the parasite's forces float in space as though they were dead. His hands clasped behind his back as ever, his eyes moved slowly across the opposing vessels, working the math in his head as to how many Adlers they could expect to lose in the upcoming struggle. In truth he didn't want them there – *Sentinel* was more than capable of dealing with even a fleet of this great size. But he wanted them on hand from the instant that the terror emerged.

"You know, for the first time in this war, I feel like we've got something like numbers on our side," Hunt remarked, watching as the assembled carriers unloaded their many craft, the latter grouping themselves into attack formations.

"They outnumber us many times over," Krancis responded crisply, though he knew the Deltan already understood that fact. "Our advantage will be quality, not quantity."

"I imagine you'll want me in the reactor?" Hunt queried, turning towards the door even as he asked, Mafalda following.

"Yes, but don't overexert yourself. Many more battles will follow this one, and we'll need you around for them."

"I'll do my best to remain both intact and operational," he replied with a little bow, his old frustration at being regarded as a weapon having softened to mere annoyance.

"See that you do. Take Wellesley with you. I want eyes and ears inside the reactor while you're working."

"Alright."

Though she followed him to the door, Mafalda hesitated. Hearing her footsteps halt, Hunt looked over his shoulder at her with a question in his eyes. When she inclined her head towards Krancis, he nodded and resumed movement.

"Sir?" she asked, walking back to where he stood.

"Yes?" he queried, his tone indicating that he'd expected such an interview. "You needn't call me 'sir,' Mafalda. Krancis is the only name I wish to be known by."

"Of course," she assented, shrinking a little now that she was alone with him. "Um," she tried to begin, but her confidence failed her.

"My ears are open to any sincerely intended contribution you wish to make." He glanced at her briefly beside him. "Provided a modicum of thought has gone into it. And given your heritage, there's no doubting that."

"My grandfather is not someone I wish to be associated with," she replied, her tone modest. "His betrayal of humanity is a shame that darkens my entire family. I only wish I hadn't been so stupid, following in his footsteps."

"We cannot escape the actions of our forebears, Mafalda. They're part of who we are, as surely as the upper part of a stream flows into the lower part. Now, tell me what you're thinking."

"I...I sense that the creature is out of sorts. I don't know how to explain it. It seems fractured, lost. I fear that its conduct in the upcoming battle might be erratic, even irrational. The Adler pilots may be taken by surprise."

"And why do you feel this way?" Krancis inquired, though his voice implied that her fears were already known to him, and indeed had been accounted for. "Was it a dream, or a faint intuition?"

"The latter, Krancis," she responded guiltily, sensing that that undercut the legitimacy of her words.

"You needn't duck your head, Mafalda," he told her, seeing her do exactly that out of the corner of his eye. "You're a potent psychic. It's only natural that you'd pick up on intelligence such as that you've just shared. The fact is the Devourer isn't well. These repeated mass detonations have wreaked terrible havoc on its mind. All throughout the empire its forces have been behaving less and less rationally as time passes."

"But why?" she asked. "Are the shockwaves damaging it?"

"No," he shook his head, watching as the parasite's craft continued to float opposite his fleet. "The masses aren't merely chunks of Devourer flesh: they're nerve centers, potent processing units for the parasite as a whole. They are, in essence, pieces of its brain. And while all the various limbs of this vicious beast can think, it requires the raw computing power of dedicated tissue to function fully."

"Then why has it been sacrificing such vital tissue?" she asked with surprise. "That's like putting a gun to its own head."

"Why does one sacrifice anything?" he asked her.

"To...serve something else?" she suggested after a few

moments' thought.

"Precisely," he said, turning slightly towards her. "That's enough questions and answers for the moment, Mafalda. You'd best get down to the reactor as well in case Hunt needs you."

"But what can I do?" she balked, fearful to be responsible for the Earthborn champion should something go dramatically wrong inside the chamber.

"Wellesley is already on hand in case he gets into any trouble. And I've stationed medical staff scarcely half a minute away. They will have reached the reactor before he's had a chance to step off its elevator. No, Mafalda, you'll merely be present to provide moral support. I'm sure he'll be able to sense your presence, and that you'll be a comfort to him."

"Yes, Krancis," she replied, instinctively bowing slightly and making her way to the door.

"Don't worry about him too much," the man in black said over his shoulder. "He's much stronger than you or he realizes."

"Yes, Krancis," she repeated, dipping her head a bit and walking out.

As Mafalda made her way towards the closest teleporter, Hunt walked into the reactor room and stood beneath the giant orb.

"This is becoming a habit," Wellesley joked, trying to make some kind of conversation with his reticent friend. "Eat, sleep, jump in the reactor."

"Tell me about it," the Deltan faintly grumbled.

"It's valuable work, Rex," the AI assured him. "Nobody else could do what you're doing."

"I'm not so sure about that," he uttered, thinking of Krancis and how quickly he'd destroyed Soliana.

"Yeah, well, he doesn't count," Wellesley said dismissively. "Besides, you don't see him jumping into this thing, do you? Must be some reason for that. You know he'd love to have you tramping around out there, hitting our enemies hard. Why would he keep you chained up here if he could just power *Sentinel* himself?"

"Maybe that's just it, Wells," Hunt responded, hearing a click over his head and looking up to see the elevator descending. "Maybe he just wants me within arm's reach."

"Aw, I don't buy that," the AI said quickly. "You're starting to sound like the colonel with his paranoia."

"Yeah? Well, I'm starting to think Philip had a point."

"You don't mean that," Wellesley half declared, half hoped, as his friend stepped onto the elevator and rode it upwards.

"If there's one thing Krancis understands, Wells, it's the value of control," Hunt said, as the elevator reached the top and the reactor swallowed him. "First and foremost, he keeps the reins in his hands. Firmly. That's what eats Philip so much."

"Pinchon needs to accept that that's the way things are now," the AI uttered somewhat defensively. "The good old days of serving multiple masters are gone and dead. He might have done valuable work as an independent agent before. But he'll be much more useful as part of a larger machine now that there are finally hands at the helm that are capable of gripping the wheel both wisely and firmly."

At once Hunt knew that the AI was speaking more of himself than of Krancis. Clearly the power he'd lately exercised pleased him enormously after so many years of dormancy. He hated to admit it, but he felt himself draw back a little from his truest friend as these words sank in. He was beginning to sound more like *Allokanah*, and less like Wellesley. Sensing this, the AI quickly followed up:

"Of course, that's not to say that the man doesn't deserve some freedom of action," he said in a reasonable tone. "The fact is he's proven himself both well-intentioned and resourceful in a scrape. I'm glad to accommodate him wherever we can to make sure he's happy. The last thing I'd want to do is lose him."

"Yeah," Hunt agreed noncommittally, a small frown passing over his lips as he moved off the elevator. Standing loosely within the reactor, he shook himself a little to loosen up and rolled his head around on his shoulders a few times. Closing his eyes, he took a deep breath and then let it out. "Alright, is Krancis ready?"

"Hold on, I'll ask him." Half a minute passed. "Okay, he'll let us know."

"What do you mean?" he snapped, opening his eyes. "Does he want me in here or not?"

"Of course he does," the AI assured him. "But the fleets haven't engaged yet. For some reason the Devourer is just sitting and staring at us, like it's in some kind of stupor." He paused for a few seconds. "In fact, according to *Sentinel's* sensors, the mass below us is giving off a lot of strange signals."

"Calling out to this friend we've been told so little about?" Hunt queried with traces of resentment.

"No, I don't think so. Seems more like random neural impulses being blasted out into space. Like the mass can't contain everything that's passing through it anymore. You know…" his voice trailed as he thought.

"What?"

"Clearly these masses are powerful psychic hubs for the parasite. What if this one is getting overloaded through the destruction of the other ones? Perhaps managing the fleet is proving a little too much for it to think about, what with it reaching out to its pal and all." Audibly he smiled. "Maybe smashing this fleet'll be little more than shooting fish in a barrel: just a giant gallery of targets without any capacity to hit back."

"I wouldn't count on it," Hunt responded, closing his eyes again and reaching out a few gentle internal fingers towards the dark realm, preparing himself for a deeper connection. "I don't think this thing is down and out. Not until every last tentacle has been turned to ash."

"Oh, sure, I wasn't suggesting that we let down our guard or anything. I just figured–," briefly he paused. "Okay, um, you can scratch that last theory. All at once their fleet has jumped to life. Krancis wants you to fire things up ASAP."

"About time," Hunt mumbled, lowering his chin to his chest and drawing deeply on the dark realm, raising his hands up and out to his sides as he did so.

As Wellesley had said, the Devourer fleet suddenly moved with the uniformity of a single thought. The fighters tore off towards their targets, intent on tearing as many of them from space as they could before their terrible warheads could wreak havoc on the frigates and capital ships. The battleships, useless against the Adlers, all moved for *Sentinel*. They had scarcely begun to move before a massive dark beam exploded from the ancient warship and collided with one of their number.

"*It's gonna be a long fight*," Wellesley thought with some anxiety, concerned for his friend given he still wasn't fully recovered from his last encounter with the shadow element. "*Just hope the Adlers take some of the pressure off Sentinel…*"

Pulling away from the enormous vessel, the Adlers waited until the Devourer's ships were just barely in range and then fired. Like teams of ancient javelin throwers, they released their warheads and then withdrew, gradually falling back as the enemy drew near, allowing successive waves of missiles to shatter whole clusters of fighters whilst staying out of reach of their opponents' deadly green shells. But even though they dealt massive damage to their foes, the parasite's craft kept coming and coming, their numbers far too great to be stopped on their first pass. As the Adlers retreated behind *Sentinel* and continued to discharge their payloads, the thick cloud of fighters swarmed it, casting a torrent of shells against its hull as they lost touch with their original purpose and turned on the seemingly invulnerable vessel.

"Keep pulling back, boys," Colonel Barnaby Moryet ordered, observing the reluctance of several of his pilots to follow orders and withdraw. They wanted to stay close, to sink their missiles deeper into the oncoming cloud and hit richer clusters of targets. But their first priority, as Minister Radik had made abundantly clear, was to stay alive.

The frigates, moving in lockstep with their larger brothers to offer some kind of protection in case the Adlers made a move for them, made an impressive sight. Their tentacles snapped and thrashed, eager to strike the warship that had savaged so many of them in previous battles.

Dispensing with the first battleship, *Sentinel* moved onto the second as its turrets blasted away at the fighters surrounding it. They were quite literally capable of shooting in any direction and striking an enemy fighter, so the captain lessened the precision of their targeting computers to allow for quicker shots. This dealt added damage to them as they swirled and swarmed around the mighty vessel, their maneuvers increasingly wooden as the parasite apparently turned its mind to other things. As their fire rate dropped and several of them collided with *Sentinel*, Colonel Moryet instantly intuited what was happening and ordered his pilots back towards the cloud. Like fireworks their missiles streamed through space, exploding all around *Sentinel* and devastating the fighters that circled it.

"*Brilliant move, Colonel,*" Wellesley reflected, glad to see such initiative. Glancing at Hunt's vitals, he was concerned to see his heart rate rising higher and higher as he channeled more of the dark energy through himself and into the ship. Briefly the temptation flitted through him to intervene, to break Hunt's concentration in an attempt to lessen the load on his body. But a quick glance through the ship's external cameras showed that, despite the loss of, by that time, three battleships, there were still just shy of fifty of them making best speed to tear at *Sentinel* with everything they had. And while they had heretofore proved incapable of dealing it the least damage, he didn't want to take a gamble with that many vessels bearing down on them. "You're doing great, Rex," he softly encouraged him.

"Mmm," the Deltan replied, his tone almost annoyed as he focused all his thoughts on the dark realm. It was struggling with him this time, intent on drawing him inside as it had before. But he resisted this, both because he didn't wish to suffer from its zealous enthusiasm a second time, and also because he had noticed a new addition to the countless floating dead during his last visit: Maximilian Hunt had at long last joined the ranks of the fallen, and the sight had shocked him down to his very marrow.

"How is he doing?" Krancis radioed Wellesley, watching as the fourth battleship disintegrated and the captain shifted *Sentinel's* cleft slightly to target the next one.

"He's holding together," the AI responded, still concerned about his vitals. "But I think we're at risk of pushing things too far. He's already been through so much."

"He'll have to do the best he can," Krancis said, calmly aware that the parasite's battleships were shortly going to slam into his vessel.

But as they neared they began to fan out. Numbly they sailed past, their tentacles only dimly aware of the warship's presence. Like great hunks of heedless meat, they paid no mind to their target as they cruised off towards the darkness of space. A few of them collided with the mighty warship, merely glancing off of it. Slowly *Sentinel* wheeled to target them again. By the time they were within sight once more, the Adlers had inflicted numerous casualties on them. But as *Sentinel* cut loose with another shot from its great cannon, the battleships finally regained their senses and began to turn in order to attempt their original plan of attack yet again. The frigates that surrounded them likewise came back to life, eager to tear at the Adlers and smash them to pieces.

The few fighters that remained also came to

themselves again, and attacked several Adlers who'd gotten too close to them as they swirled *Sentinel*. Their quick destruction reminded their comrades that the battle was not yet over, and caused them to keep their distance, letting their powerful missiles do the work.

Anxiously ignorant as she stood under the reactor's sphere, Mafalda could sense something powerful happening within the Devourer mass below. A strange feeling, like an electrical charge in the air, surrounded her. But it was more than that. Not merely an impersonal sensation, she could feel the *consciousness* of the parasite reaching out, communicating, filling the space around the planet with its thoughts. The broadcast wasn't addressed to her, that she knew with certainty. She could tell she was nothing more than a rock in the midst of a rushing stream, its water pouring around and over her. The creature's attention was on something far more important than a single ex-Fringer who stood wringing her hands. She could feel its desperation, its fear. So close to attaining its object, it nevertheless stood on the brink of failure.

Then it happened.

For a fraction of a second she saw an image of a creature so terrible that it made her scream and step back in fear. Unable to process what had passed before her mind's eye, she was shaken to her core.

"Rex!" she called upward without thinking, realizing immediately afterward that she ought to leave him alone to do his work. But the image was so vile, so hideous, that she felt she must share it with someone or otherwise burst. Putting her hands to her head as though to keep the image contained until she could unload it, she hurried from the reactor room and hustled back to the bridge to tell Krancis.

Unbeknownst to her at this time, *Sentinel* was covered all on one side by frigates which pecked and struck it with their little arms. The battleships likewise ranged themselves on its right side, intent on pushing it into the atmosphere and crashing it into the planet. Firing the engines up, the captain fought against their combined pressure. But the warship began to slide towards the beleaguered world below.

"Captain, order the Adlers to focus all fire on the battleships," Krancis instructed over his radio. "Our turrets can more easily take down the frigates than they can. It would be a waste of their ordnance at this point to target smaller craft."

"Yes, Krancis."

Quickly the Adlers broke off into teams, each of them targeting a specific battleship and pounding it with their warheads. Hollowing them out, gutting them from top to bottom, several of the capital ships saw their engines flicker and then die out. Inertia kept them moving towards *Sentinel*. But as more of them went offline, the warship's slide towards the planet slackened, and in turn it pushed back against their dead weight. Drifting helplessly, their noses pressed against the side of the huge vessel, their rears began to move up or down around *Sentinel*, sliding across its hull and then continuing past it towards the planet.

"Krancis, more Devourer forces have just entered the system," the captain informed him, causing a portion of the panoramic bridge to magnify on a modest fleet that had warped in near the original carriers. Evidently proving too much for the parasite to think about, they emerged from their rifts and then floated idly in space.

"They don't seem to be any cause for concern at this point, Captain," Krancis remarked with a faint smile, pleased that the Devourer was so mentally overloaded. Glancing around at the numerous craft that were still shoving *Sentinel*, he could see that the flames that burned from their engines had lessened, the parasite unable to keep them going at one hundred percent. Indeed, several dozen frigates and a handful of battleships had by then slipped off of *Sentinel* and were passing over it, their tentacles drunkenly reaching for it.

"Krancis," Mafalda said urgently as she entered, afraid to interrupt him during the battle, but yet more afraid not to. "I've seen something terrible."

"Something so frightening that you could barely contain yourself?" he queried knowingly, not bothering to look at her as he continued to watch the battle.

"Why…yes," she said, dumbfounded. "I've never seen anything so horrible in all my life. And I don't even know what it was! Some kind of…creature."

"Yes, I saw it as well," he told her, his hands clasped calmly behind his back. "It's what the Devourer has been calling out for, what it so desperately seeks. It's the entire reason we're here, Mafalda."

"But how can you be so calm, sir?" she asked with awe, unable to understand how he could be aware of any such abomination without quaking at the thought, as she then was.

"Fear is of no advantage to us in this struggle," he told her, as another salvo of missiles screamed towards *Sentinel* and pummeled their way into the hulls of its attackers. "Only cool rationality will see us through the crisis to come."

"Yes, Krancis," she assented, incapable of saying more. Closing her eyes for a moment, a faint memory of the creature flashed before them and made her jump with a little involuntary yelp.

"Calm yourself, Mafalda," he instructed, before pressing his finger into his ear radio. "Captain, order the Adlers to concentrate their fire yet more. They're spread out across too many targets. I want to see a battleship going offline every few seconds until *Sentinel* can once again move entirely without interference." Looking off towards the planet, he could see it still growing slowly larger. "It won't be too much longer before its gravity begins to exert an unwelcome influence on us."

Following his eyes, Mafalda watched the planet for a few seconds. Huge smoke plumes still rose up from its surface into the atmosphere. A very large world, it made her wonder what size the oncoming terror would be.

"How big is this creature, Krancis?" she asked.

"No one knows," he answered, nodding slightly in approval as he saw the Adlers form up in tighter groups and hit fewer targets. "Except the dark realm and the parasite. And neither of them are talking."

"What, even the dark realm won't say?" she queried, unable to help flinching as a trio of missiles exploded near the bridge, ripping mountains of flesh out of an already ailing battleship. "I thought it was on our side."

"It's on its own side. But it has proclivities that point it in our direction. Perhaps affections would be a better word. But that doesn't mean it shares everything with us. Some things are too terrible for it to contemplate unless it has to."

"You mean even the dark realm has fear?"

"It has aversions, like all living things," he explained, once again nodding as the Adlers began working their way in a line that ran from the front of the warship towards its middle. "Captain, tell our pilots to continue precisely as they are. This is what I want."

"Yes, Krancis."

Looking over his shoulder at her finally, he tipped his head towards the door.

"You shouldn't have left Rex, Mafalda. No matter how afraid you were. Return to your post. I've satisfied enough of your curiosity for the moment."

"Okay," she agreed, nodding a little before dipping her head and leaving him alone.

Back inside the reactor, Wellesley monitored his friend with concern.

"You're doing great, Rex," the AI said, though he was certain the Deltan could no longer hear him. Seriously tempted to try and snap him out of it, he resisted the urge and turned his mind towards the warship's external cameras. Most of the battleships were either destroyed or torn nearly to pieces, just waiting for a final missile to push them into their well-deserved graves.

"How is he doing?" the man in black radioed.

"Well, how should *I* know!?" the AI snapped, his anxiety getting the better of him.

"Is he *breathing?* Is his heart functioning properly?" Krancis specified, enunciating clearly.

"He's doing fine medically, more or less. But after last time–."

"I'm only concerned with the present, and that which lies immediately ahead."

"*Yes*, Krancis, he'll manage to be your weapon for at least a little longer," Wellesley said acidly, the bite in his voice surprising even him, though he felt no power to stop himself from speaking thus. "I'll let you know if his condition goes south."

"You do that," he replied, unphased by the AI's tone.

"*What's gotten into you?*" he asked himself critically, not wishing to jeopardize relations with Krancis through acting out emotionally. Yet something made him speak the way he had, all but forcing him to lash out. It was strange. He couldn't make sense of it. But before he could think more about it, a groan escaped Hunt's lips, and he began to slouch. "Buddy? Are you alright? Rex?" he queried quickly, but received no response. Checking his vitals, he watched his heart rate climb a little higher, but otherwise he was none the worse. Not *medically*, anyway. "*Sometimes I really wish I could see what you're seeing in there, Rex*," he thought, curious if the dark realm was interacting with him. "*See what you're feeling.*"

Unknown to the worried AI, Mafalda had returned to the reactor room and was once more standing beneath them. Squinting as she felt the Devourer's mind reaching out yet more earnestly, she rubbed her temples and then looked up.

"Rex?" she whispered, thinking she had felt some kind of emanation from the reactor. "Are you alright?" she queried fruitlessly, wringing her hands at her helplessness. "Oh, I wish I could *do* something!"

As she said this a pulse passed through *Sentinel* that made her yelp.

"Something going on, Krancis?" Wellesley radioed, picking up the pulse when Hunt likewise jerked inside the reactor.

"The parasite has nearly completed its work," he replied, watching as frigate after frigate was turned to ash, and the last of the battleships pummeled to death. "The terror is nearly upon us."

"Well, then send the Adlers to bomb the mass back to the stone age!" the AI exclaimed. "Their special warheads are perfect for that kind of job!"

"The mass has embedded itself into the planet, Wellesley. Its roots run far too deep for conventional weapons to be of any use. Only *Sentinel's* cannon could destroy it from top to bottom, and that's already been ruled out. We'd merely be wasting ordnance to send the Adlers against it."

"Well, then, tell your terror to hurry up and get here! I don't want Rex in here any longer than he has to be."

"Rest assured, it will be here soon enough," the man in black answered, closing the connection between them and rubbing his temple with a couple of fingers. *"You're giving it almost everything you have, parasite. But you know as well as I do that it will take the life of your final nerve center to call the beast home again. How much longer are you going to drag your feet before you finally pull the trigger?"*

Another pulse shortly succeeded the first one, again causing Hunt to jerk.

"Come on, buddy," Wellesley said. "Just a little longer."

The AI had no notion that his words would prove prescient. Moments later the mass exploded, casting its stinking, ugly flesh in all directions, tiny fibers of it filling the air. An incredible pulse emanated out of it, dropping

Mafalda to the floor unconscious and causing even Krancis to grimace and grip his head with one of his hands. The captain, attached via a neural link to the ship, received an incredible charge as the vessel acted as an antenna, channeling it into him and burning his nervous system to ash. Instantly made aware of this by *Esiluria*, Krancis instructed the captain's second-in-command to assume control of the vessel.

But as he spoke these words, *Sentinel* began to hum with energy.

"Krancis, something is happening within the reactor," *Esiluria* informed him. "The power level has spiked dramatically. I think something terrible has happened to Rex Hunt."

"Rex!" Wellesley shouted to his friend, as the Deltan dropped to his knees, his hands stretched above his head as he screamed unconsciously, his mind still in the dark realm. "Rex, you've got to snap out of it! You'll burn up!"

"We need to do something quickly, Krancis," *Esiluria* cautioned him. "Or the energy will damage *Sentinel*.

But they were out of time.

Before the man in black could reply, an incredibly large warp rift was torn in space a short distance from the warship. Darker than even the most foul nightmare, it seemed to consume all light around it. Out of it lumbered a terrible creature many times the size of *Sentinel*. It had the appearance of a brown tribal mask, its shape roughly that of a human face.

"All forces attack the creature at once," Krancis ordered, though the Adler pilots were stunned by the sight. As it fully emerged it began to turn, revealing the skull behind the face to be a jungle of slow, lethargic tentacles. "I repeat: all forces, *strike!*"

Drawn from their stupor, the fighters accelerated away from *Sentinel* and targeted the creature just as the great cannon cut loose. Powered by the ordeal through which Hunt was passing, it burned blacker than it ever had before.

But it produced no effect.

The moment they were within striking distance the Adlers released every warhead they had, sending a screaming cloud of missiles towards their target. Doubling back the instant the ordnance was free of their ships, they pushed their engines to the max, struck to the deepest recesses of their hearts with fear.

As the missiles hit it and exploded, the countless arms began waving more rapidly. But no harm was done.

"We need to get out of here, Krancis," Wellesley told him, watching from the ship's external cameras. "That beast isn't hurt in the least. We've lost."

"We have to burn off more energy before warp, or the ship will be at risk," he replied in a tense though calm voice, watching the creature from the panoramic bridge.

"That thing will destroy us the second it really wakes up," the AI countered, noting with alarm that the tentacles were moving more rapidly with each passing second. "We need to take our chances."

"The decision isn't yours, Wellesley," the man in black responded, closing the channel in order to devote his entire attention to the empire's new foe.

"Of course! Who would listen to me?" the AI complained inwardly, before his attention suddenly went to Hunt as the latter dropped to the floor and groaned. "Rex! Rex, are you okay?"

"I…I don't…" the Deltan mumbled in confusion. Unable to stand, he dragged himself to the lift and gripped the metal arms that raised and lowered it. Dragging himself upwards into a crouch, he nodded for Wellesley to have it lowered.

"Sure, absolutely," the AI said urgently, taking his meaning at once.

In a daze Hunt descended to the floor, rolling off the lift and onto all fours, his head hanging as he tried to collect his thoughts. He felt shaky, unsteady. And yet…powerful somehow. Gripping the floor with his fingers, he felt almost as though he could tear handfuls out of it. It was at this moment that he realized the black marks had disappeared from his arms.

Faintly aware that someone else was in the room, he slowly lifted his head and saw Mafalda laying in a twisted heap twenty feet away. Crawling awkwardly, he reached her side and felt her pulse.

"She's okay, Rex," the AI said as he withdrew his hand, though he hadn't had the time to scan her thoroughly from Hunt's brief contact with her.

"What happened?" Hunt queried, his voice sounding strange in his ears as he allowed his head to sag once more. "Did we win?"

"I wouldn't say that," Wellesley replied, his attention shifting to the ship's cameras. "I'm afraid we've lost terribly."

As this remark passed through Hunt's skin and traveled up to his brain, the creature at last came to full alertness. Moving more rapidly than it seemed capable of doing, it closed the distance with *Sentinel* as the warship turned away, still firing its cannon off into space to discharge energy. The new captain accelerated, but a massive tentacle lashed out and struck the right side of its engine compartment, collapsing part of it and sending the ship spiraling away.

"*Now* can we go?" Wellesley asked pointedly, reopening the channel to Krancis.

"You may depart, Captain," the man in black said calmly. "We can't risk staying here any longer."

"Yes, Krancis," he replied, attempting to steady the warship while simultaneously tracking the creature's advance and shutting down the cannon. Unused as he was with his role, it took him longer than it should have, and the beast managed to strike *Sentinel* a second time before he could put the vessel on a straight enough course to open a rift. Again the engine compartment took the blow, and once more *Sentinel* spiraled.

"They're never gonna escape, Colonel," one of the Adler pilots radioed to Moryet. "They'll never manage to get a rift open and fly into it."

"I can see that," he replied soberly, he and the rest of his command following the creature from a modest distance, their initial fear gone.

"What are we gonna do?" another queried. "We're out of ordnance!"

"Every pilot's got ordnance as long as he's still flying," Moryet responded grimly.

"I was afraid you'd say that," the first pilot commented, though the finality in his voice indicated he'd already settled on the same notion. "Doubt we'll even put a dent in it, though."

"No, we won't," Moryet confirmed, accelerating, as did the rest of them. "But we might distract it for a few seconds, give 'em a chance to slip away."

"I hope so," remarked another. "I'd hate to smash up this pretty little bird for nothing."

Unable to help himself, the colonel grinned at this. Activating his radio, he contacted Krancis and imparted his plan.

"You're a good man, Colonel," the man in black replied. "You and your command will always have a place within the annals of imperial history."

"Thank you," he said somewhat tensely, his attention attracted by the creature as they drew nearer to it. "We won't let you down." Cutting off the channel, the colonel accelerated yet further. "We need to watch it, boys. When this thing coils up to strike again, we've got to crash into it and try to make it miss."

Like a whale beside gnats it dwarfed them. Smaller tentacles reached out eagerly to smash the little craft, but weren't quite long enough.

"I'd say it knows we're here," the first pilot observed.

"Good. Then we've started to distract it already," Moryet answered, doubtful that that fact had much value.

Managing to struggle his way to the bridge once Wellesley had called for medical attention for Mafalda, Hunt entered on wobbly legs and made his way to Krancis.

"Status?" the Deltan asked, seeing at once that they were in deep trouble.

"Questionable."

"Can we warp away?"

"Provided we can fly through the rift. The Adlers are going to try and buy us a little time."

"When?" he asked warily, watching the creature draw closer, one of its massive tentacles coiling up.

"I'd say right about…now."

Just then a cloud of explosions could be seen erupting against the beasts' forest of limbs. The tentacle still lashed out, but it struck the vessel more squarely in the rear, merely shoving it forwards instead of tumbling it over. Seeing his chance, the captain at once opened the rift and sailed quickly into it, leaving the monster behind.

"So it's come to this, then," Hunt uttered, as Krancis turned to leave. "All the fighting – all the sacrifices we made to defeat the Devourer, just so it could call this abomination up from wherever it was hiding."

"It wasn't hiding, Rex. It was imprisoned."

"Doesn't make much difference now, does it?" he asked, pointing back down the tunnel of blackness towards the creature. "*Sentinel* couldn't do a thing to it. And the Adlers didn't even scratch it, did they?"

"Not in the least," Krancis confirmed.

"Then what are we supposed to do?" Wellesley asked over the room's speakers.

"We shall do what the Earthborn have always done: fight to survive."

"But how can we *fight* something like that?" the AI prodded. "What weapons would even *begin* to hurt it?"

Without answering, the man in black made for the door.

"At least tell us its name, Krancis," Wellesley said. "You owe us that much."

Pausing just short of the exit, his hands clasped behind his back, he turned slowly and eyed the Deltan.

"You've changed," he remarked without surprise, looking him up and down a time or two. "Your marks are gone."

"I've noticed."

"What you likely haven't noticed yet is that your eyes are aglow with shadow," he pointed out. "And that your powers have increased."

"You knew this was going to happen," the Deltan said, his voice beginning to growl. "You wanted me in there."

Neither confirming nor denying this statement, he again turned.

"The name, Krancis," Wellesley insisted over the radio, as Hunt followed him into the corridor. "I want to know its name."

"Soon everyone in the galaxy will know its name and tremble," he replied, walking.

"Yeah, well, I'm special. I like to know before everyone else."

Pausing one last time, he looked Hunt in the eyes.

"*Khelmatoth*, Wellesley," he said quietly. "The ancient terror *Khelmatoth* is upon us."

At once Hunt felt a revolt within him at this terrible name. Unable to help it, he shivered.

"The dark realm loathes this creature," Krancis explained, nodding towards Hunt. "You can feel it."

"Yes, I can," Hunt confirmed, raising his hands to his face and trying to understand the strange sensations he felt running through his body.

"But why?" Wellesley queried.

"Because," the man in black said, walking away again.

"*Khelmatoth* is the dark realm's firstborn."

    End of Book V

THANK YOU!

I hope you enjoyed The Crusade of Vengeance!
If you did, please leave a review so others can enjoy it too!

Review on Amazon

Printed in Great Britain
by Amazon